Black Rosebud

Black Rosebud: Have No Mercy II

Bobby and Kam Ruble

With love,
Kam

Global Authors Publications

Black Rosebud: Have No Mercy II
©Bobby and Kam Ruble 2003

ALL RIGHTS RESERVED
No part of this book may be produced in any form,
by photocopying or by any electronic or mechanical means,
including information storage or retrieval systems,
without permission in writing from both the copyright
owner and the publisher of this book, except for the
minimum words needed for review.

This is a work of fiction. Names, places, characters, and incidents are either the product of the authors' imagination, or are used fictitiously, and any resemblance to actual persons, living or dead, events, or locales is entirely coincidental.

ISBN: 0-9728513-1-3
Library of Congress Control Number: 2003108258

First published in 2003 by
Global Authors Publications

*Filling the **GAP** in publishing*

Edited by T. C. McMullen
Cover Art by Phillip C. Beebe ©2003
Interior Design by Dehanna Bailee

Printed in USA for Global Authors Publications

Black Rosebud: Have No Mercy II

Dedication

This book is dedicated to
Jerome T. Gacke, M.D.,
in heartfelt gratitude and deep appreciation for his friendship;
and for his free expert advice and consultation in reference to
all medical information written into the storylines
of our fiction novels.

Thanks, Doc.

In Memoriam

Sgt. Bobby G. Corsi, USMC
KIA 22 August 1966
Quang Ngai, RVN

Sgt. Robert P. Santor, USMC
Explosive accident 24 September 1966
Quang Tin, RVN

Lest We Forget

Acknowledgements

T.C. McMullen - for her editing, advice and comments, which place her at the top of the list for an author's best friend.

Captain Larry Trosper, Grand Island Police Department, Officer in Charge, CID, Department Coroner for his assistance in the duties of a coroner in the State of Nebraska.

Phillip C. Beebe - for his wonderful cover art, advice and friendship.

Dallas Hodder Franklin - for her professional and personal advice, support, encouragement and friendship.

Joan W. Lewis - for her advice and editing comments, promotional assistance and friendship.

A special "thank you" to the professional team of *Global Authors Publications* for the encouragement, enthusiasm, dedication, hard work, unconditional friendships and ever ending support.

Foreword

Bob Jensen, Publisher

The writing of a novel is an all-consuming act. To breathe life into a fictional story takes great imagination and a dogged determination to tell the story through to its logical conclusion.

Bobby and Kam Ruble have done just that with their latest book, *Black Rosebud: Have No Mercy II.* Their grand effort in completing this sprawling story, filled with its many twists and turns, comes as no surprise to me since I know the Ruble's. Or at least I know their passion for writing.

It is something we have in common. For the past quarter century I have been a staff writer at several Nebraska newspapers, the publisher of two, including *The Central City* (NE) *Republican-Nonpareil* and founder of Nebraska's only high school sports weekly publication, *Huskerland Prep Report.* Through it all, I have been given the opportunity to tell many stories. And I can tell when I am done when I've got it right – when I feel I have connected with my subject.

That connection, that passion for this story – creating its complex characters for instance – comes through in each page of *Black Rosebud.* The Ruble's willingness to explore the dark corners of this sad, twisted tale makes this book an excellent read.

Authors, novel authors especially, not only need to be able to craft a story, but also need to show a great deal of discipline in the progress. And being willing to take your investigation of your characters to great depth only makes the story you tell all the more worthwhile.

And the Ruble's do that, bringing you into the circle of memorable characters which include Mama and Farm Girl, a pair of under-educated, downtrodden drifters who find a home with the warm-hearted Jefferson Welk, on his farm located near a rural Nebraska town. Farm Girl, who was sheltered, hidden actually, from the real world by her Mama for the first 17 years of her life, stumbles into a plot set by the ruthless egomaniacal Darin Righter, who is hungry to get out of Kidwell by any means possible.

From there death, mayhem and mystery rule the day, including a shocker of an ending to this engaging tale.

You will enjoy *Black Rosebud* not only for its complex and riveting story, but also for the love of the written word, which comes through in each paragraph of Bobby and Kam Ruble's book.

Good reading to you,
Bob Jensen, Publisher
The Republican-Nonpareil
Central City, Nebraska
  May 2003

Black Rosebud

GROWING UP WITH MAMA

PART ONE

On the Jefferson Welk farm in rural Nebraska, it's a typical end of a winter's day. The trees are starting to bud. Ice has melted from the river that runs through the Welk property. The official beginning of spring is just around the corner.

Although it isn't frozen, in many places the fields are still mushy. Too wet for the area farmers to start plowing. The thawed mounds of earth are no longer miniature banks of mud. This damp earth is easy to shovel, especially when using it to fill a hole in the ground such as a grave.

The cold night air sends chills clear to the bones. Dawn is breaking. As the sun starts to make its way into the horizon, the sky turns deep orange.

Half-dazed in deep thought, Farm Girl seems unable to move. She stands above the grave she placed her mama's body in just a short time ago. Farm Girl knows that it is up to her, from now on, to do whatever she must do in order to survive. As she stands in silence, memories of how Mama raised her to be a survivor occupy her mind.

In her naivety, Farm Girl has no idea that murder will overshadow everything Mama had tried to accomplish when conveying survival techniques to her.

BACK IN TIME

Mama appeared to carry a large burden on her shoulders. Being a loner for most of her adult life, she kept her burden of secrets well hidden from the rest of the world. For her own personal reasons, even her daughter knew very little about Mama's past. According to Mama, there was not a soul alive who could tell her anything about who she was or where she came from.

Before retiring for the night, many children had parents who read to them from storybooks. For a number of years, Farm Girl never knew about storybooks. Consequently, her favorite bedtime stories consisted of small portions of the heartrending truth about Mama's background.

In her toddler years, Farm Girl would nestle her head of natural curly hair in Mama's lap. Then she listened as if she were hearing Mama's short but sad tale for the very first time. Even when Mama explained her past, Farm Girl was too young to figure out why some of the stories did not make sense.

"When I was a wee babe, someone done wrap me in a blanket and left me on a doorstep a one a them places they calls an orphanage. A note with my blanket teld them orphanage folks that I done come into this world in June a nineteen and forty."

Farm Girl said, "Tell me again when I was born."

"In April a nineteen and seventy-seven."

To say Mama led a hard life would be an understatement. In her thirties, her weathered, leather-like skin with the deep lines that dug into her face, along with the premature gray strands that wove themselves through her sleek dark hair, gave the outsider the opinion that she was twice her age. Adding to her premature aging, Mama always wore her hair swept back off her face and rolled into a chignon at the nape of her neck. In Farm Girl's admiring eyes, Mama was young and beautiful.

Running her gentle but calloused hand softly back and forth across Farm Girl's forehead, Mama continued her story. "When I was growin' up, folks was tossin' me about from home to home. Not one person was carin' about me, nor lovin' me enough to make me their own. That was 'cause I didn't have me one a them papers they calls a Certificate a Birth."

Even though she had heard Mama's story many times over, Farm Girl always managed to ask the same questions. In turn, Mama always had her own pat answers.

"Does I has me one a them papers?"

"Yes, ya does, child. Y'ur mama seen to that."

"Does I has me name F.G. on that paper?"

"Yes."

"How does I git me such a funny name?"

"Y'ur name ain't funny." Clearing her throat, Mama spoke of the past that haunted her. "Y'ur mama done name ya F.G. 'cause there once be a special love in her heart fur them initials. She was hopin' when ya be older, ya can use them initials to spell out a name to y'ur likin'. I calls ya F.G. Light."

"Was Light one a my mama's love names, too?"

"It's a nice name. Doesn't ya like it?"

"Yes, but I wanna knows why ya calls me that?"

"Ya be one a the few bright gifts God give to y'ur mama, that's why."

"Be my real mama in heaven?"

"No more talk now, child. Close y'ur eyes and git some sleep."

Before closing her eyes, Farm Girl always confessed, "I be y'ur kin now and ever, and I loves ya."

"I loves ya, too, sweet child. Now, git to sleep."

As Mama traveled across country by foot, she took her daughter with her. If people asked personal questions, Mama ignored them. When some people got too persistent in their questioning, thinking that Mama was running from something or someone, Farm Girl and her mother moved on without hesitation. Mama could never take the chance that someone might get too nosey and start checking into her background.

Whenever the mood suited her, Mama changed her name. She never made enough money or stayed in one place long enough to pay taxes. Farmers she worked for welcomed the idea of paying her in cash for the chores she performed. Never needing a Social Security Number, Driver's License, or any other pertinent identification, changing her name as often as she liked never posed a problem. She became Mary, Rachel, Sara, or whatever name suited her fancy.

When Farm Girl was old enough to ask questions about things she did not understand, she began questioning Mama's use of different names.

"I doesn't know why, but each time I gots me a new set a foster parents, them new folks would up and give me a new name from the last place I was livin'. Havin' all a them changin' names was a might confusin' when I was young," Mama admitted. "When I gots out on my own, I didn't has one given name, like most folks does. Today, I just uses all them names folks was callin' me when I was growin' up."

From the time Farm Girl could remember talking, she assumed

Mama was her sibling. Mama had an ulterior motive for making her daughter believe such a lie. Not knowing the truth, kept Farm Girl from accidentally calling her *Mama* and warranting unnecessary questions from anyone they encountered. Mama had no desire to explain the absence of Farm Girl's father. Above all costs and at all times, Mama had to protect her child. So Farm Girl wouldn't get confused with Mama's name changes, she had her daughter call her *Sister.* The name Sister needed little explanation.

When Mama did farm chores, she asked for little compensation. As long as she was working on a farm, she had but one requirement—room and board for her and the child. Room and board to Mama meant a straw bed in a barn with leftover food from the master's table. When the employment ended, Mama asked for either a pittance in wages or food to take along on the next journey. With this wage arrangement, it became apparent that none of the employers cared what name she answered to, what the little girl's name was, or if either of them had a last name.

Moving from farm to farm, seeking work, Mama was confident and polite as she approached the farmer. "Beggin' y'ur pardon, sir. Be ya the owner a this here farm?"

"I am," most farmers replied. "What can I do for you?"

"Me name be Jan." Wearing her take-pity-on-me look, she explained, "This here little one be my baby sister. Her name be F.G. Our folks be dead in a house fire, leavin' me to care fur her. With no home and no kinsfolk to help take care a us, I'd be mighty beholden to ya fur givin' me work. I can give ya my word, this little one won't be gittin' in the way and keepin' me from my chores."

After listening to Mama's unfortunate story, many farmers couldn't refuse her plea. They gave her a job, if only for a day.

There were times when a farmer didn't quite know what kind of outside chores a woman could do, especially while caring for a small child. In that case, the farmer might suggest she go to the house and talk to his missus. Perhaps there would be inside chores for her to do.

"No, sir, I ain't lookin' fur no housework where this little one can git into things when I cain't keep an eagle's eye on her. Since we been on the road fur most a her small life livin' in barns or out under God's blanket a stars, she don't 'member what inside a real house looks like. I ain't has me no chance to train her proper-like yet fur no house." Mama went on to explain what kind of outside chores she was capable of doing while at the same time keeping Farm Girl beside her and out of harm's way.

If a farmer had no need for a farmhand, but instead, offered Mama food for her and the child, Mama voiced her objection. "As hungry as we be, we ain't starvin', and I ain't in the habit a takin' without givin'. Unless ya has a small chore fur me to do in return, we'll pass on the food."

Fortunate for Mama, she never met too many coldhearted farmers that would let a child walk away hungry from his farm.

While working on one particular farm, the farmer thought F.G. wasn't a proper name for a little girl. When he started calling the little girl *Farm Girl*, the name stuck like butter to a slice of freshly made toast.

Farm Girl was thrilled to have a new name. "Now, I can play y'ur game, Sister."

"What game be that?"

"Ya changes y'ur name all the time. Now, I can change mine, too."

Shaking her head, Mama replied, "I doesn't mind if'n ya wanna be Farm Girl, but don'tcha be furgittin' that y'ur mama name ya F.G."

"I won't."

"Well, then, what does ya want me to be callin' ya now?"

"I thinks I wanna be Farm Girl."

"Then Farm Girl it be."

At a very young age, from planting seeds in a garden to cleaning out a barn, Farm Girl assisted her mother. Regardless of her small size, she did more than her share of work for a little girl.

People that Mama worked for were not always kind, like the day one farmer's wife cornered Mama in the barn. She told Mama she was going to turn her into the local authorities. This woman felt Mama was violating the Child Labor Law by making her little sister work such long stressful hours each day. Being confused, Mama asked the interfering woman to explain what she meant by such a law.

After receiving the brief, but ominous explanation, Mama verbalized her own resolute thoughts on the subject, putting the woman in her place. "If'n ya sees a rat, leave well enough alone. The rat ain't gonna bother ya, if'n ya don't bother it. Corner that rat, though, and the rat will attack ya in self-defense."

Mama seldom raised her voice and never allowed a cuss word to cross her tongue. Although she never lost her temper, she was a bit sharp with the tongue when she felt cornered, like a rat. Then she knew exactly what she was saying in her own defense. That particular day, however, Mama said something, quite by accident, which she had kept to herself for years. Her words were a significant turning point in Farm Girl's life.

"At fifty cents an hour, y'ur husband don't pay fur Farm Girl's share a my chores. She ain't workin' fur neither a ya. She's just helpin' her mama."

Farm Girl stood beside her mother, listening to every word. Her little heart felt as if it was breaking into a million pieces. Mama was too busy telling the woman off to see the tiny rivers of tears running down her daughter's face. Farm Girl turned and stepped behind Mama so she could wipe her face and dry her eyes with the bottom of her oversized apron.

"I sees y'ur two sons," Mama continued, "them seven and eight-year-old boys out there in the fields, chorin' right 'side a y'ur husband. So, if'n there be such a law, I think them authorities might wanna know and be speakin' to y'ur mister." The woman stood there, speechless, feeling the threat of her own bad intentions thrown back in her face. Mama's parting words summed it all up. "Most folks needs to pull weeds out a their own grounds befur they frets about ones in their neighbor's yard."

As they moved on their way, Farm Girl was just itching to ask Mama a question. Gritting her teeth to hold back another stream of tears, she could no longer hold her curiosity inside. Facing the ground as she walked, she asked, "Why did ya told that mean woman that I was helpin' my mama with chores? Did I do somethin' bad that ya doesn't wanna be my big sister no more?"

Even though Mama was leery of Farm Girl's reaction, the time had come for honesty. Mama stopped walking. Farm Girl followed suit. When Mama sat on the ground and placed her baggage next to her, Farm Girl mirrored her actions.

"No, child, ya ain't done nothin' bad. I was just hopin' ya be older befur I tells ya some stuff about our lives. But, reckon the time's come fur me to tell ya the truth."

"Truth? Has ya been tellin' me fibs? About what?"

"Hold y'ur tongue, child, and I'll tells ya." Mama looked toward the sky. After saying a silent prayer, she turned back to her daughter. "Tellin' lies be a bad thing, just like I been teachin' ya. Most folks that tells lies, goes to the land a the devil when they dies. Don'tcha furgit it." Sitting in silence, Farm Girl acknowledged Mama's words by shaking her head.

"To keep nosey folks from askin' us too many questions, I just teld them whoppers. Wasn't real lies. We was playin' a game." Farm Girl played in the dirt with her hands. She was getting restless waiting for Mama to get to the point. "Ya see, Farm Girl, I ain't y'ur sister. I be y'ur mama."

Farm Girl's big brown eyes widened. Rubbing her hands on her apron to remove the dust, she asked, "Ya be my mama?"

"Yes, I be."

"My mama ain't dead from no house fire?"

"No, child, that's just a story I done make up as part a the game we was playin'. Now that ya knows, ya can start callin' me Mama. But, when them nosy busybodies starts askin' questions, ya lets me do the answerin'."

"Does I has me a daddy like them other kids does?"

That question opened up an old wound, a deep hole Mama didn't want to climb into at this time in her daughter's life. "Ain't ya just happy to has ya a mama right now?"

"I sure be," Farm Girl shouted.

Even with her often-pleasant mood, Mama seldom smiled. Tears and laughter, more often than not, appeared foreign to her emotions. Inside, however, the over-whelming enthusiasm that Farm Girl expressed, when finally finding out the truth of their relationship, delighted Mama's very soul. A warm smile brightened Mama's normal unexpressive face as Farm Girl gave her a hug of affection.

That was one secret Mama no longer had the burden of keeping locked up inside. Even though Farm Girl had a million and one questions to ask, Mama had no more to say on the subject.

From April through October, Mama preferred working in the fresh air of the country. From November through March was a different story. During this cold season, when farmers no longer needed an extra hand, Mama was often fortunate to find work in town. Just before harsh cold set in for the winter, Mama would manage to find an abandoned structure to set up housekeeping. There she would often leave her daughter for the day while going to the nearest town looking for odd jobs.

With her town earnings, plus what little change she received from the farmers she had worked for, Mama was able to purchase a few groceries. Shopping was simple. Bread and cans of pork n' beans were the only items on Mama's list because both were within her price range. When she could afford it, she purchased a package of wieners. Both she and Farm Girl enjoyed eating them cold. If they were lucky enough to have a campfire, however, hot beans and a weenie roast to them was like a palace banquet to royalty.

No work, however, meant little food. There were times that Mama had to supplement their meals with bugs and worms. These became a temporary necessity for hungry appetites. Weather permitting and the season being right, Mama and Farm Girl dug for truffles close to the riverbanks or sought out edible berries.

Often times, they would help themselves to a few plumes of wheat to chew. Quite fortunate for them, since both had small appetites, having enough food to get her and Farm Girl through the winter was seldom a problem. No matter where they went, there was someone always willing to give them a drink of water to quench their thirst.

Making her way back and forth to town, during the cold months, was Mama's daily routine until the snow was too deep for her to walk. Mama rationed what food they had until she could get back to town and back to work.

Once, when Farm Girl asked why she always had to stay behind rather than go to town, Mama's reasons discouraged her from wanting to go along, or ever ask again.

"Farmers doesn't ask many questions. Ya does y'ur job, and they leaves ya alone. Now townsfolk, well, they be different. They seems to have a need to know everythin' about everybody. Maybe they means well. Maybe they doesn't. But, I doesn't need none a them to be askin' ya all kinds a them nosey questions. I trust ya to keep y'ur mouth shut, but it's just easier fur me to turn a deaf ear. Nope, don't nobody need knowin' our business."

Farm Girl could be a jabber box when she wanted to. However, when Mama was talking, she listened with care to every word.

"Ya knows what else they gots in them towns?" Farm Girl shrugged "They gots lots a them evil strangers I be warnin' ya about. Them are the peoples that hurts ya with nasty remarks or painful deeds."

Even though she had a multitude of bad experiences under her belt, Mama was referring to a time, years ago, when she had been in a town looking for work. As she walked along a sidewalk, she noticed two boys just ahead of her. They were standing with their upper bodies leaned against a building. When Mama walked past them, one of the boys had stuck out his foot and tripped her. All she could hear was their laughter when she fell to the pavement.

"Say, ya ain't afraid to be stayin' alone, is ya?"

"No, Mama." Farm Girl shook her little head of curls.

"Of course, ya ain't. Trust me, child, it's safer stayin' alone than bein' with me in some nasty old world where folks would just as soon eat ya alive as to look at ya."

Farm Girl shuttered. After Mama put the fear of God into her, she was more afraid of towns and the people in them than she was of dangerous four-legged animals.

At her young age, Farm Girl had already learned how to survive. Never was she fearful of the elements that surrounded her when left alone. Even though Farm Girl had seen coyotes, snakes, and other wild predators while she and Mama traveled, she was fortunate to have never encountered any danger from them. Since Mama had taught her how to deal with nature and all of its wild creatures, the mere thought of these beasts, large or small, was never frightening to her.

Indeed, Mama had trained her daughter well for the kind of life she lived. Unfortunate for Farm Girl, other than scaring the tar out of her about townsfolk and strangers, Mama never taught her about the dangerous, two-legged predators that existed in the *real* world.

GROWING UP WITH MAMA

PART TWO

When traveling, many women sport a purse or some sort of bag for carrying around their personal essentials. Not Mama. She always carried a rusty old coffee can with her that contained her valuables. No matter where Mama went, the can went along. Even though the can had lost its original color, the Folgers brand name was still legible. A piece of brown paper from a used grocery sack covered the top. Elastic torn from a pair of old underpants held the paper in place.

At any given time, Mama had the opportunity to dig through garbage cans and trash barrels, just as she did for clothes and other useful items, and retrieve a newer, cleaner can or carryall. She never cared to. Since her favorite tin held a special meaning, Mama refused to part with it.

Wherever she stayed for a few days or just camped for the night, Mama would dig a small hole and bury the can. To remember where she left it, she marked her hiding place with a special placement of rocks and sticks.

Farm Girl knew the rusty old tin housed her Certificate of Birth, a needle, spool of thread and a pair of scissors. However, that is all she knew. When she asked Mama what else was in the can, Mama shook her head at Farm Girl's persistent curiosity.

"My life, Farm Girl, my life. Someday, when God calls me from this life, that old can and everythin' in it will be y'urs. Then ya can look in it and find out things about y'ur mama I don't care fur ya to know yet. But, child, not till God calls me."

"If'n ya passes up to God befur ya tells me what's in y'ur can, I won't knows what them thingies in there be good fur, will I?"

"God and me has a pact. Years ago, I done promise to take care a His land and His creatures, if'n He'd let me raise ya my way until ya reaches the age of eighteen. So far, I has kept my word and so has God. So, don't be puttin' me in my grave until I fills my promise. Now, if'n ya promises not to ask me again, I'll tell ya about them personal things in my can when ya reaches that special age."

"That special age bein' eighteen?"

"Uh-huh."

"Okay, I promise." Lifting her hand and making the sign of an *x* across her heart, she spouted, "Cross my heart and hope to die, stick a needle in my eye if—"

"Stop! Where does ya learn such nonsense?"

"I hear me some kids sayin' it, so I 'member the words."

"Well, I doesn't want such baloney comin' out a y'ur mouth again. Hear me?"

"Yes, Mama, I hears ya."

"And how many times has I teld ya to stay away from other kids?"

"I wasn't with them. They was just close to me."

Many of the farm children, not of the full understanding as to how their words and actions could wound someone's feelings, called Farm Girl hurting names. Since she was dressed a bit old fashioned, like her mother, body covered with a skirt draped to her ankles and adorned by a tattered apron, sleeves extended to her wrists, and leather boots covering her feet, no matter what the weather, Farm Girl was easy pray for the other children to poke fun at.

Farm Girl soon learned to hide her presence when other children were around. Being a normal child with an inquisitive mind, however, Farm Girl could not resist spying on them. She would sneak up on other children and find something large enough to hide her tiny body. Unnoticed, she could watch them at play and listen in on their conversations.

From the time Farm Girl could remember, associating with other children was something Mama never allowed under any circumstances. However, in her little mind, listening was not the same as talking with the children. Watching was not the same as joining in and playing with them.

Mama knew her daughter had a strange way of stretching the truth.

So for the moment, she let the truth-skirting issue drop. Not that she cared to, but there were times when Mama had no other choice but to accept work on a farm that had children.

Mama continued with her pleasant but firm lecture. "I keeps tellin' ya not to be talkin' or playin' with them there kids."

"I 'member."

"Don't want none a them turnin' y'ur head with childish fancies and wild notions."

"No, Mama."

Her first encounter with words of profanity came from her being in a place she was not supposed to be. Farm Girl didn't think the words were bad when she heard them. They were just foreign to her little, virgin ears. When she repeated them to Mama, she soon found out Mama's feelings on the subject of her new vocabulary.

Before she ever again repeated any words to Mama that she didn't know the meaning of, she reminded herself, "When a young'n gits a mouth warshin' with soap fur usin' bad words, ya can bet she ain't never gonna make the same mistake twice. Least ways, not within Mama's hearin' distance."

Farm Girl loved watching the children play their games. Mesmerized, she memorized every move of two particular games that were of real fascination to her. Tag was one game that intrigued her. She called the game *It*. From a distance, her little heart yearned to join in the fun and be chased around like the other children.

The second game that fascinated her was the game of *King's X*. Even though Mama taught Farm Girl to never tell a lie, she was quick to learn that she could tell a whopper and get away with it. Just as long as she crossed her fingers behind her back, she wasn't lying. She was playing King's X.

Picturing in her mind how to play these games, gave her something to daydream about. Little did she realize, at that time, that both of those innocent childhood games would play an important role, later in her life. Sadly, one of these games would take Farm Girl down a tragic path of no return.

Without Farm Girl's knowledge, Mama was quite aware that Farm Girl spied on other children when they were around. When Mama felt that the children's way of life was filling Farm Girl's head with too much foolishness about the way they live, she packed up her daughter and moved on. Mama couldn't take any chances that Farm Girl might get wise and decide she wanted a different lifestyle. A life other than what Mama was providing.

When crossing the State of Nebraska on foot, Mama was finding that farms were either diminishing or modernizing. With progress, such as the Interstate Highway and Housing Developments, jobs for farmhands, especially for females, became fewer and far between.

Zigzagging across the countryside from farm to farm, Mama and her daughter often returned to a farm they had previously worked on. Sometimes they stumbled upon a farm where they had never been before. Such was the case when they met Jefferson Welk for the first time.

Spring was in the air. Walking up the steps to his backdoor, Jefferson took a deep breath, inhaling the perfume of the lilacs that filled the bush close to his house. As he reached the porch, he saw Mama and Farm Girl walking up his driveway. He still enjoyed good eyesight for his age, but from where he was standing, they looked like two young girls.

Always the gentleman, Jefferson removed his cap and stuck it into his coat pocket. Since he seldom received company, he watched and waited for the two females to approach the porch. As the strangers got closer, their features were much clearer to Jefferson. He realized that the two females were in fact a middle-aged woman and a child.

When they got within hearing distance, Jefferson raised his voice and commented, "Well, looks like you two are carrying around quite a load on your backs." They continued walking toward him in silence. Once again, Jefferson addressed them. "Are you two lost?"

Approaching the porch, Mama replied, "Good day, sir."

Jefferson had a sudden pain, which felt like a bolt of lightening in his chest. He grabbed for the nearest porch column for support, hoping he didn't appear sick-like to his visitors. Ignoring Mama for the moment, looking down at Farm Girl, he asked, "Is this woman deaf?"

"Ain't nothin' wrong with my hearin'."

Looking back at Mama, he asked, "Then why didn't you answer me when I was calling out to you?"

"Not in the habit a raisin' my voice, sir."

As Jefferson smirked, his eyes twinkled. "Oh, I see. Well, what can I do for the two of you?"

"I be lookin' fur work."

The words from Mama's mouth confused her daughter. *What's wrong with Mama? She ain't never said nothin' about work without first tellin' her name and mine. Maybe she don't know who she's gonna be today.*

An elderly man of color, Jefferson had more than enough money to pay for anything he wanted or needed. Because of the modest way he lived, some people thought of him as just another farmer trying to make a living. That was far from the truth. Funds set up in a trust account in his name, when he was much younger, kept him on the wealthy side of life.

Trusting very few people, and leery of most, Jefferson never took very well to strangers. That is until Mama and Farm Girl showed up on his doorstep looking for work. Not that it would matter to them, but neither was aware of Jefferson's financial status. Mama made the same deal with him as she did with all the other farmers she encountered when seeking work.

"If'n ya hires me, ya gits this child's help, too. Now, I ain't askin' fur much fur the two a us, just a place to sleep and somethin' to eat. And, if'n ya has a mind to, give me a little cash or some food to take with us when it's time to be leavin'."

A man of generous nature, Jefferson thought about just being charitable. He could give the woman and the child something to eat, a few groceries to take with them, and a little cash to tide them over until the woman could find work. That, however, was a mere fleeting thought. Since he had lost his wife after forty years of marriage, he was a very lonesome man. He was also getting up in years.

Having someone to help him with housework and farm chores sounded very tempting. Besides, he was certain that a woman and a child were not a threat to him. He felt he had nothing to lose.

"That sounds like a might decent proposition. I could use some help around here. Tell you what. I'll take you on for the season."

"Thank ya, sir. We be mighty obliged," Mama said. "We'll be doin' our best fur ya until the changin' a the season comes and it's time to move on."

"The changing of the season is just a few months away. That's not what I meant. I was speaking of the farming season which could be into October, depending on the weather this year. That is, if you want to stay that long?"

"Yes, sir. That'll be mighty nice."

Keeping silent, Farm Girl grinned as she squeezed Mama's hand.

"Problem is, I don't have any quarters set up for guests to bed down."

"We sure ain't guests, sir. Walkin' up here, we seen ya gots plenty a barns. We just needs room in one a them with a small bit a straw fur sleepin'."

"I only have one barn. The rest of the structures are for machinery, feed, farm supplies, and a garage for my pickup. None of those are suitable for living quarters. Neither is my barn. I never have gotten around to having the barn modernized. There's no electricity or running water in it."

"Does ya has a kerosene lamp and a river close by?" Mama was hoping Mr. Welk was not going to change his mind about hiring her.

"Yes, I have several kerosene lamps, and there's a river that runs behind my barn. But why would you ask about a river?"

"Fur warshin'," Farm Girl spouted.

Jefferson looked down at the young girl. "No, no, that will never do. Well, never you mind. We'll figure out something later. So, little lady, what's your name?"

"They calls me Farm Girl."

"Farm Girl? My, my, that's a most unusual, but a nice name."

"Thank ya." She waited, hoping to hear Jefferson say something else. When he didn't, she said, "Well, ain't ya gonna tell us what we be callin' ya?"

Pulling on Farm Girl's hand, Mama glanced down at her daughter. "Child, tell this nice man that just give us work how sorry ya be, then hush up."

Jefferson couldn't help but grin as he kept his eyes on Farm Girl. "It's quite all right because she's absolutely correct. I should have introduced myself. Farm Girl, my name is Jefferson Welk." He gave a quick dip of his head. "I'm very happy to make your acquaintance."

Before he could say anything more, Farm Girl looked at her mother and asked, "Mama, what do that mean?"

"He's happy to meetcha."

"Oh." She turned her attention back to Jefferson. "That's swell, but ain't ya happy to meet Mama, too?"

"Yes, of course I am," he answered, holding back his laughter. He looked at Mama and, once again, tipped his head. "I'm happy to make your acquaintance, too, Mama. And I would suggest you quit pulling on that little ones hand so much, or she'll be walking around with one arm longer than the other," he suggested with a touch of humor.

Farm Girl started giggling. Even sober faced Mama smiled.

"Well, ladies, I'm an old man who is cold and hungry. You caught me just as I was about to go in and fix myself a little supper. I wasn't expecting company, but I have plenty of bacon and eggs in the refrigerator. I bet that little one could use some hot food in her tummy. Couldn't you, honey?"

There had been little to eat during the long, cold winter. Farm Girl's mouth was watering at the thought of food. Better yet, it was hot food. Her thoughts emphasized her hunger pangs. *Yummy, bacon and eggs. Ain't never had me none a that bacon befur, but it sure do sound good. My tum-tum be sure hankerin' fur some food, since it ain't has nothin' in a few days but a spoonful a beans and some spring worms.*

When Farm Girl's mouth opened to speak, Mama gave an immediate squeeze to her small hand. Farm Girl was quick to receive the message to keep quiet—so was Jefferson.

"There you go again, Mama. I can appreciate a child with manners, but pulling and squeezing this little one's hand, all the time, can't be right when someone asks her a question. Let the little gal speak for herself," he suggested with gentle persuasion. After all, he didn't want Mama to feel that he was interfering with her motherly discipline.

Conceding, Mama nodded acceptance. Addressing her daughter she said, "Okay, answer Mister Welk. But mind y'ur manners."

Beaming, Farm Girl replied, "I sure can make myself eat some a that hot food to make my tum-tum feel better."

Mama was not very pleased the way Farm Girl answered, but Jefferson enjoyed the child's spirit. "Well, then, that's settled. Why don't the two of you come on in and join me." As he spoke, he walked to the door and pulled open the screen door. With a slight turn of his body, he made sure he was once again looking at Mama. "We can talk inside while we get a bite to eat."

"We be mighty obliged to ya, but we cain't accept y'ur offer. Farmhands doesn't sit at the same table with folks they chores fur. But, if'n ya be willin' to share y'ur food befur we start them chores ya has fur us, we can sit out here on y'ur stoop and eat."

Still holding on to the screen door, Jefferson stared at Mama, as if he were looking into her soul. Feeling a bit self-conscious, Mama remarked, "I mean no disrespect."

"No, of course you didn't. Tell me something, Mama. Can you cook?"

"Yes, sir."

"Well, then starting right now, that's one of your chores. I haven't had a decent home cooked meal since I lost my missus. After you fix supper, and you still want to come outside to eat, then that's your business."

He turned, reached for the knob to the backdoor and twisted it. With one hand holding the screen open, and the other resting on the doorknob, Jefferson took a step inside his house. He stopped, leaving one foot still resting on the porch. Keeping his back to Mama and Farm Girl, he turned his head to one side, directing his eyes toward the deck of the porch.

"We can talk while you cook. Taking care of the house will be another one of your chores. After supper, I'll show you around."

"But, sir, we be farmhands. I doesn't mind cookin' a meal fur ya, but we does outside chores."

"That's good, Mama, and I'll have plenty of them for you to do. Now, do you know how to keep house, or not?"

"Yes, sir, I does fur sure, but my daughter don't know nothin' about bein' in no house and doin' inside chores."

Jefferson still didn't look up. "Well, this is as good a time as any for her to learn. There's nothing in my house she can hurt. It will be a good teaching ground for her. Okay?"

Reading the look of plea on her daughter's face, Mama gave in. "Yes, sir, I reckon that ya be right."

"Good. I'm glad that's settled. Now, come on inside where it's warm."

For Mama there was an instant bond with Jefferson. Quite unlike most of the farmers treated her in the past, Jefferson didn't talk down to her, like he was better than she was. His gentle way of speaking to her was comforting. She could find no argument in doing household tasks and cooking, or in finally teaching her daughter how to manage inside domestic chores.

Still standing on the ground next to the porch steps, Mama said, "Since we be a might dirty from our travels, we'd like to warsh up first. If'n ya doesn't mind?"

It was already very clear to Jefferson that Mama was a woman set in her ways, believing that farmhands knew their place, and it was *not* rubbing elbows with their employers. Therefore, he knew without even asking that it would be senseless to offer use of his inside plumbing facilities.

Releasing his hand from the doorknob, he stepped back on the porch. Turning to his newly hired help, Jefferson pointed to the side of the house. "You'll find the well just around the corner, over there. I've got an electric motor hooked up to it. The switch on the side of the motor is bright blue, so you can't miss it. Primed her good this morning, so just turn on the switch and you'll get plenty of fresh water. It's going to be ice cold, but I imagine you're both use to freezing water this time of year.

You'll find soap over there, too. I don't keep any towels out there, but there are plenty of clean rags in the small metal container that sits close to the motor. Anything else?"

"No, Mister Welk, thank ya," Mama answered. "We'll be in soon to git that hunger a y'urs fed."

In no time at all, Mama and Farm Girl had washed up and entered Jefferson's house. As Mama cooked and issued orders to Farm Girl for setting the table for Jefferson, the three of them became acquainted.

"Have you been around these parts before, Mama," Jefferson asked.

"Yes, sir. Why does ya be askin'?"

"I don't remember faces well, but there is something familiar about you."

Most times, when people started asking questions, there was a warning sign that popped up in Mama's brain. Her norm was to appear too preoccupied to answer. Feeling at ease with Jefferson, she never gave her fears a second thought.

"Some years back, I done chores fur a few farmers in this area. Durin' the winter, I done inside housework fur Miss Jenkins. She be livin' on the edge a town. Does ya know her?"

"No, but I knew of her. It's funny you would mention her of all people. Heard she passed on just a few weeks ago."

"I be real sorry to hear that. Guess I won't be lookin' to her fur no winter work this year."

"I don't associate with too many in this area. Maybe you just remind me of someone else."

"Maybe."

"How is it you never came to my farm before now, looking for a job?"

"Reckon 'cause we left the area fur a while. This be our first time back."

Being quiet long enough, Farm Girl felt the overwhelming need to have her say. "Does ya knows ya be callin' my mama 'Mama'."

"So I have. I guess we've been talking so much that I've been rather rude. Please forgive me, Mama. Tell me what your name is, or what you'd like me to call you."

Before Mama had a chance to speak, Farm Girl piped in with her declaration. "Wait, Mister Welk. I likes ya callin' her Mama."

"Well, young lady, that has to be up to your mother to make that decision."

Mama was quick to agree. It would be much easier for her to answer to Mama then it would be to remember another name. Also, she liked the idea of not having to lie to Mr. Welk about who she was, or was not. Although she didn't fully understand why she even cared, Mama was starting on the right foot with their employer to employee relationship.

As much as Jefferson disliked the idea, Mama and Farm Girl sat on the cold porch and ate their supper. They weren't on the porch long enough to feel the cold. Both were so hungry for a hot home cooked meal, they did all but inhale their food.

After washing the supper dishes, Jefferson took Mama and Farm Girl on a brief tour to acquaint them with the house. At the same time, he explained the inside tasks he required. Farm Girl was in awe of everything she saw. Most of the time, she was speechless.

Jefferson built the small house with his own two hands. Since there was only him and his wife at the time he built it, there was no need for a bigger house.

The main floor consisted of a good-sized kitchen, a cozy living room, a large sitting room, one bathroom, and a large storage room. He had built the storage room with children in mind, in case there was need for an extra bedroom.

Four cement block rooms divided the basement. The largest of the four housed an old wringer-type washing machine, an automatic washer and dryer set, the furnace, and hot water heater. One of the smaller rooms was for cleaning and storing fresh eggs. What was once a coal room was now used for extra storage use.

Even though Jefferson took pride in his work, the fourth room was one he hated to use. It was a well-equipped and fully supplied tornado shelter. Living in Nebraska, he had spent more time in the shelter than he cared to. Jefferson felt fortunate the shelter had always kept him and his wife out of harm's way when a treacherous funnel would fall from the sky, ravishing every thing in its way.

In her lifetime, Mama had spent time in a few storm cellars for tornado protection. However, most of the time she had not been that fortunate. When a death-threatening tornado approached, Mama had always latched on to Farm Girl and run for the nearest ditch or culvert. She would wrap her body around her daughter to protect her from the flying debris that filled the air about them. Even though they had some narrow escapes, Mama and Farm Girl always managed to survive unscathed.

There was one room on the top floor of Jefferson's house. It was a large bedroom. Other than a double bed and a chest-of-drawers, a multitude of boxes littered the room.

"My wife had a nice dresser in here with a big mirror on it. She loved that dresser. Had no need for it, once she was gone. Now, it's stored in that room off the kitchen. Forgive the clutter, but many of these boxes are full of her clothes and personal items," Jefferson explained. "I just haven't brought myself to throwing any of it, like her clothes, in the trash."

"That's where we gits most a our clothes. Why don't ya give them thingies to me and Mama?"

Mama gasped. "Oh, my, child. Y'ur mouth be turnin' y'ur mama's face red, talkin' like that."

"It's true, ain't it? If'n he's just gonna toss them away, he can save us diggin' them out a the trash by just givin' them to us."

"Well, Mama, you can't disagree with that kind of reasoning." Since Mama appeared to be without words, Jefferson addressed Farm Girl. "Tell you what I'm going to do. I will go through all of these boxes and pull out what I don't need to be keeping. Then, I'll give all those things to you and Mama to go through. What you don't want or can't use, you can throw in the trash. How's that?"

Mama answered for her daughter. "No, we cain't ask ya to do that."

"You're not asking. I'm offering," he said looking at Mama. "It's a task I've put off far too long. Now I have a good excuse to get it done."

Prejudice was an evil in people that Jefferson had already witnessed too many times in his life. In his seventies, he didn't care to place himself in any similar situation, ever again. Knowing his bad heart might not be able to handle the stress, he still had to chance it.

"Okay, Mama, be honest with me. Do you *not* want these clothes because they belonged to a woman of color?"

"What's a woman a color means?" Farm Girl asked.

Stunned from Jefferson's words, Mama didn't know how to react. His insinuation cut at the very soul of her existence.

"Skin color," Jefferson stated. "But your mama knows what I mean."

Before Mama could speak, Farm Girl popped in with her innocence. Standing between Jefferson and Mama, she was quick to take hold of both their hands, pulling them together in front of her. Holding them up, she said, "Look, Mister Welk. Ya has skin lighter than Mama and the same color as me, and Mama likes my skin."

"Honey, skin tanned from the sun and—"

"She's right, Mister Welk. People's skin color don't tell me what's in a person's heart. I ain't never been accused a somethin' so terrible befur in all my born days. And I ain't full a shame that we digs through trash fur clothes, or takes hand-me-downs when given. I were just a might upset with the boldness a my child's mouth. We'd be most beholden to ya fur anythin' ya gives us."

Relieved, Jefferson held on to Farm Girl's hand, bent over and kissed it. "Thank you, little one. You and your Mama have made this old man very happy." Standing erect, he placed his hand on Mama's shoulder. "Please forgive an old man for being blinded by the cruelness of the world he has lived in."

Due to a past filled with heartache, and living a very solitary existence since his wife passed, Jefferson welcomed the sunshine that Mama and Farm Girl brought into his life. Because they were such an enormous help, he kept them on during the winter months that followed.

Jefferson was kind, helpful, giving, and asked very few questions. With all of those fine qualities, Mama couldn't help but admire and respect him. There were times when Mama and Jefferson would disagree about certain things, especially the way Mama was raising her daughter.

Because they were a mere exchange of opinions, neither would lose their temper nor walk away with hard feelings. Even though he didn't approve, Jefferson respected Mama's right to raise her daughter the way she deemed appropriate. Mama appreciated Jefferson's honest concern.

From the day they were hired, Mama and Farm Girl took care of Jefferson, as if he was their own flesh and blood. As close knit as they had become, however, neither Mama nor Jefferson ever confided in one another. Both were extremely close-mouthed when it came to sharing the deep, dark secrets of their personal lives before they had met. They were very much alike in that respect.

As the months disappeared, like a penny tossed into a well, Jefferson continued to keep Mama and Farm Girl around. They seemed more like family to him, not just hired hands. They had a job with him for as long as they cared to stay.

Furthermore, he requested they refer to him as 'Pappy.' A name he had hoped his own children and grandchildren would have called him. With that dream no longer possible, it warmed the cockles of his heart to have his surrogate family call him such an endearing name.

Jefferson tried every way he could to make Mama and Farm Girl comfortable. Every time he would offer a suggestion to make life a little easier for the two of them, Mama always had her objections.

When Jefferson told Mama of his plans for modernizing his barn, she squelched his ideas.

"Ya don't needs to be spendin' no money on our comfort, Pappy. With all them warm horse blankets and quilts ya give us, me and my daughter's been real cozy out in y'ur barn."

"Mama, before you go jumping to conclusions, I wish you would hear me out."

"Yes, sir, I be sorry. But sayin' what it be ya has to say, ain't gonna change my mind none."

Shaking his head, Jefferson remarked, "God love ya, Mama, but sometimes you can be stubborn as an old mule." She knew he was right. "Now, I have other reasons for wanting to install electricity and plumbing in the barn. I've been thinking how much easier it would be to buy one of those milking machines to milk my cows. Getting down on the little stool, milking them by hand, is getting harder and harder for me.

Also, I've been looking at one of those electric separators. Have you ever seen one?" Keeping her lips sealed, she shook her head. "Well, just like the milking machines, they've been around for years. It's just that I haven't ever had any interest in them before now."

Jefferson played it cool and made sure he didn't mention that any of his plans were to convenience Mama and her daughter. He felt Mama could have no objections if she thought the plans were just for him. Even though he had a right to spend his own money the way he saw fit, he respected her opinion.

"As for the plumbing, it would sure be handier for me to be able to wash up all the milking utensils right there in the barn, instead of hauling them all the way in the house for cleaning. The plumbing won't just give me running water. I can have a small bathroom installed in the barn, too. At my age, the kidneys work overtime. A stool in the barn would sure be more convenient than running to the outhouse when I'm working out there.

Now, if I'm going to go to the trouble of having the barn wired for electricity, then it will be very simple to have a few more electrical outlets installed The older I get, the colder I get. Being able to plug in one of those electric heaters in the barn when the weather is frigid would do well for the old joints. Well, I can see you're just chomping at the bit. So go on, let me hear what's on your mind."

Mama licked her lips. Her mouth was dry. She had to think about everything Jefferson just told her, and take a minute to gather her thoughts. She learned a long time ago, if she listened with a clear mind, she was really hearing what the other person had to say.

From her own experience, she knew if she had thoughts going around in her head as to what she was going to say next, then she wasn't listening to a word the speaker was saying. In that case, the one talking might just as well be speaking to a wall.

"I ain't very smart at math. But it seems to me, spendin' a whole lot a money fur fancy machines to milk six cows be as foolish as buyin' one a them electric dishwarshers when ya just gots a few dishes to warsh. Does ya plan on buyin' more milkin' cows?"

"No, I don't need any more dairy cows. Even with you and Farm Girl helping out, I couldn't handle any more. Say, how do you know milking machinery is so expensive?"

"I done chores in lots a towns and on lots a farms in my years. Befur Farm Girl come along, I was chorin' fur lots a farmers with them fancy machines on their modern farms. Didn't never ask no questions. Cain't help it, though, when I hears people talkin' with me standin' right there in the same area. Reckon a lot a them folks was thinkin' I was too stupid to know what they was talkin' about. But I done learn me a lot, keepin' my ears open and my mouth shut."

"Sometimes you baffle me, Mama. I think maybe you're smarter upstairs in that head of yours than you let on." He didn't get a response. "So, is that all you're concerned about, the money I would spend just to milk six cows?"

"I knows that ain't none a my never mind, but it just don't make no sense to me. Might I ask ya another question?"

"Don't hold back now."

"If'n ya ain't thinkin' these here barn changes be fur makin' me and Farm Girl more comfy like, then why ain't ya done all these fancy changes befur we gots here?"

Jefferson had no suitable answer. Instead, he conceded. As long as Mama and Farm Girl were happy, he discarded his plans, like yesterday's garbage.

Until settling on the Welk farm, somewhere around the age of eleven, Farm Girl had never stayed in one place for such a long time. To her recollection, she and her mother had never been happier. After two years of working for Jefferson Welk, this was like steady employment for Mama.

By living on Jefferson's farm, however, time would bring about a dramatic change in all their lives. Neither Jefferson's goodness nor Mama's protection could keep Farm Girl from the deceit and disaster that the future held.

BOUND FOR GREED

When Frank's four-year hitch was up, he had decided against the U.S. Marine Corps as a full-time career. After making a brief side trip, keeping a promise for a friend, he had returned to Kidwell to live with his parents.

For twenty-six years, Franklin Godfrey Righter had been an only child in the Righter household. With the exception of time spent in the military, an overbearing mother had kept him glued to his parent's farm with no life of his own.

When Darin George was born into the Righter family, the situation for Frank didn't change. Even as a grown man, if Frank dared to disagree with his mother, she browbeat him into the ground with her foul mouth and degrading words. Mrs. Righter tended to be somewhat easier on Darin. The few times when she had scolded him, Darin never paid any attention. To Frank's dismay, Darin always got away with murder when growing up. Because of his aggressive personality, Darin stayed in trouble.

To all who knew both Righter boys, it was obvious that Darin inherited different genes than Frank. The single inherent trait Darin had that Frank lacked was a backbone. There were times that Frank felt Darin went overboard, showing disrespect to almost every person he encountered. Quite unlike the often rude, egotistical personality of Darin, Frank was a gentle person. He was soft spoken, humble, and honest. Mild mannered Frank almost envied Darin for speaking his mind and for doing what he wanted.

Mr. and Mrs. Righter died in a car accident just before Christmas. Darin was fifteen at the time. Due to Darin's age, Frank had become his sole caretaker. This had been agreeable for them both. Having been around since the day Darin was born, Frank loved Darin. Because of his mother's constant interference, Frank had never been able to show his true affection. Now he could.

Darin relished the idea of spineless Frank being his guardian. This allowed Darin to get away with more of his antics.

After his parent's death, Frank had remained on the homestead, farming. Most of the work, he had done by himself. More aggressive than Frank, ambitious Darin wanted nothing to do with farm work.

Though excellent in schoolwork, graduating from high school just before he turned sixteen, Darin had a wild hair and had always enjoyed raising Cain, both in and out of school. Darin had gone from a mouthy, petty-thief kid into a conniving, law-breaking young adult.

Because of his pleasing personality, Frank was very likeable. He was easy to look at, but shied away from women most of his life due to his inferiority complex. As young as Darin was, his girlfriends far outnumbered the girls Frank had met in his entire lifetime.

In facial features, Darin didn't resemble either of his parents. However, he did have his mother's golden skin tone. His natural wavy, chocolate brown hair, that he combed straight back, highlighted his cold, deep brown eyes. Darin never looked at a person. He looked through them.

Since he wasn't a physical type, Darin went through life trying to get by on his good looks, intelligence, lies, and cunning ways. He was unwavering in his convictions that he would some day live like a millionaire, not a farmer.

Darin knew almost everyone in Kidwell, the town they lived in. Most everyone knew him, too, especially the local Police Chief, Lincoln "Rusty" Simmons.

Rusty's younger brother, Stu, was Frank's closest friend all through elementary and high school. Following in Rusty's footsteps, Stu and Frank had joined the U.S. Marine Corps at the same time. A tragic accident took Stu's life, two days before he was to return home. Stu's death bonded Frank and Rusty's friendship, which kept them in constant contact by mail.

When Rusty had retired from the Corps, he had returned to his home in Kidwell. Missing the wearing of a uniform, that's when Rusty joined the town's nine-man law enforcement team.

Because of the bond between Rusty and Frank, Rusty had tried to be lenient with Darin when it came to enforcing the law. Whenever

Darin had gotten into trouble, Rusty took him home instead of arresting him or locking him up in the local jail.

Mischievous shenanigans became a constant game with Darin even after Rusty became the chief of police. Insistent on trouble making, Darin had tried to find out how many times he could get away with pulling pranks on people and stealing inexpensive items from local stores without getting caught. The game had always been quite amusing to him.

Since Rusty hadn't arrested him, Darin felt he could get away with almost anything. At that time and for no special reason, Darin didn't dislike Rusty. He just didn't like authority figures.

During his last year in high school, Darin took his games too far. When Rusty had no choice but to arrest and book him, twice, Darin's dislike for Rusty turned into hate.

At the age of sixteen, after graduating from high school, Darin went on to further his education. He could have lived at home and gone to a college much closer to Kidwell, but that would not do. Not for 'get-my-way' Darin.

PRESENT

After three full years of a tough scholastic schedule, including summer classes, Darin received his college degree. Still hating farm life, he did not want to live at home. Lack of funds to live a life he felt he deserved, forced him to do so. Living with Frank on the farm was necessary until he could get a job and afford to make other arrangements.

For a short time, unemployed Darin was either out and about town, drinking and carousing, or sitting around the house drinking beer and smoking cigarettes. He never bothered to lift a hand to help Frank. Easy going Frank didn't mind. Money was never an issue.

Knowing how rumors spread in their small farming community, Frank felt his finances were his own private business. Because of this, he didn't bank in Sharpin where most of the local county citizens banked. He belonged to a savings and trust association located in another county.

Unaware of Frank's true financial status, all Darin cared about was that Frank made sure he had money for his drinking and smoking habits, clothes, and anything else he needed or wanted. Like everyone else in his life, Darin used Frank for his own personal gains.

In March, nine months after college graduation, an employment ad in the <u>Want Ads</u> section of the local newspaper caught his eye. He was not thrilled about going to work, but he believed this job offering could be his first step to getting off the farm.

As if the job was already his, Darin began planning. "Sharpin's about twenty miles from here, if I use the back road shortcut. That's not so bad. Until I have enough money saved to get out on my own, I could drive it back and forth from here. I'll hit Frank up for expense money. Then I'll ask if I can have his car. Poor, spineless Frank never says no to me."

Slouching down in his chair with his stocking feet propped on the seat of another chair, Darin fiddled with the newspaper. "What the hell am I thinking? Just because Frank buys a new car every year, doesn't mean I want to be seen driving an old-man-type car. Man, why can't he have better taste and buy something hot, like a Camero? Now that's class. Wishful thinking, Darin. Well crap, wheels are wheels when you need transportation.

Me, a bookkeeper in a bank. I'm as thrilled as polar bear in a steam bath. I didn't go to college and get a friggin' accounting degree just to work in a stinking farmer's bank. Not me. I have different plans for using my accounting skills."

Darin was still sitting at the table, drinking his second cup of morning coffee when Frank entered the backdoor and walked into the kitchen.

"Hey, sleepy-head, how's the coffee?"

Darin sat straight and placed his feet square on the floor. "Strong, as usual."

Getting his favorite mug, Frank filled it to the brim. Then he joined Darin at the small, rectangle table. "I didn't have a chance to read the paper this morning. The delivery was late. Anything new going on in town?"

"Not in Kidwell. Sharpin has an ad for a bank job. I'm thinking about submitting my application."

"What kind of job is it?"

"I'm not quite sure. All the ad says is that they have a position in their accounting department working with a loan officer. Since I don't know much about banking, I'll just have to wait and see."

After taking a drink of coffee, Frank questioned the uncertainty in Darin's voice. "You said you were thinking about submitting an application. Isn't that the kind of job you're looking for?"

Darin tore the ad out of the paper. "Yeah, I guess it's better than nothing."

"You don't sound very excited. What's the problem?"

"There are a few drawbacks to applying for this job. Or any other job, as far as that goes."

"Like what?"

"Transportation, for one."

"That's no problem. You can drive my car, like you've been doing. Heck, I use my pickup for just about everything and anything anymore. If you're not driving it, the car just sits around collecting dust," Frank admitted.

"That's true." *Cheapskate. You buy yourself two new vehicles, every year. Why in the hell don't you offer to buy me a set of wheels?*

"Okay, that settles that small dilemma," Frank said with a grin.

"As much as I appreciate the offer, I still don't know if I should check out this job, or not."

"Why? I thought accounting is what you earned your degree in."

"It's not my education that I'm worried about. It's my clothes."

"What's the matter with your clothes?" Frank wasn't upset, but he didn't understand Darin's comment. "I pay more for one shirt for you than I pay for three shirts for myself."

"I'm not complaining about the clothes I have. I just don't think my college garb is what bank employees wear, even in a small town."

"Oh, I see what you mean. Well, again, that's not a problem. If you really want the job, go for it. Then, if they hire you, we'll go to Omaha or Lincoln and buy you some new duds. How's that?"

"Sure. Hey, not to change the subject, but what ever happened to that dopey kid from across the road that was always hanging around here?"

Taken aback, Frank asked, "What on earth made you think of him?"

"Clothes. You were always giving him the clothes I grew out of, or buying him new ones. You haven't mentioned one word about him since I've been home. Not that I miss the leachy screwball."

"Darin, that's no way to talk. Henry was a good kid. I enjoyed his company."

"That's an understatement. Every time he was around, you treated him as if he was part of our family."

Frank shook his head. "I never did understand, since you two were the same age, why you couldn't have been nicer to him. To tell you the truth, I miss Henry."

"You would," Darin said with a smirk. "Damn, I use to get so pissed off. It seemed, everywhere you took me, he had to tag along. If I remember correctly, the folks didn't like him hanging around here, either. So, what happened to him?"

"His parents sold the farm and they moved out of state. Now, if you don't mind, I don't care to sit and talk about him. Henry was just a kid I enjoyed doing things with and for. He's gone and that's all there is to it."

* * *

At First People's Bank of Sharpin, Loan Officer Dodd just finished interviewing Darin.

"Darin, if you don't mind waiting for a few minutes, I'd like to take your application in to Mr. Shomond's office."

"No, I don't mind, but who's this guy Shomond?"

"That's Mr. Shomond," Dodd stated with authority. "Mr. C.D. Shomond is the bank's president. If you happen to get hired, it would be to your benefit to always mention his name with respect."

"Yeah, sure."

When Dodd left his cubbyhole office, Darin followed. Out of idle curiosity, Darin wandered around the bank.

* * *

"I'm a little concerned about this young man. He's barely nineteen. Might have an accounting degree, but the young man has no work experience. Do you think he's what we're looking for?"

"Yes, I do. I believe his age and inexperience are to our advantage."

Puzzled, C.D. said, "You lost me there."

"If we hire someone who is set in his own way of doing things, Mr. Shomond, then I'll have one heck of a time trying to train him to do things our way. Don't you remember the problems we had with Lyle Sole?"

C.D. sat back and thought for a minute. "Yes, I do recall Lyle. We had to let him go because he refused to follow orders."

"That's correct, sir. He was so set in his ways from the last financial institution employment, he was causing us more trouble than he was worth."

"Yes, I see what you mean. Okay, you have my approval with one stipulation."

"And that is?" Dodd asked.

"Place him on a thirty-day probation period. If he pans out as an asset, then we can offer him a permanent position."

Getting to his feet, Dodd thanked Shomand then left his office. As he headed back to his own domain, he spotted Darin talking and laughing with a female teller. Catching the teller's eye, Dodd motioned her to send Darin back to his office.

No sooner did Dodd sit at his desk than Darin entered the cubby. "What's the verdict?" Darin asked, reoccupying the chair he had left a short time ago.

"We would like to offer you the position, Darin, but you'll be placed on a thirty-day probation period. At the end of that time, your work will be reviewed. If you've proved able to handle the responsibilities, you will then be given a permanent position."

Darin's cockiness showed through in flying colors. "I guess that means I'll be working here permanently. I can guarantee, I'll be your top employee before you can cross those thirty days off your desk calendar."

"Then, you accept the position?"

Shit, didn't I just say that? This guy is sure dense for a loan officer. "Yes, Mr. Dodd, I accept."

"Out of sheer curiosity, I find it rather unusual you've never been in a bank before today. Might I ask why?"

"You misunderstood me. I've been in banks before, just not this one. Never had any need to."

"I see. Well, Darin, I've already briefed you on the work schedule and what the job pays. One thing I forgot to mention and that's our dress code. We're not terribly formal around here, so a suit and tie isn't required. A nice shirt, slacks and a sports coat will be sufficient. On Fridays and Saturdays, we dress casual, within reason. That means, don't show up in shorts or something inappropriate on those days."

"I won't be able to go clothes shopping until the weekend," Darin said.

"That's fine. What you're wearing will be suitable until then. Do you have any questions you'd like to ask me?"

"When do I start?"

Dodd stood and stretched his hand across the desk. Instead of answering Darin's question, he stated, "Welcome to First People's Bank of Sharpin."

Getting to his feet, Darin grasped the hand of his new boss in a firm handshake. "Thank you, Mr. Dodd."

"I won't expect you to start work today. But if you'll come with me, I'll show you around and introduce you to your new co-workers."

As he walked out of his office, Darin was on his heels. "Where will I be working?"

"In a cubby next to mine. We weren't expecting to find an employee so soon. Right now, your office space is being used for storage. I'll have it cleaned out this evening and it will be ready for you to move in at 7:30, tomorrow morning."

"Oh, that's great." *Damn, nothing like having my boss lurking over my shoulder all day long. I don't think I'm going to like that, one bit.*

"By the way, Darin, it's obvious you're a nice looking young man, and single."

Now walking along side Dodd, Darin teased his new boss. "Thanks, but you're not my type." When Dodd gave him a look of apprehension, Darin was quick to explain. "Sorry, Mr. Dodd. That was supposed to be a joke."

"I should hope so."

Doesn't anybody have a sense of humor anymore? "What did you mean by your comment?"

"We are all very cordial around here, Darin. However, taking time away from your office duties to fraternize with our single female employees is one sure way to collect bad marks on your job review. Don't get me wrong. We don't have strict rules like the banks do in the big cities. What you do on your own time is your business. But, while you're employed here, your time is our business. Understand?"

"You bet." *Spoil sport. Not to worry, Darin, you'll find a way to get around their stupid rules.*

Proving once again that he could get away with breaking any rules he felt like defying, it didn't take Darin long after he started his job to start flirting with his fellow female employees. He was careful not to let Dodd or Shomond catch him. Brown-nosing the bank's president, and conning the rest of the bank's employees, Darin had everyone eating out of his hand in no time. Going out of his way to assist co-workers, and laying on flattery so thick it almost gagged him, Darin became the bank's pride and joy—the frosting on a richly decorated cake.

Most times after work, Darin hung out at Sharpin or Kidwell's local bars with a beer in his hand and a great looking woman on his arm. To his new group of barfly friends, and some old ones from high school days, Darin was a big spender. Cash in Darin's pocket didn't last for more than a couple rounds of drinks for his drinking buddies. When the money was gone, Darin ran bar tabs.

Fun loving, and the life of the party, almost everyone who knew Darin on a social basis, loved him. However, no one knew the true Darin or what made him tick. Not even Frank.

Spending money like it was water pouring out of an open faucet, Darin's paychecks were gone within a few days after he received them. He kept borrowing money from Frank to pay his bar bills. Then he would start charging again. Frank never considered the monies he gave Darin as loans. As long as Darin needed money, Frank dished it out.

All too soon, Darin became bored and apprehensive about his future. Feeling trapped, and going nowhere, he needed to figure out some way of obtaining more money—fast.

Sitting at his desk and daydreaming about his miserable life, Darin could hear voices coming through the thin walls that divided Dodd's and his cubicles. Concentrating on his job while at his desk, Darin had never realized, nor ever cared before now that he could eavesdrop. Sliding his chair closer to the wall, he could hear Dodd speaking with another man. Darin picked up in the middle of their conversation.

"… that way, I don't have to pay taxes on it," a man's voice stated.

"I don't think that's wise," Dodd commented. "Keeping so much money hidden at home is just asking for trouble."

"When was the last time you heard of a house robbery in this county?" The man laughed. "Hell, I don't know about you, but we still leave our doors unlocked."

Not only did Darin's ears perk up, his eyes lit up as well. *That guy's bragging about keeping money stashed at home and leaving his door unlocked? What a birdbrain. Come to think of it, Frank does the same thing, most of the time. If the guy's right about others doing the same thing, then I wonder how many of those 'others' also keep cash hidden at home. If I play my cards right, that could be what I'm looking for to get me a one-way ticket out of Nebraska.*

"You've got a point there," Dodd remarked, "even if I still don't agree with you. However, it's your money."

When Darin heard the unfamiliar voice say, "Well, I've taken up enough of your time. Time to head back home," he was quick to slid his chair back to his desk.

Dodd's visitor would not have to pass in front of Darin's door when he exited Dodd's office. However, Darin wanted to make sure he looked engrossed in his work, should Dodd decide to pop in on him. Devious Darin could not wait to put his moneymaking plan into motion.

At quitting time, he stopped by to chat with Dodd. Rapping on the wall, as he stood in the open doorway, Darin asked, "Mr. Dodd, may I speak to you for a minute?"

Looking up from his deskwork, Dodd nodded. "Sure, Darin, come on in." Darin walked into the office and stood in front of Dodd's desk. "Have a seat."

"No, that's okay, sir. I just want to ask you a quick question."

"What's on your mind?"

"I'd like permission to move my office around."

Dodd tilted his head. "Move it around?"

"Yes, sir. You know how it is working with numbers all day, sometimes your eyes get crossed." Dodd smiled. "Right now, the way my desk is situated, I'm in a shadow. That doesn't help me do my work when I have to keep straining my eyes due to lack of light."

"I understand that. Have you thought about a desk lamp, like I use? I can write a requisition to order one for you."

Darin had to think fast on his feet. "No, that won't be necessary. I figured out that I can move my desk so the light from the above window will rest directly on my work."

Dodd looked up to the small window that sat close to the ceiling in his space. "You're kidding. Those little windows don't bring in enough daylight for desk work, no matter where you place your desk."

"Oh, but they do. I've been testing different areas of light in my room throughout the day. I would like to give it a shot, if you don't mind?"

"Sure, why not. Just one thing, you'll have to move things around on your own time."

"Yes, sir, and thank you."

As Darin was leaving the office, Dodd said, "Oh, Darin, one other thing."

Turning, Darin replied, "Yes?"

"How ever you rearrange your office, just make sure you keep your face to the walkthrough, at all times. With all the accounting projects you're working on, we wouldn't want anyone sneaking up behind you and looking over your shoulder."

"No, sir. I mean, yes, I will."

Overjoyed that Dodd walked right into the scheme of things, Darin rearranged his office before he left for the day. The way he placed his desk, he had his back just inches from the separation wall. Now, he would be able to hear any conversation that went on in Dodd's office without anyone suspecting he was eavesdropping, not working.

Trying to figure out a pattern, if there was one, Darin started recording information he felt was crucial to his plan. He always had some good excuse for passing by Dodd's cubical doorway so he could glance in and see the visitor's face. Being a quick study, Darin never forgot a face. Most people he saw visiting Dodd, he recognized as customers of the bank.

If the visitors were Dodd's friends, and not bank customers, Darin would get Dodd in a casual conversation. Then he would mention he had seen "Oh, what's his name?" stop in for a visit, again. The unsuspecting Dodd would naturally volunteer his visitor's name, thinking Darin knew the party but he just could not recall the name at that instant.

Utilizing the fact that he had become a fair-haired trusted employee, Darin snooped through bank files, getting addresses and financial information on the people that interested him. Any person that mentioned keeping money hidden at home, in lieu of keeping it in a bank account, had their vital information recorded in Darin's notebook.

At times, laughing under his breath, Darin's thoughts spoke out to him. *Idiots. They must think Dodd is a damn Priest or something the way they confide in him about their private stash. If they only knew these walls can talk, they'd think twice before confessing their stupidity to Dodd in his office.*

Staying ahead of his bookkeeping job, Darin started offering more of his services to Dodd. As the bank's only lone officer, Dodd was delighted to get the extra help, which made his job a little easier. He was especially impressed that Darin wanted to improve his position by learning more about the bank's business.

Darin revealed his accomplishments.

"Everyone at the bank has been easy enough to con, and in a short time. Suckers. They're all ignorant, just like everyone else that lives in these stupid, small, farming communities. That's why they're living here. Well, they can all frigging rot here. Not me. Not Darin George Righter. That's why I'm getting the hell out of here. I'll walk over anyone I have to, to do so."

PUTTING A SCHEME IN ACTION

Sitting at his desk, Darin's thoughts blurred his vision as he stared down at his accounting figures. The numbers seemed to run into one large, black blob. As he bounced the pencil's eraser on the desk with nervous energy, he continued conniving.

How am I going to accomplish my goal? I know I could change a few numbers on the accounts I take care of, but embezzling isn't my bag. Too easy to make a friggin' mistake and get caught. However, I need money. If I can make some fast bucks using my brain, I can get as far away from small town U.S.A., as I can get.

From everything I've read, New York is where the action is. It's for damn sure, this guy wants to be in on the action. Money is that one vital ingredient holding me back. Making an honest living will never get me what I want. And all this stupid information I've been collecting, hasn't done me one damn bit of good. Unless—That's it! I have to make my move. It's now or never.

Since Darin had the confidence of everyone at the bank, especially Mr. Dodd, he started asking questions about business. Then he got into a casual, 'buddy-buddy' conversation. His first such inquiry put all of his thoughts into motions.

"Mr. Dodd, I heard from an old friend the other day. He told me the Schmikel's are going on a vacation. Rumor is, they're leaving tomorrow." In total ignorance that Darin was searching for detailed information in regards to his eavesdropping, Dodd nodded. Receiving confirmation, Darin asked, "I think that's great. Do you know how long they'll be gone?"

Once Darin got his answer, he thought out his first plan of attack.

It seemed like a tradition that many of the local men between ages thirty and sixty, married or not, and those that didn't have anything else to do, got together in their own individual groups on Friday nights to play cards. Frank belonged to one of those groups. He and his friends took turns, each week, hosting the card games.

On the Friday evenings that Frank left the house to join his poker-playing friends, he always let Darin know exactly where he would be. Darin made it a point to call and check in with him before heading off to bed. This was one phone call that Frank always depended on.

Knowing that Darin spent Monday through Thursday, and practically every Saturday night out drinking at one of the local bars, Frank found solitude in Darin staying home on Friday nights to rest. Since Darin could count on Frank's Friday night card games like clockwork, just as Frank could count on Darin staying home, this would be Darin's perfect alibi.

Just three days after finding out how long the Schmikel's would be on vacation, Friday night came. After confirming that Frank would be keeping his usual poker night schedule, Darin had the perfect opportunity for putting his plan into action.

It's rather ironic that this is my sixth-month anniversary at the bank. What better way to celebrate? This will be even better than my twentieth birthday celebration at the bar a few months ago.

In order to keep Frank from being suspicious, Darin kept to his Friday night routine. He dressed in his usual around-the-house garb of faded blue jeans and sweatshirt. After opening a cold beer and lighting a cigarette, he sprawled out on the couch in front of the television. The huge difference between this night and other Friday nights was Darin's impatience, waiting for Frank to leave the house for the evening.

After Frank was gone for well over an hour, Darin telephoned him. "Frank, I didn't mean to take you away from your game. Are you winning?"

Laughing, Frank admitted, "Heck no. I think I'm down ten peanuts."

"Well, if you win them back, don't eat up all of your profits."

"That's rather a salty joke."

Each of them had a good laugh over their far from intelligent comments.

"Well, Frank, I'm just making my usual check-in with you. I wanted you to know I'm heading for bed."

"It's a might early, Darin. You sick?"

"Nope, I feel great. It's just a lousy night for TV. So, thought I'd hit the hay. You know me, I turn in early, every so often, to catch up on my beauty sleep."

"Not this early."

After giving a rather loud, fake yawn into the mouthpiece of the telephone, Darin said, "Oh, sorry about that. I'm pooped."

"Okay, Darin, I'll try not to wake you when I get home. See you in the morning."

To Frank, this didn't appear as an unusual telephone call. Darin had often called him at his poker games for the same reason. This was Darin's way of letting Frank know to be extra quiet when he got home and not disturb Darin's sleep. Since he had assured Frank that he was not sick, Frank was quick to put the earliness of the call out of his mind.

His poker buddies, however, loved to razz him.

"Damn, Frank, one would think you're Darin's old man," one man stated in jest.

"I guess I'm old enough to fit the bill," Frank responded with laughter, slapping the shoulder of the man next to him.

"Yeah? Okay, Daddy, deal the cards before it's my bedtime," another man joked.

Laughing at the teasing and ribbing from the guys, Frank admitted, "Go right ahead and poke fun all you want, you pirates. I missed the scamp when he was away at college. So I feel rather good about him checking in with me." Poor unassuming, gullible Frank fell for Darin's line of bull: hook, line and spinner bait.

It was a clear September night. A frigid, artic front had swept away the summer heat. Darin carefully planed and followed through with every move he made to be sure he covered all his tracks. Being older now, this was not one of those teenage pranks he used to pull. This was a game in the big league.

Once Darin was inside the Schmikel house, he searched through everything he could think of, looking for money. Each time he rummaged through a drawer or a cupboard, he took great care in putting things back, exactly as he had found them. Then, he hit pay dirt. As he counted out his discovery, he said, "Five hundred big ones. Not what I was hoping for, but not too shabby of a start. At least the night isn't a total wash."

At home, Darin undressed then crawled into bed. Thinking about his next caper, he heard Frank cough. This was a clear sign that Frank had come home. Closing his eyes, Darin pretended to be in a sound sleep.

As he had done since Darin was a baby, Frank opened Darin's door to check on him. When he saw Darin sleeping, he closed the door and went to his own room.

"Perfect," Darin whispered. "Good night, Frank. Thanks for my alibi."

FINDING A GOOD HOME

BACK IN TIME

With all the property Jefferson owned, he preferred to pasture his cows in the meadow closest to the main yard. This pasture was barbwire fenced on three sides to keep the cows out of crops. An abundance of trees lined the fourth side.

On a hot summer day in mid-July, Farm Girl and Mama were in the pasture doing a typical late afternoon chore. They were to locate the grazing cows in order to walk them home for milking. As they walked through the open field of prairie grass and weeds, they conversed.

"I won't be helpin' with the milkin' when we gits back."

"Why not, Mama?"

"While I was checkin' eggs this mornin'—Watch where y'ur steppin', child." With a quick downward look, Farm Girl leaped over a cow pie. Mama kept right on talking, as if the interruption never happened. "The lamp went out. I went to git a fresh bulb, but was sidewangled by Pappy. He was needin' me to sew a button on his shirt."

"Since ya was busy, why he wasn't askin' me to do it? He knows I can sew on buttons."

"Fur the simple reason ya wasn't there when he was needin' it done, and I was."

"Oh."

Keeping in step with Mama, Farm Girl bent over and grabbed at a long stem of prairie grass as she walked by. Breaking it off in her hand, she placed the broken end in her mouth and began to bite on it.

"When I was done with the shirt button, I done furgot about the light bulb and them eggs."

"When do I git to start helpin' ya inspect them eggs again?"

"When ya be old enough to tell between the chick egg and the eatin' egg."

"I 'member. Ya holds up the egg to the light sos ya can see inside the shell. If'n there be a dark spot inside, then that be a chick egg. I knows I can do that. Ain't I thirteen now?"

"Last time I let ya help me, I was endin' up with far too many a them chick eggs. I'd be makin' Pappy plum unhappy if'n I'd fry up them bloody little membranes fur his breakfast. 'Sides, y'ur age don't gots nothin' to do with egg checkin'."

"But that was a long time ago when I was a little girl. I be a woman now."

Holding the temptation to smile, Mama shook her head. "No, child, bein' thirteen don't mean ya be a woman."

"I think it's purdy silly that I can drives a tractor, but I ain't old enough to inspect no stupid hen's eggs."

Before Mama had a come back, they approached the area where the cows were grazing. The conversation about inspecting eggs had to be put aside until the cows were rounded up.

When Farm Girl and Mama first arrived at Jefferson's farm, Farm Girl couldn't count. Along with the A, B, C's, Jefferson had been teaching her to count from one to one hundred.

To practice, Farm Girl always made a game of counting everything she saw when there were two or more of the same object. Each time she gathered eggs from the hen house, she counted how many eggs she collected. To her, counting was fun. Even though she knew exactly how many cows Jefferson had, she counted them just for practice.

As they walked in a slow pace to the side of the cows, Farm Girl discovered a problem. "Mama!" she shouted in a panic, spitting the stem of prairie grass from her mouth.

Grabbing Farm Girl's arm, Mama came to a dead stop. It was only natural that Farm Girl didn't take another step, either. "Hush, child," Mama warned in a low voice. To be sure her daughter's shouting hadn't scared the cows into bolting, Mama kept her eyes on them. "Ya knows better than to be hollerin' out like that."

"I'm sorry."

"Well, stop and think next time."

"Yes, ma'am."

The shouting hadn't frightened the cows into a run, but it did start them moving. Mama and Farm Girl made sure they had the cows walking in the right direction.

"So, what was all that yellin' about?"

"There be just five cows here."

Since she hadn't paid much attention, assuming all were together, Mama made a quick count. "Ya be right. Well, no need to panic like ya did. It ain't unusual fur one to go strayin' off on its own. Take these cows on home to the barn. I'll go on up the pasture and search fur the missin' one. She cain't be too far away."

Farm Girl spotted the stray. "Wait, Mama." The cow was grazing right at the division of the pasture and the wooded area. She pointed in the stray's direction. "Look up there by them trees."

Looking in the area her daughter was pointing, Mama nodded. "So there she be."

"We must a went right past her befur. Wonder why we wasn't seein' her there?"

"No doubt 'cause we was too busy chewin' the fat," Mama explained. "Since I don't has to go searchin' fur her now, go after the stray and bring her on home. I'll herd these others on in."

"Okay," Farm Girl replied.

"'Member child, ya knows better than to run her sos she don't lose her milk, but don'tcha be lollygaggin' neither."

"Yes, Mama. I won't."

Mama continued walking behind the small herd to keep them moving.

Thinking about what to do, Farm Girl took her time as she headed toward the stray. Her decision was to get in front of the cow in order to get her moving back toward the pasture. Farm Girl headed into the small forest. Fearful of making any noise from the scrunching of twigs and leaves beneath her feet, she took one small step at a time.

As she walked through a portion of the wooded area, glancing to her side from time to time, something caught her eye. There appeared to be a small building sitting in the distance, blending into the landscape.

She turned and walked in the direction of the structure to get a closer look. When she came to a wide clearing, she stopped. "It be a house down there by the river. And this big ole space without no trees must be the road to git there. I wonder if'n that's the same river runnin' behind Pappy's garage-barn? Crimeny, I wonder if these here grounds belongs to Pappy?"

Curiosity was killing her. She felt a desperate need to investigate the house from a much closer distance, but she didn't dare take the chance. Farm Girl's thoughts danced about in her head as she mumbled, "I need to be askin' Pappy about that house. If'n he says no one lives there, then I needs to know how to git back here again to take me a closer look-see."

Focusing on the ground, she looked for small, broken tree branches. Making a carrier out of her apron, she held the apron with one hand and gathered twigs with the other. Following the road in the direction of the pasture, she came to a pile of brush and limbs.

The barricade blocked the path to the open field. She had to make her way around them. Crisscrossing around some of the trees, she returned to the pasture just a few feet away from where the cow was still grazing.

In a lazy manner, the cow lifted her head. With her big brown eyes, she looked directly at Farm Girl. Obviously content, she went back to indulging in her prairie fodder.

Since the cow seemed to be satisfied where she was grazing, Farm Girl scampered back along the front of the trees. She didn't stop until she saw the pile of branches and brush that had stopped her from exiting the forest from the large clearing.

Dropping the bottom of her apron allowed the twigs to go tumbling to the ground. "There. Now, just in case I gits to come back here again to git me a better look-see a that house, them sticks will tell me where the trail be hiddin'."

Brushing the debris from her apron, she walked back to the cow. Turning the cow with care, Farm Girl urged the female bovine to walk back into the middle of the pasture, heading her toward home. As she walked along side, Farm Girl kept her hand pressed against the cow's side.

After milking chores were completed, Jefferson was in the barn pitching straw. Farm Girl asked if that was his property that went from the pasture, through the woods, and down to the river.

"Yes, child. I own every bit of that land with the exception of the river rights. Why?"

"I was in them woods, earlier, tryin' to git y'ur stray to turn back home," Farm Girl informed.

"You did a good job. But I told you that already."

"I knows." Farm Girl scratched her head. Wanting Jefferson to hurry and finish, she started getting fidgety. She wanted his undivided attention. "Ain't that enough straw fur now?"

"Almost," he answered, swinging the pitchfork, tossing more straw onto the wooden planked floor.

"Why don'tcha let me finish that sos ya can sit a spell. I gots somethin' awful important to talk about."

"No, child, I'm almost done. I can work and talk at the same time, just like we're doing. What's so important?"

"When I was in them woods today, I saw me somethin' strange. There was this house sittin' there at the end a the trees. It was right next to the river. So, if'n that's y'ur grounds, then that must be y'ur house, right?"

"I haven't been down in that lower area since the last time I visited my wife's grave." Jefferson leaned the pitchfork against the barn. Pulling his red kerchief from the side pocket of his overalls, he removed his straw hat. He wiped the perspiration from his face then from the inside of his hat.

"You must be talking about that small shanty my granddaddy built over a hundred years ago." Farm Girl was listening, but her mind was turning circles. "Time and the weather have taken their toll on the old place. Granddaddy cut down trees and built a solid structure with the logs, boards and large riverbed rocks that he had available at the time."

It was very clear to him that Farm Girl had been some place he didn't want her to be. "I made a barricade to hide the road's entrance, rather hoping you or Mama would never discover that area of my property. But, now you have."

His normal pleasing voice turned harsh. As he spoke, he shoved the kerchief back into his pocket and put his hat back on his head. "I want you to hear me good, child. You stay away from that place," he warned. "As you are well aware of, child, it's not normal for me to issue demands, but that's an order."

For the moment, Farm Girl ignored his mood change and his harsh words. In her childish mind that seemed to sway back forth like a leaf in a windstorm, something else took immediate precedence over her interest in the small house.

"What's a granddaddy?"

"That was the daddy of my daddy."

"The daddy a y'ur daddy? Holy cattails! Does ya knows the daddy a y'ur daddy?"

"Sure did, honey," he answered, starting to feel a bit melancholy. The harshness left his voice as he spoke with tenderness of a few memorable thoughts. "My daddy was born in that small house, and so was I. To my recollection, I was close to six when I helped my granddaddy dig that old well, out behind the shack."

For one brief moment, Jefferson closed his eyes to relish the fond memory of helping his grandfather.

"Pappy, do y'ur granddaddy still lives there?"

Opening his eyes, Jefferson leaned against the barn next to the pitchfork and crossed his arms. "No, he no longer lives there. No one does."

"Wow, ya sure be lucky to has ya both a daddy and a granddaddy. I don't even gots me one daddy. Where be them now?"

Jefferson's cherished memory vanished when he felt a sudden sharp pain. His eyes popped wide as he clutched his chest, trying to take slow, deep breaths. His heart seemed to pound so hard, he felt like a pressure cooker inside him was ready to blow. Beads of perspiration formed on his forehead.

His hands turned clammy. On the floor next to him sat a bale of straw. Feeling as if he had legs like gelatin, he plopped down on the bale. Remembering the tragedy that took place near the old shack when he was a mere child was more than he could bear.

Not knowing what to do, Farm Girl asked, "Be y'ur heart botherin' ya again? Does ya want me to run and fetch Mama?"

"No, honey, I'll be fine. Don't you go and worry your pretty little head about my heart."

"Does ya want me to bring ya a drink a wader?"

"No. I just want to sit here for a few minutes."

As she stood in silence, Farm Girl kept an eyeful watch on Jefferson

When his pain subsided, he started conversing again. "You know, child, all the kinsfolk I ever had are all gone now. My immediate family is buried under that giant oak tree down by my granddaddy's old house. Did you see the tree I'm speaking of?"

"I doesn't think so. I was just lookin' at the house and wonderin' who be livin' there."

Reminiscing about his past was not the least bit pleasant for Jefferson. No matter how hard he tried to hold on to the warm and loving thoughts, they fleeted in a hurry. The horrible memories always took over.

Once again, there was harshness in the tone of his voice. "No more talk now about the past. Yesterday is gone. It's wise to leave old memories buried with the dead.

Now, as soon as I rest up a bit, I need to finish up here. Dinner will be ready before long. Which reminds me, you better scat now and go help your mama."

Many times Farm Girl's one-track mind guided her mouth. It was even more prevalent now, since the small house in question sounded like a dream come true. Paying no attention to what Jefferson said, she asked, "Wouldja let me and Mama live there?"

With more of a statement than a question, he bellowed, "What!"

"I wants to know if'n me and Mama can live—"

"Yes, I heard you the first time. Child, why you and your mama would want to live in a colored man's rundown shack like that one, especially with no electricity or running water, is beyond me," he stated, shaking his head and gritting his teeth.

She plunked herself down on the straw-laden floor right in front of Jefferson. Looking up at him, she explained what was going on in her head. "I was havin' me one a them light bulb moments ya always be talkin' about.

See, it ain't gonna make no never mind that y'ur granddaddy's shack be old, since we be already sleepin' in y'ur old barn. And no ecletic'risity ain't gonna bother us none, just like it don't bother us in y'ur barn. And ya knows ya gots plenty more a them kerosene lamps in that old storage shed a y'urs doin' nothin' but collectin' dust and spider webs. So, if'n ya be agreein', we can use one or two a them fur evenin' light.

And, and ... " filled with excitement, she stopped talking just long enough to take a quick breath, " we'd git wader from y'ur granddaddy's wader-well fur drinkin' and cookin', and, well, we won't use much. We'd still use the wader from the river fur bathin'. And—"

"No!" he growled before she could finish explaining her idea. "Besides the fact that the well is sure to be dry by now, I don't want to hear any more of your nonsense. This subject is closed."

Before now, Jefferson had never raised his voice at Farm Girl. Convincing herself that he was just overheated from too much sun, she decided to dismiss his change in demeanor. Rising to her feet, she patted him on his thigh. "That's okay, Pappy. Maybe when ya gits back in the house where it ain't so hot, ya won't be so grumpy."

"I'll have you know—" Farm Girl ran off before he could defend himself. He didn't feel like yelling after her.

Running toward the house, Farm Girl was grinning ear to ear. A few years earlier, before she ever experienced the sight of the inside of a house, she was always content when she and Mama had a barn for their living comfort. Now, the idea of her and Mama living in a house just like everyone else she had known, filled her with joy. She was determined to make that happen.

While Jefferson was not around, Farm Girl told Mama about the empty house and her idea. As she tried to convince her mother, she left out one very important factor.

"Don't it sound super, Mama? Won'tcha please come with me to see it?"

"If'n it's Pappy's grounds, we needs to ask him first."

"We didn't ask when we was diggin' in his shed last year fur another kerosene lamp to use. Or when we gots us some extra gunnysacks fur coverin' the straw to sleep on."

"Mind y'ur mouth with me, child."

"I sure don't mean to sass, Mama, but Pappy wasn't upset with us when we told him what we done. He told us," she tried changing her voice as to impersonate Mr. Welk, "I want you two to feel at home here."

"Stop that."

Ignoring the order, Farm Girl kept up with her mimicking. "Feel free to go into any of my buildings anytime, and get anything you need."

"Okay, it's not funny anymore. Stop befur Pappy comes upon us and thinks ya be makin' fun a him."

"I ain't makin' fun a Pappy. I was just tryin' to be funny."

"I know, child, but whatcha be doin' be the same as makin' fun a the way someone speaks."

"I'm sorry. I won't do it no more. But now does ya see that we already has his okay to go take a look-see at his granddaddy's shack?"

Farm Girl was hoping Mama would hurry and give her a positive answer, so she could uncross her fingers behind her back.

"I reckon ya be right. I'll go if'n ya gits that silly notion out a y'ur head about livin' there. We'll just go look at it to satisfy that long nose a y'urs."

"Oh, sure, Mama."

Once evening chores were completed, Farm Girl took Mama back to the pasture where they were earlier that day. Instead of walking down the middle of the pasture, they walked close to the trees. As they chitchatted, Farm Girl kept her eyes glued to the ground.

When she spied what she was looking for, in an excited voice she proclaimed, "Look, Mama, here they be. Them be my marker sticks."

"Sos I see." Looking toward the trees, Mama asked, "Where's that pile a brush ya told me about?"

Knowing she dropped the twigs in front of the hidden roadway, Farm Girl turned and pointed. "It's right … " She hesitated as her excitement turned to disappointment. Everything looked the same. As she scanned the area, Farm Girl couldn't tell one pile of brush from another. "Maybe them ain't my sticks?" With her chin to her knees, Farm Girl walked about, looking between trees and hoping to see something familiar.

Mama took a few steps backward toward the pasture. Tilting her head back, she looked toward the center of the treetops. "It's okay, child. Come on back."

Pivoting in place, Farm Girl looked back at her mother. "What's okay?"

"Y'ur openin'. I done find it."

"Ya did?" she yelled, running to her mother's side. "Where?"

"Look up there." Mama pointed to the top of the trees. "See that big space from one tree to the next?"

"Uh-huh."

"That must be the openin'. So, it's right where ya left them sticks."

Walking straight ahead of them so they wouldn't miss it again, Farm Girl asked, "Why didn't we see it when we was standin' right next to it?"

"I think they call that camouflage."

"Cama what?"

"Never mind."

"But ya don't never use them big words." Farm Girl was amazed. "Hows come ya ain't never told me ya knows them kind a words, just like ya never told me ya knows the A, B, C's and how to count?"

"Ain't no sense usin' words like that when ya be a farmhand. 'Sides, I don't even know where that word come from in my brain. It just sort a come out a my mouth."

"What do that funny word means?"

"I ain't sure, but I think it has somethin' to do with that pile a brush blendin' in with the rest a this area, hidin' that clearin'. Unless ya knows to look fur the spacin' between the trees, ya'd never be able to find it.

"Crimeny, ya sure be smart, Mama. I hope I be that smart someday."

"Just 'member what I keeps teachin ya. Keep y'ur ears open and y'ur mouth shut."

"Yes, Mama."

"Why did ya say Pappy be coverin' this pathway fur?"

By now, every time Farm Girl told a lie, she played her familiar game of King's X. "I didn't told ya 'cause I don't 'member."

"Well, we ain't gonna move that door a brush. That's fur sure."

Taking hold of her daughter's hand, they walked between the trees into the wooded area. Just as Farm Girl did earlier that day, they weaved in and out of a few trees until they were on the dirt road. Farm Girl let loose of Mama's hand. Without saying a word, Mama knew what was on her daughter's mind.

"Go ahead. I'll be right behind ya."

Taking the lead, Farm Girl headed down the road's slight decline toward the house.

Mama was not for the idea of settling in permanently, anywhere. They were already staying longer with Jefferson than she had ever planned. Even though it had not happened in all the time they had been on his farm, Mama was well aware that, at any given moment, an outsider could show up, unannounced, and discover them living there. If that were to happen, they would have to move at the drop of a pullet's egg.

So, looking at a house as possible living quarters was the furthest thing from Mama's mind. However, she knew how persistent her daughter could be. Had she not come along, Farm Girl would have never let her hear the end of it.

As she approached the area where the house sat, Farm Girl immediately spotted an enormous oak tree. "Look, Mama." She ran closer, stopping where the tree branched out over her head. Wanting a view of the top, she tipped her head back as far as she could without falling backward. From the angle she was standing, however, it was a virtual impossibility.

Knowing Mama was close behind her, she asked, "Crimeny, Mama, has ya ever put y'ur eyes on such a big ole tree in all y'ur born days?"

Mama had seen many trees throughout her years of traveling across country by foot, but she never took the time to admire any of them. From where she was standing, she had a much better view than her daughter. Tilting her head, her eyes followed the tree as far as they could. From her sight, it appeared the top of the tree met the sky.

Enjoying the enormous splendor that towered before them, Mama finally responded. "No, child, I doesn't reckon I has takin' in such a wonder a God's work. This here tree must be hundreds a years old."

Farm Girl's eyes got as big as saucers. "Hundreds a years," she echoed.

Approaching the tree's mammoth trunk, Farm Girl placed her hand on it. Running her fingers across the bark, she strolled around to the opposite side. Spotting something unfamiliar, she came to an abrupt stop. "What's them thingies?"

Bringing her focus back down from the treetop, Mama looked around. She could hear her daughter, but she couldn't see her. Mama called out. "Over where? I cain't see where ya got off to."

Staring at the objects foreign to her sight, Farm Girl said, "I be over here."

Walking around the tree, toward the sound of her daughter's voice, Mama called out again. "Well, where is over ... " Then Mama saw Farm Girl just a few feet away. She waited until she crept up right behind her daughter before she finished her question with a loud, "HERE?"

"MAMA!" Farm Girl screeched, as her body jerked around toward her mother. "Crimeny, that ain't nice. Ya almost make me wet my bloomers."

Farm Girl's comment tickled Mama. "Ya knows I was yellin'," she said with a faint smile.

"I did when ya was somewheres else. But that ain't the same as someone sneakin' up behind ya and yellin' 'here' in y'ur ears."

Seldom did Mama laugh. It just was not her nature to joke, tease, laugh, or have a good time. In fact, Farm Girl was so surprised that she shared the joy of the moment.

"It ain't funny," Farm Girl giggled.

When Mama covered her mouth with her fingers to compose herself, Farm Girl knew she was through having her moment of fun.

"What was ya yellin' fur, anyhow?" Mama asked, sweeping back the loose ends of hair and tucking them into her chignon.

Cocking her head, Farm Girl motioned with her eyes. "Over there. Stickin' in the ground."

Following Farm Girl's eye movement, Mama saw the objects in question. "That there be a cemetery where they bury dead folks."

This must be where Pappy teld me all a his kin be. "But what's them little pieces a wood fur with writin' on them?"

"Them little boards be what they calls head markers. The writin' tells ya the dead people's names and how long they was livin' on this earth."

"Why ain't they like them big stones ya done shows me in one a them cemeteries we was walkin' through one time?"

"Years ago, folks was markin' graves with them boards befur they gots them fancy headstones. Come on now. Let's not be standin' around here where we doesn't belong. One has to show some respect fur the dead."

Farm Girl ran toward the shack just a short distance from the grand oak tree. In rapid step, Mama was right behind. Mama intended to stick to her convictions about not wanting to live in any house. However, she began to waver once the rustic structure of large stones and logs stood before her.

Once they inspected the house, inside and out, Mama made the mistake of remarking, "This here little house looks to be in better shape than some a them barns we been stayin' in."

Those were just the kinds of words Farm Girl was hoping to hear. Now she was even more excited about the aspects of living in the small one-room shack. "I bet, if'n ya asks Pappy, he'll say we can live here."

"Ya knows I cain't do that. Outside a askin' fur some straw or a few gunnysacks to take with us fur the cold months, I ain't never ask me no favors a no one I has ever done chores fur. I sure ain't gonna start now."

"Oh, please, Mama. I ain't never was livin' in a real house befur. Cain't you ask if'n we can live in this one?"

From the look on Mama's face, Farm Girl could tell she may be wavering in her decision.

"I just doesn't know if'n it's the right thing to do. It would be another place to keep clean, and we has enough chores to do now."

"Crimeny, Mama, we spends all day doin' chores fur Pappy, from the time we wakes up till almost time to go to bed. How can it git that dirty in here if'n we ain't here that much?"

"The same way Pappy's house gits dirty when he ain't in it most a the day. All the dirt that's always blowin' around outside, finds its way into the house when a body ain't lookin'."

Farm Girl looked around the room. "We ain't gonna has all that furniture and stuff in here, like Pappy has. So, if'n I promises to keep it clean just like I keeps the barn clean, then wouldja ask him?"

Against her better judgment, Mama agreed to approach Jefferson with Farm Girl's idea. The biggest obstacle would be to convince him.

In a hurry to return to the house and talk to Jefferson, Farm Girl couldn't get her mother to move fast enough to suit her. "Hows come ya be walkin' so slow?"

"I be thinkin'."

"That's all ya been doin' since we left the house. Crimeny, my head would be plum worn out thinkin' that much."

"More thinkin' and less talkin' sure ain't gonna do ya no harm, child."

"I reckon I ain't gots that much in my head to think about sometimes. Cain't ya think while ya be walkin' faster?"

"I believe I can. But fur sure I cain't think with ya babblin' on like an old magpie. Now go on ahead and wait by the barn. I'll be there shortly."

Mama didn't have to tell Farm Girl a second time. She took off down the middle of the pasture in a full run.

"Finally, now I can put my thoughts together. I ain't never been afraid to speak what's on my mind. But askin' Pappy fur a favor, well that's gonna take some doin'. I just need to ask him straight out, I reckon, and git it over with."

Mama talked her way back to the barn where Farm Girl was waiting. It was beginning to get dark. If they didn't talk to Jefferson, right away, he would soon be heading for bed. The two of them scurried over the drive, across the yard, up the back porch steps, and to the backdoor of the main house. Mama rapped on the screen door.

After a few minutes, they saw the kitchen illuminate. Then the porch light above their heads lit up. Jefferson pulled back the curtain that covered the window on the door. When he saw who his company was, he opened the door with his usual welcoming smile.

"Thought you two had gone home without saying goodnight. Come in, come in."

Mama opened the screen door. With her arm placed around Farm Girl, Mama gave her daughter a friendly push so she would walk into the house first. Mama followed, closing the screen door behind her.

"We hate to bother ya, Pappy, but we has somethin' mighty important to talk to ya about."

Closing the main door, Jefferson replied, "You two are never a bother. This must be my day for important conversations, though," he added, giving a quick glance at Farm Girl. In turn, Farm Girl gave him a sheepish grin. "Come on in to the living room. We can talk in there."

"No," Mama said. "I mean, if'n ya doesn't mind, we be better sittin' in here."

"Okay. My, this sounds serious."

The three of them walked to the fifties style kitchen table, with its deep blue, gray flecked Formica top. Out of respect, Mama and Farm Girl stood waiting until Jefferson took a seat in one of the four chartreuse, Naugahyde covered chairs.

"You both look so grim. I hope you aren't going to tell me you're leaving? That would just about break my heart."

"No, sir. It ain't nothin' like that," Mama reassured him.

"That's a relief," he replied with a smile. "Well, then, what is it?"

Farm Girl placed one hand under the table and rested it on her lap. The other hand she nonchalantly hung over the back of her chair, as if she was just getting comfortable. She crossed her fingers on both hands. Making sure she had all the luck on her side, she also crossed her legs.

"I has givin' this a great deal a thinkin' 'cause I don't wantcha to think that we be takin' benefit a y'ur kindness."

Jefferson shook his head. "I don't have the slightest idea what's on your mind, but I think I know you well enough, Mama. You would no sooner take advantage of me then you would take your daughter to town with you."

"Oh, no. I sure ain't never gonna do that."

"That's my point, Mama. Now, tell me what this is all about."

"I needs to ask ya a mighty big favor."

"If it's something you want me to do or help you with, I'll do my best."

There was no turning back now. Mama had laid the groundwork. She just had to spit it out. "Me and Farm Girl went to take a look-see at y'ur granddaddy's house."

"You what?" In an immediate reaction, he eyed Farm Girl with a look of disappointment.

Oblivious to the reason behind the look he gave her daughter, Mama continued speaking. If she didn't, she felt sure she would lose her nerve. "If'n ya gots no plans fur that house, we can sure turn it into a place fur us to stay. Now, don't think that we hasn't been comfy stayin' in y'ur barn, 'cause we has. But it's sad fur a house like that to be just wastin' away, when there be folks like us that can be usin' it fur comfort."

"Well now, seems I remember a discussion about this very subject, not too long ago, when another female was interested in the same thing."

Knowing full well that he was speaking of her, Farm Girl hung her head, dropping her eyes to the table.

In the dark as to Jefferson's comment, Mama stated, "Since there ain't no one livin' there, I reckon ya teld that other person no?"

Jefferson didn't know whether to scold Farm Girl and tell Mama the truth, or laugh about Farm Girl's determination to get what she wanted. "Yes, Mama, I did tell that other female no. In fact, I do believe I was very emphatic about it."

Farm Girl looked up. *He didn't never emphatic me, did he?* "Pappy, what do that word means?"

Giving Farm Girl a shame-on-you look, he gave a brief explanation. "No means no."

"Oh."

"Be quiet now, child, and let me say what I come here to say."

"Yes, Mama."

"If'n ya gives me an emphatic no, I ain't gonna ask no more. But, if'n it ain't a fur sure no, then maybe ya can think real hard befur answerin'. Ya see, Farm Girl ain't never been livin' in a house befur. Well, not that she 'members. Not that I wants her to git all spoils like a rotten tomato, but it would be real nice if'n she can enjoy that time just once with her mama."

"I don't like telling either of you no, but I can't see anyone living there. Like I told the other female, I recently had this conversation with, that run-down shack is deteriorating from old age. I should've probably left the trailer there that we used for extra living space, but I sold it years ago. Maybe then I would've considered allowing you two to live in it, but not in that one room shack. It should've been torn down years ago. I just couldn't bring myself to do it. Guess I was hoping it would collapse on its own."

"Now don'tcha be talkin' that way. Don'tcha tell me everyday how y'ur legs be botherin' ya when ya be on y'ur feets too long?"

"What are we talking about my legs for?"

"Okay, I won't talk about y'ur legs. I'll talk about them heart pains ya has. All the time tellin' me that's 'cause ya be gittin' old."

"Mama, my health and my age have nothing to do with you wanting to live in my granddaddy's house."

"No, it don't. But I be tryin' to tell ya somethin'. Just 'cause somethin' be old, don't mean it ain't worth keepin' and enjoyin'."

That brought a smile to his face. "You know, for an uneducated woman, you still amaze me. You're comparing me to the old shanty, aren't you?"

"If'n I be, then maybe ya won't think no more about tearin' the house down. It needs a little fixin' here and there, but it's still too nice to make firewood out a yet."

"There's no personal facilities out there by the shanty. The two-holer we had was so old, it buckled years ago."

"We ain't had them outside portals many times, and it ain't never been a bother to us. Anyways, unless we has a real crisis, we can use y'ur outside privy befur we leaves here in the evenin', and when we comes back in the mornin'. If'n we does have a crisis, there's plenty a trees around there to be doin' our business."

Farm Girl figured she had sat quiet long enough. This was her cue to speak. "See, Pappy, even Mama thinks y'ur granddaddy's shack, uh, house can make a nice home fur us. Oh, please, won'tcha say we can live there?"

"When winter comes, considering we can get some pretty good storms dumping several inches of snow around here, how are you two going to get back here to help me? That's quite a distance from here when you're tramping through snow."

"We be use to trudgin' through snow drifts way befur we come here," Mama said. "I knows livin' there, we cain't be as close as we be sleepin' in the barn, but we'll git here and still do our chores. That's a promise."

"No, no, that's no good. That's too long of a walk in the snow." Jefferson sighed. "Let's be reasonable, Mama. Your legs and feet would be frozen by the time you got from one place to the other."

"Hatin' to disagree with ya, but we traipses through the snow when we does chores fur ya in the winters. It cain't be no different."

"Well, it is. You two are only outside for a very short time. You might get cold and damp, but it's nothing like it would be making that trip from the riverbank to here."

"Well, sir, sometimes there wasn't enough food to git us through the winter. When that be the case, I was walkin' to the nearest town in snow up to my knees to find a day's work."

Crimney, be Mama playin' King's X? With her hands hidin' under the table, I cain't tell. She ain't never been walkin' to a town in snow that deep. Least ways, not that I 'member.

"It didn't kill me then," Mama stated, "and it ain't gonna kill me now."

"What you did before I knew you, is your business. I won't have you walking that distance in deep snow while you're working for me. That's all there is to it."

After further intense discussion in regards to the pros and cons of allowing Mama and Farm Girl to live in the one-room shanty, Jefferson tried to be more understanding. Terrible recollections of the past kept clouding his mind, heart, and his emotions, but he hated to disillusion Farm Girl and Mama's persistent enthusiasm.

He did his best to bury his past heartache. Wanting to please them, he offered to clean out the old storage room off the kitchen and turn it into its original intent of use: a bedroom. With the purchase of twin beds, he felt Mama and Farm Girl would be more comfortable in his home than the shack. After all, he loved them as if they were his own flesh and blood.

"I'm mighty beholden fur the offer, but me and my daughter livin' under the same roof with ya, be out a the question. As much as we cares about ya, we ain't y'ur kin. I be tellin' ya that every time ya gives us them invites into y'ur home on a kin-like basis. We be y'ur farmhands, pure and simple. Now, livin' in that small house can be a real comfort to us. But, if'n it's gonna cause ya too much grief to allow that, then we ain't bringin' this matter up again. The barn be better than sleepin' on the ground with the sky as our roof. So, the barn's where we'll stay."

"Okay, here's another idea. Why don't I purchase one of those mobile homes for the two of you to live in? We can set it up right next to the house—"

"If'n ya wants *emphatic*," Mama said, "then emphatic be whatcha gits. Ya ain't buyin' no such thing fur us to be livin' in."

The disappointment was obvious in Farm Girl's face. It appeared as though her chin had dropped through the table and crashed on the dark tiled floor. Her look crushed Jefferson's heart.

"Okay. The small house is yours for as long as you want to live in it."

Letting out a squeal, Farm Girl jumped from her chair and ran to Jefferson's side. She attacked him with a loving hug and a kiss on his cheek. "Oh, thank ya, Pappy. Gosh, ya be just super."

"You're quite welcome, honey. I just want you two to be happy."

"I knows just what I be gonna name our new home. That be, if'n it's okay with ya?"

"I've never heard of anyone naming a house," he said, smiling. "But you can name it anything you want to."

Turning to Mama, Farm Girl questioned, "What's that favorite song a y'urs that ya hums all the time?" Mama shook her head as if she didn't know what her daughter was talking about. "Crimeny, Mama, ain't ya always hummin' that song ya calls <u>Sugar Shack</u>?"

"Yes, I reckon that's true," Mama admitted.

"Well, that's what I be gonna call our new home. Sugar Shack."

To Farm Girl's delight, she and Mama moved into the small cabin by the river.

Even with a home of their own, Mama and Farm Girl started spending more and more time in Jefferson's house. After Jefferson convinced Mama to set aside her stern belief that farmhands didn't get chummy with their bosses, the three of them started enjoying Sunday dinners together. From there, the visits extended into more of a family affair.

On different occasions, Jefferson would allow Farm Girl to watch a program on his television set, but only when he was around to control her viewing. He allowed her to watch cartoons and animated presentations that didn't have real people in them.

On rare occasions, Jefferson permitted her to watch movies, like <u>Heidi</u>, or a music show, such as *Grand Ole Opry*. Even though the show had real people performing, the fact was drummed into her head on a constant basis that these programs were just make-believe.

Wanting to appease Mama, Jefferson did everything he could to help them out and make them comfortable, Mama's way. Farm Girl didn't know Mr. Welk had made any promises to Mama. For one, he was never to tell Farm Girl about the real world outside the farm. And, he was never to allow her to watch any television program that would influence or disrupt her innocent mind.

Making one excuse after another, Jefferson would never go visit Mama and Farm Girl after they set up housekeeping, even when Farm Girl pleaded with him to see what a nice home they had made for themselves.

Other than making an occasional visit to the gravesite of his loved ones, Jefferson stayed as far away as he could from the grand oak tree and the old shack. Each time he was in the area, it brought back the treacherous visions of white-hooded men and a baby in a cradle—his reasons for mistrusting people.

LEARNING AT ANY AGE

Mama and Farm Girl were dressing for one of their Sunday visits with Jefferson.

"Don'tcha wishes we had all a them dresses now that Pappy done give us from his dead missus? If'n we did, we ain't has to be wearin' the same clothes all the time."

As if an arrow had penetrated her heart, Mama clutched her breast with both hands. She collapsed into one of the old wooden chairs that sat next to their weatherworn table.

Farm Girl rushed to her side. "Mama! What's the matter?"

"I swear, child, I doesn't know where ya comes up with these terrible words."

"What did I say wrong?"

"There ain't no need fur folks like us to have more than two sets a clothes. All we needs, be one fur everyday wearin' and one fur special invites to the main house. 'Sides, ya knows none a them clothes Pappy done give us, all them years ago, didn't fit neither one a us, except fur some a them smaller sweaters. That's why I cut them dresses up into patches to make our clothes we has now."

"I knows whatcha done, and why ya done it, Mama. I was just thinkin', if'n we has more clothes, we don't has to be warshin' so much the ones we has now."

"Quit thinking such things. Think more about how grateful ya be fur whatcha do has," Mama scolded, "and that we no longer needs to be warshin' clothes in the river. Pappy be more than generous lettin' us use his automatic clothes warsher machine. Them's the kind a things ya needs to be thinkin' in that brain a y'urs."

"Yes, ma'am."

"If'n y'ur ready, let's go. Pappy be waitin' fur us to show up and start dinner."

When they arrived at the main house, Jefferson was taking a nap. Mama prepared their Sunday dinner while Farm Girl set the table.

After dinner, Jefferson suggested, "Since there isn't anything good on TV, how about I read us another story after you two get the dishes cleaned and put away?"

Once again, because of Mama's insistence, Jefferson could only read fiction books to them. Farm Girl didn't know the difference. All she knew was that she loved listening to the stories.

"Will ya read us <u>Black Beauty</u>, again? I just love hearin' about that swell horse."

"Honey, between books I already had, and the ones I bought for you, the shelves in my sitting room are full of a wide selection for reading. Wouldn't you rather we start a new story?" Jefferson asked.

He couldn't miss Mama's immediate glare and the raising of her eyebrow. "And many of them are wonderful *made-up* stories," he stated, glaring back at Mama with a smirk. Turning his attention back to Farm Girl, he said, "There's a lot of wonderful books in this world because of all the talented authors."

As Mama drew the dishwater, Farm Girl was clearing the table.

Farm Girl asked, "What is them, Pappy?"

"Authors?"

"Uh-huh."

"They're the people who write the books."

"Where does they live?"

When a metal lid hit the floor with a bang, next to where Mama was standing, Jefferson took the hint. Unless he wanted trouble from Mama, he had to make sure he chose his words with considerable care.

"They live in the world of books," he replied, biting his tongue.

"When ya reads books, a body can pretend she lives in another world. That's why I likes to close my eyes when ya reads to us. Someday, I wanna be one a them authors," Farm Girl gleefully admitted.

"Don't be dreamin' about doin' somethin' ya knows nothin' about," Mama warned. "Book learnin' comes befur book writin', and ya ain't never gonna be doin' neither."

Even for as many years as Mama and Farm Girl had worked for

Jefferson, he still objected to the way Mama raised her daughter. Through the years, however, he tried to keep his objections to himself, to keep harmony amongst the three of them. To refrain from a heated exchange of words, he changed the subject.

"Well, ladies, I'm going into the den and get comfortable." Jefferson stood from his chair. "Come on in when you're ready."

"I'll finish up in here, child. Go on in with Pappy sos he can read ya y'ur favorite story."

"Be ya sure?" Farm Girl questioned with surprise.

"Yes, I be sure."

"We don't want to start the story without you," Jefferson stated.

"Go ahead. I have some fresh eggs in the basement to check, after I git through in here."

If he were more of a boss than a friend, Jefferson wouldn't have cared what Mama did with her time. Problem was, he did care.

"I don't need to remind you, I suppose, that it's Sunday, and it's our special time together. Those eggs can wait until tomorrow morning."

"It sometimes becomes necessary," Mama responded, "fur a body to do what they gotta do."

As much as Jefferson did not like to argue with Mama, he sometimes enjoyed the battle of words. "And who says checking those eggs before tomorrow morning is necessary?"

Lifting her soapy hands from the dishwater and wiping them on her apron, Mama turned toward Jefferson. "I say it's necessary."

"Are you the boss around here?"

Standing very quietly, Farm Girl's head moved back and forth, like a ping-pong ball, as she listened to Jefferson and Mama in one of their stubborn discussions. She could always bet on Mama winning.

"Be sortin' eggs one a my chores?"

"Did I ever tell you, for as long as you've been working for me, that sorting eggs is a Sunday job?"

"Don'tcha go to market every Monday mornin' with fresh eggs?"

"Don't I always go to town after I've got the milking done, so you have plenty of time to finish the egg sorting early on Monday mornings?"

"And does I always has to sit and listen to some book stories I ain't gots interest in, just 'cause ya wanna entertain us?"

Realizing what she said, Mama had the look of shock on her face. Jefferson, on the other hand, thought it was funny. When he burst into laughter, Farm Girl started laughing. Mama donned a timid smile at what unintentionally blurted out of her mouth.

"You know," he proceeded, still laughing, "you would have saved us ten minutes of nonsense if you would've been honest in the first place."

"If'n I'd done that, you and Farm Girl wouldn't has y'ur fun fur the day."

"No, I guess we wouldn't have. Okay, Mama, you do what you have to do. Farm Girl and I will be in the sitting room."

After reading one chapter of <u>Black Beauty</u>, Jefferson placed the book in his lap.

Sitting at his feet, Farm Girl asked, "Somethin' wrong?"

"No, honey, nothing's wrong. In recent weeks, I've been doing a great deal of thinking about you."

"What about me?"

"You know, I'm getting up in years. It won't be very long before I'm gone and you and Mama will have to move on."

She covered her ears with her hands. "I doesn't wanna hear ya talk like that."

Leaning forward, Jefferson reached out and pulled Farm Girl's hands away from her ears. "I'm going to talk, and you're going to listen. These are things that need to be said."

"Okay, but I doesn't like it very much."

"I'll tell you something else you're not going to like. There might come a time when you'll need to take over the responsibility of caretaker. That means you may have to support your mother."

"That ain't never gonna happen."

"Child, we never know what is going to happen tomorrow. You need to be prepared for anything."

"Like how prepared?"

"If you get schooled, you can do much better for yourself than being a farmhand."

"What is schooled?" she inquired, then answered her own question. "Oh, you mean like them kids I once knows that was goin' to school fur book learnin'?"

"Well, yes and no. You need a real education, which you would get by going to school. Now, I know going to school, at your age, would be more than a little embarrassing for you. So, I thought, maybe, I could purchase the books we need. Then, I could teach you."

"Y'urself can teach me book learnin'?"

"Truth is, honey, I went to school, but just through the third grade. However, my parents and my grandmama made sure I got a home education. I won't be the best teacher in the world, but I know I can teach you some basics that you really need to know. I'm speaking of more than counting and knowing the alphabet. But, we can discuss this later. It's getting late," he picked up the book, "so let's get back to our story."

All Jefferson had intention of doing, was to plant the education seed in Farm Girl's mind. He would wait for Farm Girl to discuss the idea with Mama. His only hope, since Farm Girl was getting older, was that Mama would be more obliging than she had been in the past, and see things his way.

Jefferson had a heart as big as the universe when it came to those he loved. And he loved Mama and Farm Girl. Both of them loved and respected him in return. They were always very appreciative of whatever he did for them. Jefferson felt God brought the three of them together to fill a void in each of their lives, to join them as a family.

Whatever Jefferson would suggest, which he felt was always in their best interest, Farm Girl agreed to go along with it. Mama, on the other hand, had to consider all aspects of a situation before agreeing to anything. Then, when it concerned her daughter, things still had to be her way, or not at all.

Later that day, Farm Girl informed Mama of Pappy's suggestion. Not at all pleased, Mama sent Farm Girl out of the room while the two adults discussed the idea. During the course of the conversation, Mama gave in with the condition that Jefferson not teach Farm Girl more than she needed to know to get by, living on a farm.

Since Jefferson had already taught Farm Girl to count, Mama had no objections to math lessons. Learning to read, according to Mama's way of thinking, would in all probability help Farm Girl understand one of those recipe books that Jefferson kept in his kitchen. That's where Jefferson's teaching would stop.

"Book learnin' be one thing, but quite another to be teachin' Farm Girl the ways a the outside world," as far as Mama was concerned.

"I want y'ur word that ya ain't never gonna mention nothin' stupid to her about love between a man and a woman, and nothin' about sex. Love between a man and a woman be an evil disease that kills folks inside. I don't never want Farm Girl to know none a that kind a hurt. Like I told ya befur. I don't want her learnin' nothin' more than life on a farm, as a farmhand."

"That's not true," Jefferson staunchly disagreed. "One of the greatest joys of my life was falling in love and marrying my wife. But I'm not going to argue that issue with you right now. Nonetheless, I am going to tell you how wrong you are about keeping blinders on your daughter. She needs to know what the real world is all about in order to exist in it."

Mama could tell from the tone of his voice that she was in for another long-winded lecture, leading into another debate.

"Mama, this is the Twentieth Century. We are long past the dark ages, where you seem to be living. You know, I learned a valuable lesson from your daughter. A person can't keep living in the past. She taught me that lesson that night she convinced me to allow you two to live in my granddaddy's old shack. To think it took a naive young girl to make this old man open his heart and mind, is rather shameful on my part.

You've got to do the same thing, Mama. Unlock that mind and that heart of yours. Whatever is eating away at you, or has hurt you in your past with such severity, you have to let it go. And for Farm Girl's sake, don't make her pay the price of your hurt by keeping her uneducated, and lying to her about what this world is truthfully all about.

It's wrong for her to think there is nothing in life but living and working on farms, and that everything else is just a land of make-believe. You may not like it, but you cannot shelter her for the rest of her life. It just isn't fair to her," Jefferson stated with firm convictions. "I don't much care for most of the human race myself, but a person needs to at least know what goes on in this world."

"Be ya through lecturin' me?" Mama asked in a calm voice.

"No, I'm not."

Unless she wanted to move their debate into an intense argument, Mama had to hold her tongue until Jefferson was finished defending his reasoning.

"For as long as I've known you, you have given me every indication that you are satisfied with your station in life. That may be fine for you, but that's no good for your daughter. It goes without saying that I respect your feelings, but Farm Girl lives in a nutshell. You taught her how to survive in that shell, which is extraordinary.

Not too many young ones her age, or even my age for that matter, could, to be quite frank, exist the way you have taught her to live. And, you can be real proud of that. However, when the day comes that the shell cracks, and you're no longer there to protect her, Farm Girl won't know how to survive in the real world.

You know, the older I get, I see farms disappearing right and left. Female farmhands, like you and Farm Girl, aren't going to be needed too much longer. Heck, to my knowledge, there aren't even too many male farmhands left. Plus, you have to think of all the machinery that has replaced, and will continue to replace, extra hands.

Also, I see a child growing into a young woman, but still using a child's mind. You've got to look into her future. What happens when all the farms are gone? What's going to happen when you're gone? Like I just said, but it bears repeating, your daughter cannot spend forever thinking that outside of farm life nothing else is real.

Forgive an old man, and understand that I'm just trying to help both of you." Jefferson paused and shook his head. "Okay. I can tell that I got carried away with my little sermon. I'll shut up now and hear what you've got to say."

Stubborn as she was, no one, not even Jefferson Welk, was going to convince Mama that she was not doing what was best for her own daughter.

"When I hears ya speakin' y'ur piece, like that, it makes me feel like a child gittin' a proper scoldin' from her daddy. But, ya ain't my daddy, and I ain't no child. Either ya promises what I be askin' ya to promise, or I ain't gonna allow ya to do no teachin' to my daughter. It's either that, or me and Farm Girl best be movin' on."

Having Mama and Farm Girl move away and leave him all alone, was not what he wanted. Abiding by Mama's wishes, as he wanted Farm Girl to be more educated than she was at present, Jefferson agreed. If teaching Farm Girl had to be on Mama's terms, then so be it.

Once Jefferson started working everyday with Farm Girl, teaching her how to read and write simple words, he realized she must have a learning disorder.

She remembered words that were more complicated then she did the short everyday words that were more common. It appeared that she locked big words in her mind, but would confuse their meanings. Often times, she merely used a word that sounded like the word she should have used.

Even though he was an honest man, Jefferson didn't have the heart to squelch Farm Girl's spirits. He didn't relate his thoughts to Mama, either, but wondered if she didn't already know of her daughter's learning disability. All he could do was to continue teaching his pupil the best way he knew how. He could only hope Farm Girl would comprehend even a portion of the lessons he gave her.

For the many months that followed, life on the Welk farm couldn't have been happier. Jefferson was feeling a small sense of accomplishment from the few things his student was learning.

Mama was content that Farm Girl was just learning enough to keep her young mind occupied, but not enough to give her thoughts of changing her lifestyle.

Farm Girl was in a daze of absorption. Whatever she was doing, her mind was on story writing.

Being an adventurer, Farm Girl discovered an enormous boulder across the river, not too far from Sugar Shack. Due to Farm Girl's love for naming everything important to her, she named the rock: Room to Write.

Every afternoon, right after their mid-day dinner, Mama allowed Farm Girl to have an hour by herself. Pencil and paper in hand, Farm Girl would dash across the pasture, through the trees, down to the river, cross it, run up the embankment, and climb up on her rock. There she would sit and write her simple stories.

In the main house, one evening, while practicing her spelling words for the day, Farm Girl started up a conversation with Jefferson. He was sitting across the room in his favorite overstuffed chair, reading a book.

Biting on the end of her pencil, she asked, "How does them authors knows what to write in them books?"

Closing the book over his thumb to keep his place, Jefferson answered. "Many of them write about something that has happened in either their lives, or someone else's life that they know about. Others write about scientific facts. Some just use their imagination to write about what ever they want." Fiction and non-fiction were words he didn't dare introduce to her vocabulary. "There are so many kinds of writers, honey, I don't even know them all."

"Mama always says I has an image a nation."

"An imagination— That you do," he agreed with a grin.

"If'n I has that, and I is gittin' book-learnin', then maybe Mama's wrong. I can be one a them authors. Cain't I?"

Oh, how he did not want to answer that question. However, Jefferson knew he had to say something. "Well, I think anyone can be anything they set their mind to be."

"Does all them authors really live in that world a books? Or does some a them lives on farms, like we does?"

"I would imagine some of them might live on farms. I've never given it any thought."

"No matter how I try, I cain't git my letters small, like I sees in them books. How does they do that?"

"Honey, you're walking me down an avenue I'm not at all familiar with. I can just assume they use some sort of a printing press. From there, I believe, the print goes into book form."

"Where does they git their stories put into them books?"

"I think most of the publishing houses are located back east. My guess is in New York City. But, I'm just going by what I see printed in most of the books I have in my own collection."

"New York City? Is that one a them other worlds?"

Feeling a rush of heat sweep over his face, he knew he had spoken before thinking. "Look, honey, would you mind keeping this our little secret?"

"Oh, I likes secrets. Mama told me a secret once ... " she thought a moment with a look of perplexity, "but I doesn't remember now what she told me. That's okay 'cause I cain't tell you anyways, even if'n I does 'member," she informed, giggling. "Why does ya wanna tell me a secret?"

"You don't understand. Telling you about New York *is* the secret. I promised your mama to only teach you about words and numbers. If she gets upset with me for talking about," he bit at his lower lip, "other worlds right now, she might not let me continue giving you lessons."

"Crimeny, Pappy, I needs ya to keep teachin' me, if'n I is gonna be an author. I won't tell Mama. I promise." *But that ain't gonna keep me from thinkin' about it. New York City. That's where I is gonna go someday when I writes me some books.*

Relieved, Jefferson breathed easier. He had to trust that Farm Girl would keep her word. Under his breath he muttered, "Mama, I don't know why you have put me in this position. If you would just—"

"Is ya talkin' at me, Pappy?" Farm Girl inquired, as she looked up from her paper of words.

"No, honey, just thinking out loud."

Mama, alone, knew her motives for keeping Farm Girl from knowing any other life but what she had taught her. By keeping her daughter ignorant, however, Mama was asking for big trouble. Farm

Girl was far too gullible.

The kind of people Mama was protecting her daughter from, would be the same kind that would eventually have an affect on Farm Girl's life. A greater influence than Mama could ever imagine.

THE NEAT NICK THIEF

PRESENT

Since Mr. and Mrs. Schmikel were on vacation, their house burglary went unnoticed until they returned home two weeks later.

At the Kidwell Police Station, the phone rang. The desk officer answered the phone then informed Chief Simmons the call was for him.

Sitting at his antique desk, reading a recent misdemeanor report, Rusty answered the phone. "Chief Simmons."

"Rusty, this is Ward."

When he heard the recognized voice, Rusty could almost see his old buddy sitting in front of him. Even though the two men were close in age, Ward had a head of pure white hair for as long as Rusty could remember, quite unlike his own full crop of red hair.

Ward's love for food and a good brew had settled in his stomach, as did Rusty's. Often times they stood next to each other to see whose belly protruded further. Most of the time, it was a tie.

Sheriff Ward Luden took his job serious but loved to sit and talk, and tease whenever he could. For the most part, he was good-natured, even when it came to dealing with the bad guys.

Compassionate, big hearted, and likeable, he had been sheriff for more years than Rusty cared to remember. Being law enforcement officers, living in small rural areas where almost everyone knew everyone else, Ward and Rusty were not just friends. They often assisted each other in their respective jobs.

"Ward, how are you today?"

"Fair to midland, as usual. You?"

"Other than a little indigestion, I can't complain. What can I do for you this a.m.?"

"I hate to burden you, but I need to ask you another favor?"

"So burden me. What's on your mind," Rusty responded.

"I got a call on a burglary over at the Schmikel place. Do you know him and the missus?"

"I know the name, but never met either of them on a personal basis."

"Well, this will be a good chance for you to get acquainted."

"Meaning?"

"I'm short handed, Rusty. Got both men out sick with some sort of bug, so I'm working solo. Since I already deputized you a few weeks back on that last case you investigated for me, I'm hoping you can also handle this one."

"Sure thing. It's quiet around here, so it'll give me something to do." Rusty laughed.

"Glad to hear it. I would advise you get there yesterday. These poor folks must think they're getting the old government red-tape runaround." Rusty could hear Ward chuckling.

"Why do you say that?"

"First they called over to Chief Kings in Sharpin. He told them to call my office, since the Schmikel's live out of his city limits. Now, I'm asking you to take the case. They might think we're passing the buck."

Fighting back a sneeze, Rusty rubbed his nose. "And why didn't you call Chief Kings back? He can handle this case for you as well as I can," Rusty replied, tongue in cheek.

"Because you're the one that I deputized. Besides, you know how Chief Kings and I get along. We're like two old Billy goats always butting heads." After a brief hesitation, Ward declared, "Damn, Rusty! You got me on that one."

Laughing, Rusty admitted, "I couldn't resist, knowing how you two don't get along. Okay, I'll get right on the case. We don't want those folks writing their City Fathers, saying we don't do our work swift enough."

"Thanks, Rusty. Keep me posted."

Rusty always went out on all the department's cases with one of his officers. He liked keeping his fingers in the pie. Besides, he never seemed to get enough exercise sitting around the office all day, and his waistline proved it. Fact was, he hadn't any more signs of a waistline, just an overhang that hid his belt buckle.

Once they located the directions to the victim's property, Officer

Kelly went with Rusty to begin a routine investigation. At the Schmikel residence, Kelly busied himself outside, looking for evidence. Rusty sat inside at the dining room table with L.C. and his wife Dora, asking pertinent questions.

In his mid-twenties, Officer Kelly was a go-getter, eager to learn, and not afraid of hard work. Even though he towered a good three inches above Rusty, he carried a much thinner physic. With his carrot-top hair and rich green eyes, he had 'Irish' written all over him. Not that Rusty was ever partial to the Irish, but Officer Kelly was his right-hand man.

Kelly admired his boss. If Rusty chose to sit, have coffee, and ask the victim questions while Kelly did the physical work, Kelly had no objections.

During the course of Rusty's routine inquiries, he found out how long the Schmikel's had been on vacation and how much money had been taken.

"If nothing in your house was disturbed, how did you discover it was broken into?" Rusty asked, continuing his investigation.

"When I checked the lock on the side door, I noticed all of those gouge marks on the door and the frame. Right then, I just knew someone pried the lock open and broke into our house. Let me tell you, I was in total shock. I mean you hear about that sort of thing going on all the time in the bigger cities, but this just never happens in our small, rural areas.

When I told Dora, she immediately went to the bathroom."

Rusty uttered a slight grunt as he tried to hold back laughter. L.C. stopped talking, wondering what happened. A comical thought ran through Rusty's head. *I had a spaniel like that once. Every time she got upset or excited, she peed. This is the first time I ever heard of a person doing it.*

Dora tapped her husband's shoulder. "L.C., that sounded terrible. You made it sound as though I wet my pants."

"Oh, my." Laughing, he said, "I didn't mean that, Chief Simmons. You see, we keep our petty cash in our emergency kit in the bathroom. It's kind of an inside joke."

"Oh, I see. Well, I'm certainly glad you clarified that," Rusty replied, with a half-assed grin.

When Rusty had all the information he needed, and was ready to wind it up, Kelly appeared at the doorway.

"Chief, I think I found something you should take a look at." Both

L.C. and Dora followed behind Rusty, as the officer led the way to his discovery. Outside, beside the house, Kelly pointed to a very noticeable footprint on the ground, very close to the house. "There, Chief."

"Is that your print?" Rusty asked L.C.

Taking a closer look, L.C. shook his head. "I don't think so, but I can't say for sure. Do you want me to place my foot inside the print and see if it's the same size as mine?"

"No. We'll need to preserve it until we get a cast of it."

The earth around the print didn't look like a pile of dirt. However, since the ground was frozen, Rusty didn't know for sure what the substance was that embedded the print. To get a closer view, he stooped to the ground. Being careful not to disturb the print, he picked up a small amount of the substance and rubbed it between his fingers and thumb.

"If I didn't know better, I'd say this feels like ashes."

"That's because it is," L.C. offered. "That's my spot for burning papers we don't throw in the trash."

Rusty looked up at L.C. "Do you own any footwear that would embed this sort of a design on the ground?"

"Not to my knowledge. I'll have to check before I can be positive."

"Please do."

"I'll go check real quick," Dora offered. "I need a coat anyway. I'll be right back."

Rusty returned to a standing position. As they waited, the men talked about the weather.

Upon Dora's return she stated, "None of L.C's footwear have that type of sole." Dora handed Rusty his hat. "Here you go. I didn't want you to forget it."

"Thank you, ma'am. I appreciate it." Since he was still in the company of a lady, Rusty refrained from placing the hat on his head.

L.C. lifted his foot and looked at the bottom of his shoe. "This sole doesn't look like that print either."

Satisfied that the print, in all probability, had not been made by Mr. Schmikel's foot, Rusty turned to his officer. "Kelly, get a plaster cast of this for evidence, and take some photos. I especially want a close up shot of that unusual sole design."

"I'm on it, Chief."

* * *

It took a few days for Rusty and his officers to check with neighbors who lived around the Schmikel's house. However, since the house was so secluded, no one could report anything unusual around the property while the Schmikel's had been away.

Since Rusty knew for a fact that he hadn't had any recent burglaries reported in Kidwell, he called Chief Kings to see if there had been any reported in Sharpin.

"Damn old cantankerous idiot!" Rusty declared, slamming down the phone. "I don't know why that man can't be more sociable." Trying to mimic Chief Kings, Rusty strained his voice, repeating, "If Ward couldn't take the case, why didn't he just call me back, instead of calling you?" Shaking his head, Rusty grunted, "Uuugh! That man infuriates me.

So, there haven't been any burglaries reported in Sharpin, either. And I know there haven't been any in Ward's area, other than Schmikel's, or he would have said something. Well, no leads there."

Rusty went back to his notes. From the plaster mold that Officer Kelly had taken at the Schmikel's, Rusty was surmising that the print was from a size ten shoe. The sole was similar to a waffle design with deep treads. Rusty was drawing two conclusions from the footprint. Either the thief was careless, or someone made the print on purpose. Which was it?

Rusty also knew the thief wore gloves, as there were no fingerprints on the entry door or the inside of the house other than those of L.C. and his wife.

Rusty leaned back in his chair, considering a few aspects of the case. "A professional would never tear a door up the way that one was gouged." He rubbed his chin. "Also, pros are in and out of a place with little to no clue left behind. This perp's break-in is too sloppy for a pro. He has to be an amateur.

Something else about this thief bothers me. This thief was sloppy about entering, yet, once inside, he took extremes in tidiness. Since there were no other valuables taken, it's obvious he was looking for cash. He had to have gone through drawers, cupboards, and the like, if he were only looking for money. Yet, the Schmikel's said everything in the house looked untouched. So, why leave the house looking undisturbed?

All that tells me is that the thief was very neat. Maybe that's a clue? I'm assuming this thief could be either a male or a female. But for now, gender unknown, I'll refer to this thief as a male: A male who is over cautious and somewhat of a perfectionist. I guess I would tag him a Neat Nick Thief."

Rusty yawned and stretched. Lifting his cup, he took a drink of coffee. The cup was almost empty, but the small amount of contents that remained was not to Rusty's liking. "Damn! I hate cold coffee." He slammed the cup back on the desk.

"What do I know about footwear? Not much. I think most men's dress shoes have smooth soles with small heels. It seems to me that the bottom of women's flat-heeled shoes would be pretty close to the same description as the men's. Many sports shoes, for both genders, have a designed sole with a definite ridge or tread in them. But, the suspect print doesn't look like a sports shoe design."

Frustrated, Rusty took his cup to get a hot refill. In the front office, Kelly and Seals were involved in a conversation.

Officer Seals was a slow mover and thinker. Although Rusty considered Seals to be a good officer, he was a definite follower, not a leader when it came to police work. When no outsiders were around the office, Rusty sometimes teased Seals, calling him the Don Knotts of Kidwell. Slight of body, he bore a slight resemblance to the famous actor. Also, some of his actions and deeds were almost a replica of the bumbling Barney Phyf on the famed *Andy Griffith Show*.

Seals did what he thought was right, but seemed to always botch up something. Often times, his screw-ups made his fellow officers sit back and roll their eyes in frustration. Seals would laugh and state, "Well, wouldn't Barney have done it that way?" which always brought about a roar of laughter.

Rusty kept Seals around because the screw-ups were but minor errors around the office. Out on the street, he was a good cop. Of course, this made Rusty wonder if Seals didn't pull boners in the office on purpose, just to make his fellow officers laugh. Officer Seals was also dependable. With guidance, he followed orders and always accomplished the job given to him.

In his late twenties and still single, Seals lived at home helping his folks with the farming. Since the late September weather had turned unseasonably cold and wet, Seals had ordered a pair of overshoes for fieldwork. He had taken his lunch hour to pick up the boots.

When Rusty walked by the officer's desk on the way for coffee, Seals had the boots out of the box, showing them to Kelly.

"Hey, Seals, where did you get those boots?" Rusty stopped to take one of the boots out of his officer's hand. "I didn't think you wore anything but shit-kicking boots like the rest of us around here?"

As Rusty handed the boot back to Seals, it slipped from the officer's hand and fell, bouncing from the desk to the floor. The boot landed on its side. Picking up the boot, Rusty resumed his stance.

"Holy crap! Kelly, get me that print mold from Schmikel's place out of the evidence locker, ASAP." Almost dropping his coffee cup as he placed it on the desk, Rusty grabbed the boot with both hands for closer inspection of the sole.

"What's going on, Chief?" Seals returned the other boot to its box.

"I'll tell you in a minute."

It didn't take long for Kelly to return with the cast print. After comparing the sole of the boot to the evidence print, Rusty noted it was a perfect waffle-design match. Excited about the discovery, Rusty's authoritative voice kicked into gear. "Tell me what kind of boots these are, Seals."

"Well, Chief, we call them farmer's boots."

Looking at Seals with a perturbed expression on his freckled face, Rusty heard an under-the-breath chuckle coming from Kelly. "Very funny, Seals. Now, since this has to do with a case we're working on, I prefer a no-nonsense answer."

"Sure, Chief." Seals gave him one of his irresistible smiles. "You'll notice that the rubber is thicker and more durable than the regular rubber boots are." As Rusty listened, still examining the boot, he nodded. "Those deep ridges in the sole grip the wet ground. When you trudge through mud and snow to do chores, you need that kind of traction so you don't fall on your ass.

The farmers like these boots because they're made to fit over, and protect the laced-up work shoes. Now there are some other kinds of rubber work boots on the market that work just as good as these do, and you don't even have to wear shoes inside of them. However—" Seals recognized Rusty's 'enough-is-enough' glare, so he concluded his lengthy explanation, "other than what you see there, that's about all I can tell you, Chief."

"Can anyone just walk in and buy these?" Rusty questioned.

"Gee, Chief, I need these boots, since I threw my old ones away."

Both Rusty and Kelly gave Seals a look of bewilderment. Seals kept right on talking, like nothing was wrong. "I don't want to sell them. They can order their own if—"

"Seals!" Rusty exclaimed. "I'm not talking about *your* damn boots."

Seals wrinkled his brow. Appearing innocent, he asked, "You're not?"

"No, Barney, I'm not."

Kelly pressed his lips together to refrain from laughing. Rusty felt the need to spell out his question so Seals would understand.

"I want to know if *anyone* can walk into *any* shoe store and purchase a pair of boots just like these boots?"

"Oh," Seals replied, crossing his eyes. "Sorry. Well, you can just tell by looking at that boot, Chief, that they don't wear out very easy, or very fast. So, most stores don't stock but one or two pair, if that. Most times, they have to be special ordered."

Now Rusty was getting the kind of relevant information he needed. "Good, that should narrow our search down some."

After handing the boot back to Seals, and the cast to Kelly, he walked over to the large map mounted on the wall. Making a circle gesture across the map with his hand, Rusty stated, "All right, let's check out a hundred-mile radius from here. Kelly you take Kidwell and everything north and east. Seals you take the west and south areas. I'll make calls to the shoe stores in Omaha and Lincoln."

He walked back to the desk of Officer Seals as he spoke. "I want a list of every person who has special ordered this type of an overshoe."

Rusty lifted the side of the boot box. "Now, I'm sure there will be different manufacturers of this boot. So, describe the boot, especially the sole, and give the people you talk to the brand name and item number that's on this boot box. Maybe that will help them understand which type of boot we're looking for." Letting go of the box, he continued his instructions. "Once we get our list together, then we can start narrowing it down to the buyers who live in our area. Any questions?"

Kelly and Seals both spouted, "Yes." They cast each other a questioning stare.

"Seals, go ahead," Rusty said.

"It's not exactly a question, Chief, but I thought you should know. I didn't order my boots from a shoe store. The last time I looked, we didn't even have a shoe store in town."

"Then where did you get them for crying out loud?" Rusty no more than finished his question when his somber face lit up with a smile. "You know, you're right, Seals. There hasn't been a shoe store in Kidwell for the past ten years. I let that one slip past me, didn't I?"

Seals grinned. That was the first time he had gotten one up on Rusty since he worked for him.

"Don't feel like the Lone Ranger, Chief," Kelly said. "I missed that one myself."

"Okay, Seals, tell me where you got the boots."

"From the True Value store here in town. They have the best prices for them."

"Can you purchase those overshoes in shoe stores?" Rusty asked.

"I don't know."

"Do you know if there are any other kinds of stores that either carry them or will order them for you?"

"Sure. Any number of veterinarians that carry farming supplies, farm and ranch supply stores, and several catalogs that cater to the farmers."

"Well, there shouldn't be more than a dozen or so vets, shoe stores, or farming supply stores in the area," Rusty surmised, "but I want them all checked. For the time being, we'll have to pass on catalog sales.

What's your question, Kelly?"

"How far back in time do you want us to go?"

"One year should be sufficient, since Seals says these boots last for some time before wearing out.

By the way, is Janx still out on patrol?"

Both officers nodded.

"Okay. Anything else, Kelly?"

"No."

"Seals?"

"Nope."

"Okay, let's get to work."

Rusty and his officers started burning up the phone wires. They called all of the stores in and around the hundred-mile radius from Kidwell, including Omaha and Lincoln, trying to compile the list of names they needed. At the end of the day, they met in Rusty's office.

"Talk about your dead end," Rusty commented. "According to the stores I contacted, almost every farmer in the State of Nebraska, including the surrounding states, must have the same kind of overshoe we're looking for."

"Yeah, I pretty much got the same feedback," Kelly said.

"Me, too," Seals added. "But, Chief, isn't that to be expected since we live in a farming community, or should I say, a farming state?"

Agreeing, Kelly nodded.

"Yes, I know, Seals," Rusty said. "I was just hoping we might pick up a clue."

Rusty got to his feet. Taking hold of his belt with both hands, he hiked up his pants as he walked to his office window. Kelly and Seals sat in silence, waiting for their boss to either give them more orders, or to dismiss them. Rusty didn't do either.

"You know, looking for one particular boot owner in a rural area surrounded by farms is like looking for a pheasant in a cornfield. The pheasant can eventually be flushed out, but it will take time and plenty of patience."

Rusty liked to close his cases in an expeditious manner. This one was no different. However, with his face up against a brick wall, he realized this one had to be put aside for the time being. "Officers, it might take a while, but we *will* flush this thief out of his hiding place."

GETTING TO KNOW YOU

As much as Darin was sincere about wanting off the farm, away from Kidwell, and away from his dead-end bank job in Sharpin, he was having too much fun foiling the law. Now, more than child's play, it was beginning to be a heavy-duty cat and mouse game, and he loved every minute of it.

The way Darin had his plan figured, he could play his game for at least one more year. Then, be set for his future. With enough money, he could make some sound investments, and, perhaps, never work again for the rest of his life. Building on his ego, he just knew he was born to be a wealthy playboy in New York, not some poor dirt farmer in Nebraska.

Several months had gone by. Several more burglaries had taken place. Rusty was getting extremely frustrated that he couldn't find the culprit responsible. He was, also, very irritated that the area's citizens, although warned, were still being foolish. They continued to keep money and valuables in their homes, unprotected from burglars.

Kidwell was a laid back, rather lazy sort of town. There were no city buses, no fast traffic with loud noises, and people were not in a constant rush from one place to another. Other than the rash of burglaries, crime was just a five-letter word.

In fact, all of Cole County, which included both Kidwell and Sharpin, had never before had more than candy stolen from the local grocery store. That candy-stealing, law-breaking citizen was a five-year old. The little girl's parents took her to meet Police Chief Simmons, who promptly gave her a small lecture about stealing, and a tour of the jail's lockup facility. She never took another thing since that eventful day.

Many people still left their doors unlocked when they would leave their homes. Some women still thought nothing of leaving their purses unattended in an unlocked car.

Helping to keep the town safe, Rusty made sure that his officers took turns patrolling the streets. Every now and then, when he needed to take a break from office work, like this particular day, Rusty took a turn patrolling Once he made his slow cruise down the main street of town, then through the residential neighborhood, he headed back to the department.

After arriving at his office, Rusty reclined in his old, familiar desk chair. The fact that he hadn't caught the person responsible for the burglaries around the Cole County area wouldn't give his mind a minutes worth of piece.

"Because of this perpetrator's insistent tidiness as he burglarizes these homes, he definitely earns the name I've been calling him. Neat Nick Thief will have to do until I find out his real name and catch him. Then, of course, I'll have some other choice words to call him, which will be everything but his real name."

Although he needed outside help, without any more clues than they had, there was no one to ask. "I'll have to fight this battle myself, but I'll get you, you SOB," Rusty verbalized with contempt. "Then you'll be just another mutt locked in a cage."

After going over the case information once again, an important fact leaped out at him. Up to this point, Rusty couldn't place the victims having anything in common, except they lived in the same area, and, as in most small towns, knew each other as acquaintances. Now, here it was staring him in the face in black and white. Something he had missed on previous readings of both his hand-written notes and the printed reports.

"Jumping Joe—Why didn't I catch this one before now? This bank business is as obvious as a turd in a swimming pool. I must be slipping."

Wanting to requisition all the known burglary victims first, Rusty then wanted to go to the bank in Sharpin and do some follow-up. Since Sharpin was out of his law enforcement jurisdiction, he called Chief Kings to ask permission to do his investigation in the Sharpin area. Since the Sharpin Police Chief was out of town, his officer-in-charge gave his consent, stating he and the other Sharpin Officers would assist in any way they could.

After questioning all the victims, being specific when asking about their loans at First People's Bank of Sharpin, Rusty could only draw one conclusion. Loan Officer Dodd was a prime suspect. Rusty went to Sharpin bank to meet Mr. Dodd.

At the bank, Rusty strolled over to a woman sitting behind a desk. Removing his gray, felt, western-style hat, he ran his fingers through his red hair, making sure it wasn't standing on end. He greeted the female bank employee who was an old familiar face. "Hi, Nancy. How's life been treating you?"

Looking up from her work, Nancy smiled. "Just fine, thank you, Rusty. I haven't seen you in here in a coon's age. How have you been?"

"Still kicking." He laughed.

"What can I do for you, today?"

"I understand you have a Mr. Dodd employed here."

"Yes, we—Oh, my, he hasn't done anything wrong has he?"

"No, no, it's nothing like that. I understand he's the loan officer here."

"My goodness, Rusty, he's been with us for a few years now."

"I guess I wouldn't know that, since I've never come in for a loan."

"Nor read the local newspapers," she joked.

"I do read the newspapers, as often as I can. Like to keep up on what goes on in our county. If his name was in the news, I might have seen it. Just don't remember. Getting old, I reckon," he admitted, with a laugh.

"Aren't we all? Did you want to see Mr. Dodd, or are you just asking for curiosity sake?"

"Yes, I would like to talk to him."

Receiving no answer after ringing the extension for Mr. Dodd from her desk phone, Nancy arose from her chair. "Mr. Dodd doesn't appear to be in his office. I'll go find him and see if he has some free time to see you."

Since Rusty didn't want Dodd warned that he was on official business, he let Nancy's comment slide.

Rusty turned to view the surroundings. It had been quite awhile since he paid the bank a visit. He liked the convenience of doing his banking by mail.

The wait wasn't long before he noticed Nancy walking toward him, motioning for him to join her. Rusty followed as Nancy led the way to Mr. Dodd's office. She introduced them before returning to her desk.

"Please, take a chair, Chief Simmons." Even though Rusty knew his visit wouldn't take long, he took a seat. "So, what may I do for you, today?"

"Well sir, Mr. Dodd, I'm here to give you a special invitation to come over to my office in Kidwell."

"Me? What on earth for?"

"I'd like to ask you a few questions regarding some of the bank's customers."

Dodd shook his head. He pushed his glasses back to the bridge of his nose. "I can't discuss customer information with you. If you want any of their banking history, you'll, uh, have to speak to the bank's president, Mr. Shomond. Besides, I couldn't possibly take time away from my job."

With a pearly-white grin, Rusty replied, "You know, it's funny you should say that. I called C. D. before I came over here today. I explained to him that I felt you could help me out on an investigation I'm working on. He approved your time away from the bank. So, how about next Tuesday afternoon in my office, at 2:00."

"Why can't you just ask me now what you want to know, and save me the trip?"

"It's more private," Rusty stood, placing his hat on his head, "and more convenient in *my* office."

Reaching for his appointment book, Dodd stated, "Let me check to see if I have an opening then." After flipping a few pages, and running his finger down his noted appointments, he replied, "I don't seem to have anything at that time, but—"

Not wanting Dodd to find an excuse to change his mind, Rusty remarked, "Good. I'll see you then," as he walked out the door.

Darin's luck seemed to be holding out. Earlier, when he heard Nancy introducing Chief Simmons to Mr. Dodd, he stayed out of sight. There was no way he wanted Rusty to see him. After eavesdropping on their conversation, Darin began to get a little fidgety.

What in the hell was Rusty doing here, asking Dodd to meet with him? Chill, Darin. If he suspected you, you would be the one Rusty is calling into his office, not Dodd.

Darin knew he had to figure out a way to find out what is going on. Problem was, he couldn't do a thing until after Rusty and Dodd had their meeting. Until then, he just had to stay cool and not plan any more burglaries. Patience would have to overrule wealth, at that moment in time.

Tuesday, at 2:00 p.m., Dodd walked into the Kidwell Police Department. Waiting for him, Rusty met his suspect in the front office.

"Come on in, Mr. Dodd." Rusty led the way. "Glad you could make it, and on time. I admire someone who is prompt. Have a seat and take the load off." Rusty gestured for Dodd to sit in the chair across from his desk, as he reclined in his usual high-back leather chair behind his desk.

The air was thick with anxiety. Rusty felt the uneasiness that Dodd was generating through his shaking hands and incessant moving of his mouth. To put him at ease, Rusty commented, "Say, did anyone ever tell you that you resemble Mr. Peepers?"

"Mister who?" Dodd asked with a look of perplexity. He reached up with his index finger, placed it on the ridge of his nose, and pushed his horn-ribbed glasses back in place—a clear demonstration of one of his habits.

Rusty laughed. "I guess you're far too young to remember Wally Cox, aren't you?"

"I guess so. I've never heard of either of those people before," Dodd admitted. "I do find it a bit coincidental, however, since my given name is Wallace."

Rusty almost choked. "Does anyone call you Wally?"

"Yes, but I prefer Wallace."

"Well, Wallace, you're the spittin' image of Wally Cox. You see, the character, Mr. Peepers, was portrayed by Wally Cox." Dodd sat with a blank look on his face. "You'll have to forgive me. I'm a born lover of old movies and classic television shows. I love meeting people and comparing their looks and actions to some of the unforgettable characters and actors of my time. It's just a hobby with me. Everyone I meet, I try to associate them with someone famous."

Receiving no reaction from Dodd, Rusty got down to business. "So, Wallace, how long have you been an accountant?"

"Excuse me, but I'm not an accountant," Dodd sputtered, again pushing his glasses into position.

Some people just look like their profession, and I'll be jiggered if Dodd doesn't look like an accountant. Guess I was wrong. But, I'm sure not wrong about who he reminds me of. If I didn't know that little guy was deceased, I'd swear old Wally was sitting right across my desk from me. "Oh, I'm sorry. You just appear to me as a man who is smart with numbers."

Feeling as though Rusty was complimenting him, Dodd reacted more favorably. "Well, I used to be an accountant until I got the job at the bank. A loan officer deals with figures, but is several steps above an accountant."

Rusty's eyes twinkled. *So, I was right.*

As nervous as he was, Dodd admitted, "I don't know what this is all about, Chief Simmons. You said you had some questions to ask me concerning an investigation you're working on. Could you be more specific?"

After finding out a bit of Mr. Dodd's personal and professional background, Rusty proceeded to ask about his connection to the burglary victims. Rusty's routine questioning about L.C. Schmikel and Jeremiah Hosh got him nowhere. According to Mr. Dodd, he merely knew them as bank customers. When asked about Digs Chadron, however, Wallace Dodd's information added fuel to Rusty's preconceived suspicions about him.

After Dodd exited the building, Rusty asked one of his officers to do a thorough background check on Wallace Dodd. "I want to know everything about him from the day he was born, up to and including the present. That little weasel has motive with a capital M. He's so jealous of those people with their hidden cash assets, that it's not even funny.

Also, check where he was on the days in question. I think he spilled the beans when he put himself on Digs Chadron's property before and after the burglary. Yes, I think we might have our first good suspect." Rusty sported a proud smile, realizing that they might have something real to go on.

When Dodd returned to the bank, he asked Darin to bring him files he needed for his next appointment. As Darin took the files into the loan officer's office, he almost tripped over his own nose. To satisfy his curiosity, he began his inquiries.

"Hey, man, you look a little frayed around the edges. Bad day?"

Getting papers together on his desk, Dodd barked, "No. I just, uh, had an appointment about which I don't wish to talk."

That kind of answer didn't give Darin the information he desired. As he started back to his own cubby, he turned and tried another approach. "Oh, by the way, I hear my old friend Rusty came into the bank to see you the other day. I was sorry I missed him. He's a good old guy, don't you think?"

Dodd looked up from his desk in bewilderment. "Darin, not that I really care or have the time to discuss your personal friends right now, but who is Rusty?"

"Rusty? He's my brother's best friend. Oh, I'm sorry, I wasn't thinking. Maybe you would recognize the name by his official title. He's Police Chief Simmons from Kidwell."

Dodd took a sudden interest in what Darin was saying. "Rusty is Chief Simmons? He's a friend of your brother?"

"Sure. Well, he's my friend too. Gee, I'm sorry I missed him." Then he turned, as if to be leaving.

"Wait, Darin. I guess I have a few minutes. Sit down," Dodd insisted. Turning back, Darin took a seat. "You know, that friend of yours, he, uh, called me into his office today. That's why I look so frayed, as you put it. Why do you suppose he'd be asking me questions?"

"Oh, shoot, Mr. Dodd, I wouldn't worry about it. Rusty's the nosey type. Just because he's a police chief, he thinks he has the right to pry into everyone's business. What kind of questions did he ask you, anyway?"

"He asked me a lot of questions. What it boiled down to, is just how well I know any of the men in Cole County that have been burglarized."

"Interesting. Did he say if they had any new evidence? You know, any new leads in the unsolved cases?"

"Evidently not," Dodd said. "After he got through with me, however, I think I admitted to being jealous of those guys having money and not having to work for a living, like I am. I was halfway back to the bank before I realized what I had said. I no doubt incriminated myself. That man's clever."

Dodd's appointment arrived. Darin, now with his nose back in place, excused himself and returned to his cubby. *Ha, Rusty, you old son-of-a-gun, you've got Dodd sweating bullets. At least now I know there's still nothing on me. I can relax and continue with business as usual. Let's see now, who will be next on my list of contributors?*

Getting closer to his goal, Darin had close to $100 thousand hidden away. Even though he still enjoyed the game of cat and mouse, Darin felt he'd been playing a new game of poker and someone dealt him a winning hand. What he didn't know was that another player would enter the game, threatening his odds of winning.

HONESTY AND DECEPTION

Quite unexpected, Mr. Welk started having financial problems. For no reason that he could see, he started receiving bills in the mail from creditors because his checks were bouncing. That's when his life started on a downhill spiral.

At first, going over his accounting numbers, Jefferson couldn't understand where the problem existed. Even the computer he had purchased to help him keep up with his bookkeeping was of no use to him.

Since the bank sent statements on a quarterly basis, Jefferson had no way of checking recent credits and debits of his accounts to compare to his personal record keeping. According to his last bank statement, he had far too much money in his trust account for any one person to spend in ten lifetimes. The only conclusion he could draw—The mistake had to be the bank's error.

After a couple of complaining telephone calls to the accounting department, Jefferson kept hoping whomever at the bank was in charge of his money, would get his accounts straightened out. That didn't happen.

He had no other alternative but to call the bank, once again. After briefing the bank employee on the other end of the telephone about his dilemma, he stated, "Don't put me through to accounting, again. I want to speak to someone with authority in regards to my trust account."

The major mistake Jefferson made, was not making an immediate request to speak to C.D. Shomond. However, Jefferson was under the impression that the party he was connecting with would be the right person to assist him. That's when real trouble entered his life.

"Mr. Welk, this is Darin Righter. I understand you are seeking help with your accounts?"

"Well, Mr. Righter, I've already called twice about this problem, and no one's done a darn thing to help me. Each day, it seems to get worse. For years, I never used my trust to run my farm. That all changed a few months back. With a bad crop, and the sales of milk and eggs from my farm being at an all time low, I figured it was time to let my trust money pay for my living expenses. I started—"

"Sir, if you'll—"

"Hold on a minute. I don't mean to be rude, Mr. Righter, but I'd like to finish what I've got to say."

"By all means, go ahead."

"As I was saying, I started charging my needs, knowing I could pay off the bills each month when the bank issued me my once a month funds. All of my life, I've had excellent credit. Now, I'm being plagued with creditors because I haven't been receiving my checks from you people. What's more, all my checks are being returned as insufficient funds. So you see, Mr. Righter, you have to get my accounts straightened out, right away."

"I'm sorry, but your trust fund has dried up and your checking account appears to be closed due to lack of funds. Now, if you want to make a deposit, we can re-activate the checking account."

"What do you mean dried up and closed? That was my money, not the bank's. There's no way millions of dollars could have just disappeared. That's an impossibility."

"I'm just explaining what our records show, Mr. Welk."

"You know, I'm tired of this runaround and I don't give a hoot what your records show. If you can't help me, let me speak to someone who can. Better yet, put the bank president on the phone."

"I'm sorry, Mr. Welk, but I am the only one that can help you. You see, I am the manager of your account. I can assure you, your records are in my *closed* files."

No funds and closed accounts just didn't make any sense. However, having no one in his life that could help him or give him legal advice, Jefferson had to settle for the fact he was broke. The fear of losing everything he had worked for all his life because he couldn't bring in enough income to keep his farm going, weighed heavy on his shoulders. His farm was supposed to be his, free and clear, for the rest of his life.

The financial worry and his responsibilities were beginning to take their toll on Jefferson's health. His frail body and head of white hair buried all signs of the strapping young man that he once was. Each day became harder for him to keep up with his farm work, plus spend extra hours teaching Farm Girl her lessons.

Because of all the stress, he began taking extensive rest periods to keep up his energy. One-hour morning naps, before breakfast and after his early morning chores were completed, got him through the remainder of the morning. After dinner to revitalize his strength, he took a two-hour nap.

Mama would utilize Jefferson's afternoon naptime to clean the kitchen, make plans for Jefferson's supper, or do something constructive, like hand sewing.

That quiet time around the farm was Farm Girl's allotted time to sit on her rock and write her stories and a journal of her life. Her printing was terrible, and she made-up most of her vocabulary, spelling words as they sounded to her ears. However, that never kept her from writing.

* * *

On the other side of the county, seeking comfort from his closest and best friend, Frank stopped by the Kidwell Police Department.

"Is the chief in?" Frank asked the officer at the front desk.

Rusty's door was open. Recognizing a familiar voice, Rusty bellowed from his office, "Frank, is that you? Come on in here." As Frank walked into his office, Rusty was waiting for him with a warm handshake. "I knew that was your voice I heard. Sit down. Gosh, it's good to see you. Running errands in town today?"

"Well it proves you still have good hearing," Frank tried to joke, considering the frame of mind he was in.

"Hey, why the long face?"

"Rusty, do you mind if we close your door? I have some rather personal business and I'm in dire need of your help."

Frank didn't have to ask twice. Sobriety replaced happiness on Rusty's face as he closed his office door. He walked to his desk and sat in his chair.

Frank has never come to my office to talk about personal affairs unless Darin was in trouble. But I just saw Darin, not too long ago, when he stopped in here for a surprise visit. I assumed from our conversation that he had been staying out of mischief for the past few years. Of course, knowing Darin, he could have been lying to me. "What's going on, Frank? Is it Darin?"

"Not at all. Darin has been great since he's been home. What I want to talk about is very personal."

"Okay, what's on your mind?"

"First, I have to know that what I tell you here today, won't go any further than the walls in this room. I'm asking you as a friend, Rusty, not the police chief. Can you promise me that?"

"As long as it isn't a legal matter or no one is breaking the law, then sure. What's this about?"

Frank took a seat in front of Rusty's desk. "I guess the best thing is to start at the beginning.

Oh, I didn't even stop to think that you might be busy. Maybe you would rather that I come back at another time, when I'm not taking you away from your police duties?"

"I assume this is going to take a while, so hold on a minute." Rusty got on his intercom to the front office and told his desk officer to hold his calls. Unless it was a dire emergency, he was not to be disturbed until further notice. With that done, he leaned back in his chair and settled into a listening mode.

"Okay, Frank. I'm all yours. What's on your mind?"

"Just for my own knowledge, let me ask you a question first. Did you know your brother, Stu, had a girlfriend he was very serious about before he enlisted in the service?"

"My brother? No. I thought I knew everything about Stu." Rusty had a sudden thought. "Now hold on a minute. You're not going to lay a bombshell on me, like I have a niece or a nephew—"

"No, no. Nothing like that."

"That's a relief. The thought of a poor child being raised without a father, especially my own brother's child ..." having second thoughts, Rusty said, Never mind. You know, Frank, for as long as we've been friends, this is a strange time to bring up Stu's girlfriend."

"I know it is, and I have no excuse for not mentioning it before now. Truth is, I thought Stu had told you."

"No, he never said a word. He always talked about staying a bachelor like me. I never would have dreamed he found someone to capture his heart."

"Well, he did. Not that it matters, but his girl wasn't from Nebraska. She lived out of state. Stu really loved her. They had planned on getting married when his stint was up."

As he listened, it was difficult for Rusty to believe his own brother never confided in him about falling in love and planning a wedding.

"It was like Stu had a premonition that he wasn't going to make it out of Nam. He made me promise, should anything happen to him, that I would pay a visit to his girl. It was his hope that I would be able to comfort her.

Well, we both made it out of that miserable war with no scratches. However, when Stu was killed in that helicopter crash, I remembered my promise to him." Rusty's mind flashed back to his brother's accidental death while stationed in California at the Barstow Marine Base. "So, as promised—"

"I don't mean to be interrupt you, Frank, but does this girl have a name?"

"Allison McBride."

"Allison. What a pretty name. And, McBride? Well, now, there's a good old Irish name for you. So, has she been in contact with you, is that why you've come in here to talk to me today?"

"No, that's not it. And if you'll stop questioning me like a cop for a few minutes, I'm trying to tell you something."

"Sorry, buddy. Force of habit."

"When my hitch was up, I didn't come straight home. As promised, I went directly to Allison's home state where she lived on a horse ranch with her parents. She was a very nice, wholesome, young woman, Rusty, just Stu's type. You would have approved of her."

"If Stu loved her, I'm sure I would have."

"Anyway, I stayed there on the McBride's ranch.. While I was there, I got a little carried away and drank too much liquor. It could have been that I was still mourning your brother's death, or feeling Allison's loss and her pain, or just relieved that I was out of the service. What ever the reason, I drank everyday for the few short days I was there."

Because of the lump in his throat, Frank stopped talking. He turned his head toward the window. Tears filled his eyes. He was trying to compose himself before continuing.

Rusty felt the pain himself, as he had been close to his brother. Even though it had been over twenty years since Stu's death, it was still like a knife in his heart that his younger brother had to die before he had a chance to live the better part of his life.

Rusty broke the silence. "Look, Frank, I know talking about Stu and the war is hard for you. Would you like a cup of coffee or something?"

Frank shook his head, declining the offer. Taking a handkerchief from his pant's pocket, he wiped his eyes. He turned back to his friend, somewhat embarrassed. "Who'd have thought a grown man would cry so many tears, even after all these years?"

Clearing his throat, Frank continued. "Allison's parent's had a female working for them. Her name was Carole. Not that it makes any difference now, but I never did find out her last name. She was five years older than I was, and such a pretty, little thing. Well, she was pretty in my eyes," he admitted.

"Since there was only one extra room in the main house, I felt like my stay had kicked Carole out of the bedroom she was occupying before I got there. Without one word of complaint, she moved out of the bedroom and bedded down in the barn. At the time, of course, I didn't know that's where she had moved to.

The night before I left, Allison and I were still drinking. Reminiscing about Stu, we went from tears to laughter, and then back again. Neither one of us was a seasoned drinker, but we really laid one on that night.

After Allison passed out on the couch, I went outside to get some fresh air. In my drunken stupor, I stumbled into the barn where Carole was sleeping. I guess I tripped over a broom or something. I went flying through space, eyebrows over toenails, and went crashing to the ground. My startling noise woke her up.

Carole came over to see if I was all right, and helped me to my feet. Then, as I leaned on her, she helped me over to her bed in the straw, and sat me down. I just had a minor cut on my forehead, but she got a cold, wet cloth and wiped the wound. Her touch was like an angel. Without thinking, I grabbed her and kissed her. Rusty, that was my first real kiss. I never had too many girlfriends in all my years of growing up, thanks to my witch of a mother I … " Frank hesitated.

He dropped his eyes to the floor then looked back at his friend. "Look, Rusty, I'm not going to sugarcoat anything here. I know I can be honest with you and say it like it is."

"Of course you can, Frank," Rusty agreed, nodding his approval. "I don't understand why it's taken so many years for us to have this conversation, but it's obvious something is eating away at you. Are you in trouble?"

Rusty's words fell on deaf ears. As Frank closed his eyes, wrapped in his memories, he could almost feel the passion he felt that night.

"After I kissed Carole, well, one thing led to another. I couldn't keep my hands off her. I helped her slip out of her dress. There she stood, as naked as a Jaybird. My God, I had never seen a naked woman before. My pulse was racing, my male hormones were stirring, and I don't even remember breathing. Never in my life had I ever dreamed of witnessing such a perfect body. I was mesmerized." Licking his lips in a very sensuous way, he stated, "Umm, I can still taste the sweetness of her today. My entire body was—"

Rusty cleared his throat. The noise jolted Frank. He stopped in mid-sentence and opened his eyes. "Sorry, Rusty, I guess I got carried away."

Rusty attempted to comfort him with a hint of a smile. "That's okay, Frank. I didn't mean to distract you. So, what happened next?"

"I guess I passed out because when I woke up, I was lying next to her. I never said a word, just got up and found my way back to the house. Later that afternoon, I found her out in the stable brushing down one of the horses. I apologized to her.

She never even turned away from what she was doing. All she said, was that she didn't understand why I was apologizing for having sex with the likes of her because she was nobody worth fretting over. Then she turned and walked away, leaving me standing there like a penny waiting for change.

Let me back up here, if I may, Rusty. You knew my mother, right?"

"Just as an acquaintance. Why?"

"She was a hard case. In fact, I joined the service to get away from the old bitty. She was always running my life. Shoot, I couldn't go to the bathroom without her knowing about it."

"I vaguely remember you saying something about it before, but you never went into details."

"That's because I've been too ashamed to talk about it before now. The gist of it is, I thought going into the service would give me some guts. When I returned home, I wanted to be able to tell Mother I was a grown man and had a right to run my own life without her constant interference.

Don't get me wrong, she was my mother and I loved her, but I hated her at the same time. I don't' know if that makes any sense at all to love someone yet despise them, Rusty, but that's how I felt."

After taking a short time to collect his thoughts, Frank continued. "Because I had been intimate with Carole, I had this terrible guilt feeling eating away at me. I couldn't get her out of my head or why I cared so much, especially since she tossed my apology into the wind.

Trying to make sense of it, I began to realize it wasn't guilt that I felt. It was something else. Problem was, I couldn't put my finger on it, at the time. Not wanting to believe that I had raped her, I tried to convince myself that we had made love. In all sincerity, I didn't know, right then, what it was that had happened.

That night, feeling depressed, and being drunk on my ... " Frank stopped to moisten his dry lips. "The truth is, Rusty, I had never been with a woman until that night." Because Rusty had sewn a few oats in his heyday years, he was a bit surprised to hear that Frank had not done the same. "Before I left to return home, I made it a point to find her and say good-bye. The look on her face was heart wrenching. I wanted to run. But, do you know what I did instead?"

"What?" Rusty asked, wiggling to get more comfortable in his chair.

"I held her close to me and cried like a baby. Something within the depths of my very being told me I cared for this woman. Not being experienced in the love department, I wasn't aware of the true meaning of love. Just the same, even though I didn't know this woman, my gut, my head and my heart told me I was in love with her. The sad part about that realization was that old gutless wonder here didn't have the nerve to tell her in words how I felt.

I wanted to give her something to remember me by, but I had nothing on me to give. I ran back in the house thinking I could find some little token in my luggage to leave with her. Lucky for me, Allison was bringing in a fresh cut bouquet—All that's not important, right now. Anyway, as much as a dreaded it, I returned home. I had been gone a little over four years, but nothing had changed. My mother was just as demanding as ever. That's when I made up my mind, I couldn't live that way. Not again.

Digging deep into my soul, I found the courage to tell my mother that I was in love. Using extreme precaution, I omitted who the woman was or where she lived. I informed my mother that I was going to ask the woman to marry me.

Well, one would have thought that the world had come to an end. I'll never forget my mother's rage. She called me every nasty name in the book." Frank took his handkerchief and wiped the perspiration from his face. "Well, Rusty, I have to admit it. I was a wimp. Courage or intestinal fortitude, they just weren't in my make-up. Can you believe that? I wore a uniform and went into battle, afraid of nothing, then came home and became a spineless wimp, again."

Deep within, Rusty's emotions were crying for his friend.

"As much as I hate to admit it, Rusty, I did exactly as my mother demanded. I buried myself in the farm, helping my father, but I never forgot Carole. A day didn't go by that I didn't feel more and more hatred for my mother for ruling me. I had an equal amount of hatred for my father for never standing up for me. I found Carole, once, after our meeting at Allison's, but only to lose her again.

Okay, Rusty, that was the past, now this is the present. I'm sure after boring you for the past hour, you're wondering why I've told you this long drawn out story?"

After clearing his throat, Rusty remarked, "I assume you decided to talk about something that's been bottled up inside of you for years."

"Maybe in my subconscious. But that's not the main reason I've been bending your ear. For the past few months, I've had some serious health problems. Doc Shively got my test results back, today. I came straight here from his office because his news made me realize the importance of finding Carole."

"You sick, Frank? Is there anything I can do?"

"I won't lie to you, Rusty. I have cancer." Frank swallowed hard. "Doc wants me to have surgery then follow with radiation and chemotherapy treatments. But I can't do that until I get the pieces of my life put together."

Shocked by the news of Frank's health, Rusty fought to keep his heart-felt emotions inside where his friend couldn't see them. He felt Frank needed his support, not his pity. "My good Lord, Frank. I'm sorry to hear that. I hate to ask the obvious, but I've got to. Does Darin know?"

"No! And I don't want him to know. Not yet. What I want is for you to help me locate Carole. After I find her and get that part of my life straightened out, then I will have a talk with Darin. Can you do that, Rusty? Can you help me find her?"

"Dang, Frank, you're talking about someone you met twenty years ago."

"I know. And I wouldn't ask you, if it didn't mean a lot to me to find her."

"Well, I'll do what I can.

As for your health, you know how a small town loves to gossip, especially ours. It won't take long before everyone will know what's wrong with you. So, you had better tell Darin before he hears rumors from someone else."

"Rusty, as far as my health is concerned, I trust everyone in Doc's office to keep my medical information private. I also trust you. Rest assured, Darin will not find out about my illness until I tell him.

As far as finding Carole is concerned, I want this to stay off the record. Not that I wouldn't trust your officers, but I'm hoping you can help me without anyone else knowing."

"What's the big mystery, Frank?"

"Please, Rusty, trust me. When the time is right, I'll explain everything you need to know."

"You know you're my dearest friend, but you're asking me to break the law."

"No, I don't want you to do anything illegal. I'm just asking you to bend the law, a little. Can't you do that for me?"

Shaking his head, Rusty's mind raced. He glanced around the room, allowing his eyes to bounce back and forth between his numerous law enforcement awards that decorated the walls. Torn between his love for a friend and his duty as an officer of the law, Rusty didn't like having to make such a choice.

After careful consideration, he finally consented. "Okay, Frank, but I've got to tell you," he pointed his finger, shaking it at Frank, "if you ever tell anyone that I'm using my uniform to get you personal data on someone, and I find out about it, I'll—well, I'll never forgive you and I'll deny it to my dying day."

Looking rather somber, but relieved, Frank nodded. "This goes beyond everything I believe in," Rusty admitted, dropping his hand to the desk. "Like you said when you came in here today, what is said in this room stays between you and me and these four walls. I'll do all I can to help.

Now that I've got that off my chest—" Rusty opened his desk drawer and pulled out a legal pad. Tossing the canary-yellow pad on his desktop, he closed the drawer. Once he had pen in hand, he asked, "You said her name is Carol. Is that a C or a K?"

"C."

"And you said that when you met her, you never found out her last name?"

"Yes, that's what I said."

After Rusty wrote down the name, he looked back at Frank "Well, can you tell me anything else about this woman? There must be thousands of females walking around with the name Carol. What about Allison McBride or her parents, have you asked them about this woman?"

"I've already contacted Allison, but Carole seems to have disappeared from the face of the earth." Placing his handkerchief back in his pocket, Frank took a piece of paper out of his shirt pocket. After unfolding it, he slid the paper across the desk.

"Here's all of the information I could think of to help you in your search. It is nothing more than her description, how old she would be today, the state where I met her and other minute details. That's all I can give you."

Picking up the paper, Rusty briefly scanned its contents. "This sure isn't much to go on."

"I know, but that's all I can give you, right now."

"Okay, but if you think of any thing else that might help locate her, let me know."

"Thanks, Rusty. You can rest assured that I will take this conversation to my grave. Which, in all probability, isn't too long from now," he added.

Rusty was the first one to tease and joke around, but at this moment, he was not at all in the mood. "That's not funny."

Shrugging, Frank stated, "Maybe not, but I know I don't have too much time left here on earth. That's why it's so important that I tie up a few loose ends in my life before I take my last breath."

"Why don't you tell me more about this cancer you have, and when you plan on telling Darin."

"It's like I said, I just got the diagnosis before I came over here to see you. Without going into medical details, let's just say that I know what I have is terminal. Without the proper care, Doc's given me two, three years at the most. And that's if I'm lucky." Rusty felt a lump in his throat. "However, I can't stress enough that I don't plan on telling Darin, or anyone else other than you. Not just yet."

"Damn it, Frank, Darin needs to know."

"Today is Darin's birthday. Do you really think I need to give him a birthday present like that? No, I'll just keep it to myself for the time being."

"Well, maybe not today, but you've got to tell him soon. As your closest living relative, he has a right to know." Frank gave Rusty a look of dismay. "Okay, I'll shut up about Darin. Besides, what's most important right now is for you to do like Doc suggested. If he thinks surgery and all those other treatments will help you rid your body of this life threatening disease, then that—"

"Hold on, Rusty. As much as I appreciate your concern, I have to do things my way. Now, let's change the subject before I start feeling sorry for myself and break into tears like a blubbering idiot, again. What's happening with your burglary investigations?"

"I'm not getting anywhere and it's frustrating as all get out. There have been nine burglaries over this past nine-month period, and this month isn't even over yet. That clown hasn't slipped up once, with the exception of a few boot prints. I lie awake at nights wondering who this jerk will hit next and for how much. It's enough to give a man ulcers."

Rusty clutched a sheet of scratch paper off his desk. "If I don't do anything else before I turn in my badge," with an anger even he didn't realize he had, Rusty scrunched the paper with force between his hands, "I'll get that 'dirtbag.' When I do, it'll be a slam dunk," he tossed the wad of paper into his wastebasket, a few feet away, "just like that. Cops one. Perp zero."

"I hope you do catch the guilty party. Lord knows he has robbed a lot of good people and taken their hard earned money. It's certainly the first time I can ever remember something like this happening in Cole County."

"According to what's on the county books, there never has been a rash of house burglaries in our area before this one. I have high hopes, when I catch this sticky-fingered SOB, it won't happen again."

Frank got up from his chair. "Well, I've taken enough of your time. I'll be on my way." Rusty stood and walked around his desk. "It seems rather lame to say after everything I've laid on you today, Rusty, but thanks for everything."

After the two shook hands, Rusty embraced his friend. "Anytime, Frank. I'll always try to help if you need me. Look, you take care of yourself. I'll be talking to you soon."

On his drive back to the farm, even though Frank was more than distressed about his health, he felt a bit of comfort in knowing he had finally confided in Rusty about some of his most personal secrets. Most of all, he felt relieved that Rusty would be helping him find Carole.

A short time later, he was sitting at the kitchen table, reading the local newspaper, when Darin came home from work.

"So, how was your day?" Frank asked.

"Same as yesterday, and the day before.

How long before we eat?"

"Dinner's in the oven. We'll eat a little later than normal this evening. I got hung up in town longer than I planned."

"No problem. I have to go out, but it can wait until after dinner.

Anything new in the paper?"

Removing his jacket, Darin hung it over the back of a chair. Taking a beer from the refrigerator, he popped the top and took a big swig. He remained standing, leaning against the counter.

"It seems like the only news, anymore, is about that guy that Rusty calls the Neat Nick Thief. He appears to be all the folks in town are talking about these days. I can't believe the law hasn't caught him before now, but Rusty says this guy is too dang smart. He never seems to leave any good clues that will help catch him. Oh, well, he'll make a huge goof, one of these days."

"Why do you say that?"

"Sooner or later he has to slip up. It's the law of averages. Whoever this person is, he sure has gotten a bundle of money these past nine months. Even some of my friends have lost their life's savings," Frank complained. "That no good coyote ought to have his hands cut off, like they do to the thieves in some foreign countries."

"Whoa! Don't get yourself all in a huff over some frigging idiots that don't want to put their savings in a bank where it's safe. Don't you think they are just asking for someone to rob them?"

"No way. Yes, I believe a bank is safer than stashing money away in your own home. But those people who wish to do so have that right. It's their money to do with as they please. By the way, I got out Dad's old pistol and cleaned it up. If that two-legged varmint ever comes around here, and I catch him, he won't live to tell about it."

"A pistol? I didn't even know the old man had one. Hey, what are you worried about? You don't have large amounts of money hidden around here, do you?"

"I have a little, Darin, but don't you worry about it. He's as good as dead, if I ever catch him around here."

Don't worry, Frank. I'm not about to steal from my own brother. If I did, then who could I borrow cash from until I get out of this cow town? "Why do you keep saying him? Did your friend, Rusty, get some new information?"

"No, Rusty hasn't said one way or the other. But odds are, the thief is a man. That's just my opinion.

So, what's on tonight's agenda?"

"I've got a big date."

"You don't say," Frank grinned.

"Don't go getting any ideas. It's just a date with a friend. Nothing serious."

"Since dinner's late, sit with me for a few minutes. I need to talk to you." Frank folded the newspaper and laid it aside.

Joining Frank at the table, Darin asked, "What's on your mind?"

"I haven't been feeling well. So, I was wondering if you'd mind helping me out a little with the chores? Now, I know you have a full time job. Under normal circumstances, I wouldn't ask for your help. I just thought—well, maybe a couple of hours in the evenings and on weekends you could cut down on some of your drinking time and give me a hand."

After taking another drink, Darin lit a cigarette. *Damn, Frank, I hate farm work. You know that. And I'm not out friggin' drinking all the time. I have better things to do, like financing my bankroll for my future. This farm is yours, not mine. Not that I'd want it even if you handed it to me on a silver platter. Of all the stupid damn times to get sick, why does it have to be now?* "Sick? Like the flu, or what?"

"No, not the flu. I just haven't been feeling up to par. Seems I forget a lot, like where I put things, or didn't put things. Guess I'm getting old, like you reminded me not too long ago."

"Forgive me for being thick headed, but what does absent-mindedness have to do with not feeling well?"

"Nothing. I was just rambling. Look, it's no big deal if you can't or don't want to help me. I understand., knowing how you dislike the farm."

"That's an understatement. If you want my opinion, you look good and healthy to me. Maybe you just have a bug that will clear itself up. I'll tell you what, give it a few weeks and maybe you'll feel better. If not, and if you still think you need my help, I'll plan on a few hours in the evenings after work. By the way, you aren't that old. You know me, I just like to tell you you're getting old because I enjoy pulling your chain." *You gullible old fart.*

Trying to be agreeable, Frank smiled. *If you only knew how sick I really am. It isn't a bug that is just going to disappear within a few weeks, but I can't burden you with my illness right now. You have your life and I'm not going to ruin it. God willing, I'll just have to do my best on my own.*

"Sure, Darin, that's fine. Well now, if you want to take your beer and cigarette in the other room, I'll check on my roast in the oven then get the table set for dinner. Here," he said, handing Darin the newspaper, "take this darn thing with you. It's too depressing."

Placing his cigarette in his mouth, Darin stuck the newspaper under his arm. He took his beer to the living room and got comfortable on the couch. He scanned the paper to see if there was any new information about the burglaries. There was nothing but repetitive news about the unsolved cases.

There was, however, an article of information confirming what he had heard at the bank earlier that day. Through the bank's grapevine, Darin heard that a land developer had purchased the old flourmill and all its property. The mill's buildings were scheduled to be torn down and the ground leveled. Darin didn't like what he had overheard, but until now, couldn't confirm the rumors.

As he looked over the article, he read part of it to himself. "Yeah, yeah, yeah, 'but the mayor says the deal will take at least eighteen to twenty-four months to finalize. Until then, the mill remains the property of' dah, dah, dah.

That's good, but I still need to set up my backup plan. So, when the time comes and I have to move my cash, I will know right where to hide it. I already made my appointment for this evening, so I can't be late. I sure hope Frank hurries and gets dinner on the table. It's imperative that I get out of here on time."

"Did you say something, Darin?" Frank called out from the kitchen.

Shoot! For a guy who's complaining about being sick and getting old, he sure has good ears. Obviously, I was speaking louder than I thought. "Yes, didn't you hear what I said?" Darin yelled back.

"No, but I thought I heard your voice. If you were speaking to me, you'll have to speak louder, or come in here."

Again, Darin yelled, "I said, how soon till dinner? I'm starved."

"You're always starved. I'm moving as fast as I can, Darin. Ten more minutes, tops."

Frank got the cake out of the pantry, which he had hidden there earlier. Right in the center, he placed one large candle before setting the cake in the middle of the table. He finished setting the table for dinner. After placing a one hundred dollar bill under Darin's dinner plate, he lit the candle. He had pondered giving Darin five hundred dollars as his gift, but considering Darin was always borrowing money for drinking, he figured Darin would spend it too fast on foolishness.

"Okay, Darin, you can bring your appetite in the kitchen, now. Dinner's on the table."

As Darin entered the kitchen, he couldn't help but notice the cake. A big smile adorned his face. "Hey, Frank, I thought you forgot."

"No way. Happy Birthday, Darin. Come on. Sit down. Then make a wish and blow out your candle."

Darin took a seat, closed his eyes, and made his wish. *Okay, brother of mine, my wish is that I get off this frigging farm for good, just as soon as possible.* Darin opened his eyes, and blew out his candle.

"Okay, what did you wish for?" Frank asked, wearing a sheepish grin.

"You know I can't tell you, Frank, or it won't come true."

"Just kidding. But, you know what they say? Be careful what you wish for because it may come true," Frank joked.

"I certainly hope so, or what's the sense in making a wish?"

"You're right there. Let's eat."

After dinner, Darin wasn't pleased when Frank asked him to clear his own dirty dishes from the table. Just another chore Darin always hated. *Why don't you buy a friggin dishwasher? Then you would spend less time doing dishes, which would give you more time to clean off your own damn dirty table.*

As soon as he picked up his plate and spotted the hundred-dollar bill, his frown of displeasure turned into a forced grin. He picked up the bill and waved it in the air. "Hey, what's this cash doing here?" *Oh, whoppy-doo. Could you spare the lousy hundred, tightwad?* "Did you lose this, or is it a tip for picking up dishes?" Darin joked with sarcasm, tucking the bill into his shirt pocket.

"Sorry your gift has to be money, but I didn't know what to get you."

After depositing his dirty dishes in the sink, Darin felt he had done enough. He leaned back against the counter watching Frank clear the rest of the table.

"I always seem to be buying you clothes, and keeping gas in the car for you. So, I didn't know what else you would like. You should take up a hobby or something, Darin. You used to read a lot, but you don't even do that anymore."

Reaching into the cupboard next to him, Darin took a toothpick from its holder and started picking at his teeth. "That's because my favorite author doesn't write anymore."

"Maybe you can find an active sport to get involved in?"

Right, Frank, rub it in that you gave me a lousy hundred for my birthday because you keep paying for my other living expenses, and then offer a stupid suggestion.

"Oh, sure, I can just see me on a Thursday or Friday night bowling league, like all the other hicks around here. Or, maybe I should take up golf? Then I can be like those other idiots that hit that little white ball with a stupid club, walk around in the weeds full of cockleburs and thistles trying to find it, then hit it again to try and get it into a tiny hole in the ground. How exciting! No thank you, Frank. I can do without a hobby or active sport, as you call it. Besides, I have enough to keep me occupied."

Keeping his hands busy, Frank stayed calm and listened as Darin spouted off. After Frank had finished clearing the table and washed his hands, he got small plates out of the cupboard. As he placed the dishes on the table, a nasty thought came to mind in rebuttal of Darin's last comment.

Sure, Darin, complain how degrading it is to be a small town boy and only have a few things like a local bowling alley and a backwoods golf course at your disposal. Drinking, now there's a genuine sport. A real hobby. Steady old man. Don't say one word because as soon as you do, you become your mother. Hold your opinion to yourself and forget about it. Common sense dictated, so he replied, "Nope, I sure can't see you playing with either one of those balls.

Now, how about some cake and ice cream?"

"Gee, I'm sorry, Frank, but I can't." Tossing the toothpick in the sink of dirty dishes, Darin pulled his jacket from the back of the chair and walked toward the backdoor. "Don't have time. I have a date. Remember? Hey, you go ahead. I'll have some later when I get home. See ya," Darin said, as he walked out the door. .

"Yeah, see ya," Frank echoed, as he sat down at the table. "Thanks for the money, Frank. Oh, and thanks for the birthday cake. Yeah, right.

Oh, Darin, you don't seem to have one ounce of love, caring, or consideration in you for anyone else but yourself. And you certainly don't ever act grateful for anything I do for you. I hate to admit it, but more and more, you remind me of Mother. Of all people, I'm sorry you had to inherit her cold, arrogant traits. I wish I knew what made you tick."

Darin was long gone, and out of earshot. He was on his way to his appointment. As he drove, Darin mulled over his scheme. "So, Welk, from what I've heard, you're a man who's afraid of his own shadow. Dodd did me a favor giving me your trust account to handle. Seems the trust account paid you a healthy living expense and took care of your property taxes and insurance. Well, that has all changed, hasn't it? There is no more money from the trust, is there?

It's a real shame when you called the bank and spoke with me that I had to tell you that the bank couldn't help you out. What a kick in the butt, old man. Your fortune just seemed to vanish into thin air like a breeze in the night. Sorry, but you can't be sitting around and not paying your debts. Why, that just isn't fair.

I have you right where I want you. From what I know about you, you are easy to bamboozle. To twist an old proverb into my own words—If I don't venture, I don't gain."

Parking in Jefferson's driveway, Darin took time to look around the property he could see from the car. "Damn, I figured with all his money, the old man would be living in a mansion, not a cracker box. That's good. If the outside is any indication of the inside, he shouldn't have too many, if any, valuables in there to sell for cash."

Darin ran up and knocked on the front door.

"Who's there?" a voice shouted from behind the closed door.

"Mr. Welk, is that you?"

"It might be. Who are you and what do you want?"

"It's Mr. Righter, from the bank. I called and told you that I was coming out to see you. Remember?"

Jefferson turned on his porch light and opened the door. Through the screen door, his eyes inspected Darin from head to toe. "Yeah, I remember. I thought you were coming out earlier, not after the chickens have roosted for the night. Not only have you kept me up past my bedtime, but I don't like to open my door to strangers after dark."

Jetting his arm in the air to clear his wrist of his jacket sleeve, Darin checked his watch. "I'm sorry you misunderstood, but according to my watch, I'm right on time."

Jefferson didn't want to argue about time. He had stayed up awaiting Darin's visit in hopes there was good news about his money. "Maybe I didn't hear the correct time."

"I believe you can turn your porch light off, now that you've seen me. Wouldn't want those pesky old June bugs gathering around right here at your door," Darin joked, getting Welk to shut off the light. "Although it's a beautiful evening out here, mind if I step inside to talk with you?"

"Sure, come on in," Jefferson welcomed. He walked away, letting Darin open the screen and enter. "I don't get company, so I sometimes forget my manners. Sit a spell and tell me why you wanted to talk to me in person."

Darin closed both doors behind him. Welk seated himself in a straight-back chair, and Darin took a seat on the sofa close by.

Okay, Darin, time to turn on the old charm. Play your cards right and you'll sucker him in. "This is a nice house you have here, Mr. Welk," Darin commented, looking around the cozy room. *It's rather dinky, considering the fact that you've been knee-deep in wealth for most of your life. And, look. There's not one thing in here that looks expensive.*

"Thank you, but I know you didn't come all the way out here to talk about my house. What's on your mind?"

"To be honest, it is about your house—or your property and everything on it."

"What about my property?" Jefferson questioned.

"Seems there are some problems with the trust account that was set up for you many years ago."

"If I recall, we already had this conversation when I called and asked why I wasn't receiving my scheduled checks from the bank anymore. I remember, all to well, how you told me the trust fund was all dried up and no one at the bank could help me."

In spite of being upset, Jefferson maintained his self-control. "When I had time to think about it, and called you back, you were very direct in telling me that I had no chance of getting a bank loan to pay off my creditors. You might just as well have told me to go jump in the river and drown myself."

Is he repeating that information for his benefit or mine? "Hey, I'm sorry that I couldn't help you get a loan. I was just doing my job.

Please understand, Mr. Welk, it was nothing personal."

"Well, sir, that was quite a while back. What's the need in coming out here to talk to me about it, now? Or did you bring me good news, like you found my money?"

"I'm afraid not. There were some property taxes that you didn't pay this past year. The bank paid them for you. It seems now that the bank will have to put a lien on your property to get their money back. I'm sure you understand."

"A lien? Say, what are you telling me? The bank wants to take my farm, my home away from me? That's pure nonsense. I'll have you know that I haven't paid any property or land taxes since I inherited this estate and all the wealth that went with it.

Besides, I'm not completely stupid, young man. If there were taxes to pay last year, which I doubt, you're forgetting I still had a trust fund back then. Taxes would have automatically been taken care of."

"No one is calling you stupid," *oh yes I am*, "but it's obvious you don't understand property taxes. You're not billed for property taxes for the year you're assessed until the following year. This year the bank paid last year's property taxes for you, as there was no longer money in your account."

"The local government has never once sent me a property tax bill."

"You're correct there, Mr. Welk. The IRS wouldn't bill you because the bank has always paid those taxes from your trust account, so they send your assessment straight to the bank. When the bank discovered that your account was void of funds, at first they thought there was an error in their accounting records. They paid your taxes anyway.

Then our bank's auditors discovered it wasn't a bank error. See, that was like a loan of money on your behalf. That's the main reason the bank wouldn't allow me to give you a loan when you asked because they had already loaned you money when they paid those taxes. At that time, they used your property holdings for collateral. The bank sent you the notice of this tax transaction, but you never responded."

Jefferson appeared to be calm, but he was seething inside. He was gritting his teeth so hard his head began to ache.

"Out of respect and good faith, the bank has been very patient. However, that has been several months now, and you haven't bothered making restitution. If I don't leave here this evening with cash in the amount of three thousand dollars, well, I'm afraid they're going to file for foreclosure," Darin concluded.

"What about the all the rents the bank is supposed to be collecting for me on the other properties I own? No one has ever explained to me where that money's been going each month."

"The bank continues to collect all rent and lease payments on your other properties. That money, in return, is being applied towards the taxes of each individual property. However, that monthly income doesn't even compare to what you still owe the bank."

"I have deeds to all my properties, free and clear of all debts."

Okay, Welk, I'm hoping you're not too smart in the legal department and not aware you can contact the courthouse or an attorney. Shit, I hope he doesn't call my bluff. "You may have, Mr. Welk, but remember, those deeds are sitting in our vault at the bank. There's no way you can get your hands on them until your loan is paid in full. Once we are no longer holding them for collateral, then you have the right to remove them from the bank and store them wherever you please."

"That's what I get for placing my trust in one financial institution. For your information, I never received any such notice from the bank. If there was such a notice, I want to see a copy of it," Jefferson demanded.

Obliging him, Darin pulled an envelope from the inner-pocket of this jacket. He took the letter out of the envelope, unfolded it, and handed to Jefferson. "Here you are, Mr. Welk. This is a copy of the notice the bank sent you. I rather planned on you wanting proof, so I came prepared."

Darin had taken a photocopy of an original tax statement of the Welk's property holdings. He had changed the date and a few figures to make the statement look legitimate.

Jefferson took the paper and read the contents. "I've never seen this letter until just now. What you're telling me and showing me here, well, none of it seems legal. Besides, according to my records, at the rate of repeating myself, the bank has made a huge error in their bookkeeping."

"Oh, I'm afraid it's legal." Before he had a chance to think or make a closer inspection of the document, Darin took the paper from Jefferson's hand. While talking, he folded the document, placed it back in the envelope, then returned it to his pocket.

"As far as your account is concerned, well, I'm afraid you must not have kept very good records. Once the bank puts a lien on your … Well, let's just say everything you own will be the bank's property in a matter of weeks.

Now, do you have the money to pay off the loan? Because if you do, we can get this whole ordeal straightened out first thing in the morning. Due to the nature of your finances, the bank will not accept a check. So, just give me the cash, I'll give you a receipt and get out of here. Then you'll no longer have to worry about it."

"There's no way I can give you money I don't have." Feeling a sharp pain in his chest, Jefferson tried to ignore it. He placed his hands on the sides of his chair with a firm squeeze, attempting to relieve the discomfort the pain was causing. The last thing he wanted was to appear foolish and in bad health in front of a bank official. "I don't like this one darn bit. Since I don't seem to have a choice, I can give you a fair payment, tonight."

Damn! I didn't plan on this old coot having money laying around the house like all of those other idiots I've burglarized. Now what do I do? Think fast, that's what. "No, Mr. Welk, a payment won't do. Like I said, the bank is insisting that you pay the full amount, tonight, or you lose everything."

"I don't understand any of this," Welk stated, shaking his head in disbelief. "I just don't understand."

"Gee, I'm really sorry that I have to be the one to bring you this terrible information. Ever since I was hired, well, I like my job. So, I've tried to bring all the accounts I'm responsible for, up-to-date. When I find one or two, like yours, I try to work with our bank customers the best I can. Like I'm trying to work with you, right now. Please understand, this isn't personal."

Jefferson hung his head. Letting loose of his grip on the chair, he clasped his hands, fingers between fingers, placing them in his lap. "I don't care about any of the other properties, but lose my house, and the land I was born and raised on. It just can't be. At my age, I don't know where I would go or what I would do if I have to leave my home."

"Like I said, if you have the money on hand, we can settle this right now."

"I just told you, I don't have the kind of money you're asking for," Jefferson answered in a weary voice. "You appear to be a smart young man. Don't you think I'd be paying off my creditors if I had that kind of cash on hand?"

That's just what I wanted to hear. Now for the kill. "Please, Mr. Welk, you're breaking my heart. Give me a minute and let me think if there's any way I can help you."

Giving the false impression that he was dismayed over the situation, Darin leaned forward and propped his elbows on his knees. He cupped his face with his hands as if to be in deep thought. After a brief period of appropriate silence, he dropped his hands and looked over at Welk.

"You know, I'm going to do you a huge favor. I'm going to lose that foreclosure file of yours for at least a year. No longer. I'm sure I can bury it deep in some of my other paperwork, and do a little fancy computer work so nobody will find it until the time is right. If my superiors don't have your records, then they'll never know that you haven't reimbursed them for the tax money.

Since I'm good at my job, I'm confident my plan will work, keeping my boss off my back, and yours. That should give you the time to come up with the full payment the bank needs from you. It should also give you enough time to save money to pay this year's taxes when they come due next year.

I don't think I could ever rest easy again knowing I was somehow responsible for a man your age getting tossed out of his own home," Darin stated, putting on an act that would have won him the best dramatic actor award.

"Why, sir, would you want to do this old black man a favor?"

Man, if you knew how much I despise the blacks, you would never be sitting here having this conversation with me, especially in your own home. It's precisely because of your skin color that I am here. Get your mind back to the point, Darin. Remember, lay it on thick.

"It's like I said, I'd hate to see you lose everything, at your age. You don't know me from Adam, but I'm a man with a good heart. The one thing I will ask in return is that sometime, if ever given the opportunity, that you do someone else a tremendous favor. It's like my brother has always instilled in me, what you give out, will come back to you. This world would be a much better place to live in if we all helped each other in the time of need."

"Amen to that," Jefferson agreed while nodding his head.

"Who knows, maybe I might be the one who needs a favor someday, and you could be the one to help me out. What do you say?"

Slumping back in his chair, Jefferson felt like a man who just had the air knocked out of him. He had no ammunition left to fight a losing battle. Taking a deep breath, he tried to slow down his rapid pulse.

"I don't know what kind of a favor I could do for you, but I certainly

Black Rosebud

would be in your debt if you could help me keep my farm. I still don't understand it though," he commented, still very flustered, "I thought no one could touch this farm. It was mine forever."

"Well, none of us can count on anything for sure in this life, now can we? Anyway, Mr. Welk, I will take care of this little matter for you. Oh, there is one thing I should advise you of, however."

"More problems?"

"No, not more problems, that is, if you do as I say. I wouldn't, for your sake and mine, get in contact with anyone else at the bank. In fact, it would be much smarter if you stay away from the bank, all together. You could lose your property, and I could lose my job if anyone found out I was covering your … Well, you get my meaning, right?"

"Yes, I understand, sir."

"Okay. I guess that about takes care of our business." Darin stood to leave. "Oh, one more thing. Folks in town say you have a female living out here and working for you. Is that right?"

"Those people in town should learn to mind their own business," Jefferson grumbled. "I do have a farmhand living out here. Why do you ask?"

"Oh, no special reason, I was … Well, yes, I was asking for a reason. Does she live here in the house, or close by? If I'm going to help you, I wouldn't want her to see me, and have her tell anyone I was here this evening."

"She lives on the farm, but not close enough to know what goes on around my house after dark. Besides, she's a closed-mouth person, if you know what I mean?" Welk remarked a bit sarcastic, as if to mimic Darin's earlier comment. "Personally, I keep my mouth shut and mind my own business. Unless you decide to tell someone about your coming out here tonight, your visit is safe with me."

"Okay, then, goodnight to you, Mr. Welk. I'll be keeping in contact."

Darin left Jefferson's home feeling he had accomplished his goal. Welk would make the perfect patsy in his cunning get-rich scheme.

BANKING ON HUMAN NATURE

"Good-morning, Mister Sleepy Head," Frank greeted Darin with a huge smile on his face.

"Morning," Darin mumbled, heading for the coffee.

"Happy New Year. Did you have a fun celebration?"

"Yeah, I guess."

Frank watched as Darin placed his full cup on the table, then eased his way down to the cushion of the chair, as if he were in slow motion.

Leaning forward so he could breathe in the fumes from the coffee, Darin asked, "What time is it?"

Even though Frank's health was not in rapid decline, the cancer was taking its toll. Much of the time in pain, Frank found little to laugh at. But even his health didn't keep him from finding humor as he looked at the sight before him. Darin's below-the-ear length hair was standing every which way. His eyes looked like they had a good case of pinkeye infection. The look on his face was as sour as the taste of a fresh lemon.

"It's about half past noon, Saturday, the first of January," Frank answered.

Not being able to hold it in any longer, he started laughing. "Darin, if you aren't a sight. If I had film in that camera of mine, I'd take your picture to show your grandchildren some day. I sure hope the New Year is going to be better than you look. If not, the whole world's in trouble." Frank was so tickled, he had to hold his stomach from the pain of laughing.

"Damn, Frank, do you have to be so loud? My head hurts. Have a heart," Darin pleaded for mercy.

Still roaring with laughter, Frank responded, "No way. Go look in the mirror. I'll be hog tied and branded if you don't look like the aftermath of corn when the cow gets through with it. You know, manure."

Darin cracked a smile. He sipped his coffee before commenting. "You just can't bring yourself to use the word 'shit', can you?"

"No, I think manure is what I said, but your word certainly fits you better."

"Okay, you made your point." Darin tried to ignore Frank's comical mood, but the humorous comments and belly laughter got to him. "Cut it out. My head feels like a ton of bricks fell on it. Man, I drank far too much," Darin admitted with a slight chuckle.

"Well, it doesn't take an algebra major to figure that one out. But what in tarnation did you do to your hair? Have a wild filly on the side, did you?"

"No, to be honest, I had her on her back," Darin quipped back.

"Oh, no! Stop! That's more than I want to hear about," Frank stated, meaning what he said, but still laughing. "Okay, I won't tease anymore, but I swear it looks like you were caught in a baker's mixing bowl with the beaters turned on high speed."

Darin yawned. "That's nice."

Holding his breath for a couple of seconds, Frank regained his funny bone composure. "Well, I've been up since dawn. I'm going in to lie down for awhile. That reminds me, I must have been out doing chores when you got home this morning. What time did you get in?"

"Somewhere around 9:00 a.m., I guess."

"That was just a few hours ago."

"Yeah. I don't even know why I got up now."

"I don't either. Well, if you're hungry, you're on your own."

Frank rose from his chair, put his soiled dishes into the sink, then left the kitchen. Passing through the living room, he headed down the hallway toward his bedroom. As his body was in slow deterioration, he was tiring more easily. According to Frank's doctor, plenty of rest was good for him.

Darin slept most of the weekend.

Monday morning, the first workday in the New Year, arrived. Even with as much sleep as he had, Darin still felt washed-out and exhausted as he dragged himself out of bed and into a warm shower. Letting the water pound on his head and pour over his body, he cleared the cobwebs from his mind to get his thoughts straight.

This evening I need to scope out my next victim. What was that guy's name? Dammit! Oh, Joansik. Well, Mr. Joansik, I may not be able to pronounce your name, but I have a New Year's visit for you. Uninvited, of course.

Once he was dressed for work, Darin entered the kitchen for his morning coffee. He was surprised to see Frank's coffee mug and the morning news on the table, but no Frank. "First time I can remember in a long time that Frank isn't in here fixing me breakfast or having coffee with me on a workday. Guess he's been taking too many daytime naps, so he's playing catch-up with chores this morning."

After pouring a cup of brew, and taking a brisk sip so as not to burn his mouth, Darin looked out the kitchen window. Dawn was breaking. Seeing the light on in the barn, he knew he was right about Frank being hard at work. His eyes made a quick scan of the yard area then back toward the sky. Darin shivered. "It looks like were in for more snow."

Taking another drink of coffee, he turned away from the window. "Let's see what good news the morning paper has to start off the New Year." Spreading the paper open on the table, Darin leaned in on one hand, skimming through the local news. "Weather, cold with ninety-percent chance of snow. So what else is new?" A certain article caught his eye.

"Here we go. '<u>The Neat Nick Thief Takes a Holiday</u>. When asked to give an update as to when the Cole County residents could expect an arrest, Chief Simmons of the Kidwell Police Department stated, the thief must have been in hiding for the holidays, as things were rather quiet around the county. He refused further comment on the issue.

Both Police Chief Kings from Sharpin, and our own Cole County law officer, Sheriff Luden, also declined answering questions for our news article. However, Sheriff Luden did say that all of the burglaries were under the sole investigation of the Kidwell Police Department, and he had full confidence in Chief Simmons and his officers.'

Nothing new in that hayseed article. Hey, stupid reporter, you ought to know, by now, that I always leave you suckers alone over the holidays. Shoot, everyone spends all their savings on presents. I'd be the sucker if I thought I would find any huge amount of money in anyone's house during December. Besides, I needed a holiday, too.

I still can't get over how I thought I was being so smart to stay out of both Sharpin and Kidwell city limits when I started this bankroll crusade. I never dreamed that good old Rusty would be the cop that ended up chasing me. He might be the new player in the card game, but

I hold the winning hand. The law still has nothing on me. Which proves my point that Simmons is just as lame of a cop as old Luden is."

In looking over the rest of the paper, Darin spotted another article of interest to him.

"'Mayor Gives Developer a Welcomed Holiday Gift. Mayor Dickson told the news media, before we put the press to bed (last year), that City Fathers would sign the important papers first thing Monday morning. This would finalize the sale of the old Douglas Flour Mill property to the housing development firm of Miles & Cook.

The mayor related, that the developers promised to start an immediate leveling of the old mill buildings, clean up the property, then begin their excavating. Without going into detail at the present time, the mayor informed the citizens of our wonderful community that his office has irons in the fire which will bring new, badly needed industry to our area. To all of Cole County, the housing development will be greatly welcomed.'

Shit! That means I need to get my money moved. Fast."

Darin checked the time. Running late, he made a quick fold of the paper and rinsed his cup. Once he had bundled up in his winter parka, he rushed out the door, heading for work.

The article Darin had read in the paper about the sale of the flourmill property, bothered him all day. Before he left work for the day, he made an important telephone call. He figured out when he started his eavesdropping at the bank that if he could hear Dodd in his office, Dodd, likewise, could hear him. This would have been detrimental to Darin's plans. To rectify the possibility of being overhead, Darin always made sure Dodd was out of his office before making any of his deceitful telephone calls.

"Mr. Welk?"

"Speaking. Who's this?"

"I'm glad I caught you in. This is Darin Righter from bank. I need to see you this evening in regards to a matter of extreme importance."

"There isn't any more trouble at the bank, is there?"

"I'll tell you when I see you. Do you know where the old flourmill is located?"

"Of course I do. Why?"

"I want you to meet me there in the Number Three Machinery Building, at 9:00 p.m.," Darin instructed. "The buildings are old and run down, but you can still read the painted letters on the front of each of them."

"Tonight? What on earth for? It's too darn cold for me to be traipsing all over the country, sir."

"Don't you have transportation?"

"Of course, I do."

"And, I assume you know how to drive."

"Let's don't play games. I have a truck and I've been driving more years than you've been alive. That's not the point. Why don't you just come to the farm if you've got more bad news to tell me?"

"Because I can't. I will explain everything when I see you. Oh, and Mr. Welk, just to be on the safe side, be sure to park your truck out of sight. Remember, Number Three Machinery Building, 9:00, sharp."

Darin hung up the phone without giving Jefferson another chance to comment, or back out of the meeting. Knowing Jefferson wouldn't take a chance in calling him back at the bank, Darin was confident that Welk would do as he had asked.

That evening, as was normal on most evenings in the Righter house, Frank was preparing dinner, waiting for Darin to arrive home from work. He always tried to plan dinner according to Darin's schedule. While setting the table, Frank did some heavy thinking. Several months had passed since he received the lab results, and he still hadn't told Darin the truth about his health. There had never been a right time to approach the subject.

"Tonight. I'll tell Darin, tonight." Making the decision the time was right, he placed the bread on the table.

Not wanting to spoil Darin's appetite, Frank kept the conversation light during dinner. After dinner, however, as Darin left the table, ready to walk out of the room, Frank got up his nerve. "Wait, Darin." Frank got up to clear the table. "Why don't I pour us another cup of coffee, and you sit back down and talk to me? You're always working, dating, or out drinking with your friends. It seems you never have time just to sit and shoot the bull with me."

Darin hesitated. Turning back, he stood behind his chair. Taking a firm hold of the chair's back, he leaned on it. "Look, I'm home every night for dinner. Granted, I may not be here right after work, but I do come home to eat with you," he defended his lifestyle. "We always have a chance to talk then, and I thought we did.

Besides, there are times when I'm around that you aren't available. You're either outside wrapped up in all of that friggin' farm work, running into town on errands, or playing poker with your Friday night buddies. Now, I'm sorry, but I don't have time to stand around and discuss this matter any further. I have to be somewhere very soon. It's imperative that I get ready and go."

"Sure, Darin, I understand." As he threw the silverware into the sink, his back to the table, he hadn't noticed that Darin had already left the room. "No, actually, I don't understand, Darin. How hard is it to give me some of your quality time? All I want to do is to tell you something very important that will affect your life, as it has mine."

Turning back to the table, Frank realized he had been talking to himself. "It just figures. I finally get up the guts to tell him about my health, and I end up talking to the walls. Okay, maybe this isn't the time to burden him with my problem. God knows, I'm beginning to wonder if there ever will be the right time."

Darin changed from business clothes into jeans and sweatshirt. He then headed back to the kitchen.

"I could have sworn I heard you talking when I walked out of here a few minutes ago."

Upset, Frank never turned away from the sink where he was washing dishes. He muttered, "Huh? Oh, I asked you how the roads were when you came home because there's been a lot of snow falling this afternoon."

"Not too bad."

"I see it's starting up, again."

"Say, is that your problem? I'll bet you figured if you could rope me into a bull session with you, that I'd forget about going out this evening? Well, don't worry about me. You know I'm a good driver in weather like this."

"Yeah, I guess you know me pretty well." Frank commented, clutching his jaws. He continued washing and rinsing dishes, stacking them in the dish drainer. At that moment, he didn't wish to face Darin. "According to the latest weather report before you got home this evening, they said this is going to be another one of those heavy snowfalls. I think we must have a good foot out there already."

Darin walked to the window. Standing next to Frank, he looked outside. "It's light. Probably won't accumulate much before I get home."

"They're forecasting a good eighteen inches before it quits, Darin. I wouldn't stay out too late."

Taking a clean dishtowel from a drawer, Frank commenced drying dishes. Darin walked toward the enclosed back porch.

"I'm sure I'll be in bed when you get home. So, I'll see you tomorrow. Drive safe."

"Sure," Darin remarked, rushing out the door.

All the time he was driving, Darin made plans in regards to his meeting with Mr. Welk. The abandoned mill was located about twenty miles out of Kidwell's small downtown area. The snow was getting heavier. Big, wet flakes were making the roads slippery. With low visibility, Darin almost missed his turn onto the road leading up to the mill's property.

As he drove up the drive, he could barely see the tire tracks of another vehicle. "Those are fresh tracks, and, Mr. Welk, they had better be yours. Good thing there's some moonlight showing through all this wet stuff, or I wouldn't be able to see a thing." Cutting his headlights, he drove with caution.

As Darin drove around to the back of the building, he turned on his lights. When he did, his headlights shinned on a parked vehicle. "Okay, Welk, I hope this is your pickup hidden back here. If it isn't, I might be in for a bit of trouble."

Inside the rundown building, Darin used his flashlight to look around the area, trying to locate Jefferson, or whoever else was there in the building. "Anyone here?" he called out.

Within seconds, a voice came out of the darkness causing Darin to jump two feet off the ground. "I'm over here."

With one quick movement, Darin's hand whipped around and flashed the light to where the voice had come from. The beam of light hit Jefferson in the face.

"Crap! You like to have scared me into an early grave," Darin shrieked. "You should wear lighter clothes so someone can see you in the dark. I can't even see that white hair of yours."

"It's cold and it's snowing outside, sir. I always wear a wool hat in this weather to keep my head warm. Any other complaints about the way I'm dressed?"

"No, just making an honest observation. Look, I'm sorry I'm late," Darin apologized.

"With this nasty weather, I've just been here a few minutes myself. Why did you want me to meet you here? All this secretive, mysterious stuff gives me the willies. What's it about anyhow? Is it the bank? Have they discovered that you—"

Yes, I'll bet you must have more than the willies, old man. I'm willing to bet you're afraid of your own shadow. "Easy, man, one question at a time. Things are fine at the bank. I'm here to ask you a favor."

"A favor? Look, sir, you could have asked me a favor over the telephone, or come to my farm. Why make me get out and drive on a terrible snowy night, like this, for a favor?" Jefferson complained. "What's going on?"

"Relax, Mr. Welk, or you're liable to go into cardiac arrest. Like I said, I need a favor and it isn't something I cared to discuss over the phone, or at your house. Now, I never would've dreamed I would have to ask you of all people to do me a favor, but I do. And, since I've been helping you out for the past several months, well, I didn't think you would mind doing me a good turn," Darin stated with confidence.

"Yes, I owe you one. There's no doubt about that. So tell me, what is this favor? I want to get out of here. The sooner the better."

"Patience, Mr. Welk. I'm getting to it. I have something of great value hidden in this building, but I read in today's paper that this property has been sold. These buildings are soon to be torn down. Now, I need someone I can trust who will hide that valuable something for me. I'm hoping that certain, trusting someone is you."

"It depends. What is this valuable something?"

"It's a whole lot of money. You see, I have plans, great plans. Some day, soon I hope, I'm going to be moving to the east coast. Since it's going to be a rather expensive endeavor, I'll need an extremely large amount of cash on hand for traveling expenses.

For quite some time now, I've been living off my brother. That's so I could save all my paychecks. To date, I've built up quite a healthy nest egg. Truth is, I've been afraid of that Neat Nick Thief. Have you heard of him?"

"I've heard about him. But why are you afraid of him?"

"Since he's been burglarizing a lot of people around the area, I've had to take extreme caution as to where I've hidden my money. It seemed only natural to keep it hidden out here where he or nobody else would think to look for cash, or anything of value.

With this place getting torn down and graded over, I have to move my money to another location where the thief wouldn't dream of looking," Darin admitted, hoping that he sounded convincing. "After visiting your home, and you admitting that you never get too many visitors, I figured you're place was just about as safe as this old mill has been. Will you help me by hiding my money at your house?"

As they spoke, Darin flashed the beams of his flashlight in a slow movement around the huge room. He wasn't looking for anything in particular, just messing around, as the light bounced off the walls and the old machinery.

"What makes you think the thief won't find out the money is at my house?"

"Trust me. I know what I'm doing. Everyone knows you don't have any money stashed away, or you'd be paying off your bills in town. Right?"

"Yes, that sounds true enough. But, why would you trust me with your money? Better yet, why aren't you keeping your money in the bank?"

"After having your accounts disappear into smoke, that's a rather dumb question on your part."

"Maybe dumb to you, Mr. Righter, but not to me. You work at the bank, so you'd be able to keep your eyes on your money. What's the real reason?"

"Simple, the reason is called the IRS. I already pay enough taxes, and without choice. They take more than their share out of every paycheck I get. If I put my money in the bank, then they can tax me again on interest on my savings.

As for trusting you, well, if you turn me in, your foreclosure records will miraculously be found. You'll immediately lose your farm," Darin threatened.

"So, you want me to hide your money and keep my mouth shut? For that, you'll continue to keep my files hidden at the bank so I don't lose my farm?"

"You got it. And, to sweeten the pie, when I'm ready to take my money back from you and get out of this hellhole, I'll give you a bonus for keeping your mouth sealed." *You may not like the bonus I give you, but that's another bridge to cross when I get there.*

"You see, when I leave my job, I'll have to put your records back on the computer files. You'll be able to use the bonus I give you to pay the bank those back taxes you owe. Then, my friend, the farm will be yours, again. Free and clear. Have we got a deal?"

"You might think that you're dealing with an old man who is ignorant, sir, but I don't like the idea of what you're suggesting. I've never gone against the law in my whole life." Jefferson hesitated. The tragic memories of his granddaddy came roaring through his mind like a locomotive tearing down the track in full throttle. "No, I don't want to mess with anything illegal and give the authorities any reason to come after me.

Besides, I don't know the justice system, but this sounds to me like a shakedown—blackmail. Is that what this is?"

Shivering from the cold, Darin flashed the light back at Jefferson. Jefferson raised his arm to keep the light out of his eyes.

"Now Mr. Welk, you're insulting me. Let's face it. You've been breaking the law ever since you agreed to let me work my magic and misplace your foreclosure files. That in itself is fraud. I have been covering your ass for months, threatening my own job security to do it, and you have the nerve to ask me if I'm blackmailing you. I don't believe what I'm hearing," Darin complained, hitting the ball back into Jefferson's court.

"Okay, I'm sorry. I just don't trust a whole lot of people. If you were older, you would understand. And get that stupid light out of my face." As Darin moved his flashlight so the beams floated off in the distance, Jefferson dropped his arm back to a comfortable position. "I want to think about this for a while before I give you an answer."

Getting irritated, Darin retorted, "No! I need to know right here and now. Either you want to help me, or plan on moving tomorrow. It's that simple."

"Sir, I'm a peaceful man, but I don't take light to threats. If that's your meaning."

"Well, maybe it is, but you have to admit that I'm being truthful. Take it or leave it, but I have to know right now. You have three choices. Lose your farm. Go to jail for fraud. Or, help me out."

Jefferson wanted to cry out, *No! Go to the devil!* Bitterness and fear of the law, however, prevented him in doing so. "Okay, okay. It goes against my better judgment, but I'll help you."

"Does that female farmhand still live with you?"

"She lives on the farm, not in my house. I told you that before."

"And no one else lives on your farm, right?"

"Not that it's any of your business, but no. No one."

"I just wanted to check, to make sure your farmhand doesn't find the money. How do I know she isn't a thief?"

"She's no trouble, does her chores and keeps to herself. I keep her on because she works for no pay, just a little food and board. Besides, I like having her around. But again, that's none of your business."

"I need to be sure when you take my money that no one sees you with it, or finds it. That's all. I can't take any chances. Until now, no one has known about my money. Now, you are the only one, outside of me, who knows. I want it to stay that way."

"It seems to me that you'd be more apt to ask your brother to keep your money for you. Or is it because you said you were living off him that you don't want him to know you have so much money of your own?"

"Look, Mr. Welk, I'm losing my patience with you. I'm living off my brother because he owes me. Besides, there's a chance that the Neat Nick Thief could rob his house. Then my money would be gone. Now, what about your farmhand?"

"No need to fret, sir. I can almost guarantee that she won't be a threat. How long do I have to keep this money for you, anyway?"

"For as long as necessary. It could be a few months or it could be a year. I can't say for sure. However long it takes, it can't be too soon for me to get out of this one-horse town."

"You realize, I hope, that I'm old and could meet my maker at any given moment. What happens to your money then?"

"I've thought about it. I'll be checking on you from time to time, and you'll show me where you're keeping my money. Any other questions, or can we get this matter taken care of? It's freezing in here. This snowfall is supposed to drop at least six more inches on us. I think we both ought to be heading towards home, real soon," Darin concluded.

"No, no, I don't have any more questions. I'm agreeable to leave now before we both die of pneumonia."

"I'm assuming that's your pickup sitting out there in back of the building?" Darin asked.

"Yes."

"I rather figured as much since I hadn't seen any other vehicle out there. I parked right next to it.

Say, how did you see when you came in here?"

"Like you, I brought my own flashlight."

"Now you tell me."

"You never asked. And, since you've had yours flashing around since you walked in here tonight, there was no need for me to waste my batteries."

"Okay, you've proved your point.

You go get your truck warmed up. I'll get my money and be right there."

"Since it's colder out there than it is in here, I hope you don't mind me asking you to hurry. It takes a long time to get the truck's heater warmed up again, as frigid as it is outside. If I leave soon, it should still be warm from when I arrived."

That's stupid. If you get out there and turn the engine on, now, you can keep it warm. "It's as frigid for me in here as it is for you. You're lucky you're an older man or I'd make you stay here and help me. Now go on, get out of here."

Turning on his flashlight to light his way, Jefferson headed outdoors while Darin headed for the old machine that housed his money. Outside, Jefferson cleaned the snow off his truck's windshield, got inside, and started the truck to get the heater going.

After a few minutes had elapsed, Darin appeared by the side of Jefferson's truck. Spotting him, Jefferson opened his door. "What the— What's that, your dirty laundry?"

"Nope, it's my money." One by one, Darin handed the bundles to Jefferson. One by one, Jefferson piled them on the seat next to him. "My brother always gives his old clothes to the poor, so I just confiscated some of them to hold my money. They make great bags."

As Darin emptied his coat pockets of more filled bundles, passing them on, Jefferson asked, "Won't your brother miss his clothes?"

"No, Frank won't miss them. And don't worry, my brother gives the poor his old clothes at least once every six months. There are plenty of these for both the poor and for my use.

Okay, that's it for right now. Why didn't you just roll down your window when I return? It can't be as cold as having your door open."

"It's broken. When you return? Don't tell me you have more?"

"Yes, there's more."

"Well, make it snappy. This old heater is working as hard as it can, but I'm still chilled to the bone."

As much as Darin hated taking orders from anyone, he, too, was so cold that he hurried as fast as he could to get finished.

After all the bundles were loaded, Darin said, "If you don't mind me asking, with all that money you had in your trust, why didn't you spend some of it and buy yourself a new truck, or at least one with a good heater and working windows?"

"What I did or didn't do with my money when I had it, sir, is none of your business. But, since you're throwing questions around, let me ask you one. There's a good amount of bundles full of money here. Just how long have you been saving?"

"I guess I could answer with the same attitude you just threw at me. How long I've been saving or how much I've saved is none of your business. But, I do know exactly how much is on that seat next to you, right down to the last penny."

Staring at the falling snow as it collected on Darin shoulders, Jefferson's sight got blurry and Darin's image seemed to disappear. Jefferson wondered how he was going to get the heavy bundles into his house when he got home.

As much as he trusted Mama and Farm Girl, he couldn't take the chance of asking them for help. He would have to wait until they went back to Sugar Shack each night, then carry one pouch at a time into the house. It would take him several nights to accomplish the feat, but he knew of no other way of handling the situation.

He also had to figure out a good hiding place. Somewhere neither Farm Girl nor Mama would ever happen upon the bundles of money.

Darin was right. Practically everyone in the area knew Jefferson owed money all over town. No one would think of stealing from him. So, the money bundles would be safe in his truck until he got them moved and hidden in his house.

"Hey, are you okay?" Darin asked. "You look like you're in a daze."

Jefferson blinked. "I'm cold and I'm tired."

"Okay, you can leave now. I'll come out to see you about once a month after I cash my checks to add to my savings. Drive careful," Darin warned, "and don't end up in any snow bank." Darin stepped back out of the path of the truck's door. Jefferson started to pull his door closed, then hesitated. "What are you waiting for? Go on, get out of here," Darin ordered.

"What makes you think I won't turn my back on my farm, and just leave town with your money?"

"Faith in the human race, and my trusty little tape recorder." Darin laughed, pulling a mini-cassette recorder from his coat's upper pocket. "I have everything on tape, starting with our first meeting. Should you decide to cheat me, or so much as steal one nickel from me, you're in as deep as I am.

Just a little dubbing here and there, and I believe the law would tag you as a co-conspirator to bank fraud. And, I'm sure the IRS would have a field day prosecuting you, too. Does that answer your question?"

"I think you are a low down scoundrel, sir. If I was younger and didn't care about starting my life over, I'd tell you where to take your money and your proposition, and, well, you figure out where you could shove it."

Before Jefferson had a chance to shut his door, Darin grabbed it. "Temper, temper, old man. I'm saving your hide, too. Remember that before you go off half cocked."

"Are you through yet?"

Cool it, Darin, or you might screw up a good thing. Say something to try and get on his good side. "No, I'm not. I forgot something very important," Darin said, releasing his grip on the door and rubbing his hands together for warmth. "Thank you. No matter what you think of me, I do appreciate your help. I just don't want you to go away thinking I'm not grateful. Okay? I don't mean to be threatening, as I want us to be friends. There, does that make everything better now?"

"Not even in the most exaggerated fashion. I'm helping you because it appears I have no choice in the matter. However, you remember one thing, Mr. Righter, I'm not, nor do I ever intend to be, your friend."

"Friends, or not, I do appreciate your help."

"Keep your misplaced gratitude. Anything else, or have you decided we're going to camp out here overnight? Which I don't care to do for more reasons than one. There seems to be a foul odor around here that's stinking up this fresh, cold air."

"Camp out, that's very funny. Okay, drive careful." With that said, Darin closed the door.

Darin watched Jefferson drive off before he got into his own car and started it. He wiped the moisture off his face and brushed the snow from his shoulders. After turning on the thermostat control, he sat waiting for the car to warm.

"Hey, I think that old skunk insulted me with that foul odor remark. If it wasn't so friggin' cold, and I hadn't had other things on my mind, I would have caught that ball when he threw it.

I'm glad I made recordings of my meetings with him. They'll be my insurance policies should he decide to double-cross me. Nah, he wouldn't do that. He might be a sly, white-haired old fox, but he really has too much to lose."

Consumed with greed, Darin was climbing his ladder, one victim at a time, to reach his goal. As long as he was staying two steps in front of his nemesis, Rusty, and still collecting his bankroll, he didn't care who he cheated, lied to, stole from, conned, manipulated, walked over or deceived. He refused to see the big picture. Greed was so often what sucked one down into the darkness of no return.

CAPTURING INNOCENCE

For close to seventeen years, Mama kept Farm Girl from the outside world and almost everything in it. She taught her daughter that most people were untrustworthy strangers, townsfolk were nosey, and anything outside of farm life were worlds of evil and destruction. Farm Girl believed it.

Mama had drummed caution into Farm Girl's head for so many years, the words were once like a ball of string unwinding in her mind.

"Ya keep y'ur eyes and ears open, child. We don't need nobody sneakin' up on ya."

"Yes, Mama."

"And if'n I ain't around, and ya hears one a them automobiles, ya git y'urself out a sight."

"Yes, Mama."

However, after spending six years on Jefferson's farm, Farm Girl no longer thought about Mama's warnings. In all those years, neither she nor Mama ever saw Jefferson have a single visitor. Because of this feeling of security, Farm Girl no longer worried about being cautious.

Being too secure could have as much repercussion as acute overcautiousness. No longer worrying about the outside world was bound to bring about carelessness.

As far as anyone knew, Mama was the only person who worked for Jefferson Welk or lived on his property. This was not merely to protect Farm Girl, but it also left little for Jefferson to have to explain to anyone who thought his business was their business. Jefferson didn't often concur with Mama, but he was in complete agreement that most townsfolk stuck their noses where they didn't belong.

It was March. For weeks, heavy rains pounded everything in its way. When there was a break in the weather, Jefferson drove his truck to check the muddy fields. Sloshing through the mud, Mama took the cows to pasture. The pasture was not yet green, but there was enough vegetation for the cows to graze.

Farm Girl stayed behind to chop firewood for the sitting room fireplace. A small frame of a girl, she had a good set of muscles from years of doing heavy chores. Chopping wood was just another routine, easy job for her.

Inside the barn, she grabbed Jefferson's old work gloves, as she often did to protect her hands. She tucked the gloves into her apron pocket, then proceeded outside behind the barn where there was a huge stump of a tree, perfect for chopping wood. Before Farm Girl began, she removed the rag from her head. Brushing her hair back from her face with her fingers, she then replaced the makeshift headscarf and tied it behind her head at the nape of her neck.

Most of the logs were saturated from the heavy rains. Putting on the gloves, she picked out some dry, medium size logs for chopping. As she chopped the selected logs, she burst into tunes from music Mama had taught her. Since Mama didn't know many of the words to the music, neither did Farm Girl. This was not going to stop her from entertaining herself to pass the time. At the top of her lungs, Farm Girl sang her made up words, drowning out the sounds of the axe hitting the wood.

After chopping a fair amount of firewood, she gathered some of the wood in her arms and headed for the house. When she rounded the corner of the barn, her eyes met face to face with a young man.

"What the—Who in the hell are you and where's Mr. Welk?" the stranger demanded.

Frightened for her life, Farm Girl dropped the armful of logs, spun around in the opposite direction, and started running as fast as her legs could carry her. She ran like wildfire through the mud and toward the pasture to find Mama.

As she ran, she tore off the gloves and threw them in the air, as if they were weighing her down on her fearful flight. In an attempt to free her legs so she could run faster, she grabbed at her long skirt and hoisted it to her knees.

For all the times Mama had taught Farm Girl to be a survivor, she had never once taught her daughter to scream out for help. As Farm

Black Rosebud

Girl continued to flee, her heart appeared to be pounding faster than her feet were moving.

"Hey kid, stop!" the man hollered, as he charged after Farm Girl in hot pursuit.

With a rapid twitch of her head, Farm Girl could see the stranger was gaining on her. She ran even faster. Her mind seemed to be stuck like a warped phonograph record. *Evil stranger! Evil stranger! Evil stranger!*

Almost breathless, the young man yelled again. "Stop! Thief!"

Dead on Farm Girls heels, he leaped and tackled her with the full force of his body, slamming her to the muddy ground. She twisted and fought like a wild animal. Because of the mud, the man had a difficult time trying to pin her down. His hands kept slipping away with each fighting movement.

In the struggle, Farm Girl's head cover fell off and the apron pocket ripped. Her clothes were in disarray and covered with mud.

Hands on the ground, trying to keep her face out of the muck, she reared her body like a wild stallion in desperation to get away. With steadfast determination, she managed to turn her body, face up. Petrified, Farm Girl couldn't give her offender a direct look in the face.

Ruffled and muddied himself from the struggle, he ultimately got the young girl pinned to the ground. Straddling the wildcat body as he held her wrists to the ground above her shoulders. "Mr. Welk doesn't take kindly to thieves," he stated in a winded voice.

Horrified, Farm Girl felt death was imminent. Here was one of those evil strangers Mama had warned her about, and he had her trapped, like a wild steer. "I ain't no thief!" she loudly defended with fear and anger. Continuing to keep her head turned to the side, she demanded in a frightful shriek, "Git off a me! Let me go!"

The young man fought to keep her restrained to the ground. "Before I do, tell me why you're stealing wood if you're not a thief?"

Still trying to break loose from his hold, her next instinct was to bite him. Just as she opened her mouth, like a man-eating tiger, child-like curiosity told her to first look at the evil person.

They locked eyes. In that split second, the fear of death drifted from her mind, like an autumn leaf falls from a tree. As if mesmerized, panic left her for one fleeting moment. A sudden calming voice spoke inside her head.

Even if'n he sounds a might put out, Farm Girl, ain't that the sweetest voice ya ever did hear? Even if'n he's all muddy, ain't he the purdiest boy ya ever did sees? Ya can keep fightin', I reckon, and try harder to git to y'ur feets, but y'ur body says, don't do it.

Then, within a single heartbeat, a frantic voice broke into her magical thoughts. It flashed a big warning sign of Mama's face, bringing her back to reality. *Purdy or not, Farm Girl, ya best be gittin' him off a ya, if'n ya knows what's good fur ya.*

Farm Girl knew it was bad to tell lies. Under normal conditions, it was natural that the truth would come pouring out of her mouth. This was especially true now, under a perilous situation. "I ain't no thief. I lives here. I be doin' chores 'cause he needs wood fur his fireplace. So, git off a me. Now!" Trying without too much strain to get her arms loose from the young man's grip, she asked, "Does ya knows Mister Welk?"

Thief or no thief, the young man smiled, assuming he had just captured a little girl. Before he introduced himself, he gave some serious thought as to how much he should tell her about himself. "Yes, I know him. Almost everyone who lives around these parts knows him, or about him." Still wheezing, he paused to catch his breath. "I'm Jack Trenton, a salesman of sorts. I came out here to talk to Mr. Welk about leasing a new truck."

"I doesn't know them words salesman and leasin'. What is they?"

"In simple words," *for an obvious simple mind,* "a salesman gives you something you want and you pay him for it. Leasing is when a person pays another person or business to borrow something for a certain length of time, like a new truck or an automobile."

"Ya doesn't really know Mister Welk, does ya?"

"Why do you say that?"

"If'n ya does, then ya knows he ain't gots no money. So he cain't be borrowin' nobody's new truck."

"You know what? I heard that from other people. Since you work for him, you must know the truth about his personal finance. So, I'll have to take your word for it."

"Quit throwin' them fancy words at me. And I doesn't know that person Al Fineants. Sounds like a bug's name."

"Personal finance is not a bug or a name. I'm speaking about one person knowing if someone has money, and if so, how much, or, if that someone doesn't have money."

"Well, crimeny, Mister Welk ain't gots none a them."

"So you're saying he has no money?"

Puzzled, Farm Girl simply agreed. "If'n that's whatcha been askin' me, I reckon I is."

"You're sure about that?"

"I ain't gonna talk no more about Mister Welk. What's his business stays his business. Now, is ya ever gonna let me up? I doesn't much like this mud I is bathin' in."

"When I'm ready. I told you my name. Tell me who you are."

"They calls me Farm Girl."

"Well, Farm Girl, someone gave you the right name from the looks of you and the horrible way you talk," he chuckled.

"Ya doesn't look so good y'urself with all that mud ya gots all— Hey, is ya makin' fun a the likes a me?"

Darn straight I'm making fun of you. You low-life. Look at you. Mud or no mud, I'll bet you haven't taken a bath in a month of Sundays. "Making fun of you? No, of course not.

Say, I knew Mr. Welk had a woman working for him, but I thought she was closer to her late forties or early fifties. I sure didn't know she was a little twelve-year-old urchin that should be in school learning proper speech and hygiene."

"I ain't twelve, mister, whatever ya say y'ur name be."

"Jack."

"Well, Mister Jack, I'm fixin' to be seventeen in a few weeks," she boasted. "Now, take y'ur dog paws off a my arms and git y'ur body off a me. Ya ain't what I calls light as a chicken feather."

Seems as though she knows animals better than she knows people. "You run like a panther and fight like a lion. Not my idea of what a young girl is supposed to act like. I thought feisty, wild, little girls, like you, were just in fictional books and movies. Not in real life."

Farm Girl didn't have the slightest idea what he was talking about, until he struck a cord and brought her back to reality.

"I wonder how come I thought you would be an older woman."

"Maybe 'cause ya was thinkin' I be my Mama since—Oh, Mama!" Farm Girl started fighting again to get free of the man's clutches. "Let me loose! Ya gots to git out a here. If'n Mama or Mister Welk finds ya here talkin' at me, we is both knee-deep in pig slop."

Amused with her speech, he burst into laughter. *She has to be telling the truth. She's too damn stupid to be a thief.* "So," he said, still laughing, "then your mama's around here, too?"

"Uh-huh. Me and she be workin' fur Mister Welk. But ya gots to promise not to tell no one."

"Why is your working here such a big secret?"

"Just 'cause Mama don't tell no one about me. Now, won'tcha please let go a me?"

That's strange. "Okay, Farm Girl, I'll let you up if you promise I can see you again."

I doesn't have to think twice befur answerin' that question. I is more fearful a Mama, right now, than I is a this here boy. Anyways, he ain't no stranger no more 'cause he went and teld me his name. I has to promise, or he ain't gonna never let me git up.

"Well, Farm Girl, what's it going to be? Do you want to stay here, pinned down in the mud, or promise to meet me again? I've got all the time in the world, so it's your choice."

"Okay, I promise."

"Tell me where," he insisted, not budging an inch.

"I, I doesn't know. Maybe 'cross the river where I goes to write my stories. Crimeny, a girl ain't got no chance to breathe with ya sittin' on top a her, like ya was ridin' a horse."

No matter how she pleaded or complained, he was stubborn. He stayed right where he was and would not let go, aware she could be toying with him just to be released.

"There are a million places over by the river and across it, so give me an exact place, and when. And don't be playing games with me, either. I know every inch of this land around here. Also, before you answer, just remember something. If you decide *not* to show up, you'll find me telling Mr. Welk that I discovered you on his property, and that you told me you and your mama were working for him."

Farm Girl gave directions the best way she knew how from Jefferson's main house to the shanty, and from the shanty to Room to Write. He would be arriving from the opposite direction, but knew the rock in which she was speaking.

She also asked him to make a promise in return. He wasn't to tell another living soul, including Mr. Welk, that he had seen her. After all, Pappy was her friend. Farm Girl didn't want to break the trust he had in her. Of more importance, Mama could never find out.

He had to hash over a few things in his head before making this dirty little waif such a promise. "Okay, I promise. I haven't walked these fields or the riverbank since I was a kid, but I know the big rock you're talking about.

Now, since you've been honest with me, I'll be honest with you. My real name is Darin George Righter," he admitted.

"Oh, ya has different names just like me and Mama do? Ain't that fun?"

What in the hell is she rambling on about? Maybe I don't want to know. "Yeah, right. Anyway, what time are you going to meet me there, at your special rock?"

After explaining she did not know how to tell time by using a clock, Farm Girl said that she would meet him the next day when the sun was directly overhead. Upon agreement of their meeting, Darin finally let her loose.

Without hesitation, she grabbed her headscarf off the ground, scrambled to her feet, and ran in haste back across the length of the pasture where Darin had pursued and caught up with her. Along the way, she was quick to retrieve Jefferson's gloves.

She ran to the barn and found a corner of a stall to hide in. There she stayed put, awaiting Mama's return. Farm Girl was happy Darin didn't wait around for Mr. Welk.

While Farm Girl was hiding, she replaced her muddied rag back on her head, pulling her hair out of her eyes. From the floor, she picked up a handful of straw and wiped as much mud as she could off her clothing.

In fear of what Mama would say or do should she discover what had happened, Farm Girl decided not to tell the truth. In her mind, a whopper was still different than a lie. Even though she felt Darin was no longer evil, Farm Girl didn't realize how the trauma had affected her subconscious. Because of this, playing King's X with Mama never crossed her mind. Not this time.

When she heard Mama's voice call her name, Farm Girl got up from her hiding place and brushed off the excess debris from her clothes. Then she ran out of the barn to where Mama was standing by the scattered logs on the ground.

Mama took one look at her daughter and forgot about the logs. "Child, what on earth has ya been up to? Just look at ya."

Standing brave, she proceeded to tell her lie. "My arms was full with firewood, and I was on my way from the old wood-chop tree to the house. When I come here to the drive, I hear a car comin'. I drops the firewood and runs fur my life, just like ya always told me to do. While

I was runnin' to find ya, I trips and goes rollin' in the mud."

"Ya knows where I was, but ya never come to me."

"No, 'cause I … I hurt my leg so I couldn't run no more. I crawl me back and hide in the barn until I hears ya callin'."

"What part a y'ur leg did ya hurt?"

"Oh, it's fine now, Mama. The hurt went away while I be sittin' in the barn waitin' fur ya."

"Why ya didn't hear the car befur ya gots here to the drive?"

"I was a singin' and a hummin', Mama, just like ya does sometimes. With my voice and the noise a the axe hittin' the wood, I just didn't hear nothin'. Sorry, Mama."

"Pick up that firewood and bring it on in the house. After ya stacks it, I'll be in the kitchen waitin' to talk to ya," Mama stated. "And don'tcha be trackin' none a that mud into Pappy's house." Farm Girl looked down at her clothes then back at her mother in dismay. "Okay, I can see that ain't possible, child."

At the well along side of Jefferson's house, Mama assisted her daughter. They washed off as much mud as they could. From there, Farm Girl went straight to the basement to toss her clothes into the washer.

In the remote possibility that Jefferson might return before her clothes had finished washing, she sat in a dark corner with a towel wrapped around her. Since the clothes dryer wasn't working, she redressed in the wet clothes and scurried upstairs.

Mama was sweeping the kitchen floor when Farm Girl entered the room at the same time Jefferson walked into the kitchen through the backdoor.

"I be glad ya be here, Pappy. I needs to talk with ya."

"You sound awful serious, Mama. Is something wrong?" he asked.

"Yes, there be. Sit y'urself down at the table so I can tell ya what's on my mind." Turning to Farm Girl who was standing by like a statue, Mama stated, "The firewood be all taken care of."

"Thank ya, Mama."

"Git Pappy a cup a coffee then take a seat. I wantcha to tell him whatcha told me."

Taking a good look at Farm Girl, Jefferson asked, "My word, child, why are your clothes all wet?"

"I'll be tellin' ya all about it soon enough," Mama said.

Once they had all taken a seat, Farm Girl's brain lit up. She remembered her game. Playing King's X, Farm Girl repeated the story to Jefferson that she had told Mama. To Farm Girl's delight, Jefferson was not concerned over the situation. However, the whole ordeal was very bothersome to Mama. Even though Farm Girl thought she had assured Mama that no one had seen her, Mama was convinced that the time had come to move on.

"Please, Mama, I doesn't wanna leave. If'n I promises to be more careful, cain't we stay?" she begged. "Please, Pappy, tell Mama we doesn't has to leave here."

"I wish you would reconsider your decision," Jefferson added to the conversation. "If the child wasn't seen, then there's no harm done."

Farm Girl left her chair and got on her knees next to Jefferson. As she knelt beside him, she reached up to hold his hand for comfort.

"Point is, someone might has already seen her," Mama stated. "We was feelin' so safe here, Farm Girl furgot all the warnin's I be teachin' her since she was a tot still in diapers. I blames myself fur that. Agreeing to move into Sugar Shack, all them years back, be comin' back to haunt me."

Droplets of tears made their paths down Farm Girl's cheeks. Jefferson pulled his clean handkerchief from the pocket of his overalls and wiped her face. "Don't cry, honey," he comforted. "You know, Mama, I have a better solution than you two pulling up stakes and leaving because of one minor incident."

"I doesn't think there be anythin' else we can do," Mama replied.

"There's always someone in the area whose dog has more pups than they know what to do with. I'll go out, first thing tomorrow, and see if I can get us one," Jefferson suggested.

Farm Girl's ears perked up. "A dog?"

"Ya doesn't need to be spendin' money ya ain't gots on no dog. And ya doesn't need to has another mouth around here to feed."

"First of all, Mama, most farmers give pups away just to give them good homes. Now, I'm not saying that I can find one, but I'm going to give it a try. And as for the food, we can feed it scraps from the table."

Placing her arm on the table, and leaning her chin on it, Farm Girl looked over at her mother. "Crimeny, doesn't that sound like a swell idea to has our own dog?"

Shaking her head, Mama replied, "I don't see what good a pups gonna be but more work and lots a trouble. We gots enough animal poop around here now to be steppin' in."

It was a serious conversation, but Jefferson found some humor to Mama's way of thinking. "Before you came here, weren't you ever on a farm that had a dog around?"

"Of course we was," Mama answered. "All they did was leave their callin' cards everywheres they was wantin', and barkin' every time … " Pausing, Mama thought about what she had just said. "Ya think, if'n ya has a dog, it'll bark and warn us when someone comes around?"

"Yes, I do. He can be Farm Girl's own personal watchdog."

In her excitement, Farm Girl turned to Jefferson and asked, "Me? Ya be given the dog to me?"

"Why sure, honey. You're the one Mama wants protected. Besides, it seems to me that someone has a birthday coming up real soon now. We could make the puppy your present from your Mama and me."

"How long's it gonna take befur a pup turns into one a them watchdogs?" Mama asked with the hint of a smile.

Neither Farm Girl nor Jefferson could miss Mama's indication of surrendering. They both knew how to read her facial expressions.

"I don't know for sure," Jefferson said. "I guess it all depends on how old the puppy is when we get it. So, it's settled then? I'll go find the pup and you two are staying?"

"I reckon it won't do us no harm tryin' a dog around here, as long as Farm Girl still keeps an eyeful watch fur strangers comin' around."

Jumping to her feet, Farm Girl gave Jefferson a hug. Then she dashed to her mother's side and gave her an embrace. "Oh, thank ya, Mama. And I will be more watchful. You'll see."

As promised, Farm Girl received a puppy for her birthday. Jefferson was fortunate to find a nine-month old collie that needed a home. Against Jefferson's better judgment, due to lack of originality, Farm Girl named her new pet: Farm Dawg.

When Farm Girl was alone in the main area of the farm, while Jefferson and Mama were off doing other chores, they tied the dog to the front of the barn. This way he could bark at strange noises, therefore alerting Farm Girl if something or someone entered his territory. The barking gave Farm Girl enough time to drop what she was doing and get hidden out of sight.

Before long, Farm Dawg followed his mistress almost everyplace she went except when she went to Room to Write. Unbeknown to either Mama or Jefferson, Farm Girl would lock the dog inside Sugar Shack while she went to her rock. Since Farm Dawg couldn't talk, Farm Girl knew her secret was safe.

As far as Mama was concerned, Farm Dawg was her daughter's protector from the wolves and foxes of the world, both the two and the four-legged kind.

Unfortunately for Farm Girl, her new acquaintance was one of those sly, two-legged kind of predators who preyed on the innocent and the unsuspecting. Even if she had taken Farm Dawg with her to Room to Write, he would not have been the protection she needed.

NEW LIFE THROUGH DEATH

With almost another year behind her, Farm Girl had learned as much as Mama would allow Jefferson to teach her. However, Farm Girl wanted to keep learning without Mama's knowledge. When she spoke with Jefferson, she would practice what she thought was grammatically correct speech, even though it wasn't.

"I is so proud when I speaks with all them nice words you been teachin' me," Farm Girl said.

Not at all pleased with his student's progress, all Jefferson could do was to placate her so she wouldn't get discouraged. "Well, honey, I'm proud of you, too. Just remember to keep practicing your words."

With Mama, however, it was a different story. Once, when Farm Girl tried to correct her mother's words, Mama became a trifle upset. "No, Mama, it's wash, not warsh. You just doesn't understand the book learnin' ways a this here English land gauge Pappy's been teachin' me."

"I understands more than ya thinks I does, Farm Girl. So don't be gittin' uppity with me, usin' them fancy words and all. Just 'member, when them cows needs milkin', they ain't gonna care what y'ur speech be like."

"Yes, I know you is right, but them cows is stupid. I was thinkin' they was smart, but Pappy done teld me they ain't. When I goes out in them worlds I ain't never seen befur, I wanna be smarter than some old cow."

"Go out where? Who put such a silly notion in y'ur head?"

"No one, Mama, I swear. I is just dreamin'."

"Well quit dreamin' about things that ain't never gonna happen." Mama rubbed her chest.

Crimeny, Mama's havin' one a them heart pains again, just like Pappy is always gittin'. "Is you all right?"

"Don'tcha be frettin' about y'ur mama. I just knows I should a never let Pappy teach ya so much. Plantin' all them fancy ideas in y'ur head be just plain nonsense. Be ya furgittin' all y'ur mama learn ya?"

"No, Mama, I ain't furgittin'. Don't be upset with me, Mama, please. I promise, I'll try not to do so much dreamin'. You ain't mad at me, is you?"

Even though she was still aggravated, Mama forced a smile. "No, y'ur mama ain't mad at ya. Just don'tcha go talkin' at me like ya knows more than I does. Just 'member, I be around on this earth a lot longer than ya has, and knows more than ya thinks.

I be learnin' me a lesson a long time ago that ya needs to pay attention to, child. If'n ya let folks know y'ur smart, they expects more a ya. Ya doesn't need to learn no more than ya has fur farm livn'. There's less hurt stayin' on a farm than goin' off into them scary worlds with book learnin'. Trust me, child, 'cause y'ur Mama knows what's good fur ya."

Before Farm Girl knew it, her birthday was just around the corner. The age of eighteen would be a new beginning and her day of liberation. This would be the time in her life when the window of opportunity would open wide for her to walk through. However, everything she had learned in the past few years was about to take her into a different life, a world of deadly confusion.

Opening Jefferson's mail after retrieving it from the roadside mailbox became one of Farm Girl's more pleasant jobs. If the envelope enclosure was a creditor's bill, she would throw it in the pile with the rest of the bills. Any other mail, she threw in a basket for Jefferson to look at when he had time.

Jefferson had sold most of his livestock and farm machinery in order to keep sending small payments to most of his creditors. He kept one cow so he would have milk in the house, and just a handful of laying hens for eggs. Two freezers, once packed with food, were now empty. Just a few can goods stood on the pantry shelves. Trusting in Darin, he ignored making any payments to the bank.

"Pappy, ya needs to quit doin' so much a that frettin'. That ain't one bit healthy fur ya. We're all gonna be all right."

"Mama, every month for well over a year now, you give me the same pep talk." Jefferson grinned. "I appreciate it. Never the less, it doesn't keep me from worrying about what tomorrow will bring. With most of my farming equipment gone now, I don't have too much left to sell to keep groceries on the table. I can't sell any land because ... Well, that's not a problem you need to hear."

"Farm Girl and me was use to eatin' small amounts a food befur we done meetcha. And, it ain't y'ur duty to be takin' care a us. I still say, I can go to town and gits me some day chores, like I once be doin'. That—"

"No, Mama, we've been all over this before. There's a person I know that's going to give me some money for a favor I've been doing for him. I'm just trying to get us by until that time. As long as I still have my home, and none of us are starving, we will be fine. So, you forget about going into town for some piddle job that won't pay you for what your worth."

A few days after the conversation, a letter arrived from the bank. Farm Girl did her best to read it. The letter was informing Jefferson Welk that the First People's Bank of Sharpin was going to foreclose on his properties. Farm Girl knew this was a very important document. This was not a letter to throw in the basket of other mail, or stack in the pile of bills. She had to show it to Mr. Welk just as soon as she could.

Sticking the letter in her apron pocket, she went to the kitchen where Mama had just started setting the table for Jefferson's breakfast.

"Is Pappy in his room nappin'?"

"Now, ya knows he be, child."

"I see you hasn't started fixin' his breakfast yet. Wouldja let me fix it today?"

Giving her daughter a look of bewilderment, Mama replied, "Silly girl. Ya doesn't even know how to cook."

"Crimeny, Mama, I been watchin' you cook ever since I be knee high to a turkey's butt."

"Farm Girl! Where does ya hear such talk?"

Farm Girl couldn't help but laugh. "From you. I hear you say that one time to some farmer man you was workin' fur."

"Oh, my, that was years ago. I cain't believe ya 'members that."

"So, can I fix breakfast fur Pappy this mornin'?"

"Ya really thinks ya can fry up eggs and bacon without burnin' them?"

"I doesn't know fur sure, but I has to try sometime. And ain't eighteen a good age to be tryin'?"

Slapping her hands crosswise to her chest, Mama took a deep breath. "Child, I plum furgot. Today's y'ur birthday, ain't it?" She embraced her daughter.

During the affectionate hug, Farm Girl thought, *She must be havin' one a them chest pains, again.*

"Happy Birthday, honey. I be so sorry I didn't 'member." The thought of years gone by pulled at Mama's heartstrings. "I was thinkin' this was one date I would never furgit."

Crimeny, I doesn't dare tell Mama that I knows she's under the weather. I wonder if'n her furgittin' is part a that heart sickness she's got? "That's okay, Mama. You ain't never furgot it before. I knows you just has too much on your mind. But it would be a swell birthday present if'n you'd let me cook."

"Okay. I'll go sit at the table while ya does the fixin'."

"No!" Farm Girl screeched. "I doesn't need you watchin' me, or fur sure I won't be doin' nothin' right."

Even though Mama didn't like Farm Girl's tone of voice, she had to agree with her. After all, it was time for Farm Girl to take on a few more responsibilities. "Okay. Okay." Mama picked up the egg basket from the countertop. "I'll go out in the hen house and gather eggs. Ya just be careful. We doesn't need to has ya settin' nothin' on fire."

After Farm Girl made the coffee, she filled the sugar bowl and placed it on the table. Jefferson couldn't drink coffee unless it was sweet. Encountering no problems frying the bacon while she made other preparations, Farm Girl was proud of herself. To keep the bacon warm, she placed it in the pre-warmed oven.

When she started frying the eggs, she called Mr. Welk down from his bedroom. Jefferson seated himself at the table. Farm Girl poured his coffee and added the sugar.

"Thank you, honey. Where's Mama?"

"She's out in the hen house, gatherin' eggs. I is cookin' fur you, all by my lonesome," Farm Girl proudly boasted. She replaced the coffee pot on the stove then returned to Jefferson's side.

"You are? Well, I think that's wonderful."

Throwing her arms around his neck, Farm Girl gave Jefferson a loving embrace.

Patting her on the back, he asked, "Hey, honey, what's that for?"

"Fur the same reason I is fixin' you breakfast. I love you."

"Well, honey, you know I love you, too."

"And anyhow, I was needin' me a birthday hug from you."

"Well, if that don't beat all. I thought your birthday was tomorrow. Happy Birthday, Farm Girl."

"Thank you, sir. I is much obliged," she replied with a giggle.

As he picked up his cup, Farm Girl stopped him. "Wait! I think you got somethin' you needs to see right away." Reaching into her apron pocket, she pulled out the bank's letter, unfolded it, and handed it to him. "Here you be."

Not letting loose of his cup, he reached with his spare hand and took the letter. As Jefferson read the letter, his hands started trembling. Within seconds, the tremble turned into violent shaking. The cup dropped from his hand, missing the plate as it hit the table. Coffee spilled about the table, escaping over the edge and dripping to the floor.

Never had Farm Girl seen Jefferson so upset. She knew he was going to be agitated reading the letter, but she didn't know it was going to cause such a horrible reaction. Tears welled up in his eyes and began rolling down his aged, weathered cheeks.

After wiping up the spilled coffee, Farm Girl got the pot, refilled his cup, added sugar and stirred it. *I ain't never seen him cry befur, and I sure doesn't like it*. Placing the pot back on the stove, she said, "Please, Pappy, calm down and drink your coffee."

Jefferson just sat there staring at the letter in his hand. Farm Girl rushed to the back door and called Mama in from the hen house. Hurrying back to the stove, she turned off the burner under the eggs, and turned off the oven.

Mama ran in the backdoor, and placed the basket of eggs on the kitchen counter. "Whatcha be callin' me in fur with such panic in y'ur voice?"

Without saying a word, Farm Girl shrugged and motioned with her eyes in Jefferson direction. Mama took one look at the sadness on his face, the tears in his eyes, and immediately knew something was wrong. For lack of words, they stood by waiting for Jefferson to say something.

Sniffling, Jefferson picked up his napkin, wiped his eyes and blew his nose. Displaying a face of anguish, he looked at the two women he had come to love. "I'm sorry for such an outburst. This letter was certainly something I never thought I would receive."

"You don't gots to tell us none a y'ur personal affairs," Mama replied. "We just wanna know that ya be okay and ain't havin' none a them heart pains."

"Don't worry yourself about my health, Mama, I'm okay. It's just..." Jefferson shook his head. "Well, this piece of paper is a foreclosure notice from the bank.

I've never burdened you two with any of my problems, other than letting you know that I had fallen on hard times. That's why I had to sell so much around here to keep up with my bills and keep a few groceries on the table."

"We already knows that. I teld ya, I should've gone to town and got me some chore doin' a long time ago. Then ya wouldn't be gittin' no such bad news."

"No, Mama. What little bit of money you might have made, would not have helped this situation. If you two will come sit with me, the time has come that I want to—no, I *need* to tell you everything."

Leaning back against the counter just steps away from the table, Mama said, "We can here just fine from right here. Be ya sure that ya wants to be tellin' us y'ur personal business?"

"Yes, because it now involves the two of you." Jefferson explained where his original wealth had come from, and why he no longer had financial support. Wadding his napkin into a ball, Jefferson stuck it in the upper pocket of his overalls. He pulled his handkerchief from his back pocket and wiped his face.

"I won't go into too much more detail except to tell you that I believed someone was helping me. Someone I've been doing a favor for. This person was going to give me money to get me out of debt so I could keep my farm. Well, that culprit is still around the area, but it's obvious that he isn't helping me anymore. This letter proves that."

Jefferson knew Darin would turn him into the law if he no longer held on to Darin's money and his secret. Although he felt his life was almost over, he had no desire to spend his remaining years behind bars. He thought about taking Darin's money and leaving town, but he was never a dishonest man. Now was not the time to change his values, even if the circumstances warranted such behavior.

In the pit of depression, Jefferson kept pouring out his heart. He blotted his face with his handkerchief. "After sending millions to charities, I managed to save a little cash for myself. It sounds rather ridiculous with all the money I had at my disposal, but, never the less, I did. All I can say is, thank God I never put it back in the bank."

"What's chair teas," Farm Girl asked, breaking her silence.

"Hush, child," Mama scolded.

"That's okay, Mama, I don't mind her asking questions. You see, honey, there are some very important organizations in this world that help find cures for illnesses. Some even give free medical help to those who can't afford it on their own. The organizations I support, well, I once supported when I could afford it, are the Cancer Foundation, Multiple Sclerosis, and the Muscular Dystrophy Foundation. I also sent funds to the Heart Association and to St. Jude's Hospital.

There are other worthy charities that received my donations, but I don't remember them right now." Jefferson stopped talking. No longer being able to help his favorite charities was filling his heart with sadness. "What that all means in simple terms, honey, is that I sent money to help with research, medical attention and medical supplies. Do you understand?"

"No. I is more mixed up now than I was befur."

"I'm sure when we're through here, Mama can explain it to you in words you can understand.

Right now, I need to talk about our future and the money I have hidden here in the house. In the first few years that you two were here, you brought love and sunshine into my life. You've been like the daughter and granddaughter I had always dreamed of having.

I wanted to make sure you two were taken care of when I was no longer around. So, I put money aside for you. I even changed my Will to include you. Not that it makes any difference now, since there's nothing left."

For a few seconds, Farm Girl blotted out Jefferson's voice and got lost in her own thoughts. *Why's he tellin' us this now fur? And why ain't he drinkin' his coffee so he can git peaceful-like? Pappy always tells me that a good cup a strong, sweet coffee always calms his nerves. But this mornin', he sure ain't doin' that. Crimeny, now I has to empty his cold coffee and pour him a fresh cup.*

Back to reality, and becoming very nervous, Farm Girl picked up Jefferson's cup from the table. After emptying the cup, she refilled it with hot coffee and sugar. As she listened to Jefferson, she placed the cup on the table, directly in front of him.

"I hope when you two have money, you keep it out of banks. Those bankers are wolves just waiting to gobble up everything you put in their trust. This letter is proof of that. They could care less that I'm an old man and was born and raised on this land. Now, they're kicking me out in the cold," he complained. "All they care about is lining their pockets. They want blood!

Forgive me, but I can't help my bitterness right now. With the exception of you two, I feel betrayed by the bank, the bank's employees, and almost every one in Cole County. You two have been the one shining light in my existence since my wife passed.

Now, in view of the circumstances, I believe it's time to just walk away. I will take some of the savings to tide me over until I can figure out what I can do to support myself. At my age, I may be able to find handyman jobs. The rest of the money, Mama, I want you to take."

"If'n you has money, why don'tcha just pay fur your farm and all them bills you has?" Farm Girl asked.

"Child—"

"It's okay, Mama. That's a fair question." Jefferson realized he would have to explain in simple terms Farm Girl would understand. "If you would take one of those dollar bills I showed you once and filled a room with them, you would have thousands and thousands of dollars. That's how much my properties are worth. Compared to that large amount of money, I only have a penny saved. That one tiny cent wouldn't make a dent in that room full of money."

Farm Girl didn't understand, and it showed by the frown on her face. However, Jefferson wanted to move on with his thoughts.

"You two will have to leave the farm and seek employment elsewhere. The money I'll give you should help pay for a place to live. Also, I want you to make sure Farm Girl gets a decent education."

Noticing that Mama was shaking her head in disagreement, Jefferson was quick to state, "Now, Mama, don't you be so stubborn. I've had a full life and I don't expect to live too many more years. Besides, an old man doesn't have as many needs as two women do. I can get by on the small amount that I will keep for myself, and by doing odd jobs.

For reasons I won't go into right now, I would advise you to move as far away from this area as possible. If this hadn't been my lifelong home, I would have moved on a long time ago. But my roots are here. You don't have any roots here, Mama. So, find a good town to live in where they have decent folks that are cordial and treat you with respect. Settle in a nice area where Farm Girl can attend a special school."

"School?" Farm Girl questioned.

"I know you wouldn't feel right attending school at your age, Farm

Girl. We discussed that before when you were much younger. But, there may be other possibilities. Perhaps, when you get settled, you could inquire about a specialized tutor."

Wrinkling her brow, Farm Girl asked, "What's a special eyes tutor?"

Ignoring her pronunciation, Jefferson explained. "An educated, well trained person who can work with you on a one on one basis, teaching you lessons at home. It would be like having your own personal teacher, Farm Girl."

"Ain't that what you was doin' with me?"

"In a sense, yes. But, I'm not a professional teacher, honey. With the proper tutor and the right books, you can get a real education. I don't know why I hadn't thought of a tutor before now." Jefferson had to stop and think if he was giving the right advice. After all, he still felt that Farm Girl had a learning disorder.

Then an idea crossed his mind. "Look, Mama, I don't know much about the schools today, but I think you can take Farm Girl to a school and get her tested. That way you will know what grade level she is and what kind of special tutoring she needs."

As Farm Girl continued to listen, she wished, *Please, Pappy, won'tcha just be quiet and drink your coffee so you calm down. If'n you keeps shakin' like you is, you is gonna have you one a them heart pains. I doesn't like to see you when you is in pain.*

When Jefferson realized that he was rambling on a mile a minute, and becoming increasingly distraught over losing his farm, Farm Girl got her wish. He stopped talking, picked up his cup and drank most of his coffee. "Well, Miss Eighteen-year-old, your coffee was—"

Without warning, Jefferson dropped his cup. He grabbed at his chest. It was obvious he was having trouble getting his breath. A few short gasps for air, and Jefferson fell off his chair, hitting the floor with a thud.

Mama dashed to the sink and got a cold, wet cloth. Then she hurried to Jefferson, fell to her knees, and proceeded to wipe his face.

At first, Farm Girl felt paralyzed. When her brain kicked in, she realized what she had to do. "I'll git us some help, Mama." She rushed to the telephone. Just as she picked up the receiver, she heard Mama's voice.

"Pappy ain't with us no longer."

Mama mourned in silence, but Farm Girl couldn't stop the waterfall of tears that flushed from her eyes. As Jefferson lay dead on the floor with the letter still enclosed in his hand, Farm Girl knelt beside him, sobbing her heart out. Mama walked to the sink and stared blankly out the window.

Then, in the midst of tears, Farm Girl pulled herself together. Her face lit up. Like a child's mind, Farm Girl could go from happy to sad and back again within a matter of seconds without rhyme or reason to anyone else around her.

Still kneeling on the floor next to the body, she told Mama, "We need to call someone and tell them Pappy is dead." There was no response from Mama. "Befur we does that, we has to find the money. He doesn't got no kin," Farm Girl stated between sniffles. Removing a rag from her pocket that she used as a hankie, she wiped her eyes and blew her nose. "Least ways, we ain't never hear him speak a no kin."

When she saw her mother's head shake, Farm Girl reminded her what Jefferson had said. "That old bank is fixin' to take everythin'. Wolves, Pappy was callin' them. Wolves. You was hearin' him, Mama. Why shouldn't we take the money fur us? Who would know? Besides, he said he wants us to has some a it anyway. With him gone now, why not take it all?"

Taking a deep breath, she continued, "No one knows about Sugar Shack. We can take the money there and hide it until it's safe to move on, just like Pappy was sayin' we should do."

Standing in silence and still staring out into space, Mama never once turned. All she could manage to do was to shake her head in disagreement and disbelief. Not only of Jefferson's passing so sudden-like, but also dismayed by what her daughter was suggesting they do. She knew in her heart why she couldn't shed any tears. However, it was hard for her to understand how her daughter could demonstrate a thunderstorm of tears one minute then be full of sunshine the next.

"Please say somethin', Mama."

"Pappy just died. His body be still warm. I knows one mourns in his own way, but I sure doesn't understands the way ya be actin'. First, ya cry buckets. Then the next thing I knows, ya be talkin' about robbin' the dead. Here I was thinkin' ya was lovin' him like I was?"

"Of course I was lovin' Pappy. I ain't never had me no one die befur that I loves. So I doesn't know how to act. Did I do somethin' wrong by cryin'?"

"No, honey, ya didn't do nothin' wrong. Guess I should a knows to prepare ya fur losin' one ya loves."

"Well, what about the money, Mama?"

"Just 'cause he was gonna give us somethin' when he was alive, don't mean we needs to be takin' it now that he's gone. That's stealin'. I ain't never still nothin' in all my born days but a small bit a hay or straw to make us a bed when we was needin'. Even then, I was askin' God to furgive me 'cause I was feelin' so guilty."

Farm Girl didn't want to hear Mama rationalize what was right or wrong. Getting to her feet; she walked over and turned Mama to face her. She took Mama's hands in hers. Assuming she knew what Mama was thinking, Farm Girl knew she had to convenience her.

"Why not Mama? We just been tellin' each other how we both was lovin' Pappy. He was lovin' us too. Why, I remember you tellin' me once that he was like the daddy you always was wishin' fur. You knows in your heart that he'd want us to has the money, and not let some old bank take it. You was hearin' that with your own ears. It ain't stealin'. It's ours fur the takin'. Come on, Mama, we has to look fur it, now."

Farm Girl just knew that upstairs was the place to start their search. Letting loose of one hand, she ran toward the steps leading upstairs, practically dragging Mama behind her. Mama had no other choice but to move her feet or fall flat on her face.

Once they were in Jefferson's bedroom, Farm Girl let go of Mama's hand, and began to search. First, she ransacked the drawers, taking care to put things back in place. Even though she was in a hurry, she didn't want to leave the drawers in disorder. No one could know they had been searched. After she looked under the bed, she looked up and noticed Mama was still standing in the doorway.

"Help me, Mama, please. It's okay. We ain't stealin' nothin' he didn't want us to has. Please, Mama, I cain't do this without your help."

A reluctant mother started helping her daughter with the search.

They went through the boxes that were still sitting on the floor, stacked up against one wall. Then they went through everything in the closet, including all the pockets of Jefferson's clothes. They came up empty handed. The one place they had not checked was the bed. Since Jefferson had just gotten up from his nap when called to breakfast, the bed was still in disarray.

All the bed items were removed and tossed aside. Mama was almost positive they wouldn't find the money in the bed, since they were the ones that washed the bedding, turned the top mattress, and made the bed. Yet, Farm Girl was almost certain that she was right and Mama was wrong.

"It's gotta be here, Mama, because we has been lookin' everywhere else in this room. And, if it ain't, then we'll go downstairs and search until we finds it."

With Farm Girl's insistence, they pulled the top mattress off the bed and dropped it on the floor. Farm Girl got down on the mattress that now hugged the floor, pushing down with her hands and knees to see if she could feel anything unusual from inside. She had Mama do the same to the mattress that remained on the bed. They felt and pushed on every inch of the mattresses, but nothing felt out of the ordinary.

Farm Girl sat on the mattress on the floor with a dismal look on her face. Mama, wearing a forlorn facial expression, sat down beside her. Removing the rag from her head, letting her natural curls flow loose around her face, Farm Girl placed her face in her hands. She rubbed her temples with her thumbs, as she tried hard to sort things out in her head.

"Mama!" Farm Girl squealed, jumping to her feet. Mama flinched. "Why were Pappy always askin' us to turn just the top mattress, and not to bother about the second one?" Before Mama could answer, Farm Girl demanded, "Git up Mama. Help me git this other mattress off a the bed."

"I already was checkin' that mattress."

"I know you was. Just help me."

Farm Girl took hold of the bottom end while Mama took hold of the top. Together they slid the second mattress off the bed, dropping it on top of the first mattress on the floor. Then they found something strange. Tucked snug within the coils of the metal spring mattress that still sat on the bed slats were several socks. Each coil had a sock nestled inside.

Not wanting to appear too brazen and assume they had found what they were searching for, Farm Girl asked, "Mama, has you ever seen one a these here metal mattresses befur?"

"A few. They calls them metal springs. Why be ya askin' fur?"

"Did the ones you seen has them things that looks like Pappy's stockin's in them, like this one do?"

"Maybe he was stuffin' them in there fur comfort, keepin' the metal from his body?"

"That don't make no sense, Mama, when he's got two soft mattresses between him and the metal. Cain't you think a no other reason?"

When Mama shook her head, that was all Farm Girl needed to

take action. As she attempted to remove one of the socks from a coil, she grunted as she pulled to get it loose from its hiding place. Untying the knot at the top of the sock, Farm Girl emptied its contents onto one of the mattresses on the floor.

Filled with joy, Farm Girl ran her fingers through the large collection of coins and bills that had fallen out of the sock. Her eyes lit up like a full moon. "Look, Mama! Has you ever seen so much money befur? I wonder how much this is?"

"Money's the root a all evil," Mama whispered under her breath, remembering a quote from the Bible.

Ignoring Mama's whispers, Farm Girl began counting the one-dollar bills, tossing the other, larger denominations to one side.

Still feeling a tinge of guilt, Mama suggested they not dawdle. "Poor Pappy's body be layin' downstairs on the kitchen floor. We needs to git out a here befur some unsuspectin' soul decides to show up on his doorstep."

"You sure comes up with some big words I ain't never hear you say befur, Mama."

Mama chose to disregard the comment.

The scenario of visitors showing up at Jefferson's house was doubtful, but Farm Girl agreed they needed to hurry. She scooped up the money and put it back into the sock. Mama pulled and twisted to remove the remaining socks from their nesting places.

A couple of the socks were caught in the coil-springs. So, when Mama tugged with all of her strength, their material snagged. A large hole was torn in one sock, which meant it would no longer hold the money inside. The other sock, although ripped, was still useable, if handled with care.

They opened a few of the remaining socks and added the contents from the badly torn sock. Mama tossed the empty sock aside. Then she helped Farm Girl tie the tops of the money-socks back into knots. Placing the filled socks on the floor, they remade the bed. Reclining on the bed, Farm Girl messed the bedding in order to leave it just as they had found it.

"Even though I doesn't like it, I is agreein' with ya about takin' some a this money. But, child, we cain't take it all. We might be strong, but all a them socks be just too heavy to be carryin' out a here."

"Yes, we is gonna take it all, and you is gonna take them socks to Sugar Shack."

"Just how does ya think I be gonna carry all them heavy things?"

"Mama, you ain't thinkin' right. If'n you can tote them heavy buckets a cow feed around the farm, you can sure carry this here money."

"I be sure buckets a feed be lighter than these here socks be. Even so, we ain't gots no buckets in here fur carryin'"

"Use your skirt," Farm Girl replied, trying to be respectful but becoming a tad impatient. "When we doesn't has no basket or bucket to carry things in, we always uses our aprons fur small things, and our skirts fur larger things. Crimeny, Mama, you was teachin' me that when I was first learnin' how to help you with chores."

Giving in, Mama lifted her skirt and gripped the hem with both hands, making a convenient carrying place. Farm Girl piled the heavy socks inside Mama's makeshift carrier. Neither of them had ever seen so much money, and Farm Girl was not about to leave any of it behind. The socks were so heavy, Mama had difficulty holding on to her skirt. She clutched the material between her hands as tight as she could.

To further assure Mama that what they were doing was all right, Farm Girl explained, "With no kin folks, I don't reckon Pappy had no one to tell that he was a hidin' money. We was closer to him than anyone, and even we didn't know. Anyways, it just makes sense. If'n no one knows it were here, no one ain't gonna know it's missin'."

Logical assumption or not, Mama had no more to say at that time. All she could think about was the loss of someone very dear to her, and now stealing from him.

Back in the kitchen, neither could look at Jefferson's body. Farm Girl opened the backdoor. "Is you feelin' well enough to make your way back to Sugar Shack?"

"It's a mighty heavy load, that's fur sure. I be feelin' a might puny right now, but y'ur mama will make it."

"Okay, then go. I'll wait here. When I thinks you be gone enough time to be back in Sugar Shack, then I'll be callin' the sheriff mans. I reckon it's best I stay around here in case he has him questions to ask. So, don't look fur me until after dark. I needs to be sure no one follows me when I leave here."

Other than gripping as hard as she could to her heavy-laden skirt, Mama didn't budge. Feeling confident that she could take care of everything, Farm Girl insisted. "It's okay, Mama, now go. You hurry back, dump them socks on the table, then sit and relax. I doesn't wantcha to worry about nothin'."

"I don't like it," Mama protested. "How does ya know to be callin' the sheriff mans?"

"It don't make no difference right now, but Pappy told me I has to learn to call that sheriff mans in case anythin' ever happens to either one a you."

"I be watchin' over ya fur eighteen years, keepin' ya safe. There ain't too many folks that knows about ya. How be ya gonna explain to some sheriff mans why ya be here on the farm a Mister Welk?"

"Easy. I'll say I is you and pick me out one a them names you was once be usin'."

With no further argument, Mama accepted the explanation and left the house.

As she started wrapping up the food from breakfast, she nibbled on some cookies left from Mama's baking.

"Remember, Farm Girl, you has to furgit everythin' Pappy done teach you. If'n that sheriff mans thinks you is smart, he might be askin' too many questions. You doesn't want to slip and let him knows that you and Mama is takin' that money."

After a good amount of time had elapsed, and Farm Girl was almost positive Mama was back at Sugar Shack, she made her telephone call.

When she received an answer on the other end of the phone, she stated, "I needs to tell ya that Mister Welk be dead here on his kitchen floor." Asked her name, she replied, "They calls me, uh, Janet. Janet Abbot. How does I know he's dead? 'Cause I be standin' here lookin' at him. And ya best hurry. Me? I be his farmhand." Not wanting to answer any more questions over the telephone, she hung up.

Farm Girl needed to keep herself busy until the sheriff arrived, so she did the dishes and started cleaning the kitchen. The kitchen was not very dirty to begin with, but she had nervous energy she needed to wear off.

Cautious not to disturb Jefferson's body, she got a damp rag and wiped up the small puddles of coffee that he had spilled from his cup when he collapsed to the floor. She was buffing the floor with a dry cloth when Farm Dawg started barking.

Straining to hear over the baking, she heard a car drive up outside. Figuring it had to be the sheriff, she didn't even bother looking out the window. She was positive that peering out the window might look too suspicious. As she finished wiping the floor, she heard a knock at the kitchen door. The sound startled her.

"Crimeny! Pappy always teld me visitors come knockin' at the front door, not the back one. I reckon, if'n that's the sheriff mans, he don't know no better," she muttered under her breath. "Of course, he ain't no visitor. So, maybe it's just natural-like fur him to be usin' the backdoor."

Shoving both floor rags into her apron pocket, she answered the door. There before her stood a man all dressed in brown, and wearing a badge on the front of his shirt. Farm Girl looked at him from his head to his toes. Like a sudden earthquake, she started shaking in her boots. Yet, she felt like she was glued to the floor.

"I'm Sheriff Luden."

With Mama's words of fear instilled in her, she almost didn't hear a word the sheriff said when he introduce himself. Thinking about meeting the sheriff, and actually meeting him in person, were entirely two different sets of circumstances.

Evil Stranger! Evil Stranger! Calm down, Farm Girl, and git yourself together. This man ain't gonna hurt you. He's here to take care a Pappy. Knees, quit your shaken! She felt like her heart was pounding a thousand beats per second.

When she realized she had been staring at the stranger, as if in a trance, she opened the door wide and allowed him to enter. Farm Girl pointed toward Jefferson's body. Before she could close the door, two other men entered the house.

Ward introduced them. "This is Deputy Doug Martin, and the man in the white coat is Doctor Shivley." Doc walked over to Jefferson's body. Doug removed his hat and gave a pleasant nod of hello. "Now, little lady," Ward continued, "who might you be?"

Speechless, Farm Girl's eyes widened as big as saucers as her head tilted back, scanning Deputy Martin from his belt buckle to his head. Doug, standing 6'2" with a muscular build, towered over her. Once again, she froze in her tracks when her eyes met his. She couldn't help staring at him even more then she had stared at Ward when she opened the door.

Her eyes moved from one side of Doug's face to the other, as if she were watching a game of badminton without so much as a head movement. As frightened as she was, Doug's eyes fascinated her.

When most people first looked at Deputy Martin with his baldhead, one blue eye and one brown eye, they either took a double take, or turned away and walked in the opposite direction as fast as their feet could carry them. The devil himself would have been scared, if he had run into Doug in a dark alley.

Ward noticed that Farm Girl appeared mesmerized. "Oh, don't let Deputy Martin scare you none, little lady. He's as gentle as a new born calf." Since she still didn't show any signs of movement, Ward pulled a chair over to where she was standing. He gave her a gentle push on the shoulder for her to sit. Once seated, Ward asked her questions while Doc made a routine examination of Jefferson.

I doesn't know why the sheriff mans is bringin' a doctor mans here fur. Crimeny, Pappy ain't sick. He's dead. Them townsfolk sure does weird things. Guess Mama were right. They is mighty strange folks. Ignoring Ward's questions, Farm Girl broke her silence and asked, "Why do Mister Welk needs him a doctor mans fur?"

"Doctor Shivley is also our County Coroner," Sheriff Luden answered.

"Oh," she uttered, as if she understood the answer. *I doesn't knows what am a county coroner, but I ain't gonna ask.*

"Did you put the towel over his face?" Doc asked.

Nodding her head, she admitted, "Yes, sir. I knows dead when I sees dead. But no one never told me that people dies with them eyes open. I sure didn't like him starin' at me, so I use the dish towel to hide them creepy eyes." She shook from the chill that ran up her spine. "Ain't people suppose to close their eyes, like when they goes to sleep?"

Keeping a sober face, but smiling on the inside, Doc answered. "No. Many people die with their eyes open."

When Ward questioned Farm Girl, she told as many lies as she felt she could get away with, and mixed them in with small fractions of the truth.

Holding the letter that Doc had taken from Jefferson's hand, Ward continued his inquiry. "So all you know is that Mr. Welk was upset about receiving this letter. He never told you what it was about."

"No, sir. It ain't none a my affair."

"Janet, let's go back to what you told me a few minutes ago. You said that you prepared breakfast. Then you called Mr. Welk down from his upstairs bedroom to come eat. Is that correct?"

"Yes, sir."

"Then you said, you poured him his coffee."

"Yes."

Farm Girl's eyes started tearing. The doctor covered up the body with a blanket he had brought in the house with him. Sitting there, now looking at his covered body, answering questions about his death, made it hard for Farm Girl to hold herself together.

Ward continued. "Okay, tell me what you did next."

Pig slop. Farm Girl, you is so afraid your knees is still shaken. I hope them mans cain't see them. Be brave. Come on, Farm Girl, he's waitin' fur you to answer him.

Moving, almost in slow motion, Farm Girl picked up the bottom of her apron and put it to her face. Stalling, she wiped her eyes. While the men conversed in low voices, this gave her time to compose herself and come up with some believable explanations. As she tried to overhear what the men were whispering about, she remembered something important. That thought gave her a brilliant idea.

Since she was sincere about being mournful that Jefferson was gone, real tears were being shed. However, to be convincing, in an extra put-on, sobbing voice, she said, "Excuse my takin' so long to speak, sir. It's just that it was an awful shock to be findin' poor Mister Welk like that, dead on the floor and all. It's more than a body can stand."

"I understand. Would you like a glass of water?"

"No. I is fine."

"Okay, so tell me what you did after you gave Mr. Welk his coffee."

"I knows Mister Welk always puts his mail right there on the table," she pointed, "when he brung it in from that funny metal box. After his mornin' nap, when he comes back down to eat, he'd open his mail."

Farm Girl didn't seem to be answering Ward's question. However, he decided to go along with her conversation to see where it would lead. "That seems pretty strange. Most people open their mail right away."

"I doesn't know about them most peoples, but Mister Welk was always too tired to be readin' his mail. It be a long way from here to that metal box and back. The walk plum wore him out. That's why he'd be a waitin' until after his nap to be openin' his mail."

Since the explanation made sense, Ward proceeded questioning. "What happened after Mr. Welk came back down stairs to breakfast?"

"Ain't I already teld ya that?"

"So you did, Janet. I just want to make sure that the deputy gets all of his notes correct." Ward looked at Doug and winked. "Right, Deputy?"

"That's right, Sheriff."

"After I be pourin' his coffee, I serves him breakfast. Then I gots the egg basket, like I does every mornin', and goes to the hen house. Ya can see fur y'urself," she motioned to the basket of eggs sitting on the counter, "them be the eggs I gots this mornin'."

Checking the basket of eggs, Doug could see they hadn't been cleaned. Feeling a couple of the eggs, noting they were room temperature, confirmed Farm Girl's explanation.

Once Ward got a nod from Doug, he turned his attention back to his witness. "Then what, Janet?"

"Crimeny, I doesn't rightly know how long I was out there. When I come back in, there was poor old Mister Welk layin' on the floor."

Frowning, Ward looked over at Doug and asked, "Is there something in your notes that needs explaining?" Traveling on the same wave link, Doug knew exactly what Ward meant. There was something in the girl's statements that didn't make sense. When Doug nodded, Ward stated, "Okay, Deputy, do you have any questions?"

"Yes, I do. Janet, from what you've told us, I got the impression you were in the kitchen with Mr. Welk when he opened his letter."

Oh, turkey turds, Farm Girl. You best think real heard befur you gits yourself in big trouble. "I doesn't 'member sayin' that. Be ya sure?"

When Doug squinched his face into a funny, bewildered look, Ward had to turn his head so he wouldn't laugh. "Well, you said ... " Doug paused to refer to his notes, "the letter upset Mr. Welk. Do you remember saying that?"

"I reckon I does."

"When the sheriff asked you if Mr. Welk told you what was in the letter, you told him no because it was none of your affair. Correct?"

"I reckon that's right. He never told me what was none a my business. Farmhands knows their place."

Somewhat frustrated, Doug suggested, "Why don't we try this again. If you were outside gathering eggs, how do you know the letter upset him?"

There was dead silence in the room. Farm Girl dropped her head and looked at her hands that were now folded on her lap. She could feel three sets of eyes staring at her, waiting for her answer.

Looking up at Doug, she responded, "Sir, he weren't even readin' that there piece a paper when I put his breakfast on the table. He be just about to, when I walks out the door to go gather them eggs. When I comes back in and sees him on the floor with that paper in his hand, his breakfast still sittin' there on his plate but his coffee cup empty, what was I gonna think? That he up and died 'cause a drinkin' my coffee?"

Doug turned his back to her and gave Ward another strange look. Ward, not being able to keep a straight face, turned and looked at Doc. Doc, who was also ready to crack up into chuckles, turned his head and gave a fake cough.

After taking a deep breath, Ward turned back to Farm Girl and commented, "Well, Doug, that sounded like a reasonable explanation to me." Doug had nothing for a comeback. Again, Ward took over. "Okay, Janet, after you found Mr. Welk on the floor, what did you do?"

"When I knows he wasn't breathin' no more, I calls that number 911 and talks to ya, didn't I?"

"Yes, I'm the one you spoke to. Why did you hang up on me?"

"Ain't that what a body's to do when they be through talkin' on one a them funny thingies?"

In frustration, Ward could only nod at her response. He didn't care to start explaining telephone manners or police protocol.

"If you saw Mr. Welk on the floor, and made an immediate phone call to my office, how do you know he wasn't still alive?"

"I teld ya, he weren't breathin'. I done checks him. A farmhand knows when a person ain't breathin' no more. I was helpin' Mister Welk, once, when one a his cows up and died. Sos, I sure knows dead when I sees it."

"Yes, I would imagine you would.

The kitchen looks spotless. One would never know you cooked breakfast in here this morning."

"But, I sure did."

"Oh, I'm not doubting your word about fixing breakfast. Did you do the cleaning in here?"

"Yes, sir, that's part a my chores. Besides, while I be waitin' fur ya to git here, I just couldn't be sittin' around lookin' at poor old Mister Welk layin' there dead, now could I?"

"No, I guess not." Ward realized he was not getting any more information then he already had out of the girl. A small conference was in order. "Okay, Janet, just sit tight for a few minutes."

Motioning with his eyes and a cock of his head, Ward got Doc and Doug in a huddle a few feet away from where Farm Girl sat. "Doug, I want you to check out the rest of the house. See if anything looks suspicious. I'll lay you odds, everything is just as the girl says it was."

When Doug walked away to look around the house, Ward spoke with Doc. "So, what did you find out?"

"From what I can tell right now, I'd say Jefferson died from a heart attack. He's had a bad heart for years. I imagine with the stress of a foreclosure staring him in the face, the old ticker gave out on him."

"How long do you think he's been dead?"

Doc shook his head. "Hard to say. Until I do a closer examination, I would guess he's been dead for well over an hour. Rigor hasn't set in yet."

"After you do the autopsy and have your report ready, just call and let me know. I'll have Doug swing by your office and pick it up."

They stood talking until Doug returned to give his report.

"Doug, what did you find?" Ward asked.

"Since I've never been in this house before, I would say everything appears to be normal. There's a fireplace in the other room. The coals are still hot. I took a stoker and kind of poked around, but I didn't find anything unusual. The bed upstairs looks like someone was lying on top the covers after the bed was made."

"So, the girl's story about Welk taking a nap would be correct."

"Yes, Sheriff, I would say so."

"Doc seems to think Welk died of a heart attack. I'm inclined to agree. Death by natural causes clears this young lady," Ward stated "I think we can send her on her way now."

Stepping back to Farm Girl, Ward stated, "You know, Janet, it's a good thing there are no other people living in the area with the last name Welk."

"What?"

"You hung up on me before you gave me an address. Now, if I hadn't known Jefferson Welk, or if there were another Welk family living in our county, I would have never known to come to this particular farm."

"Who be Anna Dress?"

"An address," Ward emphasized. "The name of a street where somebody lives. Speaking of which, do you live around here?"

"I lives in the barn with my dog."

"You can take your dog, and what other belongings you have, and head on your way. The letter that Mr. Welk was holding states the bank will now own this farm. I imagine, as soon as we contact the bank, they'll be sending some people out here to take over. So, you'll have to leave. Doctor Shivley says it appears that Mr. Welk simply died of a heart attack. So, we won't have any more questions for you. You're free to go."

Farm Girl did not move. The shaking knees that earlier wanted her to run away, now felt like lead weights as her curiosity got the best of her. "Sir, what be a heart attack?"

Ward glanced over at Doc to allow him the pleasure of answering her question. Understanding Ward's look, Doc gave a brief explanation. "It's when your heart just stops beating, Janet."

"Oh, y'ur heart just stops beatin'," she repeated, as she focused her attention in Doc's direction. "Do that mean he was dyin' peaceful-like?"

"I would say so," Doc stated in an appeasing voice.

Then her mind skipped into a very different pattern. Looking back at Ward, Farm Girl asked, "Do the food in the house belongs to them folks at the bank, or can I take it fur me and my dog?"

The sheriff smiled, giving her shoulder a gentle pat. "Janet, I don't think the bankers are going to care that a young lady and her dog take something to eat."

"Farm Dawg and me is much obliged, sir."

"Farm dog?" Ward stated with a question.

"Yes, sir, that's my pet's name."

Ward had no comment.

As Farm Girl arose from her chair, she retrieved the thermos and the small, foil-wrapped package of food from inside the cupboard. She turned back to the sheriff.

"This here thermos gots the coffee leftover from breakfast. Hot coffee will be pleasin' to me on a cold day like this. And I wraps some food in this here foil while I was waitin' fur ya to git here.

Out a respect fur Mister Welk and all, I feels it my duty to stay around and finish my chores. I can sleep in the barn, as usual. Then I'll be leavin' first thing in the mornin' after Mister Rooster wakes me."

Farm Girl almost dirtied her bloomers from fright as Ward, without warning, reached out and took the thermos from her small hand.

Her immediate response was to proclaim innocence. "I wasn't tryin' to steal that old thermos."

Ward opened the thermos and handed it to the doctor. "No one thinks you're trying to steal anything. We just need to check out these items before you leave with them," he replied.

After Doc smelled the contents of the thermos, he stuck his finger in the coffee and tasted it. Shaking his head with a sour look on his face, shuttering from the distaste that lingered on his tongue, he handed the thermos back to the sheriff. "That coffee not only smells strong, but it's so sweet, it tastes like syrup." Addressing Janet, he asked, "Don't tell me you drink this stuff?"

With a blank look on her face, she nodded. "Yes, sir, just like Mister Welk done." *Crimeny, I doesn't drink coffee. I upchucked the day Mama let me taste some a hers. I hopes he doesn't make me drink none a it.*

"I would certainly advise giving it up. Drinking a cup of that concoction would darn near kill a healthy man," Doc joked with a somber face.

Ward fought hard not to chuckle at Doc's deadpan humor. He closed the thermos and gave it back to Farm Girl. Then he took the foil-wrapped food from her, opened it, and again handed it to the doctor. Once Doc had smelled and tasted bits of the contents, he gave it back to the sheriff with his approval.

"Ya sure doesn't think I be puttin' somethin' bad in the coffee and food, does ya?"

"This is just a precautionary measure, Janet," Ward said, closing the foil and returning it to her. "There you go.

Now, about those chores, I wouldn't worry about them. Under the circumstances, I'm sure Mr. Welk will still rest easy even if you don't complete the work. Like I said, collect your belongings and be on your way."

No! I has to stay so you cain't follow me to Sugar Shack, Mama, and all that money. "But, sir, Mister Welk done pay me fur a day's wages, which I'll be needin' fur more food till my next farm job. Takin' his money without earnin' it, just ain't right. And with him dead and all, I sure cain't give the money back."

Sheriff Luden, now just wanting Farm Girl to leave the house, agreed she could stay outside and do chores, sleep in the barn that night, then leave the following day. Allowing her to stay in the house and do any inside chores, however, was out of the question. He was already a trifle displeased that she took it upon herself to do up the breakfast dishes and clean the kitchen before they had arrived on the scene.

Farm Girl smiled, knowing she had done a good job with her lies, but she still wasn't ready to leave. "Sir, I doesn't think Mister Welk gots no livin' kin. So, I knows he'd sure wanna be with his love ones.

Black Rosebud

I'd be mighty beholden to ya, if'n ya'd sees that he gits a decent bury with one a them marker boards with his name on it."

Ward was beginning to feel like he was never going to get rid of her. "I can assure you, Janet, Mr. Welk will be taken care of in the proper manner."

Satisfied she had all of her questions answered, Farm Girl finally left the house. As she closed the door, sandwiching herself between it and the screen door, she placed her ear against the wood. She could hear the sheriff relate his feelings to the other two men.

"Good Lord! Have you ever in your whole life met anyone more fitting for the expression 'backwoods hillbilly'? I'd have promised her the moon just now to get her out of here. I didn't realize in this day and age that a person could be so illiterate. That's so sad," Ward commented. "I'm a patient person, but good gosh almighty, I believe it would be easier communicating with a four-year old."

Doc nodded in agreement. Doug added his opinion. "I can't quite figure out if she's illiterate or if some of her speech was a spoof, Sheriff."

"Why do you say that?" Ward asked.

"She appeared to give a good deal of thought to everything she said. Plus, she used many correct words then threw in a word, here and there, like *ain't* or some other bad English. It seemed as if she was trying to throw us off balance with her answers."

"Well, you could be right. On the other hand, I knew Jefferson. For a man who didn't get a schooled education, his speech wasn't all that bad. It could have been very easy for her to pick up some of his correct words."

"Yeah, I guess that would make sense."

"You know, that just reminded me of something," Ward remarked. "Welk was said to have a female farmhand working for him. Did either of you hear that rumor?"

With a negative response, Doug shook his head. However, Doc responded with a nod. "I heard it straight from the horse's mouth," Doc stated. "But somehow, I got the impression it was an older woman working for him when he mentioned her to me. This Janet sure doesn't fill that bill."

"I, too, heard his farmhand was an older woman," Ward admitted.

To add his thoughts to the conversation, Doug said, "Maybe you're both right? It could be that the older woman left and this Janet took her place. We didn't ask her how long she was working for the deceased."

"You know, I'll bet you're right," Ward agreed.

There was a lull when no one spoke. Ward broke the silence. "I should have gotten to know him better after all these years."

"Know who better?" Doug inquired.

Realizing he had verbalized his thoughts, he shrugged the question by responding, "It's not important.

Say, Doc, shouldn't that ambulance be here by now to pick up the body?"

Doc looked at his watch. "Yes. I'll go call and see what the hold up is." Looking about the kitchen, he asked, "Anyone know where the phone is?"

Pointing, Doug said, "Over there on the wall, right next to that cupboard. It's kind of hidden out of sight from here. During my walkthrough, I noticed it when I came back up from the basement."

Looking rather glum, Ward commented, "I can't believe that poor soul has been living in the barn. If I weren't supporting one young lad as a foster child already, I'd take that little lady and help her. Tomorrow morning, Doug, let's get out here before she leaves.

I'm assuming old Mister Rooster," he said with a chuckle, "will wake her at daybreak. So, we'll have to be here by then, and take her into town. The least we can do is to get her something decent to eat. It was all I could do to give her back that packet of cold food. God, what a way to live."

Ward had a sudden flash. "Good gosh almighty! I didn't even ask her for any ID. She might be under age or hiding out from someone. Shoot, she could be one of those missing kids we always get reports on. As soon as we get back to town, Doug, call in her description and see if there's a Missing Persons Report on her."

"Sounds good to me, Sheriff, but then what?"

"If she's on a wanted or runaway list, we'll follow legal procedures. If no one is looking for her, maybe we can help find the little lady a job somewhere around the county."

"I swear," Doug replied with a smile, "you've got the biggest, most generous heart of anyone I've ever met before." Doc ended his phone conversation at the same time Doug asked, "Why wait, Sheriff, when I can go out now and ask the kid for an ID?"

"No. We'll worry about that tomorrow, since this isn't a crime scene." As the doctor walked back to where they were standing, Ward added, "Right Doc?"

"Not as far as I'm concerned. Jefferson had a bad heart for years, and I warned him about cutting down his intake of caffeine. Dang, from the smell that reeked from that thermos, that coffee was so strong that it—" He gave a quick glance in Doug's direction. In a very serious manner he related, "I'll bet it was strong enough to keep your head smooth, Doug. A good cup of that hair remover every morning, and you wouldn't need to use a straight edge on it."

Doug gave an instant chuckle. "Very funny."

Doc went on to say, "In all seriousness, Ward, I don't think there was any foul play here. Considering his age and health history, I believe Jefferson's heart just gave out."

"Well, Doc, that's good enough for me," Ward responded.

"Say, Sheriff, do you know what that girl was talking about when she mentioned that Mr. Welk would be happy being with his loved ones?" Doug asked.

"Yes and no. She might not have meant anything in particular, other than meeting them in heaven. On the other hand, I'm sure there must be a graveyard on this property where Jefferson's wife and immediate family members are buried. But, I'm not positive. To my understanding, there's acreage after acreage on this property. It would take days to locate any graves, and that would only be true if the graves were marked."

"So, should we start looking?"

"No, Doug. The county will see to it that Welk gets a descent burial in our local cemetery. Considering everything that's happened, they owe the man that much."

Doug hadn't the slightest inclination of what Ward meant, but now was not the time to ask for an explanation. Doc knew the meaning behind Ward's comment, but he, too, let Ward's comment pass.

Scratching his head, Doc remarked, "Well, I would have thought two intelligent lawmen, like yourselves, would have thought of this. But, since you haven't, I have a suggestion." His comment was a definite attention getter. "Go ask the girl what she meant. Maybe she knows the location of the Welk's family private resting place."

Ward smirked as he looked at Doug. Doug's eyes flashed to the ceiling and back to Doc. "Maybe you should pin a badge on him, Sheriff," Doug joked.

Shaking his head and raising his hands in a stop gesture, Doc responded, "Not in your life."

"Well, Doug, all joking aside, Doc is right. Before we leave, we'll ask Janet if she knows where the graves are.

Doc, we need to get this body out of here before the bank people arrive. Is the ambulance on its way?"

"Yes. Seems they had a flat tire of all things. They should be here real soon."

"Good. Now I need to contact the bank. Doug, after the body is out of here, I want you to take Doc back to town. Then come back and get me. I'll wait here for the bankers."

"That's not necessary, Ward," Doc responded. "I'll hitch a ride back in the ambulance."

Before she got caught listening, Farm Girl scampered away.

Oh, I cain't tell them where to bury Mister Welk under that oak tree. If'n I does, they might go there right now. Then they'd find Sugar Shack and go snoopin' around. I is sorry, Mister Welk, but I just cain't tell them.

Now I gotta think how long I has been workin' here. Maybe I can just say the same as what one a them mans was sayin'. Crimeny, I doesn't want to answer no more a them questions. But I is gonna has to because I cain't be goin' on my way, not yet.

Before leaving the farm, Doug found Farm Girl and asked her about a graveyard on the property.

"I doesn't know nothin' about no graves," she responded. "Mister Welk told me once that most a his kin be dead. I just wants him to has a nice bury, sos he can join them in heaven."

The explanation was not what Doug was expecting. He had no other choice but to accept it.

"Have you been working here for very long?"

"I doesn't know how long very long be."

"Okay, I'll word the question in another way. How long have you worked for Mr. Welk?"

"I doesn't know how to read one a them paper clocks."

"You mean a calendar?"

"If'n ya says so."

Before Doug's frustration got the best of him, she finally gave him an answer he could live with. "One day I be here lookin' fur a job. Mister Welk done told me, I got here just in time 'cause the other farmhand workin' fur him up and left."

As the day went on, Farm Girl performed various chores to keep busy, always keeping an eye on the farmhouse. She watched the removal of Jefferson's body from the house, and waved her fingers as the ambulance drove away, disappearing from her sight.

When the sheriff's car left the property, Farm Girl breathed a sigh of relief. However, she checked the driveway, now and then, making sure that the law officers did not return. She also watched the men that came in trucks and boarded up the windows and the doors of the house.

Realizing she couldn't take Farm Dawg with her when she left the farm, she needed to tell him goodbye. Kneeling next to him, she threw her arms around his neck. Holding on to the dog with the side of her face snug against his hairy body, she said, "I wishes I can take you with me, Farm Dawg, but I just cain't." As she started sobbing, a tear rolled down her cheek. "I ain't never gonna furgit you, and I hope you ain't never gonna furgit me. Always remember that I love you." Giving her pet a quick kiss and an extra tight squeeze, she jumped to her feet and ran for the barn.

After wiping her eyes, Farm Girl started looking around at the different, small objects in the barn. Deciding to take some of Jefferson's items with her, she grabbed four empty gunnysacks from a stockpile on the floor. Using one as a carrier, she placed the other three gunnysacks inside along with a pair of work gloves, a ball of different rope lengths, a hand trowel, a small stack of newspapers, a knit hat and a flashlight.

Evening came. It was time to check on Mama. Farm Girl approached the man who had been left to guard the house. After convincing him that she had to take the cow to pasture before turning in for the night, she went to the barn.

Hiding the thermos and foil of food in her apron, she headed the cow to pasture. Once she was at the clearing that led to her home, she left the cow and took off running. When she entered the door, Mama was sitting in her chair next to the table. The money-filled socks covered the table.

"Good gracious, child, it's about time. Ya has y'ur mama plum frettin' out a her mind."

"I teld you not to worry about me. I bring food fur the trip, and some sweet coffee fur you to has while I is back at the farm."

After Mama cleared a small space on the table, Farm Girl placed the foil packet in the space available. As she was about to set the thermos down, Mama reached for it. Farm Girl yanked her hand back, pulling the thermos out of Mama's grip.

"Child, what's the matter with ya?"

"I is in a big hurry. You can enjoy your coffee after I leave. I has to talk to ya real fast, then git back befur that guard mans comes a lookin' fur me."

Mama leaned back in her chair. "What guard mans?"

"Just someone that sheriff mans has watchin' me. Don'tcha worry about him. I did just fine talkin' to that sheriff mans. You'd be proud." She snickered. "He thinks I is you. Oh, a doctor mans was there too. He told me Pappy died a what he calls a heart attack. I knows Pappy was havin' him a sick heart, but I sure didn't knows that a heart can attack you. That means it just stops beatin'."

"Don't be silly, child. Hearts don't attack nobody. That just means the heart ain't workin' no more."

"Okay. Anyways, the sheriff mans told me Pappy will be gittin' a decent bury."

Mama slid to the edge of her chair. "They be bringin' Pappy down here fur buryin'?"

Farm Girl wasn't ready to answer. She placed the thermos on the table. Walking behind Mama's chair, she placed one hand on Mama's shoulder. Since she was now out of Mama's view, her other hand went behind her back with crossed fingers. She had told lies all day, but not to Mama.

"Sit back and relax, Mama. They isn't gonna bring him down here because—I think they said the ambulance has it a flat tire."

"What?"

"Uh, the ambulance will come tomorrow to git Pappy."

"You mean his body's still layin' on the kitchen floor?"

"Ya but they was covernin' him with a blanket. And, they gots that guard mans sittin' on the back porch so no one will bother him. So, there ain't nothin' to worry about."

"That's a mighty strange way a doin' things."

The time for playing King's X was over, for now. Farm Girl stepped back in front of her mother. "Well, ain't that good news? Besides, we'll be out a here tonight. So, we doesn't has to worry about none a them findin' us livin' here in Sugar Shack."

With a forlorn look on her face, Mama slowly shook her head. Farm Girl was concerned. "What's the matter? Is ya still feelin' puny?"

"Child, I don't feel right in my heart nor my head. Stealin', lyin', and sneakin' around ain't gonna bring us nothin' but trouble. 'Sides, how we gonna hide all this money when we gits to the next farm fur chore doin'? We'd be havin' to dig us a mighty big hole to hide it in. That's too much extra work fur us to be doin' every time we moves around from farm to farm."

"Now who's bein' silly? Why does we want to be doin' chores fur when we gots all this money? There ain't no reason, no more, to keep workin' fur no more farmers."

"Just listen to y'urself, child. I hope ya doesn't think we can settle down in some town fur ya to go to school or git some fancy tutor, like Pappy done told us? It ain't possible. While I be waitin' fur ya, I opens me some a them socks to take a look-see. Good heavens, child, ya'd never understands how much money there be in them socks. Some a them paper monies be big dollars like ya ain't never put y'ur eyes on befur.

Ya cain't just go to a town and start spendin' that money without no one askin' where it comes from. If'n them nosey busybodies don't start trouble, that sheriff mans or one like him, be sure to. Folks like us just don't show up in any town and start livin' like rich folks. 'Sides, ya just don't know nothin' about livin' in the world a wealthy folks with all them fancy clothes and phony ways."

"Ain't I eighteen now? And ain't I gots the right, now, to say what I does, or doesn't do?"

"I just doesn't understand what's gotten into ya, Farm Girl. Ya only be eighteen fur a matter a hours. Does ya thinks that makes ya old enough to be tellin' y'ur mama what to do and what's best fur ya?"

"I thinks I is old enough to be helpin' ya make some important *incisions* about my life."

Farm Girl knew she didn't have time to debate the issue with Mama, right then. She dropped the subject. Mama dropped it, too. Although she didn't like Farm Girl's new forceful attitude, she was too tired to fight back. She had always protected her daughter the best way she knew how. Maybe now it was time to allow Farm Girl a little more freedom in making some decisions about their lives.

"I has to git back, Mama, but I'll be back here after dark. Why doesn't you relax and quit frettin'." She embraced her mother. "I didn't mean to be disrespectful. You know I love you, don'tcha?"

"Yes, child, I does. Y'ur Mama loves ya, too."

Farm Girl walked to the door. She stopped and turned back. "You has taken care a me since I come into this world. Now, it's my turn to take care a you."

As Farm Girl headed back to the main area of the farm, a sudden thought swept into her already heavy-burdened mind.

I is the age, now, when Mama is gonna show me them secrets she keeps in her old can, and tell me why that can is so important to her. I are waitin' all these years, then I goes and furgits because I is thinkin' too many other things. Crimeny, I wish I has time to go back and ask her right now. But, I cain't, lesson I wants that Mister Jason comin' after me.

If only Farm Girl had taken the time to go back to Sugar Shack and asked Mama. She could have headed on a different, more pleasant journey than the dangerous one she was about to encounter.

Back at the main part of the farm, Farm Girl's chores were completed, the chickens were roosting, and the cow was already resting in her bed of straw.

The barn had enough light from the moon so she could see her way around without running into anything. Getting together her gunnysack of items and the small milking stool, she walked deep into the shadows. After placing the stool where she felt safely out of sight, she sat on the stool and placed the gunnysack at her feet. Tired, Farm Girl rested her head against the wall.

As her eyelids became heavy, Farm Girl spoke to herself in a low voice to stay awake. "Mama's wrong. All strangers ain't evil. So, maybe bein' out in them other worlds ain't gonna be so scary. And she's wrong about all that money, too. After a journey far away from here, a body has the right to have money and spend it on anythin' they wants.

Crimeny, I sure knows what I wants with my part a the money. I wants me a house to live in, runnin' water, an inside pooper and electricity. Then I is gonna have me all a them appliances like is in Pappy's house. Once you figures out what buttons to push, they sure does make inside chores easier.

I wonder why God done give that deputy man two different color eyes? Maybe God likes both a them colors and couldn't make up His mind, so He give him one a each. And that poor man," she uttered while yawning, "don't got one stitch a hair on his head."

When she felt the time was right, she pulled the flashlight out of the gunnysack. Confident she was ready, she made her way to the open door, staying hidden in the darkness. Lifting her skirt, she tore out of the barn in a full run. She kept running and never looked back.

SAYING FAREWELL

Since the trees of the wooded area blocked out much of the moonlight, Farm Girl used her flashlight to help light her way down the path toward home. When she got there, Sugar Shack was dark. "I guess Mama was fearful someone might see the light, so she never light a kerosene lamp."

As she opened the door, she shined the small beam of light in front of her. The light illuminated the table. The socks were still sitting where Mama had placed them earlier that day. Moving the light to the area where she and her mama slept on the straw-laden floor, she saw Mama reclining. The thermos was sitting upright on the floor next to Mama, and the small metal cup was laying on its side, close to her hand.

"Mama, I is here," Farm Girl said, a bit winded from her run.

When Mama didn't answer, Farm Girl stepped inside the shack and closed the door. There was just a hint of light coming through their small window. Propping the lit flashlight on top of a money-sock, gave her enough light to see what she was doing and allowed the use of both hands.

Knowing she only needed two sacks, and they had to be strong enough to carry everything she considered necessary to take with her, she doubled them, one inside the other, for extra strength. Unrolling the small ball of rope, she whispered, "Four long pieces and three short ones. Well, I gots to make them work."

Rope in hand, she proceeded to tie several socks to it, spacing them as she went, as if she were hanging them from a clothesline. She made sure to wind the rope tight, two to three times around the neck of each sock before tying. With two long pieces of rope left over, she tossed them on the table.

"Now I gots me a stringer line, almost like that one Pappy done has fur holding fish we was catchin' in the river. Only mine holds money."

Holding on to the two loose ends of the rope, she attempted to pick up the stringer. "Crimeny," she continued whispering, "Mama was right. This ain't even half a them money-socks and they is heavy. Well now, let's see if them knots Pappy was teachin' me works." Putting the stringer back on the table, she tied the two shorter pieces of rope, one to each end.

Once she had finished, she picked up her flashlight, walked over to where Mama was reclining, and knelt next to her. As she shined the light on Mama's face, looking straight into her glaring, almost glass-like eyes, Farm Girl let out a scream. The hair stood up on the back of her neck.

"Crimeny, Mama! If ever I was gonna use one a them cuss words, I'd sure like to use one now. Why didn't you told me when I be flashin' the light and callin' out to you that you was awake?" Mama didn't answer. Farm Girl kept the light shined in Mama's face as she tugged at her arm. "Mama? Mama, ain't you gonna answer me?"

There was still no response. Then, Farm Girl realized that Mama's eyes didn't blink. They bore the same distant and frozen stare as Jefferson's eyes when he died. Dropping her flashlight, Farm Girl placed her head on Mama's chest. There was no heartbeat. Mama was not breathing.

Resting on her mother's chest, she began whimpering, "You knows I love you, don'tcha, Mama?" Cradling her beloved mother in her arms, she began rocking her body. Although she cried on the inside, her weeping never brought about a single tear. "You was my only kin, Mama. And Pappy was the only man I was ever lovin' like kin. Now I ain't gots neither one a you. I knows you was ailin', and I should a been here with you. I'm sorry that I couldn't be. Please furgive me."

Farm Girl sat there on the cold floor, holding the body of her mother in her arms, rocking to-and-fro, back and forth. Soon she realized the time had come to let go. Mama had always talked about having a decent burial. In turn, Farm Girl would always promise that she would give her one. Due to the circumstances, however, Farm Girl had to break that promise.

Time was, in hopes of getting supplies and lumber from Jefferson,

Black Rosebud

when Farm Girl had dug a big hole in the ground between Sugar Shack and the old well. Since she had learned from Jefferson how to build things, Farm Girl was going to build her and Mama an outhouse over that hole. Farm Girl wanted more privacy than a tree or a bush when nature called.

Of course, due to Jefferson's financial situation after the hole was dug, there were no funds for supplies to build anything. Since the hole in the ground would no longer serve the purpose for which it was intended, Farm Girl felt it would be fitting to bury Mama there, temporarily.

Deciding her mother needed to be buried in her good patchwork dress, Farm Girl undressed her mother. She noticed a pin attached to Mama's slip, but decided to live it in place. When Mama was clothed in her best dress, Farm Girl placed a blanket on the floor. After pulling Mama's body onto the blanket, she rolled Mama in it.

Grasping a hold of one end of the blanket, she dragged the body, one baby step at a time, out of the shack. Once outside, there was enough moonlight glimmering through the tree branches to aid her sight. Slow and sure-footed, she crept backward.

"I knows you understand that I is doin' what I has to do. Survival. You teach me well, and I ain't never gonna furgit it. I will never furgit you, Mama. You ain't never has a name to call your own, but you is always gonna be my Mama."

When she got to the hole in the ground, Farm Girl rolled Mama's body, blanket and all, over the side and into the deep cavity. She picked up the old shovel that laid on the ground next to the hole. With little effort, she began to cover the body with the cold, damp earth. As she filled the grave, Farm Girl commenced jabbering in fast forward speed.

"I cain't even give you a proper name on one a them head markers. With no real name, you was just a nobody." She swallowed hard. "Well, I is gonna has me a real name. No one is gonna call me Farm Girl the rest a my life. I ain't gonna be ig—ignore—well, I ain't gonna be stupid the rest a my life. I has learn a lot, and I knows I has a lot more learnin' to do. But I ain't gonna keep workin' fur farmers and end up like you. Does you hear me, Mama?"

Finished, Farm Girl tossed the shovel on the ground close to Mama's grave. She scraped the edge of her boot across the ground in search of a rock. When she found one big enough to write with, she picked it up. Kneeling next to the mound, she wrote the letters *N O B O D Y* deep into the soil, across the top of the grave.

The light from the moon was not bright enough for her to spot small items on the ground. She ran back inside the shack, got her flashlight, then ran back to Mama's grave. With the light, the ground was searched for stones. After gathering as many stones as she could find, they were placed in the dirt, outlining the etched letters. Once finished, she repeated the only prayer she knew. "Thank you, God, fur everythin'. Amen.

I is glad you'll be able to see that big oak tree from here." She didn't have to have night vision. After living in the area for the better part of five years, she knew her bearings. "Crimeny, I ain't never pay me no attention till now, but you isn't very far from them other graves. Layin' here, you is gonna be even closer to Pappy than I was thinkin' befur."

Before standing, she kissed the damp ground that covered Mama's body. Then she stood, dazed and in deep thought. Her mind forgot about how important time was to her. The petite frame of her body didn't notice the frigid temperatures of the early morning air.

Indeed, Farm Girl had lost so much, all in one day. Loved ones she would never see again. Her emotions whirled around inside, like a tree caught up in the treacherous winds of a Nebraska tornado.

Happy about starting a new life, yet sad about leaving behind the one real home she had ever known. Mournful about both Pappy and Mama's passing, but heartfelt they were both peaceful in an eternal sleep. Although frightened about meeting new people, she was excited about venturing into new worlds.

Tears gushed from her eyes when Jefferson died. A few tears were shed when she said farewell to Farm Dawg. However, for some unknown reason, there were no tears left for her mother.

Coming back to the moment, after thoughts of all her years with Mama had rushed through her head, Farm Girl realized the sun was making its way into the sky. Daylight was sparking. The present, seemed to slap her in the face, making her aware it was time to hurry and get out of there. Get away from Sugar Shack and away from the farm. Almost everything had to be behind but her memories and the money.

She ran inside shack and started turning, first one way then another. Her mind seemed muddled. Collecting her thoughts, she knew what had to be done. No one could turn back the clock. Plans for her future had to be carried through.

Black Rosebud

Before leaving, items needed to be packed for the long journey. She had to make a few good choices, and dispose of the rest.

Looking at the extra pieces of rope left on the table, gave her an idea. "I cain't hardly lift the line a money socks. So I knows it ain't gonna stay in place around my waist. If'n I makes me some shoulder straps, like Pappy's suspenders, that'll help hold it on my body. I has to remember not to throw them away."

Utilizing one of the doubled gunnysacks for a necessity bag, she filled it with survival and personal items.

As she tightened the lid of the thermos, she remembered something. "Wait. I doesn't see Mama's old can. She must a gotten it from her hidin' place because she wouldn't go nowhere without it." The thermos was placed on the table as she glanced about the room. Nothing could be hidden or have gotten lost in such a small area.

Within a matter of moments, she spotted the missing can under Mama's chair. "Come on, Mister Can," she muttered, picking it up, "you is goin' with me." Taking care not to tear the can's paper cover, she placed the can into the necessity sack.

Remembering her own hiding place, she dashed out of the house, across the river, up the embankment and to her favorite rock. Once she retrieved her treasures from her hole in the ground, she rushed back to Sugar Shack and flung everything into the take-along bag.

Then, the money from the torn sock was emptied into the other reinforced gunnysack along with the socks that were not tied together. The torn sock was tossed on the floor.

From the small pile on the floor, she picked up the clothes she had taken off Mama's body, and draped the two sweaters over the back of a chair. The skirt from Mama's body was spread out flat on the floor. Almost with a vengeance, she threw just about everything left, including the partial-filled thermos, onto the floor atop the skirt. She didn't want to leave any evidence behind that might link her or Mama to Mr. Welk.

In a slow turn, she looked over every inch of the room, making sure that the only thing left for anyone to find would be the old furniture and the kerosene lamps. Spotting the torn sock on the floor, she uttered, "If'n anyone finds that, who'd be carin' that they finds an old sock belongin' to Mister Welk in a shack that were his granddaddy's? Nobody, that's who. Not even that sheriff mans."

The skirt was rolled around everything she had dropped onto it. This bundle was then carried outside with every intention of disposing of it in the well. In a hurry, she didn't get very close to the well before hurling the bundle of items. It flew through the air, harshly scraping the well's edge as it disappeared from her view.

"I reckon throwin' all them twigs fur Farm Dawg, gives me a mighty good throwin' arm."

Back in the house, she retrieved the old quilt and horse blanket from the sleeping area. After folding them, they were both draped across the back of the empty chair. The extra gunnysacks from their straw-laden bed went into the necessity bag. Both packed gunnysacks were placed next to the door.

Each end of extra rope pieces was tied to two separate areas in the middle of the makeshift stringer. Using the table for balance, she butted up against it, almost sitting on the edge. Wrapping the stringer around her waist, she tied the ends together. Reaching behind, the two loose ends were brought across each shoulder then tied to the front of the stringer. Now, she had a belt with shoulder straps.

Standing straight, inching away from the table, the socks plummeted, almost pulling her to the ground from the sudden drop of heavy weight. They dangled about, surrounding her stomach, hips and rear.

Hoisting the makeshift belt, leaning back against the table, the rope around her waist was retied. Just to make sure she could move with the extreme weight, she walked around the room. The socks were heavy and bulky, but Farm Girl felt she could manage.

Taking her nice dress from the shelf, putting it on over the clothes she was already wearing, she covered the rope of socks. For added warmth, she dressed in Mama's two sweaters. Even though the shanty was cold, she was dying of heat.

Folding the quilt in a diagonal shape, it was wrapped it around her shoulders. The horse blanket was folded and draped across her arm. After putting on Jefferson's gloves and hat, she was ready for traveling.

"Bye, Sugar Shack. Maybe, someday, you can be a home to someone else who needs one, just like you was to me and Mama. Ain't nobody should ever be without a home."

Ready for her walk into a new life, she opened the door. She twisted the tops of the two gunnysacks tight around her hand. Garnering every bit of strength she had, the bags were swooped in the air in an attempt to sling them over her shoulder, which promptly sent her flying backward. Lying on the floor stunned, she stared at the ceiling.

"Crimeny, Farm Girl, that wasn't suppose to happen. You has to be strong enough to do this. Now, git yourself up and try again."

Letting go of the bags, she rolled over, facing the floor. First, she got up on her hands and knees. Then, she raised her body to a kneeling position. With a bit of effort, she got to her feet. Dragging the two gunnysacks to the table, they were hoisted to the tabletop, one at a time.

Turning her back to the table with a tight grip of the tops of both bags, she draped them over her shoulder. In a slow movement, she took one step away from the table. Bracing herself, a second step was taken, allowing the bags to slide off the table. This time she kept her balance.

"I remember a cartoon picture I seen one time on Pappy's TV. It was a Santee Clause carryin' a bag full a goodies. I feels just like him," she stated in a light-hearted nature. "I knows I ain't Santee Clause, but I sure gots me a bag full a goodies."

Farm Girl had a difficult time walking from all the weight, but the word *survival* kept running through her head. Since heading back toward the farm was not an option, so she took off in the opposite direction, following the riverbed as the sun popped up into clear view.

As Farm Girl headed out on her journey to a new life, the bags of money were not the only heavy burdens she carried with her.

OPERATION IVY

Darin was ready to make his final plans and get away from his small town life, even though it seemed forever to get here. No one suspected him, and to play it double safe, he hadn't burglarized anyone in a couple of months. He had even surprised himself.

Sitting tight for such a long time without blowing his top was not in his normal makeup. Even if he felt as though he had spent forever setting the wheels in motion, he had to remain calm and cool. Having a little over $350 thousand in cash plus the gold and valuable coins, he was almost home free. Wallowing in his success, Darin was patting himself on the back.

"It sure is funny that Coyt guy never reported to the police that his gold coins are missing. He either stole them himself, or he didn't want the IRS to know. Whatever his reasoning, it sure was a blessing for me. Oh," Darin snickered, more than pleased with himself, "and that coin collection was another great take. Lucky for me the newspaper said old man Alt didn't have his collection insured or recorded anywhere.

Wow, I can't believe how fortunate I've been. If there is such a thing as 'Lady Luck', she sure has been giving me a favorable smile.

Ha! And stealing all of those friggin' chemicals from Reeves was ingenious. I'll bet that sure fouled up old Rusty's law enforcement mind. I'd bet he doesn't know what to think now about his Neat Nick Thief. I can just hope it throws him enough off base that he'll start looking for clues somewhere else. Any place, other than my front door."

As the time to leave his Nebraska home drew near, Darin was very excited. But he wanted to do one last burglary before he cashed in on his jaded life. Since he didn't need the extra money, this last job would be just for the thrill of getting one more over on Rusty.

In the meantime, after a thorough investigation, the Kidwell Police Department cleared Wallace Dodd as their number one burglary suspect. Dodd checked out to be a model citizen, a Sunday school teacher, and a community volunteer for any worthwhile function that needed him. All of Rusty's premonitions about Dodd, proved to be wrong. This disappointment did not sit well with the frustrated police chief.

The Neat Nick Thief was still on the loose. Rusty felt as if he was butting his head up against a cement block wall. "Come on you miserable excuse for a human being. One slip, that's all I need. Just one. Then your thieving ass is mine."

As Rusty sat in his office, going over his numerous files on the reported burglaries that spanned a period close to three years, he received a call on his intercom from his desk officer.

"Chief, a nurse from Farmer's Community Hospital is on line two. Says it's urgent that she speaks with you."

"Got it," Rusty responded. Putting a fast two and two together, hospital plus Frank's health, Rusty could feel a lump in his throat as he answered the phone. "Chief Simmons."

"Good morning, Chief Simmons. This is Mrs. Williams. I'm the head nurse over here at Farmer's Community Hospital."

"Yes, ma'am. What can I do for you this morning?" Rusty asked, hoping the urgency in his voice didn't come across on the other end of the telephone.

"I hate to tell you this over the phone, but Sheriff Ward Luden is in our intensive care unit."

"Ward?" he blurted out in his astonishment. "What happened?"

"The sheriff was brought in late last night by the emergency unit. He suffered a severe heart attack and his condition is critical." Rusty was relieved that the phone call wasn't about Frank, but he still didn't like hearing the bad news about Ward. "As weak as he is," the nurse continued to explain, "he's been in and out of an unconsciousness state. However, he's lucid now. The sheriff says he doesn't have any blood relatives for us to contact for him, but he's asking for you. I told him I would call you."

"I'll be right there."

Rusty seldom ran his siren, but as he sped down the highway, the siren roared at full blast. He rushed into the hospital only to find out he was too late. Sheriff Luden died just a short time before he arrived.

Rusty stood at the front desk of the Intensive Care Unit with a blank look on his face when he heard the news. With a sudden twinge, he felt a vast emptiness in his gut.

Not being able to maintain his normal congenial mannerism, he raised his voice a pitch above his usual tone. "No! It couldn't have taken me more than fifteen minutes to get here. He can't be gone. There's got to be a mistake. Where is Nurse Williams? I want to speak to her. Please."

Rusty walked over to a wall where he could keep an eye on the nurse's station. Leaning back, he braced his body against the wall, waiting. When Nurse Williams arrived at the ICU desk, she had brief words with the desk nurse. Rusty was so involved in his own personal thoughts, he didn't noticed the maternal looking woman when she approached him.

"Chief Simmons?"

Hearing the woman's voice, Rusty was quick to stand at attention. "Yes."

"I'm Nurse Williams. You wanted to speak with me?"

"Yes. I came to see Sheriff Ludin, but the nurse at the desk—" Rusty stopped speaking. Quite unusual for him, he had a difficult time getting the words out of his mouth. At any age, death was never easy to accept.

Nurse Williams placed her hand on his arm with a comforting touch. "I'm sorry, Chief Simmons, but he didn't make it."

Had Rusty not been in such a state of shock, he would have used his own good common sense. Death could be as quick as a strike of lightening. Unfortunately, losing a friend and colleague hit too close to home for him to think straight. Anguished, Rusty questioned, "How could Ward go so fast when you just called me not fifteen minutes before I arrived here? I don't understand."

"I was informed that Sheriff Luden had gone into cardiac arrest while I was on the phone with you. I'm very sorry, but the doctors did all they could to resuscitate him."

"That fast? I can't believe it."

"You must have been very close."

"We were friends for as far back as I can remember."

"I'm so sorry for your loss. Why don't you come over here and sit down." She gestured to a small grouping of chairs lined up against one of the walls. "May I get you anything?"

"No, I don't care to sit down, and I don't want anything. Thank you. I'm sorry for all of the questions. I know you informed me that Ward's condition was serious, but I guess I didn't think he would go that sudden. It's just a bit hard to swallow."

"I understand. If you would like to come back in about an hour, you can pick up his personal belongings. The sheriff mentioned before I called you that he wanted you to have his things. He said you would know what to do with them."

Rusty barely heard a word the nurse said. "Was Deputy Martin called?"

"No. I was just asked to notify you."

"Yes, of course," he stated, not even aware that he had said anything aloud.

Still in a dazed state of mind, Rusty left the hospital. As he sat in his car, he rested his forehead on the rim of his steering wheel. "I thought you were in perfect health, Ward. You were going to retire next month and do that traveling you always talked about. I'm sure going to miss you. Cole County has lost a good law enforcement officer, and I've lost one heck of a good friend. We are all going to miss you."

After Rusty pulled himself together, he notified Deputy Martin of Ward's death. Doug was as shocked as Rusty was when he heard the news.

Later that day, Rusty went through Ward's belongings that the hospital had given him In Ward's billfold he found a small key and piece of paper folded into the size of a dollar bill. When he unfolded the wrinkled paper, Rusty saw it was a letter addressed to him. He also recognized that the letter was in Ward's handwriting. Making himself comfortable, he began reading.

"'Rusty, if you are reading this, I guess I'm not around to shoot the breeze with you anymore. Since I don't have any immediate relatives left, I hope you won't mind doing me one last favor. I'm writing this just in case something happens to me before my young friend graduates from high school.

You know how they always show those ads on TV about those hungry kids overseas, and ask help to feed, clothe, and educate them? I figured that we have enough of those poor kids right here in our own country. Several years ago, through a charity program, I became pen pals with a young black lad in Tennessee. In my own way, I guess, I was trying to make amends for the horrible atrocity my prejudicial grandfather committed.

This young man, who I've been supporting, will graduate two weeks after I retire. To top it off, he turns eighteen the same day he graduates. I had planned to be there for his graduation ceremonies and give him a nice birthday celebration. But, if I'm not around to follow through with my plans, this is where you come in.

Remember that bank form I had you sign with me for my safety deposit box?'"

Rusty stopped reading as he flashed back to years earlier when a day of coincidental circumstances stood out in his mind. On that particular morning, Frank had asked Rusty to sign financial documents. These legal documents gave Rusty full control over Frank's financial accounts should anything happen to Frank. Rusty didn't hesitate to honor the favor.

At the same time, Rusty made Frank the beneficiary of his financial accounts, also. In the afternoon of that very same day, Ward contacted Rusty. In the event that anything should happen to Ward, he, too, wanted Rusty to be his beneficiary, therefore having access to all his accounts.

Rusty remembered feeling honored that two of his friends had such high regard and trust in him. He also remembered feeling a little depressed that none of the three of them had ever found love in their lives. To him, they were over-the-hill, confirmed bachelors, depending on one another like family members.

The unusual coincidence of the day was almost mind-boggling to Rusty. It was also quite strange, due to the fact that Ward and Frank knew each other but not as well as Rusty knew both of them.

The brief thoughts had brought a smile to his face. As the past dissipated, Rusty continued reading Ward's letter.

"'The key to that box is in my billfold along with this letter. In my deposit box, please get out the information on this young man, my Will and my insurance policies, which have all been made out with you as beneficiary. Also, take the loose cash I have placed in there. I have your name on everything because I felt you could handle any legal issues that may come up.

I'm counting on you to see that this kid gets the money so he can get a college education. Because he had a bad start in life, he's older than the rest of the kids in his class. There's plenty of money in there, even after taxes, so it won't take a cent out of your pocket, just your time. Give the young man my badge and my fond affection. I'm just sorry I never got to meet him in person.

Since it appears that I'll get to heaven before you, I'll be waiting to greet you when your day comes. I'm hopeful that won't be for a long time after I'm gone. That's assuming, of course, that you walk as straight as you do now so you don't end up going in the opposite direction. Thanks for everything, Rusty. Your friend, Ward.'"

Even though he was a bit weepy-eyed, Rusty had to smile at Ward's sense of humor. The letter was not dated so Rusty had no way of knowing when Ward had written it. Had he written the letter just as an assurance that his affairs would be taken care of, or was he aware that he had a bad heart? Rusty would never know.

Rusty followed Ward's last wishes. The young man's name was John Daniel Hobart. Since there was no phone number for this young man mentioned in Ward's letter, and no way of contacting him other than by mail, Rusty wrote him a beautiful letter explaining Ward's unexpected death.

In the letter, Rusty also wrote of a few cherished memories about Ward, hoping it would help the young man know more about his benefactor, and long-distance foster parent. He also explained to John Daniel about the funeral arrangements he had made, which included day, date, time, funeral home's name and address, and the name of the cemetery where Ward would be buried.

Pacing the floor, Rusty deliberated about what he should do. "Most kids in high school, or fresh out of high school, aren't mature enough to handle large amounts of money. It's too tempting to be foolish and spend it on a hot car and fancy clothes." He scratched his head. "No, I guess that's what they would have done years ago. Today, the big money is spent on booze and drugs.

Damn, I don't know why I'm even debating the issue. When it comes right down to it, this isn't my call. If Ward trusted this John Daniel, then I need to follow through with his wishes. Besides, if the kid's going to be eighteen, or is already for that matter, he'll have every legal right to the money."

At that time, Rusty was not at all certain how much money he was talking about. He could only assume that Ward's modest home, his furnishings and his car would bring in at least $70 thousand. The estimated sale plus the insurance money would total quite a large inheritance. He was a little apprehensive about sending over $100 thousand to a young man who had not yet graduated from high school.

Under no circumstances did Rusty want any of Ward's inheritance. He was more than pleased to help a friend, but he was certain he didn't want payment for it. So, he explained to John Daniel that as soon as the insurance company paid the $50 thousand on Ward's policy, and after the requirements of Ward's Last Will and Testament were met, that all monies would be forwarded to him for his college education. There would be plenty of money left to invest or spend wisely. Rusty mailed the letter along with Ward's badge to John Daniel.

The next few days, even though Rusty still did his job, he felt like he was in limbo. Ward had not been just a fellow officer, but he had been Rusty's friend for over fifty years. A friend like that was hard to let go.

Then came the day of the funeral. Police Chief Simmons, his uniformed officers, and the new Cole County Sheriff along with his new deputy, were Ward's pallbearers.

After the gathering of mourners left the gravesite, Rusty lingered, alone, for a few minutes longer. With his head bowed, Rusty bid a last farewell. "Rest in peace, pal. I'll see you again, someday. I'm sorry that John Daniel couldn't be here today. I wrote him, but I guess he just couldn't make it."

Through his grief, Rusty felt a warm glow surround him. Ward's teasing and laughter echoed in his ears. His wide grin flashed before Rusty's eyes. Rusty turned his head upward and looked at billowy clouds that seemed to float through the sky.

"You always said you were a stauncher Catholic than I am, you crazy German, so now's your chance to prove it. You had better put in a good word up there for this Irishman, since you got there before me.

And, I expect you to lead me to the Neat Nick Thief, since you have a clearer view on things from up there than I do from down here. Don't ask me how, but I know you're in the right place to figure it out." With a wink and his warm Irish smile, Rusty had closure in his friend's passing.

Back on the job, Chief Simmons showed up at the sheriff's office to meet with the newly appointed sheriff, Doug Martin.

"With Ward gone now, I'm not sure how this works," Rusty admitted. "Since he deputized me so I could work on the county's burglary cases, am I still deputized, or do you have to deputize me all over again? I've been a law officer for years, but this is a whole new fishing hole for me."

"Same fishing hole, just a new fishing pole," Doug offered with a smile. "You are still legally deputized. I will work as close with you as Ward did. Just let me know if I can help."

"Okay, let's get right down to business concerning this Neat Nick Thief case I'm working on. I'm toying with the idea of planting someone in the bank. I have ruled out Wallace Dodd as a suspect, but every one of those victims is somehow connected through the bank in Sharpin. I would like your input."

"Planting someone you can trust in the bank sounds good to me, but do you think the thief is still around these parts? There hasn't been a burglary for quite a few months now."

"That's the same question I keep asking myself, over and over. I haven't come up with an answer. But if he is, I need to flush him out," Rusty stated, rather perplexed.

"I agree. In regards to this plant, who do you have in mind?"

"I don't know yet. I know I have to be careful of entrapment, so I have to play it smart. Let me think on it for a few more days and I'll keep you abreast of what's going on." As Rusty turned to leave, he added, "You know, Doug, it seems a bit strange coming in here and talking to you as I did with Ward."

Doug nodded his head in agreement. "Believe me, Rusty, I understand what you're saying. I feel strange sitting in Ward's chair."

Rusty's departing words were, "Well, it seems to fit you, and I know you'll do a great job."

After returning to his office, Rusty called in Officer Kelly to join him. "I've got all of the local politicians after my you-know-what because we haven't caught that no good thief yet. We have over twenty reports of over $300 thousand stolen from our good neighbors. That's one hefty pot full of money!"

"You've got that right, Chief. And who knows how many people were burglarized but were too embarrassed to report their thefts to the authorities?"

"True. With all the other unanswered questions staring us in the face, I still can't figure out why anyone would want to take exterminating chemicals."

"Yeah, Chief, that's a puzzle to me too. Maybe this was just a prank someone played on Reeves to throw us off base?"

"For what ever reason, it sure doesn't fit the bill of our Neat Nick Thief. With the containers scattered all over the garage floor, like they were, the perp we're after would have never left the place in such a mess. That is, unless he's playing with us. Did Reeves ever get you an inventory list of the chemicals that were stolen?"

"After Reeves cleaned up his garage and put the scattered items back on their shelves, he claims almost everything is accounted for except few containers of poisons along with his petty cash.

It could have been just some kids tearing up the place and taking the containers for kicks. Maybe they didn't even realize they were taking containers of poisons. In their mischievousness, I'll bet they just stumbled across the money, took it, and ran. My guess is that those missing containers will show up in someone's dumpster."

"It's a good theory, Kelly, and you could be right. We'll do some further investigating into The Reeves case later. For now, I want to concentrate on that no good Neat Nick." Rusty shook his head. "As you are well aware, it's been too quiet around here. That clown is sitting somewhere on that small gold mine he's been accumulating."

"It doesn't make sense that people would leave so much cash unattended, does it."

"No. You know, if I would have sold my farm for $90 thousand cash, like Boyd did last September, you can bet your life that money would have gone straight into the bank."

"Yes, but Chief, Boyd said it was a private deal in his house. The banks were closed by the time they worked out all the kinks in their hand-written contract with the buyers."

"Kelly, let's be smart. If you had that kind of money in your home, even if it was midnight, wouldn't you think about making a night deposit at the bank?"

"Now, that you mention it, yes. I'm sure that's what you or I would have done. But are we sure Boyd banked in the area?" Receiving a questionable look from Rusty, Kelly laughed. "Okay, I retract that question. I forgot that he banks in Sharpin."

"You got it. I can't believe that old man Boyd didn't consider that option. What gets me is the fact that not only didn't he think about a night deposit, but like some idiot who was born yesterday, he goes out drinking and celebrating, and has the stupidity to brag about the deal for all to hear.

Our mutt just happened to be at the right place at the right time to hear the good news that the money was just waiting for him. Hells bells, why didn't Boyd just wrap it all up with a big red ribbon and hand it to the mutt as a gift."

As bad as the situation was, Kelly had to snicker at Rusty's humorous remark. Ignoring Kelly's unmistakable sounds of amusement, Rusty continued venting. "Then we've got that screwball Alt, who sits on a valuable coin collection and doesn't have the good sense to insure it.

I just don't understand these people. After all the warnings they've had, they still insist on acting like village idiots. You know, it's no dang wonder that people in other states think the good citizens of Nebraska are all backward farmers that don't know a damn hole in the ground from their a—"

"That's okay, Chief," Kelly interrupted, grinning. "I get the picture. But you know, you're right about a lot of people not taking heed to a warning that will protect them. It's like telling them that drinking and driving don't mix. Yet, they insist on getting behind a wheel of a car after they've had a few under their belts. I guess it's that syndrome that they're indestructible, and bad things just happen to someone else."

"Let's get back to the situation at present. Either our thief is laying low because things got too hot for him, or he's left town. My guess is he's still around just waiting for another juicy ripe apple to be dangled in front of him. He's played us for fools far too long. How much money do we have in our funds to set up a sting?"

"Right off the top of my head, I don't know, Chief. I can find out in a hurry."

"Yeah, as soon as we're through here. We need a plant in the bank. Someone who isn't known in these parts. Got any ideas?"

"Not right off hand," Kelly said.

"On second thought, maybe I don't want a plant in the bank. Maybe I just need someone to get to know and confide in Dodd. Whoever is pulling these thefts, knows something about every one of those bank customers who takes out a loan.

Maybe we need an older, retired man with lots of money that just wants to … " Rusty stopped talking. An idea rushed into the forefront of his mind that he had to give more attention to. Kelly sat waiting for Rusty to speak when he noticed a twinkle in the chief's eyes.

Rusty snapped his fingers. "That's it. I just had a brilliant idea. Tell me what you think. Somehow, we'll get a rumor started that a wealthy man is moving to town. Rumors are easy to start in these small farming communities, especially ours.

Oh, I've got the perfect person in mind to spread the word. We'll have this guy get in contact with Jesse over at Town and Country Realtors. I'll bet she's the president of Cole County's rumor mill," he remarked with a grunting laugh. "With her gossiping big mouth, everyone will know within twenty-four hours that this guy is pretty well-to-do and he's looking for a modest house to rent in Kidwell."

Kelly laughed. "Shame on you, Chief."

"Well, if the shoe fits—Anyway, we'll also have our guy go over to Sharpin and introduce himself to Dodd. He can lay the groundwork, saying he just wants to meet the bankers he'll be doing business with when he has moved into the area. One thing, I want this to stay under our control and in my jurisdiction. That's why I'm going to insist that our man lives here in Kidwell.

Once this guy has moved into his house, we'll have him go back to the bank to take out a small loan, just to establish credit in his new community. We'll have him brag, more than a little, about having money stashed around his house because he doesn't trust putting all of his cash into the bank. He will need to do that bragging to our friend, Wally Dodd. How am I doing so far?"

"I'm with you, Chief, but why Dodd? I thought we ruled him out as a suspect?"

"We did. But, it appears he's still the main party most of these victims seem to have been in contact with. I'd bet my life that the bank is tied into this in someway. That didn't come out right. What I mean is, Dodd still appears to be the burglary victims single contact at the bank. Many of the victims have had contact with the tellers and other bank employees, but Dodd seems to be the one person that these people sit and talk to, like friends do.

Maybe Dodd likes to gossip and confides in a fellow employee about his clients' personal lives? Or, maybe there's someone in the bank that has a bad habit of eavesdropping on private conversations between Dodd and his visitors? Who knows. But if we set this up, I'd lay wager that whoever the leak is in the bank, the information will get passed on to our Neat Nick Thief.

Boyd's is the one burglary in our files, since the rash of break-ins started, that we can't tie in to Dodd, even though he banks there. It was his own big mouth that set him up for his loss."

Wrapping his upper lip with his lower one, wrinkling his chin in the process, Rusty shook his head. Conscious of what he was doing, he wiped his mouth off with the back of his hand. "I know I sound like an instant replay, but I still can't get over one person losing ninety thousand big ones. Can you imagine it."

"Lose it, hell, I can't imagine even having that much money in my possession. Question. Doesn't it sound reasonable that Dodd would know Boyd, since he banks there?"

"True. But, according to both men, they have never met."

"Getting back to your idea, Chief. If this man you want as a plant is supposed to be wealthy, why would he want a modest rental house? Wouldn't he want to purchase a big, prestigious one?"

"Nope. We want him to be the modest sort. We'll leave it up to Jesse to spread the word around town that he's wealthy. She'll be led to believe that he keeps his wealth tied up in investments and the rest in his many bank accounts. When he informs her that his financial status is to be kept private, you can bet Jesse's ears will perk up. That's going to be like giving a bank robber the combination to the safe," Rusty stated with a chuckle.

"The only one he will confide in about the stashed dough in his house, will be Dodd. It would defeat our purpose if we had our guy living in an expensive house, giving the perception that he has valuables inside waiting to be stolen. He would be like a sitting duck for any thief. It's the Neat Nick Thief we're after.

We, also, need a single man for this sting. I don't want any lifestyle interference, or someone who has to keep secrets from his wife just to help us out. Are you with me so far?"

"Sure, Chief. Now I understand where you're going with this idea."

"Good. Now, we need a code name for our plant should we have to mention the case in front of any office visitors. On second thought, a code name should be used at any time, here in the office or out in public. One never knows who could be eavesdropping on our conversations. Then our plan could go up in smoke. You're going to laugh, Kelly, but the first thing that comes to mind when I think of a plant is ivy. How about, 'Operation Ivy'?"

At first, the officer snickered, but after a few seconds of thought, he added to the chief's remarks. "Now that I think about it, that isn't so far fetched. Ivy seems to grasp hold of everything it touches, just like Chief Simmons always gets his man. I like it."

"I'm sure you're too young to know, Kelly, but, years ago, on television they had shows like *The Man From U.N.C.L.E.* and *To Catch*

A Thief. Man, those titles were all so original. Now, the best I can come up with is Operation Ivy.

Oh, well, let's get back to my plan. We'll keep Operation Ivy under twenty-four-hour surveillance. If the thief tries one of his capers, our stakeout will be ready to nab the mutt. To keep things short and simple, we'll call the person we hire to help us Clinger."

"Klinger? As in the TV show *M*A*S*H.*?"

"No, that never crossed my mind. I was thinking of ivy being a clinging vine. Clinger with a C just sounded more fitting than Clinging. So, what do you think?"

"I think you've been reading too many of those cheap detective novels, Chief," Kelly said with a laugh. "To be honest, it sounds good, but who do you have in mind that can pull this off?"

"Well, Kelly, that's why this is called brainstorming. So far, I've done most of the talking. Don't you have any ideas?"

There was complete silence in the room as both men were in deep thought. Officer Kelly broke the silence. "I don't know if he'll do it, but I have a brother-in-law over in Clayridge. That's about eighty miles from here." Aware of the town, Rusty nodded. "My sister died about two years ago, so he's alone now. He always calls and says he wants to move here to Kidwell, but he always finds one excuse or another for not doing so.

Before he retired, five years ago, he was a cop in Chicago. He isn't young but his law enforcement background would be a benefit in this sting. Maybe he will be willing to help. Do you want me to call him?"

"He sounds perfect, Kelly. I knew I could count on you to come up with something. Okay, first things first. You find out what our funds are so we know the amount of finances we have to work with. Then get back to me before we go any further. Make it fast. I have a gut feeling this Neat Nick Thief is ready to strike again, and I want to be ready."

Walking to the door, Kelly turned and asked, "Chief, we didn't complete our discussion on this possibility that the thief has already left town. What if—"

"Our sting should prove that, one way or another. If he doesn't take the bait then we'll know he's left our area." With a somber look on his face, Rusty commented, "I'd sure hate to leave my post as police chief knowing I let this clown get away. That's something I don't care to consider right now. I'm hoping the perp's still around so we can recover the stolen money."

"Okay, then let me throw something else at you. What if the thief is planning to leave town? With so few of us around the county wearing a uniform of the law, how in the world would we stop him?"

Shaking his head, Rusty replied. "We wouldn't, Kelly. Besides, even if we did have the manpower to cover all the roads out of town, we don't have any idea what this mutt looks like."

"I know."

"We'll just have to hope that the breaks start moving in our favor."

"Yeah, Chief, I guess you're right."

Once Kelly looked up the department's finances in the bookkeeping records, he reported to Rusty. "We show a balance of three hundred. That won't be enough, will it?"

"Hardly. Get me Mayor Dickson on the horn. Tell him it's vital that I speak with him, ASAP."

After Rusty received permission from the mayor to do what he had to do to catch the Neat Nick Thief, and he allocated a small amount of funds at Rusty's disposal, Officer Kelly was given the thumbs-up to call his brother-in-law, Oscar Denton.

Oscar was thrilled to help and arrived in Kidwell the following day. Arriving at the back door of the Kidwell Police Station, cautious so as not to be noticed, Officer Kelly escorted his brother-in-law into the chief's office. Rusty made sure the door was closed to the outer office.

Not that the other officers weren't aware of what was going on, but it was for safety reasons. No one outside the department could know that the new man in town would be working undercover with the police. If they were to find out, it could blow the whole sting operation.

Operation Ivy was soon to be a reality.

Rusty was impressed even before he spoke to Oscar. Before him stood a man with a head full of silver-gray hair, a small gray mustache, warm eyes and a pleasing smile. He was nicely groomed, dressed in casual clothes, and looked the part of a man of wealth.

Officer Kelly made the brief introduction. "Chief Simmons meet Oscar Denton." Rusty and Oscar shook hands.

As the three sat in their respective chairs, Rusty started the conversation. "Oscar, I assume Kelly, here, told you what we needed?"

"Yes, he did, Chief," Oscar answered, looking over at Kelly who was nodding in acceptance.

"Look, my officers have to call me chief out of respect," Rusty remarked with a laugh. "You can call me Rusty."

"Okay, Rusty, I'll just do that."

"How long were you on the force in Chicago?"

"Thirty long years. When my wife took ill, she wanted to come back to Nebraska where she grew up. She had always been the perfect cop's wife, handling the strain well. But when she took ill, my job started stressing her out. And, at my age, I was beginning to slip a little, too. I wasn't doing the department any good by sticking around. So, I retired and brought my wife back here to Nebraska so she could die in peace."

"I'm sorry to hear of your loss."

"Thank you, Rusty, that is mighty kind of you. It's been two years, now, and each day it gets a little better. But, I must tell you, I was thrilled when my brother-in-law called me and asked if I would be interested in helping you out. It gives a real boost to an old cop's ego."

"I don't know what kind of boost it will give you, but I understand, once a cop always a cop. Now, do you have any questions about what we want you to do?" Rusty asked.

"None that I can think of."

"I know Kelly is a very thorough officer, but I would like to hear in your words what you know is expected of you. I'm sure you understand that if something goes wrong, I'm the one that takes the full responsibility. So, I have to know that you have an exact understanding of the details."

"Okay. To anyone concerned, I state my correct name, Oscar Denton, from Clayridge. I'm retired. Only I say I'm retired from farming in Clayridge, not from the Chicago Police Department. If anyone should inquire into my past, my background will check out since my wife owned a small farm in Clayridge. We sold the farm about a year before she passed, but my name was on the paperwork.

Anyway, I will go to the realtors around this area and tell them I'm looking for a modest house to purchase here in Kidwell. I'll make a special point to meet with the owner of Town and Country Realtors. I think her name was Jesse." Receiving a receptive nod and a grin from Rusty, he continued. "I confide in this woman about my wealth. When I find a house I like, I will make a cash offer. Then I'll go to the bank in Sharpin and ask to speak to the loan officer, Mr. Dodds. I will—"

"No. Oh, I didn't mean to interrupt, Oscar, but his name is Dodd, without an s," Kelly stated, correcting his brother-in-law.

"That's quite all right. I want to get the name correct, and I had

Black Rosebud

Dodds locked in my head. I'll try and remember Dodd. Anyway, I will act real palsy-walsy with him," Oscar joked, "and tell him I want a small loan, just to establish credit. I can give him some bonds to cover my loan. So, there won't be any need for him to check out my banking background. Even if he does, he won't find anything out of the ordinary. Nothing that would tip him off that I'm not on the level.

I'll mention to this Dodd fella that I want to put some of my money in his bank. However, I'm a great believer in keeping a lot of my money in my own home, where I can put my hands on it without having to go to a bank every time I need cash. Of course, since I'm new in town, I won't know anything about this Neat Nick Thief. If Dodd happens to mention the thief, I'll just tell him no petty thief frightens me. How am I doing, Rusty?"

"I think you got the story stretched a might," Rusty answered with a smirk on his face, looking over at Kelly.

Officer Kelly looked back at the chief with an innocent look on his face, and shrugged. "Don't look at me, Chief. I didn't tell him to do all of that."

"Let's back up here, Oscar. We got permission to fund the rental of a house, and stash five hundred cash in it to bait our trap. No more, no less. Where did this other nonsense come from, like purchasing a house for cash?"

"Well, Rusty, it isn't nonsense. I've told Pat ever since his sister died, that I wanted to move to Kidwell. I'd like to be closer to his family since I don't have any blood relatives of my own."

"Pat? Oh, you mean Kelly." Rusty chuckled. Kelly was tickled at Rusty's temporary look of puzzlement. "I've called him Kelly for so long, it took me a second to think who this Pat was you were talking about. Look, Oscar, while we're on this case, if you don't mind, could you refer to Pat, here," Rusty joked, "as Kelly?"

Oscar agreed then continued his explanation. "As we speak, the realtor back home is listing my house for sale. I do have the money to make a cash purchase on a house here in Kidwell, and I plan on doing so. I also cleaned out my bank accounts in Clayridge and have the money with me.

I figure your only risk, money wise, is to give me the five hundred to, as you said, bait the trap. I didn't think my extra personal plans would cause a problem. It gave me the excuse I needed to get off my duff and move, like I kept saying I was going to do.

I also think that Kelly and I should be careful. If your thief should find out I'm related to a cop, he might not want to chance burglarizing me."

"Good point, Oscar. I know it'll be difficult but best that you two either keep in contact by phone, or plan on meeting from time to time here in my office until Operation Ivy is concluded." Rusty looked over at Kelly for a look of acceptance. When he received it, he asked Oscar, "Is there anything else?"

"Not from me, except to say that I don't mind being called Clinger in this Operation Ivy sting."

"As a retired police officer, I'm sure you're aware that the code name will just be used when we speak of this sting or write up our reports. Out in public, after you move to town and we have met as Kidwell citizens, you'll still be called by your given name."

"Understood."

"It sounds like you're well informed and fit the bill for what we're looking for. Okay, then it's official."

"Look, Rusty, I don't want to throw any water on this fire, but I need to tell you something. I didn't handle details real well before I retired, even though I feel confident that I can do this for you without screwing it up. Having said that, do you still want me in on this case?"

Believing Kelly, that Oscar was once a good cop, Rusty was willing to take the chance with him. If there perp was a dangerous criminal or murderer, Rusty might have had second thoughts, but not for a two-bit thief. Besides, Oscar appeared to have all the details of the present case down pat.

Rusty stood and walked around his desk to Oscar. He extended his hand. Oscar, knowing a gesture for a handshake when he saw it, got to his feet and shook hands with Rusty. "From now on until our thief is caught and convicted in a court of law, you will officially go on the case file as Clinger." Rusty added, "Thanks for your help and welcome aboard."

"Don't thank me yet, Rusty. Let's just see if your plan works. It sounds good to me, but let's hope the bait sounds good enough to this thief you're trying to catch."

The ball was rolling. Once Rusty introduced Oscar to the rest of the law enforcement crew, he confirmed that Operation Ivy had a green light. As far as Rusty was concerned, it was a definite red light for the Neat Nick Thief.

FIRST ENCOUNTERS

As Farm Girl journeyed, following the riverbank, the changing temperatures were taking a physical toll. The days were getting warmer but the nights were still very cold. She started getting the sniffles, which soon turned into sneezing and coughing. In her head, she just knew she was catching her death.

In the many times that she and Mama had traveled about, it was rare that she was ever sick. Although used to being outside doing chores, no matter what the weather, she hadn't been without some sort of shelter in years. Sleeping on the cold, damp ground, not getting a good night's sleep, coupled with the fact that she'd been living on nothing but bugs, worms and berries for days, she was losing her strength.

In her solitude, Farm Girl had no verbal interruptions. This allowed her time to practice some of the grammar Jefferson Welk had tried teaching her. Even though she didn't remember everything, she did improve her speech—somewhat.

Feeling she had walked far enough away from Jefferson's farm and Sugar Shack, she started walking inland, away from the river. Making her way through wooded areas and across fields, traipsing through weeds and mud, she finally came across a graveled road.

After looking in both directions, she had to make a decision. "I reckon either way is gonna take me to another world."

Not giving a thought that she might end up back where she had started from, she made her decision as to which direction to go, and started walking again. As she followed the road, her sneezing and coughing seemed to get worse.

Lucky for her, it wasn't long before a farmer on his tractor came upon her. He slowed down. When Farm Girl stopped walking, he stopped along side of her.

Being neighborly, like most Nebraska farmers, he yelled over the noise of his tractor, "Can I give you a lift?"

If he be an evil stranger, why are he talking nice to me? Well, maybe he be nice like them other mans I meet like Mister Carl and Mister Jason. But, what's that he wants to do, lift me? Since he's on one a them tractors, you is still in farm world, isn't you? So, if you is, he cain't be speaking a foreign language. Maybe I best ask what he means.

Becoming impatient, the farmer commented, "Can't offer you more than a lift in the manure wagon, but take it or leave it. Just give me an answer because I have to get going."

"I doesn't know what a lift are," she yelled back in response, "but I thank you fur asking."

The farmer smiled. "I'm offering you a ride. I can take you as far as I'm going."

You is too plum tired and too hungry to go any farther on your own two feets right now. Besides, you doesn't know where you is going. So, be brave, Farm Girl, and take the ride. "Can you tell me where is the closest world that has them townsfolk living in it? Because that's where I need to be going."

With all the racket of the tractor motor, the farmer was sure he didn't hear what the girl asked. Instead of wasting time, asking her to repeat it, he hollered, "I'm heading towards town. If you want a ride, hop on board."

Deciding to take the ride, Farm Girl walked to the back of the wagon. The farmer watched. She tossed her two gunnysacks and her horse blanket into the wagon. Not being able to jump, due to her excess baggage, she clumsily climbed aboard. Seating herself on the edge of the wagon, she dangled her feet over the side. When the farmer saw she was aboard and seated, he put the tractor in gear, proceeding down the road.

Weary, Farm Girl leaned back and enjoyed the ride as if the manure pile was a field of daisies. She rode all the way to the edge of town.

Coming to a halt, the farmer turned and yelled, "This is where I turn off. You'll have to get off now."

Dropping her bags and the blanket to the ground, Farm Girl jumped from the wagon. With the heavy weight around her waist, she hit the ground with a thud. The farmer drove away. Getting to her feet, she picked up her belongings and headed toward the buildings in her sight. Even though she was now within spitting distance of a new world, she was far too exhausted to pick up her slow moving pace.

"With all my practicing, nobody's gonna know that I aren't gots me no school learning when I speak. I need—Ah-chew! I need to remember everything Mama teach me about manners. First, I need to git myself cleaned up, feed my poor tummy, then find me somewhere to sleep. Ah-chew!"

Stopping to take in the breath-taking view, Farm Girl stood in awe. The site before her was surreal to her innocent eyes. She had seen pictures of towns, cities, even countries in Jefferson's books and on a map that Darin once showed her, but those were just pictures.

She had seen images of towns and their different shaped buildings on Jefferson's television, but was told those type buildings weren't real. All on television and in books, according to Mama and Mr. Welk, were just make-believe—figments and fantasy of someone's imagination. However, this was no longer make-believe or fantasy.

Walking, once again, and not paying attention, she stepped into the street right in front of traffic. The blast of a horn almost scared her to death. Realizing that she was in a road and almost run down by a car, she dashed, as best she could, to the other side of the street.

At the first building on the corner, she meandered up and planted her face snug against the store's large, plate-glass window and gazed inside. Spotting a sign inside, she read, "Wood-ees Pe-har-ma-see." Her eyes wandered around the store's interior from top to bottom, wall to wall.

"Look at all them boxes and bottles in there. This must be one a them stores where you gives them your money and they gives you store-bought stuff. But why wouldja wanna buy bottles and boxes fur? Don't be a silly goose, Farm Girl. Pappy always had boxes and bottles a different stuff in his house. So a course folks buys them. They comes with all kinds a little surprises inside."

When her sight landed on a man, she stared at him. He was leaning over a counter, writing. In his present stance, all she could make out was his salt and pepper hair, the little round glasses that seemed to fit on the tip of his nose, and the smock he was wearing.

With a mixture of fear and excitement running through her body, all at the same time, Farm Girl had almost forgotten how tired and hungry she was. "You best git in there and ask that stranger to help you, or you'll be standing out here all day."

Opening the door, she stepped inside. Walking up to the man behind the counter, in a polite way she asked, "Pardon, sir. Could you tell a—

Ah-chew! Excusy. Could you tell a girl where she can git herself washed up and git her some store-bought clothes? Ah-chew! Ah-chew!"

Raising his head back with a rapid turn of his face, he attempted to keep out range of her sputtered germs. Turning back to the front of the counter, and standing erect, Woody looked at the filthy urchin standing in front of him. From his immediate observation, it seemed obvious that whatever she was carrying in the gunnysacks draped across her back, made her bend forward like a little old lady.

Good heavens this child is grubby. She looks like she's been wallowing in a pigpen. Oh, yuck! What is that foul odor? PU! Mercy, I believe she smells of cow manure. It's no wonder she wants to wash up. It's obvious no one ever taught her to cover her mouth when she sneezes.

Store-bought clothes? What kind of question is that? Maybe she's one of those autistic people. No harm in helping the poor thing. Besides, the sooner I help her, the quicker she'll leave. That stench is almost unbearable.

He responded to Farm Girl's sneezes. "Gesundheit."

Crimeny, it's just like Darin told me about these here other worlds. There's one a them foreign language words they speaks here. Because he hadn't answered her question, thinking the man didn't understand her, Farm Girl asked straight out, "I sure doesn't understand that word you just told me. So, maybe, you doesn't understand my words either."

"Yes, of course I understood you. I'm sorry you didn't understand me. I guess I assumed everyone was familiar with the German word that means, God bless you." *German?* Farm Girl silently questioned as Woody continued speaking. "To answer your initial questions, first, a girl has to have money. If she has that, then she can go about three blocks down the street and purchase herself new clothes in the clothing store.

If she goes five blocks to the west …" He stopped in the middle of his sentence and asked, "I'm assuming this girl we're speaking of is you?" Farm Girl gave a quick nod. "I thought so. Okay, do you know which way is west of here?"

"Most times," she blurted out, as she started coughing. After a quick sniffle she added, "I does when the sun sets. But, at this time a day, sir, I is afraid I doesn't. Ah-chew! Excusy. Besides, I doesn't wear me none a them…" Farm Girl couldn't think of the correct word she was searching for. So, she reverted to a term more familiar. "I doesn't has one a them arm clocks."

Black Rosebud

Taking a second to ponder her statement, he repeated his blessing. However, this time he wanted to make sure she understood. "Bless you, child." *She can't mean a wristwatch if I asked her about directions, can she? I don't think so.* "You do mean a compass, don't you?"

"I doesn't think I do, seeing as how I doesn't know what is a compass."

"No, probably not. " Gesturing with his hand, he explained. "That way is west. Okay? There is a motel … You do know what a motel is, don't you?"

"No, sir, I don't reckon I does."

Woody detected the confusion on the girl's face. Tipping his head, he peered over the top of his glasses. Enunciating every word, as if he was in a slow motion movie where the speech is slowed almost to a standstill, he attempted to explain. "A mo-tel is where you go and pay a lot of mon-ey for the pri-vil-ege of stay-ing in a room. You get a bed to sleep on and fa-cil-ities for show-er-ing. Do you un-der-stand?"

"I think so, sir. Ah-chew! Ah-chew! Excusy." *Crimeny, they might not has any barns to sleep in, Mama, but they has a sleeping room you pay money fur. Aren't that super?*

"God bless you, a-gain."

"Sir, how come you is speaking so funny like that?" *I doesn't mean to be hurtful and all, but he didn't talk that way when I first come in here. Maybe that's how they speak in this world? First all normal like, then funny. Jiminy Crickets! I wonder if he's one a them people that don't know they has a sick problem? Maybe that's why he's talking at me so strange like? Poor man. I hope he's got kinsfolk at home to git him some medicine.*

While Farm Girl stood quiet, listening to the voice in her head, Woody had thoughts of his own. *I guess I messed that up. Big time. I forgot that one doesn't have to be condescending or talk down to autistic people. Ha! I must have sounded like a grown idiot talking to her that way.*

After another healthy sneeze, once again, Woody blessed her. "Thank you again, sir. I need all a them blessings you can give right now. But I hope you keep a few a them fur yourself."

Keep a blessing for myself? How quaint. Although she hasn't asked for anything, yet, she looks like a beggar. I'll bet this poor kid hasn't got a cent to her name. He heard a strange gurgling sound. Even though Farm Girl paid no attention to the noise, Woody was quick to figure out it was her stomach growling. "I know you haven't asked, but would you like a couple bucks to get yourself a nice hot meal?"

"What means your word bucks?"

"Dollars. Would you like some money to get something to eat?"

Behind Farm Girl's smile was a befuddled mind. She didn't understand why a perfect stranger wanted to give her money. "I doesn't be needing your money, thank you. I might has my own money fur food. In fact, I might even has enough money to buy me some a them store-bought clothes.

You know, I doesn't need me no facilities because I doesn't know what them are. But if'n I gits me one a them motel rooms, does them showers has hot and cold runnin' water?"

I think I've misjudged this girl. I don't think she's autistic at all. I think she is uneducated and very naïve. "Yes, young lady, that's hot and cold runnin' water," he mimicked.

"Sir, is you making fun a the likes a me saying runnin'? Cuzz, if'n you is, I reckon your mama didn't learn you no manners." *Oh crimeny, Farm Girl, you is trying so hard to be smart but your mouth's making you stupid. Cuzz? You ain't been using that word in a long time. Think first befur you say one word you isn't sure of. No wonder he's making fun a you.*

Feeling a tad guilty that she took his teasing as an insult, Woody apologized. "No, I wasn't making fun of you, I was having fun with you. You know, young lady, you're like someone right out of a storybook."

A sudden thought flew into his head about national news' reports. Maybe he was overlooking the obvious. "Say, you're not one of those runaways, are you?"

Farm Girl sneezed a couple of times then threw in a couple of fake sneezes. *Oh, no, there's one a them nosey questions. Runaways? Nope. Mama always told me there was just me and her. And how come he cain't see that I isn't out a no storybook? Oh, shame on you, Farm Girl. I reckon he don't see so well. Maybe that's why he's wearing them eye specks, like Pappy was wearing fur reading*

"No, I isn't no kin to them Runaways, and I isn't out a no storybook, neither. Ah-chew! My friend told me them storybooks are plum make-believe. I is sure sorry that you cain't see me very well, but as I stand befur you, I is alive and very real. Nope, there aren't no storybook make-believe about me," she reiterated with a sort of dignity in knowing exactly who she was, and who she was not.

It was all Woody could do to contain himself. To hold back his laughter, he clenched his teeth.

"I thank you fur your time, and I is beholden to you fur your offer to buy me something to eat without even asking me to do chores fur you first. I hope you doesn't mind me asking, but is you one a them doctor mans?"

"No. Why, do you need a doctor?"

"No. I just think you was one because you is wearing one a them doctor man's white coats."

"Oh, my smock. Yes, most doctors do wear them, but I'm not a doctor. I'm a pharmacist."

There's some more a them foreign words. I cain't remember them all, but I hope I remember smocks means coats in this new language.

After Woody gave her directions to the clothing store, he also told her how to get to the motel. "You know, this isn't a very big town, so it's not too easy to get lost in it. However, if you feel you are lost, stop in any place along the way and ask for directions. People are very nice here. Anyone will be more than happy to help you."

After hearing the girl's stomach gurgling again, Woody told her where to locate the local restaurants. He also gave her a briefing as to what other shops were around the area, just in case she would be staying in town for a few days. "Now you know where to go to eat, and … "

When he noticed that Farm Girl was looking around and not paying attention to him, anymore, he realized he was telling her things she probably didn't want to know. "I'm sorry, young lady. I have a tendency to get carried away with diarrhea of the mouth."

Farm Girl's head made a rapid jerk as she turned her attention back on Woody. She stared at his mouth. *Diarrhea a the mouth? Crimeny, the folks in this world be awful strange. Wonder what part they eat with? I best be leaving befur I sees me something I doesn't wanna see.*

On her way to the door without turning back, she said, "Good day to you. Ah-chew! I is mighty beholden to you fur all your help."

She exited the store. Before the door closed behind her, she swirled around and headed right back inside. "After what you told me, don't suppose folks like you has an indoor privy with one a them water cleaning poopers I can use while I is here? Ah-chew! This here town world are sure purdy, but it doesn't has too many trees or bushes to squat behind."

Having just sprayed his counter with disinfectant, Woody was caught off guard from her sudden return and comical declaration. He had to bite his tongue so Farm Girl wouldn't be aware of how amused he was. Pointing toward a door just a few feet away from him, he responded, "The public restroom is back there.

By the way, in case you don't know, as a pharmacist I can recommend a great over-the-counter medicine until you can see a doctor for that cold you've got. You might have money for new clothes, but it's more important to spend some money and take care of your health."

Not knowing what to say, Farm Girl gave him a quick nod. Heading for the bathroom, she mumbled, "Wonder why they put a privy in a room to rest in? Oh, that's got to be their word fur privy. Ah-chew! They must has pooper rooms fur folks like me.

I might git me some a that medicine he calls over-the-counter, but I isn't gonna see me no doctor mans. The one doctor mans I ever seen were that one who come to see Pappy. And Pappy were dead. I sure doesn't plan on being dead. Not yet."

Even with the pungent smell of the disinfectant he had used to clean the counter, Woody realized that the overpowering stench from Farm Girl was still lingering around him. As he held the can of air-freshener in the air, spraying its contents wildly around the area, he stated under his breath, "I wonder if she dirtied her drawers? No wonder she needs to use the bathroom.

Goodness, I hope she cleans it up when she's done in there. I'm sure I'll have to disinfect it for a week to get rid of her foul odor." No longer able to contain himself, he started chuckling. "I've never heard of a privy with a water cleaning pooper before. And what a strange thing to ask if folks like me have a—Wait. After what I told her? Oh, my God, she thinks—" Realizing what the girl was referring to, Woody's chuckles turned into laughter. "That's just plain disgusting."

As Farm Girl entered the bathroom, she made sure the door was closed tight so no one would enter. With the immediate realization that the room was pitch black, she dropped the sacks to the floor. Bending over, she felt around inside the sacks until she found the flashlight and turned it on. The batteries were weak but the beam gave enough light to view the small room.

As the dim light shined on a mirror, bouncing back an eerie reflection, the brief glimpse of her image was startling. "Yikes!" In one quick movement, she opened the door for more light. Looking toward the ceiling, she spotted an overhead light-fixture. Searching for a way to illuminate it, she looked for a switch or pull-chain.

"Hey, are you all right back there?" Woody called out after hearing her screech.

"I is fine, sir," she yelled back. "I didn't real eyes, uh, real-a lies—I just didn't know I look such—Ah-chew—a frightful mess. Sorry. You know it's mighty dark in here and my flashlight are dying on me. I see one a them electricity lights in here on the ceiling a this room, but I doesn't know how to turn it on. I need to see when I close the door."

"The light switch is on the wall behind the door," Woody answered.

Once she found the switch and turned on the light, she closed the door. Turning off the flashlight, it was placed on top one of the gunnysacks.

Farm Girl removed Mama's sweaters and tossed them in the garbage along with her filthy horse blanket and muddy quilt. She knew in her heart that someone else might go through the trash, just as she and her mother had done, and retrieve the old clothes for their own use.

She slipped out of her good dress and wrapped it over the doorknob. After untying the stringer from her waist, and slipping the twine off her shoulders, she let the heavy belt drop to the floor. Aching from the heavy load, she rubbed her back and shoulders.

The constant sneezing, coughing and sniffles were becoming very annoying.

Every item in her necessity bag, no longer needed, was discarded. All that remained was one gunnysack of money, the stringer of money socks, and an almost empty gunnysack with just a few necessities left in it.

While sitting on the commode, she kept staring at a clear glass container attached to the wall above the sink. Her curiosity got the best of her. Right after flushing the toilet, she moved closer to the container and started feeling, pulling and pushing on it. When her pushing allowed a rather large spurt of liquid to spill out and drop to the sink, she quickly released her hands.

"What's that stuff?" After dipping her finger into the solution, she tasted the substance. "Yucky!" Gagging, she leaned over the sink spitting and sputtering. Turning on the cold water to wash out her mouth, she bitterly complained, "Someone needs to tell these townsfolk how to make soap.

You is s'pose to let it set and git hard, not use it while it's still all gooey. Lessen, of course, it's that kind a soap Pappy done had fur washing dishes. But if it is, what's it doing in a privy? Crimeny, Farm Girl, if they poops and eats different than farm folks, maybe they has their own reason fur washing dishes in a privy."

Leaving the water running, she took her toothbrush and tube of toothpaste out of the sack. As she brushed her teeth to get rid of the soap taste left in her mouth, she had to laugh as more flash backs flew through her head.

Every time I were brushing my teeths with this here white stuff, my mouth were tasting fresh as spring. Mama use to think I were chewing on mint leaves all the time. I were sure lucky Pappy had him that small patch a wild mint growing next to the barn. I was feeling real bad, though, when Mama was thinking them mint leaves was making my teeths so white. She be chewing on them leaves everyday fur a week and didn't know why her teeths weren't turning white, too.

Pappy had him one of them little brushes in his bathroom that I was using to clean out his pooper with Until Darin done give me my toothbrush, I didn't know it was fur teeths cleaning. I remember asking Pappy if that little brush in his privy was fur brushing his teeths. When he said yes, I were feeling kind a bad. Oh, well, Pappy was never complaining about nothing, so I guess the taste a that privy cleaning powder didn't bother him none.

Finished brushing her teeth, Farm Girl bent forward and slipped the top sweater over her head, removing it, and allowing it fall to the floor. The remaining soap left on the sink was used to wash her face and hands. Looking about, she didn't see anything for drying her hands and face. Out of necessity, she pulled up the bottom of her skirt and used it as a towel.

Recovering the heavy sweater off the floor, she proceeded to slip it back over her head. In doing so, her eyes peeked through the neck opening, seeing herself in the mirror. The sight looked so funny, she got the giggles and started playing peek-a-boo in the mirror.

Then she stuck her head through the neck opening, but didn't place her arms through the sleeves. Acting goofy, turning to get different views of her image in the mirror as she flopped the loose sleeves in the air, her foot caught the end of a gunnysack. With her arms pinned inside the body of the sweater, she lost her balance and went crashing into a wall.

Suddenly, she heard a loud roaring noise and felt hot air blowing down her back. Jumping with fright, she made a quick turn to see what she had fallen against. In her eyes, she saw a strange looking machine mounted on the wall. Preoccupied with everything else she had been doing since entering the room, she hadn't even noticed the strange, metal machine with its large black button. Having never seen a hand dryer before, she was befuddled. "What's that funny contraption fur?"

Black Rosebud

Keeping an eye on the machine, she stuck her arms into the sweater's sleeves. When the machine stopped, she bent in a position that allowed her to look into the spout, wanting to see where the air came from.

To make sure she didn't fall again, standing in such an awkward position, she reached up to hold on to the machine. Her hand hit the *on* button. Without warning, she got the full force of the warm air straight in the face. Pulling her head away from the machine, she hurriedly took a step back.

"Crimeny! Does that thing go on and off all by its lonesome?" After closer examination, she remarked, "No, Farm Girl, I think it were that big ole button what's on the front a that machine."

Once the noise and air ceased, she stepped back to the hand dryer and pressed the button. Once again, the machine started operating. Moving her hands so the air hit them, she was reminded of the summer breeze.

"Oh, I just got me one a them light bulb moments again." Picking up the bottom of her damp skirt, she held it up to the warm air. "So that's what this is fur? After you uses your clothes to dry off the water from washing, you don't has to walk around with wet clothes. What other reason are there fur not having nothing in here to dry with? This machine be just as neat as the big appliance Pappy done had fur drying lots a clothes at the same time.

Darin were right about these townsfolk being smart. Mama were visiting towns, but she never told me about none a these fun thingamabobbies." Retrieving her horse brush from the sack, she commenced brushing her filthy hair. "Could be Mama didn't know about all these smart thingies. Could be the world of farm folks don't know about them, either."

Plopping her body to the floor, Farm Girl tossed her brush back into the necessity bag. Then she untied one of the money-socks, emptying the contents onto one of the gunnysacks. Keeping her voice to a whisper, she tried to figure out how much money she needed for her purchases.

"Pappy done told me he had to pay some two hundred dollars, one day, just to buy himself a good pair a work boots and some store-bought overhauls. So maybe three hundred dollars ought a buy me a good pair a shoes and maybe two pairs a them overhauls.

Then, I need to git me food and that motel place. If'n I hasn't gots enough money, I'll just has to find a private place to go so I can git me more out a my sack. I best be listening to Mama about townsfolk asking too many questions about me having money."

After shoving the socks that came off her waist into the necessity bag, she got back on her feet. Feeling a slight light headed, Farm Girl grabbed the sink with both hands. She held on with a tight grip to keep from fainting. As the room started to spin, she let loose of her grip with one hand to turn on the faucet and splash cold water on her face.

"I teld you to git some food, Farm Girl. You hasn't had a decent meal since you left the farm. You need to listen when your tummy speaks at you. Then you won't feel so funny."

Leaning over the sink, she waited a few minutes until her head quit swimming. When she felt better, she removed her dress from the doorknob. "I reckon, since I aren't wearing my stringer a money bags no more, I doesn't need me this dress." After drying her hands and face with the dress, she tossed it atop the other items that now filled the trashcan.

Once she opened the door, she stuck her head out and yelled. "Mister Pharmacist man, how much money does you be wanting fur that medicine you calls over-the-counter that you says are good fur this here cold I has floating around in my body?"

"Up to five dollars," he called back with a chuckle in his voice. "Depending on what kind you want."

"I just told him I wants that over-the-counter kind, didn't I?" she mumbled to herself, closing the door. "How many medicines are there anyway? I only knows a…" She hesitated to count on her fingers. "I knows four, and now this new one makes five.

Crimeny, I hope that over-the-counter aren't this townsfolk word fur caster oil. Pappy always said it cleans out a body's system when nature won't take its course. Ain't no wonder. After Mama make me take some, I was thinking I were gonna has to live in Pappy's outhouse privy. I sure doesn't want me some a that nasty tasting stuff, ever again. Yuck! It makes me sick to even think about it. I best be finding out first what over-the-counter tastes like, befur I goes and buys it."

After picking up the two gunnysacks, she promptly dropped them back to the floor. Even though she had thrown quite a few objects and clothes in the trash, the load seemed much heavier now.

"Maybe that weren't a smart idea to be carrying the money instead a wearing it. Toting around one bag might be easier than trying to hold on and carry two a them."

She placed one sack inside the other. Using her full strength and a grunt, she swung the heavy sack up to the sink's ledge. Twisting the top of the bag, she used the same technique that she had used before leaving

Sugar Shack to secure the gunnysack over her shoulder. Now, facing the door, she attempted to take a step. The bag stayed in place, pulling her back against the sink. Letting loose, she turned back toward the sink.

"Crimeny, I was carrying me more than this gitting here, and now I cain't even lift what I has left. Well, Mama always teach me, there are more than one way a skinning a cat. You just gotta use your brain."

Wrapping the sack's top around her hand, once again, she yanked. The filled bag went crashing to the floor. She opened the door and turned off the light. With both hands behind her, gripping ever so tight to the bag she was now dragging, she headed toward Woody's front counter.

"What the … " Woody tried to find the proper words to express his amazement, "Where in the world did you come from?"

Oh, rat tails! How can he know I is from another world? Maybe he don't mean that, Farm Girl, or he would a been asking you befur. Maybe with his sickness, he just don't remember. "I is walking right out a your … " *Crimeny, what did he call that room? Oh, I remembers.* "I were in your public restroom because that's where you done send me."

Before Woody could respond, Farm Girl's mind switched gears, again. "I need me some a that medicine, but … " It was obvious to her, Woody wasn't paying attention. From the strange look on his face, she wondered if he wasn't feeling well enough to hear what she had to say. She decided to keep quiet and wait.

His eyes scanned her body from head to toe. Bewildered by the change in Farm Girl's appearance, Woody hadn't realized that his bizarre customer had quit talking.

That's weird. She's no longer wearing that cruddy old blanket across her shoulders. That winter hat and the dark brown gloves are gone. And where's that dirty blanket she had folded over her arm? Her face is a bit cleaner. On top of all that, she seems to have lost weight. All this in the course of twenty minutes in the bathroom. Yes, indeed, very strange. Her outer appearance may be different, but she still carries a distinct foul odor.

If I recall, correctly, she had two of those filthy bags before she went into the bathroom, and she was carrying both of them. Oh, I'll bet she put all those other items into one bag. No wonder she's dragging it. That gunnysack must be her suitcase. This poor urchin. My heart goes out to her.

Feeling she had waited long enough, Farm Girl broke the silence. "If'n you is feeling puny, maybe you ought to sit a spell."

Her voice made him realize he had been staring holes through her. "Puny? Why would you say that?"

"You is acting mighty strange like."

"Oh, I'm sorry. I feel fine, just have a lot on my mind. Now, let's get you that medicine."

After making the decision about which cough medicine was best for her, due to a strong recommendation from Woody, she listened to his list of instructions as to the how and when to take each prescribed dosage.

I doesn't know how my brain is gonna remember all that. But, at least he done promise this stuff in the bottle aren't going to taste like castor oil.

Farm Girl was impatient to get on her way. However, Woody had one last word of advice. "Make sure you don't take this on an empty stomach."

As she was paying for her purchase, Farm Girl noticed something familiar on the wall behind where Woody was standing. "Would that be one a them calendars you has hanging there?"

"It is, and my name is Woody."

"Mister Woody, you got the wrong month on it, doesn't you?"

Smiling, he replied, "No, this is definitely the month of May."

"This is May?" *Crimeny, where did April go to?* "Is you sure this be May?"

"Yes, I'm sure. Why, what month did you think it was?"

"April. Could you be pointing out fur me which date it be right now, please?"

Being obliging, Woody took a step back from the counter. With a slight turn, he pointed out the present date on the calendar. "You appear to have lost a month somewhere," he remarked.

"No, I didn't lose it. I just don't know where it went. I'd be mighty beholden to you, if'n you was to give me that there calendar fur awhile, Mister Woody. I need to count some days from it."

"I have a better idea." He stepped forward, stooped down, and reached under his counter, disappearing from Farm Girl's view. When he reappeared, he extended his hand with something in it. "Here, you can have this pocket-size calendar to take with you."

"You is giving that to me as a gift?"

"Yes. Take it."

Oh, I almost furgot that it don't has to be Creesmas nor my birthday to git me a gift. Farm Girl reached out and accepted the item from Woody's hand. "Thank you."

"You're quite welcome."

Alas, Farm Girl exited the store. Outside, she dropped her change from her purchase in the same small bag that carried the bottle of medicine. Thinking this was such a good idea, she removed the money from her sleeve and put it into the same pharmacy bag.

"Wonder why Mister Woody give me back so much money? I think I give him the five dollars he told me that medicine was gonna be. Maybe I should go right back—No, Mister Woody's smarter than you is, Farm Girl. You just needs to be paying better attention next time you is paying fur something."

Struggling with every step, she stopped every now and then for a moment's rest. There were several puddles of water on the sidewalk. Farm Girl didn't know if they were from melted snows or if it had rained before she had arrived in town. Not that she really cared. Her boots and her gunnysacks were already wet and muddy from her foot-journey. However, she tried to walk around as many puddles as she could.

Walking on the sidewalk, she encountered a few passersby. Some gawked at her while others didn't seem to pay her any attention. Too busy watching where she was walking, while looking into all the windows of the buildings she passed, Farm Girl never noticed anyone else around her.

Finally, she approached the place she was looking for. Here eyes lit up when she peered in the window. "Here's that place fur store-bought clothes that Mister Woody told you about, Farm Girl. Crimeny, I ain't never seen me so many clothes in one place befur."

Inside the clothing store, Farm Girl strolled from counter to counter, rack-to-rack, looking at everything. As she moved about, she continued to drag the gunnysack behind her, making a dirty, wet track that followed her every step. She was in wonderment at the selection of different styles, colors and fabrics.

Across the room stood a tall, slender, gray-haired woman, who was keeping her eyes on her new customer. Farm Girl saw the woman staring at her but chose to ignore her. The saleslady didn't mean to appear critical of the way Farm Girl looked, yet her facial expressions gave her away.

The woman knew there were poor people in the world, and many were living in a farming community, like theirs. She certainly had seen her share of people in dirty clothes. However, in her mind, most folks, no matter how poor, at least cleaned up before coming in town to shop for clothes.

I wonder if this young girl has enough money to purchase any of these clothes? Or, maybe she's here to steal an item of clothing? It would be real easy for her to take something real quick like and hide it in that filthy gunnysack she's pulling.

Too bad my boss doesn't have the same rules they have in some of the big city stores. Have your baggage checked at the counter, or don't take it into the store at all. I'm not taking my eyes off this one. It's for certain we don't need vagrants or thieves in here trying to shoplift.

Not caring to get too close, the woman approached Farm Girl from the opposite end of the counter. Forcing a smile, she greeted, "Welcome to Clothing Corner. May I help you?" Before Farm Girl could answer, she followed with a firm but pleasant order. "And please, unless you have the money to purchase those items, let's don't touch the merchandise."

"Help me?" *Ain't this nice, Farm Girl, having these folks helping you instead a you helping them, like you done as a farmhand?* "Yes ma'am. Help me, please," Farm Girl replied. *Wait. Why does she tell me don't touch unless I has money? It don't make no sense that I has to show her my money first befur buying something. Mister Woody didn't make me do that. Oh, I has me a light bulb idea..*

In a very deliberate movement, Farm Girl swung the sack of medicine around in space, as if to say—I do have money. See. I just bought something at the pharmacy.

"I is afraid I be traveling too long, and, uh, some thief stole most a my clothes. So, I need to buy me some new store-bought ones." Farm Girl opened the gunnysack and tossed the pharmacy bag inside. Holding her empty hand in the air, she turned it from back to palm for the woman to see. "My hands is dish soap and water clean."

"Yes, of course they are, dear. It's lucky for you the thief didn't take your money, too."

"Huh? My money?" Farm Girl almost panicked since she didn't understand the woman's comment.

"Yes, your money. It just appears very strange that someone would steal your clothes and not take your money, too. I'm assuming, of course, that you do have money to make purchases today?"

"Oh, well, I" ... *Assume? Purchases? What a funny way to ask if'n I has money.* "Yes, I does has my money. I always be burying my money so no thief can find it.

Does you do chores here?"

Buried? Chores? "If you mean, do I work here, the answer is yes. I'm the saleslady."

"Well, Missus Saleslady, Mister Woody—he teld me I can call him that—says a pharmacist mans sells people medicine, like he done sold me. What do a saleslady do?"

Dear Lord, what does it look like I do in here, sell groceries? "I sell the clothes in this store. Customers call me Dora. If you plan on making a purchase, what size clothing do you wear?"

Deciding a little honesty, now and then, wouldn't hurt, she responded the best way she knew how. "Well, Missus Dora, since I be eleven, my mama was making my clothes fur me. So, I doesn't know fur sure what size I be wearing. Ah-chew! Ah-chew! Excusy."

Her sneezes discharged mists of fluid across the counter of clothes. Even though Dora was on the other side of the counter, she still backed up a step and cupped her hand over her nose and mouth.

Girl, you are disgusting. Your mother should've been teaching you manners and hygiene along with making your clothes. Cover your mouth when you sneeze.

And, if you're going to pass gas, at least have the common courtesy of stepping outside or do it before you come into the store. Pew! I can smell that disgusting odor clear over here. Oh, I wish I had the guts to tell her what I'm thinking. If I didn't need this job, I would. I hate to get any closer to her, but I'm afraid I'm going to have to do my job.

Removing her hands from her face, Dora commented, "You're a lucky girl. Not many mothers make clothes for their children any more. Of course, it is very obvious from the rather unique way that you're dressed that ... " she paused, refraining from further comments of the way the girl was dressed. "Well, dear, I'm sure we can fix you up once we get your correct measurements."

Taking hold of the tape measure that had been dangling about her neck, she headed in Farm Girl's direction. As she got closer, the rank order coming from Farm Girl was overwhelming. The saleslady stopped and backtracked a few steps. In an attempt to block the stank order, she placed her left elbow in her right hand for leverage, giving the impression that she was politely rubbing her nose with her left hand.

My word, I can't stand it. She smells like feces. Oh, I've got to get rid of her, and quick. For two cents I'd yell fire, but I doubt she'd know enough to run out of a building, even if it was true. I know, I'll speak fast and throw all kinds of prices at her. Maybe then she'll get upset with me and leave. Sale or no sale, I have to send this dirty little, street kid swiftly out the door.

The nerve of her coming in here, passing gas and smelling up the place. If any other customers should come in here right now, they would make haste leaving. I just know I'm going to have to spray the whole area to get rid of that disgusting odor she's emitting. I might even have to put the closed sign out and lock the doors for the rest of the day, if I can't get rid of it. Deciding finesse wasn't called for, she asked, "Do you need to use the bathroom?"

I aren't got my legs crossed, and I aren't wiggling around, like a worm on a hook. So why's she asking me such a question fur? "No. I went already in that Mister Woody's privy. Oh, I mean public restroom. But, thank you fur asking."

So, that's what I smell, dirty pants. My guess is, she didn't wipe. I know Woody keeps a clean bathroom and he always has toilet paper. It's obvious, she doesn't know what toilet paper is used for. Whatever it is that smells so rank, I'm not taking one step closer to her.

Keeping her distance as best she could, the woman managed to help Farm Girl select a few clothing items. Disappointed that the store didn't have overalls, Farm Girl ended up purchasing a pair of jeans and a long sleeved sweatshirt. These items were suitable until she could get a decent shower.

After getting directions to the shoe store, Farm Girl tossed the bag of new clothes into the gunnysack, and headed out the door.

"Overalls, huh? I was always thinking Pappy were calling them overhauls." Mimicking Dora, Farm Girl stated, "You overhaul a car. You wear overalls." Farm Girl shook her head. "Crimeny, that's nice to know, but she didn't have to be so prickly about it. Reckon she's having one a them grumpy days. I need to go to that motel and take me a shower befur I goes anywhere else."

Remembering Woody's directions, Farm Girl headed for the motel. She hadn't walked very far when she spotted a large sign next to the sidewalk: Motel Starlite. Inside the office, after paying for one night, she received a room key.

In search of the door with her room number on it, Farm Girl tried to sort out her muddled brain. "Pappy teach me what is a penny, a nickel, a dime, a quarter and some a them dollar bills. But he never told me what no credit card is. I wonder what kind a money that looks like? At least now

I know what pay-in-advance means.

I be learning me some more new words in this foreign language they speaks. Ain't it funny, though, that these here townsfolk speaks a lot a the same words we speak in the farm world." As she jabbered away, she kept walking past the numerous doors.

"I sure has to remember I is Fran Good.

Where is room number—Ah-chew! Oh, here it is, and not too soon. This old gunnysack fur some reason keeps gitting heavier and heavier. Ah-chew! Ah-chew! Ah-chew!"

As Farm Girl opened the door and looked inside, her mouth dropped open. In her eyes, she didn't see a dingy little room of chipped-paint walls and worn-out carpet.

"Crimeny, would you look at this! In one little old day I has gone from the farm world into the town world, and now into the motel world. Look at them beds. Them looks like someone cut one big bed into two pieces, like Mama cut a sandwich in half. Wait, I doesn't want no one else sleeping in here with me. So why did that woman give me two beds?

Farm Girl, you is being a dumb bunny. That woman told you that you was paying fur this whole room with your cash-in-advance money. You doesn't have to share with no one. I reckon you gits to sleep on either bed you want."

It didn't take long for Farm Girl to experience everything new to her from the texture of the carpet to the softness of the bed. After a warm shower, another new experience, and washing her hair, she dressed in her new clothes. They were far too big for her small frame, but they were clean. The old clothes went in the bathroom wastebasket.

Untying the stringer of socks, she used part of the rope as a belt to hold up her new pants. Before heading back to the clothing store, she stuffed her pockets with money for more purchases. After hiding the socks of money between the mattresses, it was back to Clothing Corner.

Dora spotted Farm Girl just as soon as she entered the store. *Oh, no, not again! I already emptied two cans of spray disinfectant around the store to get rid of the stench the first time she was in here.* Her thoughts quickly changed when she noticed Farm Girl's wet hair, and her new clothes.

The rolled up sleeves of the sweatshirt, the shirt hanging below her knees, and the legs on the pants dragging on the ground, didn't exactly make Farm Girl a walking advertisement for the clothing store.

Quick to approach her return customer, the woman said, "I can see those clothes don't fit you at all. Oh, my, did we guess wrong. We should have put you in petites."

With her sensitive nose, she detected the smell of soap. Getting closer, Dora commented, "Well now, don't you smell nice. Seems to me that you've taken a bath and washed your hair." Farm Girl nodded. "It's amazing what a little soap and water can do, making a body smell fresher, and how new clothes can make you feel better."

"Yes," Farm Girl replied, "you is right about soap and water, but not these here clothes. I sure doesn't feel better when they doesn't fit my body very well. Even hand-me-down throwaways fit—" *Be careful, Farm Girl.* "Never mind. All I mean is, these here clothes ain't fur a small body like mine."

"Yes, so I see."

"I cut off all a them little tags. Ah-chew! Ah-chew!" With a rapid turn, the saleslady spun her face away from Farm Girl. "Ah-chew! Excusy."

She might smell better and look clean, but she still doesn't have any manners for Pete's sake. Hoping the sneezing episode was over, she turned back to Farm Girl with a definite frown of aggravation.

Farm Girl continued talking. "I was thinking some a these other clothes you got—"

Anticipating what Farm Girl was going to say next, Dora interceded. "No, no." S*he's certainly not going to pull a fast one on me and get away with it.* "I'm sorry I sold you the wrong size. But, since you've removed the tags and you're wearing the clothes, we can't take them back and give you a refund. That's against our store policy."

"I doesn't know what you mean by a refund or store policy," *accept that they is more new words to learn,* "but I sure knows you cain't take these here clothes back. I recall that I was paying you real paper money fur them. They is mine. I just was thinking since I'm clean, put on my new store-bought clothes, and no longer smell like the manure wagon I ride into town on earlier today, that you could guess a little smaller fur what size I'd be wearing."

"Oh, my, so you rode to town on a manure wagon? Well, no wonder you ... " Recognizing that words may come out of her mouth that she would be sorry for, the woman ceased talking.

Farm Girl paid no attention to what the saleslady did, or didn't say. She started wandering about the store as she had before. This time, however, it was in search of what she really wanted. As the woman followed Farm Girl through the store, they conversed.

"Does you has any smocks?"

"Smocks? Good heavens, I haven't seen women wear smocks in years."

"How does they keep warm when it's cold outside? Does they just wear sweaters, like I done?"

"The last time I knew, no one ever wore a smock to stay warm. Are you sure you aren't confusing a smock with some other type garment? Perhaps, since you mentioned sweaters, you're speaking of a jacket?"

Afraid of saying the wrong thing, Farm Girl just shook her head in response.

Dora measured Farm Girl. Finding out her correct clothing size, Farm Girl selected two dresses, several pairs of panties, and a sweatshirt. "Is there anything else I can show you?"

"I is real unhappy you isn't having no overalls," Farm Girl said with a grin, proving she remembered the correct word. "So, I best be gitting me some more a these here long pants in a size that fits me."

"Many people call them denims. I call them blue jeans."

"Blue jeans," Farm Girl repeated. "That's what Mama was calling them. Is you from the farm world?"

"No, I live in town, but I don't recall ever hearing the term 'farm world' before. Although I can imagine, to an outsider, farming must seem like a world all its own."

With Farm Girl's short attention span, the saleslady's words fell on deaf ear when she spied a rack of coats on a back wall. As she rushed over to them, she remarked, "There's some a them smocks. You teld me you didn't have none."

Following right behind her, Dora clarified, "But those are coats. What gave you the idea that coats were called smocks?"

Crimeny, she must be from farm world, like me. "You calls these coats, too?"

"Of course I do."

"If'n you is learning this here language, like I is, then you need to be calling them smocks."

Completely frustrated, the saleslady replied, "I'm sorry, but I don't really know what you're going on about. I'm not speaking any foreign language. A coat is a coat."

"When I asked Mister Woody about his white coat, he teld me it were a smock."

Turning away and rolling her eyes, Dora decided it was better to agree than to disagree if she wanted to sell a coat. "Oh, I see. So, do you want to purchase one of these smocks?"

"If purchase means buy, I sure does. I like me that purdy blue one," Farm Girl replied with a smile, pointing out a coat. "It's the same color as a summer sky when there ain't no clouds."

After finding her size, the saleslady took Farm Girl into the dressing room with her selection of dresses.

"What's this room fur?"

"This is where you get undressed and try on clothes before you buy them."

"Why? Didn't you say them dresses is my size?"

"I did, but I want to be sure this time so you don't come back—uh, to return them. Just go on in. I'll close the curtain and wait right out here."

Farm Girl tried on the first dress and it fit fine. While attempting to try on the second dress, she got her hair tangled around a button. "Help me! I is stuck!"

The saleswoman rushed into the dressing room. As she untangled Farm Girl's hair, she noticed her customer had nothing on but a pair of underpants with baggy legs that hung to her knees.

"There you go."

"I is mighty beholden to you fur freeing me. Reckon I doesn't want this here dress with all them tiny buttons on it for hair catching."

Dora went back to the main part of the store. Moments later, she returned with female undergarments. Standing outside the curtain, she asked, "Honey, are you decent? May I come in?"

"What does you mean, is I decent?"

"Are you dressed yet? I brought you some brassieres to try on." Handing the selection to Farm Girl through the split in the curtain, Dora said, "I will be happy to come in and help you with them. That is, if you aren't too modest."

"Crimeny, what kind a clothes might them be?" Farm Girl quizzed, looking at the strange contraptions the saleslady held in her hand. *This must be something these townsfolk wear because I aren't never hear a no brazy-zere befur. And I doesn't remember Mama wearing one a them. Mama just was wearing her a petticoat.* "I doesn't think I need me any them."

"Take my word for it, dear. You do."

Taking the bras, Farm Girl placed them on the dressing room chair. Still standing on the opposite side of the curtain, shaking her head in disbelief, Dora explained, "Like I told you, they're called brassieres. Almost everyone today calls them bras, but I prefer to use the correct term for the support garments. I just brought you three to see which style you would prefer to wear."

Listening, Farm Girl removed the last dress she had tried on, hanging it on a hook. Then she picked up the bras. "I may have guessed your other clothes wrong, but fitting foundation garments is my expertise. I'm pretty sure I brought you a size that will be a perfect fit. Are you modest, or may I come in there and help you?"

Muttering to herself, Farm Girl remembered, "Mama always told me, naked is fur the bold and modest is fur the innocent. Crimeny, Mama use to git purdy upset when I didn't leave some a my clothes on when I was washing in the river. She could sure scold me good, telling me I was still innocent, so I should act like it.

If'n I lets this here saleslady come in here, does that mean I aren't no longer innocent? I could stand here all day and wonder about it, but I has other things to be doing." Hearing her stomach rumbling, reminded her she hadn't eaten yet. "Yes, tummy, I hears you.

Let me try this alone first," Farm Girl responded. "Then, if'n I need your help, I'll be asking fur it."

"Okay. Try the different styles. Select the one that fits you snug without being too tight. You want a nice uplift with good support. Let me know if you do need assistance."

What do that mean, uplift with a good support? Farm Girl scratched her head as she stood there looking at the unusual items of clothing, trying to decide what to do with them. After selecting a lacy one that took her fancy, she dropped the other two back on the seat of the chair.

Not having the foggiest notion as to how to wear the garment, she stuck her head through one of the straps, pulling at the hooks that hung down in front of her. Then she bent over and pulled hard, stretching the material to get the other end between her legs. She tried to hook the two ends together.

"Crimeny, that hurts my neck," she whispered. "Guess this contrap— constrict—This thingie aren't long enough to go through my legs and up my back to hook together, lessen I wants to walk on my knees with my head between my legs. I reckon it don't go this way. Besides, it sure don't make no sense what a body would be wearing it fur."

After removing the strap from her neck, she put her legs through the straps and pulled the bra up as far as it would go. Peering in the mirror at her back side, she quickly covered her mouth as she muffled her giggles.

"Even with my bloomers on, I can see my butt cheeks is too big to fit into them funny cups." Raising her voice louder than she thought, she said, "Maybe it don't belong this way, neither?"

"Did you say something?"

See, Farm Girl, you shouldn't be talking to yourself or just like Mama told you, people is gonna think you is touched in the head. "No," she called back. "I were just clearing my throat."

Stepping out of the straps, she decided one last try would be to wear the bra just like one wears a jacket. She put her arms through the straps and hooked the bra in front of her chest, just under her breasts. Once again, she turned to look in the mirror.

This time, playing it safe, she communicated through her thoughts. *Now aren't that the strangest thing. Wonder what you is suppose to carry in them funny cups when they hangs on your back like that?*

Starting to get a little impatient as she waited, and a bit curious, Dora inquired, "How are you doing in there? I know putting on a brassiere for the first time can be very difficult. Trying to get the hooks fastened behind your back, takes practice. If you need assistance, that's what I'm here for."

Farm Girl raised her breasts and looked down at the hooks fastened in front of her. "Behind my back? I doesn't care to lose my innocence, but maybe you ought to come in and help me. Because I must has this darn thing on cockeyed."

As the saleslady entered the dressing room, she had to bite her tongue to keep from laughing. "I can see you really don't know what a brassiere is for, honey. Let me show you."

Dora unhooked the bra and slid the straps off Farm Girl's arms. After placing the straps back on her arms in the correct direction, the woman cupped Farm Girl's breasts with the bra. "Now," she stated, "cross your arms, hold on to the cups, and turn around." Farm Girl did as asked. Once Dora took hold of both ends of the bra, she ordered, "Bend over a little."

With a slight bend from the waist, Farm Girl began to wonder, *Crimeny, what is I gitting myself into?*

"Okay, unfold your arms and let loose of the cups." Just as soon as Farm Girl followed directions, Dora pulled the bra ends back and forth, shaking Farm Girl's breasts into the cups. Pulling the ends together, she attached the hooks.

Now I know what a horse feels like when he gits a saddle on him, Farm Girl complained in silence.

"Okay, stand straight and turn around. Let's get a look at you." As Farm Girl turned, Dora commented, "Perfect. Well, how does it feel?"

"Terrible! I feel like someone is tying me up and trying to squeeze the breath out a me."

"Well, it's not too tight. It will just take some getting use to." As Dora stepped aside, Farm Girl looked at her new image in the mirror. She couldn't believe her eyes. Admiration took over discomfort. Running her hands over the lacy cups, turning to get different views of herself, she listened to the saleslady.

"When a young lady starts developing a bust line, she should make sure those growing breasts receive firm support. From the size of your breasts, you should have started wearing a brassiere some time ago. If you want my professional advice, you should give serious consideration about purchasing this one."

Although fascinated with her new look, Farm Girl had some gigantic doubts about such a suggestion. "Maybe I want me a petticoat, like Mama had. I ain't gonna have no one around to be helping me, and I ain't has another set a hands behind my back. Or is I suppose to wear this thing forever?"

"No, of course you don't wear it forever. Fastening the hooks behind your back will get easier. Just like anything else in this life, practice makes perfect. Of course, it is acceptable to hook it in front of you first. Then turn it around before putting your arms through the straps. Whichever way you decide that works best for you, always make sure you position yourself in a slight bend to fit your breasts proper-like into the cups. Oh, and one other thing."

"There's more?"

"Yes, just another word of advice. As your breasts increase in size, make sure you get yourself a larger brassiere.

Where do you come from?"

The warning antennas lit up in Farm Girl's brain. "Why is you asking?"

"I was just curious. Most females, I know, shave under their arms. I noticed that you don't. Not that there's anything wrong with that, you understand, it's just that I heard some women in other parts of the world like hairy underarms."

Still looking in the mirror, Farm Girl lifted her arm. "Is you talking about them hairs in my armpits?" she asked, pointing to her underarm. From the image in the mirror, Farm Girl saw the woman nod her head. "What's shave? Oh, wait." Farm Girl remembered Mr. Welk telling her how men got rid of facial hair. "You means like a man do to his face with a racer?"

"Yes, that's what I mean, only we call it a razor."

Aren't that what I said? Shaving under her arms would be something she would have to give considerable thought to before attempting such a function. And, perhaps, if she seriously thought about doing such a thing, she would have to find out how to go about it at another time. Right then, she just wanted to get her clothes purchased and get out of there.

Once her selection of clothing was paid for, Farm Girl headed for the next shopping experience.

"I wonder why that there Missus Dora was so nice to begin with, then turn out to be one a them nosey busybodies? She were keeping on asking me all them questions. Is you sure you can pay fur all a them clothes? Where's your handbag, honey? Does your parents live close, or does you have relatives in town? Is you staying in town or just passing through? Why didn't your mother ever told you that you need to wear a brazy—a bra? Doesn't you know petticoats is an old fashion name?

She sure fool me when she suggest I git me a thing she calls a handbag to carry my money in, instead a keeping it in my pant's pockets. I sure doesn't know how she know that. Oh, yes I do. When she put that funny yellow ribbon with all them numbers on it around me to git my size. Don't make no never mind now. Crimeny, I sure is glad to git out a that place and git away from her. At least she told me where I can buy me some store-bought shoes and that handbag."

Feeling washed-out, Farm Girl was finding it difficult placing one foot in front of the other. Consequently, she was moving in a slow pace, stopping to look in windows of various shops. She had forgotten where Woody told her she could get something to eat. While she was curious about what each store contained, she was searching for a place to find groceries. That is, until she remembered something.

"Flying ladybugs! I better quit my dillydallying. The saleslady says them stores is gonna close soon and lock their doors until tomorrow. Sorry, tum-tum, but you is gonna have to wait fur a while longer befur you gits food."

The shoe store was another adventure for Farm Girl. Even though the store was not very big, it had chairs sitting about the room. Looking around, she noticed a man sitting in a chair, and a young girl putting a shoe on his foot.

Following suit, Farm Girl seated herself in one of the chairs. Filling her eyes with everything in the room that surrounded her, she noticed several shapes and colors of shoes displayed all over the walls, on different kinds of shelves, and on all shapes and sizes of tables and floor displays.

Within minutes, a young man approached Farm Girl. "What can I do you out of today?"

"What do that mean?"

Great! Another customer with no sense of humor. "It means, do you need help?"

"Maybe. Is you the saleslady of these here shoes?"

Because of his outspoken and often brash attitude toward customers, Tom's boss had called him on the carpet many times in the past. In spite of his sarcastic mouth, he kept his job in the shoe store because of the limited employee pool in the area. In spite of the warnings, however, it wasn't in Tom's makeup to use a bedside manner with customers.

"I don't know whether to be offended or laugh," Tom commented. "In case you haven't noticed, I'm not wearing a skirt. So, you either don't know the difference, or you need your eyes checked. P.S., I'm not a woman."

"Crimeny, I know that. But, if you ain't a saleslady because you sells things, then what does folks be calling you?"

Oh great, a whacko! "Some refer to me as a salesman or a salesperson, and some prefer to call me a shoe clerk. If it's easier to remember, my name is Tom. Now, if we're through playing your name game, how may I help you?"

Crimeny, ain't that super? He knows about playing the name game, like me and Mama use to play. "I sure likes to play games, but I hasn't got time right now, Mister Tom. I need me some shoes, but—Ah-chew!" Even though he was standing, the young man dodged to one side to get away from her unexpected and rather moist sneeze. "Excusy. I is afraid I doesn't know what size fits my feets," she confessed.

"Do you have anything special in mind, like maybe another pair of boots?" Farm Girl shook her head. "Would you like casual, sporty or dress shoes?" Farm Girl shrugged. "Are you looking for any particular color?" Again, Farm Girl shook her head. Frustrated, Tom asked, "Do you know if you want low or high heels?"

Farm Girl raised her hands, palms up, and shrugged. "I just want me some shoes that fits my feets. And, maybe, I want black ones."

This ought to be fun. I should sell her a pair of clodhoppers to go with her pea brain. Tom slid a stool across the floor and seated himself in front of his customer. "Since I have to sit down here in front of you, please have the courtesy of covering your mouth if you sneeze again. I don't much relish the thought of having a customer's slimy germs spewed all over me."

Frowning, she asked, "What do that courtesy means?"

"Polite. Covering your mouth so you don't sneeze or cough on other people is called good manners. They don't pay me enough around here to have customers spitting in my face."

"Oh, them words courtesy and polite both means manners in your language?"

Oh, brother! Tom nodded and uttered, "Uh-huh."

How come Mama or Pappy didn't teld me to cover my mouth? And why is folks always saying bless you all the time if coughing and sneezing aren't the mannerly thing to do?

As Farm Girl was trying to figure things out in her mind, Tom picked up her foot. She yanked it back. "Hey!"

"Look, I have to remove your boot to measure your foot in order to find out what shoe size you wear. Don't you know anything about buying shoes?"

"I reckon I doesn't or I wouldn't be asking fur your help, now would I?" *Well, well, Farm Girl, you is gitting a might brave with your mouth. Darin told you when you was eighteen that you need to be your own self and not let Mama or no one—*

"Look," Tom stated, growing impatient, "I don't have time to just sit here. Are you going to let me measure your foot, or not?"

Farm Girl didn't relish the idea of having another stranger touch her. However, she needed a pair of shoes. Begrudgingly, she placed her foot on the stool in front of Tom. He removed her shabby, water-soaked boot. Unbeknown to Tom, the boots exterior bore a mixture of everything imaginable around a farm and a riverbed, which gave the worn leather a slimy texture. From the look on his face, Farm Girl could tell her wet boot displeased him.

With his elbows at his sides, Tom held his hands up with a slight backbend of his wrists. His fingers were spread apart and bent at the knuckles. In his mind, he had just touched the grossest thing ever imaginable.

To top it off, the foul odor the boot omitted was more than disgusting. Without a doubt, he was not looking forward to touching the moist foot that came out of the boot.

Farm Girl felt she had to defend herself. It was as if she were back on the farm trying to explain something to Mama so she could stay out of trouble. "I reckon a body cain't help gitting her boots wet with all them puddles a water sitting around everywhere you walk."

"It might help to wear socks in your boots," he replied in a sarcastic tone. "They do help to absorb some of the moisture."

"I always does, but they was too wet and dirty to put back on after my hot and cold running shower."

No, don't even ask. In his typical brash way, he declared, "It looks like you didn't just step in the puddles. As soaked and as stinking as your boots are, one would think you were wearing them while swimming in a cesspool."

Cesspool must be this town world's word fur river. But I doesn't go swimming in my boots. "You know, Mister Tom, when you walks in as much water, muck, chicken dung, dog doo and cow pies as I be walking in, you cain't has no clean, dry boots. Least ways, that's what Mama always teld me."

Chicken shit and Cow crap? Now she tells me. I'm certainly glad I just have to remove one of those rotten boots. If she wants to try shoes on both feet, she's going to have to remove the other boot herself. Damn, I need to go wash my hands, pronto.

Without even excusing himself, Tom left the stool and walked away. Going into a back room, he disappeared from Farm Girl's sight. When he returned, he had a towel in his hand. Sitting back on his stool, he wiped her foot with his towel. Tom reached into his pocket, pulled out a soft material object and placed it on Farm Girl's foot.

Aren't that the funniest shoe you ever did see, Farm Girl? You sure doesn't want them to walk around in. You might as well be walking around in your bare feets.

Looking down at Tom's foot, and pointing, she said, "Mister Tom, I wants shoes like you be wearing that keeps a body's feets off the ground. Not," she pointed back to her foot, "this here kind a shoe."

"That's not a shoe. It's a footsie. And before you even ask, we use it to protect our shoes from customer's feet when they're trying on our shoes."

Satisfied, Farm Girl gave him one of her innocent smiles.

Next, Tom had her stand on a cold, metal gadget that he said measured her foot for shoe size.

Farm Girl knew she would never need to wear leather boots again, just as she knew in her heart that there wouldn't be rattlesnakes in the book world of New York City. Not knowing dress from sport, canvas from suede, or ties from Velcro, she took the very first pair of black shoes the young man showed her and tried on her foot.

"So, is this what you want?"

The shoe fit, had a flat heel, it was black, and all she had to do was to slide into it. "Uh-huh. What does you be calling this here kind a shoe?" she asked, admiring the shoe on her foot.

Making fun, he answered, "We be calling them there shoes, loafers."

"Ain't that funny. Where I comes from, loafers is a body that don't do nothing." She chuckled.

"Yeah, ain't that funny. It's the same word we use in my language."

Misunderstanding Tom's meaning, Farm Girl's eyes widened. "Oh." *Reckon he be from another world, too.*

With one shoe remaining in the box that sat on the floor next to Tom, he placed the lid on top the box to pick it up. As he lifted the box, Farm Girl expressed, "Sir, I doesn't care what I pays fur them shoes, but I'd like to git me one fur each feets."

Thank God, it's almost closing time. "For your future knowledge, when you purchase shoes, they all come in pairs. You get one for your right foot and you get one for your left foot. Now, do you wish to wear the shoes or do you want me to put them in a bag for you to carry?"

"I want to wear them."

"Will this be cash or charge?" he asked, removing the shoe from the box and handing it to his customer. "Here, you can put this one on yourself. Oh, and keep the footsie." *No way would I want to it use again.*

As he waited for an answer, Farm Girl took the shoe. *I wonder if them purdy gold coins is one a them charges or cashes? Don't be sitting here thinking, Farm Girl, ask.* "Do charge mean gold in your language?"

What the hell! I can't even qualify for a regular credit card and she has a gold card? No way! I wonder if she stole it? "I don't care what language it's in, is the card in your name?"

"What card?"

"Your gold card."

"I aren't got no gold card. I just has me different kinds a money."

Good grief! Talking to her is like trying to find your way out of a maze. No way can I accept foreign currency. "We only accept U.S. dollars?"

"I doesn't know what am 'you es', but I has dollars."

"Well, that settles that. Dollars it is. I'll go ring up the shoes and get you your receipt."

As he started to walk away, she stopped him. "Wait, Mister Tom."

Oh, Lord, save me. "Now what?"

"I needs me one a them money carriers they calls a handbag."

I should have known I wouldn't get rid of her that easy. "Sure, follow me."

With an old boot on one foot, a new shoe on the other, Farm Girl latched on to her bag of clothes and her other shoe. She hobbled behind Tom to the back of the showroom.

"This is our selection of purses," he offered, standing in front of wall hooks with an assortment of purses dangling from them. "Pick out the one you want."

"But I doesn't want me no purse. I know I ask you fur a handbag because that's what that saleslady at that 'coroner' place told me about."

What does a saleslady have to do with a coroner? Looking down at the floor, counting to ten so he wouldn't lose his temper, he noted the name on the side of Farm Girl's shopping bag. "Clothing Corner," he projected, looking back at her.

"Yeah. That's where Missus Dora is that told me about the handbag."

As a loud bell sounded off in his head, Tom scanned the surrounding area for a hidden camera. For one strange moment, he thought Farm Girl was a setup. He halfway expected the crew from a television program to be lurking somewhere about the store, taping his reactions to his bizarre customer.

Turning his head, Tom looked in every direction, including the ceiling. Seeing nothing out of the ordinary, he finally turned back to Farm Girl.

"Okay, I get it. You're from *Candid Camera* or one of those kinds of shows that like to catch people off guard, aren't you? I should have guessed it right off that this was a setup. You're from," bent at the elbows, Tom raised his arms. Both hands went up with pointer and middle fingers extended and wiggling, as if to represent a quote before he concluded, "the world of television. Right?"

Uh-oh, he knows I is from another world. But, I aren't from no television world. I sure doesn't know why he keeps looking all over the place and asking me all them questions instead a helping me find my handbag.

And, what's that funny thing he's doing with his fingers? Maybe there's something wrong with him. Mama always told me to never make fun a nobody like that because God make them special. So, I need to pretend I doesn't see how he's acting.

"Well, are ya?" he insisted, making sure he got her attention.

Crimeny, they says ya for you in this here world. Reckon it's okay now if'n I says it too. "No, I isn't from no television world. Now, is ya gonna tell me where is them handbags, or not?"

Realizing he was wrong, he felt let down, somewhat stupid, and infuriated to an extreme. *Why couldn't I have been right? Man, what did I do to deserve a first class numbskull like this for a customer? Maybe I should consider myself lucky that I didn't ask if she wanted a shoulder strap or clutch purse. I'd be here until morning trying to explain everything to her.*

I should have listened to my mother and stayed in school. If I had a decent education, I wouldn't be standing here dealing with the world's dumbest female right now.

Tom was so perturbed, he couldn't look at Farm Girl. Instead, he turned away and kept his eyes on the display wall of purses. "These are handbags. Purse is just another, more common word used for a handbag."

"Oh! Like smocks is coats?"

"Girl, if you want a smock to be a coat, that's your business. I don't sell clothes. Now, if you want a purse, pick one out."

"It sounds to me like you is having one a them grumpy days, just like that saleslady was having when I was there."

Shaking his head, he remarked, "I can see why." Tom walked away and found refuge behind the counter. That is where he stayed until Farm Girl was ready to pay her bill.

After looking over the selection, Farm Girl chose an extra large purse with a long strap on it to carry over her shoulder. She also liked the idea that the handbag was black and matched her new shoes.

As she counted out her money, Tom stopped her. A hundred dollar bill appeared between the smaller denomination bills. "Wait. That's not a one dollar bill you have there." *Fool! You could have pocketed that if you weren't so—*

"Oh, I uh, I know that. I were just confused." In one quick movement, the larger bill was stuffed into her pants pocket.

Tom, not believing his customer looked like she had enough money to pay for her shoes, let alone have a hundred dollar bill, just shook his head in amazement. *Man, never judging a book by its cover certainly applies here.*

Returning to her chair, Farm Girl removed her other boot and put on the new shoe, leaving the old boots sitting on the floor next to where she sat. She took her time and the advantage of sitting in a nice comfortable chair.

Opening the new purse, she discovered it was full of wadded-up paper. She removed the paper, placing it on the floor next to her. Pulling her new clothes from the shopping bag, she rolled them up. Then she stuffed them all into the huge purse.

Placing her old boots and the wadded paper into the now empty shopping bag, she took the bag to where Tom was standing. "Does you have a place to be throwing trash?"

"Yeah."

Placing the shopping bag on the counter, she said, "I'd be a might beholden to you, if'n you'd throw this bag in the trash. Might be someone in your world are needing a pair a boots. They can has mine." While Tom was thinking what to say in response, she commented, "You needs to keep a better eye on folks that comes in here and uses them handbags fur gitting rid a their trash."

"Excuse me," the befuddled clerk stated. "What in the name of— What are you talking about?"

"This here handbag had a whole lot a funny paper stuff inside a it, like an old Tom turkey on Thanks-be-given Day."

"That funny paper is stuffed in there on purpose to help the purse keep its shape." *Oh, I know I'm going to hate myself for this, but I'm dying to find out.* "I love that Thanks-be-given Day. How do they say Christmas in your part of the world?"

Farm Girl gave him a forlorn look and pretended she never understood the question. With an abrupt turn, she headed out the store before the clerk asked any more questions she didn't wish to answer.

Back in her motel room, Farm Girl removed her clothes from her handbag. She couldn't wait to try on a new pair of her underpants. The old bloomers and the new baggy jeans and sweatshirt went in the trash— another one of her donations to the needy.

After dancing about in her bra and panties, it was time to pack for traveling. Before she did however, she removed her shoes. Just a few blocks of walking in them, and dancing around the room, hurt her feet worse then she could ever remember her feet in pain. Also, her feet were freezing, which brought about thoughts of her recent visit to the clothing store.

"Instead a buying me some warm socks, wonder why I let that saleslady talk me into buying them funny thingies she calls pantyhose? I just know my feets wouldn't hurt so bad right now, and they'd be lots warmer with socks on them."

As she took off the one footsie she was wearing, and threw it in the trash, she said, "One aren't no good without the other. Now about them there pantyhose, Farm Girl. Reckon you should try them on first and see what they is like befur complaining about them. They might be warmer than you think. Okay, but later. I aren't has time right now."

Her stomach growled. She ignored it. She stopped to admire herself in the mirror. Running her hands across the bra, she felt the way it curved across the top of her body.

Talking to her image, she praised, "Crimeny, Farm Girl, just look at you. Looks like someone take those young female boobies a yours, tie them up in a mighty purdy package, and set them up on a shelf right there on your chest. They does look a might better, like that, than dangling from your body, like them big ole teats hanging on them cows.

Mama would not approve a this look. Wonder why Mama never be wearing one a these here bras? Maybe because no one was never throwing one away fur her to find. I know you isn't never gonna throw yours away, Farm Girl."

She sat on the bed. Struggling vigorously, verbalizing the many cuss words she remembered hearing others say, she finally got into the pair of pantyhose. "Must be some sort a mean spirited person that make this here pair of funny stockings connecting to panties," she interjected into her voiced obscenities, stepping into her half-slip.

"It's bad enough that I doesn't remember all them words Pappy was teaching me, but this foreign language is confusing me." Covering her mouth, she sneezed, then wiped her moist hand down the side of her slip. She continued airing her confusion. "Bloomers is underpants or panties. Petticoats is slips, and slips can be whole or half. Shoes has too many names fur me to even remember. Blue jeans is denims.

And, overhauls is for cars but overalls is fur wearing. Overalls. No wonder Pappy was laughing at me every time I said that word. Crimeny, it almost take me my whole trip from Sugar Shack to remember to put in-g on the end a my words. Well, I aren't gonna worry about it because I is gonna leave here tomorrow and go to a new world. Ah-chew! Ah-chew! Oh, I almost furgot about my medicine."

She hung her coat and two dresses on the hangers in the motel's small closet, just like she had always hung Jefferson's clothes after Mama had ironed them. Gingerly, she set her new shoes and purse next to the chair in the room.

After removing her socks of money from under the mattresses, she remade the beds. Picking up the necessity bag from the floor, she pulled out her pharmacy bag and placed it on the nightstand. Making the decision which bed she wanted to sleep in, she pulled back the covers then sat on the edge of the chosen bed.

Taking the bottle of cough medicine out of the bag, she twisted and twisted until she removed the top. At that moment, she didn't remember what Woody had told her, and she was too tired to even attempt to read the directions. She tipped the bottle and took a big swallow. Replacing the cap, she set the bottle back on the nightstand.

Off the bed and down on the floor on her knees, she dug through her necessity bag until she found her pencil and all her notebooks. Flipping through the notebooks, she came to one that had some unused paper in it.

"I almost has all a these here books Pappy done give me, full a my stories. I reckon the next time I goes to one a them stores, I need to buy me some more writing paper. I cain't write no stories without no paper. Need to buy me a knife, too, fur sharpening my pencil, like Pappy always done fur me. Maybe I'll also buy me a new pencil, since this one aren't got its erasure no more."

Taking the notebook with the blank paper and her pencil, she climbed into bed. "Farm Girl, ever since you learn how to write, you has write a story about every day and every thing you can remember since you was knee-high to a toadstool. You has so many stories now, that New York City, fur sure, will know you is a real good writer a books.

Just like Darin having him that job in a bank because he's good with money and numbers, I is gonna have me a job writing in a book place."

As she wrote about the day's adventure into her new worlds of a town, a motel, various shops in town, nosey townsfolk, the people who had helped her, spending money, and, every little detail as she remembered it, she started yawning. Her extreme exhaustion was both mental and physical.

Until her stomach growled, gnawing at her insides, she hadn't realized that she had forgotten, once again, to eat. It no longer mattered. Farm Girl didn't have the energy to get dressed and go out again. As her eyelids started getting heavy, she ended her story for the day.

"I wonder how many times Mama was playing that King's X game I teach her when she was talking with me? Crimeny, you and Pappy sure told me some whoppers, Mama. No, I think they was lies. Maybe you two isn't having dinner upstairs, after all. With all them lies you done told me all my life, I wonder if you two is burning in the fires a the devil's land? Or was that a lie too? These new worlds sure is a might scary, but at least they is real."

Dropping her paper and pencil to the floor, she crawled under the blankets, snuggled inside, and fell fast asleep, oblivious to the dangers that the future held in store for her.

FACING CHALLENGES

Bang! Bang! Bang! A woman's voice followed the loud pounding on the door. "Hey, you in there? Miss Good, if you can hear me, it's past your noon checkout. You just paid for one night, you know."

Farm Girl sprang up as if someone from beneath the bed had pushed her up toward the ceiling. For a split second, she was in a daze as to where she was, who was hollering, and who was Miss Good?

"Mama?" she blurted out. After hearing her own voice, she wiped the sleep from her eyes. Taking in the surroundings, she remembered exactly where she was and yelled back. "I is mighty sorry. I reckon I oversleep too long."

"I would say so. It's 1:00 in the afternoon," the woman yelled. "You owe for another night. Make sure you stop by the office and pay up. I'm warning you, Miss Good, don't try to sneak out on me."

"It's 1:00 in the afternoon, why, that's one whole hour after high noon," Farm Girl muttered to herself in her drowsiness before yelling back. "I won't. I'll be gitting my clothes on and be right there."

The voice on the other side of the door sounded vaguely familiar. Farm Girl ran to the window and peeked out the curtains, as she watched the woman head toward the motel's office. "It were that motel woman who was banging and yelling at me."

Farm Girl walked back to the bed and sat on the edge. "Wonder how these here townsfolk wakes up in the morning without no roosters to be crowing them awake? Crimeny, like Mama done told me, I doesn't dare be lollygagging. Hurry and git your clothes on and git out a here, Farm Girl, or should I say, Miss Good. You best remember the name you give her yesterday.

Oh, I don't feel so good," she moaned, grabbing at her stomach.

"Crimeny, this aren't no time to be feeling under the weather. Git moving." As bad as she felt, she forced herself to move in high speed.

Since Farm Girl had gone to bed with all of her underclothes on, she just had to put on one of her new dresses to be fully clothed. In her excitement of purchasing clothes the day before, she had forgotten that the new dresses were shorter than the ankle length clothes she was use to wearing.

"Mama always teld me a young lady shouldn't show too much a her legs nor her body because she's plain asking fur trouble. Crimeny, I know Mama was always telling me things to protect me, but I reckon I doesn't has to worry now about none a them thistles, burrs or other weeds to scratch up my skin. Besides, I got these here thingies they calls pantyhose to protect my legs. See, Mama, my skin's gonna be just fine without no long skirt, long sleeves, long stockings and high boots. I is dressing fur the new worlds."

While she was brushing the tangles out of her hair, she turned sideways to look at her figure in the mirror. "This dress didn't fit me this way yesterday. Wonder why? Oh, goofy gander, it's that bra lifting you up that's filling out the top a your dress that a way. I reckon I has to git use to looking like this."

Keeping expense money aside for her trip, she packed a few of the money-filled socks into her oversize purse. Emptying her necessity bag out on the bed, she discarded the remaining items she knew she would no longer need for on the next leg of her journey. They went back into the now empty gunnysack. The waste can in the bathroom was very small, and already overflowing. She placed the gunnysack of discarded items on the floor next to the waste can.

Mama had always taught her, if she didn't waste anything, she would want for nothing. However, she justified tossing the items in the trash as not being wasteful, but helpful to others. Almost everything she had left, she packed into her purse and the one remaining gunnysack.

One of the few items left to pack was her second new dress. After careful consideration, she put it on over the top of the one she was wearing. Farm Girl was used to wearing many extra clothes, especially during her foot journey. Therefore, wearing two dresses at one time didn't bother her.

After she hurried to clean the bathroom, she made the bed. "Sleeping on a bed with a mattress was just like I always dream it would be. It were just like sleeping on a cloud made a cotton. And them pillows—well, I is gonna have me some a them pillows someday. Someday soon."

Without warning, she doubled over with severe stomach pain. "Crimeny! Ooh! Ooh!" she moaned, grabbing at her mid-section. Hurrying, as fast as she could, she raced to the bathroom, pulled up both dresses, her slip, and, "Oh, drats!" she let out a holler. She had to hold up both dresses and the slip while trying to pull down her pantyhose, followed by her panties.

Sitting on the commode, she shook her head in agitation. "A body needs two sets a hands to go to the bathroom with these here cockamamie pantyhose. Out on the farm, all a girl has to do were to lift her skirt, pull the leg a her bloomers to the side, and go.

Mama always would scold me fur waiting too long. Guess with these new kind a clothes I'll be wearing, I is gonna have to remember Mama's warning and go as soon as I feel the urge. Because I sure doesn't has me four hands. Now that I put my mind to it, you need four hands to attach one a these bras I is wearing.

If'n bras and pantyhose is townsfolk clothes, maybe they has extra hands I ain't seen? Maybe they hides them in their clothes? Anything is possible, I reckon, fur folks who gits diarrhea a the mouth."

The thought struck her funny and she got the giggles, which immediately turned back into groans. "Ooh, my stomach hurts, bad. Come on, Farm Girl, you cain't sit here all day. Bellyache or not, that motel lady is already losing her temper at you fur sleeping late."

It was another struggle for Farm Girl to get her clothes back in order. She rushed to put on her coat. After slipping into her new shoes, she grabbed her purse. Her purse was so full of items, she had a difficult time getting the top closed and snapped to secure everything inside. As she slipped the purse straps over her shoulder, she prayed they wouldn't break from the extreme weight.

Collecting her spending money, she stuck it into her coat pocket. As she tried to pick up the gunnysack, she could not budge it. "I throw most a them things away that I no longer need, pack me my handbag full, and I had me a good night's sleep. So, why cain't I lift this old gunnysack today? It should be lighter, not heavier. You ain't has time to be wondering. Git yourself out a here." Dragging her gunnysack behind her, she left the room and headed to the motel office.

"Ooh! My stomach is sure talking out loud to me. Crimeny, that's my problem. I need something to eat. I was so busy yesterday worrying about everything else, that I plum furgot all about eating until I was too sleepy to care. No wonder you is barking at me again, tummy. I promise to git you food, real soon. Oh, how does I find me something to eat when I need to git my body to an airplane? Sorry, tummy. I reckon you is just gonna have to wait a might longer."

When she got to the office, money in hand and very apologetic, the motel clerk had cooled down.

"I thought you were going to stiff me, honey. Sorry I had to be so boisterous in getting your attention this morning, but you were a hard one to wake up. I had to pound on your door since you never answered when I called you on the phone."

"I is the one who's mighty sorry fur sleeping so long. I sure didn't think to ask yesterday how folks here in your world gits up in the morning without a barnyard rooster to wake them."

"Surprisingly, in my world," the woman commented, tongue in cheek, "alarm clocks were invented a long time ago. Some people carry their own alarms with them. If not, all you have to do is ask for a wake-up call."

"Where I comes from, stiff means hard like one a them boards. And I know what clocks is, but I sure aren't never heard a no alarm clock. Since I doesn't know much a your foreign language, I doesn't understand what you be telling me. But, I doesn't have time to stay here and learn all them new words."

The woman started to make a comment when Farm Girl offered, "Here's your money fur me sleeping late. It's the same count I be paying you yesterday."

Rather confused herself, a little voice in the woman's head was asking, *Who's the dumb one here, her or me? She says she doesn't understand me or my language. What in the hell is that supposed to mean? If I believed in flying saucers and aliens, this might make sense. But, I don't.*

She doesn't have a foreign accent, otherwise I'd think she was from another country. Wherever she's from, someone that ignorant shouldn't be traveling alone. I'll just give her a break and get her out of here.

"Keep it, honey," the woman finally replied. "It's slow this time of year, so no one's waiting to rent the room you were occupying. I just didn't want you to think you could stay longer than what you paid for. Stiff, by the way, is an expression that means to cheat someone out of what is owed them." With the look of total bafflement written all over Farm Girl's face, the woman remarked, "Never mind, no harm done."

Farm Girl put her money back into her coat pocket. "I is mighty beholden to you, ma'am. Now, can you tell me where I gits me one a them airplanes to fly me to the world a New York City?"

"You're kidding?" With the expression of a lost child on Farm Girl's face, the woman answered her own question. "No, I guess not. Okay, our largest commercial airport is over a hundred miles away."

"This, uh, airport, what is it?"

"Didn't you just ask me about an airplane, or are you pulling my leg?"

How come she tells me I is pulling her leg when I ain't even touching her?

"Well?" the woman asked.

"Yes, I wants me an airplane. I just doesn't understand how come you wants to give me an airport when I doesn't know what that is?"

"Look, Ms. Good, it's none of my business, but if you don't know what an airport is, you shouldn't be asking about where to catch a plane."

Crimeny, I doesn't want to catch one. I wants to ride in one. Besides, if'n I had wings to be catching airplanes, I'd be flying my own self to New York City.

Not knowing how to react to the woman's last remarks, Farm Girl thanked her then walked away. She would either have to be brave and find someone else to ask, or walk until she found an airplane on her own. As she started out the door, someone approached her from behind, placing a hand on her shoulder. Farm Girl froze.

"Pardon me, Miss."

As soon as the man removed his hand, Farm Girl didn't know whether to turn around or to run for her life. A quick decision told her to turn and see who was speaking to her. Besides, she wouldn't be able to run very fast, or too far, dragging a gunnysack full of money behind her.

As she turned to the stranger, he said, "I couldn't help but overhear your conversation with Mable—"

"Mable?" Farm Girl interrupted in a loud voice.

"Yes, Mable. She's the owner of this motel. You were just speaking with her at the desk. Anyway, I'm heading to Omaha. That's our closest airport where you can catch a commercial flight. I don't know if they have direct flights all the way to the east coast, but I'm sure you can find out when you get there. My car is right outside in the parking lot. Would you like a ride to Omaha?"

I sure doesn't care what all them other words means, but I is starting to think them airports has something to do with airplanes.

Oh, that must be like a barn is a home to barn animals, or, like the garage-barn were to Pappy's tractor and truck. Maybe an airport's a home to them airplanes? Crimeny, I can has me a ride in a real car. And, this cain't be one a them evil strangers, so maybe it's okay to say yes. I reckon I was lucky and walk me into a nice world.

Jay waited for a response. Noticing the peculiar and distant look on the girl's face, he assumed she was leery of riding with a perfect stranger. With all the kooks in the world, he didn't blame her.

As a father of four children, and a grandfather of seven, Jay was a devout family man. He was personable, easy-going, friendly, and loved helping his fellow man.

"Please forgive my manners. I'm Jason Schmidt. Folks call me Jay. Mable can vouch for me since I'm a regular here at the motel. Look, take your time and think it over. However, I can assure you, there aren't even any buses that come through this burg. And, it's a long way to walk, which might get you there next month, if you're lucky," he joked. "I'll just go over and check out of my room. You can let me know when I'm ready to leave if you want a lift."

Farm Girl gave a brief nod as she watched Jay walk back to the motel's counter. *It's over a hundred miles to an airplane? I doesn't know how far that be but I reckon I can walk there. No you cain't, Farm Girl. That was when you was dressing fur the journey, and your boots was a might more comfy then these here new shoes. You cain't walk a long ways in these clothes, either.*

Besides, you got rid a them thingies you needs to go walking and camping outside. And, how can you be furgitting that you is dragging a heavy gunnysack behind you? I know now what lift means, thanks to that farmer that done give me a ride, but what do he mean by leery? And, what's a burg? Crimeny, my head's too full. Furgit about them new words fur now, Farm Girl. Worry about how you is gonna git to that airport where that airplane be, if'n you doesn't say yes.

As if in a stupor, Farm Girl continued to stare into space. *I always want to ride in one a them cars, so now's my chance. Mama never let Pappy give me a ride in his truck because she were afraid someone might see me.*

She felt like her body jumped two feet in the air when she heard, "Well, what do you say."

"Oh!" she squealed. "You scared me."

"Sorry about that," Jay said with a smile. "Okay, do you want a ride, or not? This is my last offer because Mable just informed me that a good spring thunderstorm is headed this way. So, I'm leaving right now."

"Yes, I'd like that ride. I is mighty beholden to you fur asking."

As they started on their way to Omaha, Jay began asking questions. He wasn't the nosey type, but wanted to get to know a little about his passenger. To Jay, it was just friendly conversation. Each question, however, sent up a small warning flag in Farm Girl's mind. Using her imagination, she spun a tale about being held captive, all her life. Jay wasn't the gullible type, but he listened with an open mind.

"And, Mister Jay, when that mean old man wasn't looking, I just up and run away."

After listening to Farm Girl's tale of woe and feeling sorry for her, he commented, "Dang, Fran, that's quite a story. Oh, and you don't have to call me Mr. Jay. It's just Jay."

"Ooh!" she suddenly moaned from a terrible stomachache. The knife-like pain was worse now than it had been before she left the motel room.

"Are you okay?"

Oh, I doesn't dare tell him I is feeling a might "Sure I is, Justjay."

"No, Fran. My name isn't Justjay. It's Jay." The way Farm Girl was rubbing her stomach, it was clear to Jay that she was in pain. "What's the matter with you? Are you sick?"

Turning to look out the car window so she wouldn't have to face Jay, she answered, "No. I teld you, I feel just fine."

"You know, Fran, I already feel like I've been lost in the twilight zone since I've met you. So, don't give me any more of that hot air I believe you've been filling me with since we left the motel in Jasonville. Now tell me the truth. Are you feeling sick?"

"No, I ain't sick."

"No, I am not sick," he corrected.

As she continued staring out the window, she expressed, "That's good, Jay. I is glad you ain't sick, too."

"If you're not sick, why are you moaning and holding your stomach?"

"I reckon my tummy just thinks my throat got slit."

"What in the name of creation is that supposed to mean?"

Turning to Jay, she clarified her statement. "Someone told me that once when they be a frightful hungry. This awful bellyache I has, well, I think that's from no food inside it." Making her next explanation as colorful as possible as to why she hadn't eaten a good meal in days, Farm Girl spun more lies.

Jay didn't have to believe any of her nonsense. Just one look at her face that had suddenly turned pale and he could tell she was in dire need of nourishment. As soon as he spotted a Wendy's sign, he exited the highway and drove straight to the drive-through. Engrossed with the fast food restaurant and its service, Farm Girl observed everything.

Never having food served to her in such an unusual form, she watched as Jay removed the paper from part of his cheeseburger. Just as soon as he took that first bite, she copied his every move. She tried to take small bites, as she had been taught. However, the food tasted so delicious and she was so hungry, she stuffed her mouth like a ravenous animal.

Pretending not to notice, Jay watched her out of the corner of his eye. When it came to her drink, Jay did his best to try to teach her how to drink from a straw. He finally gave up, removed the lid from her chocolate frosty, and had her drink from the cup.

When they were finished eating, they headed back on the highway. Continuing their conversation, Farm Girl threw in a bit of truth. She told Jay she was on her way to New York to be an author.

As much as he didn't believe one word that came out of her mouth, Jay gave his advice about the importance of an education before pursuing any career—especially one of an author. Also, he convinced her to take a cross country bus instead of traveling by air.

"Here's the Greyhound bus terminal where you get out, Fran," Jay said, pulling up to a large building. "Hold on and I'll come around and get your door." Jay unhooked his seat belt, leaned over and unhooked Farm Girl's. Out of the car, he walked around and opened the door for her.

As Farm Girl got out of the car with her belongings, she turned to Jay. All of a sudden, she felt like a lost child. "What does I do now, Jay?"

"Go inside this building. Look for a sign that says Ticket Window. Tell the person behind the window where you want to go. That person will tell you how much your ticket will cost. You pay that person. That person will give you a ticket. Then, you will be told where and when to get on your bus."

"Okay. Thank you, Jay. I is mighty beholden to you. You know, you ain't one a them evil strangers or like most a them nosey busybodies I hear about."

"The who?" Jay asked in bewilderment.

"Crimeny, don't pay me no never mind, Jay. Like I teld you, I'm plum beholden to you fur everything. Does I pay you fur my ride, like one a them taxi drivers you told me about?"

Jay smiled and shook his head. "No, Fran, just consider it my good deed for the day. *Maybe even for the year.* Look, I have to go. Fran, take care and have a nice trip. I have enjoyed having you along on this drive. Believe me, I will never forget you. Good-bye and good luck."

Farm Girl watched as Jay drove away. Turning toward the building, she walked inside the bus terminal. She roamed around trying to read the various signs. There were people all about, sitting, standing and walking from one place to another. When she found the ticket window, she told the ticket agent where she wanted to go.

According to the ticket agent, the bus ride would take approximately twenty-seven hours. It was the stops and layovers in Des Moines and Chicago that she didn't understand. After hearing the schedule from Omaha to New York City, she commented, "Jumping jackrabbits. That's as confusing as an earthworm trying to go two different directions at the same time."

Having already missed the bus that left at 3:35 p.m., she had to wait for the 10:05 p.m. departure. Her ticket paid for, and having quite a few hours to spare, she walked around and found a small gift shop. With such a cumbersome purse, and dragging the gunnysack behind her, she had to be very careful not to bump into anyone or anything. Inside the shop, she discovered an assortment of items she had never before seen. Farm Girl was like a child at Christmas who had received entrance into Santa's workshop.

Because of their beautiful pictured covers, the magazines caught her attention. "Them are the purdiest books I ever did see. I need to come back here and git me some." Scanning the array of knick-knacks and miscellaneous gifts, her stomach dictated her brain when she spotted the snack section.

Standing in front of shelves filled with a variety of foods and sweets, she salivated. With both hands occupied, she was in a split second dilemma. *Now's when I wish I still had me an apron. How does I git everything I wants together? This am another good reason to have me four hands.*

Then she remembered she was wearing two dresses. She pulled the gunnysack around in front of her until it sat between her feet.

The top of the gunnysack went between her knees, freeing one hand. Managing to get the hem of her outer dress pulled up, she gathered the hem snug into the hand that was gripping the purse. Now she had a free hand to collect the items she desired, and a makeshift basket. Since she was so involved in what she was doing, she never saw the strange looks she was getting, nor heard the snickers from other customers in the small shop.

After careful eye inspection of the food items, she grasped hold of an assortment of candies and dropped them into her makeshift carrier. When she spotted a familiar package of M&M candies, she took every package from the shelf.

When she saw the big letters that spelled out Lay's on the brightly colored packages, she had a quick flashback. "Yummy. I remembers when Mama buy us a big sack a them. They is potato chips." She added several packages of the chips to her candy selection.

Pushing with one foot at a time, she slid her gunnysack across the floor and back to the rack of magazines. Two magazines were selected because she liked the beautiful flowers on the covers.

Looking around, Farm Girl wondered why someone had not come forth to assist her. A service she was getting use to while shopping. When she noticed someone giving money to a woman behind a counter, Farm Girl approached the same counter. Placing the magazines on the counter, Farm Girl inquired, "Does you take my money here fur these goodies I wants to buy?"

"Yes," the cashier replied with a cheerful smile.

Just as she started to empty the items from her dress onto the cashier's counter, Farm Girl felt a huge sneeze approaching. Remembering what to do, she was quick to raise her hand, covering her mouth as she sneezed. In the sudden movement, she dropped the hem of her dress. The small bags of candy and chips flew everywhere.

Before she could say, "Excusy," several customers voluntarily picked up the items for her, and placed her selections on the counter. Standing by like a fish out of water, Farm Girl could not believe everyone was being so helpful. She squeezed out a smile and a nod, but words failed her.

"My, someone sure has a sweet tooth," the cashier remarked, as she started ringing up the sale. "Did you want anything else, or will this be it?"

"I see some folks drinking something out a them purdy bright blue cans with red and white colors on them. What's they be drinking?" Farm Girl asked, pointing out one woman in particular.

After looking at the item Farm Girl pointed out, the cashier didn't quite know what to think. It wasn't very often that she received foreigners in her small shop. However, she thought every part of the world was familiar with a can of soda. "That woman you're referring to is drinking a soda beverage. That particular soda is a PEPSI. It's a refreshing soft drink that's very popular in this part of the world."

"It must be a might tasty fur all them cans I keep seeing people drinking out a?"

"Yes, it is. Would you like to buy one?"

"Nope, I reckon I'd like to buy me two a them. I has a mighty healthy thirst right now. And, if I like it, I'll buy me some more later."

After paying for her large selection of items, Farm Girl strolled back into the main terminal. She felt fortunate the cashier had given her a bag with handles on it, making it easier to carry the extra package around her wrist.

Being an outdoors-type person, Farm Girl headed for a plate-glass door leading to the outside. When she noticed the pouring rain, she decided to stay inside where it was dry. Standing next to the door, watching the rain, she spoke softly so no one else could hear her. "Jay were right. That spring thunderstorm is here and it's pouring buckets out there."

She was tickled, remembering a saying from childhood. "One day, after a big rainstorm, I remember listening to one big boy teasing his little brother. He said, 'Tommy, it rain cats and dogs, last night. Make sure you doesn't step in any poodles this morning on your way to school.' I didn't understand what he mean until we went to live with Pappy, and I ask him to explain it to me. Now, every time it rains, I always think a them goofy words."

Decided to sit for a while, she selected a chair in an area where no other people were sitting. After placing the gunnysack and purse between her feet on the floor in front of her, she placed her bag of snacks and magazines on the empty chair next to her.

Digging around in her gunnysack, she retrieved the calendar Woody had given her. "On the day Pappy died, I look on his calendar so I could remember that day always in my mind. I need to remember it forever because Mama died on that same day. Now, what did Jay say the name a that town world was where I staying?"

Scrunching up her face, squeezing her eyes tightly closed, she tried to remember. "Jasonville," she mumbled, opening her eyes. Since Jay had mentioned the current date during their lengthy conversation, she knew what day it was. Looking at the calendar, she counted the days backward to the date she remembered leaving her home.

"Crimeny!" she stated, somewhat astonished. "I was walking fur twenty-eight days from Sugar Shack to Jasonville. Now I know why I lost me a month. No wonder I was so tired and hungry."

After tossing the calendar back into the gunnysack, she took the small plastic bag off the chair next to her and held it in her lap. Taking a soda from her bag, she made a close examination of the can. "Maybe I should a ask that woman how to open this thing." As thirsty as she was, she didn't feel like hauling everything back into the gift shop just to find out how to open the can. The can was put back into the bag. Retrieving a package of her favorite candies, she began eating the delicate, candy coated chocolate morsels. As soon as she emptied one package, she opened another.

The wait seemed extremely long, but Farm Girl passed the hours away looking at the pictures in her magazines, watching the people in the depot, and running words through her head. Finally, she heard the announcement over the loud speaker that the bus headed to Des Moines, Iowa, was boarding. This was her ride out of Nebraska.

Into her gunnysack went the magazines. The edible items and sodas remained in the plastic carrying bag. Securing her purse and her bag, and getting a good grip of her gunnysack, she headed toward the boarding area.

There weren't too many people in line. In no time, she approached the bus driver. As the driver checked Farm Girl's ticket, he couldn't help but notice the gunnysack she was dragging. When he asked if she wanted him to place her gunnysack in the baggage carrier under the bus, she politely refused.

"Okay. Watch your step," he warned, as he did all passengers boarding the bus.

The bus driver tried to help Farm Girl. Insistent she didn't need his assistance, she declined. Entering the bus, she hoisted the heavy bag and plopped it down on the bottom step. She stepped up on the first step with her bag. Then she heaved the bag to the second step. A thought of encouragement helped her along. *One more step, Farm Girl. You can do it*. While people behind her were becoming a bit impatient, waiting for her to get on board, Farm Girl took one last heave-ho, and managed to get the bag to the bus floor.

That last step was just a bit steeper than she had anticipated. When she lifted her foot, the toe of her shoe caught the edge of the top step, sending her smashing to the floor of the bus. She held on to her purse and gunnysack for dear life, but her goody bag went sailing through the air. The bag's contents were scattered everywhere.

Black Rosebud

The bus driver helped Farm Girl to her feet. A few on-board passengers helped by collecting the packages of potato chips, candies and sodas that were strewn about.

"Are you all right?" the bus driver inquired.

Now I know why he tells folks to watch your step. Like Mama says, the last one is a doozy. "I are peachy fine," she answered without looking at him. She was more interested in her treats. When one passenger handed back her the bag, Farm Girl gave a gracious nod.

"You're sure that you're all right?" the bus driver repeated.

Even though her knees stung from the fall, she answered, "Yes, I are fine. But if'n this be your bus, maybe you could lower that top step a might, so people doesn't has to stretch so far to reach it. There's some folks like me that never done grow very long legs."

Smiling, the bus driver replied, "Yes, ma'am."

Farm Girl made her way to the back of the bus and found a seat next to a window. She placed the gunnysack on the floor between her feet, holding on to it as she did in Jay's car. After laying her gift shop bag in her lap, she cushioned her purse between her and the side of the bus so she could lean against it, securing it at the same time.

Pulling up the hems of her dresses and slip, she bent over and looked at her knees. They were a bit skinned, but that didn't worry her. What did bother her, however, was the fact her new pantyhose now had holes in the knees and the legs were full of runs. Appearance was not why she cared.

Oh, turkey turds! I just bought me these here pantyhose and now they is old already. I look like I has me a skin disease on my legs. They look like chicken legs. Next time I go store buying, I is gonna git me some real socks. They might not be as purdy as these things, but they sure do last longer.

Knowing she had money enough for other purchases, her concern was quick to fade. She put the hem of her slip and dresses back in place, and sat upright. Feeling chilled, she overlapped the sides of her coat to cover her chest.

Now, having an intense thirst, Farm Girl pulled a can of soda from her bag and held on to it. As much as she wanted to taste the contents, she didn't know if she was bold enough to ask someone on the bus to help her. When the bus driver walked through the bus to make sure everyone was seated and ready to travel, Farm Girl got an instant twinge of bravery.

When he approached her seat, she held up the can and asked for his assistance. "Mister Bus Driver, I would be mighty beholden to you if'n you'd show me how to git inside this here can."

Standing in the aisle with a fixed smile on his face, the bus driver felt it necessary to clarify her request. "You want me to open that soda for you?"

Farm Girl nodded. To oblige his passenger, the bus driver took the soda from her hand. When he snapped the tab, the soda squirted out in a fine mist, hitting him in the face. Handing the can back to Farm Girl, he took a hankie from his back pocket, wiped his face, and walked away.

Tipping the can to her lips, Farm Girl took her first taste of the beverage. Finding the taste refreshing, she took several huge gulps. Not ever drinking a soda before, she was not aware of what the carbonation, especially at room temperature, would do to her. She let out a huge belch before making the proud proclamation, "Hot diggidy! This here Pepsie must be fur peoples what a flower's nectar is to bees."

Her immediate response raised snickers from some of the other passengers. Others in her area, looked at her in disgust for displaying such bad manners. Realizing she was drawing attention to herself, she stopped voicing her opinion in such a boisterous manner and continued enjoying her newfound drink.

Then, without warning, her stomach started acting up again. The mixture of the food Jay had bought her, the several packets of candy she indulged in, and now the warm soda gave her pangs of discomfort. As she leaned toward the window, raising one side of her buttocks off the seat, she let out an enormous roar as she broke wind.

Sitting back in a comfortable position, looking back toward the aisle, it was hard to miss the unpleasant glares she was receiving from those passengers sitting across the aisle. With a swift turn of her head, she dropped her gaze toward her feet.

The rotten fumes, her body explosions produced, were more than the people around her could handle. As she sat in her own little world, she was oblivious to the fact that people around her were either holding an item of clothing over their faces in order to keep from smelling the stench, or they were moving to seats further away from her. Farm Girl was used to bad odors, so the smell didn't bother her in the least.

She was unaware that it was very uncouth to expel gas in public. Due to this lack of knowledge, it was just natural that she placed full blame on the soda for making her erupt from both ends. *I sure didn't know that drinking this here soda was gonna cause them piggy-like burps and butt-boppers.*

Feeling bloated and uncomfortable, she positioned herself on one side of her buttocks so she could expel the unwanted gas, at leisure, without any extreme body movement.

Since the bus left Omaha in the evening, it was a dark trip to Des Moines. Because of the darkness, she was unable to see any of the scenery she expected. What she could see, other than the occasional distant lights, was that the storm clouds had disappeared, leaving an array of diamond-like stars filling the sky.

During the two-hour and fifteen-minute journey, most passengers napped. Others had the small lights on above their heads and read books, magazines and newspapers. Farm Girl just sat there, leaning her head against the window. Mesmerized by the stars as they sparkled and twinkled in the night's sky, she thought about some of her meetings with Darin. So other passengers around her wouldn't hear, she began whispering.

"When I start meeting Darin, I were so happy when he'd show up at Room to Write and surprise me. Sometimes, when I was hoping he'd be there, he wouldn't show up at all. I remember how he brung me a gift on his first visit.

Once he brung me my very first taste a chocolate candy. He call them M&M's, just like the ones I buy me today. I was always wishing that he'd bring me more a them sweets, but instead he'd always brung me more toothpaste when I told him mine was all gone.

He didn't come to visit me just to be bringing me presents though. Mostly, he like to ask questions. Boy, Darin was sure one a them nosey busybodies. But I like him, so I just answer his questions. That is, unless they was personal questions about Pappy. Darin sure did want to know all about Pappy's business.

He were so surprise when I told him Pappy done let me git his mail and let me open up all a them envelopes. Pappy told me reading them envelopes and pieces a papers inside were good practice fur my reading and learning new words.

I remembers, too, one time, I was telling Darin about all them neat appliances and tools Pappy had. I memorized three a them names that Pappy told me come from the Sears parent company. There was May Tag, Ken More, and Crafts Man. Them Sears folks was mighty nice parents to put the names a their kids on them appliances.

Darin didn't believe me when I told him I didn't never know about electricity until we work fur Pappy. I was plum excited when I seen me all those appliances and so many other thingamabobbies fur the first time."

Thinking about those days, made Farm Girl snicker. "Darin thought he were smart telling me I had all them appliance names wrong, and Sears parent company didn't has nothing to do with being parents to no kids.

Everybody know about electricity and modern appliances, he teld me, unless they was born under a rock and raise in an old-fashion cow barn, or still lives in the dark ages. He never explain to me what that all means."

Farm Girl took time out from her thoughts to yawn and rub her eyes. She was getting very sleepy, but she didn't want to close her eyes in fear of falling asleep. She lay her head on the backrest of the seat. As she stared at the back of the seat in front of her, she drifted back to her thoughts.

"It were sure funny that day when Darin teld me he were planning on moving to New York City. When I teld Darin I be going there, too, someday, that's when he teld me that I had to do more book learning first.

He teld me the world I live in were a lot different than them other worlds outside a farm life. That's when he also teld me that I didn't talk the same language as them people who live in those other worlds."

Since he find out I like to play games, he teld me that he was playing a game a It with someone. Only, he call the game Tag. I was wanting to play, too, but Darin teld me he had to think about it because he didn't think I was smart enough to play with the grownups.

I know I write me stories about everyone a them meetings with Darin. But daydreaming about them times, like Mama were calling it, sure do pass the time away, especially on this long, old bus ride to the world a Des Moines, Iowa."

DISAPPOINTMENTS

Just as Oscar said he would do, after he purchased a house to his liking, he headed to the bank in Sharpin. He met with Mr. Dodd. As the two men conversed, Cole County's favorite scoundrel was eavesdropping on the other side of the cubical. By this time, Darin had already made his plans to get out of town with his small fortune. However, his snooping allowed him an unlooked for opportunity. Something too good to ignore.

Fresh meat. Looks like it's time for me to come out of retirement, just one more time. I'd almost given up hope of finding one last victim before I flew this chicken coop. Well, Mr. Oscar Denton, welcome to my world. Hmm, no family, no dogs, and new in Kidwell.

Kidwell! Shit! I wish you would've moved to the country or to Sharpin. Well, I can't sweat the small stuff. You can bet I'll have your address before I leave work today. Darin the mouse is going to enjoy getting another good one on that old Tomcat Rusty.

Not moved in yet, but hope to be by the end of the week, huh, Denton? And, you're just another idiot who enjoys bragging about keeping money around the house. Fool! That's like sending me an engraved invitation. I'll be paying you a visit after you get completely settled.

Just call me the one man unwelcome-wagon. Darin stifled a snicker. *Then, hot damn, I'm out of here. I was going to give my two-weeks notice. That won't do now. It would be too conspicuous. I've been smart enough to lay low for months, so I don't want to blow it. Not now. Not when I'm so close to getting everything I want.*

Fortunate for Darin, Oscar's house was located on the same route that Darin took to work. During the workweek, this gave Darin the opportunity to drive past the house twice a day. Sometimes more often, depending on what Darin did on his lunch hours.

Taking every opportunity to spy on his next victim, Darin made special trips to town during the evening hours and on the weekends. Other than witnessing a few repair men, coming and going, and Oscar's furniture moved into the house, it appeared Oscar was a recluse.

Not that he could watch Denton's house twenty-four hours a day, but from all his surveillance trips, Darin was getting agitated. "Damn, Denton! Don't you ever go anywhere?"

Believing his new scheme would never work, Darin gave up hope of giving his final jab at Rusty before leaving town. However, since he wasn't going to get the chance to do so, Darin made up his mind that it no longer mattered. In Darin's mind, it was time to move to his final plans.

Darin gave his notice at the bank, explaining he had a better job offer in another state. Before he could leave the bank, his books had to be audited. Knowing he had to account for every penny, he went through all the accounts he had handled.

As his last official act, he sent out notices to all the severely delinquent accounts, informing them that the bank was foreclosing on their properties. This was a task he was used to performing with or without the bank's knowledge. Confident he had covered all his tracks, Darin wasn't surprised when the audit of his books checked out to the letter.

His last day on the job, his co-workers gave him a small farewell party. According to the bank officials, they were losing a down-to-earth, hard-working, honest employee.

"So long, suckers." Darin laughed, as he drove home. "You did me a good service, and I will never forget you, especially Dodd. It blows my mind how some people can be so educated, yet so stupid. Dodd sure fit that bill, lucky for me."

When Darin arrived home, he immediately went to his bedroom. First thing he did was to change from his suit into jeans and sweatshirt. Taking his suitcase from the closest, he started packing. "Let's see, I can pack light. A couple pair of blue jeans and a few shirts should tide me over until I can get me some classy clothes in New York. Then, I can dress like a real human being. A rich one." Going through his dresser drawers, he selected the few personals to take along, tossing them into the suitcase.

"I can't forget to take my tapes and mini-recorder. Damn! Did I leave those things in the car or ... " Darin had to take a moment to think. "No, I remember. I put them back in their hiding place. I couldn't take the chance that Frank would use the car and discover them under the driver's seat. Since I'll no longer need the tapes, once I leave, I'll dispose of them somewhere between here and the east coast.

Hiding my money with Welk was one of the smartest moves I made, outside of collecting the money. If my hiding space would've been big enough, I never would've needed old man Welk. But, the space is so small, I don't think I could have gotten one more tiny tape squeezed into it. Oh, well, it worked out okay. I just have to remember to pack the tapes before I leave.

Leave. What a fantastic word. Sure wish I could leave town on an airplane instead of riding some stupid travel bus. The bus could work to my benefit, though. Less suspicion on Frank and Rusty's parts if I don't spend a lot of money for plane fair.

Speaking of Frank, I wonder where he is?" Just then, he heard the backdoor slam. "Speak of the devil."

Exhausted and in excruciating pain, Frank was near collapse as he sat down at the kitchen table.

Wanting to talk to Frank, Darin left his packing and hurried to the kitchen. "Frank!" Darin exclaimed, as he rushed over to his chair and knelt beside him. "You're as white as a ghost. You sick again?"

"Just tired."

"You look awful. Can I get you a glass of water or something?" Darin asked, showing a bit of concern to hide his aggravation.

Under normal conditions, Frank didn't take his pills with anything but orange juice. Time was of the essence, so water would have to suffice. "Sure. Water would be great. I need to take my pills."

"Pills? Where are they?"

"Right here." Frank reached into a side pocket of his overalls.

While Darin dashed for a glass of water, Frank removed the container's cap, and shook out several pills into the palm of his hand. Up until this point, Frank had always hidden the pills from Darin. Right then, however, he was in too much pain to think with a clear head. With the glass of water in hand, Darin rushed back to Frank. "Here."

To thank him, Frank nodded. Downing the pills with water, he placed the half-empty glass on the table.

"What are those pills for?"

"That bug I got a couple of years ago. The stupid infection just seems to come and go. No big deal. I'll be fine, Darin. Just need to sit a spell. I don't have enough energy to remove my boots. Help me with them, will you?"

As Darin removed the rubber boots from Frank's shoes, Frank stated, "When I came in from the north field, I was surprised to see the car in the drive. What are you doing home so early?"

"I quit my job. That's what I came in here to tell you. That I—Well, it appears this is not the right time to talk about it. You look like you're going to pass out, Frank. I think you should lie down." After placing the boots on the porch, he washed his hands at the kitchen sink.

Returning to Frank's side, he reached out and took hold of Frank's arm. "Come on, let me help you to your bedroom." Frank felt too weak to move. "You know, Frank, this is utterly ridiculous. I've never heard of an infection that keeps coming back, like this. I'm going to call your doctor."

"No, don't call the doctor. He's doing all he can. That's why I'm taking these pills," Frank stated, returning the pill container to his pocket. "I think I'll take you up on your offer, though, and let you help me to the bedroom. I'm sure I'll feel better after a cat nap."

Darin helped Frank to his feet. "Put your arm around my neck." Needing all the support he could get, Frank followed Darin's suggestion. Darin placed his arm around Frank's waist and walked Frank to his bedroom.

"The fields are a muddy mess. Sure hope we get a few more sunny days, like today, to dry everything out," Frank said.

"Forget the fields for now."

With Darin's assistance, Frank sat on the edge of his bed. As soon as Darin let loose of his support, Frank started wavering. Limp as a dishrag, he fell back in a reclining position. After removing Frank's shoes, lifting his legs onto the bed and making him as comfortable as possible, Darin covered Frank with a blanket. "You rest, and I'll check in on you later." On his way out, Darin partially closed the bedroom door.

Rushing to the kitchen, Darin telephoned their family doctor. Doc Shively didn't tell Darin anything except that Frank was under his medical care and needed as much rest as possible. Dissatisfied with the uninformative explanation from the doctor, Darin had no alternative but to accept the fact that Frank was telling him the truth.

Not knowing the truth about Frank's health, rest to Darin had a far different meaning than it did to the doctor. The way Darin figured it, there was sufficient time to give Frank a decent twenty-four hours of rest, and he could still catch the Friday bus out of town.

For the remainder of the day, Darin lounged around the house watching television, drinking beer, snacking, and smoking cigarettes. Upon Frank's beckon call, Darin helped Frank to the bathroom and back to bed a few times during the late afternoon and evening hours. With the television as a lullaby, Darin fell asleep on the couch.

The next morning, Darin awoke to the aroma of fresh coffee. Leaping off the couch, he ran to the kitchen where he found Frank standing at the stove preparing breakfast. "What the—Frank, what in the hell do you think you're doing?" Darin scolded.

"Now, what does it look like I'm doing, milking cows?" Frank joked. "Coffee's ready. Get your cup."

"You gave me a scare, yesterday. How are you feeling?"

"To be honest, I've felt better. But, I'm going to live, at least for today," Frank replied with humor. Frank began to feel a bit out of sorts, but was quick to determine the feeling was due to his intolerable pain. After taking his prescribed medication when he got out of bed that morning, he was hoping for a little pain relief.

"Doc Shivley says you need plenty of rest. I don't think cooking breakfast qualifies as resting."

Annoyed, Frank snapped. "What in Sam hill did you call Doc for? I told you *not* to."

"Hey, don't bite my head off. I was worried about you."

"What did Doc say?"

"Only that you need plenty of rest and to take your medication, as needed, and drink plenty of liquids. Why? What did you think he was going to say? What are you keeping from me?"

"Nothing. Look, I'm sorry for getting upset, but you worry too much." *You must be sick, old man, or those words wouldn't have come out of your mouth. For years, you've complained silently how Darin doesn't care about you or anyone else. Now, he's proving your wrong. Maybe it's time—*

"Frank, did I lose you?"

"Huh? Oh, uh, no. Come on, get your coffee. Breakfast will be ready soon."

Both Darin and Frank had favorite coffee mugs. For as long as Darin could remember, whenever Frank made coffee, he always placed the two mugs on the counter next to the coffeemaker. This morning, there was but one mug in view. As Darin filled his cup, he inquired, "Where's your coffee cup?"

"Still in the cupboard."

"Why? Aren't you drinking coffee this morning?"

"Nope. That caffeine will kill you, you know," he said with a laugh. Pointing to his empty juice glass sitting on the counter, he requested, "You can pour me another glass of juice, though, if you would?"

"Sure, Frank." Darin set his mug on the counter. Once he had Frank's glass filled with juice and placed within Frank's reach, he picked up his coffee. Standing within close proximity of the stove, Darin butted up against the counter and watched Frank crack eggs into a skillet.

Making small talk, Darin asked, "Did you hear the rain last night?"

"Guess not. Just what we needed, huh? The fields are already too muddy to work in.

Sit down, Darin, you're making me nervous."

"Yeah, that'll be the day." Darin laughed.

"You know, Frank, I can count the times on one hand that I've ever seen you fixing breakfast in your robe and pajamas."

"I've got good reason. I've gotten behind on the laundry. Seems I don't have any clean shorts. Thought I'd wait until after breakfast, then put a load in the washer."

Now I suppose, the lecture starts about spending so much on me that he can't afford extra skivvies. With all his money ... Well, I'll ward that off in a hurry. Anyway, I'm not taking everything with me. "They might be a little big for you, but I've got several extra pairs. I'll give you some until you get yours washed. Better yet, you can keep them. After all, what are brothers for if they can't share?"

Giving a chuckle, Frank replied, "Sharing is good, but no thank you. If I wore your skimpy little jockeys, I'd be walking around, all day, pulling cotton out of my butt. I'll stick to my boxers, thank you very much."

"Very funny."

Checking the eggs with a pancake turner, Frank stated, "Sausage and toast are warming in the oven and the eggs are almost ready." He laid the pancake turner on the counter. Reaching for his glass of juice, he suddenly collapsed to the floor on his knees.

Slamming his cup to the counter, coffee flying in the air, Darin launched forward to catch Frank from going down on his face. Helping Frank to his feet, Darin walked him to the kitchen table and sat Frank on a chair. "You're scaring the shit out of me. Dammit, Frank, don't give me any more baloney about an unknown bug. Tell me what's wrong," Darin demanded.

"Guess Doc was right about that rest. I should've stayed in bed. The old legs suddenly feel like rubber," he responded, forcing a grin. "Just help me back to my bedroom and I'll lie back down for a while."

Darin took a firm hold on Frank, and walked him back to his bedroom. After removing his robe, he put Frank back to bed.

"Bring me my orange juice and get my pills out of my pocket," Frank requested, pointing to his robe Darin had thrown over the bedroom chair.

"Haven't you taken your pills this morning."

"Yes."

"You're not taking too many of those things, are you?"

"Darin, I'm a grown man. I know how many pills I can, or can't take. You know, I'm too weak to argue with you, right now. Just bring me my pills."

Displeased over the situation, Darin got the pill bottle and handed it to Frank. While Frank sprinkled pills from the bottle onto his hand, Darin ran for the glass of juice. Once Darin returned to the bedroom, he raised Frank's head to assist him taking his pills. When Frank had emptied the glass, Darin took it and the pill bottle from Frank's hands, placing them on the nightstand. Then eased Frank's head down on his pillow.

As Frank closed his eyes, he complained, "I'm cold."

After making sure Frank was covered, Darin picked up the pill bottle to read the label. To his dismay, half of the label had been removed. He returned the bottle to the nightstand.

Opening his eyes, Frank looked up at Darin towering over him. "I'll be fine. Just let me sleep for a while."

"The label on your prescription bottle doesn't tell me much. Is there a reason the portion with the name of the pills and the dosage has been removed?"

As his eyes flickered, trying to stay awake, Frank answered with a logical excuse. "The darn thing started coming loose from the container. It was a dang nuisance. Every time I went to pull it from my pocket, the raised corner of the label kept getting caught. I finally just ripped if off."

"What's the name of these pills?"

"Darin, for Pete's sake. I don't remember."

"You've taken them on and off for years, and you don't remember?"

"No, I haven't taken the same pills for years. When this infection flares up, Doc gives me a new prescription, hoping to find one that will work. Look, I don't feel well and I've got a short fuse right now, Darin. So drop it."

"I'm just trying to find out if this is serious, this condition of yours, or if it's really just a bug."

Frank felt as if he had to force himself to speak. Even with his mind becoming a bit fuzzy, he still had to choose his words with care.

"Sometimes, certain antibiotics don't cure what ails a person. In that case, I think, most doctors will prescribe a different kind of medication until they find one that works. Doc can't say, as yet, what my problem is. So, I can't tell you whether or not this infection is serious."

"Do you think what you have is contagious?"

"Of course, not. If it was, you would have caught it before now. I really don't feel like talking anymore, Darin." Frank's eyelids grew heavier. "Why don't you go in the other room, now, and let me rest."

Maybe Frank's figured it out and knows I'm leaving? As long as he's sick, he holds me here. "I'll leave in a minute. Tell me, if you knew you needed bed rest, what were you doing up this morning?"

More questions? I'm running out of answers. Oh, my—"The eggs!"

"They're fine, Frank. I turned off the stove when I got your juice." Darin paid no attention to the fact Frank was starting to drift off into slumber land. Out of pure selfishness, he continued his third degree. "Answer me. Why were you up fixing breakfast, when you knew you should have stayed in bed?"

Taking his time, forcing the words, Frank said what he could to satisfy Darin's questions. "I thought when I woke up that I felt good enough to make breakfast and get outside to do chores."

"Are you sure you'll feel better after resting? Because all the hours you've slept, already, didn't seem to help."

"Of course, I'm sure. That is, if you get out of here and leave me alone."

"Okay. *Go ahead, Darin, volunteer. Maybe it will help get him back on his feet, sooner.* Don't worry, Frank, I'll do the chores. Might as well, since I don't have a job anymore. You just worry about getting healthy."

"Thanks, Darin. That will help me a lot."

Before starting toward the door, Darin inquired, "Oh, I know this is the wrong time to ask, but what ever happened to our newspaper delivery?"

"I cancelled it a month ago. I'm surprised you hadn't noticed before now."

"What on earth for?"

"Does it really make a difference, right now?"

"I guess not. Okay, Frank, I'll leave you alone. I'd tell you to call out

Black Rosebud

if you need me, but I won't hear you while I'm outside." Darin walked to the door, still talking. "I guess I'll just have to check on you, every once in a while."

Darin's words fell on deaf ears. Frank was already asleep.

Having slept in his clothes, all night, Darin went to his room to put on a jacket. A shower and clean clothes could wait until after he was finished with the outside work. The half-packed suitcase still sat on his bed. He slammed it closed, and slid it under his bed.

"Crap. Of all the freakin' times for Frank to get really sick! Postponing my trip, again, ticks me off. Well, I'm sure Rusty, or any of those other cops, have no idea where the money is. So, at least I'm sure it's safe until I'm ready to take it back into my possession."

Before heading outside, Darin peeked in on Frank. Since Frank appeared to be in a sound sleep, Darin closed his door.

On the back porch, Darin picked up Frank's mud-caked rubber boots. Opening the porch doors, he stepped out on the top step and banged the boots together to remove the major part of the dried mud. Since he hadn't done farm work in years, not even to help Frank, he didn't own boots of his own. Back inside, Darin put on the boots and Frank's work gloves.

Grabbing a clean milk pail, he walked outside, leaving the porch door open and taking care not to slam the screen door. "These old boots don't fit as well as they did when I was wearing Frank's work shoes inside them, but at least this is the last time I'll have to wear them. Of course, that depends on the weather and how long I have to do chores. As much as I hate wearing these hideous farmers' boots, they sure kept law off my tail, especially Rusty.

Wow! Soon I'll be out of here. Hallelujah!" he yelled, jumping in the air like a small child, causing the milk pail to swing back and forth in the swivel that connected it to its wire-like handle.

Darin took care of the livestock, making sure they were all fed and had plenty of drinking water. After milking the cows, he separated the milk. The milk was poured into the clean milk pail. Cream was poured into a clean jar to take into the house. Then he took the milk suds from the separator and slopped the hogs.

As he was pitching hay for the cows, a police car drove up the drive. Darin walked to the barn door and saw Rusty behind the wheel. Rusty spotted Darin and rolled down his car window.

"Hey, Darin," Rusty said in a loud voice that carried to where Darin was standing, "I thought you were Frank for a minute there. What the devil are you doing out here? Get a day off from the job?"

Turning off the engine, Rusty got out and stood beside his car. Darin heard him clear enough but chose to ignore Rusty's curiosity. He put down the pitchfork, and strolled over to where Rusty was standing. Trying to make light of the fact that Rusty showed up uninvited, Darin asked, "What are you doing here, Chief Simmons? Lose your way to town?"

"No. Just driving around, checking out a few things. Thought I would beg a cup of coffee off of Frank, since I was in the neighborhood. Is he around?"

"Frank is sick in bed." *If you think I want you nosing around here, you're mistaken, big time. And, I'm not going to offer you a cup of coffee. So, take the hint and leave.*

"Sick? Then I need to go in and check him out," Rusty said, starting toward the house.

Since when did you get a medical degree? Check him out, my ass. Darin dodged in front of his unwanted visitor. Like a traffic cop gesturing *stop*, he blocked Rusty with his body. "Wait a minute, Chief Simmons. My brother is real sick and he's sleeping right now. I don't want you disturbing him. The doctor says he needs his rest, and I'm going to make sure he gets it."

Why, you little—Cool it, Rusty. He's just protecting his brother. I wonder if Frank told Darin, yet, just how sick he really is? Just in case he hasn't, I better be careful and not give it away. I've got to get in there and talk to Frank, though. I've got some news for him.

"Calm down, Darin. I don't want to bother him if he's sleeping. Say, you don't mind letting an old guy with weak kidneys use your bathroom before I head back to town, do you?"

Town isn't that far from here so you're not ... Don't be stupid, Darin. If you act suspicious, the chief will think you're up to something. Let him use the bathroom, then send him packing. Wait. He doesn't suspect you're the one he's been chasing, so by acting gracious you can keep it that way.

"Darin, is it okay?"

"Huh? Oh, sure." Darin lowered his hands and took off his gloves. He reached out and clutched Rusty's arm, giving it a cordial squeeze. "Look, I'm sorry for being so over-protective of Frank. Come on in. I was just thinking, I'm ready for coffee break. How about having that cup of coffee with me before you leave. While you're here, I'll check and see if Frank's awake," Darin offered, hoping he was doing the right thing.

"Hey, Darin, that sounds mighty good on a cool June morning." Darin started toward the house, walking in the mud as he had done all morning. Not wanting to get his western boots too muddied, Rusty lingered behind, attempting to walk on the harder ground where there was less mud. "Where in the blazes is that sun and warm weather we generally get by now?"

"Who knows. We're in Nebraska, remember? It's the one place I know where you can wear a fur coat one minute and a pair of swim trunks the next."

"Yeah. As unpredictable as a turtle race," Rusty laughed. "Say, I've got to … " Rusty hesitated, then suggested, "Look, Darin, you go on in." Rusty stopped walking. "I'll catch up to you in a minute."

Turning, Darin asked, "Something wrong?"

"No, nothing's wrong. I just want to call the station and tell the guys I'll be here for a while. I'll call from the car radio."

"You're welcome to the use the phone in the house."

"Thanks, but the radio's fine. It'll just take a minute."

As Rusty checked in with his office, Darin went inside the house. After Rusty made his call, he headed back toward the house. Once again, watching where he walked, Rusty happened to spot something familiar on the wet ground. That familiar something was so suspicious, sirens went off in his head. He only paused for a second in case Darin was watching from inside the house.

Turning, Rusty meandered back to his car. On the radio, once again, he said, "This is the chief. Can you read me?"

"Affirmative, Chief. Did you forget something?" the officer responded.

"I need Officer Kelly to get a search warrant and get out here to the Righter place, ASAP. Tell him to bring the camera and cast kit. There are some footprints out here in the mud that lead from the main livestock barn to the back porch of the house, south side.

I want pictures taken and a mold of a couple of these prints. I'll try to keep the suspect occupied in the house. Tell Kelly to drive up behind the main barn and get the samples from the fresh prints closest to the barn. That will, I hope, keep any unforeseen noise away from the main house. Kelly's been out here before, so he'll know which barn I'm speaking of. 10-4."

"10-4."

On the seat next to him, laid his shoulder radio. Rusty was about to pick up the radio when he had second thoughts. "Maybe it's best I just leave this in the car for now. This was supposed to be a social visit, not an official one. Oh, Darin, I hope for Frank's sake that my suspicions aren't right." As he headed toward the house, his thoughts kept churning. *Dammit! Now I've got to be the enemy, when I came here as a friend. Sometimes, I don't like my job, at all.*

Entering the back porch, Rusty noticed the muddy rubber boots that Darin had been wearing were now sitting on the porch floor. He wiped his boots on the throw rug, making sure he didn't carry any mud into the house. As he entered the kitchen. Darin was just pouring the coffee.

"I just reheated the breakfast coffee. Hope you don't mind?" Darin apologized, placing two filled mugs on the kitchen table. "I just checked on Frank. He's still sleeping."

"Maybe we can check in on him again later," Rusty suggested, "before I leave."

Picking up his cup, Rusty remarked, "Thanks, Darin, warmed over is fine. Ha! Any coffee has to taste better than that mud we drink down at the station. Then again, that mud is better than what we had to drink when I was in the service."

Realizing that he had used the excuse to use the bathroom as his means for getting in the house, he figured he had better follow through with it. Just as Darin took a seat, Rusty placed his cup on the table. "Oh, just let me empty these old kidneys first, then I'll be right with you."

"Go right ahead. I guess you've been here often enough. You know where the bathroom is."

Nodding, Rusty headed toward the bathroom. Since the bathroom was in the hallway where the bedroom doors were also located, Rusty looked in on his friend. Just as Darin said, Frank was sleeping. Once he closed Frank's door, he dilly-dallied around in the bathroom, trying to kill time.

When Rusty returned to the kitchen, Darin joked, "You took so long, I thought you might have fallen in."

"Sorry about that, but when nature calls—Well, let's just say I was glad to be on the toilet and not driving around in my car." Rusty laughed.

"Darin, you didn't tell me why you're home today?" Rusty persisted with his previous question.

Man, you have a one-track mind. Well, I guess I had better tell you the truth, or at least some of it. "I got a job offer in another state, so I quit my job. I planned on leaving today, that is, until Frank collapsed."

Rusty didn't like the term, collapsed. It made him extremely concerned about Frank. However, since Frank appeared to be in a peaceful sleep, he needed to keep Darin in a calm and lengthy conversation. "Hey, Darin, that's great about the new job offer. What state, or is that some military secret?"

"As a matter of fact, it is. I want to make sure it pans out first. No one likes to brag about such a great opportunity, then fail. So, I decided I would tell Frank where I'm going, no one else. That way, if it doesn't work out, I can come home and not feel ashamed that I didn't make it.

Being the little brat that I was, getting into trouble all the time, it has taken a lot of effort on my part to prove I'm not still wet behind the ears. Now, I have to go a step further. I need to prove to myself that I can work and live in some place bigger than Kidwell and Sharpin, and not have Frank around to assist in my financial support. Does that make sense to you?"

Darin had lied through his teeth, and Rusty knew it. *Whether it makes sense to me or not, Darin, it doesn't matter because I don't believe you. Just keep talking, though. The longer I keep you in here and occupied, the more time Officer Kelly has to get that search warrant, get out here, and get those prints.* "If it makes sense to you, Darin, then that's all that matters, isn't it?"

Darin was in whole-hearted agreement. "You've got that right."

"So tell me, Darin, will you be doing the same kind of work, whatever that is, in, well, wherever you're going?'

"Uh, sort of. I'll be working for a big corporation. It's a great opportunity for me, and the best part is the pay increase."

"Oh, I'm sure you're right there. Big cities pay a lot higher wages than small towns do. Of course, you have to take into consideration that the cost of living is much more expensive."

I didn't say anything about going to a big city. Damn him, he's fishing. "Well, I don't know about a big city. But, where I'm going, it's certainly bigger than Cole County."

After a rather lengthy conversation about nothing in particular, Darin stated, "Well, enough of the small talk. This has been a good break for me, but I better get back out to my chores. I promised Frank I would get them done for him while he gets his bed rest."

Darin started to get up from his chair hoping Rusty would take the hint and leave, when Rusty reached out and clasped hold of Darin's wrist. "Hey, you and I have never had a man-to-man, one-on-one conversation like this before. Is there a reason you're trying to get rid of me so fast?"

"Of course, not," Darin answered, sitting back in his chair." *Of course I'm trying to get rid of you, you badge-wearing, over-the-hill idiot. You've been here for over an hour, drinking one lousy cup of coffee and asking me too many questions. Now what?*

Rusty let loose of Darin's wrist, and got up from his chair. Getting the coffeepot, he poured Darin and himself more coffee. As he replaced the coffeepot in its stand, he glanced out the window. Noticing that Officer Kelly's patrol car was parked at the side of the barn, and visible from the kitchen window, he had to keep Darin inside for a while longer. Rusty sat back at the table.

Just what I need, another cup of coffee and more bull with the pitiful police chief. When a noise interrupted his train of thought, Darin got to his feet. "Did you hear something?"

"Nope." Rusty had to think fast. "Say, if you heard something, maybe it was Frank? Should we go see if he is awake? If it was him, maybe he needs something."

When Darin turned toward the window, Rusty quickly got to his feet again, as if to stretch. He commenced twisting his shoulders around, and rotating his head. He acted as if he was trying to get the kinks out of his body, when he was actually blocking Darin's view.

"Drat this arthritis," Rusty complained, "sure gets the old joints tightened up with all this damp weather."

"I thought the noise came from outside, but I'll go check on Frank, just in case it was him." Giving Rusty a fake smile, Darin headed to Frank's bedroom. When he returned, he shook his head, as he sat back in his chair.

Sitting back at the table with Darin, Rusty picked up the conversation again. *I'm almost positive those are Darin's prints. However, I should find out if there's been anyone else around.* "So, with Frank sick, I can assume he hasn't been outside this morning."

"You assume right."

"I imagine, since you've had a day job for a few years now, doing the chores, alone, is a little rough on you?"

"Alone and rough are the key words. That's for sure. It would be great to have help, but no such luck. Just me, myself, and I doing the chores. I know it doesn't bother Frank to do chores by himself, but he likes farming."

"Yeah. It's a shame a neighboring farmer didn't just happen over this morning to help you out."

"No such luck."

"It poured in town last night. Did you get any of it out here, or is all that mud out there from the last rain?"

"Yeah, we got the storm last night." Darin frowned. "That's rather an odd question, since I can't remember a time that we didn't get the same weather as you get in town. What's your point?"

"Yeah, I guess that did seem a bit odd. Reckon I was just thinking how much easier it would be for you walking around out there in all that mud, if you could walk in a path already made by Frank. That's all."

"Oh. Well, again, no such luck. The rains washed away most of Frank's tracks. The remaining tracks, the deeper ones, were filled with too much water to step in."

Well, Darin, thanks for confirming what I already knew. Now to find out how much you know about Frank's health. "So, tell me, how sick is your brother?"

"Can't say as I know for sure," Darin answered before taking another drink of coffee. "He's been taking a prescription that the doctor gave him. All Frank will tell me is that he has a bug. You should have seen him yesterday. He was as white as a ghost. After he took his pills, I took him straight to bed.

I phoned the doctor, but he wasn't what I would call an encyclopedia of information. Anyway, I figured Frank would sleep in today. But, when I got up this morning, the screwball was fixing breakfast. One minute he was fine. The next thing I knew, he collapsed to the floor. That's when I put my foot down. I took him back to bed and gave him strict orders to stay there and get well."

"So, the doctor didn't tell you much, huh?"

"That quack. He just told me that Frank needs plenty of bed rest—" Another noise caught his attention. "Are you sure you don't hear something outside? I could swear—"

"Relax, Darin. It's possible you're a little jumpy because you're worried about Frank. Can't say as I blame you. I'm worried about him, too. Drink your coffee and calm down. Trust me. I don't hear a thing and I have good, police-trained ears." *Shit! That was without a doubt the most stupid statement I ever made in my law enforcement career. Police-trained ears! What for the love of Mike does that mean?*

Come on, hurry up out there, Kelly, then get out of here. I can't stall much longer, and I don't want Darin to even think that I'm checking him out. He could be as clean as the morning wash, but if he thinks he's a suspect, Darin will bolt, like a wild stallion.

Empty mug in hand, Rusty stood and walked to the sink. As he did, he glanced toward the window and noticed Officer Kelly's car was gone. After rinsing the mug, he placed it on the counter. Relieved, he turned to Darin, who was still sitting at the table.

"Well, I want to thank you for the coffee and pleasant chat. Now, if you don't mind I would like you to check on Frank just once more before I go. He's like my brother, you know? Ever since I lost Stu, well, Frank has always been there for me and me for him. I'm sure you understand."

The main thing I understand, you snake in the grass, is you treat me like a wicked stepchild. Yes sir, Chief Simmons, sir. Kiss my royal, naked ass, sir. "Oh, of course I understand. Come on, we'll go to the bedroom together," Darin stated, heading toward the back hallway. *Anything to get rid of you.*

As they got to Frank's room, Darin opened the door so they could look in. Frank just happened to be opening his eyes at the time. Rubbing the sleep from his eyes, he cleared his vision. Frank smiled as he focused on the two figures standing at his door.

In a hoarse whisper, Frank said, "Rusty, is that you?"

"It sure is, Frank," Rusty answered.

"Hey, and Darin. Come closer, you two."

Darin stepped aside, allowing Rusty to enter the room first. As he walked to Frank's bedside, followed by Darin, Rusty sat down on the edge of the bed. As he spoke, he kept his head turned toward Frank so Darin couldn't see his face. "How you feeling, buddy?" With quick eye movements, Rusty was silently indicating to Frank that he wanted Darin out of the room.

Even in his sleepy state, Frank caught the obvious hint. Feeling like he was in slow motion, he chose his words carefully. "Darin, have I been ah-sleep long?"

"A few hours."

"It's time for my pills'n juice, and a cup a coffee? That should help me get ah-wake."

"Sure, Frank, I'll get your juice but there's no coffee left. Chief Simmons and I emptied the pot from breakfast. Wait. Didn't you tell me this morning that you quit drinking coffee?"

"Changed my mind. Make some—"

The difficulty Frank was having, speaking, was quite obvious to Rusty. His immediate reaction was to take over. "Yes, Frank, that sounds like a great idea. How about it, Darin? Brew a fresh pot for your brother. I'll stay in here and keep him company."

You don't give me orders, Rusty. I have half a mind to—You're damn lucky I've got too much to lose, right now. Darin had a hard time hiding his anger, as he stated, "Fine. But don't overdue it, Frank. You *need* to get well."

Turning to Frank, as Darin left the room, Rusty leaned down, getting as close as he could to Frank's ear. "What's wrong with your voice, Frank? You're barely speaking above a whisper, and your speech seems a bit abnormal. Is this due to the cancer?"

"Just tired. Nothing to worry ah-bout."

"Okay, I'll take your word for it. I'll say what I have to, then get out of here and let you get back to sleep. The last time we spoke about that woman you're looking for, I told you how ironic it was that her trial led right here to Kidwell." Frank gave a slow nod. "I contacted an organization that specializes in finding long lost relatives and friends. Another big fat nothing, I'm afraid," Rusty whispered. "It doesn't look good, Frank."

"Don't give up."

"I have to be honest. I've worked on this for two years now. With just a first name and being a farmhand to go on, the chances of finding her are slim to none. My sources are running dry. It seems like your ladyfriend just fell off the end of the earth. I won't give up, not yet," Rusty assured him. "But I was kind of hoping you could give me more information to go on."

Hearing the sound of Darin's footsteps coming down the hallway, Rusty sat straight. In an immediate switch of words, he got into a normal conversation. "You're one lucky guy having a brother, like Darin, around to help you out."

"He's a good boy."

Darin walked in, carrying a glass of orange juice. "Hey, is that all you two have to talk about is me?" He placed the juice on the nightstand. "How many pills, Frank?"

"Two for now."

As he took two tablets out of the prescription container, Darin commented, "I've decided that coffee will just keep you awake. So, you're not getting any until you're feeling better. Orange juice and pills will have to do."

Rusty chuckled. "Well, Frank, you can't argue with a man when you know he's right."

Holding the pills while picking up the juice glass, Darin requested, "Chief Simmons, if you'll help Frank raise his head, I'd appreciate it."

Rusty was more than happy to assist. After Frank took his pills, and was resting comfortably back on his pillow, Frank said, "Okay. Go on now, you two, and let a man rest."

"Okay, Frank," Rusty said. "If there's anything you need, you just tell Darin and he'll call me. Anything, Frank. I mean it."

Leaving the pill bottle on the nightstand, Darin picked up the empty glass.

Answering Rusty, Frank replied, "Thanks, Rusty. I'm in good hands."

"You stay in bed and get lots of rest, like the doctor ordered, and get your strength back," Rusty stated. "I'll be checking on you."

Echoing Rusty's sentiments, Darin commented, "Chief Simmons is right, Frank. It's a good idea to go back to sleep and get your strength built back up."

As Darin followed Rusty to the back porch, Rusty stopped before going out the screen door. He focused his attention to the floor. "Those your boots, Darin?"

"No, they're Frank's. I just wore them to do chores. Why?"

"They're pretty muddy. Looks like you might want to clean them up for Frank before he wears them again. I know how picky he is. Of course, with all this rain we've had, everything seems to be staying muddy."

"Yeah. Well, I don't have boots of my own, so I have to wear his. I'll probably wear them again when I go back out to finish chores. You don't have to worry, Chief Simmons, I'm more persnickety than Frank. When I'm through, those boots won't have a trace of mud on them.

Thanks for stopping. I'll keep you informed as to how Frank's doing," Darin said, as Rusty walked out the door.

So you're persnickety, huh, Darin? Well, so is my Neat Nick Thief. I need to get to the station to see what information Kelly has for me. I hope for your sake, Darin, as well as for Frank's, that I am dead wrong about my suspicions.

At the Kidwell Police Department, as soon as Rusty walked in the door, he could tell by the look on Officer Kelly's face that what he dreaded to hear was going to knock him for a loop. "Kelly?"

"I'm sorry, Chief, but they're an exact match."

"Dammit! Why? Why do they have to match? What in the hell is wrong with this world today, Kelly? Damn that kid! Come into my office."

As Rusty took a seat behind his desk, Kelly sat in the chair on the opposite side. "You're sure, Kelly? I mean, one hundred percent positive? There can't be a mistake." Rusty hoped against hope that there might be just a small margin of error.

"No. No mistake. The prints are an exact match for foot size and sole design. Whose prints did I pick up out there?"

"Darin's."

"I rather assumed as much," Kelly replied.

"Actually, they're Frank's boots, but I know darn well that Frank isn't our Neat Nick Thief. Heck, most of those burglaries took place on Friday nights. I know for a fact that Frank has never missed a Friday night poker game. That conniving little punk walked right in front of me, so I knew he made those prints in the muddy ground."

"It's a good thing you've got a good eye for details."

"Well, that definite waffle-like print wasn't hard to spot in the mud."

"That's what I call being at the right place, at the right time."

"Amen to that, Kelly. Darin has got to be the thief we've been looking for."

"I'm sorry, Chief. I know how close you and Frank are." The chief sat quietly, pursing his lips. "So, what do we do next?"

"In order to be proof-positive, we'll send all of the casts we've accumulated to the FBI Crime Lab. After we get their report of the comparisons, then we'll know for sure. Dammit! This will kill Frank. He's so sick right now, I don't know how he'll take it if we arrest Darin."

"Frank's sick?"

"Yeah. He's in bed with … " Rusty paused. He had to think of what to say so he wouldn't give away Frank's secret. "He's got some kind of a bug, like the flu or something. Why couldn't Operation Ivy work so we could make an official arrest, not one based on suspicion?"

"Chief, may I offer a suggestion?"

"Of course you can. I value your opinion, Kelly. You know that. What is it?"

"I've been just as frustrated about catching up with this thief as you have. So, I was going over the case files, again. It's plain that this Neat Nick Thief only struck when the victims were away from their homes for a good length of time. My point being, Clinger is always home."

"You're right." Rusty made a fist and pounded it on the top of his desk. "We missed that."

"I don't think we missed it, Chief. We have to remember that it's been a few months since the last burglary occurred. I don't think either one of us even thought about the homes being vacated by the victims when we were setting up this sting."

"Yes, maybe you're right, but that's an important fact neither of us should have forgotten. It's a darn good thing you decided to go over the files, for what, the umpteenth time?"

"Something like that," Kelly responded with a grin.

"Okay, maybe we won't arrest Darin, yet. Let's get Clinger to join some kind of club, or something that gets him out of the house for a few hours in the evening, at least once a week. It has to be for the same amount of time on the same day, like a fixed schedule. You know, since Frank is sick, that means Darin will be staying in town for a few days. So, if Darin is our suspect, he may go for one last take."

To Kelly, everything was adding up. Instead of jumping right in with his information, he wanted to find out first what Rusty had to say. "Who told you Darin was leaving town?"

"Darin did. Seems Darin quit his job because he has some big job offer out of state. He said he planned on leaving today, but Frank's collapse detained him. He's just staying around long enough to help out on the farm. I sure hate to see Frank down like that, but maybe it's a blessing in disguise. It gives us one last chance for Operation Ivy to work. We'll either prove our suspicions wrong about Darin, or bury him. As soon as were through here, get on the horn and tell Clinger what we need him to do."

"Chief, I know you and Frank are like brothers," Kelly said, looking rather worrisome.

"Point being?"

"Did Frank ever tell you where Darin worked?"

"Let's see," Rusty responded, giving the question a lot of thought. "I don't believe he ever mentioned it, and I never bothered to ask. In fact, even when I spoke with Darin earlier, he said that he quit his job. However, he never mentioned where he worked. Why?"

"Hold on to your shorts. When I reread the Dodd report, there was mention of him having an assistant. This was earlier, before you called me out to the Righter place. Just out of curiosity, I called the bank and spoke with Dodd. Guess who is assistant was?"

"Darin?"

"Darin. Actually, Darin was a top accountant, but Dodd had considered him his right arm. Dodd also told me that, as of yesterday, Darin no longer worked for the bank because he got a better job offer out of state."

"What a lamebrain I am. In all this time, I never gave one thought about checking out any one working in close association with Dodd. Damn, maybe it's time to hang it all up? It seems there are more holes in this case than a sieve because of facts I've been overlooking."

Kelly shook his head. "Hey, Chief, we all make honest blunders. Shoot, I'm the one who wrote up the report, and it never dawned on me to check out who the assistant was to Dodd. Nor did I ever suspect Darin worked at the bank. So, we both made a mistake. So what? Do we throw in the towel, or do we catch our mutt?"

There was no doubt as to what to do.

"For almost three grueling years, this conniving, thieving piece of trash has been jerking us around. Look, I've got to go to the can. Use my phone and call Clinger. Tell him what we need."

When Rusty returned to his office, Kelly said, "Okay, it's all set. Clinger says he needs to lose a few pounds, so he'll join the athletic club in town. He'll set up a schedule so he'll be out of the house one night a week for at least two hours. He said he would start right away. And, he'll contact us with his new schedule."

"Sounds good. Now we have the trap and the bait. All we have to do is to get the rat to take the bait. Think I'll stop by Frank's, again tomorrow. I'll see how he's doing and find someway to mention our newest Kidwell citizen for Darin to hear, accidentally on purpose."

The next afternoon, as planned, Rusty stopped by the Righter farm. Even though Darin greeted Rusty with a smile, he was not pleased to see him again so soon. Once the forced greetings were over, Rusty asked if Frank showed any improvement.

"Frank's about the same," Darin said.

"Is he awake?"

"No, and I don't want to disturb him. I'll tell him you stopped by."

"I wanted to ... Look, Darin, why don't you call me next time Frank wakes up. I can get out here in no time at all."

"What's so important?"

"Well, I wanted to talk to him about his weekly poker games."

Shit! I hope Rusty isn't here to question Frank about my Friday night whereabouts during the burglaries? I've got to find out. "I've sat in on one or two of his games. Why don't you tell me? Then I can pass the information on to Frank, and save you a trip."

"Say, that would be a great."

"Would you like a cup of coffee? I've got about enough for two cups left over from this morning."

"Sounds good." *Perfect, Darin. Now, I can dangle the bait in front of your nose.*

"Have a seat and I'll heat the coffee." Rusty sat at the kitchen table. "So, what is there about the games that you want to know?"

"Oh, I don't want to know anything about the poker games, Darin. This morning, I met a newcomer to Kidwell. When he mentioned that he liked to play poker, I thought of Frank. I thought maybe, when Frank was feeling better, he could ask this new guy to join their Friday night poker games."

Is that all? I'm stuck with having another BS conversation and a cup of coffee with the chief just because he wants Frank to meet some new guy in town? Shit! Well, might as well make the best of it. "I hope you told this new guy that the old poker farts only play for peanuts. Wouldn't want the law after them, thinking they played for money. I hear that Chief Simmons can be a real son-of-gun if someone breaks the law around here," Darin teased with a grunting laugh.

Rusty didn't know if Darin was joking or being sarcastic. However, he decided to play along which would help him deliver the bait. "You got that right, Darin. Of course, if they did play for money, I'm sure as a widower, who inherited quite a healthy estate, money would be no object to this fellow."

"Oh, well-to-do, is he? Well, he could take pistachios in place of peanuts." Darin laughed. "Who's the new guy?"

"His name is Oscar Denton." That got Darin's undivided attention. "It seems he lost his wife about two years ago. He moved here from Clayridge. Older fella, retired, and, like the rest of us older men in town, says he's overweight. I told him about our great athletic club, so he said he was going to join. He thinks if he goes for a couple of hours a week, he'll be able to shed a few pounds. I told him, lots of luck." Rusty patted his stomach. "Many of us have tried it without good results."

"It sounds to me like this guy ... " *careful or you'll let on that you know about him,* "ought to get settled before he's bombarded with poker nights."

"Oh, he's been here long enough, according to him, and he's anxious to get acquainted in town." After all his years in law enforcement, Rusty was pretty good at reading faces. As he spoke, he was hoping to get some reaction from Darin's face. "That was his other reason for joining the athletic club for a couple of hours each week. He wants to get to know some of the older men around town. Say, Darin, is that coffee warm, yet?"

"Should be." Since Darin was still standing, leaning against the counter next to the coffee machine, he reached over and felt the pot. "Yeah, it's ready." After pouring the coffee, he served Rusty.

Coffee mug in hand, Darin remained standing. "So, tell me more about this guy. I want to be sure to give Frank all the details."

Good, Darin. If I'm correct in the way I'm reading you, my bait is tempting you. We'll soon find out. "Well, Darin, I told Mr. Denton that there are still a lot of us old timers who have to work for a living, during daylight hours. So, he's sure to meet a lot more guys at the club in the evening."

Noting that Darin seemed to be out in space, Rusty knew he had definitely sparked a flame in Darin's head. Allowing Darin to collect his thoughts, Rusty sat in silence, drinking his coffee.

Darin's thoughts raced through his mind like the Indy 500. *Wow, that's the same guy I was going to hit before I left my bank job. This is great news. Chief, you just gave me a one hellava gift for my twenty-third birthday, and you don't even know it. I could kiss you, you old fool.*

Maybe it's a good thing Frank took to bed? I gave up hope. But now, I'll be able to rattle Rusty's cage and get a little extra money, all at the same time. With Frank sick in bed, he'll never know if I sneak out of the house while he's sleeping. Or, maybe, with some extra help, just to be on the safe side ... Um, that's something I'll have to think more about.

This one will be for you, Rusty old man. One final kick in that old ass of yours, just to let you know how much I care. The one nicest thing you ever said about me, and you weren't even aware of it, was to call me a Neat Nick Thief.

Figuring he had waited long enough, Rusty's voice broke into Darin's devious thoughts. "You know, Darin, I just happened to think about something."

"Huh? Oh, sorry. You'll probably think this lame on my part, but you have to remember that it's been years since I've done chores. I was just trying to remember whether or not I fed the chickens this morning."

Chickens—my Aunt Lucy's china. You're making plans already, aren't you, Darin? "It doesn't look like Frank is going to make Friday night's poker game." Getting to his feet, Rusty took his cup and placed it in the sink as he spoke. "So, tell your brother that I'll introduce him to Mr. Denton just as soon as he's up and around."

"Sure, I'll do that."

"Thanks for the coffee, Darin. I best get back to town."

"Yeah, sure. Thanks for stopping by."

After Rusty bid his farewell, Darin closed the kitchen door. "Hot damn!" He laughed with excitement.

Darin took what he wanted from those around him. He was as cocky as a Banty rooster. Although he would keep strutting around, like the rooster in the barnyard with full confidence that he was in charge of his own life, that cockiness would blind him.

TAKING TIME OUT

Although the bus ride from Omaha to Des Moines was just a little over two hours, it seemed like an eternity to Farm Girl. She was used to walking, which kept her body active and her mind alert. Between the car and the bus rides, Farm Girl was listless and sleepy.

The bus pulled into the Des Moines bus terminal and all transfer passengers were to leave the bus to make their next bus connections. Those passengers who were continuing their trip would have a thirty-minute layover before they departed for Chicago, the next leg of the long trip to New York.

Farm Girl was tired of sitting. As nice as riding was, compared to walking, she didn't want another ride for quite sometime. It was dark outside. Wanting to see more of the new world she had ventured into, she decided not to continue on her trip, at that time. Nebraska had posed a threat to her, but since she was now safely away from there, she wanted to stay put for a while.

The exploration into the world of Des Moines would have to wait until the next day. Now, under the assumption that ticket agents were safe to talk to, Farm Girl found the ticket window.

Behind the small window glass, the man inquired, "Destination, please."

"Does you have them motels in this world a Des Moines, Iowa?"

"Do you want to purchase a ticket, or not?"

"No, I doesn't. I already has me one a them," she answered, pulling her ticket from her coat pocket and holding it up.

"May I see it?" Farm Girl slid the ticket through the small space under the widow. After looking at it, he stated, "According to your destination, your bus leaves in less than thirty minutes." He gave her back her ticket. "You don't have time to stay in a motel."

"I doesn't want to go nowhere on the bus again, right now. I just want me a motel. Does you got any a them?"

The ticket agent knew there was an information booth in the terminal. However, since he wasn't busy, he didn't mind being helpful. "Yes, we have plenty of motels. Do you want to stay close to the terminal?"

"Is that here?"

"Yes."

"Uh-huh."

"I don't know how good it is, but there's one just a couple of blocks from here."

"Where does I go to git me there?"

"Turn around and walk straight back." He gestured. "That will take you to the front door. Go out the door and turn to your left. It's about two blocks down. You can't miss it."

Placing the ticket back in her pocket, she thanked him and walked away.

The walk from the bus terminal to the motel was a short distance. Once she arrived at the motel, she realized how exhausted she really was. Not wanting to have another motel owner waking her in the morning by pounding on her door and yelling at her, Farm Girl checked into the motel for a week's stay.

While staying at the motel in Des Moines, Farm Girl took advantage of writing short notes about her journey, since the television in her room wasn't working. Other than loafing around her room, she walked to the bus station three times a day. The depot's small restaurant, which was the nearest place from the motel to eat, was where she ate breakfast, lunch and dinner.

Just before her week at the motel was over, Farm Girl was having her daily lunch at the food counter. Her waitress asked, "Say, honey, do you live around here? By the way, everyone around here calls me Floss."

"I is living in a motel just a short ways from here. Ain't staying there long because I is on my way to New York City."

"You're not speaking—By the way, what's your name, honey?"

"Uh, Martha. They calls me Martha."

"It's nice to meet you, Martha. Now, as I was saying, you aren't speaking of that rat-trap a few blocks down the street from here, are you?" Not sure of what the woman was referring to, Farm Girl nodded to be polite. "You're kidding? If you're going to New York, why are you staying in that dump?"

I know what it is to take a dump, but it don't sound like that's what she means. That word must be different in this language? "I ain't never seen me no rats where I is, and what's a dump?"

"That motel's a dump, for one thing."

"I doesn't rightly know what you mean by a dump."

"That roach-ridden, hole in the wall they call a motel. Then they have the nerve to charge people to stay in one of their shabby rooms. Now that's a first-class dump."

As she spoke, Floss proceeded to wipe the counter with a damp cloth so her boss would think she was busy. Farm Girl listened, but she still didn't comprehend. The motel she was staying in was a whole lot better than Sugar Shack.

"Look, Martha, it's none of my business, but if you need money, there's a dish washing job here."

"Why does you think I need money?"

"I've noticed that you've been wearing the same dress for almost a week now. And if you're staying in that rundown motel, well, I assume you need money. Admitting you're poor or down on your luck isn't shameful. Even I have money problems. That's why I'm working at this grease pit," she smirked. "Speaking of which, I better make like I'm really busy. I'll get your glass of water."

On the way to the water container, Floss dropped the wet rag in a pan of dirty dishes. When she returned and placed the glass of water in front of Farm Girl, she picked up her conversation.

"To say you're going to New York is a nice dream. Unless you're hitchhiking across country, it costs big bucks to get there. Staying there is expensive, too. And take my word for it, kid, unless you're a homeless person, one dress won't make it as a wardrobe in a big city."

"But, I does has me another dress. I just wear this one so I can keep the other one fur a special invite somewhere. I has me lots a new clothes. I'm saving them fur New York City."

"Sure, kid, and that gunnysack you keep dragging around with you is your expensive leather suitcase."

"A what?"

"Nothing. Look, I better get back to doing my job." She took her pad and pencil from her pocket and started writing. "So, Martha, do you want your normal burger and fries luncheon plate with your usual drink?"

"Yes, but don't furgit my dessert."

"Oh, I'm sorry, kiddo. We're fresh out of chocolate pie today. We've got cocoanut cream, lemon meringue, banana cream, cherry, apple and blueberry."

"But I like my chocolate."

"Look, do you like bananas and ice cream?"

"Yumm, I sure does. But I like my chocolate bestest."

"How about when you're through with your lunch plate, I make you a banana split with chocolate ice cream and lots of chocolate syrup and whipped cream. How does that sound?"

Farm Girl's mouth was drooling. "I doesn't know is what splittin' bananas, but it sounds like I want to eat it, right now. I'll has it befur I has me that burger and fries."

Floss chuckled. "Okay, one banana split coming up, but I'll hold the lunch plate. You might not be hungry for it after you've eaten the split."

As Farm Girl enjoyed her new tasty treat, Floss kept busy with her lunch-rush customers. After the lunch crowd had diminished, and Farm Girl's appetite was satisfied, the two continued their previous conversation.

"What's this here hitchhiking mean that you teld me about?"

"Thumbing a ride." *God, doesn't she know anything? From the look on her face, she hasn't the slightest clue what I'm talking about half of the time.* "You stand out on the highway with your thumb extended this way," she gestured with her hand, "until someone picks you up and gives you a free ride."

A free ride is like Jay give me. But I didn't stand on no highway pointing my thumb. I reckon I doesn't need to know anymore about this here hitchhiking.

"Hey, earth to Martha. Are you still with me?"

"I doesn't need me no free rides. I has money to git me to New York City and live there for as long as I want to."

"Well, if you've got plenty of money," *which I'll just bet you don't,* "then why aren't you staying in one of those fancy hotels here in town? Better yet, why don't you buy yourself some more clothes so you don't have to save a dress for special occasions?"

"Since I doesn't understand your language yet, would you tell me what a fancy hotel means?"

"Ha!" Floss laughed. "Martha, you're a stitch. Well, in plain language, it means you pay more for your room. However, you get clean sheets on your bed every day. And, that's not all. In a fancy hotel, they also have room service."

Crimeny! I doesn't even know this Des Moines, Iowa's language, yet, and she gives me plain language words. "You is sure confusing me," Farm Girl confessed. "In your plain language, what are room service?"

Grief, this kid must have been raised in Podunk City where nobody knows anything. I dropped out of school when I was sixteen, but next to her, I feel like a college graduate. Why did I get myself into a conversation with her? All I wanted to do was to help the poor kid by telling her we had a job opening. This should teach me to keep my big mouth shut and mind my own business.

"You call on the phone from your room and order your food. Then, someone delivers your order right to your door. I stayed in a fancy hotel once, and believe me, it was heaven. The food sure is a lot better in those hotels than eating these greasy plate specials in here. Of course, it costs a lot more money to stay in one of those ritzy places. But if you can afford it, it's worth it."

"Someone brings you food right to your door?"

"They sure do. There's nothing better than having someone else clean the bathroom, make your bed, and having three squares delivered right to your door. Now that's what I call first class. But, if you aren't staying in town, I guess it doesn't matter where you stay or where you eat."

"In your plain language, what am squares?"

"That's just another term for three meals a day."

Crimeny, a motel's got a bed and running water, but a fancy hotel has food right to your door. That means I doesn't have to drag my gunnysack back and forth all day long to go eating. I need to find me one a them fancy hotels.

Farm Girl was intrigued. All her life, she had to work along side her Mama, doing hard farming chores. Although she never complained, now it was her chance to do nothing but sit around and let others wait on her. She couldn't pass up the opportunity to find out what that was like. After getting directions to the nearest hotel, she returned to the motel, checked out, and headed down the street.

The hotel was a long walk from the motel. Following the easy directions, and in no hurry, Farm Girl moseyed along, dragging her baggage behind her. She still had somewhat of a fear of strangers, but it never once crossed her mind that someone one could hurt or steal from her. Even though it was daylight, she had to walk through an unsavory part of town.

Farm Girl walked the streets like she didn't have a care in the world.

When she reached the hotel, the desk clerk debated about sending her back out the door. Although Farm Girl looked neat and clean, it was the filthy gunnysack is what shot up a warning sign that she might be a vagrant. The clerk had second thoughts when Farm Girl said she wanted to check in for a month and would pay cash-in-advance.

Once Farm Girl had the key to her room, she asked, "I didn't see me a whole lot a them doors to rooms outside your building, like them motel's has. How does I git to my room?"

"That's because this is a hotel and the doors to our rooms are inside," the clerk explained, attempting to retain a pleasant attitude. "Take the elevator behind you. Go to the second floor. Your room number is on the door."

Farm Girl looked behind her then turned back to the clerk. "I is new to your fancy hotel world, so I doesn't know your language yet. What's an elevator?"

Instead of explaining, the desk clerk asked a bellhop show Farm Girl to her room. Farm Girl felt a tinge of fear when the elevator doors enclosed her and the young man into such a tiny space. As soon as the elevator started moving, her fear turned to giggles. As the elevator stopped and the doors opened, she exclaimed, "Wow! That was fun. Can we do it again?"

"I'm afraid not," the bellhop answered.

"Now what does we do?"

Rolling his eyes, the young man asked, "What's your room number?"

Looking at her key, she responded, "2-1-3."

"Room 213 is this way."

The bellhop walked down the hall. Farm Girl followed, trying to keep up with his pace the best she could. When he arrived at room 213, he stopped, turned, and waited for Farm Girl to catch up. "If you'll give me your key, I'll unlock the door for you."

"I knows how to unlock a door, but I is mighty beholden to you fur leading me the way. You can leave now."

Farm Girl waited in the hall until the bellhop disappeared behind the elevator doors. Unlocking the door, she entered into a dark room. She felt around the walls until she found and flipped on a light switch. A dim light went on overhead, but it was enough light so she could see. After closing the door, she let loose of the sack and dropped her purse to the floor.

Within a matter of minutes, she discovered how to turn on the lamps in the room. After she did, she turned around in circles, looking at everything. Pulling back a drape, she peered out the window. Deciding she liked the glow of the room much better without daylight shining in, the drape was placed back the same way she had found it.

"Crimeny, Mama, look at this here bed. It's so big that you and me and Pappy could all fit in it, and still have room left over. Wow!" Removing her shoes, she crawled to the middle of the bed, and sat with her legs folded in front of her.

"Almost everything in here is red, Mama. The same color as them poppy flowers we was growing in Pappy's flower garden. The only color that's different is them two pink chairs over there by that little table. I reckon that's where I eat when I git me some a that room service.

Oh, look," she said pointing, "all them pieces a furniture is white. And I even has a white telephone. Ain't this fancy room just bountiful, Mama? No, maybe that word am beautiful. Oh, I doesn't remember, but it sure am purdy.

I could sit here forever talking to you, Mama, but I is too tired. I know it ain't night yet, but I has a lot to do. I been spending all week in this new world, all wore out from going back and forth to the bus depot. Now, I doesn't have to do that no more.

Tomorrow, I need to find me some a them stores to buy me some more dresses. Folks doesn't need to be knowing I has lots a money, but they doesn't need to be thinking I need me a job washing dishes, neither. I ain't doing me no more chores fur nobody."

Pulling back the bedcovers, she climbed into bed, fully dressed. Her eyes were closed before her head hit the pillow.

The next morning, Farm Girl was up before the sun was. Having already learned how to use an in-room telephone, she knew how to call the front desk. After calling the hotel operator to find out how to order room service, she was a trifle upset to find she was too early. Room service wouldn't be operational for close to two more hours. However, she was informed about the small coffee maker in the dressing area of the bathroom. Problem was, she didn't drink coffee.

Utilizing her time, Farm Girl unpacked her personal belongings. Almost everything but the money went into the dresser drawers. Taking her time, she soaked in her first hot bath. She didn't get out of the water until it was cold and she had prune-like skin. After dressing, she made the bed. Taking her gunnysack and purse, she headed down the stairs to the lobby. As much as she had enjoyed the elevator ride, she wasn't sure if she knew what buttons to push. There would be plenty of time to learn, but not just then.

With assistance from the front desk clerk, Farm Girl took her first ride in a taxi, and experienced shopping in the main area of the city. Everything she had seen in the stores intrigued her. However, she limited her first day of shopping to items she considered necessities. The new dresses were forgotten about when she spied so many other items she thought were more important.

Just for kicks, one day, Farm Girl spent the whole day venturing through a large department store. Everything amazed her from escalators to elevators. She spent hours checking out the cosmetic department, electronics, and the bedding department.

She was having fun looking and touching everything in sight. Never once had it occurred to her, she was in the midst of evil strangers and nosey busybodies. Like kids in a candy store, oblivious to everything but the treats before their hungry eyes, Farm Girl was in hog heaven.

On one of her shopping expeditions, she discovered suitcases. She purchased a large suitcase with a retractable handle and wheels, several smaller travel cases, and a briefcase for carrying her stories. Now, she would be able to push or pull her heavy items with ease.

When she returned to her room with the suitcases, she emptied the gunnysack and handbag contents onto the bed. The gunnysack went in the small waste can next to the desk. Travel expense money, along with a new comb and brush, went back inside her purse.

Opening the dresser drawers, Farm Girl took out her belongings and placed them on the bed. When she emptied the contents of Mama's old coffee can onto the bed, a ring rolled out along with some pictures, Farm Girl's birth certificate, what was left of a dead flower wrapped in a piece of wax paper and Mama's scissors.

"Just think, Mama, if'n you had one a these handbags, you wouldn't had no need fur your old can."

Now was her chance to look at her birth certificate. No longer curious, she didn't bother. The piece of paper was nothing more than verification of what she already knew. She wasn't even curious about the ring or the dead flower that she found.

Since Farm Girl was more intent on learning new experiences, studying her vocabulary, and reading and writing her stories, the contents of Mama's can held no significance to her anymore. Mama's life was in the past. Just like the items from the can, they were to be put away and forgotten about.

All the suitcases were filled with various items and the money. Now, she could comfortably pull most of her items while carrying her half empty purse.

Since the television was broken in the last place she stayed, Farm Girl didn't bother turning the TV set on in her hotel room to see if it worked. Neither Mama nor Pappy could tell her what she could, or could not watch. However, she knew that once she got to New York, she would have plenty of time to watch television.

While staying in Des Moines, she not only wrote more stories about her new adventures and the people she had encountered along the way, but she also enjoyed reading her stories. On one typical lazy evening, making herself comfortable on the bed, she selected a story for reading. Her words took her back to more reminiscences of Darin.

"Fall come so early, it was like there wasn't no summer," Farm Girl read aloud. "Pappy be complaining it be a bad year fur his crops since there be little to no sunshine, what with the dark rain clouds and all. There just wasn't no warm weather to help his corn and wheat grow. But the sun be shining on me when I gots to my Room to Write that day 'cause Darin be waitin' fur me."

As Farm Girl was reading, she closed her eyes. In her mind, she could visualized that day, like it was yesterday.

BACK IN TIME

"Ah-ha, I beat you here today," Darin joked.

"What kind a howdy does ya call that?" Farm Girl asked.

"My, aren't we grumpy today? Wake up on the wrong side of the bed, did you?"

"I did not. 'Sides, I doesn't sleep on no bed. There ain't no wrong side and no right side to straw that's layin' on the floor. And, I ain't grumpy. Seems ya be taken y'ur own sweet time in comin' back to pay me a visit."

"So that's your problem. You're aggravated because I haven't been around."

"Aggregated? What do that mean?"

"Aggravated. It means upset, like you are with me, right?"

"On the calendar, it be many months since I see you. All a summer's been goin' by already. I be thinkin' ya plum furgot about me."

"We haven't had much of a summer this year. The constant rains keep making things harder for me."

"What things? Whatcha goin' on about, Darin?"

"Nothing, just verbalizing my thoughts. Forget it. Hey, are you still getting the mail everyday for Mr. Welk?"

"No, goofy gander, there ain't no mail on Sundays. But, I gits it every other days a the week."

"Yeah, silly me. Have you any new secrets to tell me about Mr. Welk?"

"Secrets? I doesn't tells ya no secrets about Pappy."

"Well, now's the time to start. That's what buddies do. They share all kinds of secrets. Now, you and I are buddies, aren't we?"

"I reckon so, but I doesn't know no secrets about him."

"But if you did, you would tell me, right?"

"I reckon. When is we gonna play It?"

"I told you, right now I'm playing the tag game of cat and mouse with someone else. So, I still don't know when you can play."

"Please tell me who's gonna be It," she insisted, jumping up and down like a small child filled with uncontrollable excitement.

"Okay, how about one of those evil strangers you're always talking about?"

Farm Girl stopped dead in her tracks. Her sudden joy turned to apprehension and anger. She doubled up her fists and commenced rapping her knuckles together. "No! I doesn't want to play with no evil strangers."

Although Darin was amused by her temperament, he tried to calm her. "Look, even if an evil stranger chases you, that stranger can be It for a long, long time. If you're smart, you can always stay one step ahead of your pursuer. That's what you want to do. Take my word, Farm Girl, it's no fun to be It. The fun in playing tag is to be chased, and never getting caught."

"I likes me them Tom and Jerry cartoons. When you plays your game, is ya the cat or is ya the mouse?"

"I'm the mouse, of course." *And, Rusty is the stupid cat.*

Bending down, Darin picked up a few stones that were close to his feet. He began to throw the stones into the river below. Facing the river, Farm Girl leaned against her big rock. She watched the stones hit the water.

"Do that evil stranger has a name, that one ya says is gonna be It?"

"I don't think you should play this game," Darin declared.

Loosening her fists, she crossed her arms in disgust. "Why cain't I play?"

"You're use to the tag game for little kids. This is going to be a tag game for grownups. I just don't think you're big enough to play with the adults."

With bitter objections to being compared to a child, she said, "Hey, ya teld me that once befur. I be seventeen and big enough to play with them adults."

"Okay, okay. But when the game starts, don't say I didn't warn you," he smirked. After throwing his last stone, he walked over to the boulder and leaned against it, next to Farm Girl.

"Listen closely, and I'll tell you the rules. There isn't just one It in this game, there are several. They are called authorities. There are sheriffs, policemen, cops—Well, there are a lot more names for them, but those are the main ones you need to know for now. Part of this game is to tell lies without getting caught."

Farm Girl's ears perked up. "Oh, like Kings-X?"

"Sort of," he answered, wondering if Farm Girl would comprehend any of what he was saying. "Now, if you get caught lying to the authorities, this makes you It. But, in the adult game, you don't get a chance to chase anyone. Instead, It will lock you up until you tell the truth. If you decide to confess, then they may let you out of lock-up, if you're lucky.

Of course, if you're not lucky, they may lock you up forever and forget where they put the key."

Suddenly, Farm Girl started singing. "Take the keys and lock her up, lock her up—"

"Say, what's the matter with you? Are you even listening to me, or do you want me to leave?"

Farm Girl's head was swimming with curiosity. She could have cared less that Darin appeared frustrated with her. "Why, Darin? Why would they lock me up? Lock me up how? Like a horse in a barn stall when ya doesn't want him to git loose in the pasture? Is that whatcha means?"

Darin doubled his fist. He rapped his tightened knuckles against his forehead to keep from losing his temper. *Don't lose it now or you might botch everything.*

"Why's ya doin' that fur? Is ya mad like I was?"

"No. It clears my head." He unclenched his fist. Sticking his hand into his pant's pocket, he began to play with this loose change and car keys. He was hoping the fidgeting would help him contain his temper.

"Yeah, like a horse in the barn, but worse. They would put you in a cage like a wild animal, with iron bars for doors and windows. So, the lies you tell them, have to be better than any lie you've ever told before in your whole life. The authorities have to believe you are telling the truth. In fact, to be extra convincing, you have to almost believe your own lies."

"I can tell some whoppers if'n I needs to."

"Telling a whopper is just stretching the truth. Lies are not telling any truth."

"Whoppers is lies 'cause Mama teld me so."

"Okay, if you say so," Darin agreed, against his better judgment.

"Since Mama and Pappy doesn't know about my Room to Write, all them stories I writes, or about me meetin' ya, I reckon I has me lots a practice tellin'…" she paused. Deciding to use Darin's word, she said, "lies." Darin smiled. "What kind a thingies does I needs to be tellin' them author a'tees?"

"All kinds of things. Like, you don't know me and never heard of me. The authorities can't ever find out that I know you or Mr. Welk, or that I've ever been around his property. Could you tell fibs like that without ever getting caught?"

"If'n fibs means lies, then that ain't nothin'. Crimeny, didn't I just teld ya I ain't never teld Mama or Pappy about ya? Them kind a lies ya wants me to tell will be easy fur me when my fingers is crosswise. But why does ya need me to tell them peoples I doesn't know ya fur?"

"It's like I said, I don't have just one It chasing me. I consider all of the authorities to be It. It's very important to me that I don't get tagged. So, if you don't tell them about me, they can't tag me. Now, if you want to play grown-up games with me, then you have to lie like you never lied before."

"I wants to play 'cause I know I can lie, real good. A course, I'll play Kings X when I tells them author-a-tees I never knows ya, so it won't really be a lie. That'll be a whopper," she stated with a giggle.

"Whatever. Look, sometimes it might not be possible to play Kings X. Could you still tell a lie without your fingers crossed behind your back?"

"I doesn't want to burn in the fires a that devil mans."

Darin stepped directly in front of Farm Girl. He was so close to her face, she could feel his breath. "Would you rather be caged behind iron bars like an animal?"

He had threatened with such a fierce facial expression, Farm Girl shuddered in her shoes. She was so nervous her head was shaking. One option seemed as frightening as the other. Right then, she wasn't sure which one she would choose. Neither, of course, sounded like the ideal

Black Rosebud

reward for lying for Darin.

Darin assumed he had Farm Girl buffaloed enough that when the time came, she would protect him. He no longer felt the need to keep jingling the items in his pocket to calm his nerves. The seeds of deceit and fear were planted.

He moved back, next to the rock. Bracing his head with his arms behind his head, he leaned back and looked toward the sky. *As dumb as she is, she'll be my perfect ally when and if I need her. No one will ever find out that I ever knew old man Welk. Ha! That ought to cook the old man's goose if he ever decides to rat on me.*

"I bet you don't know where this boulder came from, do you?"

"I reckon God put it here, just like Mama says he puts everythin' else on the earth."

"People say the man that use to own this property before Mr. Welk owned it, built a mansion somewhere close to where we're standing. One time, so I heard, this man was in Colorado when there was a tremendous rockslide. This boulder broke off the side of a mountain.

He brought it all the way from the Colorado mountains and placed it right where it is now. I'm really just guessing that he placed it here. But the darn thing is so huge, I don't think it's been moved since he brought it to Nebraska."

"Crimeny, my Room to Write rock come from somewheres ya calls Colorado? What be that place, Darin?"

"Let me put it this way, it's a whole different world from what you know, Farm Girl. I've never been there myself, but I know they have mountains as high as you can see."

"Wow, another world, just like New York City? How many worlds be there?" Not saying a word, and without taking his eyes off the sky, Darin shook his head. His silence didn't stop Farm Girl's questions. "What's a mountain?"

"It's an enormous hill made of rock."

"Why did that mans put this big rock here fur?"

"I don't think anyone knows for sure, but my guess is that the boulder was placed here for yard decoration." Looking around, Darin said, "The original mansion used to sit somewhere up here on this hill, overlooking the river."

"What's a mansion?"

"It's a huge, very expensive house. The owners, from what I've been told, had so much money, they didn't know what to do with it all. Folks around here called them multi-millionaires. That's what I'm going to be, soon. A multi-millionaire."

"What's a multi-mill in air means?"

"A multi-millionaire is when a person has so much money that they can buy anything they want, and they never have to work."

"You ain't gots to do no chores, never?"

"Yeah, that's what I mean."

"Wow! Is that one a them other worlds, too?"

With a smile and a grunt, Darin answered, "Boy, you can say that again. Being that rich would be like living in a whole new world compared to farm life."

"Where'd that mansion and them folks go?"

"The people have been dead for years. Some people in town are afraid to come out here. They say that couple's ghosts haunt this area late at night with their loud screams of agony. The rest of the people seem to stay away from this area so they don't get in trouble for trespassing."

"Ghosts? I see me ghosts on the TV. One a them names be Casper. Does them peoples see Casper?"

"Don't be foolish. There are no such things as ghosts. Of course, some people believe in them, but I don't."

"I sure be happy to hear that, Darin, 'cause I doesn't want to believe in them neither. Mama told me a ghost story once, but I gots so afraid that she promise never to tell me one again. But you didn't told me where that mansion go to."

"The old mansion had a fire and burned to the ground. Some folks say the fire wasn't an accident. Others say it was struck by lightening one night during a storm. I don't think anyone knows the real story, or if they do, no one talks about it."

Exploding with doubts, Farm Girl placed her hands on her hips. Turning to Darin, she spouted, "I think y'ur tellin' me one a y'ur lies, Darin George Righter. Pappy says he live on this here land with his daddy and his granddaddy fur years and years. If'n that were a true story, Pappy would a told it to me."

Why do I even bother to explain anything to this numbskull?

Not everything about Jefferson Welk's past was clear in Darin's mind. Nor did he know the whole story about the deceased wealthy couple. Most of what he knew was based on years of town gossip. On the other hand, maybe the town gossip was in actuality folklore. Not knowing for sure, he changed the subject.

"If you had a horse and you knew it was dying, what would you do to help it?"

Removing her hands from her hips, she let her arms drop to her sides. Clenching the sides of her skirt, Farm Girl began twisting the material with her fingers. "I guess I'd has to git someone to shoot the poor thing so it won't suffers no more. That's what them farmer's done that I know once. Why?"

"No special reason, just curious."

Farm Girl's hour was over. As she ran back to the farm, her mouth was racing.

"Listen, Farm Girl, maybe ya doesn't want to play them grown-up, adult games with Darin. Then again, ya knows ya been playin' games already, tellin' Mama all them whoppers and lies ever since ya meet Darin. Don't guess it makes no never mind tellin' stories to them peoples who is gonna be It.

Darin ain't gots to know if'n ya crosses y'ur fingers, or not. And, if'n ya be smart, them author-a-tees cain't catch ya. So, ya doesn't has to worry about no iron cage. Maybe it'll be fun? Yeah, it'll be fun.

Wonder why Darin was actin' so silly-like today, like he was all mad and all. Crimeny, you knows why he weren't himself today. Poor Darin must has himself a dyin' horse, and he needs to shoot it to put it out a its sufferin'. Poor Darin."

PRESENT

Tossing her story on the hotel room floor, Farm Girl stretched. "Boy, I sure is glad Darin warn me about them authorities. I know when they find out that I has all this money, they is gonna be chasing me. All I need to do is to git myself and the money to New York City without gitting tagged to be It. And, so far, I is doing a purdy good job."

Finally, she floated off into slumber land. Enjoying, perhaps, one of the few nights left in the artificial world in which her mind lived.

IMAGES OF LIFE

Due to her lack of worldly knowledge, Farm Girl was limited as to what she did and what her thoughts consisted of on a day-by-day basis. Other than writing and the times she had spent with Mr. Welk when he was tutoring her, she was never given the opportunity to have a hobby, learn a craft, join in any sports, have any friends, or get involved in anything fun and exciting with children her age.

Once she left the farm, all she had to occupy her mind were her stories; memories of Mama and Pappy; thoughts of Darin, the one person she considered her buddy; and, her eagerness to learn more words. As dull as it was, these were the few elements that controlled her mind.

Each morning when Farm Girl awakened, she remembered falling asleep the night before thinking about Darin. This morning was no different.

"Crimeny, I could think about you all day long, and dream about you all night, Darin George Righter. Where ever I go or whatever I do, I is always gonna carry you in my heart. But now, I need to git my morning chores done, so I can has my breakfast. Then I need to write more on my stories."

After her shower, she was looking in the mirror while brushing her hair. She started talking to her image. "Farm Girl, Pappy said you was the spitting image a your Mama. You be weighing the same as her and being as short as her. Petite, that's what Pappy was calling me, just like the saleslady called me in Jasonville. Pappy told me that meant tiny. I even has Mama's brown eyes. The one difference between me and Mama was our hair. Mama's hair were straight. Mine is natural curly. Remember that day when Darin was talking at you about your hair?"

As that day came rushing back to her mind, the mirror before her magically turned into a view into her past. She could vividly see the picture of her and Darin talking.

BACK IN TIME

"How do you make all of those waves in your hair? Do you use one of those curling irons?" Darin questioned.

"I know a brandin' iron fur markin' livestock, and a clothes iron to git them wrinkles out a Pappy's clothes, but what's a curlin' iron?"

"Females use it to put curls in their hair. It's obvious, you don't use one."

"Mama calls me a river blonde with natural curly hair."

"A river blonde with natural curls. That's a new one on me. Why don't you let the length grow longer? I'll bet it would look better because it looks nice and thick."

"Mama says shorter hair be fur boys, and real long hair be too hard to manage. When my hair's wet, it gits them thingies Mama calls frizzies. Them frizzies be too hard to brush out with long hair. So Mama—"

"Mama! Mama! Mama!" he exclaimed. "You're seventeen, for rat's sake. Don't you have a mind of your own? What is Mama going to do to you if you let your hair grow longer, punish you?"

"No, Mama don't never punish me. It's just I respect Mama. So what she says, I do. Don'tcha respect y'ur mama?"

"My mother's dead. But, even when she was alive, I still did what I wanted to do. I am my own person," he declared. "My hair is longer than yours, and I dare anyone to tell me I have to wear it shorter or I can't wear it any longer than it is. Nobody tells me what I can, or cannot do."

"Maybe, someday, I'll let my hair grow long. Fur now, though, I agrees with Mama. Most times, I be warshin' my hair in the river. It takes two hours a brushin' to git them frizzies and the sand out after it dries. Sometimes, if'n I is lucky, I gits to use well wader or wader from the horse tank to warsh my hair. Then it turns out purdier 'cause there ain't no sand to brush out. But, that ain't too often that I gits to do that. So, long hair, I reckon, takes longer than I cares to spend brushin'."

"Well water, river water and water from a horse tank? Doesn't Mr. Welk have running water in his house?"

"He do, but I ain't allow to use it. Farmhands has to know their place, Mama says. So, I doesn't dare use Pappy's runnin' wader."

"I'm sure if you asked him, he would let you use—"

"I ain't gonna ask, lesson I wants a good scoldin' from Mama," she pounced back, giving Darin no chance to finish his statement.

"What do you use for shampoo? Never mind, I'm sure shampoo is another word you don't know. What do you use for soap to wash your hair?"

"Me and Mama makes our own soap."

"I guess I better not bring you any shampoo. That would be a hard one for you to explain to your mama."

"What is it?"

"Shampoo is a special soap for washing your hair. May I touch your hair?" Instinctively, she dodged, like someone was going to take a swing at her. "I'm not going to hurt you."

Deciding it would be all right, she consented. "Okay. If'n ya be a mind to."

Taking her time, she moved her upper body toward Darin, and turned face down. Darin reached out and touched her hair with his fingertips. He was quick to pull his hand away and rubbed it on the side of his pants. It was as if he were trying to clean away the repulsive texture that lingered on his fingertips.

Gross! That's disgusting! Her hair feels like a mixture of dried muck and steel wool.

As Farm Girl's head flipped up to look at Darin, he was hoping she didn't see the shocked look on his face. Conscious of the intensity in which he was rubbing his hand, he immediately stopped and stuck his hand in his pocket. "Yes, I was right. Your hair is sure thick. I bet some good shampoo and hair conditioner would do wonders for it."

"Why does I need to be usin' one a them machines like sits in Pappy's window on my hair fur?"

"What machine?"

"Didn't ya just told me I needs me some a that air-conditioner."

"No, you stu—You misunderstood me. Air is like wind. I said hair, like the hair on your head."

"What's that conditioner gots to do with my hair?"

"After shampooing your hair and rinsing it real good, conditioner makes your hair smell good and feel almost silky. In simple words, it makes ugly hair soft and easy to brush. It may even help you get rid of those frizzies you mentioned. Maybe, someday, you can try some. I still think you should let your hair grow longer."

"I sure doesn't know why ya cares, but maybe, someday, I will. And maybe, someday, I can try that there shampoo and conditioner ya be talkin' about. If'n it gits out them uglies and them frizzies, like ya says, I knows I is gonna like it."

BACK TO THE PRESENT

Farm Girl smiled as Darin's image disappeared from the mirror along with her memories, as she finished brushing her hair.

"I remember how Darin use to scold me because I was saying warsh and wader. I reckon I speak better now with all them words I been learning. I know I doesn't say ain't and if'n no more, since I been studying real hard. Maybe sometimes I furgits and does, but not much. I still gits plum confused with them *is's* and them *are's*. Ain't just fits better than those words does."

Admiring the length of her hair, she pointed a finger at her mirrored reflection. "You is eighteen, so you has a mind of your own, just like Darin. So, now you can has your longer hair and isn't no one gonna stop you."

After cleaning her mess in the bathroom, she got dressed. Hungry, as usual, she ordered breakfast from room service. Knowing New York City would be waiting for her, she enjoyed staying put and being lazy. After all, other than getting up at the break of dawn to start farm chores, and meeting Darin when she had her private time, she never comprehended the meaning of time.

She enjoyed the comfort of her room so much, that she extended her stay from one to two months. Other than her shopping trips, she seldom ventured outside of her room. The exception was for an occasional can of soda from the vending machine.

Still believing she knew how to write, she continued to write her stories. In order to practice her grammar, she would read both her new and her old stories aloud, over and over. With no one around to correct her, she was still using incorrect grammar when she spoke.

On occasions, if she could sound out a word, she tried to look it up in her dictionary, as spelling and pronunciation were important to her. Most times, she wasn't successful. When she couldn't find a word she was looking for, she complained in a loud voice. "How's a body suppose to look up a word to see how it's spelled, if you doesn't know how to spell it in the first place?"

Even though she had written many stories about Mama and Pappy, those stories became secondary. The stories about Darin were her favorites. On this day, she selected a particular story to read that took place on one of Darin's visits in the middle of winter.

After looking at her written words, she set the paper aside. "I doesn't need to read this story again. I remember that day in my head.

Pappy and Mama was talking earlier that day about Old Man Winter acting kind of strange, giving us cold temperatures but hardly no snow. I sure didn't care. Unless there were a terrible snowstorm, weather never keep me from going to my Room to Write.

I were sitting on my rock when Darin show up. He were bundle up in a coat and hat with gloves covering his hands. As warm as he should of been, he were complaining about being cold. He thought I was crazy sitting up there with no coat on. But, I was wearing three long sleeves of sweaters under a heavy sweater jacket. I were warm enough.

That's when we start in talking about me being a survivor. At first, he didn't believe me when I told him I could live out in them woods down by the river or in the fields, fur days, weeks and even months, if I had a mind to. I'd know what to eat, where to sleep, how to hide from strangers, and how to be safe. Mama teach me."

Farm Girl broke up her verbal reminiscing with laugher. "It were funny to see Darin's face when I told him that if me and Mama couldn't find nothing to eat, not even berries, that we'd eat bugs and worms. He be turning green as a bullfrog.

That were also the time that he hurt my feelings. He went on and on about how I couldn't survive outside the farm world. He also told me, unless I learn more about words than I already know, I won't never be a writer of books. I reckon I had me a sourpuss face from his hurting words, as he told me he was sorry. Mama was always saying that everybody has a right to be wrong once in a while, so I was forgiving him that day.

That sure were a good story."

Farm Girl put the story back with the others. She searched through the stack of papers and notebooks until she found another one. This time, she selected one that she wrote just prior to turning eighteen.

"I doesn't remember all about this day, so I best read it."

As she read, that day became more familiar to her. After reading a few pages, the words seemed to bounce off the paper and dance around in her mind. Farm Girl realized her eyes were getting tired. With the pillow cushioning her head, she closed her eyes, allowing her mind float back in time until she could actually visualize that day.

BACK IN TIME

"Hi, Darin, I ain't seen you fur a while. Where has you been?"

"I've been busy, and isn't always easy to get out here to see you on my lunch hour."

"How come you do sometimes, and sometimes you doesn't?"

"Most times, when I show up here, it's because the bank thinks I'm out running errands. I can't use that excuse all the time or I'll get caught. If I get caught, then I can't meet you here anymore. Understand?"

"Yeah, I reckon I does, but I didn't till you teld me."

"So, do you have anything new and interesting to tell me?"

Farm Girl grinned. "Maybe I does, and maybe I doesn't." Receiving no response, she asked, "Crimeny, ain't you gonna say nothin'?"

"If you don't have anything new to tell me, that's okay. But if you do, you need to tell me. We're buddies, remember? And, buddies tell buddies all of their secrets," Darin expressed.

"I know. You already told me that befur. Well, I doesn't got no secrets fur you."

"You're sure you have nothing new to tell me about Mr. Welk? Like, how's he keeping up with his bills?"

"What means keepin' up?"

"How's he paying them."

"He be sellin' everythin' he owns, and he ain't gots too much left."

"I see. Well, I'm glad he's still hanging in there."

Farm Girl's mind fluttered back and forth like the wings of a butterfly. She had already forgotten about their conversation concerning Mr. Welk, and thought about one of Darin's earlier visits. "Did your horse git better, Darin?"

"What?"

"You be askin' me, one time, what I be doin' if'n I has me a dyin' horse. Don'tcha remember?"

"Oh, yeah. I'm going to have to kill the poor thing to put it out of its misery. Some ailments just can't be cured any other way."

"What kind a horse is it?"

"What does it matter? If you really care about something or someone that's suffering, you have to take it upon yourself to do what's best for them. Horses can't talk, so they can't tell us when they hurt anywhere. Did you know some people are like that?"

"What does you mean, that there's people that cain't talk?"

"Of course there are people who can't talk, but that's not what I mean. I mean a lot of people may be in pain, but they won't say anything because they don't want others to know."

"Why doesn't they?"

"They don't want sympathy—Oh, Farm Girl, quit looking at me that way. What I mean is, they don't want their loved ones to feel sorry for them or worry about them."

"Why not?"

"If your mama was in pain and she didn't want you to worry, do you think she'd tell you and let you fret about it? Or would she keep her pain to herself?"

"How do a body knows if'n someone be sick when they ain't tellin' ya?"

"Sometimes, their actions give them away. Like breathing too fast or not being able to catch their breath. Maybe they rub their chests or grab at them from pain. They might feel too weak to stand on their own two feet, and bingo—they'll fall down. There are so many actions that give them away, I can't even begin to tell you all of them."

"You be right, Darin. A horse cain't tell you none a them things."

"I don't want to talk about sick people, anymore.

You know what? I think you need to do a lot more studying. You still have a long way to go before you can ever fit in the world outside of farm life. Unless you had someone with you, holding your hand, you'd never make it living in another world."

Darin hurt Farm Girl's feelings, and he knew it from her facial expression. Before he got in any deeper than he already was, it was time for him to leave. "Look, I've got to get back to my job." Darin walked away, yelling, "See you sometime."

Even though her feelings were stepped on, she called out, "Wait, Darin. Doesn't you want me to answer your question?" Darin ignored her and kept walking. "Maybe I doesn't have an answer to give yet, anyways," she complained. "If'n I were sick, I doesn't think it would be no secret from no one, but sure not from Mama. Is that wrong to has Mama worrin' over me? Maybe it ain't me and Mama he's talkin' about? Maybe it's him or someone he loves that's sick? I sure hopes who it be, he don't shoot them."

PRESENT

When the story in her mind disappeared, Farm Girl opened her eyes and sat upright. She looked at the notebook she still held in her hand. Disgusted, she threw it on the floor.

"Well, Mister Smarty Darin, I is in the world of Des Moines, Iowa, all by myself. Me! Farm Girl! And, there aren't no one here holding my hand," she boisterously proclaimed.

Then, for one fleeting moment, she felt like a scared four-year-old child, as a shroud of fear came over her. "Oh, my, did I just say I is all by myself?"

Other than the tears when she mourned the passing of Pappy, she couldn't remember shedding any tears when Mama passed. She knew Pappy and Mama were deceased because she had witnessed both of their dead bodies. Being so excited about getting to New York, and so intent on surviving every new experience she was encountering, reality hadn't come to the forefront until that very minute.

However, as quickly as sad memories and the fear of loneliness came, they left just as fast. Farm Girl's mind blocked out the fear as she gave herself a good lecture. "Hold on to your bloomers, Farm Girl. You've been doing just fine. So, don't go gitting afraid just because you has one awful thought that you blurt out loud. You know you isn't alone because Mama are watching over you.

You should be mighty proud that you've done so well on your own in these new worlds you've been visiting. And, you writes better stories now than you ever write befur. So, just calm yourself down.

I is surviving, Darin. I has to admit, at first I are thinking that surviving outside by the river were easier. But now, after sleeping on a soft mattress with clean sheets, pillows fur my head, and blankets that smells as clean as springtime, well, I doesn't. You know what else, Darin? You was right about money. It can buy me anything I want.

Okay, Farm Girl, don'tcha think it's high time you quit dillydallying around? Darin aren't listening to you anyway. Git yourself back on your journey. Yes, that's what I is gonna do.

On my calendar it is eleven days into July, already. Time for me to travel, again. Tomorrow, I is gonna go to the whole new world of Chicago, Illinois. What them bus depot folks told me, that'll make me closer to New York City.

You know who I miss and want to see again? My buddy, Darin. Darin told me he were gonna be there, someday, when he leaves his home. I doesn't know how big is the world of New York City, but sure hope I can find him when I gits there. Won't he be happy to see me. I need to remember to tell him about poor Pappy and Mama."

After a gaping yawn, she continued making plans. "One of these days, real soon, I need to go through all my stories and make sure they all has titles. Then I need to put my name on them so everyone will know I were the writer. I be starting to do that befur I meet Darin, but then I didn't has me so many stories to write. I reckon I is gonna keep my name Farm Girl, since I has that name already on some of them.

I is ready," she yawned, "to cross me another one of them bridges, Mama. As soon as I gits to Chicago, I is—" In mid-sentence, she talked herself to sleep, once again, into the land of sweet dreams—unaware of the nightmare she would face in the future.

DEFYING THE ODDS

It was a beautiful sunny day in July. After weeks of solid bed rest, Frank was weak but finally feeling well enough to get out of bed. Darin was seated at the table having his morning coffee.

"Hey, I thought we discussed this yesterday. What do you think you're doing up?" Darin scolded, as Frank meandered into the kitchen." *It's about time you got out of that damn bed. I was beginning to think you were going to spoil everything for me.*

"I know I promised you, yesterday, to stay in bed a few days longer. There's just no way." Rubbing his lower back, Frank joked, "Never realized how sore a person can get just lying around.

Besides, I'm hungry as a bear, Darin. It seems like I've been in that stupid bed for an eternity, eating nothing but that soft food crap that you've been feeding me. I want something more wholesome. Now, instead of yelling at me, how about you fix me a hearty breakfast," Frank requested, smiling at Darin.

As Frank took his favorite seat at the table, Darin stood.

"Do you want a cup of coffee?" Darin asked, heading for the cupboard to get Frank's cup.

"Well, that's a start. Then, I want three eggs, scrambled, a couple of sausage links, some fried potatoes, and toast with lots of apple butter."

"Wait a minute, Frank. First of all, I don't think you are supposed to eat solid foods yet. Also, I'm no short order cook," Darin replied. "Laugh, Frank. That second part was a joke."

"I'm so famished that I'm too weak to laugh. It's a fool shame when a body gets starved to death just because he isn't feeling well. You told me, I just had to stay on that tasteless liquid and bland soft food diet until

I felt better. Well, I feel better. Now, are you going to fix me some real food to eat, or do I have to fix it myself?"

"Okay. Okay. Don't get your shorts on backwards, Frank. I haven't been to the store, so you'll have to settle for eggs and toast. Okay?"

"Why haven't you been to the store? That's part of the chores around here. Just because you put me on that no account diet didn't mean you shouldn't have food in the house for you to eat."

"Don't worry about me. I had plenty of snacks to keep me full. Besides, I didn't want to leave you alone, not to mention the fact that I don't do grocery shopping. You know that. Every time Mother would send me to the store, she complained I never got what she asked for. She always sent me back two or three times to get *exactly* what she wanted. That was so aggravating to me, I gave up grocery shopping, years ago," Darin stated, rather irritated at Frank for even mentioning it.

"I'm sorry, Darin. I didn't mean to bring up miserable memories. Mother sure was a real pain in the neck, most times. *Actually, she was a real tyrant.* Hey, eggs and toast would be great. Give me some solid foods to eat and I'll be as good as new in a few days, just you watch."

While Frank chatted away about the farm, Darin fixed the eggs and toast. Not listening to a word Frank was saying, Darin made plans for the evening. He had to make sure he had every detail covered, and his schedule was timed down to the second. His last job had to be as smooth and as clean as all of the others he had pulled. Now was not the time to get sloppy and get caught.

As long as Frank had been sick in bed, he could never take the chance of being away from home for very long. That's why his evening trips to town to check on Oscar's house were made as swift as possible. Now, with Frank better, he felt safe in leaving Frank alone for a longer length of time. But, it sure wouldn't be to go grocery shopping.

I've got the perfect plan, even if I do say so myself. And, the best part, since Frank is feeling better, I can plan on leaving town in the next couple of days. Hello, Big Apple!

" … and maybe he'll come over and help. What do you think?" Frank ended his lengthy one-man conversation.

"What?" Darin asked, coming out of his daze.

"Where's your mind, Darin? I swear, you're burning my eggs, the toast is probably cold by now, and you haven't heard a word I said, have you? It's like you're spacing out. What's going on?" Receiving no response, Frank kept talking. "Maybe you've been working too hard. Perhaps you should go to bed and let me take care of you?" Frank couldn't help but notice the intent look on Darin's face as he busied himself, so he waited for Darin to start talking.

Keeping silent so he could concentrate on what he was doing, Darin looked down at the skillet he was frying the eggs in. Turning off the fire, he moved the skillet to a cool burner. With his spatula, he lifted the eggs to look at the bottom of them. They weren't burnt, but close to it. Placing the eggs on a plate, he set the plate on the table in front of Frank.

Retrieving the toast from the toaster, Darin noted the toast wasn't cold, but in fact, still hot. He put the toast on Frank's plate, got him the apple butter out of the refrigerator, and then got the pot of coffee.

As he refilled Frank's cup, he apologized. "Look, Frank, I'm sorry. I don't do these things well, not like you do, but the eggs aren't burned and the toast isn't cold. I wasn't talking to you because I was concentrating on fixing your breakfast. I don't know how you do everything at one time, like you do, without burning something." Darin hoped his explanation would satisfy Frank. Frank rolled his lips together, holding back laughter. "Can I get you anything else?"

"I would like some butter for my toast. And, maybe a fork and a knife would be nice, so I can eat. Oh, and how about a smile. That would really be great," Frank said in jest, giving a weak chuckle.

Darin had to laugh at his own meager efforts. He got Frank his silverware and the butter, then refilled his own coffee cup. After replacing the coffee carafe on its hot plate, he sat back at the table. "Okay, my mind is clear now. What did you say about someone coming over to help?"

With a mouthful of eggs, Frank repeated his earlier comments that Darin hadn't listened to. "I turned my radio on this morning before I got up the energy to get out of bed. According to what I heard, the sun has been shining, drying up all that moisture the rains dropped on us a few weeks back.

I hadn't realized I had been bedridden for so long. Anyway, it sounds like the ground might be dry enough to get out and check the crops. If we keep getting some good sunshine now after all that moisture, we should have some real good crops this year." Frank hesitated long enough to swallow and scoop in another mouthful of food.

"I'm not capable of getting on a tractor, yet, and I know how much you hate it. I was saying that I bet Casey would come over and help out. Unless he has been around since I've been laid up in bed, I don't think you know Casey, do you?"

"No, I don't, Frank. And no one but Chief Simmons has been around here since you took to your bed. Who is he?" *And, where in the hell has he been these past few weeks? He could have been doing the chores instead of me.*

Frank gulped down some coffee to wash down his food. "When Henry's folks sold the farm, Casey is the fella that bought the place. Not long after that his brother moved in there with him. Both are nice young men.

Anyway, Casey has come over and helped me do the fieldwork for the past few years since they just live across the road, and you were never available. I thought I'd give him a call and see if he could come over and help you out with the fieldwork. What do you think?" Frank said, gobbling up his food, like he hadn't eaten in years.

"Help me out? *Me*, do fieldwork? Come on Frank, no way. I mean, I've been here for weeks now doing the everyday chores, but you know I hate driving that stupid tractor and doing field work," Darin complained with venom in his voice.

Frank swallowed his last drop of coffee. He knew Darin hated farm work. However, since Darin had been so great at helping out these past weeks, Frank really thought that he would be more than happy to help in the fields.

"I'm sorry, Darin. Bad assumption on my part. Hey, I think I'll give Casey a call anyway. You know, at least he could keep an eye on the crops for me, right? And soon, well, I'll be as good as new, like I said before. Then I can get out there in the fields myself and not have to depend on you or anyone else to get my chores handled.

Heck, I didn't even think about asking for Casey's help until now." Darin grunted. "Sorry, I wasn't thinking straight before, Darin, or Casey could have taken over the chores instead of you doing them." Frank lied through his teeth to try and cheer up Darin's look of disdain. "Anyway, the way I feel right now, I know I'm on the mend."

"You know, Frank, I agree. You do look better and you ate, no, you inhaled a good breakfast." Darin chuckled, looking down at Frank's plate. Frank wiped it clean with his last bite of toast. "Anyway I need to talk to you, serious like, and no time like the present. How about I get us some more coffee first?"

A serious talk? That's wonderful. This is the opportunity I've been waiting for. Finally, I can tell Darin the truth about my health and ease this burden I've been carrying around on my shoulders for years now. "Okay, fill me up." Darin left the table and returned with the coffee carafe. "You know, Darin, when you're through telling me what's on your mind, I've got something important to talk to you about, also."

"We have just enough for one more cup each," Darin said, pouring the coffee. After he put the empty pot in the sink and sat back at the table, he started his heart-to-heart talk. "Frank, you know I love you, and you know I despise the farm. It isn't just this farm, it's farm life in general. I hate all farming communities like Kidwell and Sharpin. I went to college to learn something that would get me off of farms and away from small towns and small-minded people.

I worked real hard at that bank, and hardly got paid enough to buy hay for one of those friggin' cows out there that you milk. It might have been a dream, but I always knew, someday, I would get out of here and move to a big city. That day has come. I saved a little money and I have enough for a one-way ticket on the bus to go to Detroit, Indianapolis, New York, or wherever I decide to live. I was going to ask you for the bus fare, but I think I have enough to get by.

Just before you took sick, I quit my bank job. I had already started packing my suitcase, Frank, but I put my life—I put everything on hold to help you out. So, now that you're feeling better, I'm leaving. It's time to follow my dreams."

Frank drank his coffee. Although his heart was breaking, he knew he had to let go. It was the first time he could remember in twenty-three years that Darin said he loved him. He had to lie to Darin or he knew he would feel guilty for the rest of his life if he kept him from leaving.

"Sure, Darin. Gees, I feel terrible that I spoiled your trip. But, you're right, you know. I am feeling better, thanks to you taking such good care of me. Say, I missed your birthday. It's a little late, but what would you like for a gift, this year?"

"In all honesty? I just wish you would stay well so I don't have to postpone my trip, again."

"I'll do my best. Oh, you just reminded me of something. Remember that birthday wish you made one time and wouldn't tell me about?"

"I sure do," Darin answered with a smirk.

"Well, can you tell me now? Did it ever come true?"

"Not yet, but it's close."

With a smile, Frank begged, "Oh, come on. Pleeeeeze."

"Okay. My wish was to get off this farm, and away from hick towns and ignorant people, permanently."

"I see." Darin word's cut Frank clear to the quick. Permanently, meant Darin had no intentions of ever returning. Not even for a visit. "You must have thought me a lame brain when I told you to be careful of what you wished for or it may come true?"

Bored with the subject, Darin answered, "No."

Sick or not, no one had to hit Frank in the head. Disappointed or not, he forced a smile. "Hey, there's nothing I like better than to hear someone has a wish come true. Especially when that someone is you. So, to make this wish happen for real, when do you plan on leaving?"

"The bus stops in town every Friday around 3:30 p.m. I've not checked it out yet, so I don't know if I have to make a reservations, how many transfers I'll have to make, or how long of a ride it will be to my destination. It's not a problem because I can do all that tomorrow. If I can just purchase a ticket and board at the same time, I would like to be on it this Friday. I'm sure you'll feel even better by then."

"Shoot, I don't even know what month it is, let alone what day it is."

"We're into the second week of July. Today is Tuesday."

"July? What in Sam hill happened to June? I couldn't have been in bed that long, was I?"

"You sure were. I got so scared, I had Doc Shivley make a house call. All be damned, Frank, I thought you were dying on me for a while there. I had never realized that a person could sleep that much, wake up groggy, then go right back into a deep sleep. I've had some lost weekends, but they were nothing compared to the way you slept." Inside, Frank was amused by Darin's comment. Wanting to hear all of what Darin was reporting, he continued to sit in silence.

"Doc said the hospital couldn't do much more for you than I was doing. As long as you kept waking up, and your vital signs were okay, he said you just had to let your body get all the rest it needed. You also needed to keep some nourishment in your body. So, when you were half awake, I held you up and forced fed you broth and hot tea. It appears pneumonia will set into your lungs if I would have just let you lie there.

Oh, and Doc had me take you off your pills until you were alert enough to swallow more than liquids. He didn't want you choking on anything solid. When you were more conscious for longer periods of time, that's when I started giving you your medicine again, and feeding you soft foods. I got a little irritated when Doc told me to follow the prescribed dosage on the prescription bottle. Of course, he withdrew his comment when he discovered the label had been removed."

"It's funny, I kind of remember some things. Others are just a shadow in my mind, but I sure don't remember seeing Doc. I thought you told me no one's been around but Rusty?"

"You were pretty adamant about me not contacting your doctor before, so I didn't want to upset you. That's why I didn't mention it. Old Doc Shivley couldn't, or wouldn't give me any straight answers, either. I think you should try to find a specialist in Omaha or Lincoln. Two years is far too long to be sick with a so-called bug."

"I'm sure Doc knows what he's doing, Darin. Please, let's not rehash this conversation. At the rate of repeating myself, thank you, again, for taking such good care of me." Darin rolled his eyes and gave a slight nod. "Let's get back to your trip."

"Okay, is Friday all right with you?"

"Oh, well, if today is Tuesday, then that's just three days away." Before Frank gave Darin an answer, he had some questions floating around on his brain. "What do you plan on doing in any of these big cities, once you get there?"

Now I'm screwing up. I told Rusty that I had a big job offer. If he and Frank start talking they will know I lied, then wonder why I lied. I had better get things straight. Some outlaw I am. I can break into people's houses and walk away with their money without getting caught, but I get caught in my own lies.

Darin took a drink of his coffee. Careful not to spill the remaining contents, he tipped the edge of his cup on the table and stared into it, like a Gypsy reading tealeaves. "Okay, Frank. I didn't want to tell you the truth, just in case I failed. You have to understand, I want you to be proud of me. So, here's the real truth. I'm going to New York. I got a great job offer from a big corporation there, working in their accounts department. I'm real excited about it, but I don't want anyone to know.

Since gossip is the name of the game around these small towns, I would just as soon you don't tell anyone. Then, if I don't make it, I won't feel like a fool if I have to come back home with my tail between my legs. If I do make it, well, then you can tell everyone and brag all you want to. Do you understand?"

"Sure do, Darin. Hey, I'm already so proud of you that I could burst. Okay, you do what you have to do. I hear New York is pretty expensive. How are you going to live until your first paycheck? Heck, where will you live?"

"Like I told you, I've been saving a little cash. I know it hasn't been very fair to you, but that's why I was always broke and borrowing money from you. Anyway, I hear they have a YMCA there in New York where I can stay cheap. Like I said, I have enough to get my one-way ticket. But, if you can help tide me over until I earn my first paycheck, well—"

"How much?"

"Whatever you can spare."

"How long do you think you'll have to work before you'll get a paycheck?"

I just knew it. I never should have asked. Now, I've got to put up with twenty questions. He knows damn well I get my trust fund in three years, so why not just give me some money without all of the malarkey that goes with it? I'll have more than enough money to spend in New York, but I thought asking him for a loan would throw good old Rusty off balance.

"I don't know how much I'll need or how long before I will get paid. Look, just forget it Frank. I sure wouldn't want to put you out." Darin tried to be nice but he knew he came across a little too harsh and rather sarcastic.

"I didn't mean to upset you, Darin. I was just trying to figure out how much to give you." Frank sat for a moment in silence, figuring out what to do. "Here, let's do this. I'll give you two hundred in cash before you leave. That should help you out with what you have saved to pay for your trip and have money left over.

After you get to New York, take a few dollars and open up a savings account. I think that would be better than a checking account until you get a permanent address. Let me know the name of the bank that you will be doing business with.

Once I have the information, I'll have my bank wire funds to put into an account for you. Do you think fifteen hundred will keep you going until you can get your job established and start earning wages?"

His enthusiasm was apparent when his eyes lit up. "Sure, Frank, that would work. And, don't you worry about me. I'm going to do just fine."

"It sounds like it to me. Okay, so Friday it is. How about you get a couple of those thick T-bones out of the freezer and we'll have a going away dinner," he said, smiling, "for you on Thursday night."

"No, that's not necessary."

"Oh, stupid me. I bet you'd rather spend the time with your buddies down at the local bar before you leave town. What can I do to help you get ready?"

I guess that would be a bit selfish on my part, spending my last night out on the tow. I don't have any respect for Frank as a man, but one last celebration dinner with him won't kill me. Anyway, who cares about those guys down at the bar. Certainly not me. They aren't my real buddies anyway. These small town hicks were good for a laugh and an alibi when I needed them, but nothing more.

I shouldn't have hit Frank up for more money. But if I hadn't, I just know he would've said something to Rusty. Then, snoopy Rusty would have gotten too suspicious and started checking me out. I'll take the two hundred from Frank when I leave. I can always write him or call him later and tell him I got an advance on my new job so I won't need the other fifteen hundred. That should keep both him and Rusty convinced I have money because of a new job. If either asks me where I'm working ... Well, I won't worry about that for now.

I've already called and made reservations. Needed to make sure I could stay at the YMCA in New York, at one of the Manhattan facilities. So, if anyone decides to check up on me, my backend is covered. I'll just have to remember to call the Y every once in a while to change my reservation dates. I could care less whether or not they get upset with me because I don't plan on staying there anyhow. They're just another step in covering my tracks.

"Yoo-hoo, Darin, did I lose you again? Boy, you're beginning to scare me," Frank commented, as he sat and waited for Darin to speak.

Darin smiled. "I'm sorry. It's just that I'm so excited about my trip that it occupies my mind."

"No wonder you've been in such a daze every time someone is talking to you."

"Everyone?"

"Me, I'm everyone," Frank joked. "But, that's okay. I guess I can understand how you feel." Frank remembered how much he too wanted to leave the farm years ago.

"You know what, Frank? Truth is, I wasn't going to go out drinking Thursday night. Actually, I was planning on going to bed early. I figured staying home and saving my money was a better idea.

Even though I've got this trip burning a hole in my head, I've been sitting here thinking about your offer. I've decided that I can sleep on the long bus ride. If the offer is still open, I would enjoy spending my last evening with you."

"Are you sure, Darin?"

"Of course, I'm sure. I wouldn't say it if I didn't mean it."

Grinning, Frank said, "Okay. I will need a big favor, but I don't think you'll like it."

"What kind of favor?"

In a rapid manner, Frank spit out the words, "Grocery shopping." Squinting his eyes, he wrinkled up his face and shrugged, as if he expected something to be thrown at him.

"Very funny, Frank. You can open your eyes now."

"Well, you said we didn't have any groceries in the house, and I would like this to be a special night. If I write you a list, would you get us a few things at the store for our last dinner together? And I don't care what color, what brand, what size or whatever. I promise I won't send you back to return or exchange anything you bring home. Deal?"

"Deal," Darin agreed, turning a pretentious smile into a grin of relief.

"Okay. Get me a pen and paper. I'll start making the list, right now."

This is good, Frank. As long as I keep you busy today, you will sleep better tonight.

Getting a pen and a writing tablet, Darin brought them to the kitchen table. While Darin did up the morning dishes and made a fresh pot of coffee, they talked about the groceries they would need for a celebration dinner plus a few other things that were needed around the house. Frank threw out suggestions as he wrote out the list. After pouring them both a fresh cup of coffee, Darin joined Frank at the table.

"Okay, Frank, what did we end up with for our celebration menu.

"I wrote down everything you said you wanted. Fresh salad, steak, baked potato, a good mushroom sauce, some French bread toasted with butter and garlic, and a good glass of red wine. Darned if that don't sound like a condemned man's last meal," Frank quipped.

Darin shivered. "That's not funny."

"It was just a joke, Darin."

Ease up, Darin. "Funny or not, I don't want anything to jinx my trip."

"That's superstitious bunk."

Even though he was managing to keep a smile on his face and excitement in his speech, Frank's stomach was starting to cramp. Hiding his pain, he kept talking and writing.

"Well, Darin, that's about it. Unless there's something else you can think of?"

"Not right now. Shopping will have to wait until tomorrow. I still have a lot of packing to do. What say, we leave the list on the table. As we think of other things we need around here, we can add them to the list. That way, you won't have to go shopping for a few weeks after I've gone. Might as well make it easy for you," Darin suggested.

"Now that's real thoughtful of you, and much appreciated. Oh, and remind me later, I'll get you some money. I'm paying for the groceries. I've also decided, along with the two hundred to have in your pocket, that I'm paying for your bus ticket. I want you to leave town with every cent you've saved."

"That's awfully generous, Frank. Thanks."

As Frank's cramps were getting worse, he was afraid he wouldn't be able to keep the agony from showing on his face. Darin's plans couldn't be spoiled, especially by Frank. "You know, that breakfast hit the spot, but I'm feeling rather tired, again. I think I'll go in the bedroom and rest a spell."

"No! I mean—Why don't you go in and relax in the living room. There's a basketful of clothes in there just waiting to be folded. I haven't had a chance to get that task done. It was very difficult trying to keep up with everything else, including your soiled bedding. Don't take this wrong, Frank, but I hope I never have to be a nursemaid to anyone, ever again. *Now, through in the guilt trip.* Cleaning up after someone who pees or craps the bed is—"

"Okay, Darin. I get the picture. I'm sorry I put you in that position."

"Oh, hey, I'm just talking through my ear. I did it, and it's over. So, if you wouldn't mind helping, you can sit nice and comfortable on the couch and do that for me. Besides, I want to change your sheets, again, and clean your room. I planned on straightening up the house today but didn't want to disturb you. However, since you're up, now I can get a few things done and not worry about making any noise. Do you mind?" Darin questioned with a hidden agenda.

"You know I don't mind. I know I'm repeating myself, but I do appreciate all you've done and continue doing around here. Even though I know how much you're despising every minute of it. Okay, I'll go in and fold clothes. While I'm at it, I'll see what's on the boob tube. Isn't that what you kids call it today?" Frank joked.

"Maybe in your generation, Frank, but not in mine. Okay, I'll finish up in here." *Once the clothes are folded, he's sure to stretch out on the couch while watching TV, then fall asleep. I can't afford to let him do* that. I'll have to come up with some good reasons for keeping him awake all day, if I want my plan to work.

While folding clothes, Frank couldn't help but agonize over Darin. *I understand your wanting to leave farm life, Darin, but I don't understand your selfishness at times. You have a one-track mind. You were so busy telling me how you hated everything and how you could hardly wait to get out of here that you didn't even care that I had something important to tell you.*

Maybe it's best you leave here and not know the truth about my health. Yeah, it's best this way. I would have a guilty conscience for the rest of my life if I did or said anything that would keep you from following your dreams. I could never do anything to make you hate me as much as I hated my mother for ruining my life. I know I'll take that hatred to my grave.

Meanwhile, at the office of Chief Simmons, the chief and Officer Kelly were conversing over coffee.

"I don't understand it, Kelly. It's been weeks since Clinger joined that athletic club and since I baited the trap for our thief. The guys haven't seen anything suspicious around the Clinger house while he's gone. Other than my last visit when I baited Darin, I've stayed away on purpose from visiting Frank so Darin wouldn't ask me any questions. I've even refrained from phoning Frank in fear Darin would answer the phone.

I could have sworn I was right about Darin. Anyway, we're going to have to pick him up and bring him in for questioning. We can't put this off any longer," Rusty commented.

"I don't think you have a choice," Kelly admitted in agreement.

"Something just crossed my mind."

"Spill it."

"You've known Darin a lot longer than I have, but you know how small town gossip is," Kelly stated with a question in his voice.

"That's an understatement, Kelly, but what's your point?"

"I go to Yank's Bar, occasionally, for a few beers after work. It seems Darin frequents that bar and is pretty well known with the crowd that hangs out there."

"If that were a crime, Kelly, we would all be locked up," Rusty admitted.

"True. The short of it is, the guys at the bar like to talk. It doesn't seem to be any secret that Darin brags about how, someday, he will have more than enough money to get out of Nebraska and move to a big city and live like a king. Seems he has a passionate dislike for farming communities, calling them small hick towns and small-minded people."

"And I ask you again, your point being?" Then, like a bolt out of the blue, Rusty was struck with an enlightening thought. "Kelly, that's why you're my main man. Damn, I've always known Darin hated Kidwell. That was obvious when he was growing up always getting in trouble. Now, working at a small bank, well, he could never make enough money to get out of here. He'd have to find other resources. Is that what you're insinuating? Am I on your wave length?"

"It makes sense, doesn't it? That bank job was a dead end job for someone with ambition like Darin has. The one thing I can't figure out though, is why he would steal to get the money? Why not just ask his brother for some money?"

"Those are good questions, Kelly. First off, if there wasn't so much money involved, I would have to say he stole for the sport. However, since our suspect has built up quit a healthy sum from these burglaries, then it has to be for financial gains.

As for Frank, I know he inherited from his parents and an uncle. Now, I never really asked him, but I figured he ended up with quite a tidy sum. Of course, I'm basing my assumptions on the fact that Frank buys a new car and a new truck every year, and has nothing but new top-of-the-line farm machinery."

"I heard the Righter's were dirt farmers, like Frank."

"Yeah, but don't be fooled by the term *dirt farmer*, Kelly. Some of them make a darn good living. The elder Righter's were a perfect example. They spent money like water."

"If you don't mind me asking, Chief, where did the Righter's get all their money to begin with?"

"I don't know. Frank always confided more in my brother when it came to his parents, but neither of the boys ever said a word to me. And, I never thought any of it was my business. Frank and I are the best of friends, but there are some things we just don't talk about.

Hey, we're getting off the track here and wasting time, Kelly. Let's get back to the present. Frank always seems to have money for whatever he wants, so you have asked the key question. Why didn't Darin borrow from his own brother if he wanted a large sum to leave town?"

"If we can find out the answer to that question, we may have a motive," Kelly commented.

"Yeah, you're right. It seems like a month of Sundays since I paid

Frank a visit. I've been keeping in phone contact with Darin, but it's high time I see for myself how Frank's getting along. If Darin's there, I'll just have to dodge his questions.

If I'm lucky, and Darin isn't glued to the house, I can get some answers from Frank. Frank isn't stupid. When I start throwing questions at him, he's going to wonder why. But, I don't have any other choice.

Darin is smart enough to have been playing mind games with us these past three years. Burglarize the community until he has enough money to live, like a so-called big-city king, then sit tight for a few months so no one suspects him. It sure sounds like something he would do. I'll go right now and have that talk with Frank before I do any more speculating," Rusty stated as he stood from his chair.

"Nope, sorry Chief, but you have to be in court in an hour. I don't think you can get out to Frank's place, have your talk, and get back in time."

"I forgot. Thanks for reminding me. Okay, one more day isn't going to make a difference, not after three years of chasing this mutt. I'll put off talking to Frank until tomorrow. We'll let Darin have one more day before we pick him up as a suspect.

You know, Kelly, I'm retiring real soon. In all probability, this will be my last big arrest. That is, if I make an arrest. In all my years I have never, not once, hesitated in picking up any suspect. This is going against everything I have believed in and worked for to give a friend's brother the benefit of the doubt. I should, perhaps, hand in my badge right now."

"Don't talk that way, Chief. I believe I'm a good officer of the law also. I also know, as well as you do, if we don't have all of the facts, including a motive, the D.A. won't have a case. We could pick up Darin for questioning right now but that would warn him we're on to him, which might send him running. I don't think we want to tip our hand until we find that motive."

"Kelly, you're going to make an excellent chief of police, someday. Well, I had better get my files together for court." As Officer Kelly stood to leave the office, Rusty said, "Just to be on the safe side, until I can get some answers from Frank tomorrow, tell the guys to stay on the stake-out. Operation Ivy is to remain officially in progress until further notice."

"Will do, Chief."

That evening, just as Darin had planned, he prepared dinner and had it on the table at 7:00 p.m. While setting the table, he placed two pills just under the side of Frank's plate. To make sure his plan worked, he also crushed one of the same kind of pills, mixing it into a pre-poured glass of orange juice. He placed the glass in the refrigerator and called Frank to dinner.

Because of his all-day bout with stomach cramps, Frank wasn't really hungry. Just to appease Darin, he sat at the table and forced himself to eat. Conversation over dinner was rather one sided. Darin carried on and on about the move he was about to make.

Leaving small portions of food on his plate, Frank leaned back in his chair. Wiping his mouth with his napkin, he declared, "I'm so stuffed, I feel like a Christmas goose. That was might tasty for a guy who says he doesn't like to cook, but I just can't eat another bite."

"I didn't expect you to eat as much as you did." Darin admitted.
"Thanks for the compliment, but how hard is it to ruin pork chops. Anyone can fry them."

"Okay, you got me there, but they were good. How about some coffee?"

"Nope. You've been up all day and had far too much coffee, already. Speaking of drinking something, it's time for your pills." Getting the glass of juice from the refrigerator, Darin took a spoon out of the drawer and commenced stirring the juice.

"What on earth are you doing, Darin?"

"Oh, ah, the pulp was floating on the top. I thought it would be easier for you to drink if I mixed it up."

"Very thoughtful of you. Thank you."

Placing the juice in front of Frank, Darin said, "There you go. Take your pills, then get your butt into bed and call it a night."

"Bed? Heck, not even the chickens roost this early. You trying to get rid of me?"

"Be serious, Frank. This is the first day you've been out of bed in weeks. I don't want you to overdo it. Now, please, for me," Darin pleaded. "I want you healthy so I can leave with a clear conscience on Friday,"

"Okay, you big bully." Frank laughed. "But, Mr. Pill Keeper, where are you hiding my pills."

"I'm not hiding them."

"If you're not, then give them back to me. I feel like a child having you dole them out every time I want one."

"The pills are on your nightstand. Right where you I put them. For your information, I wasn't doling them out. I was just trying to be helpful. Their yours. Take them any darn time you want."

"Good. I'll just take my juice into the bedroom with me, and—"

"That's not necessary, Frank."

"Why not?"

"Before dinner, I brought a couple of your pills in here," Darin looked around the area by Frank's plate, "and I could have sworn I put them next to your dinner plate."

Frank moved his plate, first to one side, then to another before he found them. "Here they are." He popped the pills in his mouth, followed by a couple of big gulps of juice. Scrunching his face into the weirdest shape Darin had ever witnessed, Frank slammed the glass to the table, loudly complaining, "Good Grief! That was the most bitter tasting juice I've ever had the misfortune of drinking." He grabbed his napkin and wiped the access saliva from the corners of his mouth. "Fooey!"

"You all right, Frank?"

"Yeah, I'll be fine. Let's get rid of that juice. I don't know if it's sour or rancid, but I sure don't want anymore of it." He rubbed his stomach. "Sure hope it settles all right. What I don't need is ptomaine poisoning."

"Gees, I'm sorry, Frank. You drank the same juice all day today, and never said a word about it tasting funny. Naturally, I assumed it was good."

"It was. Oh, I don't know. Maybe my taste buds are wacky. Call it psychological, but since you mentioned bed, I am feeling a little tired. That is, my body feels tired, but I don't feel sleepy."

"Fine. Go to bed and I'll bring you in a magazine to read. Reading will help you fall asleep. I know it does me. Now, up with you," Darin said, "and into bed. Doctor's orders."

"Okay, okay, I'm going." Frank turned sideways in his chair. He braced one hand on the table and one on the back of the chair for support in standing. Before he got to his feet, he said, "Oh, I clean forgot to ask you. Where've you been going after dark?"

"What? I haven't gone anywhere in weeks." *Blast it! Those times I checked on Denton, I didn't think Frank woke up and noticed me gone. He never said anything before. Why now?* "You know, Frank, even when you were awake, you weren't alert. Are you sure you're not just remembering a dream? You could have been hallucinating, too."

"Those weeks in bed did make my mind a little fuzzy. I remember, though, two or three times being lucid enough to call out for you. You didn't answer. I'm almost sure I wasn't dreaming."

"If in fact you did call out to me, did you ever stop to think that I've been so exhausted from all the physical work I've been doing around here, plus taking care of you, that I fell into a deep sleep when I finally dropped in bed? I'm sure I wouldn't have heard a bomb go off, let alone your voice."

"Oh, well, that makes sense. I guess at the time it seemed real enough to me. I just figured maybe you had gone out drinking or something."

Darin licked his dry lips. His nerves were getting the best of him. "Shame on you, Frank. I wouldn't go gallivanting around while you're sick in bed. You know better. In fact, I had a difficult time leaving the house to do chores in fear you might wake and need something.

You know, I read once that a person's mind can play tricks on them when they're as sick as you were. Now, that's enough of this hogwash for tonight. Get yourself to bed."

Satisfied with Darin's explanation, Frank went to bed. Darin took him a magazine. Once the kitchen was cleaned, Darin sat in the living room and turned on the television for noise. Waiting, impatiently, he kept an eye on the clock. Just after dark, he checked on Frank. Frank appeared to be sleeping. The nightstand lamp was on and the magazine was laying on the floor beside the bed.

After picking up the magazine, Darin needed to find out if the pills had worked. In his normal voice level, Darin asked, "Frank, do you need anything?" Receiving no response, he raised his voice. "Frank." When Frank didn't so much as flicker an eyelid, Darin picked up his hand, then let loose. Frank's hand fell limp to the bed. After turning off the lamp, bidding, "Sweet dreams," he left the room, closing the door behind him.

"That worked faster than I thought it would. I think by keeping him up all day helped to get him good and exhausted. Enough contemplating about Frank. I need to get into my dark clothes for my evening raid. My farewell to Kidwell." Darin checked the clock once again. He was right on schedule. After changing clothes he went back into Frank's room, removing Frank's shoes from the closet. In the kitchen, he put on the work shoes. Then to the back porch, where he put on Frank's rubber boots. Grabbing the ski mask and the gloves, even though he knew he would die wearing them in the July heat, he was off to town.

Unless there was a close location full of brush or trees in which to hide his car, Darin never burglarized a house. Oscar Denton's house was located next to such a lot, making it another easy target for Darin.

As he neared Denton's house, Darin realized he was faced with problem. On all of his scouting trips, there was always a light on in the house. Now, there was no illumination, at all. "Damn! Now I don't know if Denton is home, or not. There's always the possibility that he stayed home and went to bed early. I'd get caught for sure, going in there if he's in bed.

I could call his house and see if he answers the phone. No, that's not a good idea. If he answers, I wouldn't know what to say. If I didn't say anything, he's libel to get suspicious. Now, if I call the club and pretend that I'm a friend, it might work."

In town, Darin pulled into a gas station that was closed for the night. Hiding his car out of sight behind the building, he used the outside pay phone.

"Club Kimball," a man's voice answered on the other end of the line.

"Hello. I'm an old friend of Oscar Denton's. I wonder, could you tell me if he's there tonight?"

"Yeah, Oscar's here this evening. If you'll give me your name, I'll page him to the phone for you."

"He's there? Great." *My name?* "My name isn't important because I don't want you to call him to the phone. I'm an old friend from out of town. I want to come to the club and surprise him."

"Visitors are only allowed in the main lobby. I'll be at the front desk until closing, so just remind me when you get here that you're the one who called looking for Oscar, and I'll get him for you."

That's a laugh. Since when did Kidwell's athletic club become so exclusive? We used to always come and go as we darn well pleased when I was in school here. Well, I'm not going to show up anyway, so I don't give a rat's ass. "I'll be sure to do that," Darin replied."

"Oscar is generally here until after 11:00, if you want to catch him before he leaves," the man volunteered. "His regular routine has been to sit at the bar and have a fresco before he heads for home. Since I'm the last man out of here, I pretty much know the members' schedules."

Fresco? What a great idea. "Say, is a guest allowed in the bar area with a club member?"

"Of course."

The bar used to be for mixed drinks and beer. "Oh, I forgot to ask. By fresco, do you mean an alcoholic beverage or a health drink?" Darin inquired, trying to set an idea in motion.

"They serve mixed drinks, beer and health drinks."

"I haven't seen my old buddy, Oscar, in a few years. The last time I remember, he was a beer drinker," Darin laughed to throw in some realism.

Joining the light-hearted spirit of the conversation, the man replied with a bit of laughter in his voice. "He still does. Some things never change. Right?"

"Right. Look, is it possible to give Oscar a couple of beers on me until I get there? I'm calling from a filling station right now, and from my map, it looks like I've still got quite a few miles to go before I get to Kidwell. I don't want Oscar to leave before I can get to your club and surprise him."

"Well ... " When the man hesitated, it was obvious to Darin that his idea might not be acceptable but he waited for a response. "I can't do that without a name and a credit card number. I hope you understand, but if you didn't show up for some reason, there's no way—

"Hey, I know where you're going. So, let me give you my name and credit card number. I'll pay in cash when I get there, but that should at least take care of a couple of beers for Oscar, should something unforeseen happen that I don't make it. Can you do that?"

Since Darin's idea was acceptable, he gave the man a fake name, a credit card number and included an expiration date. He was counting on the fact that a small athletic club in Podunk, Nebraska, wouldn't have the means or the know-how for checking out credit cards that late in the evening. After Darin ended his phone call, he grinned from ear to ear, relishing in the fact that he had set Oscar up.

"Just in case it takes longer at Denton's house then I plan on, at least now I'm sure that he won't come home unexpectedly and catch me in his house. Since he hasn't lived in town very long, it's a sure bet he has out-of-town friends. So, he'll wait to see who shows up. It's a good plan, even if I do say so myself. Shame, shame, Oscar Denton. You shouldn't be working-out to lose weight, then sit and have a few brews when you're through. That's bad for your health. But, oh, so good for mine, especially tonight."

Back in his car, Darin headed for Denton's house. He turned off his headlights about a block away from the wooded lot. Driving directly over the curb and onto the lot, he parked in the midst of the high brush.

Once he had his ski mask and gloves on, he grabbed his screwdriver and flashlight, and exited the car. He knew the greenery and small wooded area would hide his car, but he still needed to use the tarp. Once the car was covered, he crept as close as he could to the house.

Darin didn't dare use his flashlight or walk around the house to check it out. Even though Denton didn't have neighbor's living close, his house was still situated on a rather busy street. Finding the backdoor, straight away, Darin felt it looked like easy access. As he started prying at the lock with his screwdriver, he was unaware he was being observed.

Keeping his voice low, Janx made a call on his walkie-talkie. "This is Officer Seals. Get a hold of the Chief, ASAP, and tell him Operation Ivy is going down. Suspect about to enter."

Rusty didn't normally ride around in his squad car at night. However, he had a strange gut feeling that night that something was going down. He was right.

"Seals, Chief here. Let the perp get inside. Stay where you are. We're on our way." Rusty immediately contacted his other officers to join him at Denton's residence.

After Darin jimmied the door and got inside, he turned on his flashlight. Looking for pictures that might cover wall safes, he ran the flashlight's illumination up the walls. The walls were bare. As he walked around, he discovered there wasn't a throw rug in sight, just wall-to-wall carpet. In Darin's mind, it became obvious with no throw rugs that there wasn't a floor safe.

"I thought by now you would've installed a safe of some kind to hide that money you keep here, Denton. Guess not. From the looks of things, you haven't even gotten settled quite yet. Now where have you hidden that money? Because of your own big mouth, I know it's here. Somewhere."

As he flashed the light into the dining room area and up over the furniture, he saw a gray metal box sitting right in the middle of the dining room table. Keeping his light shined on the box, he walked over to the table. "My, my, what have we here, a strong box not yet put away. It's very careless on your part, Mr. Oscar Denton.. Let's just take a look and find out what's inside."

Darin picked up the metal box and laid it on the floor. He got down on his knees. After propping the flashlight between his thighs so he could see what he was doing, he examined the outside of the box. "With any luck, my screwdriver will pop this lock, or, Oscar my friend, I will just have to take the box with me and find out its contents later."

Just for kicks, Darin decided to see if the strong box opened first. To his surprise, it did. He laid the screwdriver on the floor. There, inside the box, sat a stack of bills all nicely bound together with a rubber band. He picked up the bundle of bills, and—

All hell broke loose. As the front and back doors flew open, lights went on, and Darin was suddenly facing Chief Simmons and his law officers.

Black Rosebud

They were fully armed and ready to shoot, if necessary.

"Get your hands up where I can see them and lay flat on the floor," Chief Simmons ordered.

Darin made an immediate sweep with his hand, as if to dramatize the procedure before putting both hands in the air. Making sure he cleared the strong box so he wouldn't get hurt, Darin fell to his stomach thinking everything but religious thoughts. *Damn! This was a trap! Rusty, you friggin' piece of shit, you set me up.*

As the chief and other officers held their guns on Darin, Officer Kelly returned his gun to his hip holster. He knelt to the side of their perpetrator. Bringing the thief's arms behind his back, one at a time, Kelly handcuffed him. Officer Seals, after returning his gun to its holster, assisted Officer Kelly in getting their thief to his feet.

Rusty holstered his gun and walked over to the masked thief, and stood in front of him. After placing his hand on the perp's head, Rusty grabbed at the top of the ski mask. "Dear God, don't let this be you, Darin," Rusty remarked in a somber voice, yanking the mask off. Even though Rusty was almost positive it was Darin they had captured, revealing his face was hard for Rusty to swallow.

With a huge grin, as if it were a joke, Darin sang, "Hi ya, Rusty. How's it hangin'?"

Angry and forlorn at the same time, Rusty stood there shaking his head. He could feel the steam of his Irish temper rising, as he ordered, "Get this piece of garbage out of here. He's stinking up the place."

Darin was read his rights then taken to the police station. There he was told, he could make his one phone call. Darin opted not to call anyone. Soon after he was fingerprinted, booked and mugged, Rusty had Darin brought to his office. Officer Kelly joined them. Officer Janx stood guard at the door.

Sitting at his desk thoroughly disgusted, Rusty looked at his prisoner. "Sit down, Darin," Rusty demanded in a harsh voice.

Not liking to be ordered around, not even a little bit, Darin glared at Rusty. Taking his own sweet time, he begrudgingly took a seat.

"You've waived your right for a phone call and to have an attorney present. So, I want to ask you a few questions. I guess the first question is," Rusty gritted his teeth, "why?"

"Why what?" Darin smugly asked in return with a cold, self-righteous look on his face.

"Look, Darin, don't be a smart ass. You're in hot water up to your eyeballs, and that's putting it mildly. We caught you red-handed, tonight, burglarizing that house. I want to know why?"

"Maybe I needed a little extra spending money? Maybe I was just playing a joke?" Darin admitted without changing his cocky attitude.

"Playing a joke? I don't think so. With close to $300 thousand hidden away, you needed a little extra spending money? What kind of stupid answer is that?"

So, some idiots were too embarrassed to report their thefts to you, right Chief Simmons? Ha! If you only knew how much money I really did have, you'd dirty your pants. "Three hundred thousand dollars? Shit, Chief, you need to learn to count. There couldn't have been that much money in that metal box," Darin stated with a smirk, keeping up his facade.

"Let's don't play any more of your stupid games, Darin. You know darn well that I'm not speaking about tonight. I'm talking about all of the burglaries you've pulled off for close to three years now."

Darin laughed as if Rusty had told him a joke. "I get it. You think that I—Oh, that's rich. You think that I'm your Neat Nick Thief, don't you? Come on, Rusty. I thank you for the compliment, but you've got to be kidding."

"That's Chief Simmons to you, Darin, and don't you forget it. Look, I know you think I'm some old lawman that doesn't know his business, but let me tell you something, you little son-of-a—" Rusty bit his tongue to hold the name calling. "You think you're pretty smart, don't you?"

That's good, Chief Simmons. Now, you're a mind reader because yes, I do consider you an old, worn-out lawman. And, I don't think it, I know I'm smarter than you. Well, read my mind now. Screw you!

Leaving his chair, Rusty walked around to his desk front where Darin was seated. He bent from the waist, placing his face within inches of Darin's face. "You weren't smart enough, sonny boy. We've got you dead to rights. We know you pulled off those other burglaries. You might as well give it up. The ball game is over."

Not turning away, Darin laughed in Rusty's face. "Myself, I prefer to play poker." *You think you know something, Rusty, but you don't know jack-shit.*

"Yeah? Well, I'm calling your bluff." Rusty stood upright. With anger in his voice, he demanded, "Lock him up, Officer Janx. Get this piece of filth out of my sight before I do something I'll regret."

Still exploiting his arrogant attitude, Darin remarked, "You've been watching too much TV, Rusty. No cops make an arrest with their guns pulled unless they're after someone armed and dangerous. Gee, were you threatened by my flashlight?"

"Janx, take him out of here," Rusty bellowed. As Officer Janx escorted their prisoner from Rusty's office, Rusty picked up a book from his desk. With a heave, he threw the book against a wall. Even though he could empathize with Rusty's physical outburst, Kelly cringed. "Sorry, Kelly. I know I seldom get out of control and show my bad side, but that kid infuriates me."

"He sure is a cocky one," Kelly replied.

"Look, I'm going to drive out to Frank's place. It's late and Frank's been sick but I need to talk to him. This matter can't wait. You go home and get some sleep. I'll need you here bright and early in the morning," Rusty said, on the way out of his office.

Knowing what a cruel turn of fate could do to a healthy person, Rusty worried how the bad news was going to affect Frank in his unhealthy state. As he approached the Righter farm, he felt as if his heart was in his throat. Darin brought this whole ugly mess upon himself, and now, as sorrowful as it was, Frank would have to share the burden of Darin's evil ways.

BLINDED BY LOVE

Seeing Frank's pick-up parked in the drive, Rusty knew Frank had to be home. The normal yard lights were glowing. Walking up to the backdoor, Rusty noticed there were no lights on in the house. After entering the back porch, Rusty knocked on the kitchen door.

"The last time I saw Frank, he recognized me, but he was still in pretty rough shape. That no-good Darin either lied to me about Frank getting better and he's still sick in bed, or already in bed for the night."

After pounding on the door several times, getting no answer, he tried the door. It was unlocked. Opening the door, he yelled, "Frank. It's Rusty." There was still no answer. Pulling his flashlight from its secured loop on his belt, Rusty turned it on to light his way. He walked into the kitchen. Once he found the wall switch, he turned on the overhead light.

Flashlight in hand, he proceeded through the house, making his way to Frank's bedroom. In hopes not to frighten Frank, he continued calling. "Frank. It's Rusty. Frank? Frank, are you here? It's Rusty, Frank."

When he got to Frank's bedroom door, he opened it and turned on the ceiling light. Frank was in bed in a sound sleep. Turning off his flashlight, he replaced in his belt loop. When he got to the bed, Rusty sat on the edge of it, next to Frank. *Darin, I could just kick you to from here to kingdom come for leaving Frank alone in the house, like this, when he's been so sick.*

With a gentle touch, he shook Frank's arm. "Wake up, Frank. Frank." Frank didn't budge. "Frank, it's Rusty. Can you hear me?" With still no response, Rusty shook Frank's arm a bit harder. "Please, Frank, wake up." Just as Rusty was ready to call for an emergency unit, Frank moaned and barely opened his eyes. "Frank, thank God. I need to talk to you.

Can you hear me all right?" Rusty asked in a worrisome voice.

Frank rubbed his eyes. Squinting from the bright overhead light, he raised his hand to his brow, shading his eyes from the glaring light. Through blurred vision, he tried to hone in on Rusty's face. "Rusty? Are, are you really here, or am I dreaming?"

"I'm here, Frank," Rusty assured him. Touching Frank's arm, he asked, "Can you feel that?"

"Yes. What are you doing here? What time is it? Where's Darin?" Frank questioned in his daze.

"Thank God, you're alert. Look, I wouldn't have awakened you, but this is urgent. Do you feel well enough to sit up and talk to me?"

"Sure, Rusty, but what's going on? Why are you here?" Not giving Rusty a chance to answer, he stated, "Move and I'll get up."

Rusty didn't budge. "Stay in bed, Frank. Just sit up and talk to me."

"Oh, it's okay. I've been up all day. Let me clear my mind first, Rusty. What time is it, and where's Darin?"

For good reason, Rusty ignored answering questions about Darin until he was sure Frank was clear headed enough to comprehend what he was about to tell him. "It's after eleven."

"Since my light's on, I assume that's eleven at night.

"Yes, it's night, Frank. I know it's late, but it's important that we talk."

"Talk—Yes." Running his tongue over the front of his teeth, Frank commented, "I feel like I've cotton in my mouth.

Darin can't still be sleeping? Oh, I'll bet he is." Rusty bit his tongue to keep from interrupting and telling him of Darin's actual whereabouts. "We just had a discussion earlier this evening at dinner about how sound he's been sleeping. Poor kid's been worn out. Well, let's let him sleep. I'll get up. Then you and I can go in the kitchen and make some coffee. We can sit in there and talk."

"That's not necessary."

"My brain doesn't seem to be functioning right now, Rusty. Coffee will help get out the cobwebs. Just give me a second here to get oriented." Frank scooted his body into a sitting position. "Today, I thought I was getting up a little more strength and feeling better. Evidently, not. I can't believe how tired I am."

"It's a cinch I no nothing about what you're going through, Frank, but according to what Darin told me, Doc says you overworked yourself. In your condition, I can see why your body is calling for extra rest."

"You know, I've never locked my doors until that Neat Nick Thief of yours started burglarizing everyone in the county. Since that time, Darin has had strict orders to keep the house locked up tight. He's been so exhausted, lately, that I'm assuming he forgot. Especially since he's still sleeping and you're here in my room. That rather bothers me. The door was unlocked, wasn't it? That's how you got in here, right?"

"Yes, Frank, both backdoors were unlocked. For a man who's been sick, you sure are a gabby one. Why don't you take a breather, come up for air, and we'll go make that coffee?"

"The least you could do, Rusty—Oh, bring me my robe over there," he pointed to the Queen Ann chair. "Like I was saying, the least you could do is to tell me what's so darn important to talk about that you have to wake me up in the middle of the night for."

Retrieving the robe, Rusty watched as Frank took his time moving to the edge of the bed. "I want to talk to you about your brother."

"My brother? You woke me up to talk to me about Darin? Good gravy, Rusty, what on earth for? Wait. Don't answer that. Let's go get Darin up, and you can say what you have to say in front of both of us. And, it had better be good."

"Darin's not in the other room sleeping."

Shocked, Frank responded, "He's not? What happened?" Before Rusty could get a word in edgewise, Frank was attempting to stand on his unsteady legs. Rusty took a hold of him to keep him from falling over. "Did somebody break into the house while we were sleeping?" Helping Frank with his robe, Rusty never said a word. "Is that why the door was unlocked and why you're here? Oh God, is Darin hurt?" Frank turned toward Rusty with a look of shear despair. "Where is he? I need to go to him."

"Calm down. No one broke into your house. Darin's in town right now, and he's not hurt."

"In town? Dang it all, Rusty, you like to have scared me to death. Why is Darin in town?"

"Look, before I give you any of the details, let's go make that coffee. Right now, I could use a little caffeine myself."

Frank insisted on walking to the kitchen, unassisted. Rusty followed close behind in case Frank's unsteady legs decided to give out. Breathing a sigh of relief when they entered the kitchen, Rusty pulled a chair away from the table, "Here. Sit. I'll make the coffee." Once Frank was seated, Rusty asked, "Where do you keep the coffee filters?"

Frank pointed to a cupboard above the stove. "Filters are up there. In all the times you've been in my home when I've made coffee for us, I'm surprised you don't remember."

"I was always too busy talking to pay any attention, I guess."

"It's still hard for me to get use to these new coffeemakers," Frank rambled. "I miss the good old percolators."

"Personally, I prefer these new machines. Convenience. You can't beat it." As Rusty opened the cupboard door and took out the box of coffeepot filters, he spotted a small bottle of pills sitting on the shelf. In Rusty's suspicious mind, the pill bottle appeared out of place. Out of a lawman's curiosity, Rusty picked up the clear glass container to read the label. At the same time, he noticed that not too many pills appeared to be missing from the contents.

"Sleeping pills?" Rusty questioned.

"What?" Frank asked, rubbing his hands over his face in an effort to be more alert. "What sleeping pills? What are you talking about?"

"These," Rusty said, holding the bottle up. Rusty butted up against the kitchen counter. "Do you or Darin have a difficult time sleeping?"

"Don't be ridiculous. Darn it, Rusty, what makes you think I need sleeping pills? Didn't you just wake me from a sound sleep? Besides, Darin and I keep all of our medicines in the bathroom. Wait … " He stopped for a moment to gather his thoughts.

"I remember now. I bought some, well over a year ago. That was when I had a light case of insomnia. I never took the darn things though. They looked so much like my prescription pills that I was afraid I would mess up and take the wrong ones."

"I've seen your prescription bottle, Frank. It's not even close in resemblance to this one."

"No, of course it isn't. Whether I'm in the bathroom, or in here, I have a tendency to lay my pills out on the counter before taking them. Something might come up that draws my attention away from them, like the phone ringing. With my memory, it would be my luck to forget which pills I had laying out if I were taking both of them. No, I couldn't take that chance."

Can't imagine why they would be up there in the kitchen cupboard?" Frank asked, not necessarily directing the question to Rusty.

"You know, I keep misplacing things around here. Maybe I stuck them up there and thought I put them back in the bathroom. Oh, well, what does it matter anyway?"

"Frank, you've been in bed for weeks. I couldn't come out and visit you everyday, but I did keep in contact with Darin by phone. The last time I was here, you weren't coherent enough to do any visiting."

"I vaguely remember when you came to visit me. I wasn't aware, though, that you kept in contact by phone. Darin's been so busy that I guess he forgot to tell me. But what does that have to do with anything?"

"You said you were up and around today, right?"

"Yeah, I was. I was feeling a lot better. In fact, I ate a good breakfast, had a light lunch, and I had a good dinner. Why all the questions, Rusty? What does any of this have to do with Darin?"

"Please don't get upset with me because I'm only guessing, but from the sound sleep you were in, instinct tells me these pills were given to you. In all probability, the bottle was hidden out of sight up here so you wouldn't find them," Rusty surmised. "I have to tell you, Frank, it took a good shaking and a lot of yelling on my part to wake you up."

"What? Rusty, have you gone loco on me? Of course I was in a sound sleep. Good Lord, man, didn't you just hear me say that I was up all day?"

"Yes, I heard you. That doesn't change the fact that I still believe this bottle was hidden on purpose, not placed there by mistake."

"What are you implying? You think Darin gave me some of those pills to deliberately make me sleep then hid the bottle?"

"I don't know, Frank. Instinct tells me, if we were to draw blood from you right now, you'd test positive for barbiturates. I would stake my reputation on it. Now, I know you're ailing, but it's like you've been in a hypnotic state for weeks. It's very possible that you've been drugged all along. I ser—"

"You wait just—"

"No, you hold on, Frank. Before you get angry or say another word, let me make coffee. I want you clear headed and calm when I explain why I said what I did. Please, as a friend, don't draw any conclusions until I've finished."

"Gosh darn it, Rusty, if you weren't my friend, I'd muster up enough strength to throw you out of here on your ear, police chief, or not."

"Yes, I'm sure you would. I'm just asking you to hear me out before you make any judgment calls."

"Okay, Rusty, make the darn coffee. Then sit down and tell me what this is all about," Frank insisted. "But whatever you've got to say had better be good."

"May I take this bottle with me?"

"I don't know why, but take the darn thing."

Rusty sat the bottle of sleeping pills on the table out of Frank's reach. He didn't want Frank to put any more fingerprints on the bottle than it, assumedly, already had. "Where are your plastic sandwich bags, or do you have any?" Rusty asked.

"In that bottom drawer, over there," Frank motioned with the flicking of his wrist and his shaky pointer finger. "Why?"

Opening the drawer, Rusty took out a small plastic bag. "I have to take the bottle as evidence," he explained. Rusty sealed the bottle in the bag. "I want the bottle tested for fingerprints."

"We now know for sure that your prints are on it." Frank was trying desperately to make light of the situation. After he realized his comment wasn't very funny, he got serious again. "You know, Rusty, you're the policeman here, not me, but any fool knows both Darin and I live in this house. It makes common sense that both of our prints could be on that bottle. So, what are you proving?"

"That's good, Frank," Rusty replied with a smile. "I could have used you on the force. You would have made a great officer."

"Okay, so neither one of us is good at making jokes, right now. Sorry, but I think your theory about Darin is way off base.

In case you haven't noticed, the coffee sits right there next to where the filters were. If you can't talk and make coffee at the same time, I'll get up and do it."

Chuckling, Rusty stated, "I know where the coffee is. That's why I left the cupboard door open."

As he prepared the coffee, Rusty wrestled in his mind how to break the news to Frank. He knew he was prolonging the inevitable by asking questions about the sleeping pills, but that was part of his job. Investigative procedures, even when it came to a friend, were instilled in him. Once the coffee was made and the coffeemaker turned on, Rusty focused his attention on Frank.

"Does, or did Darin ever have a reason to take any of these sleeping pills after you bought them?"

"Back to those stupid pills, are we?" Rusty nodded. "No, not to my knowledge, but I wouldn't swear to it," Frank said. "What difference would it make if he did?"

"Maybe nothing. We'll just wait and see what prints come up when we have the bottle dusted."

Too agitated to sit, Rusty remained standing by the counter. He rubbed his nose. The time had come. "I have to tell you, Frank, this has been one of the worst nights of my life. We finally captured the Neat Nick Thief. He's in jail, as we speak."

"That's great, Rusty, you—Hey, wait a minute. That should mean a good night, not the worst. From the comment you just made, it must be somebody you know. Was it that much of a disappointment to you to find out who it was?"

"More than you know."

"Do I know him?"

"Probably better than anyone."

Frank smiled. "That's pretty funny, Rusty, considering I don't know too many people that well. I know a lot of people, but not what I'd call on a personal basis. On the other hand, you—" A sudden force of reality wiped the smile off Frank's face.

"Shoot! You think it's Darin, don't you? That's why you're here waking me up out of a sound sleep and giving me that trash about Darin giving me sleeping pills. Friend or no friend, Rusty, this is where I draw the line. Who in the Sam hill do you think—"

"Hold on, Frank. Don't say something you might be sorry for, until you hear me out. I need to ask you to take a blood test."

"A blood test?"

"Yes, to verify my suspicions that Darin drugged you."

Frank took a deep breath. This upsetting conversation wasn't sitting well with his failing health. "Is this test mandatory? Because if it's not, I'll have to think about it."

"No, it's not mandatory. The test would ease my mind," Rusty stated, trying the optimistic approach.

"Like I said, Rusty, I'll have to think about it."

"Make a quick decision. If the drug is in your system, it will dissipate within twenty-four hours. You could take the test, you know, and prove me wrong," Rusty insisted.

"Say, you never answered me, Rusty. Where is Darin? Oh, don't tell me. You've got him locked up, don't you? When you said he was in town, you meant in jail."

Rusty hated the position he was in at that very moment. There was no choice. He had to be honest with his best friend, like it or not. "Look, Frank, we set a trap to catch the Neat Nick Thief. There's no way of sugarcoating this, Darin is the one we caught. He swallowed the bait, and we hooked him."

Frank glared at Rusty in total disbelief of the nonsense that was oozing from Rusty's mouth. He didn't believe a word of it.

"Dang it all, Frank. Don't look at me like that. I would have given anything, anything," he stressed, "if I didn't have to be here giving you this bad news. Darin is the perp we caught tonight. Red-handed. You're door was unlocked because Darin forgot to lock it when he sneaked out of here, after he made sure you were in a sound sleep."

"Don't you give people you arrest their one phone call anymore?"

"I gave him a chance to call you. He wouldn't do it. Look, Frank, I can imagine how this is all very unsettling to you, even more so now considering your ill health. Would you like me to call your doctor?"

"No! I don't need any doctor, right now. Who I need to call is my attorney. Isn't that coffee done yet?" Frank barked.

"Almost. Do you still keep the cups up here," Rusty asked, turning to open a cabinet door.

"Yes." Getting two coffee mugs off the shelf, Rusty placed them on the counter. "You never answered me, Rusty. Darin is in jail, right?"

"Yes, he is."

"Can I see him?"

"There's no reason you can't, but I would prefer you didn't. I would like him to cool his heels in there overnight. When I was questioning him, he was being a real smart-aleck. I think a night in lock-up might take that chip off his shoulder. You can come to the jail first thing in the morning. If you feel up to it."

The coffee was ready. If there were barbiturates in Frank's system, Rusty had to be sure Frank didn't consume too much caffeine. He didn't want to comprise the blood test, should Frank agree to one. He filled Frank's cup half full. After serving Frank, Rusty took his coffee and sat at the table.

"Tonight, well, this could be the first burglary Darin committed. If it was a burglary," Frank said, stopping to take a sip of coffee. "Well, you still know how to make a good cup of coffee, Rusty."

"Thank you, my friend."

"You know, I remember you telling me there hadn't been any reported burglaries in this area for several months. I assumed your thief left town. What makes you think Darin is that Neat Nick Thief you've been chasing all these years?"

"Truth is, I can't tell you right now, Frank, but we do have some evidence that points to him. Let me ask you something off the record, and hypothetically speaking. If Darin is our infamous thief, why would he feel he had to rob other people to get money? Why wouldn't he just ask you if he needed extra cash?" Lifting his cup, he took a drink, waiting for a reasonable answer.

"He does borrow money from me. Not that I ever expect him to repay me. In fact, just today, I decided to loan him a couple a thousand," Frank admitted.

"I won't ask you why you were loaning him money. That's none of my business. However, that's penny-ante compared to what I'm trying to get at."

"Two thousand dollars is not penny-ante. Not in my book."

"Not in mine either, Frank. Look, a good thief would be smart enough not to be throwing money around that he normally wouldn't have. That would cause too much suspicion. But, that's not my point. Let me rephrase this. Let's say Darin wanted or needed a much larger amount, like ten thousand dollars. Would he feel confident in asking you for that amount?"

With the continuous rubbing of his eyes and the nape of his neck, Frank fought hard to stay awake. Neither man cared for the conversation they were involved in, but they both enjoyed their coffee, as they talked.

"Well, no, but that's a long story."

"I've got plenty of time. Fill me in."

"Not having any expenses of my own, I set up a trust for Darin, back when he was about eleven, I guess. At that time, of course, I figured my folks would be around for a long time and take care of him. So, I made sure Darin couldn't touch the trust money until he reached the age of twenty-six. You know how young people are, as soon as they hit the miracle age of twenty-one, they think they're grown-ups. Most of them aren't.

Add to that the fact that Darin was always a bit on the wild side when he was younger, I figured if he got his trust money at twenty-one, he would just blow it and have nothing to show for it later in life. I don't know why I picked that age, but that's neither here, nor there.

Anyway, the trust was in Darin's and my name. I kept control. If need be, I could cancel the trust at any time I had a mind to before he reached twenty-six. Darin figured, I guess, if he borrowed a great deal of money from me, like a large sum all at one time, that I would take it from his trust. In that case, he would have less to receive once he turned twenty-six. Have I confused you yet?"

"Anything about trust funds is Greek to me. Guess that's why I'm a police chief, not a lawyer. Look, Frank, I assumed your parents left you pretty well off. What about your money? Why couldn't, or wouldn't you loan Darin some of your money instead of taking it out of the trust fund?"

"You're right about my parents. They left me a substantial amount of funds, and the farm. Also, I had very wealthy uncle who favored me with a rather healthy inheritance when he passed away.

If Darin would have asked for a large amount of money, I would have loaned it to him without question. But he never asked." Frank stopped to drink down his coffee until his cup was empty. "Since Darin's been home, he's always borrowed, here and there, just to have spending money. I never questioned why he needed it, even though I knew he earned a paycheck.

On top of that, he lived here with absolutely no expense out of his own pocket, including his clothes. To my knowledge, he has no bills, so he doesn't owe anyone. He always drove my car, so he had no car payments. The gas and insurance, also, came out of my pocket." Even though his eyes were on Rusty, Frank appeared to be looking through him.

"I even paid for Darin's college, and all of his expenses while he lived away from home for those three years." Frank rubbed his eyes. "Well, now, getting back to the present, I didn't care what Darin did with his earned wages, or why he never seemed to have any money of his own. Shoot, I had plenty for both of us. By the way, your memory must be failing you, Rusty."

Rusty had just finished the last of his coffee. He placed his cup on the table. Raising an eyebrow, he asked, "Why do you say that?"

"If you think back to the day I added your name to all of my financial accounts, you'd remember that Darin's trust was one of those accounts."

"To be quite honest, Frank, I didn't pay much attention to the information I signed that day. I figured I was doing you a favor by signing all of those forms and signature cards, but I sure didn't need to know your business."

"My mouth is getting dry, Rusty. Don't suppose a man could have another cup of coffee, could he? And don't be so stingy. Fill the cup."

"You can have more coffee, but too much caffeine isn't good for you," Rusty offered, getting up to get the coffeepot.

"So now you're playing doctor?" Frank quipped.

Rusty laughed, as he poured the coffee. "Just be grateful I'm allowing you a refill."

"Yeah, like I really need to worry about coffee killing me."

"Sorry, Frank, I wasn't thinking."

Frank changed the subject back to Darin's finances. "You know it's funny, but just today, Darin told me that his pay at the bank was very little. I had always assumed it was, but never felt it was my place to ask." After acknowledging Rusty's kind gesture, with a nod of his head, Frank took a brief moment to take a drink of hot coffee

"Anyway, Darin said he had been saving what little he could, to better himself. According to him, that was why he was always borrowing from me. Heck, Rusty, it's just not possible for me to live long enough, as fast as I'm ailing, to spend what I have put aside. Darin might as well enjoy some of it.

Now, I know Darin is a whiz when it comes to accounting, but his dollars and sense, if you'll excuse the pun, don't add up to his way of living. Darin has, and always has had, a rich appetite. The scamp has always lived beyond his means without taking into consideration where the money comes from. He always saw my folks spending a lot of money, and would get very upset if they didn't just dole it out to him every time he wanted something.

When he was little and I gave him a nickel to buy a candy bar, he would pick out a candy bar for a quarter, knowing I'd pay the difference. That's precisely the reason I will loan him all the money he needs, as long as I keep the books. I just won't release his trust fund to him yet."

"In my opinion, you spoiled him, Frank, always giving, and giving, then giving more. Other than the past several weeks that you've been almost bedridden, I've never known a day that Darin has helped you out."

Frank nodded, knowing Rusty was right on the mark. He was guilty of spoiling Darin. "Well, that isn't my business either," Rusty admitted before going any further with his unsolicited comments. "I still don't understand. If Darin would borrow spending money while all the time earning his own pay, no matter how little, then why wouldn't he ask you for a larger sum if he needed, or wanted it so badly?" Rusty kept asking, digging for answers.

"You mean a large amount, like that ten thousand dollars you asked me about?"

"Yes."

"Are we still speaking hypothetical?"

"Yes, Frank."

"Well, okay then. I just wanted to make sure. Now, what was that question again?"

"I want to know why Darin would not borrow ten thousand from you if he wanted it so damn bad, for what ever reason?"

"I think it was because of my folks. Truth is, it was my mother. Back when Darin turned fifteen, he wanted to buy a car. I wanted to give him the money. My folks forbade me to do so. Then my mother told Darin that if he wanted money for a car, it would be taken out of his trust. Even though it was my money that went into that trust, Mother used that as a leverage to threaten him with. That was so Darin wouldn't ever ask for a large sum of money again.

Remember when I told you how spineless I was when it came to my mother?" Rusty nodded. "Yeah, well, I just kept my mouth shut. That was easier for me than going against her demands. I guess Darin still remembers that conversation with my mother, so he never approached me for anymore than pocket money. That is, until earlier today when we talked about the small loan."

"What about college?" Rusty asked.

"What about it?"

"I have a distinct memory of you telling me that Darin had come to you and asked you for the money to go to college. When you said yes, he turned around and asked if you would also foot the bill so he could live away from home."

"I think you need more caffeine," Frank remarked, in jest. "You're just repeating what I told you a few minutes ago."

"I know. I'm trying to get everything clear in my mind about your money and Darin's knowledge of it."

"Darin never knew the truth about my financial status. Sure, he knew I paid for everything, including sending him a rather healthy weekly allowance when he was away at college, but he was under the assumption that the money came from a rather large insurance policy the folks had. Darin believed part of that insurance money was his. That wasn't true of course, but I never told him any different."

"Wait, Frank. If Darin thought part of the insurance money belonged to him, why not ask for the remainder in cash? Wild or not, he is over twenty-one."

"Because I made it very clear to him, his funds from that policy was a limited amount. After his college expenses, his portion was all spent.

Everything came out of my pocket.

"I'm just guessing about some of this, mind you, but I think I know Darin pretty well and the way he thinks. After all, Rusty, he is my flesh and blood."

Rusty didn't care to comment on Frank's statement. Ever since Darin was arrested, Rusty was wishing that Frank wasn't even remotely related to his perp.

"Okay, everything you've explained to me makes sense. We're assuming, here, that Darin didn't ask you for cash from the insurance policy based on the fact that you told him his money was used up."

"Assuming would be correct," Frank agreed.

"I'm still puzzled, though," Rusty admitted. "Why wouldn't he just wait for a few years until he turns twenty-six to get the trust money? Why go out and rob other people of their savings? On the other hand, you said twice that you would loan him the money, not give it to him. Maybe he didn't want to have to repay you."

"Listen, Rusty, I don't think you're talking hypothetical, anymore. You're assuming it was Darin who robbed all those other victims. Just because you caught him burglarizing one house, tonight, still doesn't prove he's your thief. I don't care what evidence you say you have. It wasn't Darin.

As for that stupid idea of Darin drugging me with sleeping pills, well, you're dead wrong. Darin told me that Doc Shivley was out here to check when I was laid up in bed. I'm sure he would have known if I was drugged, or not. Shoot, I've just been up one lousy day. No wonder you had a hard time waking me tonight. I'm sick, Rusty, can't you get that through your head instead of making wild accusations about Darin."

Frank shut down. Here he had been sitting and talking about Darin, while all the time feeding into Rusty's law officer's questions. To think things through before making any more snap judgments, he held his cup to his mouth, taking several long drinks of coffee.

He concluded that under the circumstances, he had no doubt said more than he should have said at that point. Frank placed his cup on the table. "With all this caffeine, my head is much clearer now, Rusty. Until I can talk with Darin, I don't think we need to have any further discussion about this."

Rusty drank the last swallow of his coffee. He then rinsed his cup in the sink. "You're right, Frank. Maybe I shouldn't have come here, tonight. As a friend, well, I wanted to talk to you and try to get some insight as to what's going on with Darin. Thanks for the coffee. About tomorrow morning, do you want me to send one of the squad cars to give you a ride to town?"

"No. I'll get there on my own steam."

"If you change your mind, just call me. I'll see you in the morning."

Rusty picked up the plastic bag that held the bottle of sleeping pills and stuck it in his shirt pocket. As he left, he felt utterly depressed that he had to be the one to upset his friend with such heart-wrenching news. Not having Frank believe him was disheartening to Rusty. However, he understood blood was thicker than water. It was natural that Frank would choose to believe Darin over anything he had to say.

Frank stayed seated at the table. Once Rusty was gone, Frank lost it. Although he wasn't a cursing man, he screamed obscenities with fire he hadn't felt in years. "Dear God, don't let it be true. Darin just can't be this Neat Nick Thief. Dammit all! I've given that kid everything I could to give him a better life than the one I had. Blast you, Mother! The fires of hell aren't good enough for you!" he yelled, pounding his fist on the table.

"I hope you're listening because my anger is aimed at you. You did this. You wicked bitch! If Darin is guilty, then it's all your damn fault! If you had let me have the life I wanted, things would be different now. My life wouldn't be in such a turmoil. If you hadn't raised Darin the way you did, he would have turned out to be a decent, loving, respectful human being. Now look at him. He's in jail! Damn you! Damn you! I hope you're happy, you bitch!" Slumping over the table, Frank broke into tears.

ANOTHER WORLD

Farm Girl had already called the front desk to let them know she was checking out within the hour. From a customer they had almost turned away on the first night of her arrival, they were sorry to see her leave.

Before she packed to leave, she searched everywhere for her bus ticket. After going through her belongings, she sat in a chair trying to remember what she had done with it. Nothing came to mind. Realizing it was lost, she decided not to worry. All she had to do was to purchase another one.

"I is ready to go to the world a Chicago, Illinois," Farm Girl sang in cheer. Hearing a knock at her door, she clamped her lips together. When she heard a second knock, she rushed to the door. Putting her ear to the metal she yelled, "Who's that?"

"Bellhop," a man's voice called from the other side of the door. "I came to get your luggage."

"I aren't has no luggage to be giving."

A bewildered voice replied, "The desk said you were checking out, today. They sent me up to help you with your suitcases."

"I can git my own suitcases. Thank you fur asking."

She listened quietly to see if she could hear any movement on the other side of the door. Hearing nothing, she opened the door a crack and peered out. Not seeing anyone, she closed the door. "That was mighty nice of them desk folks to send someone to help me. But no one's gonna take my stuff, but me."

Once she was at the bus station, she went directly to the ticket window. Since she had already lost one ticket to New York, she just purchased a one-way fare to Chicago. She could always buy another ticket to New

York when she arrived at the Chicago bus terminal.

Finding out the bus to Chicago was already boarding, Farm Girl hurried to the boarding area. After showing the driver her ticket, she boarded with caution. She stepped high to reach the last step. The scab on her knee was a good reminder that she didn't want to trip and fall, again. On board, she looked around. The bus wasn't too full, yet, so there was still a good selection of seats.

After finding a seat by the window, Farm Girl compressed the suitcase so the wheels and the handle were retracted and out of the way. The suitcase stayed on the floor between her legs. As she had done before, she propped her purse between the side of the bus and her right arm. This not only cushioned her from the hardness of the bus's hard interior wall, but also protected its contents from any thief that may be lurking about.

Since her briefcase hadn't fit into the suitcase, as planned, she ended up carrying it. She placed it on her lap and secured it by resting her hands atop its leather exterior. Settled in, she rested her head against the window and watched the large amount of people board her bus.

Crimeny, all them people cain't be gitting on this bus, can they?

Before the bus left the depot, Farm Girl was aware that the bus was crowded. Someone sat in the seat beside her. Keeping her eyes toward the window, Farm Girl chose to ignore whomever it was sharing her space. Because there was an empty seat next to her on the last bus ride, she wasn't bothered about other strangers that were on that bus. This time was different. She was a bit frightened, now, that another body was sitting so close to her and all the money in her possession.

Taking no risk, she clenched her legs against her suitcase until she thought for sure that her legs would drop off from lack of circulation. She picked up her briefcase and nestled it against her chest. As an extra added security, she leaned as close as she could possibly get to her purse. Without a doubt, she was crushing everything inside the purse, and she was very uncomfortable.

She was on the 8:55 a.m. bus, and wouldn't get to Chicago until 3:30 p.m. It was going to be a very long ride, but for safety sake, she would just have to tolerate the unpleasant position.

Why did someone has to sit next to me? So far, I be meeting so many nice strangers, Mama. So let this people next to me be one of them nice ones too.

The bus driver boarded and they finally got under way.

So engrossed in her own thoughts, Farm Girl felt as if she jumped a foot off her seat when she felt an elbow poke her arm, followed by a voice. "Hi, my name is Micky. What's yours?"

Crimeny, what's that person has to jab me fur? Maybe it were an accident. I wonder if this be one of them busybodies? I reckon I can just give my name. No harm in that. Think, Farm Girl, what's your name this time? You doesn't want no one to know your name is Farm Girl until you git to New York City.

Daisy's a good name. I aren't never use it befur. That weren't a name Mama was ever using, but it's one 'a my favorite flowers. Yes, Daisy will do me, just fine. Also, if I give her my name, maybe she'll leave me alone. Refusing to turn away from the window, Farm Girl was rather curt as she answered, "They calls me Daisy."

Enjoying the passing scenery, something she had missed on the ride from Omaha to Des Moines, Farm Girl heard, "Hi, Daisy. Glad to meet you. Are you getting off in Chicago, too? Or do you transfer buses there and travel further across state?"

Maybe I should take me a peek at this person. It's gotta be a she person from the sound of its voice, but aren't the name Mickey a boy's name? Yes, it is. Because I remember when I were little. Befur we moved to Pappy's farm, one little boy on a farm we was working on, his name were Mickey.

Her curiosity got the best of her. "I is going to New York City," Farm Girl replied, turning toward the unknown passenger. She saw a young woman sitting next to her. The woman had blonde hair. She wore it pulled back and hanging in one large braid that swept around and draped down across the front of her shoulder. Her jade eyes appeared to be accentuated with the heavy eye shadow she was wearing.

Mama, just look at all them paint colors she's wearing on her face. She looks just like that Floss woman who was serving me food in the Nebraska world.

Farm Girl didn't pay any attention to the clothes the girl was wearing, but she couldn't help noticing the large gold earrings hanging from the girl's ears. As the girl moved her arms, straightening her ankle length skirt, the multiple gold bracelets dangling around each arm, jingled like a wind chime.

"The Big Apple, huh? I've been there. I like Chicago, much better. Why don't you like Chicago?" Micky inquired, noticing that Farm Girl was soaking her up with inquisitive eyes.

"I aren't sure why you be talking about an apple fur when I are talking about New York City?"

"Apple fur." Micky chuckled. "New York City is called the Big Apple."

"It is? What fur?"

"How do I know? So, why don't you like Chicago?" Micky asked, once again.

"I doesn't reckon I teld you that I doesn't like Chicago. I doesn't know Chicago. Not yet."

"Oh, I see. Well, Debbie, you would. Like it, that is. Everybody does. There's lots to do for young adults. How old are you?"

I reckon it's okay to tell her how old you is. Besides, she don't look like no authorities. If she aren't It, she cain't be catching me. Well, if she can ask me all them questions, I guess I can ask her some. Besides, it'll be nice to talk to someone other than myself fur a change.

"I is eighteen How old you is?"

Feeling more at ease, Farm Girl scooted to the middle of her seat. From pushing so hard against her purse, her arm was cramped. Moving her purse atop the briefcase in her lap, she rubbed her arm in an attempt to relieve the pain.

"You're eighteen? Hey, that's great. I'm nineteen. Are you a runaway or just on the loose?"

"Why do everybody keep asking me that goofy question fur? Them Runaways isn't no kin of mine. I doesn't even know any of them folks."

Micky burst into laughter so hard she could barely manage to talk. "You're so funny, Daffy. You're no kin to the runaways, huh? Oh, no!" In a sudden movement, she crossed her legs. Micky started rocking nervously, as she tried to quit laughing. "Man, that was a close one. You almost made me wet myself. Wow. You're too much."

"I aren't never use it befur, but there's a privy at the back of the bus," Farm Girl said.

"A privy?" Micky stated, once again with laughter in her voice.

Not knowing what to make of the girl she had just met, Farm Girl sat in total confusion, watching her strange actions.

"You know, Dixie, my daddy used to have a saying that would be perfect right now. It was … " Pausing for a few seconds, she said, "Oh, I remember. I ain't never laughed this hard since the cow's teats got caught in the wringer and whitewashed the fence." Micky started laughing, again. "Have you ever heard anything so stupid, yet so funny in all your life? My daddy spoke better English than that. But, he was a stitch, just like you."

"What kind of cows are them that can whitewash a fence with them teats? We didn't have them kind a cows in my world. I had to paint me them fences with a bucket of whitewash and a brush when I—" *Crimeny, Farm Girl. Mama would be saying you has a big mouth. Better watch what you says.*

Exploding into laugher, once again, Micky pleaded, "Quit! You're cracking me up. Man, did I pick a nut to sit next to, or what?"

Farm Girl didn't find anything funny in what she said. "I aren't no man. Is you making fun of me, laughing all the time when I say something?"

Realizing that was a serious question, Micky reached over the chair arm and took hold of Farm Girl's hand. "Oh, no, Dahlia. I'm not making fun of you by laughing. I'm laughing because you're hilarious. You know, ha, ha, funny."

As Farm Girl jerked her hand from Micky's grasp, she responded, "Does you mean, like one of them jokes?" *Pappy told me and Mama a joke, one time, but I doesn't know me no jokes to tell. So, I are sure I didn't teld her one.*

"Sure, like a joke. The name runaways isn't a relative of anyone. Oh, maybe, if your last name happens to be Runaways. Then it is. The word I'm talking about is the name they use for kids that run away from home. Like I did. We run away. So, we're dubbed runaways. Got it? Now, do you see why you made me laugh?"

Crimeny! I run away from my Sugar Shack home. I are one of them runaways and didn't even know it. I cain't tell her I are. She might tell somebody else. Farm Girl tried to act like it was all very funny to her, too. "Oh, now I know what you're talking about. Runaways. Ha! Ha! Ha!"

I don't reckon I'll ever understand them jokes. And I doesn't think Micky's joke is funny since now I know I are one of them runaways. Maybe only them that's telling the jokes finds them funny? "What is loose a name fur in your language?"

"Stop, Daphne." Micky flicked Farm Girl's arm with the back of her hand. "You're killing me. Loose isn't a name either. I asked if you were on the loose. In slang language, it means, no ties. You know? No adult supervision. No one to tell you what you can, or can't do."

Oh, Mama, now I gots to learn me Chicago language and slang language. "Do all the peoples in Chicago speaks slang language, too?"

"Stop! My sides already hurt from laughing," Micky remarked, holding her crossed arms tight against her rib cage, rocking with laughter. "Now I've got the giggles and can't stop. You know they're going to kick us off of this bus if we don't settle down."

"I aren't doing nothing, Micky. Please don't git me off this bus," Farm Girl complained with a touch of fear in her voice. Then, her survival upbringing came to the surface. "If anyone has a mind to kick, I can kick back hard as a mule."

At the point of hysteria, Micky doubled over. Burying her face in her hands, as she sandwiched her hands between her face and her knees, she tried to muffle her intense laughter. Farm Girl stared at her until Micky calmed herself and came up for air. "Okay. Okay, Ducky, I'm going to be fine now. Please, don't make me laugh that hard anymore, or at least not for the rest of the trip. My poor sides can't take any more." Micky wiped the tears of laughter from her eyes. "I think I'll go use that privy before I have an accident," she teased, as she left her seat.

Farm Girl stared at the back of the seat in front of her. When Micky returned to her seat, she said, "I can't let you go to New York City, not yet, DeeDee. You have got to stay in Chicago with me, at least for a few days. You're too roaring hilarious to let go. Just too funny for words."

You is pretty funny yourself, Micky. You is calling me names that even Mama never was using. And even Mama just use one name at a time. I lost count how many names you is calling me already. You has me so confuse now, I doesn't even remember what name I teld you was my name.

Crimeny, since I cain't remember, I best just let her call me any name she wants to, or I might be in big trouble. She might not remember my name, but she seems nice enough. Maybe I might stay with her in Chicago. Like she says, fur a few days. She kind of makes me want to laugh too.

Look at her. Wonder why she was wailing so loud like a coyote befur, and now she comes back from the privy and has her eyes shut. She's as quiet as a cockroach. Cain't be asleep that fast, can she? Oh, I hope all that laughing didn't make her sick. I sure doesn't want me meeting no more sick peoples. They ends up dead.

"Micky, is you all right?" Farm Girl asked, touching Micky's arm. Opening one eye and turning it in Farm Girl's direction, gave Farm Girl an eerie chill up her spin, making her shiver. "Eke!" she yelped.

Micky swiftly raised her arm, placing her hand over Farm Girl's mouth. "Shush," Micky whispered. Farm Girl's eyes widened with sudden fear. Before she could react, Micky explained, "You really will get us kicked off of this bus, and it will be the bus driver who'll be doing the kicking.

What's the matter with you screeching out loud, like that?" As she took her hand away from Farm Girl's mouth, she put her finger to her lips and mouthed, "Shush!"

Swiping her hand across her mouth to wipe it, Farm Girl whispered, "If you doesn't want me to yell out from fright, why does you go and make them creepy faces at me fur? You likes to be scaring me plum into another life."

"Hey, Darla, I'm on a roller coaster ride. Can't you feel it?" Micky replied, grinning.

"No. I doesn't know what no roller coaster ride is."

"Oh, that's so sad. I tell you what, when we get to Chicago—I live with my boyfriend—he'll fix you right up. Trust me, Delores, you'll experience the ride of your life in Chicago. I'll see to it."

Micky pushed her seat back into the lounge position. Once again, she closed her eyes.

Noticing how Micky got her seat to recline, Farm Girl followed suit. Releasing her leg vice on her suitcase, she marveled at the comfortable position. Lying her head against the headrest, Farm Girl turned toward the window. Watching the scenery move swiftly by, she allowed her mind to wander at will. In so doing, she sat and talked in a muffled voice, hoping Micky or no one else could hear.

"Just how many rides is there in these worlds? In the farm world we has tractor rides, car rides, horse rides, truck rides, cow rides, mule rides and, oh, piggyback rides. Darin are the one who told me about airplane rides. Then, Jay told me about them taxi and cab rides, and bus rides.

The world of Des Moines teach me escalator rides, and the fancy hotel world teach me elevator rides. Now, Chicago gots them roller coaster rides. I doesn't know what that are but it sounds like fun if I gits to laugh as much as this Micky girl's been laughing.

Mama hardly never were laughing. Pappy were laughing sometimes, but most times when I read him my stories. They was both too sad all the time. And Darin, well, he were almost as bad as Mama, being all serious-like and all. I like it when someone laughs because it makes me want to laugh too, even though I doesn't too much. I think laughing makes a body feel good all over. I guess the Chicago world must be where the funny peoples live.

This Micky girl's words are almost like mine. So, maybe Chicago's foreign language won't be so bad to learn. I think it's them words from that Slang language that's gonna make me have to work harder at learning.

Black Rosebud

Well, what I doesn't know, I'll just ask like I been doing."

Just the thought of Mama sent Farm Girl's mind bouncing like a rubber ball to a different channel of her verbal thought pattern.

"I hasn't been talking with you much lately, Mama, but that don't mean I doesn't still love you. I been thinking about you. With you gone, I aren't never gonna know nothing more about you.

You died not ever knowing your real name. But, I know it. I figure it out when I remember my name on my birth certificate. No, I didn't look at that old paper. I didn't need to. If my last name are Light, like you told me it were, then you had the same last name as me.

Darin told me once that he had the same name as his mama, which come from his daddy. You never told me about no daddy, but I think his name were Light, too. And, since you remember some of them orphanage peoples calling you Cheryl when you was little, then your whole name were Cheryl Light. See how simple that are, Mama, when you is book learn like I is?

You never had no friends or kin but me and Pappy. Maybe you wasn't lonesome, but there is times when I are. Maybe that's why I are thinking about staying in that Chicago world with this here Micky girl. She's real nice, Mama, so she could be my friend. I aren't never had a friend befur. With a friend, then I won't feel lonesome no more.

I doesn't think that old coffee can mean anything to you, Mama, like I think it did when you was around. You was just using it fur carrying things. Too bad you didn't know about a handbag, like I got. Know what else? I thinks all them things in your old can aren't has no meaning. I think you find that stuff in the rubbish just like we find our clothes. And, like you always told me—Well, you knows what you always told me.

Even though them things don't mean nothing to me except my birth certificate, if I ever needs it, I will keep them always because they is all I has left of you. So, now I think I know all a your secrets.

Now, I need to tell you my secret. I were waiting until now because I want to be sure that you and Pappy had you a chance to talk. When he told me about New York City, and that's where people like me need to be if I want to write books, I promise him I would never say nothing to you. He didn't want you to be mad at him because you would make us move again.

If Pappy aren't told you that secret yet, now I has. I are sorry, Mama. I didn't mean to hurt you. Please forgive me. There, now I feel better since you know the truth about all them whoppers and lies I told you. I didn't teld you before now because I had me an awful lot of learning to do.

Okay, now I need to decide on what to do. Chicago with funny people and a roller coaster ride sounds like—Yes, that's what I are gonna do. Don't need no more thinking about it. I fur sure is gonna stay in Chicago world fur a few days with my new friend, Micky, and gits me some of that laughter and ride me a roller coaster."

Once in Chicago, Micky took Farm Girl by the hand after they departed their bus. Nature calling, she led Farm Girl to the nearest public bathroom.

"I've got to pee so bad, DooDah, that my eyes are turning yellow," Micky quipped, tugging at Farm Girl to hurry along. "Come on. Come on. Let's move." In her rapid pace, she happened to glance down at Farm Girl's legs. "Say, are you wearing panty hose?"

Moving in a quick step along side of her new friend, Farm Girl answered, "Yes."

"I thought so. With all the stuff you had packed into the seat with you, I couldn't see your legs on the bus. When we get to the bathroom, take those disgusting things off and throw them away. They look terrible all snagged like that with your knees hanging out," Micky explained with a chuckle.

"They was new store-bought ones until I fell gitting me on the bus. They is real hard to be gitting into when they is in one piece. With all them tares in them, they is even worse trying to put on. My toes keep gitting stuck in them holes."

"You mean you didn't just do that when you boarded the bus we just got off of?"

"Nope. I done it weeks and weeks ago on another bus."

Micky shook her head. "Why didn't you just throw them away?"

"Because, they is the only ones I has me to wear. It ain't … I mean, it aren't like I want to buy me any more of the dumb things. I doesn't really like them. Every time I goes shopping, I keep furgitting to buy me some stockings."

"Excuse my French, but they look like hell. You're better off not to wear anything, like me."

Trying to look at Micky's legs, which she couldn't do because of the long skirt Micky was wearing, Farm Girl asked, "You doesn't wear nothing on your legs?"

"Nope. I don't even wear undies."

"No undies? Ah!" Farm Girl exclaimed. "Don't that mean you ain't wearing no bloomers?"

"Darn you, Dip-Stick. Don't you make me pee all over myself. Now quit talking and get a wiggle on it."

Farm Girl was pulling her suitcase behind her, moving as fast as she could. She didn't understand what it meant to put a wiggle on it, but she certainly understood when someone pulling her was in a big hurry. Once they got inside the bathroom, Micky let loose of Farm Girl's hand and headed for a stall.

From behind the stall's door, Micky yelled, "Hey, why do you pull that suitcase around with you? It's nice, but very square. You need to get with the program and get yourself a backpack, like I have. No, I take that back. You don't need a backpack. Heck, your purse is big enough to carry a horse.

And, why in the world would someone like you need to carry around a briefcase? Good grief, the way you lock onto those things, it's like you were carrying around your own Fort Knox."

Farm Girl looked around to see if anyone else was in the bathroom. Not seeing anyone, she got down on her knees and looked under all of the stall doors. Since there were no other feet to be seen, only those of Micky's, Farm Girl went inside the stall next to Micky. She had to go to the bathroom, too, but didn't want someone to reach under the door and steal her suitcase away from her.

After placing her suitcase sideways, fitting it snuggly between the toilet and the stall wall, she took care in balancing her briefcase and her purse on top of it. Finally, she responded to Micky.

"You're plain goofy," Farm Girl yelled back through the middle divider that now separated them. "Not even a baby horse could be fitting in my purse. I carries all my treasures in my suitcase and my briefcase. Are a backpack that funny thing you is wearing, like a jacket with no arms?"

Micky's laughter rang through the bathroom and seemed to bounce off the ceramic tiled walls. After Micky regained composure, her inquisitive nature kept verbalizing. "Yes, this jacket with no sleeves is called a backpack. It's a heck of a lot easier to transport then some old stupid suitcase. Treasures, huh? So, I was right about Fort Knox. What kind of treasures, Dottie?" Micky asked, as she flushed the toilet and left her stall, allowing the metal door to slam closed.

You be careful, Farm Girl. You knows you cain't tell her what kind of treasures you be carrying. Well, maybe a few things, but not everything. Crimeny, I couldn't carry everything I need in one of them backpacks. Funny thing, though. Ain't that like I made me from twine fur carrying them moneybags on me. Mine carried them socks around my middle, so maybe I had me a backpack and didn't even know it?

"Micky, does they have them backpacks to be wearing around your middle?"

"Do you mean fanny-packs?"

Does I? Since them socks kept always hitting me in the fanny when I were walking, reckon that's what I had me. A fanny-pack

"Yes, I reckon that's what I mean, Micky."

Farm Girl never said another word until she was through in the stall and had joined Micky by the sink. She placed the raggedy pantyhose on the small ledge above the sink. Micky watched in wonderment as Farm Girl wiggled her body around until she had straddled her suitcase, then edged her briefcase between one foot and the suitcase.

Finally, with her arm through the strap of her purse, she propped the bulk of her purse on her back. Carefully, she leaned over the sink to wash her hands. As if it were an everyday occurrence to Farm Girl, she proceeded talking as if nothing ever interfered with her conversation. Micky sat on the edge of the sink next to Farm Girl, shaking her head in merriment.

"I feel half naked without my leg covers," Farm Girl admitted.

"Hey, naked's good," Micky replied with a grin.

"Micky, what do French mean?"

"French is a foreign language."

"Aren't that funny. Mama told me hell were a very bad word. I got my mouth washed with soap once, when I were using that word. Reckon she didn't know it were a French word."

Shaking her head, Micky covered her mouth with both hands. She took a deep breath, counted to ten, then removed her hands. "Are you for real or am I hallucinating." She giggled. "Wait, don't answer that because I don't want to know. Tell me about your suitcase."

"I has my store-bought clothes in my suitcase. And, I are real."

"Store-bought clothes? Oh, Dewdrop, you have to quit. I don't think I can take any more, right now."

"I aren't doing nothing to you, Micky," Farm Girl replied, rinsing the soap off her hands. "Why doesn't you tell me the meaning of them foreign words you be saying, like what do Fort Knox mean?"

"Foreign? Yes, I guess Fort Knox would be foreign to a lot of people. Actually, it's a huge building that has a whole lot of money in it. But in slang, if anyone seems to be glued to their carry-alls, like you are, we joke that they're carrying around their own Fort Knox. You know, like you had a whole lot of money you're packing with you."

Wow! I just learned me another one of them new words. Oh, no, does she know I has all this money with me? No, she cain't know. Maybe she are just guessing? I'll bet it's just another one of her jokes she thinks is so funny. To be nice, Farm Girl pretended to laugh. "Ha! Ha! Ha! I sure aren't gots me no Fort Knox, but you sure is funny, Micky."

"Aren't gots?" Micky sputtered, tilting her head back and letting out a loud squelch of laughter. "We've got to get you to my friend's house. He's going to love you. Come on, Dinky. Let's go."

Micky headed out the bathroom door. Not wanting to be left behind, Farm Girl shook the water off her hands the best she could. With wet hands, she grabbed her belongings and followed Micky. They walked outside and down the street, side by side, for quite a few blocks. As they walked, Micky did most of the talking. It seemed like every time Farm Girl did have something to say, Micky would laugh so hard she could hardly walk.

"There you goes laughing again, Micky. It's like my mama once told me, you must of swalered a feather fur breakfast," Farm Girl chuckled. "All I wants to know are one thing?"

"Swalered? Damn, that's a word I've never heard before."

Still listening to Micky, Farm Girl had a quick thought, *That's because you probably doesn't know them foreign language words in my world.*

"Okay, Dippity-doo-da, what's the one thing you want to know?"

"How come you has a boy's name?"

"Ha! My real name is Michelle. I don't like it. Everyone calls me Micky. Now, you've got to swear on your life that you won't ever tell anyone my real name, or call me that. Promise? Because if you don't promise, I'll cut your heart out and feed it to the wolves. Promise me, right now."

Farm Girl stopped dead in her tracks. She was so terrified with fear that her body wouldn't move. Her mouth wouldn't work. *Oh, Mama, she are an evil stranger! I swear, I will never tell no one her name. Mama, please, don't let her cut my heart out!*

Noticing that Farm Girl was no longer walking beside her, Micky turned. She saw Farm Girl standing with a petrified look on her face. Returning to her side, Micky took hold of Farm Girl's purse clutching hand. "What's the matter with you, Duchess? You're as white as a sheet.

Hey, you're not getting sick on me, are you?"

It was all Farm Girl could do, as she forced, "No," out of her mouth.

"Well then, what's wrong?"

"I—I promise, I will call you Micky. Please, don't cut my heart out and feed it to them wolves!"

"Oh, no," Micky laughed. "That's a joke, Ducky. I can't believe you thought I was serious. Yes, I guess you would. Come on, let's go," Micky insisted, pulling on Farm Girl's purse.

Feeling relieved, Farm Girl started walking again with her new friend. Micky was giggling but Farm Girl wasn't even smiling. *I doesn't like all them jokes peoples tell me. I still doesn't think none of them is funny. Reckon if I stay in this Chicago world, I'll get use to it. I hope so.* Still being pulled along, she asked, "How long does I have to live in this world before I understand the funny language?"

Micky let go of Farm Girl's hand and started running. Farm Girl didn't know what else to do but follow, almost losing her suitcase a few times as its tiny wheels hit the cracks and holes in the sidewalk. It was all she could do to keep pace and hold on to her purse and briefcase.

Micky ran into an alleyway, stopping at the door of a large, brick structure. Pulling a key from her pocket, she unlocked the door, as Farm Girl caught up to her. As if Farm Girl was a rag doll, Micky latched onto Farm Girl's arm, yanking her inside the building with her.

Since the day she left Sugar Shack, Farm Girl always walked into each new adventure a bit fearsome, but wide-eyed and ready to take on each new discovery. By now, she had totally forgotten most of the words of warning that had been drummed into her head. Mama's words of caution seemed to be dead and buried, just like Mama.

Poor, naïve Farm Girl was not aware of the ultimate dangers lurking in the corners of the new world she just entered. Dangers that were ready to pounce on her when she least expected it.

STICKING TO YOUR CONVICTIONS

Once Frank had composed himself after receiving such devastating news about Darin, he went back to bed.

The following morning, a strange noise crept into Frank's dream. When he realized the noise was coming from his alarm clock, reality of the night before came to the forefront. Managing to drag his tired body out of bed, he got ready for his trip to town.

While the coffee was brewing, he called his attorney's office. John was out of town for the day, so Frank left a message with his secretary, Betty. She promised to have John return Frank's call.

With the sour taste of rancid orange juice vivid in his memory, Frank took his pain pills with water. After pouring a cup of coffee, he sat at the kitchen table in deep thought. Once he made the decision as to what to do, he called and made an appointment to see Doc Shively. Due to another patient's cancellation, he felt fortunate to find the doctor could see him right away.

In town, at the doctor's office, Frank was blown away when he discovered the reason for his weeks in bed was due to his own foolish blunder. Because of his extreme pain, Frank had overdosed on his pain pills. This information eased Frank's mind, proving Rusty's intuition wrong about Darin being the cause of his cataleptic state.

However, there was still the doubt of the previous evening, whether or not Darin had fed Frank sleeping pills in order to slip out of the house without Frank's knowledge. Having complete confidence in Doc, Frank explained Rusty's suspicions. Doc ordered a blood test with the promise that Frank would have the test results within twenty-four hours.

After Frank left the doctor's office, he headed for the police station.

He went directly to the police chief's office where Rusty was waiting for him.

"Good morning, Frank. I've been expecting you. I see you made it town with no problems."

"Yeah."

"Come on in and have a seat."

"Don't care to. I want to see Darin."

"Okay, Frank." Rusty got on the intercom and requested Officer Janx to come to his office.

While waiting for his officer, Rusty explained, "Officer Janx will take you to lock-up. He'll have to pat you down first before he takes you to see Darin. Sorry, Frank, but rules are rules."

Janx entered the room. "You wanted to see me, Chief?"

"Yes. Mr. Righter is here to see his brother. Make sure he's clean, then take him down to see Darin."

Although Frank was very upset that Rusty had Darin in custody, he understood that Rusty was just doing his job. That didn't mean that he had to like it. After Frank emptied his pockets, and was shook down to make sure he hadn't any concealed weapons or contraband on him, Officer Janx escorted him to lock-up.

As they walked down the long, gray corridor, Frank felt a cold chill run through his body, all the way to his bones. The few windows in the hall were all barred with steel. The only sound was the pounding of his and Officer Janx's shoes hitting the cement floor as they walked. Once they reached the end of the corridor, a large barred door stopped them. Janx unlocked the heavy door and waited for Frank to enter the lock-up area.

Making small talk, Janx commented, "In general, we don't have an officer on duty in here, even when we have customers." Janx turned and locked the barred door behind them.

"That's quaint. Since when are prisoners called customers?"

"Sorry, Mr. Righter. Unless we have a hardened criminal locked up in here, such as a murderer or rapist, we call our detainees customers. It's just a private joke around the department."

Frank wasn't the least bit amused. "Anyone locked behind steel bars is a prisoner in my book."

"Yes, sir."

As Frank followed, Janx walked to a door opening and entered a room of cell blocks. He showed Frank to Darin's cell.

Seeing Darin behind bars, broke Frank's heart. He could barely speak. Feeling a lump in his throat, he asked, "Officer, aren't you going to unlock this darn thing so I can go in and have a personal talk with Darin?"

"Sorry, Mr. Righter, but I can't do that. You can talk to him through the bars. Chief's orders." Janx walked a few feet away, stopped and turned toward Frank. He then stood at ease.

Darin was seated on a cot. When he saw Frank, he turned toward one of the cell walls with a quick turn of his head. In his situation, Frank was the last person he wanted to face.

Talking to Darin through steel bars, was extremely aggravating to Frank. He turned to Janx. "Can't we at least have some privacy? Or is that against the rules, too?"

"I'm not allowed to leave the area when a prisoner has a visitor, sir. But, I can give you some space," Janx responded. He walked to the end of the room and waited while Frank conversed with Darin.

Frank grasped a firm hold of the bars in front of him. "Darin, are you all right?"

Darin took a deep breath, his nostrils flaring, as he turned and looked at Frank. The sadness in Frank's face was hard to ignore. Getting to his feet, Darin walked to the bars and cupped his hands around Frank's hands. "I'm fine, Frank. I should have known good old Chief Simmons had to run and brag to you that he locked me up."

"He wasn't bragging, Darin, but I'm glad he told me. He said you wouldn't call me last night. I wish you would have."

"No need to bother you. You need to think about getting well, not worrying about me."

"Are they treating you okay? Have you eaten anything?"

"Other than wanting to get out of here, I told you, I'm fine," Darin insisted. "Did you bring me any clean clothes?"

"No, Darin, I'm sorry. Clothes were the last things on my mind.

I called John Johnston. He's out of town today but he'll be back tomorrow. Then we'll get you out of here."

"I don't need an attorney, Frank. They can't keep me in here for very long," Darin stated with confidence.

"What's the matter with you? Rusty said they caught you red-handed, stealing money out of someone's house. What in the blaze of glory were you thinking?"

"So, I broke into one man's house. They can't give me life for that, Frank," Darin joked.

"Look, this is no laughing matter. Rusty seems to think you are the

Neat Nick Thief. Are you?"

Frank struck a cord and Darin did not like the sound of the music. Letting loose of Frank's hands, Darin stuck his hands in his back pockets. Perturbed, he stepped away from the bars. "No, Frank, and you hurt my feelings by even asking such a lame question. Why don't you just go back home."

"Sorry if you think it's lame, Darin. But, listen to me. Rusty said they have evidence. We've been friends far too long for him to lie to me. Think of all the times when you were growing up that he kept you out of jail. If it weren't for him, you would have more than just a couple of breaking and entering arrests on your record.

Lucky for you, that record was sealed because you were a juvenile. You promised Rusty, before you went away to college, that you would straighten up your act."

Darin didn't like it that he had nowhere to go. He was a captive audience. There was no other choice but to listen to Frank.

"About a year, after you were working at the bank, I was proud to tell Rusty how you've kept your nose clean. I don't know why you had to go and ruin everything by starting this breaking and entering escapade all over again, and at your age. I know I sound like I'm lecturing, Darin, but I'm not. I'm just confused. Do you know what kind of evidence they have on you?"

"Oh, come on, Frank, the chief is just baiting you. Something he's good at doing. He hasn't got a thing on me. Wise up. Your alleged friend is bluffing."

As Frank shook his head, not knowing what to believe, or disbelieve, he happened to look down at the floor, noticing Darin's feet. "What happened to your shoestrings?"

"Oh, the cops took my shoestrings and belt." Darin replied, lifting his shirttail and glancing down at his empty belt loops on his pants. "They want to make sure I don't hang myself in here. Right. Like suicide's on my agenda. Ha! That's a joke." Changing his demeanor, he blurted, "Damn!" *Keep your voice down, stupid. The cop can hear you.* Moving back to the bars, he lowered his voice, asking, "You haven't said anything about my trip Friday, have you?"

With his eyes still glued on Darin's feet, Frank replied, "No. I promised you, I wouldn't tell anyone." Looking up, he met Darin eye-to-eye. "Why are you wearing my old work shoes?"

With a quick look at his feet then back to Frank, Darin thought fast.

"I couldn't find my old ones last night. I didn't think you'd care if I borrowed yours. Why? What's the big deal?"

"That's kind of funny, you know." Frank forced a laugh. "You haven't tried to wear my shoes since you were a little boy. I remember you playing with them, traipsing all around the house." Darin gave a half-cocked smile. "I won't promise, but I'll try to get back here later today with some clean duds for you."

No! I don't want Frank in my bedroom. Damn! You're the one that opened your big mouth. "There's no need to go searching around in my room for clothes, Frank. I didn't get all of my clean clothes put away yesterday. I believe they're still on the chair in the living room."

"Yes, I seem to remember seeing them there this morning. Well, I'm sorry you have to spend another night in here. I promise, I'll get John to get you out first thing in the morning."

Those words finally sunk into Darin's head. "Tomorrow?"

"I told you John is out of town today. You're going to have to spend another night in here."

Hitting the bar with the butt of his hand, Darin cursed, "Damn!"

"Take it easy. We'll get you out just as early tomorrow as possible. Until then, you stay calm and don't be a wise acre with that mouth of yours. Understand?"

"Sure, Frank. You go home and get some rest before you come back to town with my clothes. A few more hours in these dirty things won't kill me."

Frank returned to Rusty's office. Noting the open door, Frank didn't wait to be announced. He walked right into Rusty's office and took a seat.

"Want me to close the door," Rusty asked.

"No. There's nothing I have to say to you that's private."

"How's Darin doing?"

Instead of answering the question, Frank had his own agenda for the visit. "You know my attorney, John Johnston, don't you?" He noted Rusty's nod. "Well, he'll be here in the morning to get Darin out of jail. I assume Darin can get out on bail if I take full responsibility for him."

"Look, Frank, this isn't like one of those kid's pranks, breaking and entering just for kicks, like Darin used to enjoy doing to stir up some excitement around town. This is serious business. Here's how it plays. Darin will be arraigned in court tomorrow morning. The judge will set bond. If Darin can post the bond, and there are no objections from the district attorney, then Darin can and will be released. If not, he will remain in jail until his trial."

"That's not a problem. I've got the funds for posting bond, and I'll take full responsibility for him. How long before Darin will go to trial?"

Rusty rubbed his chin. At that moment, he was wishing he could speed up the judicial process and give Frank different information then he had to tell him. He couldn't. "It could take up to twelve months."

"Twelve months?" Frank repeated. *Shoot, Darin isn't going to like the idea of having to stick around the farm for another year. With bond, at least that will be twelve months not locked behind bars.*

When Officer Kelly entered the doorway, he caught Rusty's attention. With a slight wave of the paper he was holding, and a significant motion with his eyes, he let Rusty know the paper was an important document. With a nod, Rusty motioned for Kelly to enter the office.

Aware someone was behind him, Frank turned his head. His eyes followed as Kelly approached Rusty's desk. Kelly placed the document on the desk in front of his boss, then he returned to the outer office.

After making a quick read of the paper, Rusty shook his head. "Frank ... Darn it all, this just keeps getting more and more complicated."

"What's the problem?"

"This here," Rusty said, holding up the paper. "Hell, Frank, I'm sorry, but it's a Search Warrant."

Feeling the hair at the nape of his neck stand on end, Frank questioned, "A Search Warrant? For what?"

"Your property. We have to search it for the stolen money. If Darin is the Neat Nick Thief, he might have hidden the money on your property." Clenching his teeth, as he listened to Rusty, Frank could feel his blood boil. "It's our job to find out. As an officer of the law it is my official duty to tell you ... " Rusty shook his head. He felt like he was adding another wound to Frank's heartache.

"Look, Frank, if you know of any stolen goods or anything that might be hidden on your property that would or could be used as evidence in this case against Darin, and you are protecting him, you could be held as an accessory after the fact. So, for your sake as well as Darin's, if you do, tell me now before we go searching your property."

Outraged, Frank got to his feet. "That's enough. I'm just about to lose my patience here. I know of no such thing. If you want or need to search my property, then darn it all, just ask me. Don't be playing this law game with me. Darin is innocent, and I don't know of any stolen money. You'll not find anything like that on my property. No sir, not on my property."

Black Rosebud

With that said, Frank stormed out of Rusty's office and headed home.

Leaving one uniformed officer to man the station, Rusty and three of his men went to the Righter farm to search for the stolen money and other incriminating evidence against Darin. While the officers searched the property, Frank got together some clean clothes for Darin and sat them on the kitchen table. To stay out of the way, Frank sat at the table.

Coming up empty handed, especially in Darin's room where they found nothing but a bookcase full of soft cover thriller books, the search continued outside. Finding absolutely nothing that would help them build a case against Darin, Rusty sent the officers back to town. Wanting to talk to Frank, Rusty returned to the backdoor of the house. He rapped on the screen door.

Responding, Frank yelled, "Come in," He got to his feet, picking up Darin's clothes. As Rusty entered the back porch, he was stopped dead in his tracks by Frank. "No sense in coming any further, Rusty. You're not welcome right now, and I'm not in the mood for any more conversation. Just tell me what you found, if you can, then be on your way."

"Nothing."

"Nothing. Just as I thought," Frank smirked.

"Look, Frank, I'm sorry things have to be this way. You know I would give my right arm for this not to happen. But it has. I have to be a police chief first. A friend, second. Please understand that Frank," Rusty pleaded.

"Yeah, I'm trying real hard. Now, if you don't mind, I'd like to be left alone. But, I would appreciate it if you would see that Darin gets this change of clothes."

"Sure, Frank." Rusty took the clothes, then left.

The next morning while Frank paced back and forth in his kitchen, waiting to hear from his attorney, the telephone finally rang. It only had to ring once before Frank snatched it up and answered. "Hello."

"Frank, this is John. Heard you have an emergency."

"I sure do. Darin is in jail and I need you to get him out of there, ASAP. How soon can I meet with you?"

"Darin's in jail? What for?" John inquired.

"We're wasting time on the phone. Rusty said that Darin would be arraigned in court this morning. So, do I meet you at your office or the court house?"

"Let's see, it's 8:00 now. Court won't start until 10:00. Okay, I'll have Betty clear my schedule. Come on into my office and fill me in with the details. In the meantime, I'll call Rusty and see what's up. See you when you get here."

"Thanks John. I'll be at your office as soon as I can get there."

In John's office Frank explained everything he knew about Darin's arrest.

"Darin couldn't deny that he broke into some guy's house last night," Frank stated, shaking his head.

"Why couldn't he deny it?"

"Because Rusty said they set a trap for that Neat Nick Thief. Darin's the one they caught. Rusty says he has other evidence, but he wouldn't tell me what it was. On the other hand, Darin thinks that Rusty is bluffing. I know in my heart of hearts that Darin can't be the infamous thief, so I'm beginning to think Rusty is pulling a bluff. Now, tell me what you found out."

"Wait a minute, Frank. I am your attorney and I want to help Darin, but you know even better than I do that you and Rusty have been best of friends for many years now. Heck, the whole town knows that. I can't believe you would even think that Rusty would try and frame Darin. Rusty, bluffing? Never. If he says he has evidence, then he's got something vital to connect Darin to these other cases.

Rusty wasn't in when I called the station, earlier. So, I haven't found out anything yet. All I know right now is what you just told me. Look, why don't you go on home. I'll go over to the jail and have a talk with Darin. Then, if Rusty's available, I'll talk to him and see what's going on." John paused to look at his watch.

"Look, I need to get going before court is in session." John had written a few notes while talking with Frank. He finished putting his notes into his briefcase and readied to leave.

Standing from his chair, Frank refused to be dismissed like a school kid. "No, I can't go home and just sit there. I'm going with you," he insisted.

"Sorry, Frank, but I would prefer you didn't. I know Darin is your brother, but I think he will talk to me more openly without you present. I promise, I will call you just as soon as I find out something. Now, go home."

"No! Okay, I won't go with you to talk to Darin or to Rusty's office, but darn it all, John, you aren't going to keep me out of court."

"Damn, you're persistent, Frank. Okay, you win, but, I have to caution you. Sit in the back of the courtroom, and no matter what you hear, don't say one word. Keeping your silence in court right now is for Darin's best interest. Understand?"

"What do I look like, an imbecile? Of course I understand." Frank headed for the door. Even though he knew John was in a rush, he still conversed. "John, whatever it takes, I want Darin out of that jail, today. You know your fee and whatever the bail is, that I'm good for all of it, don't you?"

"Yes, of course I do, Frank. Now, let's go, or I won't be any good at all in helping Darin. He'll have to stay another night in the slammer because of your lip smacking," John quipped, as they headed out the office door.

After John had completed his consultation with Darin, he went to the police chief's office. During their meeting, Rusty told John what evidence the D.A. had against Darin. John wasn't impressed.

In court the judge set bail, John took care of the legal papers, and Darin was released in Frank's custody. Since Rusty had obtained a warrant to keep the rubber boots Darin was wearing the night he was arrested, they were held in evidence. Also, on the night of Darin's arrest, the car had been impounded and was being searched for any clue that might tie Darin into the other twenty-six reported burglaries. After Darin received the rest of his belongings, Frank took him home. There was complete silence all the way from town to the farm. Once inside the backdoor, the silence ended.

"Sit down, Darin. I need to make a phone call. Then, you and I are going to have a talk," Frank stated.

"No, I don't want to sit down. After spending two nights in that fleabag, all I want to do, right now, is to shed these clothes and take a hot shower."

As Frank called Doctor Shivley's office, he reiterated with fatherly authority, "I said, sit down. Rusty told me you were allowed to shower in jail, and I know you got the clean clothes I sent because you're wearing them."

Blast it! Another lecture, no doubt. Haven't I had enough lectures, listening to the chief and the attorney, and then that monkey-faced judge? Well, I might as well let him have his say now. Maybe then I can get my shower. One with some privacy. What's so friggin' important that he has to make a phone call as soon as he walks in the door? As

Frank waited for an answer on the other end of the phone, Darin pulled out a kitchen chair and flopped down on it.

"Good morning. Shivley Clinic. Sherry speaking."

"Sherry, this is Frank Righter."

"Hi, Frank. Doc just asked me, not five minutes ago, to get you on the phone. Hold on and I'll connect you."

After a few seconds Frank heard, "Hello, Frank."

"What's the word? Did you get my results?"

"You were right, Frank," Doc replied. "Your blood test shows you had a trace of barbiturates in your system."

Frank's eyes bored holes in Darin as he listened to Doc's news. "Thanks for getting me the results so quickly. I sincerely appreciate it."

"Thought you'd like to know, all of your other blood work looks as good as can be expected in your condition."

"Thank you."

"Okay, bye for now."

"Bye." Frank hung up the telephone with a lot of questions on his mind. *What is going on? Why would Darin want to give me sleeping pills? There has got to be a logical explanation. There has to be. And it better be good.*

Noticing that Frank was still standing with his hand on the telephone, even though he had disconnected his call, Darin was tired of waiting. He got to his feet. "I'm exhausted. All I want is that hot shower and maybe a good nap on a real bed. Talk to you later, Frank," Darin said starting to leave the room.

"Stop right where you are, Darin, and sit back down. I told you, I want to talk to you," Frank ordered.

"Come on, Frank, we just went through this. I just spent two nights in a cold, cement hole with bars on it. Now, I sat here like you wanted, but you seemed to be preoccupied with a phone call to some babe named Sherry that, obviously, couldn't wait. Give me a break. We can talk later."

"Now!" Frank demanded. "I've never spoken a mean word to you in your whole life nor ordered you around, Darin, but this time you are going to listen to me. Now sit."

Darin's hands flew up in front of him. "Okay, okay. Hang loose, will ya. No sense in getting your water hot."

As much as he didn't want to, Darin returned to his seat. Frank sat next to him at the kitchen table.

"This isn't easy for me, Darin, but I have to ask. Why would you give me sleeping pills?"

Darin's eyes widened. "What? Sleeping pills? I don't know what you're talking about."

"Don't you dare lie to me, Darin. The bottle of sleeping pills was up there in that cabinet." Frank pointed to the cabinet above the stove. "Furthermore, it was hidden behind the coffee filters. I had a blood work-up done. The results proved that I had that sleeping medication in my blood. Doc Shivley just confirmed that on the phone.

Now, I know I didn't take those pills on my own, and there isn't anyone else in this house who could have given them to me. So, give me a straight answer."

"Okay, I'm guilty as charged," Darin admitted. "Look, Frank, you had been in bed for weeks, then, all of a sudden, you're out of bed and want to stay up all day. I figured you were up and around too soon, so I wanted you to get a really good night's rest. Actually, I felt a little guilty for asking you to fold clothes, and keeping you up all day so I could get some house chores done that I had neglected. Remember?"

"I remember."

"So, I gave you a couple of sleeping pills. Big deal. I just did it to help you rest."

"You don't think week after week in bed gave me enough rest?"

"To be honest. No. You were sick then. I'm speaking of a good night's sleep. There's a big difference in my way of thinking."

"Why hide the bottle if it was all so innocent," Frank continued to question.

"I guess, I was in a hurry to get the house cleaning done so I just stuck the pill bottle up in that cupboard. I made coffee for us for dinner that night, so the bottle just got pushed behind the filters. So now what, I'm in trouble for giving a damn?"

That explanation of Darin's concern sent Frank on a guilt trip. "Oh, dear God. Darin, I'm sorry. Here you're worried about me and I jump all over you. It's just that—well, never mind. Look, Darin, please accept my apology. God knows you have enough on your mind without me thinking the worse.

Look, go in, take your hot shower and get some rest. I think I'm going to lie down for a while, also. Later we'll have a bit to eat. Okay? Forgive me?" Frank asked as he placed his hand on Darin's hand in a warm, loving gesture.

"Sure, Frank. No harm done."

Darin stood and headed toward the doorway into the living room.

"Oh, Darin, one more thing. Don't plan on that trip Friday."

"Yeah, I know the routine," Darin spouted, walking away from Frank.

Why didn't I get rid of those friggin' sleeping pills, or put them back in the medicine cabinet. In too big of a hurry, I guess. Dumb! Really dumb! Get in a hurry and you get careless, Darin. Well, thank heavens Frank believed my story. Pretty good one too, even if I do say so myself.

All the time Darin was showering, he kept his mind active. *If they haven't found the screwdriver yet that I used to enter Denton's house, they shouldn't find it until after I'm free and clear of all charges. Man, that was so cool. One little sweep of the hand, and that little baby rolled right out of view. And the best part, it was right under Rusty's nose.*

After a short nap, Darin got up, dressed, then went looking for Frank. When he found him, he was in a sound asleep on the living room couch. *Good. Now I can take his truck without a hassle. But, where did he leave his keys. Oh, I remember.* Darin headed for the kitchen. *He was so hell bent on calling Doc Shively when we first walked in the house, that he dropped the keys by the phone. Ah, ha. There they are. Now, for some moola.*

Frank always kept a rather healthy amount of spending money in an old plastic butter container, sitting on a shelf with the can goods. After opening the container, Darin helped himself. Not bothering to count it, he stuck the money in his pocket. After scribbling out a note to Frank that he was making a beer run and would be right back, he propped the note next to the coffeepot. Being as quiet as he could, he left the house, careful not to let the screen door slam behind him.

In town, Darin went to the KWIK Stop, which was also the local Greyhound bus stop. He took his time driving onto the property, making sure he didn't recognize any of the vehicles that were sitting around the parking area.

When he pulled up to the front of the building, he parked in front of one of the large plate-glass windows. This gave him a clear view inside the building. He didn't want to run into anyone he knew, especially Rusty or any of his officers. Seeing that it was all clear, he got out of the truck and went inside the station.

"Afternoon," the attendant behind the counter greeted, tipping the bill of his cap. "Haven't seen you around here before."

Like I care. Without so much as a smile, Darin nodded at the man. Heading to the coolers, Darin acted like he didn't have a care in the world.

Up front, in the meantime, the attendant was straining his neck to see the license plate on the front of Darin's truck. There were so many items in front of the window blocking his view that he couldn't see the plate.

After getting a cold six-pack from the cooler, Darin took the beer to the attendant. He placed the beer on the counter.

Curious, the attendant asked, "I've been admiring your Ford truck. We don't see too many of them around here with four doors on the cab, like that. You new around these parts?"

Getting no response from Darin, who was completely ignoring him and looking at a shelf of cigarettes, the man decided to change the subject. "Somebody's got a thirst. Man, I don't blame you on a day like today." With still no response from Darin, he asked, "Will that be all?"

"No. I need a pack of cigarettes and your bus schedule," Darin replied.

The attendant couldn't resist throwing in his three-cents worth of advice. "I know it's your life, but you need to quit smoking, son. Do you know cigarettes can—"

Assuming he was about to get an unsolicited lecture about smoking, Darin abruptly cut in finishing the man's sentence with his own words. "Taste great with a cold beer? Yeah, I know. And you need to mind your own business." The attendant had no response. "You shouldn't be selling cigarettes if you're going to give lectures on the hazards of smoking. Give me a pack of those," Darin stated, pointing to a soft pack of Carlton 100's.

After checking out the bus schedule, Darin paid for his beer and cigarettes. He, also, purchased his bus ticket for the following week. Darin put the ticket in his hip pocket, put the package of cigarettes in his upper shirt pocket, picked up his cold six-pack, and left the building.

He sat in Frank's truck for a few minutes to open his fresh pack of cigarettes, and lit one up. Darin started the truck to get the air-conditioner going. To allow the smoke to filter outside, he cracked the window. Because it was a hot, humid, miserable summer day, he thought about opening a cold beer. *Nah, I've got my backend in enough hot water. I guess the beer will have to wait until I get back home.*

Off duty and driving his own car, Kelly drove to the gas pumps just a few feet away from Frank's truck. Kelly exited his car to fill his tank. As he was pumping gas, he noticed Darin sitting in the truck. It was no big deal to Kelly because Darin wasn't doing anything wrong or unlawful by sitting in the truck, smoking a cigarette. Darin left the station's lot without even noticing Kelly's presence.

After taking a twenty-dollar bill out of his billfold, Kelly went into the station to pay the attendant. Inside, at the counter, the attendant was looking through a brochure. As he looked up, he greeted his customer, tipping his cap. "Afternoon, Pat. It's a hot one out there today, isn't it?"

"You can say that again, Jerry," Kelly replied. "Pump 2, and I believe it's eleven dollars. You know me, I always try to round off those numbers."

"Pump 2?" After checking his computer, Jerry answered, "Yes, sir, eleven even."

The attendant took the twenty-dollar bill from Kelly. Like many small town folks, each loves to tell the first person they see about the business of the last person they had talked to. Naturally that's how gossip always got started, especially in Cole County.

Jerry was no different. Whatever his reason, either bored, lonesome, or wanting to let someone else know what he knew first hand, Jerry proceeded to tell Kelly about his last customer.

"Man, that poor fella that was just in here is in for quite a ride. He sure is lucky those buses have air-conditioning on them," Jerry stated as he rang up Kelly's bill and handed him change.

"Yeah, how's that?" Kelly asked, wondering what in the world this guy was talking about. Plus, he was curious, since he knew Darin had just left the station. He stuck the change in his pocket as he listened to the attendant's scuttlebutt.

"This guy just bought a ticket to New York. My goodness, Pat, you can't believe how complicated his trip is going to be with all of them transfers he'll have to make. I don't think I envy him at all. Nope. Any place I go, I drive myself. That way, if I—"

"Sorry, Jerry, but can you tell me something about the guy who bought that ticket."

"Like what?"

"Was that him that was sitting by the window in the white pick-up?"

"It sure was. A brand new Ford, too. Why?"

"This ticket he bought, when does that bus leave Kidwell?"

Raising his cap, Jerry scratched his head. "Well, the bus stops here every Friday on its way through town," he replied, replacing his cap. "That young fella bought his ticket for next week."

"You're sure it was for next week?"

Reaching down under the counter, Jerry brought up his bus reservation schedule. Since Darin's name was at the top of the list, Jerry glanced at it to recall the name and reservation date. "Yeah, next week. Here it is, D. Right. He said he couldn't be ready in time to leave on tomorrow's bus, so next Friday would have to do. Say, Pat, why all the questions? I'm not going to get in trouble for telling you all this, am I?"

Patting his hand on the counter, Kelly said, "Thanks, Jerry. I'll talk to you later."

Rushing out the door, Kelly jumped in his car and headed straight to the police department. He rushed into Rusty's office. "Chief, I'm sorry to barge in here this way, but I've got to talk to you," Kelly said with urgency in his voice.

Rusty was reading over some papers at his desk. Looking up at his off-duty officer, he was quite surprised. "What the heck are you doing here? Can't stand having a day off from this place, or is the heat getting to you?" Rusty joked.

Kelly placed his hands on the front of Rusty's desk, and leaned in. With a smirk on his face, he shook his head. "Okay, Chief, cut the jokes for now. Want to hear what I just found out?"

Rusty laughed. "Okay, get out of my face and tell me."

Kelly stood erect and stuck his thumbs in his pockets, leaving his hands hanging loose. "Our good friend, Darin, is planning a little trip to the big city of New York."

"That's good. He can plan all he wants to, but—"

"Sorry to interrupt you, Chief, but hear me out. He purchased a ticket, not twenty minutes ago, to leave on next week's bus."

Rusty got to his feet, like he had been shot out of a canon. "Next week? Kelly, do you know that for a fact?"

"Shoot, Chief, I wouldn't come in here on my day off just to pull some stupid prank on you. I was over at the gas station where the Greyhound buses stop on their way through town."

"Yes, I know the place. KWIK Stop. Jerry's the manager there, right?"

"I don't know, Chief. I thought he was a service attendant. Anyway, I'm filling my tank when I see Darin sitting in Frank's pick-up. He wasn't doing anything wrong, so I just minded my own business. When I went inside the station to pay for my gas, Jerry starts telling me how this fella, meaning Darin, is going to have such a confusing trip because of all of the bus transfers from here to New York City.

Oh, and Darin didn't use his correct name for his bus reservation. He used the name, D. Right. Now, is someone planning on skipping town, or what?"

"Janx, get in here," Rusty yelled. "Thanks, Kelly. Go home now and we'll take care of it."

As Kelly left Rusty's office, Officer Janx entered.

"Janx get the district attorney on the horn, and stand by. You and I are going out to the Righter farm and pick up Darin."

After Rusty informed the D.A. about Darin's scheduled trip, the D.A. got Darin's bail rescinded based on the grounds that Darin was a high flight risk. The D.A. didn't have to do much convincing to the judge after he brought up the fact that in a recent discovery, Darin already had an arrest record.

Darin had purchased a bus ticket under an alias name, and he had made reservations to leave town before he was to appear in court. Since there was the possibility that he was the real Neat Nick Thief and have the stolen money hidden somewhere, this would enable him to have traveling expenses. As a flight risk, Darin needed to be locked up so he wouldn't jump bail.

Out on the Righter farm, Frank was in the bathroom. Darin was sitting in the living room, watching TV and drinking a beer.

Legal papers in hand, Rusty and Janx rushed to Frank's farm. The backdoor was open, but the kitchen door was closed. Rusty opened the screen door, walked into the porch area, and knocked at the kitchen door. Beer in hand, Darin walked to the door and opened it. As he did, Rusty stepped inside with Officer Janx right behind him. Darin didn't get a chance to say anything before Rusty started talking.

"Sorry, Darin, but you are going to have to come with us. Your bail has been revoked. Now, if you come with us real peaceful like and don't cause any trouble, we can do this without the cuffs." Darin grinned with a look of defiance in his eyes. As he tipped the beer to take a drink, Rusty grabbed the can away from him. "Ignoring me doesn't help my temper right now, Darin. Now, are you coming quiet like, or do we use the cuffs?"

"I don't know, Rusty," Darin said with more than a touch of contempt, especially knowing he wasn't one of the privileged few to call Chief Simmons by his nickname. "What's this all about anyway?"

Rusty ignored Darin's sarcasm and smart mouth.

Just then Frank entered the kitchen. "What's going on out here?" Frank demanded.

"Your dear friend, Rusty is hassling me, Frank," Darin complained. In almost the same breath with bitterness, he expressed, "Get his butt off of our property."

Frank was baffled. "Rusty—"

"Now wait a minute, Frank. There's a explanation for what's going down here." Holding the can of beer, he offered it to Frank. "Here, if you will, please take Darin's beer."

Frank took the can of beer. After Rusty reached into shirt pocket, he pulled out a piece of paper and held it up in front of Darin. "I have a court order here, signed by the judge, revoking your bail and ordering us to take you back into custody, Darin." With a jerk of his head, Rusty turned in Frank's direction as he explained. "It seems like Darin purchased a bus ticket, today, to leave town next week, and under a fictitious name. Right, Darin?"

Frank was shocked. He looked at Darin and asked the obvious. "Is this true, Darin?"

"Yeah, I bought a ticket. So, what's the big deal? I figured your attorney friend could get me in and out of court in a few days. Then, I'll be free to go where and when I please," Darin defended his actions.

"Sorry, Darin," Rusty interceded, "but you were told it might take up to a full year before you even get to court. I find your story a little hard to swallow. Besides, even if you are telling me the truth, why use the name D. Right instead of using your real name?"

Frank backed up and sat in a kitchen chair. He was very weary and confused with Darin's actions. "Oh, Darin, how could you be so stupid? I don't know how I'm going to help you this time."

Rusty motioned to Officer Janx, who in turn took hold of Darin's arm and escorted him out the door and into the squad car.

"I'm so sorry, Frank," Rusty said, as he turned and walked out the door.

Before Rusty's police car even left the drive, Frank was on the phone to the attorney's office. "Betty, this is Frank Righter. I know it's getting late in the day, but is John still in?"

"Hi Frank. Yes, John is in his office, but he is with a client. May I have him call you back?"

"Please do that, Betty, and as soon as possible. Thanks. Bye."

As weak as he was, Frank was too upset to sit and save his energy. He paced back and forth across the kitchen floor, waiting for John to return his phone call. After what seemed like an eternity, the phone rang.

"John?" Frank barked, as he answered the phone.

"Yes, Frank. What's up?"

"Rusty was just here with a warrant and arrested Darin again. Said the judge revoked bail. Can they do that?"

"Whoa, hold on. What in the—What did Darin do to get his bail rescinded?"

"All he did was to purchase a bus ticket to leave town next week, thinking you could get him in and out of court right away on a misdemeanor or something. I guess he also shortened his name to D. Right, whatever that means. Oh, I don't know, but darn it, John, it's not like he just took off or tried to be sneaky about it," Frank defended Darin.

"Why that little son-of-a beachcomber! I'd say that was pretty sneaky, Frank. You know, that's all the D.A. needed. Up until now Darin's past arrest history was not supposed to be brought up with this case. This cute trick gives the D.A. the perfect opportunity to use it against Darin. That is, if the D.A. has Darin's past records by now. Knowing him, he probably does."

"What are you talking about, John?"

"A past record for breaking and entering, like Darin's record, could not have been brought into court since he was a minor when those arrests occurred."

"Right. I remember Darin's juvenile record was sealed."

"Was, is the key word here, Frank." John proceeded to inform Frank why Darin's bail was rescinded and why he was rearrested.. "Now his past juvenile record could be entered into the case against him. If this happens, I don't think he's going to walk out of court on a misdemeanor charge."

Bewildered, Frank asked, "So what do we do now, John?"

"There isn't much we can do now but to let Darin sweat it out in jail. I'll go over my paperwork, have a talk with Rusty, and get back with you in a few days. Also, I'll see if the D.A. is going to use Darin's past arrests against him in court."

"John, you never did tell me what kind of evidence Rusty has on Darin, if he does have any."

"Hold the phone a second, Frank," John said. Placing the receiver on his desk to free his hands, John looked for Darin's case file that was buried under more recent paperwork on his desk. Finding the folder, he scanned through his notes. He picked up the receiver. "Okay, Frank, sorry to keep you waiting. You know, I already told Darin about the evidence. It's funny he never said anything to you."

"If he did, John, I wouldn't be asking you."

"I know. That was just a matter of speech. Okay, here it is."

As John explained the evidence against Darin, Frank gazed at his kitchen wall. The pale yellow paint seemed to fade into a strange color of pink then turned into a deep red as Frank's temper enraged. Overridden with a loss of patience, and nothing John was saying making any sense, Frank cut in, "So what does that have to do with Darin? Besides, he doesn't even own a pair of rubber overshoes."

"Hold on, Frank, and let me finish. He had rubber boots on that day Rusty was at your place and first noticed the footprint in the mud."

"Does that, alone, prove that Darin is the county's so called Neat Nick Thief?"

"Well, it is a pretty good piece of evidence, Frank. Never the less, I will try and throw a wet towel on the fire by mustering up some doubt. I'll need to get a copy of Kidwell Police Department's report that has all of the dates and exact times that the victims were burglarized.

Then I'll get with Darin and see if he can remember where he was on those dates, and if anyone can vouch for his alibis. Once I've done that, I can use that information to knock some holes in Rusty's and the D.A.'s case against Darin. However, I will need some time to do all of this."

"So while you're finding out all of this information, Darin will have to sit in jail for a whole year? He'll never make it, John."

"In answer to the first part of your question, yes. Darin does have to stay in jail now, but that is his own fault, Frank. As for court, well, the dockets are always so booked with cases anymore that we will be lucky to get to court in a year. Times are changing and criminal behavior is on the rise. I'm more sorry than you'll ever know, Frank, but Darin was given his chance. He blew it.

As for your last statement, Darin has to make it. Go visit him as often as you can and try to stay optimistic. Keep his spirits up. If Darin knows you are on his side, backing him one-hundred percent, and that we are doing everything we can to get him cleared, then he should be fine."

John thought a moment, then added, "I need to clarify my statement, Frank. You need to understand that I cannot get Darin off on this Oscar Denton break-in, since he was caught in the man's house with the money in his hands. All I can do there is to ask that Darin pleads guilty when the time comes, and beg for mercy of the court. But, I will try my best to see that he isn't charged with all of the other burglaries."

"John, tell me honestly ... " Frank was hesitant to ask, but he needed to know, "do you think Darin is telling the truth when he says he isn't the Neat Nick Thief?"

"Hey, an attorney never defends a client he doesn't believe in, Frank, you know that," John answered with encouragement.

"Okay, John, I'll take your word for it. Thanks for your time, even though I know you're going to charge me for it anyway," Frank said, trying to put a little humor into their very serious conversation. "Keep in touch."

"You know I will, Frank.

Hey, you didn't look too hot when I last saw you. Are you in poor health?"

"No. I've just been so worried about Darin that I haven't eaten or slept in days." Frank lied, since he still hadn't told Darin about his illness.

"Okay, Frank. Listen, I'll talk to you soon. Bye for now."

As Frank hung up the telephone he verbally ran through his conversation with John and the things that were confusing to him.

"Overshoes? Footprints? What the—None of this makes any sense to me. Wait, what was the real reason that Darin was wearing my old work shoes when I went to see him in jail? He lied to me about not being able to locate his own shoes because they sat right there on the back porch in plain sight.

If he was wearing my work shoes to do chores, then why in Sam hill would he wear rubber overshoes on top of them? One doesn't wear both at the same time. It's either one or the other. At least the kind I have which are well insulated. Now, if he were wearing an ordinary shoe, then I can see wearing the rubber work boots over them. Shoot, I do that all the time. But, that's not the case with Darin. Wait, something else is screwy. Darin doesn't even own a pair of rubber overshoes."

Frank walked out on the back porch and spent a few minutes looking around. "Well now, where in the devil are my boots? And where are my work gloves and ski mask? That's crazy. I couldn't have misplaced those things.

Doesn't matter if I've been sick or not, I have a clear memory of wearing my rubber boots over my shoes, the last day I was out in the field. Yes." Frank nodded, "I had Darin remove my boots for me because I didn't have enough strength to do it myself. Darin, something smells like a trapped skunk. You need to start giving me some straight answers."

Frank immediately headed for jail to see Darin. After being checked out by the officer on duty, Frank was allowed to visit with Darin on the opposite side of the bars, as usual.

Excited, Darin asked, "Hi Frank. Did you talk to John? Are you here to get me out of this dump?"

Frank looked beyond Darin, more like through him. When his mind and eyes focused back on Darin, he replied, "No, Darin. I'm afraid you are in here for the duration. That is, until you go to court."

Outraged, Darin slammed at the bars with his clenched fists. "Screw you! What do you mean I have to stay in here until I go to court?"

"Calm down, Darin," Frank insisted, as he flinched from Darin's outburst. "Look, I'm sorry but you brought this on yourself. If you had listened when John and Rusty told you to stay at home, and to definitely stay out of trouble, then you wouldn't be in here. They also told you that you wouldn't be going to court for a good twelve months. So why would you want to pull a stunt like buying a bus ticket to leave town next week?"

"Put a sock in it, will you, Frank. You sound like a television re-run. Change the channel," Darin spouted, turning his back to Frank.

Frank turned, also. He leaned back against the bars. Suddenly, he started chuckling to himself. He remembered what John had suggested about him supporting Darin and the thought struck his funny bone, even in the middle of all of the chaos.

Hearing Frank's muffled laughter, Darin turned. He put his hands up through the bars and grabbed the back of Frank's shoulders. "Sure, Darin, the no good wayward kid is behind bars. Right where he belongs, right Frank? Is that what you're laughing at, Frank? Turn around and talk to me."

"I'm afraid you wouldn't find it amusing, Darin. I was just thinking as we were standing here, back to back, how I was here backing you up."

Releasing his hands from Frank's shoulders, Darin threw his arms in the air in disgust. "You're crazy, Frank, and I'm the one that's locked up. No wonder this world is screwed up." With a throbbing headache, Darin rubbed his temples, massaging the areas of pain. "Look, I realize that you've been a little under the weather, and now a bit stressed out, but you have to figure out how to get me out of here instead of standing there laughing at some dumb joke you thought up."

"Of course, Darin," Frank agreed, walking away.

"Hey," Darin yelled, "Frank? Frank! Come back here, Frank! Frank!"

Frank just kept walking until he could no longer hear Darin's pathetic voice. It was virtually impossible for him to even get close to asking Darin any imperative questions. Darin was too hot-tempered and too full of rage. Frank's questions would have to wait. He walked into the main office of the police department. Rusty's door was closed.

Stopping to speak to the front desk officer, Frank requested, "If the chief is in, would you tell him I would like to see him, please?"

"He's in a meeting right now, Mr. Righter, but I'll let him know you're out here waiting," the desk officer replied. The officer buzzed Rusty on the intercom.

"Yes," Rusty responded.

"Chief, sorry to disturb you, but Frank Righter is here to see you," the officer announced.

"Tell him to please wait. I'll be through here in about five minutes. Oh, and see if he wants a cup of coffee, will you?" Rusty's voice echoed through the intercom speaker.

Inside Rusty's office, he, Officer Kelly and Officer Seals were discussing Darin's case.

"Okay, men, we need to wrap this up because, as you heard, Frank's in the outer office waiting to see me.

Now, Kelly, go on over to your brother-in-law's house and check out that backyard area. Then get permission to check inside his house. Whatever kind of tool Darin used to break into Denton's house, can't just have disappeared into thin air.

I want you to take Janx with you. If he isn't back from his patrol in the next ten minutes, radio him to meet you at Denton's house. Let's get this taken care of tonight. On your way out, tell Frank I'm sorry but I will be with him as soon as I can. Okay?"

"Sure, Chief," Kelly said as he left the room.

"What about me, Chief? I could go with them," Seals suggested.

"No, you're due over at the D.A.'s office to give him your statement, not that he's going to like it. Just for my knowledge, tell me one more time where you were and what you were doing when Darin broke into Denton's house. The D.A. is a stickler for details so don't leave anything out." Rusty checked the time on his watch. "Let's make this quick because you have to be at the D.A.'s office around six and it is getting close to that time."

"You know I don't mind repeating this, Chief, but I've got every detail written up in my report."

"I'm aware of that, Seals, and I know you've already verbally told me everything. I just want to make sure you haven't left out anything when you're questioned by the D.A."

Seals moistened his lips with his tongue then began explaining. "Well, Chief, it's just as I told you before. I was on stakeout inside the garage. I had my hand radio with me to use instead of my shoulder radio, just like you told me to do." Seals stopped reporting. Since they were on the subject of stakeouts, it seemed like a perfect opportunity to clear up a question in his mind.

"Chief, since I've never been on a stakeout before you started Operation Ivy, it was a new experience for me. Now, I hate to appear dumb, but why did I have to use the hand radio instead of the shoulder radio? I'd like to know for my own knowledge, but I should also know in case the D.A. asks me."

"Simple, you have to have the volume louder on the shoulder radio. And you're not dumb just uninformed, which is my fault. Okay, back to your report, and try to talk a little faster."

"Even though it was a moonlit night, it was dark in the garage. From where I was standing, I could see clear as a bell out of the garage window, directly to the backdoor of Clinger's house." Noticing that Rusty was shaking his head, Seals stopped, once again. "Something wrong, Chief?"

"I would prefer that you drop the Clinger and say Denton's house when you talk to the D.A. Okay, continue."

"Sure. Now the way I was standing at an angle to the wall, if anyone happened to look in, they couldn't have seen me. This was around 9:00 p.m., or a little after. I remember because it had just turned dark when I saw something run out of the shadows, moving towards Denton's backdoor. It dawned on me that I was looking at a human being, dressed in dark clothes.

I turned away from the window, backed up flat against the wall of the garage, and I called in what was going down. You were quick to respond to my call."

Seals mouth was dry. As he stopped to clear his throat and swallow, this gave Rusty the perfect opportunity to add, "I believe this is where my statement will fit into sequence with yours. The reason I responded so fast to your call was because I was already in the vicinity of Denton's house. Oscar Denton had just notified me about a possible setup to detain him longer then his usual stay at the athletic club.

Of course the rest of what Denton told me will be just here say on my part. Denton can verify what happened on his end, like the telephone call message that was relayed to him, and how he checked out the credit card number with the name he was given, just to find out that it was bogus. Those were all sure-fire clues that someone wanted to keep Denton away from his house that night. My bet is, Darin is that someone.

Lucky for us, Denton has a lot of law enforcement friends, or he wouldn't have been able to get that information so quickly that night. Okay, Seals, then we get back to you and what you did next."

"I stayed put in the garage until I saw your car and the other squad car pull up to Denton's house. And, like they say, the rest is history."

"Very funny. Why, if no one could see you, did you decide to change your position at that window?" Rusty quizzed.

"Simple, Chief. Have you ever seen the windows in those old garages? They're thin as paper. No one could have spotted me, unless they placed their face directly on the window to look in. On the other hand, if anyone would have flashed a light towards the window, I'm sure the beam would have bounced off my badge. Also, I'm dead sure someone would have heard me if I had radioed in from where I was observing. I didn't want the noise of my voice to scare anyone away or tip off my presence to the suspect."

"Now you understand why I didn't want you to use the shoulder radio," Rusty stated. Seals nodded. "Carry on."

"By the time I got through talking with you and looked back out the window, the suspect was already inside the house."

"How did you know the perp was inside Denton's house?"

"I didn't at first. But, as I kept watch on the house, waiting for you to arrive, I saw a brief flicker of light from one of the windows. The house had been totally dark since Denton had left. So I knew someone was inside with, I assumed, a flashlight."

"Thankfully, you assumed right. Darin had to have jimmied that door to get inside. According to Kelly, Denton swears he locked his backdoor before he left that evening. But without you seeing him, Darin that is, and without any kind of tool, we can't prove it."

"He didn't have any tools on him that night, right?" Seals asked.

"Not one damn thing."

"To change the subject, is it okay if I go back on my dayshift schedule, Chief? Or, do you need me for more night work?"

"Get back on your regular shift. I think we've all put in enough overtime lately. The night owl crew will be happy to get their shift back to normal, too. I won't take Kelly and Janx off the overtime list until we get more evidence on Darin."

"Thanks, Chief."

"Okay, Seals, you best be getting over to the D.A.'s."

As Seals exited, Rusty followed him to the outer office. Frank was seated on a bench, his clasped hands in his lap, rolling his thumbs.

"Frank, I'm sorry I had to keep you waiting. Come on in to my office and have a seat." After Frank entered the office, Rusty closed his door. Frank took a seat.

"How are you holding up?" Rusty asked, taking his seat behind his desk. He crossed his arms and leaned to one side so his elbow could rest on the chair's arm.

"Okay, I guess. I'm just exhausted, Rusty. I don't know what is happening anymore. You know, one minute you have the world by the tail, and then, wham! Everything turns upside-down and backwards. Just think, a few years ago I had my health, Darin had just come home from college, and I thought life was grand," Frank rambled.

"Shoot, Rusty, I am forty-nine years old and I'm dying. But that's not what hurts so much. It's Darin. He is barely twenty-three and he's locked up behind bars. He has his whole life ahead of him. What am I going to do?"

"I feel worse than you can ever imagine about this whole ordeal with Darin. Even though I'm just a little over a year away from retirement, I've been giving serious consideration to retiring, right now. The stress of—"

"Boy, aren't we a pair. Poor me, poor you. Is this what happens when you get older or terminally ill, Rusty? Do we turn into cry babies?"

Rusty shook his head and shrugged. "Life. What a carnival ride, huh, Frank?"

"Well, now that we've cried on each other's shoulders, I just came in to find out if you've received any further information on the woman I'm looking for?"

"Sorry Frank. I have hit nothing but dead ends," he admitted. "I don't know any more now than I did when I spoke with you last month when you first took to bed. Without any more information than you have given me—"

"I know. Well, you tried and that means a lot to me. I guess it's up to me now," Frank stated, getting up to leave. "Rusty, I know putting Darin behind bars makes him some sort of a criminal in your eyes, but see that he gets fair treatment. If you would, I would appreciate it."

"Frank, I give all of our inmates the same good treatment. They eat three squares a day, are permitted hot showers and phone calls, and sleep on clean cots. I have no mercy for law breakers, and I might not respect any perps I have locked up, but they are all treated like human beings."

Rusty stayed seated as Frank opened the door. Waving goodbye over his shoulder, Frank left the office.

Frank felt like he couldn't take another step, but he knew he had to. He had to push and push to convince himself to keep going for Darin's sake. However, he would have to push tomorrow. For now, he had to lie down and get some rest before he collapsed again. He drove home and virtually dragged his worn-out body into the house where he took his medication, then fell, fully clothed, into bed.

Between cancer and his deep worry over Darin, Frank didn't know which ailment would kill him first. The way he felt, Frank knew he was closer to death's door than he cared to be. He wasn't sure if he would even wake up, again.

HOSPITALITY

"Daniel?" Micky hollered. "Danny, baby, your lover's home."

Micky pulled her arms out of the backpack straps and placed the carrier on the floor. She kneeled beside it. After unzipping the main pocket of the backpack, she started rummaging through it. "I'm dying for a smoke. I know I've got cigarettes in here, somewhere."

Oblivious to anything Micky was doing, Farm Girl stood like a statue in awe of the space around her. Still catching her breath, she took in everything in sight. Finally, she unconsciously started chattering under her breath.

"Crimeny, this is sure a giant house. Mama, would you just look at this big old room I are standing in. This room looks bigger than the whole house that Pappy live in. It's way bigger, I'll betcha, than one of them fancy hotels I was staying in. Maybe I are in that beanstalk house of Jack's, like in one a them storybooks Pappy buy and done read me. Look over there. There's a bunch of steps going way up towards the sky."

Moving in a slow, inch-by-inch turn, Farm Girl continued describing what she viewed, as if Mama was listening. "There is steps and doors going everywhere. Over there is a big old fireplace with purdy white rocks all around it. Look at them windows, Mama. They is so big, neither me or you could clean all the way to the top, even if we was on one of Pappy's big ole ladders."

Enclosed in her own mental space, Micky found her cigarettes. She continued digging through the pockets of her backpack, trying to find her lighter. When it dawned on her Farm Girl was talking, Micky gave a slight turn of her head to see if anyone else was in the room. Realizing there were just the two of them, Micky got to her feet.

"Did you say something to me, Diana, or are you talking to yourself?" Micky asked.

Farm Girl was so preoccupied with looking around the vast surroundings and talking to Mama, that she didn't hear Micky. Instead, she continued to be engrossed in her amazement. "Oh my, Mama, can you see them purdy purple colors in here? Them walls matches the rug, just like they done in that fancy hotel in the world a Des Moines."

"Hey, Dawn, you off in la-la land or something?" With still no response from Farm Girl, Micky raised her voice. "Okay, enough, already, Dresden. Get a grip. I'm no your mama."

The elevated volume of Micky's voice caught Farm Girl's attention. "What?"

"Are you calling me Mama, or is that a ghost you're talking to?"

Wide eyed, Farm Girl asked, "Does you gots a ghost in here?"

"No, Dimwit." Micky laughed. Taking a cigarette out of the pack she was holding, Micky inquired, "Say, don't suppose you smoke, do you?"

"No. I try it once with my buddie. Didn't like it. All that smoke make me cough so much, my throat fill like it were on fire."

"You just need a little practice, that's all. Once you get the hang of it, it won't burn your throat. The trick is to inhale, not breath in the smoke. Look, you stay here. I'll go find Danny. He works nights, so he's probably sleeping up in his room."

"This are sure a big house your friend has," Farm Girl stated, still in awe.

"Yes, it's very spacious but it's not a house, Diamond. This is an old warehouse. Make yourself comfortable," Micky stated, as she ran up a flight of steps, disappearing from Farm Girl's view.

Other than turning in place, Farm Girl didn't move from the entranceway. "Wear house? Maybe this am one a them slang words? I'll bet Chicago world peoples calls a house a wear house, like Mama were calling Pappy's house a farmhouse."

A sudden fear encased Farm Girl's entire body. Chills ran up her spine. "Crimeny, if this be a beanstalk house, and Micky comes back bringing a giant with her, I just doesn't know what I'll do. Oh, yes I does. But, I'll sure need me some clean bloomers if that happens.

Oh, Farm Girl, should you stay here, or should you leave and git yourself back on that bus to New York City? Nope, don't want to do that. I want to go on one a them roller coaster rides first. Wonder if they has one a them fancy hotels here in Chicago? Maybe I need me to go find out."

As Farm Girl opened the door, ready to leave, Micky hollered, "Hey, Dakota, where you going?" Farm Girl turned toward the sound of Micky's voice. "Wait, Danny is coming down to meet you." The jingling sound of Micky's bracelets, as she ran down the flight of steps, reminded Farm Girl of the money that jingled around her waist when she made her long journey on foot. "Come on, you don't want to go anywhere."

"I, I thought, maybe, Chicago might has one a them fancy hotels with room service and a privy. I are gonna find me one," Farm Girl expressed. "You has too much room here. A body like me might git herself lost.. I aren't never seen so many steps befur in one wear house. Crimeny, I aren't never see me any wear house befur."

"There you go," Micky said, exhaling the smoke from her cigarette. "You're going to get me going on the giggles, again. I don't know how much more I can take, today. My sides are killing me now.

You don't need any fancy hotel to stay in, 'Dinky-doo.' Yes, we've got plenty of space here for you, and I can guarantee, you won't get lost. Most of those steps lead to different levels of rooms. If you go up one set of them, you come back down the same ones. Except for Danny, and he has two sets of stairs from his room. Later, I'll give you a tour of the place so you can learn your way around."

"What's a tour?"

"Micky, who's your friend?" a deep voice asked, as a man appeared at the top of one of the flight of steps.

Standing with the door open, Farm Girl raised her head to see who the voice belonged to. Her mouth fell open in amazement, as she backed up a step.

Crimeny, I doesn't know if he's a giant, or not. He sure am big. And look, Pappy, he's got him some of that purdy color skin, just like you. There aren't no hair on his head, just like that deputy man. Guess he don't care though because he gots some growing out a his chin.

Looks to me like he's wearing more of that fancy stuff than Micky's wearing. There's one in his ear, and all them purdy color stones on—Does you see them, Mama? Them stones is on all his fingers.

That thing around his neck is as purdy and shiny as them gold-colored monies I has. It looks mighty heavy. Wonder how he can stand up carrying that big thing on his neck, like that? Since Micky has all them same shinny things hanging all over her, maybe this here giant's gots him one a them hens that lays them gold eggs?*

Dressed in navy pants and an open collared navy shirt that hung over his belt, Danny walked down the steps with the glow of confidence and a stride of masculinity. Casually, with each deliberate step, he headed to where Micky and Farm Girl were standing.

"Look, baby, I told you I brought home a surprise." Micky explained, snuffing out her cigarette in the nearest ashtray. "This is my friend Daisy."

"Hi, Daisy. I'm Daniel. Don't mind Micky, she's on one of her trips." As he turned and started walking away, he offered, "Close the door so you don't let the flies in. Then, come on over here, Daisy, and make yourself at home. You know the saying, mi casa es su casa."

"You look pretty silly, Daisy, standing there with your mouth wide open. Close it," Micky suggested with a grin.

Farm Girl closed her mouth and swallowed. She closed the door but stayed standing next to it. *Speak, Farm Girl. Micky are your friend, so this Mister Daniel aren't gonna hurt you. I doesn't think so anyway.* "No, I doesn't know that saying, but I reckon if I stay a while I can learn me some a your foreign language."

"Oh, we don't speak Spanish either. So it's no big deal if you don't," Micky admitted. "Danny just knows a few words and phrases. He likes to use them when the opportunity arises."

Danny seated himself in a plush-velvet, lavender chair in close proximity to the sofas. His arms resting on the chair's wide armrests, Danny stared at Farm Girl. "Micky, bring your friend over here."

Micky took her puzzled guest by the arm and walked her toward one of the two gray velvet sofas in the room. Being led across that vast floor to the seating area, Farm Girl was still trying to figure out what Micky told her. *Spanish must be what they calls this here Chicago language. I are hoping Micky's right and I doesn't has to learn it. What with that French and slang I gots to learn, I doesn't need to be learning Spanish, too.*

Aren't that funny, now she's calling me Daisy. I think that's the name I give her on the bus ride.

"Let loose of those cases, Daisy, and sit down," Micky said, smiling. "Your arms have got to be worn out the way you're always clutching everything. There isn't anyone here that's going to take that stuff away from you."

"No, I is fine," Farm Girl replied. "How come you know my name now, Micky? You hasn't called me Daisy since I teld you that were my name."

Micky started laughing, but Danny didn't find it amusing. "Micky likes to play games with people's names, Daisy. She likes to see how many different names she can call you, using your first initial," Danny explained. "I'm sorry if she insulted you.

I don't like it either. She is only allowed to call me Daniel or Danny. You can feel free to call me either."

"Games? I like to play games, Mister Either. But that one sure am plum confusing to my mind. For a while I be furgitting what name—I mean, I furgot who I are with all them funny names," Farm Girl admitted. "I had to constipate real hard to remember."

"Stop, you're killing me," Micky squealed, getting the giggles, again. "I hope you meant to say concentrate? Come on, Daisy, relax. Let go of the suitcase, drop the briefcase and that piece of luggage you call a purse. Sit and take a load off," Micky insisted.

"Micky. Cool it, darling, will you? Can't you see you're scaring this poor girl half to death. Come over here, sit by me, and leave her alone," Danny ordered. "Daisy, my name isn't Mister Either. I meant, you could call me either Daniel or Danny. Now, if you want to hold on to your things, you just do so."

Directing his attention toward Micky, he asked, "Give it to me straight. What's going down?"

Leaving Farm Girl's side, Micky joined Danny and sat on the floor at his feet. Expressing a pouty face, she looked up at him. "Come on, baby, please don't be angry at me. Nothing's going down. I just brought her home because she makes me laugh." In a low, almost whisper voice, she added, "She's close to the same age we are, but I think she has a child's brain. The way she speaks and the words she uses—'What fur? Does you gots wanna them?'—cracks me up."

"Truth." He demanded, glaring at Micky with his cold eyes, while all the time keeping a smile on his face for Farm Girl's benefit.

"I said you would take her on a roller coaster ride," Micky admitted. "Please?"

Danny turned to Farm Girl who was still standing next to the sofa, watching and listening. "If she keeps you happy, then I guess one or two days won't hurt," he replied. "Does Daisy know what a roller coaster ride is?"

"You doesn't have to ask Micky, when I are right here. I sure doesn't know, Mister Danny. But if it makes me laugh as much as Micky be doing, then, fur sure, I wants to take me that ride."

Micky was so tickled, she fell back on the floor, rolling with laughter. Farm Girl still hadn't seen anything too funny to laugh at. Just the same, she smiled at Danny to show she was trying to enjoy whatever made Micky laugh so hard.

Even Danny found himself chuckling at Farm Girl's naivety. "You have never had the pleasure of such an amazing ride, Daisy?" Farm Girl shook her head. "The ride will take you slowly up an incline one minute, then the next thing you know, your going down and around curves so fast, it will take your breath away. You have to hold on tight, or you'll—"

Micky, still reclining on the floor, said, "Come on, baby, you're only confusing her. She's oopid-stay."

"Really?" he replied, giving Micky a cockeyed look. "Don't you think I've already figured that out on my own? I'd say she's more than oopid-stay. Perhaps i-eve-nay."

"What are I?" Farm Girl asked.

Micky sat upright. "I assume you don't speak Pig Latin, do you?" she asked, keeping her eyes on Danny, hoping Farm Girl didn't understand that they had just made some derogatory remarks about her.

"Pig who? Oh, am that another one a them foreign languages?"

"N-O," Micky silently mouthed to Danny before turning to Farm Girl, saying, "No, Daisy It's just another game."

"Wait, Micky," Danny said, "be honest with her. Yes, Daisy, it is a foreign language. Do you speak any foreign languages?"

"Crimeny, I speaks farm language. I learn me some words of that Omaha language. And I reckon I picked up a few a them words they speaks in Des Moines. Oh, and Micky teach me one a them French words."

"Micky taught you French?" Danny asked, looking at Micky with a raised brow.

Laughing, Micky explained, "We were talking and I said, pardon my French."

"The word was hell. It were easy fur me to remember because in my language, we calls them cuss words. But, Mister Danny, I doesn't want to learn much more of them languages. Not right now, because I are going to New York City. I reckon I can only constipate—uh, consummate one language at a time."

When Micky started to correct Farm Girl's word, Danny gave her a slight kick to silence her, allowing Farm Girl to keep talking. "When I gits me to that other world, then I wants to learn me that New York City language.

It's purdy funny, though. I doesn't know you can speak pig talk. All the time I were on them farms, I be just talking regular farm words to them pigs. Aren't that funny I has to come to Chicago to know them pigs has a language all them own. Crimeny, wouldn't Mama has her a surprise if she know that?"

Micky looked up at Danny, crossing her eyes. Pointing her index finger at her temple, moving the finger in a circular motion, she muttered, "Crackers!"

Micky has her one a them strange finger problems, just like that Mister Tom was having. I best not let her know that I see it. Poor girl.

After lighting a cigarette, Danny deeply inhaled the smoke. Farm Girl watched as the whiffs of smoke came flowing from his mouth with each word he spoke. "Yes, we do have some crackers," he replied, kicking Micky, again. "Daisy would you like some crackers?"

Not knowing what they were, Farm Girl asked. "Crackers?"

"If you don't want crackers, what would you like to eat?" Danny inquired. "I should ask first, are you even hungry?"

"I sure are. You gots any burger, fries and a chocolate shake? That's what I really has a hankering fur."

Once again, Micky started rolling around on the floor in laughter as she mimicked Farm Girl's words. "Hankering fur?" Attempting to gain a bit of composure, Micky took a few quick breaths. She sat upright, again, and looked at Danny.

"Didn't I tell you she was a stitch? Now you know why I brought her home." Directing her attention to her guest, Micky suggested, "How about we show you to your room, Daisy, and you can rest. Later, we can get you something to eat. How does that sound?" Turning back to Danny, she asked, "Is that okay with you, baby?"

Danny nodded in acceptance.

Forgetting about food, Farm Girl asked, "My room?"

"Sure, your room. You didn't think I was going to share one with you, I hope?" Micky joked. "I can guarantee you that it is bigger and better than some old hotel you've ever stayed in. It even has its own bathroom."

Farm Girl didn't answer because she didn't really know what to do. The thoughts in her head were still swaying between staying and leaving.

Holding her head between the palms of her hands, Micky groaned. "Oh, my roller coaster ride has come to a dead stop. I want to take a shower and crash. Hopefully, you want to do the same, Daisy."

After putting out his cigarette, Danny got to his feet. Bending over with outstretched arms, he pulled Micky to her feet and wrapped his arm around her waste.

"What do crash mean?"

"That means to take a nice long nap, Daisy." He focused his attention back on Micky. "Yes, your trip is over. I agree, it's time for you to rest now." Under his breath he whispered, "Did you use everything you had with you?"

"Yes, but it got me home, didn't it, baby?" Micky whispered.

Danny walked Micky toward a three-step set of stairs. Glancing back in Farm Girl's direction, he reiterated Micky's earlier suggestion. "Come on, Daisy. We'll show you to your room."

Missing constant companionship, such as Mama had been all her life, this was an experience Farm Girl decided not to pass up. *New York City can wait. I need my new friends to take me on one a them roller coaster rides, first.* Once she made her decision, Farm Girl followed Micky and Danny.

This time there was no doubt that Farm Girl had entered into another world. As far as she had journeyed on her own, surviving every step of the way no matter what the odds, Farm Girl's fate now rested in the hands of strangers. Hungry for friendship, Farm Girl had forgotten Mama's constant warnings about strangers are evil.

Black Rosebud

REACHING OUT FOR LOVED ONES

Starting his own search for the woman who had stolen his heart, Frank phoned an old school chum, Rob Janzon. Rob was the owner and editor of his own newspaper in one of the larger rural areas in Nebraska. Frank called his friend for assistance. After Frank explained about the missing woman he was looking for, Rob agreed to help. Along with Carole's picture that Frank would be mailing to him, Rob volunteered to write a small article, <u>Looking for Lost Love.</u>

"If you can, Rob, I want coverage in the entire state of Nebraska, border to border," Frank insisted. Once Rob received the photo of Carole, he promised to send the information to the Nebraska Associated Press.

Not all newspapers from Omaha to Scottsbluff or from Vermillion to McCook received the press wires. He would have to personally contact the smaller periodicals. He warned Frank, not all newspapers would carry the picture and the article. All Frank could do was hope for the best.

When the phone call ended, Frank felt he was following through with his last option. "I couldn't give Rob anymore than Carole's first name. There's just no way in knowing what last name she is using, today." If plastering Carole's picture all over the state didn't help locate her, nothing would.

After completing everything he needed accomplished at home, Frank headed for town. At the police station, an officer informed him that Darin was unavailable. Darin was in one of the client-attorney conference rooms with his attorney. Frank could either wait or return at later time. Frank opted to sit in the hallway and wait.

Inside the conference room, John was trying to get his facts straight according to what Darin was telling him. John was sitting on one side of the banquet-size table, asking questions and taking notes. Seated opposite him, Darin was answering with his lies.

"Darin, I need you to tell me one more time why and what you were doing at the Oscar Denton house the night you were arrested."

"It's like I told you before. Around the first week in June, I quit my job. Planned on leaving town. I've lost all track of time, so you can check at the bank as to when my final day of employment was there. Frank got sick. So, I didn't want to leave town, right away. I love Frank, you know. He's been a super brother. Ever since our parents died, Frank has been like a father to me."

Great, Darin, throw in the mush. Make yourself look like the loving, caring, can-do- no-wrong, all American guy. "I just couldn't walk out on him when he was sick in bed. After weeks of doing nothing but farm work—what a drag that was—and taking care of Frank, I got bored. I might have worked outside doing chores, but I felt like the walls were closing in on me. Frank can tell you, in fact anyone who knows me can tell you, I like to play pranks on people. That's what I do to break up the monotony in my life, when I start feeling restless."

"Get to the point, Darin."

"I am. Frank was planning a celebration dinner in honor of my leaving. Since he was barely out of his sick bed, he asked me to get a few things from the store. On my way to do the shopping, I passed by this particular house. I used to pass this same house on my way to work. For the past six months, there was a For Sale sign in the yard. That night, I not only noticed the sign was gone, but I saw a guy in a new Chrysler pulling out of the driveway. I didn't recognize the driver as a local citizen. Who was he?

Then I remembered hearing about this Kidwell newcomer. Putting two and two together, I figured this had to be the new guy I had heard about. Since he was leaving, his house was dark, and I was looking for that bit of excitement in my dole drum life, I decided, right then and there, this guy would be perfect for one of my old tricks. It was a spur of the moment decision."

"Okay. According to what you told me before, you followed Mr. Denton to the local athletic club. Why did you follow him?"

"Easy. I just wanted to know where he was going. See, if he went some place just to run an errand, like pick up something at the KWIK Shop, then he wouldn't be away from home for very long. No one I know of goes to the athletic club unless they plan on staying an hour or so. I needed to be sure I had enough time to scout out the house without him coming home, ruining my fun."

John was actively taking notes, as he kept up his inquisition. "The need for a few kicks directed you to drive the car onto the lot next to the house, hiding the car out of sight?"

"Naturally. It would have been dumb on my part to park in the guy's drive or out on the street. Most people in town don't drive a brand new Ford, John. Also, most of Kidwell know Frank's car and that I drive it."

"After hiding the car in the lot, why cover it with a tarp?"

"Couldn't take any chances. Headlights from approaching traffic could have reflected off my car. That might have set off an alarm in a suspicious-minded driver. Since I always carry a tarp in my trunk, it seemed natural to cover the car and prevent that from happening. As I covered the car, I couldn't help but laugh that I still had the old balls of fire still in me." Darin laughed, making his lie appear humorous.

Annoyed that Darin thought his so-called prank was funny, John stated, "This isn't a game, Darin. Breaking the law is a serious business."

"Cut me some slack. I wasn't going to burglarize the place."

"You followed Mr. Denton to be sure, in your mind, that he'd be away from his house for an ample amount of time, giving you time to play a so-called prank. In addition, you take precautions to hide your car. That sounds to me like you planned on burglarizing Mr. Denton's home."

"You got it all wrong. I was just going to see what kind of mischief I could do. Just to let him know someone was messing with him. For example, if he had any outside furniture and a garden hose sitting out on the lawn, I was going to stack the furniture and tie it up with the hose. He didn't have anything sitting outside.

So, I decided my mischief making would have to be inside the house. Surprisingly enough, the backdoor was wide open. An unlocked door is always a great invitation to me, or anyone else. I walked on in. That's all there is to it.

Oh, except one vital detail. Before I got a chance to exit the house, Chief Simmons and his two-bit officers came rushing in with guns pointed at me. Scared the friggin' life out of me. I hate to admit it, John, but I almost soiled my pants. Thought for sure they were going to shoot me. Next thing I know, Chief Simmons accuses me of being his Neat Nick Thief. Then they locked me up." Darin felt satisfied that he had told a convincing story. He stuck to the same story, only in more detail, as he had told John once before.

"It is my understanding, Mr. Denton doesn't go to the athletic club until after 9:00 p.m. You're telling me that you went grocery shopping that late?"

"Yes, I am. Grover's Market is open twenty-four hours a day, in case you didn't know. With Frank sick, I had to make sure he was in a sound sleep and wouldn't need me for anything before I could leave the farm. That's why it was late when I went shopping."

"Let's back up a minute to the tarp."

"What about it?"

"For what reason do you carry it in the trunk of the car?"

"Simple. Like I said, the set of wheels I drive belong to Frank. Since I'm always on the go, I don't have time to keep the car in the garage. Covering the car with a tarp protects it from tree sap, bird dung and stuff like that. Plus, I don't always have time to wash the car.

You know Frank gets a new car every year?" John nodded. "It's he least I can do to keep it nice for him. Keeping the tarp in the trunk is easier then keeping it in the shed. That way, it's always quick and easy to get to when I need it."

John kept hammering away with his questions. It was imperative that he got every detail straight to be able to defend his client in court. Any loop holes, and the D.A. would be sure to find them to use against Darin. If John decided to put Darin on the stand in his own defense, Darin had to give the same detailed information. Just in case Darin wasn't telling the full truth, John was trying to trip him up.

"I want to get back to Denton's house. Just because you follow someone and watch them enter a place of business, another house, or wherever, why would you think the person left their house unoccupied? Let me rephrase that. Why didn't you think someone else was in the house that night? Unless you knew, of course, that Oscar Denton lived there alone. Did you?"

"To tell the truth, I did know he was living alone. Shoot, everyone in town knows when someone new moves into a small town, like Kidwell," Darin responded rather belligerently. "Not just is gossip at its best about a newcomer in this community, but within hours, everyone knows their business. At least they think they do.

I knew weeks ago when Denton first moved to town that he was a retired farmer, wealthy, a widower and lived alone. What I didn't know, until that night, was where he lived."

John looked up from his note writing. "Wait. Now you're telling me something you never mentioned before, Darin. You told me you didn't recognize him. What you're stating, now, is that you had already known about Mr. Denton."

Calm and confidant, Darin proceeded. "It's not like anyone ever showed me a picture of him. I knew about him, as I said, but I had never met the man." Darin paused for a moment to think. Then, an instant replay in his brain refreshed his memory. "Wait! Chief Simmons told me about Denton. The chief wanted Frank to invite this Denton guy to join the Friday night poker parties Frank belongs to."

John's eyes rolled with his own flash of lightening. "Now I understand how you got baited. Never mind. Let's go back to the car tarp."

"Again?" Darin asked, quite bored with having to repeating his story.

"Yes, again. Why did you cover your car with the tarp the night you were arrested at Mr. Denton's home?"

"For crying out loud, John. I've told you why, twice or three times already."

"Tell me again."

"To hide the car from oncoming traffic. You don't get to be known as Kidwell's Bad Boy without knowing all the tricks, John. If I had left the car uncovered, it wouldn't have been any fun. I could've been caught, right away. All it would've taken was one headlight to bounce off the car, some nosey person to investigate what was shining amongst the trees, and my car would've been discovered. The challenge of a prankster is to *not* get caught."

"Unfortunately, Darin, that is also the challenge of a crook," John replied, not taking his eyes off Darin. He was hoping for a facial reaction. Since he got no change of expression from Darin, he continued.

"Okay, let's move on to the ski mask you were wearing the night you were arrested the first time. Had the burglary taken place in early to mid June, when we were still experiencing cooler temperatures than normal, there may have been some stupid excuse for wearing a knit ski mask. However, we're talking July weather. Hot July temperatures. Why would you have a ski mask with you if you hadn't preplanned this prank, as you call it?"

"When I found the hat in my pant's pocket, it seemed only natural to wear it. I used to do that, years ago. It kept light rays from bouncing off my skin. You know, like the car. That way there's no reflection to attract unwarranted attention." Receiving a look of doubt, Darin knew John wasn't buying his explanation. "Okay. To be honest, I used to wear it to hide my identity when I pulled my pranks. I didn't want to take the chance that someone might recognize me."

"Darin, that is probably one of the most honest statements you have made to me, today." *Sucker!* Darin thought. "Now that you're on the right track of honesty, explain how you just happened to have the ski mask in your pant's pocket on the night in question."

Feeling offended by John's remark, Darin wanted an answer of his own. "Look, you told me earlier that you know I'm telling the truth. Now, you say my last statement was the first honest thing I've said. Are you telling me that you've done a complete change in midstream? Now you're not believing my whole story?"

"No, I didn't say that. I'll admit some parts of your story are a little more believable. Nevertheless, there are, also, far too many questionables in your story. Makes it smell a little fishy. Answer my question. What is the real reason you had the ski mask with you in the night of question?"

"Just a coincidence. I haven't worn those pants since February, when it was still cold outside. As soon as I put the pants on, I noticed there was a bulge in the pocket. When I removed the bulge and saw it was the ski mask, I stuck the stupid thing back in my pocket. At the time, that seemed easier than putting it back where it belonged.

Don't forget, John, Frank was sick in bed. It was imperative that I hurry to town, shop, and get back home, as soon as possible. When I decided to pull my prank, I remembered I had the ski mask in my pocket. I put it on. Just like the good old days." Darin laughed.

Irritated, John remarked, "Just because I'm a small town attorney, doesn't mean I don't have intelligence. What do you take me for, a lamebrain idiot?"

"I don't know what you mean."

"What could it have taken you, five minutes tops, to put a ski mask away? And if you were so blasted worried about not leaving Frank alone for very long, why would you take the time to pull some stupid prank?"

"I don't have an answer for that."

"Why am I not surprised?"

Thinking fast, Darin found an answer. He hoped it would satisfy his attorney. "Let me draw a parallel here. It would be like the kid that knows he has to be home by dinner. If not, he'll get in trouble for being late. On his way home, a giant mud puddle catches his eye. Suddenly, he isn't thinking about home, dinner, the time, or the consequences for being late. The mud puddle is so fascinating to him it takes over all common sense thoughts in his mind. So, he stops to play in it.

My mind was on Frank, at first, but when I saw the opportunity to pull my prank, all of my original worries about Frank vanished. I certainly didn't forget about Frank on purpose. It was just one of those crazy impulses that draws a person to spontaneity."

"That's good, Darin. The D.A. is going to be trying to make you angry and have you say things that might incriminate you. You have to keep your cool. Think smart. Then give a clear explanation, as you did for me just now. Now, they caught you with Mr. Denton's money in your hands. Theft is not a prank. How did you get from wanting to stack lawn furniture to stealing money?"

"Looking around the inside of the house, I was checking things out to see what mischievous act I could do. Bam! There it was sitting right on the dining room table. A small metal box. Since it's my nature to be curious, I opened it. They can't throw the book at me for being curious. And, there's one major detail. I was just holding the money in my hand, trying to figure out how much was there.

Actually, I was thinking about how stupid this guy was for leaving money in an unlocked strong box with the Neat Nick Thief on the loose. My other hand was holding the s—stupid lid of the strong box. So you see, I had every intention of putting the money back. If I had wanted the money, I would've jammed it in my pocket, and gotten the hell out of there. Not just sit there, looking at it." *Damn, I almost told John what I was holding. I've been doing so good. Can't mess up now.*

"Let's not be juvenile, Darin. One hand or two, you still got caught holding the money." After looking over some of his previous notes, John kept grinding away at his client. "Why were you wearing goulashes? It certainly wasn't muddy outside that night."

"Do we have to keep going over the same frigging questions and answers? I've already told you—"

"Hold it, Darin. I'll keep asking questions and you'll keep answering them for as long as it takes to get every aspect of your story covered. A mind can be a funny thing. We can do something or say something which plants a memory in our subconscious. Many times when we draw on that memory, we think everything comes back to us exactly as we remember it."

Darin sat in silence, but his thoughts were active. *Oh, great. Now I have to get a frigging lecture on the human brain. He's as bad as those professors I had in college. Boring. What I wouldn't give for a cold beer and a cigarette right now.*

"However," John continued, "there are times when just one minute detail is missed because for some reason it got lost in the subconscious. That detail might not come to the forefront unless the memory either thinks about it or by verbally repeating it, several times over. Then, from our subconscious, that little detail reappears. Suddenly, our memory is even more vivid then it was before.

I can tell from the look on your face that I'm boring you, Darin." Darin gave a distinctive nod. "Understanding how the mind works, should help you understand why we need to go over your story, again and again. Now, let's try this again. Why were you wearing goulashes on the night you were arrested?"

"Why can't I smoke in here?"

"Because I prefer you don't. When you get back to your cell, you can smoke all you want. Now quit stalling."

Screw you, John! Speak up, Darin, or you'll never get out of here. "In case you haven't been on a farm in a while, there's lots of mud holes around, especially after all the rain we had at that time. Not to mention the cow manure and other crap to step in. Since I was doing chores for Frank, I wanted to keep my shoes clean. I don't own a pair of rubber boots. So, I borrowed Frank's. Dammit, John, I don't care what you say about the memory and the subconscious, I feel like a frigging magpie, repeating myself all the time."

"Forget your nasty little comments, Darin. In all probability, we will go over the same information a hundred times before you go to court. Get use to it. Now, finish answering the question."

"After chores, since I was in a hurry to go shopping, guess I forgot to take them off. I wouldn't bother him because he's been pretty sick, but if need be, Frank can verify about me going to the store to get those groceries, and about me doing chores for him. I'm sure you can check the archived weather reports. They should confirm the rain we had back then, and why it was necessary for me to wear boots."

"I'm well aware of all the rain we had then, Darin. There's no reason for your sarcasm. I'll be talking with Frank. You can bet I'll be checking every witness as to your whereabouts on all the nights in question. Moving on, let's go back to a few years ago. I'm going to give you some dates. Take your time and think, very hard, before answering. I want to know where you were, what you were doing, and names of those who can backup each story," John stated, raising his eyes for a momentary glance at Darin.

"I want clean witnesses, too. Not some friend that thinks he owes you a favor. We're talking serious business here. Not some kid's prank. Perjury is a federal offense."

"Okay, John, but my hat goes off to anyone who can remember where they were and what they were doing a year ago, let alone two or three. All I can do is try."

After an hour of John asking Darin about certain dates, which were the exact dates the reported burglaries in Cole County had taken place, and getting as many answers as Darin could remember, John asked Darin if he had any questions.

"Other than the fact that I think this is all malarkey, I do have a some question. Rusty and his uniforms appear to have no motive and no witnesses, so they can't pin this rap me. They have no proof that I'm that Neat Nick Thief, right?"

"Right now it does seem circumstantial for the most part. However, I'm sure they'll have some concrete evidence before we get to court. It's hard to know what kind of ace in the hole the district attorney might be holding. Before we go to court, I'm supposed to have all of the facts. So far, I haven't received even a preliminary report from the D.A.'s office because it's far too early. What's more, I might not get said report until the day before we go to court. Which, as I told you, could be a year from now."

"Wait a minute, John. When I first went to court, last month, you told me then, it might be a year. Now it's August, and you're telling me it could still be a year from now? That sucks!" Darin complained.

"I think being locked up has gotten you a little confused. They just arrested you yesterday, for the second time, not a month ago. It's still the month of July, the last time I looked at my calendar. So, don't try to pull any of your nonsense on me. And settle down. Nothing is ever etched in stone.

Talk about being repetitive. I have told you many times that it could take a year, possibly less, but in all probability, longer. The court is pretty booked up with previous cases. You're just one little fish in an ocean full of other offenders. You just have to wait your turn."

Scanning his notes, John used his pencil to put check marks by several items on his list. When he came to topics he hadn't discussed yet, he proceeded to give Darin instructions. "I don't care who comes to visit you, keep your mouth shut. I'm the one you confide in. Nobody else. I know Rusty is your friend, but I don't want you to get into a conversation with him. You might accidentally slip and tell him something he doesn't need to know. That could jeopardize your case. If he wants to talk to you, you insist that I be present. Understand?"

"What about Frank?"

"Yes, you can talk to Frank. That goes, without saying. Frank is on your side. I must warn you, however, when Frank comes to visit you, you will still have bars between you. I'm sure you're aware by now that an officer of the law stands watch just a few feet away. He can hear every word you say. So, be very careful.

Actually, I would rather you not talk about the case with Frank for that very reason," John warned, having second thoughts. "Also, I wouldn't want you to confide in Frank about anything you haven't told me. If you do, the D.A. could call Frank as a witness against you. I don't think you want to put him in that position."

"How do I talk to Frank, if I can't talk to him? Hey, why can't they put him and me in a room, like this one, so we can talk? That way, no one could hear our conversation."

"Darin, you had the chance for private conversations with Frank when you were home on bail." John stood and tossed his pencil down on his papers. "Look, you are a prisoner. You have no rights when it comes to sitting in a private room talking with a relative or anyone other authorized person. The main reason you're in here with me is because I am your attorney and an officer of the court."

"That doesn't make any freakin' sense. I see it in the movies, all the time, a prisoner has a visitor and is taken out of his cell and—"

"Stop right there, Darin," John ordered. "First of all, you're not in prison as a convicted felon. You're in a local jail, awaiting trial. Also, this is *not* a movie. This is real life. At the rate of repeating myself, get used to it."

John rolled his head around to ease the pain in his neck from leaning over and taking notes for so long.

"Before I forget, it wouldn't hurt you to clean up your mouth. I'm not just talking about words like frigging and freakin', which I deplore. Uniforms? Call them policemen or police officers. A little consideration and respect coming out of your mouth would be a plus.

Let's get back to what we were talking about a minute ago. I don't know if you're aware of it or not, but attorney's do have a code of honor. This means, what you say to me, stays between the two of us. However, I would like to suggest that I'm the one who keeps Frank abreast of what is going on, instead of you conferring with him.

Then, there's no chance for an outsider to overhear any of our information. That will also eliminate the chance of putting Frank in the hot seat by telling him things they can use against you in the courtroom. I'll only feed information to Frank that I think is important for him to know. Nothing more. Do I have your permission to work that way?"

Darin nodded in agreement. "You know, John, you mentioned earlier about Rusty being my friend. Well, you're dead wrong. Rusty is Frank's friend. A few months back, there was a rumor going around. Seems our illustrious police chief is supposed to retire, real soon. If you want my opinion, I think he's trying to make a big name for himself by saying he caught the Neat Nick Thief. In plain English, I think he is using me as a patsy."

John started putting his legal pad and other papers into his briefcase, pretending he never heard Darin's last remarks. After closing his briefcase, he walked to the door.

"Darin, your time is up. I'll stay in touch." After opening the door, he informed the officer guarding the door, "I'm through with Mr. Righter for today. You can take him back to his cell now."

As John entered the hallway, he noticed Frank sitting in a chair with his head leaning against the wall behind him. His eyes closed. John sat in the chair next to Frank and gently touched his arm. "Frank."

Frank opened his eyes and sat upright. "John? Well now, I must have dozed off. Sure don't know why though after a good night's sleep. Are you through talking with Darin?"

"Frank you don't look at all well, and don't tell me it's all because of Darin's mess. That has only been for a short time. You look like you've been sick for a long, long time. Also, Darin mentioned to me that you had recently been bedridden."

To keep from looking John in the face, Frank looked around the hall. As he did, he saw the police officer with Darin heading down the opposite end of the hallway.

"Look, John, I appreciate your concern but I'm doing fine. Is Darin going back to jail right now?"

"Yes. I'm through questioning him for the day."

"I want to know everything you know about Darin."

"It's clear you're ignoring my question about your health. Okay, have it your way. Just know I'm concerned." After a cordial pat to Frank's arm, John got up from his chair. "Okay, Frank, if you have the time, you're welcome to come over to my office. I'll fill you in on everything I've discussed with Darin." He glanced at his watch. "As a matter of fact, we can do it right now. If you want?"

Frank was so exhausted, he didn't want to have to get in his truck and drive anywhere else but home after he visited with Darin. "Why can't we talk right here?"

"Too many ears, Frank. Look, if you don't want to come over now, call Betty and make an appointment for next week. Or, when you feel up to it."

As John walked away, Frank slid to the edge of his chair, pushed himself to a standing position by using the arms of the chair as a crutch. "Wait, John. I need to know what's going on or I don't think I can stand it. I'll follow you over in my truck."

At John's office, John informed Frank of everything he had found out from Rusty. Then he filled Frank in on all of the information, minus a few details, that he had gotten from Darin.

"I'm sorry, John. Just don't know what I'm going to do about Darin. His mouth and his attitude are bad enough without him badmouthing Rusty," Frank said. "I hope you scolded him for what he said? Shoot, I'm a little upset with Rusty, myself, but he's my dearest friend. That's the very reason I know he wouldn't try to frame Darin. You know, Rusty kept Darin's little tail out of jail so many times, I lost count. Darin's darn lucky he only has two strikes against him from those days."

"Who do you think you are talking to?" John asked, smiling. "I'm the guy that helped you, remember? I was pretty busy back in those days when Darin was sowing his wild oats. I couldn't be Darin's legal council, but I recommended a great attorney to handle things for you. Right?"

"Yes. That was that Thames fella that moved to Michigan a few years ago. You're right, John. Darn, I must be losing my mind. It seems I can't remember too much of anything anymore. The older I get, the shorter the years and the memory seem to be."

With a grunt of laughter, John commented, "You're mind seems to be better than mine is, Frank. I had forgotten that attorney's name, until you said it."

Frank didn't appear to be in the mood for smiles and small talk. John returned to the subject in hand. "To get back to your question, no. I didn't say a word to Darin about his acid little comment in reference to Rusty. I did, however, tell him to clean up his language and to speak with more respect for the law. You're right, he's got quite a mouth on him and he knows all the angles. At least he thinks he does. He's hiding something. I just don't know what it is, yet. All I can say is, he had better not make a fool out of me," John warned.

"That'll be two of us if he does," Frank remarked.

When their discussion of the case concluded, Frank left John's office and went directly to see Darin. Tired, and his mind filled with uncertainties, Frank made his visit short. On his way home, he couldn't help but worry about all the things that John had told him. He had his truck radio on, but his own words drowned out the sounds coming from the broadcast.

"Those darn boots, again. Darin told John that he put my overshoes on to keep his shoes from getting muddy. That would explain where my overshoes went, since John said that Rusty kept them for evidence. Question is, why did Darin even need to wear overshoes when he was already wearing my old work shoes? That stupid question keeps plaguing me. Wish I knew the answer.

For some reason, I don't remember it being muddy enough outside to wear rubber overshoes. Oh, wait. That was my first day out of bed in weeks. I remember when I got up that morning, I heard the weather report on the radio about the extreme temperatures and blazing hot sunshine. In fact, if I recall correctly, I even discussed the weather with Darin that morning. Yes, I even talked about getting Casey over to check the crops since the fields were dry.

Why, Darin didn't even go out of the house that day. Yeah, that's right. It's all coming back to me now. I was up all day. In fact, he insisted on it while he straightened up the house. So, he didn't have my overshoes on to do any outside chores. I know darn well he wasn't wearing them around the house. No, he had to put them on after I went to bed. As a matter of fact, I even recall that he was wearing his own shoes all day.

John read me the list of clothes Darin was wearing that first night Rusty arrested him. That was weird, too. Darin doesn't own work gloves or a ski mask. Darn it all, those are mine from the back porch, I'll bet. That's why I can never find them. He told John that the ski mask was in his pant's pocket. That can't be right. I wore that ski mask almost all winter when I went out to do chores."

After considerable thought about other things that made Darin look guilty, Frank stated, "Oh, I've got to stop this before I start believing Darin is a liar.

Just look what your joking around got you into, you crazy kid. All this time home from college, you've been great, working hard and staying out of trouble. I thought you had finally grown up, Darin. Why did you have to go and mess it up for one stupid night of kicks.

As for the Neat Nick Thief, I know that's not Darin. Being a prankster is one thing, but I know in my heart that he isn't a law-breaking crook. So Rusty, I'm sorry. You're going to have to keep looking elsewhere for your thief.

Since John thinks the district attorney probably doesn't have a concrete case against Darin for any more than breaking and entering, I won't tell John what I know. No sense in me poking holes in Darin's defense. I'm sure Darin is innocent anyway. I'd bet my life on it. Or, am I too darn blind to see the truth?"

SEEKING THE PAST, SURVIVING THE PRESENT

It was early in the morning when Chief Simmons met with Officers Kelly, Janx, and Seals for coffee and rolls at the local Waffles 'N' More restaurant. Once they were on their second cups of coffee and the affable chatting was out of the way, it was time for serious conversation.

"Enough of me being sick in bed for a week with that nasty flu bug, but mark my word, those flu shots are worth getting. You guys ought to consider getting one."

"Sure, Chief," Seals laughed, "then we can all get the flu and stay home for a week, just like you."

"Yeah. What a way to spend some beautiful summer days. Flat on your back," added Janx.

After the guys had their laugh at Rusty's expense, Rusty commenced with the early morning meeting. "Okay, okay. As much as I love your cheerful attitudes and funny remarks this morning, let's get down to business. I believe Operation Ivy was a success.

If not, and we end up with the wrong man in custody, which I doubt, then we'll have to find a new name for a new sting. So for now, no more codes. It's back to real names. On that note, Kelly, tell me what you two found out that night you searched around Oscar's house?"

Placing his coffee cup back on its saucer, Kelly started fidgeting with his napkin. "Well, Chief, Janx and I looked everywhere around the backdoor of Oscar's house, with no luck. Then Janx," Kelly glanced over at Officer Janx to acknowledge what he was saying, "came up with an idea. While I kept on searching the back area, outside the house, Janx went home and got his metal detector and brought it back to Oscar's place. We searched the backyard until dark, but again with no luck."

"Nothing, huh?" Rusty asked.

Both Kelly and Janx shook their heads, and Janx added, "Well, other than a few nails."

Kelly proceeded with his report. "You and Oscar must have gotten your flu shots from the same needle, Chief, because he, also, got the flu." Rusty gave him a half-cracked smile while the others tried to muffle their chuckles. "It's a cinch Janx and I didn't want to catch it.

We've stayed clear of his house since then. Anyway, Oscar called me at home, last night. Said he was feeling better. Janx and I are going back there this morning to look around inside the house."

"Did you already get permission from Oscar to go in and nose around?" Rusty asked, making sure everything they were doing was legal.

Nodding his head, Kelly stated, "We did. That night after we got through out back, Oscar invited us in for a glass of iced tea. Of course, that's when we found out that Oscar was not feeling very well. So, we declined the invite. However, we briefly told him that we were looking for some kind of a tool that our suspect jimmied the door with to gain entrance on the night in question.

Of course, being a retired cop, Oscar knows how important that piece of evidence is to the D.A.'s case. Oscar offered to move his furniture and start the search himself, but I told him, since Janx and I are much younger, we would do the heavy duty stuff when we returned."

"Younger is good," Rusty laughed. "If we find the tool laying around Oscar's house, which matches those marks on the wood we took from Denton's home on the night we arrested Darin, then we'll send it along to the lab with all the other wood pieces we've collected.

Now, if we don't find a tool, then we'll have to have the lab do some other testing and give us their best educated guess as to what kind of a tool made all of the pry marks. That horrible flu bug can sure stall an investigation, so we need to start moving ahead again, at full speed."

Rusty turned his attention back to Kelly. "Take Seals with you this morning. He can help you look inside the house. Don't forget to tell Oscar how much we appreciate all of his continued help on this case. Next time I see him, of course, I'll personally thank him, too."

Having finished their morning discussion, Kidwell's best left the restaurant.

A few hours later, just as Rusty was just getting off the telephone, Officers Kelly and Seals walked into his office. Carrying a screwdriver inside a clear plastic evidence bag, Kelly laid the item on Rusty's desk.

Just one look at what was placed in front of him and Rusty lit up, like the sky on the Fourth of July. Beaming with excitement, he blurted, "Hot damn, it's Christmas." Once in a blue moon, a law officer might slip and forget to take the right precautionary measures at a scene of a crime, or in evidence gathering.

Rusty had to make sure this was not one of those times. All it takes is one mistake from a law officer, and a judicial system can throw a good case out of court on a technicality. "Tell me you both wore gloves when handling this evidence."

After getting the of-course-we-did look from both of his officers, Rusty chuckled. "Okay, men, I can read your minds. So, Kelly," Rusty picked up the evidence bag, "tell me where you found this baby."

"We had to move Oscar's dining room table before we discovered it. The tool had, obviously, rolled from where Darin was kneeling when we caught him, and lodged itself under the leg of the table," Kelly explained. "If we hadn't moved the furniture, we would never have found it."

"Great. I'm proud of both of you."

"Don't be too proud, yet, Chief," Kelly warned.

Rusty looked at Kelly as if he knew something was about to spoil his good fortune. "Okay, Kelly, lay it on me. Where's the rat in the woodpile?"

"There's no rat, Chief. We do have this screwdriver, and you did say you were going to send it along with all of the other evidence blocks of wood to the FBI Crime Lab to see if the marks match up, right?"

"That's a mouthful," Rusty joked. "Sorry. That's all true. But? Come on, drop the other shoe."

"Oscar says he doesn't want to throw water on your fire, but he had painters, electricians, carpenters, and then the furniture movers in and out of that house before he moved into it. That screwdriver could belong to any one of those workers."

"Of course, it could, Kelly. And, the marks on those pieces of wood that came from Oscar's house could have been there, unnoticed, when your brother-in-law bought the house. In our line of work, everything is a possibility. Oscar is absolutely correct. That is the precise the reason we need to get expert comparisons.

Janx, when we're through here, I want this screwdriver, and all of those blocks of wood out of the evidence locker, packed up for mailing to the FBI Crime Lab. Make sure you address the package to the attention of my friend, Special Agent Leo Coats. He did such a great job matching those footprint casts we sent him that I would like him to continue working on this case for us. Get Seals to help you.

Kelly, you can handle the paper work. Remember to enclose the evidence receipt so the chain of custody doesn't get broken. Also, we'll need a return receipt on these items. I've got a good feeling about this tool. If my hunch is right, it will match those pry marks left on all the wood evidence. We might, also, get lucky and have Agent Coats find some fingerprints. It's obvious our perp wore gloves since we never found any latent prints at any of the victim's houses, but our suspect might have slipped up when handling the screwdriver. Wouldn't that be nice?"

The officers stood by, waiting, as Rusty played with the evidence bag, turning it in different directions to get a clearer view of the screwdriver inside. "Did you guys look at this handle? This looks like a handcrafted, made-to-order tool. I haven't seen scrollwork like this on a wood-handled tool in years.

I'll bet this was a special order back, um … " Rusty stopped to think about past years. Then he placed the screwdriver to the front of this desk in front of Seals, since his train of thought really had nothing to do with the matter at present. "Never mind. You guys are far too young to remember.

Okay, I want these items to be shipped, ASAP, overnight express. I'll place a call to Leo and alert him to expect this package tomorrow. Thanks, again, Officers, you did a good job."

Back at the Righter farm, Frank woke up later than he had planned. Sitting at the kitchen table, drinking his morning coffee, he made plans. "Outside of locating Carole, it's about time I make a decision as to what I've been contemplating this past week.

With my health, I'm only fooling myself if I think I can get back into the routine of farming. I can't keep asking Casey to do my outside chores for me. After all, he has a farm of his own to run.

Time to go forward. As much as I'm not looking forward to speaking with big mouth Jesse, she's the only one who can help me."

"Town and Country," a female's cheerful voice answered.

"Good morning. This is Frank Righter. I would like to speak to Jesse, if I might?"

"This is Jesse, Frank. Say, I haven't seen you around town in quite a spell. Has the farm been keeping you busy?"

"Yeah, you know farm work. There's always chores to be done. The reason—"

Jesse talked fast and she talked a lot. Before Frank could get out one word as to why he was calling, Jesse beat him to the punch. "I was sure sorry to hear about Darin getting locked up in jail, Frank. Is it true—"

"Nothings true about small town gossip," he snapped. "I swear, I don't know how anyone tends to their own lives with their noses in everyone else's business." Getting complete silence on the other end of the phone, he explained the reason for his call. "I want to list my farm for sale, Jesse. Can you handle that for me?"

Jesse was a little put out by Frank's curtness and insulting gossip comment but over-looked it as she welcomed his business. After all, any property she could sell meant money in her pocket. Moreover, she was very much aware that Frank's farm was prime real estate and would go for big bucks.

"Yes, I can handle the listing for you, Frank. You will have to come in and give me all of the particulars. I'll need to have a list of everything that will be included in the sale, your asking price, your terms, and other pertinent information. If you have a current appraisal, you can bring it with you. I'll go over my contract with you, explain some other details about listing your property, then we can go from there."

"Look, Jesse, I'll write you up a list of everything I think you'll need, and drop it off at your office in a couple of days. Then you can look it over and call me, if you have any questions. I don't have an appraisal but I believe I know the market value of my place. If and when someone is interested and needs an appraisal by an official appraiser, I can get one then.

After you get all of your paperwork together, and only then, will I come in to sign a contract. I don't like contracts anyway. It used to be that a man was as good as his word or a handshake. Paper contracts weren't needed."

"Times change, Frank." After a brief pause, she said, "Okay, that would be suitable for you to drop off your information. If you have a free and clear title, and a record of the last property taxes you paid, bring them in with you. If not, I'll have to have you sign some papers so we can do a title search and get your tax records from the courthouse."

"I have the deed to the property and my tax records."

"Good, that will save us time, and save you some added expense. Now, if I'm not in when you stop by, just leave all of your information at the front desk with my secretary. Let me ask you something, Frank. Are you in a hurry, or are you just going to put the farm on the market and see what develops?"

"What difference does that make?"

"Well, a citizen of our fine community mentioned to me that you look like you've lost some weight. In fact, the word sickly is—"

"Stop right there, Jesse. It's pretty sad when a man can't go on a diet without the whole town thinking he's got one foot in the grave. Just proves my point about gossip."

"I didn't mean anything, Frank."

"Drop it. Look, I'm in no big rush to sell out, however, the sooner the better. Then I can move to town. Darin doesn't care much for farm life, and it's getting too much for me to handle alone."

"That's good. What I meant to say, Frank, is that's good you aren't in any rush. That gives you the leading edge in sticking by your price. Many times, my clients wait until the last minute to decide they want to sell their property and move. Then they get in a big hurry. Let's just say that the buyer takes advantage of a rush situation and makes an offer that is far below the asking price. Then it's only natural that the client takes the low offer just to sell and get out. That ends up a lose-lose situation."

"Look, Jesse, I have to go now. Thanks for the information."

"Bye, Frank."

"Okay, now I need to get in touch with Casey."

Feeling as if he needed to go back to bed, Frank made his phone call to Casey very short. He arranged with Casey to do the farm chores and fieldwork, each day, for a fair weekly salary. Since Casey lived so close, he was more than happy to help his neighbor.

Casey didn't want to take any payment, but Frank insisted. He would either pay Casey, or have to ask someone else to do the work. Helping out a friend was one thing, but practically running the farm was more than just a helping hand. Casey agreed and would start right away.

Frank didn't go out of his house again for several days. He made sure he ate soup and crackers, drank plenty of liquids, took the proper dosage of pain pills when he needed them, and got plenty of rest. Gaining a bit more strength, he went to town. After running a few errands, Frank went to see Darin.

Darin spotted Frank being led to his cell. Running to the bars, Darin grabbed them with both hands. "Where in the devil have you been, Frank? I thought you deserted me." Darin raved. "It's been days since you've bothered to visit me in this hole. Get me out of here."

"Calm down, Darin," Frank stated, as he approached the cell. "You know full well I can't get you out."

"I can't stay locked up in here any longer." Darin's hands were turning white from the tight grip he had on the bars. "I'm going stir crazy. Looking at three cement block walls and a wall of iron bars, all day, isn't what I would call my favorite view. Can't that attorney of yours get the judge to get me in court right away?"

"Listen to yourself, Darin. You're not making any sense. John can't just call a judge and ask him to set a date for your trial. The courts have a schedule. Otherwise, there would be complete chaos."

Frank didn't know for sure what he was talking about, but he hoped it gave Darin something to think about while he changed the subject. "How's the food they bring you? Are you eating okay?"

"Food? Is that what they call it? Have you ever eaten jailhouse food before, Frank? It's slop you wouldn't feed to your pigs. No, I'm not eating okay."

"Why don't I go get you a hamburger, or something?" Frank asked, trying to stay calm.

"Yeah, that sounds good. I want a big juicy burger with everything on it, an extra large order of fries and a chocolate malt with a beer chaser. Oh, and while you're at it, how about some smokes? With you not showing up for days, I've been ready to chew nails and spit rust."

"I thought you only smoked when you drank beer."

"Past tense. There's nothing else to do, sitting around in here all day. Might as well smoke," Darin remarked.

"I don't think they'll let me bring you a beer, but I'll go get you a hamburger and return just as quick as my body will allow."

There was just the one fast food restaurant in town with a drive-through. That's where Frank went. After getting the food, he stopped at the local food store and bought a carton of Carlton 100's. He threw them in the bag with the food, tossed in a book of matches, and returned to jail.

The officer in charge, according to rules and regulations, had to open the bag and check out its contents. Finished with the food, the officer opened the carton of cigarettes and removed one pack. Then he opened and emptied the pack on his table, examined the loose cigarettes, then replaced them into their package.

He informed Frank that they would allow Darin no more than one package of cigarettes at a time. The department would lock up the rest of the carton with Darin's other personal belongings. All Darin had to do when he wanted more cigarettes, was to ask. The officer also confiscated the book of matches. Every time Darin wanted to have a smoke, he had to ask the officer in charge for a light.

"I have to search you again, sir."

"What? You just searched me not more than thirty minutes ago, when I came in here the first time."

"I realize that, sir, but you left the secure area. Rules are—"

"Rules. I know." Raising his arms, Frank mumbled, "Come on then. Let's get it over with so I can get that food into Darin before it's ice cold."

After a quick pat down, the officer escorted Frank back to Darin's cell. The officer gave Frank the go-ahead to hand the food and cigarette items through the bars to Darin.

Darin grabbed the open pack of cigarettes and threw them on his cot, scattering cigarettes all about.

He snatched the bag out of Frank's hand, opened it to get the hamburger, and started chomping at it as if he hadn't eaten in a month of Sundays. His mouth was still full when he reached back into the sack, grabbed a handful of fries, and stuffed them into his mouth too.

"Slow down, Darin. If you don't choke to death, you'll certainly end up with indigestion. You don't need to be in here and get sick, too," Frank warned, standing with his hand through the bars, still holding on to Darin's drink. "I'll talk to Rusty and see if he can't get some better food in here for you."

With a mouthful of food and his head filled with hatred, Darin spewed, "Screw Rusty. Screw the whole freakin' police department. They don't care if I get decent food, or not. Your frigging friend, Rusty, isn't going to change things just because you ask. Wise up, Frank." Darin shut up long enough to grab the drink from Frank's hand. He took one sip. "Hey, what the—This isn't a chocolate malt. It's a soda."

"They didn't have anything but sodas today, Darin, I'm sorry," Frank apologized.

"Where did you go?"

"I went to the drive-thru. They normally have malts and milk shakes there, but their ice cream machine was broke down today. All they had were soft drinks. I thought you might settle for a soda."

"That was your first mistake. I told you, I wanted a chocolate malt. Not a friggin' soda. There's a big difference, Frank. Ned's Ice Cream Shop is the only place in town that serves a real malt. You should know that, since you're the one who introduced me to the place when I was younger."

"Look, I'm sorry, Darin. I wanted to get you your food as quick as I could. I just don't have the energy to go into the ice cream shop. Sitting in the truck and ordering is much easier for me."

Almost through with his hamburger, Darin spouted, "Thanks for nothing. I can get a freakin' can of soda from the guard."

Ignoring Darin's temperament, Frank stated, "Look, I can't come visit you every day. You'll have to make do with what they bring you to eat in here."

"What do you mean you can't come *every day*?" Darin bitterly complained, sputtering particles of food.

"I'm sick, Darin. I've been in bed for these past few days, trying to get my energy level back. These trips, back and forth to town, are wearing me down. I can't even do the chores anymore. It's a cinch you aren't in a position to be of any help. I've contacted Casey and he agreed to help out with the livestock and the fieldwork."

"Yeah, now blame me because you've had a relapse and can't take care of the farm. Like it's my fault that your friend, Rusty," Darin wadded up the paper from his hamburger and threw it with rage against a cell wall, "has a hair up his ass and has it in for me."

"Look, Darin, get as angry as you want. Saying I'm blaming you for my health, is nonsense. And Rusty isn't framing you." Frank shook his head. "I can't stand here and use up my energy fighting with you. I'll see you in a few days."

As Frank turned and walked away, he heard Darin yelling. "Sure, Frank. Go ahead. Walk away and leave me here. You've done that before. Haven't you, Frank? You've been a wimp all of your life. Go on. Who needs you?"

The officer went into the cell area in an attempt to quiet Darin. Frank stood around the corner leaning against a wall, out of Darin's sight.

Oh, Darin, if you only knew how your words hurt me. If you didn't always think of yourself, I could have told you the truth about my declining health by now. On the other hand, I wonder if it would even make a difference.

Back to the main part of the building, Frank walked passed the desk officer, directly to Rusty's office door, and peered in. "Rusty, may I come in?"

Looking up from the document he was reading, Rusty smiled. "Frank, you're always welcome. Come in and sit a spell. May I get you anything?"

"No, I'll just stand. Thank you. I won't stay long."

"Have you been in to see Darin?"

"Yes. He's complaining the food here stinks. Can I have some food delivered so he eats well and keeps up his strength? I don't want him getting sick."

Rusty glanced out his window then turned back to his friend. "Let me ask you something, Frank. Have you ever eaten across the street at Dan's Diner?"

"You know I have."

"Think Dan's restaurant food stinks?"

"Of course, not, Rusty. Dan makes the best homemade dishes I've ever eaten in a restaurant. It's one of the few places in town that serves decent food. In fact, I use to hear some guys joke with Dan and tell him, if he wore a skirt under his apron instead of pants, they'd marry him. Why?"

"Darin receives breakfast, lunch and dinner from there. Everyday."

"I'm sorry, Rusty. Guess the kid's so angry for being locked up that he just has the need to complain about everything. Should have known better."

"Look, Frank, please sit for a few minutes," Rusty offered once again. "I haven't seen you for over a week and Darin, obviously, hasn't seen you in days. Damn, he sure put up a hissy-fit when you didn't come back to visit him."

"Yeah, he let me know how displeased he is. Look, I have a few things to take care of before I head back home. Just wanted to talk to you about the food Darin was getting. Now that you've straightened me out, well, I'll be going. Thanks."

Once he left Rusty's office, Frank stopped by the realtor's office. He signed a thirty-day contract with Jesse, and gave her the documents she needed to sell his farm. Stopping at the Post Office, Frank checked his mailbox in case he had any word on locating Carole.

Returning home, Frank made himself a cup of tea and a slice of toast. His appetite wasn't good, but he knew he had to eat something. Besides, every time he went to town he would always forget to buy groceries. There wasn't too much wholesome food left in the house.

While drinking his tea, he read the letters from his Post Office box. The first letter mentioned the possible whereabouts of Carole, some 22 years ago. Wadding up the letter, he set it aside. The second letter, one from Canton County, was of interest to him. With the use of the magnifying glass and a red marker pen, Frank circled the area on the map.

It was difficult, but Frank tried to stay positive. "Canton County, eighteen years ago. That's a long, long time. Hopefully, it's a good start. It beats twenty-something, that's for sure. At least I know people are seeing her picture, reading the article, and responding. But, I need someone who has seen Carole in the past couple of years.

What if I was wrong? Maybe I should have had Carole's picture sent to the newspapers in the surrounding states, not just Nebraska. That was rather stupid on my part, since I met her in Missouri. That's her home state, so I can't imagine what I was thinking. Fact is, she could be anywhere, if she's alive. No, I'm not going to think that way. I know finding her would be a miracle, but I have to pray for the best. Miracles do happen."

A week later, as Frank entered lock-up, Darin was standing at the bars. When he saw Frank, he began his usual mouthing off in a very loud voice. "Hey, world, look. The big man, who is supposed to be my brother, decided to show up."

Ignoring Darin's venom, Frank asked, "Hi, Darin. How are you doing?"

"Hi, Darin. How are you doing?" Darin mimicked. "Well, that's rich. You walked out on me the last time you were here. Now you waltz back in here, and that's all you have to say to me? Why did you even bother to show up? Want to put me on a bigger guilt trip about your no-account life?"

Frank had taken as much as he could stand. "Look, Darin, I have had enough of your smart mouth. *You* are the one who decided to break the law. *You* are the one who got caught. *You* are the one who has to pay the penalty for what you've done.

So, if you want to put the blame on someone for your being locked behind steel bars, I'll gladly bring you a mirror on my next visit, which might not be for another week." Frank left the area, leaving Darin speechless.

Later that same afternoon, Rusty called Frank at home.

"Frank, this is Rusty."

"Is Darin all right?"

"Yes, but I am calling on his behalf."

"Darin's behalf. What does that mean?"

"I stopped by a few minutes ago to see how he was doing. He said he'd been quite rude to you."

"That's putting it mildly. He was petulant to say the least," Frank interjected. "So now he's crying on your shoulder. That's a first."

"No, nothing like that. He did ask me to call you and tell you that he wants to apologize. He wants you to come back and visit with him. I told him he had phone privileges, but he insists in talking to you in person. Darin says to tell you that he'll act like a human being, not a horse's ass. Anyway, I told him I would pass the message on."

"Okay, I appreciate it, Rusty. Problem is, I can't come back into town today. That ride just wears me down. I hate to make you the messenger boy, but can you get word back to Darin that I will try to visit him tomorrow?"

"You know I will, Frank. I wish you would come in and visit with me."

"I was there earlier."

"That's not what I mean. You know, like you used to do before all of this Darin business started. In all our years as friends, we've had some good heart-to-hearts. Gotta tell you, Frank, I miss that," Rusty remarked. "I'm so sorry you don't understand that I'm just trying to do my job."

"You know Rusty, I try to understand. It's just that, well, having Darin in jail doesn't make it easy. It adds salt to the wound, knowing you're the one who put him there.

Now, even when I have my good days and try to look at this from your point of view, well, then I have the attorney's words jumping around in my head. John's afraid I might slip and tell you something that would help your case against Darin. Not that I know any more than you do, but I have to protect Darin." *Talk about shading the truth. If Rusty knew the doubts I had in my head about this whole business—*

"Sure, I understand Frank." As much as he wanted to, Rusty didn't understand. Being in a sticky situation where he had to separate his job from his personal life was new to Rusty. He didn't like it. Frank had too many things on his mind to worry about right now. Rusty didn't want to add to those worries by stating what his true feelings were. "Okay, buddy. Take care of yourself. So long for now."

"Yeah. So long."

Early the next morning, Frank returned to lock-up. He prayed that Darin was being sincere when he had told Rusty that he wanted to apologize for his childish actions and smart mouth the day before. As he approached Darin's cell, Frank waited for Darin to speak first.

"Hi Frank," Darin greeted, acting excited to see him. "I'm sure glad you're here."

"Good morning, Darin. How are they treating you? Or is that, too, a bad question to ask?"

"As well as any jailbird can expect, I guess," Darin answered in a pleasant voice. "I guess I don't really need to ask you how you're feeling. You look terrible."

"I'm hanging in there." Frank knew that he looked as bad as he felt. However, this wasn't the time to dwell on how he looked or felt. "Can I get you anything?"

"Yeah. You can tell me the truth. What's going on with your health? That business of having a bug doesn't wash anymore. So, what's the truth?"

The timing was wrong. The best Frank could hope for was to lie with a straight face in hopes Darin would believe him. "Doc thinks I have low blood sugar. That's what he's been treating me for. I don't understand much of what Doc explained to me, but it seems low blood sugar zaps the energy right out of you. I'm mentally exhausted worrying about you.

Compound the worry with my physical problem, and my whole body is worn out. But, hey, don't you worry about me. Just be a little more understanding as to why I can't be here, as often as you'd like me to be."

"Low blood sugar? Never heard of it. That isn't what you told me those pills were for when I asked you before. You lied to me," Darin stated with a sharp tongue.

"When was that? Oh, you mean that time I spent in bed just before you got in to all of this bird dung?"

"You could have chosen a better way to put it, but yes, I do."

"What is that saying you're always using, give me a break? Well, I'd like to apply that here. I was so bad off, back then, my mind wasn't thinking straight. I might have said or told you anything. I'm sorry if I misled you but it wasn't intentional. *I'm not use to telling lies, so I sure hope he buys this.*

Anyway, Doc gave me some new pills. I'm hoping they'll do the trick. Before you know it, I'll be back to my old energetic self. Listen, I spoke with Rusty about the food they serve you, and—"

"I know, I know. Rusty told me. Look, Frank, I'm sorry about the way I've been acting. It's just that I hate being caged up like this. I'm sorry for everything. Okay?"

"Okay. Apology accepted. Now, do you want me to bring you anything on my next visit?"

"I would appreciate some more cigarettes. Oh, and how about a few girly magazines to help me pass the time of day. At least I can get a thrill, or two, looking at the nudies. Then enjoy a smoke afterwards," Darin remarked with a devious laugh. Watching the color of Frank's face turn flush with color, he added, "Don't give me that holier-than-thou look, Frank. Hey, I'm a young stud with hormones. Can't help it if I miss the girls."

Turning, Darin leaned against the bars. "Of course, I don't think you even know what that's like, do you? Have you ever had a woman in your whole life, Frank?" Dying to see the look on his brother's face as he answered Darin's provocative questions, Darin made a quick pivot. To his dismay, Frank was gone.

"Idiot, you did it again. You took one foot out of your mouth then inserted both of them. You know, Frank isn't stupid. If he ever starts adding things up, he'll turn on you if you don't start showing him some respect. You need to keep your cool. Patronize him, like you did with old man Welk and that stupid excuse for a female.

Oh, yes, Farm Girl. Now there's a real piece of work God should've rejected straight from the get-go. I said things to her that gagged me. If she knew the truth that she turned my stomach, well, I couldn't have pumped her for information, like I did. Hell, that dog blew my mind with her back wood's speech and misuse of words. The only good thing about her ignorant, childish mind was the fact I could manipulate her.

And what a joke, telling me how she and her mama loved old man Welk so much that they considered him kin. Then they were dumb enough to call him Pappy. Welk was of a different race than she was. I couldn't believe she didn't know the difference. Damn, I can't imagine anyone in their right mind wanting to consider someone of a different race, creed, or color as their family. That's the key here. Farm Girl is not in her right mind."

Darin paced back and forth in his cell. He could walk three steps from the back wall to the bars, turn, then take three steps back to the wall. The five by six cell barely left enough space for the cot. At times, Darin felt as if he were doing nothing but walking in circles.

"That Farm Girl has serious mental problems. Anyone who sits on a bolder, writing in below freezing temperatures, has got to be nuts. She sure could get her nose bent out of joint because I wouldn't show up at her stupid Room to Write everyday. Every time she made me promise to be there when she was, it irritated the hell out of me.

Knowing her, she's worrying over why I'm not showing up to meet her, like I said I was going to. Well, as long as she's known me, she ought to know by now that any of my meetings with her have been in my own good time. She's so stupid, she'll wait forever for me to show up. No one dictates to me. Well, not until I ended up in here. Damn, instead of wasting time thinking about some lame brain female, I should be concentrating on holding my temper with Frank.

I need a smoke. Damn! I forgot. The friggin' guard told me Frank bought me a carton of cigarettes. All this time, I've been having a nicotine fit when all I had to do was to ask for another pack of smokes. If I hadn't offended Frank, I'm sure he would've reminded me when I asked him to bring me some more." At the top of his lungs, he yelled, "Guard!"

Receiving no answer, Darin knew right away there was no guard on duty. Often times, since it was such a small jail, the officers would be busy with other responsibilities around the department. They took turns checking in on their one and only jailbird from time to time to see if he needed anything.

"It just figures," Darin complained. "There's never a cop around when you need one."

HANGING ON TO HOPE

As the next few months passed, the changing of the season was dressed in all its glory. Adorning the trees were brilliant colors from gold to orange, and red to purple. Lawns were still green and seemed to highlight the fall flowers in full bloom. During the day, air was brisk. There was frost on the pumpkins, as soon as the sun went down. A few trees that stood alone, unprotected by wind, were beginning to lose their leaves.

As he kept losing more and more of his hair, Frank felt like an autumn tree. There was a huge difference between him and the somewhat baron trees. Frank would not grow back his loss as the trees would with the coming spring.

Keeping up his visits to see Darin was getting even more difficult. Frank could only make it to town, once or twice a week. Each time he was in town, he stopped by the post office, always hoping for information that would lead him to Carole. Frank had received numerous postcards and letters in the past months, but nothing helped his search or got him any closer to locating his lost love.

Since there appeared to be no potential buyers for his farm, Frank never signed another contract with Jesse. He had almost given up hope of selling out and moving to town, when he had a knock at the backdoor.

"Hi Casey."

"Frank. If you've got a few minutes, I'd like to talk to you."

"Sure, come on in. I've got some coffee made, how about a cup?"

"That would be mighty neighborly. I take cream and sugar, if you've got it?"

Frank headed back to the kitchen, leaving Casey to close the door and follow him.

"Have a seat," Frank offered. Once they both had coffee, and were seated at the table, Frank asked, "Do I owe you money again?"

"No, Frank, we're square. I didn't come in here to talk to you about money. Well, not money for farm work, anyway. I wanted to ask you about your farm. I might as well get straight to the point. I'm interested in buying it. That is, if the price is right."

"You, Casey? Shoot, it wasn't too long ago that you bought the farm you're on now."

"Time slips away faster then we think, Frank. When I met you, Darin had just gone off to college, I believe."

"It's been that long?" Frank asked, raising his eyebrows. Casey nodded. "My, it seems like yesterday."

"Sometimes it does. You know my brother lives with me, right?" Receiving a nod from Frank, he continued. "It's been great, but it's time for him to get a place of his own. We agree on farming, but man, we are as opposite as hot and cold water when it comes to living together. That house just isn't big enough for the two of us anymore." Casey laughed. "We're like those guys, Oscar and Felix, from that TV program *The Odd Couple.*

Anyway, you having your place for sale could solve our dilemma. My brother and I had a long discussion about this last night, after you called. He could buy my small farm from me, if I bought your farm. Besides, I really need more space for my milkers. My brother wants to raise chickens. The small acreage we have now will be perfect for him, once I get my dairy cows out of there. And, living right across the road from each other, well, we can help each other out with the farming when needed. Just like I've been helping you."

"Shoot, Casey, that would be great."

Once the details were worked out, Casey offered his and his brother's assistance in getting Frank moved to town. After Casey left, Frank was elated. It had been a long time since he had reason to be excited about anything in his life.

"Son-of-a-gun! Who would have guessed it? Here I'm wishing I could sell this place, and Casey comes knocking at the door, walks in, and presto, he's buying the farm. Well, I'll make it right with him." He looked up. "Thank you, God. I know you had a hand in sending Casey to my backdoor today and I do appreciate it."

As the days passed into weeks, Frank sold his farm and purchased his new home in town.

Struggling for the energy to keep going, Frank's days continued to fly by. After packing each box of his personal belongings, he labeled them with a black marker. With the kitchen and living room completed, Darin's was the only large room left to be boxed and labeled.

Taking a couple of empty boxes to Darin's bedroom, Frank placed them in the middle of the bed. He sat on the edge of the mattress and stared at the vast amount of books on Darin's bookshelves. Most of the paperbacks were thrillers and mysteries.

While packing the books, some slipped out of his hand and fell to the floor. As he bent over to pick up the fallen books, he noticed that many of the pages had been *dog-eared*. In checking out the marked pages, he found highlighted items in different areas of the books. Out of curiosity, Frank scanned the dog-eared pages and read the highlighted sentence fragments.

"'Call in my marker—Look behind pictures on walls, and throw rugs on the floor for hidden safes—Copy cat crimes—Wear shoes or boots, preferably not your own, and larger than your normal size to disguise footprints—Wear gloves to hide your fingerprints.'

What in Sam hill would Darin mark these passages for and ruin perfectly good books? Oh well, he must have had his reasons. After all, they're his property to do with as he pleases."

Feeling he was wasting time scanning any more of the books, Frank went back to packing. While he was getting more books from the bookshelves, one slid behind a shelf and fell to the floor behind the bookcase. After boxing the books, the bookcase was empty. Frank slid it away from the wall to retrieve the fallen book.

When he picked up the book, a loose floorboard caught his eye. From where he was standing, he could see that the nails to the board were missing. "Wonder how that happened?"

Since the board was loose, he figured he might as well lift it and check for signs of termites. It was a real chore getting down on his knees. When he did, he got his fingers under the edge of the board and pulled. What Frank discovered was a total mystery to him.

Picking up the items nestled just beneath the board, he questioned every reason he could think of as to when, why, who and what. "What in the world is this stuff? It looks like a mini tape recorder and tiny tapes. Where in blue blazes did they come from?"

The wood floor was getting hard on Frank's knees. He moved to a sitting position, and leaned up against the wall to further inspect the mini-recorder. It looked easy enough to figure out how to work it, so he picked up the cassettes that were still nestled beneath the floor. As he turned one of the cassettes over to place it in the recorder, he saw Darin's name written in black marker.

"So, Darin, these are your things. Why in the heck would you hide theme under the floor? I can't believe you hid them because you didn't trust me."

Frank was never the nosey type. For as much as he wanted to listen to the recordings, he believed, Darin's business was Darin's business. Getting to his feet, Frank walked over and sat back on the bed. Placing the recorder and the cassettes on the bed next to him, he had a sudden heart-wrenching thought.

"Passages marked in books that only a thief would be concerned with, and now a hidden recorder with cassettes. Darn it, Darin! Are you the Neat Nick Thief, or is this just another coincidence? I don't know any more. It just seems like every time I turn around there are one too many coincidences. I want to believe in you, but finding stuff like this doesn't make it easy. Dear God, help me find the truth because I don't know what it is."

Frank didn't want Darin to even know that he had been in his bedroom. Most of all, he didn't want Rusty to know that the recorder and the tapes existed. Reopening one of the packed boxes of books, Frank unpacked the box. Then he placed the recorder and the cassettes in the bottom, repacking the books on top.

The rest of Darin's personal items were then packed. As he finished filling the last box, including the few clothes he found in the suitcase under the bed, Frank sat on the bed for a moment to relax.

"I'm worn out. I never come in here, so I didn't know Darin had so much accumulated junk. Everything was put away, nice and neat like, but so much stuff. Well, it's done now. If I packed anything Darin doesn't want, he can throw it away when he gets out of jail. When the time comes that he can leave town, he can repack his suitcase, too."

Trying to get everything done, feeling he had an obligation to get out of the house as soon as possible, Frank didn't take the time to rest that he should have. The strain on his health was too much. He collapsed on the living room floor.

In town, even though Rusty often thought about his friend, he had a strong inclination something was wrong with Frank. He hadn't seen or heard from his close friend in quite a few weeks. Although Rusty never professed to have ESP, he felt an irresistible urge to check on him. At first, common sense won out.

"This is ridiculous. I'm sure Frank's just fine," Rusty stated, trying to reassure himself. Convincing himself, however, wasn't easy. To ease his mind, Rusty made a special visit to see Darin and find out when he had last seen his brother. When Darin boldly complained that Frank had abandoned him, since he hadn't been in for a visit in weeks, Rusty became worried. He began to listen to his earlier feelings that something was wrong.

Rusty tried contacting Frank by phone. When he didn't receive an answer, he decided to drive out to the farm and find out why. Although he didn't speed, Rusty kept the speedometer right at the speed limit, pushing it to the nth degree.

"Frank, I hope you're okay, old friend. I've stayed away because I know how painful it is for you that I had to be the one to arrest Darin. As sick as you've been, I should have checked on you anyway. You've got to be sicker than a dog not to have visited Darin for weeks on end. I should have listened to my gut instinct, instead of my head this time. Be okay, Frank. Just be okay."

Once Rusty arrived at Frank's, he didn't wait to knock. Opening the screen and the backdoor, he walked in. "Frank, it's Rusty. Hello, Frank." With no response, Rusty assumed he would find Frank in bed, just as he was on the first night Darin was arrested. As he walked from the back porch into the kitchen, calling out Frank's name, he was surprised to see boxes sitting all about.

"What in the world? It looks like Frank is packing up to move."

Walking from the kitchen into the living room, Rusty spotted a body on the living room floor. Because of the boxes blocking his view, he could only see the legs. Assuming they were Frank's, he shouted, "Frank!" as he rushed to the body. He was right. It was Frank. Rusty shoved some boxes out of the way and knelt next to Frank's limp body. He placed his fingers to Frank's neck. His pulse was faint.

Rusty's law enforcement training governed his immediate reaction. Reaching for his shoulder mike, he made an emergency call to his dispatcher. "This is Chief Simmons. Get the EMS unit out to Frank Righter's farm. Frank is on the floor in a cationic state. He has a pulse but we need help. 10-33."

Taking hold of Frank's limp hand, Rusty started rubbing it. "Frank, it's Rusty. Can you hear me? Blast it, Frank, how long have you been lying here? Help is on the way, my friend. Just hang in there. Come on Frank, hang on."

Rusty sat there holding Frank's hand when the EMS crew arrived and rushed into the house. They checked Frank's vitals then rushed him to the Farmer's Community Hospital. Rusty followed behind the emergency unit with his siren loudly screaming, all the way.

At the hospital, Rusty paced the floor of the emergency room. It was shear agony as he waited for news about his buddy. Each minute of waiting, felt like an hour. Once he spotted Doctor Shivley, Rusty approached him with great haste. "Okay, Doc, the truth. Frank told me all about the cancer so don't pull any punches."

"He's in bad shape, Rusty. I'm having him admitted," Doc stated, shaking his head.

"May I go in and see him?"

"Let's give the nurses time to move him to a room in intensive care and get him settled first. He's conscious but very, very weak. We have an IV going and we're monitoring his heart. After close examination, I don't think he's been eating or resting, like he should.

Of course, I warned him right from the start that without proper medical attention, which he refused, he would physically deteriorate until it was too late for any form of treatments or medications to help him. Any stress, strenuous work, or overworking without the proper rest he needs, is like another nail in his coffin. He didn't listen to a word I said," Doc concluded.

"No, that's quite obvious. He's been very upset about Darin's ordeal. And with a trial in the future, well, I think he cares more about Darin's life then he does his own. Frank will get well enough to leave here, won't he Doc?" Rusty asked, concerned about his friend.

"He's in grave condition right now, but I'm not going to speculate how he will be doing one way or the other, Rusty. With complete bed rest and the proper nourishment, only time will tell. We'll be monitoring him closely since the next forty-eight hours are critical.

Frank has seldom complained about his pain, but I know it has to be excruciating. I'm going to change his pain medication and put him on Oxycontin. If nothing else, we can make him as comfortable as possible."

"Sickness and death are always hard to handle at any age, Doc, but he's not even fifty yet. He's still a young man, at least compared to my age. I don't know what's worse, dying like Stu did before he had a chance to live his life, or dying like Frank, working hard so he can have a good retirement, then suffering and dying just a few steps away from getting there?"

Rusty knew he had been rambling on and on, but the thought of Frank dying was too overwhelming for him to think and talk straight in his present state of mind.

"Hold on, Rusty. I didn't mean to give you the wrong impression. The situation is grim but Frank's not dead, yet. Quit being so pessimistic and morbid. I know you're concerned about him, but let's look on the brighter side of things, right now, and hope for the best. He's hung on longer than I ever thought he would, so I know he's got a lot of fight left in him."

Doc placed his hand on Rusty's arm and excused himself. He walked to the nurse's counter. After he spoke to a nurse, he returned to Rusty's side. "They've moved Frank over to the ICU, Room 102. I told them no visitors until he gets out of ICU and into a regular room. However, I'm making this one exception. Go on now, but please, no more then a couple of minutes," the doctor cautioned.

"Okay, Doc. Thanks."

Rusty walked down the hallway toward the intensive care unit. When he found Frank's room, he entered and approached the bed. Rusty looked around at all the machinery connected to his friend, probing into many parts of his body. With a gentle hand, he touched Frank's arm. Frank opened his eyes and tried forcing a smile.

"Hi, Frank. Damn, you gave me quite a scare. How are you doing, buddy?"

Breathing was difficult. Frank took a deep breath from the oxygen tubing that was resting in his nostrils. He licked his dry lips. Rolling his head to one side, Frank looked at Rusty. In barely an audible voice, he said, "I know I've been better. Where … What happened?"

"Listen, you shouldn't be talking. I should've known better than to ask you anything, right now. You're in the hospital, Frank, where they're going to take good care of you," Rusty explained, as he patted Frank's hand. "I'll let you get some rest now. I'll be back tomorrow."

Over a month had passed. Frank was still in the hospital. He was no longer connected to the wires and tubes that were helping to keep him alive, weeks prior. Doc Shivley had Frank moved from ICU to a private room in the cancer care unit. As much as Doc wanted to, he did not believe Frank would ever leave the hospital on his own two feet.

In Frank's mind, he had put death on hold. Only Frank knew why he was still hanging on to life, defying the odds. At the top of his priority list, he had to find Carole. He had to see that Darin was out of jail. Also, Frank needed the chance to tell Darin the secrets he had been keeping from him. Being hospital bound, Frank couldn't check on Darin, other than through phone calls and information from Rusty.

* * *

"Knock, knock," Rusty verbalized, entering Frank's room.
"Come on in, Rusty."
"That looked like an empty lunch tray they just took out of here, and look at you, sitting on the edge of the bed. This is sure good news. Feeling better?"
"Sure. Find me a date and we'll go out dancing." Frank laughed.
"Hey, he's joking and laughing. You just don't know how that does my heart good, Frank. Do you need anything?"
"No, thanks, Rusty. How's Darin doing?"
"He's had his nose bent out of shape because you've been in the hospital so long. However, considering the fact that he's been in lock-up for five months now, he's okay. I guess."
"You guess?" Frank snapped. "Oh, I'm sorry Rusty. Scratch that. Okay?"
"Sure, Frank. Hey, other than checking on you daily, we haven't had a chance to visit since you've taken up residency in this place."
"Residency? Oh, yeah. I guess you're right. What a rotten way to spend my big 5-0. Lord knows I've been in here long enough," Frank agreed. "I don't know where the time goes. I swear the older I get, the faster time goes by. By the way, did I thank you for the flowers and the birthday card?" Rusty smiled and nodded.
"Has it been five months since Darin's been in jail?"
"Well, we arrested him the first time around the first week in July. The second time was just a few days later, and it's darn near Christmas right now. That makes his jail time a little over five months. If we can forget about Darin for a minute, tell me about your decision to sell everything and move to town," Rusty requested. "You vaguely mentioned it in passing the last time I was here."
"You know that I can't visit with you on a personal basis, not yet. As much as I appreciate your concern about my life, I have to respect John's wishes. I just can't jeopardize Darin's case."
"Look, Frank, we're both grown men. I have just as much to lose as

you do, if I were to have an accidental slip of the tongue and give you some vital information that you could pass on to John. What do you say, we just decide to stay away from the subject of Darin and have a comfortable friend-to-friend conversation. We can do that, you know."

"Okay, Rusty, you're right. Well, between the financial strain, and that trip back and forth to town for one thing and another, especially to visit Darin, I figured the best thing to do was to sell the farm and move to town. Another important factor in my decision was my health. Since Darin was jailed, I was paying my neighbor Casey to do all the farm chores. I was darn lucky that Casey—Oh, I don't know if you've ever met him, have you?"

"No, not personally, but go on."

"I bought the house in town and that's it. Now don't get me wrong, Rusty, I don't want you going off and worrying about my financial status. I still have plenty of money. I just prefer not digging into my savings unless it's a dire emergency."

"I understand."

"Speaking of finances. A person has a lot of time to think when they're just lying around in a hospital bed for days on end. To be more precise, I was thinking about my financial affairs. No matter how much we disagree about Darin, you're name is still on my financial accounts."

"After all these years, Frank? Why haven't you replaced my name with Darin's?"

"Because you have a more level head than he does. When the time comes, I know you'll do right by Darin."

Frank's words eased Rusty's mind. *That's got to mean he doesn't believe I tried to frame Darin?* "I don't want to discuss such a morbid subject. Say, you certainly didn't expect to move your things all by yourself, did you?"

"No. To be honest, I wasn't going to move any of it. I was just boxing up the stuff I wanted to take with me, and throwing away the junk. Casey offered the services of himself and his brother to move everything to my new house. Now, well, the poor guy is just waiting for me to get out of here so he can move my belongings out of the farmhouse and his stuff in. According to Doc, I'm stuck in here for a few more weeks. That's a dilemma. I have no one to help me."

"Thanks for the slap in the face. But if you think I'm going to turn the other cheek, think again," Rusty stated, half serious and half joking.

"What in the Sam hill are you talking about?"

"Dammit, Frank, I'm still your friend. When will you ever get that through your thick head? Now, what do you need done?"

Frank explained that he had one more closet in the farmhouse that needed packing. He also wanted his father's toolbox from the tool shed. After giving Rusty two sets of keys, one for the farmhouse and one set for the house in town, Frank gave him Casey's telephone number.

"Let me get this straight, Frank. You want me to get the tools out of the shed, finish packing, oversee the move, lock up your new house when everything is moved in, then give this set," Rusty held up the set of keys for the farmhouse, "to Casey when were done. Right?"

"That's it," Frank acknowledged. "Oh, I almost forgot. Darin has a set of keys to the farm, but you have them locked up. Can I get those to give to Casey?"

"Sure you can, Frank. I'll personally go see Darin and ask him for his permission to release the keys to you. That reminds me, we've been finished with the inspection of your car for quite some time now. Since the title is in your name, it can be released to you as soon as you get out of here."

"See? Gosh darn it!" Frank grumbled, pounding his fist on the bed.

"Hey, Frank, don't get so worked up. What's the problem? See what?"

"Without Darin to help me, I just can't get this all handled. I can't keep asking and depending on everyone else to do everything for me," Frank replied, shaking his head in disgust.

"Like what?"

"How in the devil am I going to get the car moved from the police station to my house?"

"Easy does it, buddy. We don't need you having a relapse. Look, I'll get Darin to release the keys. Then I'll drive the car to your new house and lock it inside the garage. Assuming you have a garage at your new place?"

"I do."

"Good. Then I'll have one of my men follow me to your house and get a lift back to my car. Now, see how easy that was?"

"Yes, that sounds feasible. Thanks. You know, Rusty, you guys sure had my car long enough. Did they find anything in the car that was incriminating?"

"Oh, no, Frank, now you're out of line," Rusty remarked with a chuckle.

"I know, I know, but I had to ask. Oh, my truck has to be moved, also."

"I assume it's still sitting out at the farm?"

"Yes. If you have the guys load it for you, you could drive it to town. Once it's unloaded, park it in the drive next to my garage and lock it up. Then, if you don't mind, you could ride back to the farm with Casey and get your vehicle. Does that sound okay with you?"

"Sounds like a good plan. I imagine it will take a few trips anyway to get all of your stuff to town."

"I appreciate you're help more than you'll ever know, Rusty."

"Yeah? Then prove it by getting well and getting out of here. Hospitals make me sick." After a wide grin in reflection of the smile he put on Frank's face, Rusty offered, "Well, is there anything else?"

"Just let me know when the move is complete."

"You know I will, Frank. Anyway, I have to bring back your keys. By the way, where are your truck keys?"

Frank had to think of the last time he had driven his pick-up. "Look in that closet over there," he pointed. "They're probably still in my pants pocket from the night I was brought in here."

Finding the keys, Rusty said, "Yup, here they are. Well, guess I better get out of here and put some time in for what they pay me for. You get some rest and don't worry about your things getting moved or your vehicles taken care of. Everything is as good as done. It's great to see you looking better. Talk at you later."

"Wait, Rusty. There is one other very important thing."

"Anything. You just name it."

"Darin still doesn't know about the move, so please don't say anything."

Rusty shook his head. "How many secrets are you going to keep from that boy?"

"Look, he has enough on his mind. After this is all over and he's out of jail, I'll hit him with both barrels, telling him everything he needs to know."

"That will be quite a blast. Do you think he'll be up to it?" From the forlorn look on Frank's face, Rusty was quick to request, "Don't answer that. You know, I used to give Darin credit for being a smart young man. Not any more. And I'm not talking about the trouble he's in. It beats the crap out of me that he can't just look at you and see you are seriously ill. I swear, Frank, you two are as different as night and day. I'm sorry, I guess I let my mouth rule my head sometimes."

Rusty walked to the door. "When I get Darin to release the keys the keys to the farm and the car, I'll just tell him that you want the car taken home, and leave it at that."

With Rusty gone, Frank called his attorney to see what was happening, if anything, in regards to Darin's case. John reported news unsettling to Frank. Amongst other things, John told him that Darin's case wouldn't go to court until May.

"Listen, Frank, if you're going to call Darin, you can save me a trip if you tell him everything I just told you. If he pleads out on the Denton break-in, we get him off easy. If I hear anything new from the D.A., I'll let you know. My schedule is tight. In all probability, I won't be in contact with you for a few months. If you need anything in the interim, just call and let Betty know."

"Sure John. You know, time has gotten away from me. I can't believe that the holidays are just around the corner. Have a very Merry Christmas, and tell your lovely wife, Joan, to have a Happy Chanukah. Talk to you next year."

"Thanks, Frank, and you have a good Christmas, also. Get better and get out of that hospital. Bye for now."

Later that afternoon, Rusty headed to Frank's farm. A snowstorm was due in the area within twenty-four hours. So, he and Casey decided they had better make the move while the weather was still decent.

After all of Frank's belongings had been moved into his house in town, and his pick-up was parked in his driveway, Casey drove Rusty back to the farm to pick up his truck and the toolbox.

In the tool shed, Rusty didn't have to look very hard. The old toolbox was sitting on a shelf just inside the door. Rusty assumed he found the correct item. It seemed to be the only object sitting on a shelf. The rest of the room looked like a tornado hit it. Taking hold of the handle, picking up the toolbox, Rusty hadn't realized that the latch was open. The entire contents of the toolbox emptied out on the floor.

Verbalizing a few choice words, Rusty stooped down and retrieved the items. "Sonavabitch! The damn lock must be broken. Either that, or someone forgot to latch the box closed the last time they used these tools. It must have been Frank. He said he keeps forgetting things. Guess I can't be upset with him."

As Rusty gathered up the tools, he took a good look at what he was holding. "Hmm, have I ever seen these tools before? I don't remember ever borrowing any from Frank or his father. Frank is always working with tools. Maybe on one of my visits I saw him using one of these tools."

Rusty admired the workmanship. "These tools might be old but I'll bet they were beautiful in their time. From the looks of that scroll design on the handles, my guess is they were special ordered or handcrafted."

Standing, Rusty proceeded to put every tool back into its respective slot inside the case. "Dammit all! Something's missing." Since there was one definite empty slot that appeared to be missing its own tool, Rusty knew he had to keep searching the floor. As much as he didn't want to get filthy from the dust and debris, Rusty got down on all fours. He began searching underneath everything on the floor. "Okay. If I were a tool, where would I have rolled?

An instant thought was like a stick of dynamite exploding in Rusty's brain. He almost fell flat on his face when the explosion hit. "That's it! I'll be a son-of-a-butcher! Now I remember where I've seen that beautiful crafted handle before." Getting to his feet, Rusty went back to the toolbox. "That empty slot is the definite shape of a screwdriver. If this matches what I think it does, then Darin, I gotcha."

Deep inside, Rusty still wanted to give Darin the benefit of the doubt. So, he went back to his search for the missing screwdriver. When his search came up empty, Rusty closed and latched the toolbox and placed it in his pick-up. He headed to the hospital.

Even though it was late, the nurse at the desk allowed Rusty to go to Frank's room. Once there, he stuck his head around the corner of the door. With the over-the-bed light on, Frank was lying in bed, reading a magazine.

"Frank, may I come in?"

Frank looked up. Surprised to see Rusty's face peering around the door, he replied, "Sure." As he placed his magazine on his bed table, Rusty approached the bed. "It's after 10:00, isn't it?"

"Yes it is. Look, Frank, I hate to bother you this late, but this can't wait."

"Is it Darin?" Frank asked, fearing the worse.

"No, Darin is fine."

"Oh, don't tell me one of you guys had an accident moving my things? Was anyone hurt?"

"No, Frank. If you'll be quiet a minute, I'll get to the point. Those tools you wanted me to get for you out of your tool shed, well, when I picked up the toolbox I didn't know the latch was undone. Everything inside spilled out, all over the floor."

In a hushed tone, Frank started laughing. "Is that the reason you came up here this late at night, to tell me you spilled the tools?"

"Look, Frank, this is no laughing matter. There's a tool missing. I think it's a large screwdriver."

"Is that all? Well, to tell you the truth, I noticed it was missing when I checked the toolbox. I just didn't get time to go back out and look around the shed for it. I'm sorry. I guess I'm the one that forgot to latch the box. Look, I'll just call Casey and tell him when he gets around to cleaning out that shed to look for the missing screwdriver. Honest, Rusty, it's okay. And certainly no reason to be chasing back here late at night to—"

"You aren't making this easy for me, Frank. Please, just be quiet and listen."

Frank raised his brow. "Okay, I'm listening."

"I need your permission to take those tools, or one of them, to compare it to a tool we already have as evidence from the Denton house. Now, you can give me permission to take the tools, or I can get a court order to seize them. Of course, I would rather you make this easy and just give me your verbal permission."

"What?" Frank sat up in bed. "You have a screwdriver in evidence and you think it came from my father's tools?"

"Yes, I do, Frank. Now, I wouldn't swear to it, but I believe the screwdriver we sent to the FBI Crime Lab has the same design on the wooden handle as your toolset. If it doesn't match, then that helps Darin's case."

Searching for the other end of the spectrum, Frank asked, "How does it help him if it doesn't match?"

"It may prove that Darin had the screwdriver we found at Denton's house, but, that it wasn't used to jimmy the door."

Confused, Frank questioned, "Is there any other reason that Darin would be carrying around a screwdriver?"

Rusty pondered before answering. "I can't think of any good reason, Frank. Seems that's a question only Darin can answer."

"Give me the negative if it does match."

"Then we'll be able to prove that Darin jimmied the door with the screwdriver to gain entrance into the Denton house. Sorry, Frank. Well, what will it be, your permission or a court order?"

"Take the whole box, Rusty." Lying back on his pillow, Frank turned his head away so he no longer had to look at Rusty. At that point, he didn't know if he was angry or ashamed. Once again, Frank wondered, was Darin guilty or innocent? "Now leave me alone. I need my rest."

After placing Frank's keys on the bed stand, Rusty honored his friend's request.

Early the next morning at the Kidwell Police Station, Rusty was holding a meeting with Officers Kelly, Janx and Seals. With the toolbox sitting on his desk, Rusty had just informed his officers about how he happened to have the tools in his possession.

"So, if the screwdriver found at Denton's, matches the pry marks on the wood evidence, we can tie all of our evidence up into one tidy little bundle, then—Bingo. We'll be able to tie Darin to every one of these burglaries. Then, that means we *do* have our Neat Nick Thief.

Seals, you can do the honors of packaging up this tool kit for overnight shipment to Special Agent Coats. I don't have to remind you to protect our chain of custody. I'll call Leo and tell him to expect this package. Any questions?"

Seals and Janx shook their heads, but Kelly stated, "I don't have a question either, but I wanted you to know that the D.A. called yesterday while you were out. He said that Darin's court date was set on the May docket."

"Great. That should give my friend at the lab enough time to get these items, analyze and compare them to the last shipment of evidence, and get a report back to us before court.

Okay, let's get to other business. We've all been so busy working on this Neat Nick Case that some of you have let your paperwork get behind. I'm not complaining, mind you, as this case has been our priority. But Christmas is just a few days away, so I would like all completed reports on my desk before then." Holding up a few paper-filled manila file folders, Rusty added, "And, Janx—"

"Yes I know, Chief," Janx answered before Rusty could finish his statement. Taking the files from Rusty's hand, Janx cracked a smile. "Kelly and Seals are busy. So, since you hate writing, it's my turn to write up your reports from your notes."

"Oh, no. I was only going to ask you to write my reports for me, Janx. But, if you insist, thank you," Rusty joked.

Everyone in the room had a good laugh. Rusty excused his men so everyone could get their assigned jobs taken care of, as soon as possible.

"Well, Darin, I'm on your wave link. Your little game of cat and mouse is over, and this cat has you trapped. I have a sneaky suspicion, though, that you've also been playing a fierce game of poker. With high stakes, you've thought all along that you were playing with a stacked deck. Not this time, punk. This time I've got an ace up my sleeve. When the time is right, I'll play it."

Rusty had to prove beyond a shadow of a doubt that Darin was the Neat Nick Thief. Only time would tell whether, or not, the law held the winning hand.

TALES OF WOE

    Winter had swiftly passed, like a puff of smoke that seems to evaporate into nowhere. Spring was willowing its way into Nebraska. The April showers were more like a slight mist as the spring flowers enjoyed popping up their beautiful new heads in colorful displays.
    Nothing out of the ordinary had happened in Kidwell over the cold and snowy winter months.
    Promising Doc that he would rest more and stay less stressed, Frank received his release from hospital. Since Darin's jailhouse visitors were few to none, proving what kinds of friends he had, no one made mention to Darin about Frank's health or his move. Frank was fortunate to keep the same telephone number, so Darin was still in the dark as to what had been happening in Frank's life.
    Darin was still sweating it out in jail. He had resigned himself to the fact that making waves didn't help his situation, angry as he was, so he became sedate. As long as Frank kept him supplied with magazines and cigarettes, he tried to keep a low profile. To keep track of time, he marked an x on a wall of his cell each evening when he put out his last cigarette for the day.
    Back in December, when Frank had informed Darin that the district attorney didn't have a case against him, other than the breaking and entering charge, Darin felt he had pulled the proverbial wool over Rusty's eyes. He was positive that he just had a few more months before he could get out of jail for good. Darin was still confident that his money was safe and would be waiting for him. He knew with brazen certainty that Welk hadn't told anyone about the money, and Rusty had never found it.
    Not until Frank's hospital stay did Darin finally wise up and realize

Frank had a serious illness. He didn't know what the illness was, but he didn't much care. As far as he was concerned, staying around Kidwell would not help his brother's health. He still had plans of moving east.

As the May trial drew near, Rusty was still waiting for the FBI Crime Lab report from Special Agent Coats. Confident as he was about his theory that Darin was the Neat Nick Thief, Rusty still had to convince the D.A. In order to do so, the evidence needed to be in the department's hands, along with the FBI report, by court date. There was the distinct possibility of jeopardizing the case against Darin without this vital information.

* * *

Rusty answered the telephone in his office. "Chief Simmons."

"Rusty, this is Doug Martin."

"Yes, Doug, what can I do for you today?"

"I've found something I think you need to come take a look at. That is, if you can spare the time to come over to my office?"

"What is it you've got, Doug?"

"Some of Ward's files."

"I thought I took care of Ward's personal affairs. What did I miss?"

"It's not personal, Rusty. This concerns—Look, I would rather not discuss this over the phone."

"You sound quite serious. Tell you what. I don't have anything that can't wait until later today. How about I come over now."

"Sounds good," Doug responded.

"I'll be there within the hour."

Kidwell's city limits made up the vast majority of Cole County. The county had no lock-up facilities, and Sharpin's jail only consisted of three cells in lock-up. Whenever the Cole County Sheriff would make an arrest, most times he would have his suspect locked up in Kidwell's jail. The Sheriff's Department consisted of one small front office, the sheriff's office, and two storage closets. Under lock and key, one closet held evidence and other important law enforcement items. Staffing was the same as the office space—limited. There was the sheriff, and he had one deputy.

When Rusty arrived at the sheriff's office, Doug personally greeted him since the deputy wasn't in at the time. "Thanks for coming over so soon, Rusty," Doug stated. The men shook hands.

"You had a certain urgency in your voice. Piqued an old lawman's curiosity."

"Urgent, no. Important, I'm not sure yet."

"That doesn't tell me much." Rusty grinned.

"Go on in my office and make yourself comfortable. I was just going for coffee. Would you like a cup?"

"Sure. Black." Rusty took a seat in Doug's confined office. "Hey, Doug," he yelled, "what happened to the bell on the front door? Damn, I couldn't ever sneak in this place and surprise Ward because that darned thing would warn him."

Doug, laughing at Rusty's comment, entered his office with two coffee mugs. After handing Rusty a cup, he closed his office door and took a seat behind his desk. "It's funny you should mention that old bell. One screw attaches it to the door. Just this morning, the screw fell out—stripped threads from age—and the bell hit the floor. I sent my deputy over to the hardware store to get a new screw. We'll have it back up in no time," he explained. "That old bell was Ward's watch dog when he was back here in his office and I was out on patrol.

Here's the trick that Ward taught me. When my deputy is going to be out of the office, he turns on his intercom to output. In turn, I make sure my intercom is turned on for input." As Doug spoke, he pointed to the intercom on his desk. "Then, if I'm in here with my door closed, like now, and anyone comes in the front door, I can hear the bell as clear as day through the intercom. It works quite well."

"With the bell broke and your deputy out of the office, maybe we should keep your door open?"

"No, that's not necessary, Rusty. I'm not too worried about it right now. My deputy should be right back. If not, he'll call in."

After a drink of coffee, Rusty had a question that was bugging him. "Let me ask you something, Doug."

"Shoot."

"I always voted for Ward to be our County Sheriff, but I'm not quite sure how a sheriff's shoes are filled when he passes, like Ward did. Is it official that you're the sheriff now?"

"You know, Rusty, not all of us have the distinct pleasure of being appointed by the mayor," Doug stated with a laugh. "Yes, like Ward, some of us have to get voted into office."

"Well, smarty, when are the next county elections? I may just want to vote for someone with a good sense of humor," Rusty retorted with humor. He was more than pleased that he and Doug could have the same good-natured rapport as he and Ward had enjoyed.

"Elections are this November. Take a good look at me. Do you think I'll have anyone running against me for this seat?" Grinning from ear to ear, Rusty shook his head. "Okay, then, I'll count on your vote. All joking aside, Rusty, when Ward died, the governor appointed me to complete his term. That's why, when I stepped into Ward's shoes last year, I immediately had the official title as sheriff. So, I hope I get elected this fall by our fine folks in this community."

As Rusty squirmed around in his chair to get comfortable, Doug pulled a file folder from his desk drawer. He laid it atop his desk.

"Now that we're on a more serious note, I want to tell you why I've asked you here. Let me start, Rusty, by apologizing that it took so long to find this file." As he spoke, he tapped his fingers on the manila folder. "I don't know how well you knew Ward, but he was a pack rat. I mean that guy—God love him—collected and saved everything. He also loved people, found good in everyone, and tried to protect the people he cared about."

Rusty nodded in complete agreement. "That was Ward all right."

"I've spent the last eleven months—can you believe it—almost a year trying to get this office cleaned up. It's small enough in here without mounds of papers piled everywhere. I have burned more midnight oil reading every scrap of paper Ward accumulated than I did the nights I hit the books hard attending college. Before I get to the file I found, let me ask you first if you know a person by the name of Jefferson Welk?"

Biting his bottom lip, Rusty sat straight. He placed his now empty cup on Doug's desk. "Yes, I do. Why do you ask?"

"Man, you were either thirsty or you like our coffee," Doug remarked. "Do you want a refill?"

"No thanks, I'm fine, and yes to both of your comments. I was thirsty and your coffee was strong, just as I like it. Now, back to the reason you're asking me about Jefferson Welk."

"Before I answer your question, please bear with me. Were you aware that Mr. Welk died exactly, uh … " Doug paused to look at his desk calendar. "It will be one year tomorrow. That was just a month before Ward left us."

"I generally make it my business to know just about everything that goes on around Kidwell. But, with things still up in arms around town last year concerning all of the burglaries that were going on, I don't believe I even heard that Welk had passed on. I'm sure sorry to hear that. Now, one cop to another, are you going to skip to the chase?"

"Okay, here's a note I found in Ward's own handwriting." From the folder in front of him, Doug took out a sheet of paper. "Let me read it to you. It says, 'Welk is a partner in a money racket of some kind—Computer disk is evidence—Talk it over with Rusty for his advice—Do I owe it to Welk to keep my mouth shut and let the dead rest in peace, or do I investigate and cause more shame?'" Doug laid the paper on the desk and looked at Rusty. "Does any of that make any sense to you?"

"Nope. Well, maybe, some of it. You see, Jefferson Welk is part of Kidwell's history that the old timers around here would just as soon forget. There's just a handful of us left that know the story as told to us by our grandparents or our parents.

Most of us who know about the Welk family, do our best *not* to keep the story going. Then something happens, like this situation of you asking me about. So, instead of it getting buried, the story gets told, once again." Rusty hesitated then asked, "I don't know if it's relevant, but since you're trying to make sense of Ward's notes, do you want to hear the story?"

"Yes. I'm all ears." Doug leaned back in his chair and folded his arms.

"I'll have to start at the very beginning, or you won't have a complete understanding of this story," Rusty stated. "Many years ago there was a very wealthy man by the name of Edgar Kidwell. He and his wife moved from the State of Georgia to settle here in Nebraska. Upon arrival, Edgar Kidwell purchased acres and acres of land. He and his wife called their place the Kidwell Farm. Mrs. Kidwell was a former socialite, Loretta Sharpin, and, it seems, the single heir to the Sharpin estate from somewhere in Georgia. Combining their wealth through marriage—it goes without saying—both Mr. and Mrs. Kidwell were well off in the financial department.

After more and more folks settled about this region, Edgar Kidwell became the patriarch of the area—hence the name of the town 'Kidwell.' And, of course, 'Sharpin' was named out of respect for his lovely wife. The Kidwell's had one son. Even though he died at birth, they named him Cole. Now you know why we live in Cole County. That's just a little background history for you," Rusty added with a smile.

"Okay, I'm intrigued, Rusty. Keep going."

"Jefferson's grandfather, Moses Welk, was the Kidwell's slave. The Kidwell's brought Moses with them from Georgia. Now, the people of

Nebraska didn't have slaves but the Kidwell's didn't know that until they had moved here. So, they gave Moses his freedom and some money to go to wherever he wanted to live and make a new life for himself.

At first, Moses rejected their offer. With the Kidwell's insistence, he changed his mind. Moses took the money and left Nebraska. Within a few months, he returned to the Kidwell's with his new wife. She was a white woman. Grandpa said he never knew her real name because she preferred people call her Mrs. Moses.

Moses told Edgar Kidwell that he didn't know anything else in life but to have Kidwell as his master. Edgar had taught him how to farm, but Moses wasn't confident enough to farm on his own. He felt as though he still needed his master's guidance. Moses also explained that, other than his new wife, he had no other living relatives. It's a mere assumption on anyone's part that Moses considered the Kidwell's as family.

This devotion leads one to believe that the Kidwell's had been good to Moses, slave or not. Moses took it upon himself to ask if he and his new wife could live on the Kidwell property. It seems they would both work free just to have a home around people Moses respected and cared for.

The story goes that Edgar Kidwell was so appreciative of the dedication that he gave some of his riverfront property to Moses and his wife. Kidwell had papers drawn up saying that particular piece of property was the legal property of Mr. and Mrs. Moses Welk. Mr. Kidwell also hired the couple so they would have an income.

On top of a hill, close to the river, is where the Kidwell's lived in their huge mansion. The property they gave Moses was across the river, a few hundred yards away from their fabulous home. I've never been on the property so I'm just repeating what I've been told. With his own two hands, Moses built a small shanty on the riverfront property for him and his wife. Edgar offered to build them a nicer home, but it seems Moses was too proud to accept any more gifts or handouts from his boss.

Cole Kidwell's death was more than either Edgar or Loretta could take. So, as years went by, they never had any other children. However, Moses and his wife did. I'll try not to confuse you here, Doug." Intent on listening, Doug nodded. "Okay. Moses had one son. That would be Joseph. Then Joseph married and gave Moses one grandson. That would be Jefferson. Both Joseph and his son, Jefferson, were born in the small shanty Moses had built. When Joseph was old enough to work, Edgar put him on the payroll.

You know what? I think I'll have that refill now, if you don't mind. My mouth's getting a bit dry with all this storytelling, and I've just begun," Rusty quipped.

"Sure, just when you get me all enthralled in your story, you get thirsty," Doug teased.

After Doug replenished Rusty's coffee, he sat back in his chair. Rusty wetted his thirst. Then he continued telling the story. "Folks around the Cole County area didn't like the Welk family because some of them were black. In fact, they were the only black people in the immediate area. The area folks also hated the fact that Moses had a white wife. Mixed marriages, in their eyes, were a sin of the Bible. You have to understand, Doug, folks were still damn prejudice back in those days."

Doug shook his head. The thought of prejudices angered him.

"One day, some deranged person broke into the Kidwell's house. Edgar Kidwell was murdered, and the no-good SOB raped and beat the hell out of Loretta. It's been said, whoever did it, thought they had killed her. However you look at it, fortunate or unfortunate for her, she survived the horrific attack. Folks in town were quick to blame Moses.

Area folks wouldn't believe that one of their own kind could have committed such a heinous crime. So it was easier to blame a black man." Somber faced, Rusty shook his head. "If my memory serves me right, I think Jefferson would have been about seven or eight then, but don't quote me. Better yet, don't quote me on any of this. I'm just telling you what I remember being told to me when I was a small boy.

Anyway, a group of vigilantes got together, went out to the Kidwell farm, and found Moses. They drug him out of his shanty. At the same time, they forced the rest of the family out of their home. Then they strung Moses up from a nearby oak tree. They made Mrs. Moses, Joseph and his wife Sarakaye, and young Jefferson watch the hanging."

"My God, Rusty, what a terrible and sad story. Was he guilty of the murder and assault?"

"No. It seems when Loretta Kidwell regained consciousness, she named the man that had attacked her and killed her husband. It wasn't Moses Welk. Loretta knew she was in such serious shape from the beating she took that she wasn't going to live very long. And, of course, she was devastated over her husband's murder.

Even in her physical and emotional pain, she suffered mental anguish over what had happened to Moses. She summoned a solicitor—Whoops. Guess that's my grandpa speaking." Rusty smiled with warm memories of his grandfather. "Loretta Kidwell hired an attorney. She had papers drawn up that gave every inch of property she and her husband had owned, to Mrs. Moses and her immediate relatives. In turn, it was to be passed down through the generations—or to anyone else of their choosing—as they saw fit.

My Lord, the Kidwell's owned all the business and government buildings in both Kidwell and Sharpin, plus some investments Edgar Kidwell had made back on the east coast. So, the fortune that Loretta Kidwell owned in her own right, plus the estate she inherited from her husband, she was leaving a bank of wealth in the Welk name.

From what I was told, that vast amount of money would have lasted for generation after generation after generation. Well, you get the picture. I tell you, Doug, that financial well would have never run dry unless some family member, along the way, was a heavy gambler and squelched millions at one shot. The proceeds from the Sharpin estate, together with the property the Kidwell's owned, well, we're talking multi-millions.

Loretta Kidwell was an intelligent woman. She knew Mrs. Moses was uneducated. Even though her son, Joseph, had graduated high school, Loretta didn't feel either of them could handle such high finances without assistance. Mrs. Kidwell was in fear of someone stealing large amounts of the monetary estate away from the Welk's. To prevent this, Loretta Kidwell had a fund set up wherein the vast fortune of money was set-aside in a sort of trust fund at the Sharpin bank.

Over and above paying for all the Welk's living expenses, the bank was to personally hand deliver a certain amount of money to Mrs. Moses, or her descendents, once a month for as long as the money lasted. To sum it up, they became the Sharpin and Kidwell heirs after Loretta Kidwell died."

"Money sure couldn't have taken the place of such a travesty," Doug commented.

"This whole story is a tragedy. An innocent man died for nothing. Poor Jefferson Welk had to witness his grandfather's execution. Just think what he had to live with for the major share of his life. Dreadful. Just dreadful."

After stopping for a drink of coffee, Rusty continued. "Okay, back to my story, but I need to back up here. Years before the hanging, with a suggestion and a gift of money from the Kidwell's, Moses had sent his son away to school. Because of the hateful ways of the area people, including the children who listened to the bigoted remarks of others—up to and including their parents—Edgar Kidwell felt Joseph should get his education elsewhere. After graduation, and like his father, Joseph fell in love and married. Not that it makes any difference, but since it's part of the story I have to tell you that Joseph married a black woman."

"Why would that make a difference?" Doug had a quick thought that answered his own question. "Oh, I see. Since his father was black and his mother was white, Joseph was of mixed blood."

"That's correct," Rusty confirmed with a nod. "Joseph felt a black woman was more suitable to be his wife since he was dark skinned like his father. When Joseph returned to the Kidwell farm with his wife, Sarakaye, they lived with his parents in that tiny one-room shack. Moses and Joseph continued working on the Kidwell's farm, and their wives took care of Kidwell's mansion.

Then, like I said, Jefferson was born. The Kidwell's got after Moses to build a bigger house. They felt four adults and a baby living in a one-room shack just wouldn't do. Both Moses and Joseph convinced the Kidwell's they were very comfortable. Using his influence and his money, Edgar Kidwell had a special two-bedroom house on wheels built. Today, of course, we call them trailers or mobile homes. Horse driven, Kidwell had the unit delivered to Moses as a gift. Moses accepted the gift, but he drew the line at having inside plumbing and electricity connected."

"Why?"

"I was never told why, so I can't answer that," Rusty said, shrugging. "When Jefferson was old enough, his parents allowed him to attend the local school. Seems Jefferson didn't want to live away from home, but he wanted to go to school. He wasn't accepted very well by the other students, but he toughed it out for the first few years.

However, Jefferson never attended school again after his grandfather's horrible death. I believe my grandpa said that Jefferson was in the second or third grade then. It's my understanding that Jefferson's mother taught him school studies at home. Sarakaye must have done an excellent job because Jefferson was an intelligent man."

Rusty stopped speaking when he heard the familiar bell tinkle over the intercom. Without saying a word, both Doug and Rusty knew the deputy had returned and replaced Ward's bell back on the front door. They smiled at one another.

"I was so involved listening to your story, Rusty, I didn't even hear my deputy come in."

"Don't feel bad. I didn't either."

"Guess that proves the point that the bell is still a good watchdog. Just a second, Rusty." Flipping the intercom switch to off, Doug excused himself and went to the outer office. He requested that his deputy stay in the office. The sheriff was only to be bothered if there was an emergency or if Rusty received a telephone call. Back in his office, Doug insisted that Rusty continue with his story.

"Joseph, his mother, his wife, and their son pretty much kept to themselves after the hanging. Using all the expertise the Kidwell's had taught them, they farmed and raised everything they needed for food from vegetable gardens to livestock. The Welk women made all of the family's clothes. In other words, there wasn't too much they needed from the outside world. A visit in town from any of them was rare, according to Grandpa.

Those that knew them could never figure out why they continued to live in that one-room shack and the house on wheels. Why didn't they move up to the big house where the Kidwell's had lived. Who knows? Maybe it was the painful memories from what had happened to the Kidwell's in their own home that kept them away.

Like his father and his grandfather before him, Jefferson left the farm for a short time, and returned with a wife. To everyone's amazement, except for his family members, Jefferson had followed in his grandfather's footsteps. Mrs. Jefferson Welk was a white woman."

"Well, I guess that makes sense," Doug remarked. "I saw the man when he was deceased. He did appear to have light skin color."

"Wait, wait, wait. What do you mean you saw him when he was deceased?"

"If you don't mind, Rusty, I'd rather you finish your story. Then I'll tell you what I know."

"That's fair," Rusty replied with a nod. "Yes, Jefferson was light skinned, not that it made any difference. Grandpa use to always say, love has no color."

Doug nodded. It all made perfect sense to him.

"Jefferson's grandma passed, then his father, followed by his mother. No one ever knew where any of them were buried, but talk was that they were all put to rest somewhere on the Welk property."

When Rusty stopped to take another drink of coffee, Doug took advantage to voice a question. "With all that money, why weren't they buried in Kidwell's cemetery?"

"Back in the days when Moses was executed, no black people were allowed to be buried there or in the Cole County Cemetery—money or no money. Grandpa told me that everyone assumed Moses was buried on his own property, close to his home. It would be only natural that the others were buried close to him."

"I can't imagine living in an area where people hate you. I sure give them all credit for not running away."

"Well, Doug, that's just part of this sad tale."

"Part of it? You mean there's more?"

"Yes, I'm afraid there is. Do you have time now to hear the rest of it?"

Doug didn't have to look at the time. "Look, Rusty, unless I get an emergency call, my time is yours right now."

"Well," Rusty said, standing and rubbing his back with both hands, "let me water the dog first and I'll be right back."

When Rusty returned to Doug's office, the saga continued. "Jefferson and his wife didn't have any children until after his grandmother and parents were deceased. Jefferson's wife wanted to have the baby at home, so Jefferson summoned Doc Shivley. According to Doc, as a new doctor in town at that time, Jefferson's daughter was the first baby he brought into the world.

Since they had a newborn, Jefferson didn't want such a large amount of cash being delivered to his door. Not that anyone ever bothered coming around their shanty again after the hanging travesty, but Jefferson didn't want to take the chance of being robbed. He set up a checking account at the bank in Sharpin. That way, the bank just transferred funds for him and he could write checks, when and if needed.

No one cared to work for Jefferson. Even though he was the richest man in the area, I assume most people felt it was beneath them to work for a black man. Refusing to part with the land, Jefferson let most of the fields go to weed. He just farmed what he could handle by himself.

On one particular day, Jefferson was working out in the field. His wife was outside hanging up wash on a makeshift clothesline behind the house. Their baby girl was sleeping inside the shanty. When Mrs. Welk went back into their home, their one-month-old daughter was gone—kidnapped."

As he listened, Doug didn't think his heart could get any heavier.

"Jefferson and his wife went to the local authorities for help, but the Welk's baby was never found. And, I might add, they never found the kidnapper. Again, I don't know this for a fact, but some say the Welk's house was—and may still be—surrounded on three sides by a small forest of trees. This, of course, made trailing anyone next to impossible. Whoever took that child, knew what they were doing.

How Jefferson and his wife ever got through their pain is beyond me. I guess the deep love they had for each other made their bond together even stronger. When his missus passed on, it broke Jefferson's heart. I believe they were married some forty years, maybe longer. I don't recall right now.

Jefferson pretty much stayed to himself. Just like his family before him, Jefferson wasn't seen in town but once a month when he needed supplies for either himself or the farm. I had heard that he was still farming for a living, selling eggs, milk, hay, and farm goods of that nature. Lord knows, he didn't need the money. He liked to keep himself busy, I guess.

Not too many years back, I heard that he had found a farmhand to live out there on the farm and help him with chores. I was a little surprised, knowing that some folks around here are still pretty much living in the dark ages. It was nice to hear that someone befriended him and was willing to work for him. As with many citizens of Cole County, I spoke with Jefferson on several occasions throughout the years. But I can't say I really knew him. Well, Doug, that's it. I might have a few dates wrong, but I can tell you the story is true," Rusty concluded.

"Dear God, Rusty. I've never heard anything so depressing in my life. It's hard to even imagine what Jefferson Welk went through, or any of his family for that matter.

Tell me, why would a man who owns acres and acres of property, and have oodles of money coming in from a trust fund, be involved with a partner in a money racket? And what did Ward mean when he wrote, 'Do I owe it to him to keep my mouth shut and let the dead rest in peace, or do I investigate and cause more shame?' Ward was always—to my knowledge—an officer of the law, first and foremost. It doesn't hold water that he would pull back from an investigation. Does any of this make any sense to you?"

"Like I said earlier, part of it does. Ward confided in me at one time about a heavy guilt he carried. I guess, since he's gone now, I can tell you. But out of respect for Ward, I don't want this information to go out of this office."

"You know you don't even have to ask."

"I know, Doug. I guess that's just a figure of speech to make me feel better about telling you," Rusty remarked with a grin. "This all fits into the

Welk's story. Ward's grandfather was a part of that vigilante group that lynched Moses. A few men in town had turned themselves in. They paid the price of hanging an innocent man. I'm sorry to say, Ward's grandfather was one of them. Before those few confessed men were put to death, they never ratted on who the other men were in the hanging party. They took that secret to their graves. Even though he was a true-blue lawman, maybe Ward felt he still owed for what his grandfather had done, all those years ago."

"Owed who, Rusty, Jefferson?"

"All people of color."

"Okay, Rusty, you've given me one hell of lot to digest here. Let me see if I can lump this all together. Years ago, something horrible happened to a black man. Ward's grandfather was in on it. Ward may have carried this guilt of his prejudiced grandfather. Knowing his grandfather was wrong, and Welk was a black man, Ward was debating whether or not to investigate him. Or, he could turn his head the other direction and forget about any law breaking information he had uncovered. Am I close?"

"Yes, you're close. Back to Ward's note. If Ward wanted to discuss with me the information he had discovered, it must have been pretty damn important. Tell me about the computer disk you mentioned."

"Let me give you some other information first, Rusty, about my knowledge of Jefferson Welk."

"Oh, right. About the fact that he was deceased when you saw him."

"Correct. Last year an emergency call came into our office. Ward took the call. He said a female told him Mr. Welk had died. She didn't give him too much information before she hung up the phone. Ward had me call Doctor Shivley. Then the three of us went out to the Welk farm. I never met nor had even seen Welk before then. In fact, because of his skin color, I didn't even realize the man was black until Ward told me. Hell, I didn't even know we had black folks living in the area."

"Could be because you're a new comer to our area, Doug. I assume you aren't one of those prejudicial people who gives a damn what a person's skin color is. Am I right?"

"You're right on the money. I come from back east where there's a melting pot of race, creed, color, language and you name it. Where I grew up, everyone was treated the same. Just look at me. I'm a perfect example of what some people call an outcast in society because of my two different color eyes, my god-awful face, and my monstrous build. Other than a few kids who teased me in school, I got along just fine with everyone. Prejudice wasn't a word in my vocabulary."

"Mine either, thank God," Rusty interjected.

"Anyway, when we got out to the farmhouse that day, we were met at the door by this little gal. From everything she told us, we all assumed she was the deceased's farmhand."

"So, the rumor about him having a farmhand was true."

Doug nodded. "This gal told Ward that she had been outside gathering eggs. When she went back inside the house, Mr. Welk was on the floor, dead. I have to tell you, Rusty, that girl was—without a doubt—the most naive person I have ever encountered in my whole life. Neither Ward, nor I, could figure out if she was uneducated, or one of those gifted people who are mentally challenged."

Nodding his head, Rusty offered, "I think I understand. Go on."

"Ward asked her a whole lot of questions. Doc checked out the body and informed us the man had perished from a heart attack. I checked around the house for anything unusual. We did it all by the book, just in case there was foul play. Everything checked out okay so Ward let the girl go. At the time, I voiced my opinion. I felt the girl was play-acting. I had a hard time believing anyone could be that ignorant. However, Ward showed me where I was wrong. So, I dropped it. The funny part was that after she left the house, Ward had second thoughts. He wanted us to go back the next morning, bring her in for more questioning, and check her ID. Ward wanted to cover his ass in case she was wanted for anything."

"That's understandable. Was she?" Rusty asked, starting to squirm a bit more than usual in his hard chair, which was now giving him a sore butt from sitting so long.

"We never got to find out. She was already gone when we arrived back at Welk's farm the next morning. Since we never saw any fliers or wanted information that fit her description, we accepted the fact that she was just a runaway who no one cared about looking for."

"I heard the old Kidwell mansion burned down back in the sixties. I was just wondering, since you say you were out there, if Jefferson ever rebuilt it?"

"I never saw a large house, or what you're calling a mansion when we went out there, Rusty."

"I guess he was like his father and couldn't bring himself to move into the Kidwell home. But I just can't believe Jefferson stayed living in that old shanty for all those years."

"I don't think he did. The house we were in was small and very modest for a man you say was very wealthy. It certainly wasn't a one-room shanty.

"You don't say. Maybe he built a house where the Kidwell's place once stood. Does Jefferson's house sit up on a hill close to the river?"

"You're asking the wrong person some of these questions, Rusty. I'd never been to Welk's place before his death. I don't know where the mansion used to sit. I can tell you that Welk's house does not sit on the river. There are just a few rooms on the main floor, one bedroom upstairs, and a full basement. Boy, you'd think with all that money he inherited that he would have wanted something bigger and nicer to live in."

"Some people don't like big changes in their lives, Doug. Did you see anything resembling a cemetery while you were out there?"

"No. Why?"

"I was just a little curious about where the rest of his family ... " Rusty paused. After licking his lower lip, he asked, "Where was Jefferson buried?"

"He's in the Kidwell cemetery. So you think the Welk family really does have a cemetery plot on the property?"

"It would sure make sense."

"If Ward were here, I'm sure he'd agree with you."

"Wait. If you're telling me that Ward knew—for a fact—about the cemetery on the property, then why was Jefferson buried in Kidwell's?"

"It was just conjecture on Ward's part. He didn't know for sure if there was, or wasn't. When I asked him if I should go look for one, he told me something to the effect that it would take too long. At the time, I got the distinct impression that he knew how large the property was that the deceased owned. So, you think there really is one out there?"

"You know, we could sit and speculate all day. However, we have better things to talk about. Now about that computer disk."

"I found an envelope in our evidence locker that had the name Jefferson Welk on it. Inside the envelope was a computer disk. Since I saw a computer in the house on the day Welk died, I'm just assuming the disk came from that computer."

"How did it get in the evidence locker?"

"I don't know for sure, Rusty, so this is just a guess. After Ward called the bankers, I went outside to ask the girl more questions. Doc was in the house with him. Chances are, if Ward decided to look around the house, Doc wouldn't have followed. Perhaps Ward picked up the disk at that time. Either he spotted the disk laying around somewhere, or maybe it was in the computer. Once again, I assume that he put the disk into computer first to see what was on it. There was plenty of time for Ward to do such a thing before I returned to the house."

"Ha!" Rusty gave out with a deep grunting laugh. "That's stretching the imagination some, saying Ward knew anything about computers."

"Excuse me? Oh, I guess I know something you don't know."

"I'm sure that's plenty, Doug, but what are we talking about?"

"Ward. Before he died, didn't he tell you he was taking night courses over at the junior college in Liptin?"

"What?" Rusty questioned in astonishment. "You're kidding me."

"Nope. It's the honest to God's truth. Ward told me that young man he was supporting had talked him into learning about computers."

"Well, I'll be. Damn, that's rich. You know that young man you just mentioned, John Daniel Hobart?"

"I know of him, Rusty, but I've never met him."

"No, I haven't either. I corresponded with him right after Ward's death. Once I sent him that rather large sum of money that Ward left him, I never heard from him again. I tried to locate him, just to see if he needed anything. Seems to have dropped off the face of the earth. Oh, well, that's not important now."

Doug wasn't paying much attention to what Rusty was saying. He had questions on his mind of greater importance. "I'm having a hard time understanding this. If Ward did find this disk at Welk's house, why didn't he ever mentioned it to me?"

"According to his note, Doug, I would venture to guess that he wanted to discuss it with me first, out of respect for the past. There were just a handful of people in these parts that knew the Welk's story. He was of them. Okay, at the risk of repeating myself, what's on the disk?"

"I haven't the foggiest idea. I want to take the disk out to Welk's house and see if it is in fact from that computer—like I think it is—then see what's on it. But I didn't want to go alone. Everything about this is rather strange. So, I thought maybe someone—like another law officer—would be good to have by my side. That's you, Rusty. Plus, Ward was going to contact you about this matter before his sudden death. Those were a couple of the reasons I called you."

Rusty chuckled as he joked, "Hey, you afraid Jefferson's ghost is still in the old farm house?"

"No." Doug stated, laughing in his own defense. "Are you just going to sit there and tease me, or are you interested in going with me?"

"Sure I will. Tell me about these bankers. Why were they called?"

"Welk was clutching a foreclosure statement in his hand. When Ward read it, he contacted the First People's Bank of Sharpin. It made sense that the property belonged to them."

"It's hard for me to believe the money well dried up. No damn wonder Jefferson died from heart failure. What's happened to the property this past year?"

"After I found this note from Ward, and the computer disk, I called the bank in Sharpin and spoke with the president. According to him, the property is still standing vacant. It seems there is some big probate issue between the government and the bank as to who takes possession of the property. Not just that, but I was told there is a list of creditors a mile long that have put a lien on the property. It looks like everyone and his brother wants a piece of what's left of the estate. Anyway, we can go out there now, if you want to?"

Rusty checked his watch. "Holy rotten tomatoes, Doug. I can't believe I've been here all morning. No wonder my hindend feels like it's part of this chair." Rusty chuckled.

"I've got a good crowbar if you need me to pry you loose."

"I might. Let me check in with my office. Then, how about a bite to eat before we head out there?" Rusty suggested with a pat to his stomach. "I'm starved."

"It sounds great, Rusty, but I'll have to take a raincheck on the meal. Why don't I meet you out there in about an hour? Maybe we should both drive our own cars anyway. Just in case we're needed someplace else in a hurry."

After Rusty stood, he put his empty cup on Doug's desk. Placing his hands behind him, Rusty pushed into the small of his back as he tilted backward to work out the kinks. Doug stood and stretched.

"I'm getting too old to sit for so long in one place. By the way, how are we going to get into the house?" Rusty inquired as he walked to the door.

"I took the liberty of getting the key from the bank yesterday. Lucky for us, they've been holding on to it until probate's settled. I told them we still have some investigating to do, which is true. They gave me some song and dance about why we are still investigating after a year. Then they wanted to know *what* we're investigating. But, I nipped that in the bud, real quick, when I mentioned the fact that the bank and the government hadn't come to terms yet as to who really owns the property.

Seems to me that the government red tape takes just as long as the law enforcement system to get anything completed—maybe longer. They gave me the ammunition by telling me about the probate, so I threw it back at them. After my diplomatic come back, they handed over the key and never pursued their questions any further."

Rusty laughed. "You'd make quite a politician."

"Oh, bite your tongue," Doug said with a shake of his head. "Oh, I also had to make sure the electricity was still on in the house. One of the bankers told me they left all the utilities connected. They didn't want the pipes to freeze up in the winter."

"Wonder who's footing that bill? The taxpayers?"

"Who knows," Doug responded.

"Say, didn't Welk have livestock? What happened to it?"

"I didn't ask, Rusty. I just assumed they sold any livestock that would have been there so they wouldn't have to take care of it themselves or shell out for boarding expenses. I do know there was a dog, and maybe a few chickens, when I was out there. Can't say I paid much attention to any other kinds of animals."

"Okay, Doug. Well, I'll see you later."

Rusty left Doug's office. One hour later, Rusty pulled in the drive of the farm. Doug was already there, sitting in his car, waiting. Doug got out of his car and stood beside it as Rusty joined him.

"No one told me the windows and doors were all boarded up," Doug declared. "Thank heavens I have a crowbar in the trunk."

As Doug walked to the back of his car, Rusty teased him. "Do you always carry a crowbar with you?"

Opening the trunk, Doug got out his crowbar. "Yeah, right." Doug laughed. "Seriously, we had a call from the MacIntosh farm the other day. Their little boy wandered inside their shed and, somehow, managed to lock the door from the inside. They couldn't get him out. I had to use the crowbar to get the door open. I just forgot to take the tool out of the car and put it away.

The bank gave me the key to the back door so we'll go in there. Here," he said, handing a large flashlight to Rusty. "From the looks of the boarded windows, we might need this to find a light switch once we get inside."

"Maybe not." Rusty took the flashlight as he tilted his head toward the sky. "The sun is pretty bright. There may be light shining through the cracks of the boards."

The two of them chatted as they walked the short distance from their parked cars to the backdoor of the house.

"Was the MacIntosh boy all right?"

"Yes, he was fine. Scared to death, but happy to get back into his mother's arms."

"By the way, did you bring nails and a hammer with you to board the door back up?" Rusty inquired.

"If I didn't know the place was boarded up, why would I have thought to bring a hammer and nails?"

"Just thought you might have them in the trunk, too." Rusty chuckled.

"Yeah. Well, I wish I did. Then I'd given you that job."

Once they removed the boards, Doug unlocked the door and the two of them went inside the farmhouse. Rusty was right. There was plenty of daylight creeping through the boarded windows. They could see without the use of a light. Careful not to touch anything, they walked around looking at everything.

"The computer's in there," Doug said, heading toward the large sitting room.

"Damn, it looks like the spiders and field mice have taken over this place," Rusty observed, following Doug. "Look at the rocks and glass on the floor. Wouldn't you think kids would have something better to do with their time then throw rocks through the windows of empty houses?"

"I'm not surprised by the broken glass, but I am shocked that no one has tried to break in. At least it doesn't appear so." After entering the sitting room, Doug headed to the computer. "Well, it's definitely a big difference in here from when I was here a year ago. At that time, this place was spotless. It looked as though that little gal may not have had too much in the brain department, but she sure knew how to clean."

Looking around the room, Rusty commented. "According to all these books, Jefferson must have loved reading—either him or his wife. I imagine all of these things will go at an auction when the property ownership gets settled."

Rusty walked to the computer, where Doug was standing.

Doug was silent as he searched for a start button on the computer. Finally locating it he said, "There we go. This is an old model. It'll need a minute or two to warm up. Either Welk had this machine for a very long time, or someone took advantage of him and sold him a relic."

"Why do you say that?"

"This model is an antique by today's standards." Doug wiped his hands together to brush off the dust his fingers collected when he touched the dust-laden computer.

"I'm sure glad you know how to run one of these things because it's totally foreign to me," Rusty admitted. "The mayor wants to put one of these complicated machines in our office. I keep hoping he'll wait until after I retire this year."

"Come on, Rusty. Don't tell me you let a machine intimidate you?" Doug joked, followed by, "I can't believe you're ready to retire."

"Yeah, come September."

"Hey, look," Doug said, picking up a small opened box of computer disks that sat next to the computer. After checking them out, he handed them to Rusty. "There's some luck." Doug removed the computer disk from the envelope in his hands. Look. They're the same brand as this one."

Checking over the disks in the box, and looking at the disk Doug was holding, Rusty agreed. "You're right, they are, Doug. There appears to be just one missing from this box. That means we are closer to the possibility that disk did come from here. Say, excuse my computer ignorance, but I'm curious about something?"

"What?"

"There's all kinds of computers over at the Sharpin bank. Why didn't you just ask to use one of them to see what was on that disk your holding?"

"Good question, Colombo. Long noses. Is that a good enough answer for you?" Before Rusty could come back with a comment, other than his guttered laughter, Doug informed him, "Okay, the computer's ready."

"Do all computers use the same kind of disks?"

"Can't say as I know for sure. To be honest, I'm still learning about computers. But I can tell you, this one doesn't look like the other type disks I've seen. Let's see what's on this disk."

"Do they all take time to warm up?"

"No, not the newer models. Say, that's a good point."

"What is?"

"This computer is an older model. So, the disks it uses should just be formatted for this computer model. That would make this disk easier to match to the ones in that box your holding."

"Good thinking, Doug. Not that I have the slightest idea what you're talking about, but I'll take your word for it."

Rusty stood by, watching over Doug's shoulder. Doug inserted the disk he had brought with him into the computer slot. He played around with the keyboard until he brought up the disk's information onto the small computer screen. As the information unfolded, Rusty leaned in to get a clearer look.

"I'll be a monkey's uncle," Rusty roared with joy, almost breaking poor Doug's eardrum. Rusty placed his hands on Doug's shoulders, then in his excitement, started shaking him. "Doug, my friend, you have just hit the *mother-lode!*" Rusty exclaimed.

"Hey, let go, Rusty. You're hurting me."

"Oh, I'm sorry, Doug. I didn't mean to get so carried away."

"I was only kidding, but wait until you get my doctor's bill."

Knowing that Doug was pulling his leg, Rusty gave Doug a friendly slap on the back. "I haven't been this excited since I don't know when."

"Do you mind telling me what all these dates and figures mean?" Doug asked, wanting in on the excitement Rusty was illuminating.

"You bet. See the name Darin? In case you don't remember, that's the kid's name that I've got locked up in jail right now."

"Yes, I recognize the name."

"I've thought all along that he's the Neat Nick Thief, and this may help me prove it. See those amounts of money?" Rusty asked, pointing to the screen. "With the exception of that first amount and a couple of other items, the rest of the entries are the individual amounts taken in each of the burglaries from that three-year period before I arrested Darin. Come to think of it, I bet the first amount recorded there would equal the same amount of money taken from the first burglaries totaled together. That would make sense, since the first few thefts aren't recorded there."

"Are you sure, Rusty?"

"I've never worked on such a big case before, Doug. Believe me, I've got those amounts engraved in my brain. I don't understand that one entry that says 'undetermined amount of gold coins', but I bet I know where that coin collection came from. Oh, the D.A. is going to love this. Hot-diggidy damn, Doug. If you were a woman, I'd kiss you."

"I'm not, so don't even think about it," Doug stated with a grin. "How does Welk fit into this?"

"Beats the devil out of me. But, if I were to take a wild guess, it looks like he must have been the hideout person—the banker. And, if that's the case, the money is still around here someplace." Rusty thought a minute then changed his mind. "Wait, when did you say that Welk died?"

"It'll be one year, tomorrow."

"Well that was in April ... " Rusty paused to figure in his head. "Darin quit his job and was ready to take off around the first or second week of June, last year. So my theory wouldn't be right. That means that Darin would have probably already been here to get the money so he could have left town with it. I sure would like to know where that money is hidden.

We searched Frank's house and all of his property. Came up empty. Which, of course, is to Darin's advantage. Let's check out the rest of the house while we're here," Rusty suggested. He snapped his fingers. "Say, I just had another thought."

Removing the disk and placing it back in the envelope he had carried it in, Doug turned off the computer. Turning to Rusty, he asked, "What's that?"

"If the bankers were here when you and Ward left, maybe some dishonest person with sticky fingers found the dough and took it for themselves."

"Damn, Rusty. Do you think so?"

"It's possible. It would be mighty tempting to find that much money just laying around somewhere. Someone could have found it. Then come back, alone, and taken it. None of it can be traced. So, who would be the wiser? It certainly would make sense as to what happened to the money if Welk was stashing it for Darin."

Rusty rubbed his forehead. "I sure wish I knew if I was right, or not. I'd love to see the look on Darin's face when he found out his stolen money was stolen from him. He'd be spending a whole lot more time behind those bars paying for his crime, while some unknown person was out spending the money—free and clear. Wouldn't that be a wonderful quirk of fate."

"On the other hand," Doug remarked, "the money might still be hidden somewhere around here. Right?"

"That's a possibility."

"Then again, you told me how vast this farm is. The money could be buried almost anywhere."

"I don't think so, Doug, and I'll tell you why I say that. Assuming that computer disk proves to be legit, and Jefferson was hiding the money, I don't think he would have hidden it too far from his immediate reach. Of course, the outside barns and sheds will have to be searched, as well as here in the house, but the vast acreage of farmland might be a different story. I think that would be like searching for a lost gold mine in the mountains. No, as elderly as Jefferson was, my bet is he kept the money close enough to keep an eye on it."

"From the excitement you displayed a few minutes ago, you do believe this disk is legitimate, don't you?"

"You bet I do. But it will be up to the D.A. to convince a jury that it is."

As the men walked around they were careful, at that point, not to do any extensive searching. That would have to wait until they got the official legal go ahead through the judicial system. They were legally in the house, now, to check out the computer disk. Searching the premises was a different story. After they finished walking around the house, they exited.

"Maybe we should look around to see what we can find to put the boards back up," Rusty stated.

"You might need back in the house to look for the money, Rusty. Let's wait. The door can always be boarded back up later, when your investigation is complete. We'll just make sure it's locked up tight for now. I'll have my deputy come out tonight and keep watch on the place."

They walked back to Doug's car. "Boy, you were sure right about a small, modest home, Doug. The whole house would have probably fit in two rooms of the old mansion."

"You mean you got to see inside this Kidwell mansion you told me about?"

"Never. I just remember Grandpa telling me about it. He had the honor of visiting the Kidwell's on a few occasions. He said the mansion was a true vision of opulence. It could have been anyplace around here." Rusty looked around, taking in all his eyes could see. "There's a lot of history here. What a shame it all had to be bad. Sometime, I would like to come out here and walk around this property to find those graves. If Jefferson is buried at the Cole County cemetery, I think he should be moved here to be with the rest of his family.

Well, no sense it standing around here chewing the fat. Look, Doug, I think you made a mistake earlier when you said *my* investigation. In all sincerity, how do you want to handle this information we have?"

"No mistake, Rusty. It's your baby. Here." Doug handed the envelope to Rusty. "Take the computer disk with you. Since you think this is all connected to your Neat Nick Thief and the kid you have in jail, well, it's your ball. Run with it. If you need any help with anything, just give me a holler. Oh, and here, take the key to this place, too. I'll tell the bank you have it."

"If that's the case, then don't send your deputy out here. I'll have one of my men stand vigilance on the house."

"Sounds good to me. See you around."

Doug tossed his crowbar and flashlight into the front seat of his car. Rusty watched as he drove away. Then he got into his own car and left the property. Driving back to town, Rusty felt ecstatic. He had gotten some very important evidence against Darin. That pleased him because he knew Darin was sitting in jail laughing at the law. Nevertheless, the other half of the coin had to show up. When Rusty thought how this would hurt his dear friend, Frank, his joy turned to despair.

In the next few weeks, Rusty received his Search Warrant. Sticking to the main grounds of the property, he and his officers scoured every inch of Jefferson's house and all other buildings on the property. They came up empty handed as far as hard evidence was concerned. They picked up and bagged several odd items that they thought might be important. The small box of computer disks and the computer were confiscated. As an officer lifted the computer from its dusty tabletop, he discovered a large brown, sealed envelope underneath. Rusty took the envelope.

Back at the police station, the officers recorded everything into the evidence files. Then they locked the box of disks and the bag of miscellaneous items, taken from the farmhouse, in the evidence locker. The computer was placed in Rusty's office. Rusty had opened the sealed envelope. When he assumed that it just contained personal papers of Jefferson Welk, and nothing to do with his case against Darin, he placed the papers back into the envelope. He placed the envelope and the disk on top the computer so he would know exactly where they were.

Rusty had already told the D.A. about the computer disk, so, he phoned him. As Rusty waited for an answer, he could picture George in his kaki wash-n-wear pants and wearing a dress shirt with the sleeves rolled up. The D.A. never wore a tie and jacket unless he had to appear in court. Because he thought it was the 'in' thing to do, he always wore white athletic shoes. George parted his brown hair down the middle, but every hair on his head was always neatly in place. Rusty swore that George used a gallon of hair spray on it. With this image of the D.A. in his mind, Rusty was laughing under his breath when George answered his phone.

"District Attorney's Office."

"George, since it's after 7:00, I'm glad I caught you still in your office."

Recognizing Rusty's voice, George's laughter resounded into Rusty's ear. "*Still* is right. My wife is beginning to think I live in my office. What can I do for you, Rusty?"

"A couple of my officers and I spent the whole day searching the Welk farm from top to bottom, and every nook and cranny in between."

"Any luck?"

"Not too much, just a bag of debris. I don't think any of it will amount too much in the way of evidence, so we just locked it up for now. If we don't get a solid case against Darin, I'll ship the whole bag to the FBI Crime Lab and see if they can find any prints or hairs on any of the stuff that can help us," Rusty reported.

"I see." George replied, showing his disappointment in the tone of his voice.

"It's all going to be a long shot, as the place had already been gone thorough by those banking people I told you about. Who knows, maybe some government officials have been in there also."

"Sorry you guys wasted a whole day for nothing, Rusty, but I think we're in good shape as far as a case against Darin is concerned. Say, did you get me that computer so I can look at the disk you told me about?"

"Yes, we got the computer. We also found an envelope full of paperwork. I just scanned through some of the documents, but I noticed a Last Will and Testament is amongst the papers. The papers don't seem to have anything to do with Darin, but I still think you should look at them. Do you want to view the disk and the papers here, or do you want everything at your office?"

"I'd rather have them here, Rusty. As far as the envelope of papers is concerned—since you said you only scanned them—I'll go through them real careful-like just to make sure there isn't any evidence in them. I can send someone from my office over tomorrow morning to pick everything up."

"That'll be fine, George. Make sure it's a strong somebody," Rusty said with a chuckle. "That computer isn't any featherweight."

"I know. We have a couple of those heavy mothers in our office. If you'd stop by more often, you'd know that."

"True," Rusty agreed. "I know we work on small town protocol, but just to cover my back-end, I'll have a Chain of Custody form ready to be signed when the items are picked up."

"Okay," George replied in agreement. "Now, unless you have something else, Rusty, I don't mean to cut you short but I've got to get back to work. I'd like to go home sometime tonight."

"No, nothing else. Talk to you tomorrow."

Rusty was so close to nailing Darin that he could almost taste success.

Black Rosebud

He was just steps away in keeping Darin behind bars for a few more years. All Rusty had to do now was to get Darin to tell him where he had hidden the money. Locating the missing money would solve the Neat Nick Thief mystery. Then it would be just another closed file. Unfortunately, there are no guarantees in life. Not even for the good guys.

GUILTY OR INNOCENT

Inside the courtroom, John took his seat at the defense table. Removing his notes for trial from his briefcase, he placed them on the table for easy referral.

Just behind the defense table, Frank sat waiting. This would be the first time in almost a year that he would see Darin without bars separating them.

Sitting at the prosecution's table, the D.A. and his assistant were engaged in conversation.

In the spectator's seats, behind the prosecution's table, sat Police Chief Simmons, Officer Seals, Wallace Dodd and Special Agent Coats. Sheriff Martin was on hand in case the court needed his testimony. Victims of the burglaries, news media, and curiosity seekers filled the rest of the spectator's section.

An officer of the court escorted Darin to the defense table where Darin took a seat next to John. Since John had already met with Darin early that morning for last minute consultation, there was no need to exchange greetings. Wondering what the people looked like who would be sitting in judgment of his innocence or guilt, Darin fixed his eyes on the empty jury box. Frank reached forward and patted Darin on the back. Darin ignored him.

The bailiff addressed all those present in the courtroom. "All rise." As everyone rose to their feet, he proclaimed, "Here ye. Here ye. The Superior Court in the State of Nebraska is now in session. Judge J. J. Swanson, presiding. There will be silence in the courtroom. No talking. No reading. No eating. No smoking. No cameras."

Judge Swanson entered from his chamber door and took the bench.

"You may be seated," the bailiff stated.

The judge put on his glasses and glanced through paperwork in front of him. Somberly he looked at the courtroom of people. Then he made his opening announcement. "The trial of the State of Nebraska versus Darin George Righter in the matter of burglary is scheduled to be heard today." The judge tapped his gavel. "Is the State ready?"

"Yes, your Honor, the State is ready," answered the D.A., rising briefly then sitting back in his chair. Having already met with the D.A. before court, Judge Swanson smiled in recognition of the district attorney's response.

"Is the Defense ready?"

Standing to address the bench, John offered, "The Defense is ready, your Honor."

"Good morning, John. Good to see you in court this morning. How does your client wish to plead?"

Still seated, Darin blurted, "I plead not guilty."

John grabbed Darin's arm and gave him a look of annoyance. Focusing back to the bench, John pleaded, "Forgive the outburst, your Honor. I can assure you, it will not happen again. With the Court's permission, I would like to have a moment to confer with my client."

After getting the green light from the judge, John leaned in to Darin and whispered, "Shut your big mouth or the judge will hold you in contempt of court, and I'll walk, leaving you on your own."

Turning back to the judge's bench John requested, "Your Honor, I wish to ask for a continuance due to the fact that I was not given vital information in this case from the District Attorney's Office until after 10:00, last night. Now, I won't be as imprudent as to say that the D.A. did this on purpose so I would come to court this morning unable to defend against their so called last minute discovery. However, it does appear a bit suspicious considering the time line."

Rushing to his feet, the D.A. responded, "Your Honor, I object."

"Overruled. Sit down, George. I will get to you in a minute. Now, John, just how long do you figure you'll need to go over the D.A.'s discovery information and ready your rebuttal?"

"I'll need at least thirty days, your Honor," John answered.

"Okay, George, your turn," Judge Swanson said as he nodded at George, adding, "Sit down, John."

"Now your Honor, in response to Mr. Johnston's request for continuance, I submit that in a 1979 case, the State of Florida versus

Hendrix, the Third District Court of Appeals ruled that a late discovery, in and for itself, was not sufficient grounds for a continuance. Therefore, your Honor, I feel Mr. Johnston has no grounds for continuance and the trial of Darin George Righter should continue without further delay."

"You are correct, George," the judge agreed. "The motion from the Defense is overruled."

Displeased with the ruling, John jumped to his feet. "Your Honor, with all due respect, I highly object and wish my objection to be noted in the trial records."

"Let it be duly noted at this time that Defense Attorney, John Johnston, objects to his motion of continuance being overruled." John sat back in his chair as the judge addressed the courtroom. "At this time, all witnesses, and those having any information in this trial, will follow the bailiff to the witness room where you will remain until called to give testimony, or be dismissed. You will not discuss this case or your part in it with any other person or witness. Bailiff, escort these people from the courtroom, please."

As Rusty stood, others who had information essential to the case, including Frank, also got to their feet. They followed the bailiff out of the room. The rest of the court sat in silence until the bailiff returned.

"Bailiff, bring the jury in and start opening statements," the judge requested.

The bailiff opened the door to the jury room and motioned the jurors to enter the courtroom. As they took their seats, one by one, Darin took a good look at each of their faces. He was curious if he knew any of them. His chin fell to the floor when he realized each jury member was a complete stranger. The short time it took for the jury to file in, the D.A. scanned through the pages of his legal pad, going over his notes for his opening statement.

With the jury seated, Judge Swanson gestured a short nod to the D.A. "Mr. Prosecutor, your opening statement." In an energetic mannerism, George rose from his chair and faced the jury. Therein the case of the State of Nebraska versus Darin George Righter began.

"Good morning, Ladies and Gentleman of the Jury. For those of you who don't know me, let me introduce myself. That will also give the news media and the court reporter an excellent opportunity to spell my name correctly."

For those present who knew the D.A.'s name, a roar of laughter broke out in the courtroom. The judge, expressing a brief chuckle, tapped his gavel to regain silence and control of the courtroom. "Okay, Mr. District

Attorney, let's not forget that we are in a court of law."

"Yes, and I apologize, your Honor."

My name is George Smith, and I am the district attorney here in Cole County." He cleared his throat. "In this trial we will prove beyond a reasonable doubt that the defendant, Darin George Righter, within a time span of twenty-nine months, did commit more than twenty burglaries, all of which took place in Cole County. We will show you motive and opportunity."

Darin smirked as he listened to the D.A. *There were a total of twenty-eight burglaries, thank you very much.*

"The State will show you evidence that puts the break-in tool in the hands of the defendant. The State will also show that this defendant in an effort to mislead wore his own brother's boots when he committed these burglaries. We will introduce to this court a computer disk that will connect a direct link between Darin George Righter and all reported burglaries in this case.

The State will not only prove, but also show that the Kidwell Police caught the defendant red-handed in his final burglary. After the State introduces its evidence, there will be no doubt that you, Ladies and Gentlemen of the Jury, will find the defendant, Darin George Righter, guilty."

Having completed his opening statements, the D.A. turned away from the jury. He briskly walked back to the table and took his seat.

Judge Swanson asked, "Mr. Johnson, do you have opening remarks at this time?"

John stood. "Yes, your Honor." Dramatizing his every movement, John approached the jury box. Somber faced, he greeted the jurors. "Ladies and Gentlemen of the Jury, good morning to you. You have just listened to the words of my esteemed colleague. I must say after hearing his accusations toward my client, he should have had an extra cup of strong coffee this morning so he could remember the difference between circumstantial evidence and fact," John stated, getting a bit of muffled snickers from the courtroom.

"Ladies and gentlemen, I know you are fair and impartial, and will do your duty according to the law and not your personal feelings in this case. We have an innocent young man here," he pointed and looked in Darin's direction, then, once again, focused his attention to the jurors as he continued, "who is an intelligent, loving, caring person, but still a kid at heart.

Anyone from this area that knows the defendant, Darin Righter, can tell you how he loves to play harmless pranks on people. Let me emphasize the word *harmless.* We will show that on the night the police arrested the defendant, he was in the process of playing one of his harmless pranks on the victim in this case, Mr. Oscar Denton. This, in fact, is Darin's unique way of welcoming a new citizen to the Cole County area. Because the police caught Darin playing this one-minute prank, the State would like you to believe that he is their, so-called, Neat Nick Thief."

If you'll bear with me for a moment, let's take a trip to Hawaii. Just because a Hawaiian native jumps off an island cliff into the ocean, and creates an enormous wave that rushes up smashing against the rocks, does not mean that native was responsible for or caused the tidal wave that destroyed the island, months later. This analogy can be compared, apples to apples, in this case against my client. One night, and one night only, the defendant was in the wrong place at the wrong time. He admits that. Darin admits that he is a prankster. But because he is a prankster, that doesn't make him responsible for the rash of burglaries in Cole County."

Standing in one place as he spoke, John scanned the juror's faces, watching for any kind of affirmative facial expression. "We will prove through testimony that the defendant couldn't have, and *wouldn't have,*" he stressed, "committed the burglaries in question, nor could he even remotely be connected with the Neat Nick Thief burglaries."

John stopped talking and walked back to the front of the defense table. In very deliberate moves, he poured himself a glass of water. After a long drink, he placed the glass back on the table. Taking his handkerchief from lapel pocket, he dabbed his mouth ever so gently, displaying good manners. When replacing his handkerchief, John made sure the ends were protruding neatly from the lapel pocket. He was hoping his dramatic actions gave the jurors time to consider his every word. After walking back to the jury box, the defense attorney concluded his opening statement. "Ladies and Gentlemen of the Jury, as this case is presented, there will be no doubt that the evidence against my client, the defendant Darin George Righter, is totally circumstantial. Thank you."

In slow but deliberate steps, John meandered back to his table, returning to his chair.

"Do to the hour," the judge commented, "I would like to break for lunch and reconvene at 1:00 p.m., sharp."

After the judge gave the jury their orders for not discussing the case until the court had a chance to hear all evidence, he dismissed them. The judge tapped his gavel for dismissal. Upon the bailiff's instructions, everyone stood silent as Judge Swanson left the courtroom. Once the judge was out of sight, it seemed everyone started talking at once as the scramble began to exit the courtroom.

Darin started throwing questions at John when a court guard approached to escort him back to lock-up.

"I'll talk to you later, Darin," John stated as he packed his briefcase.

Out in the hallway, Frank pushed his way through the crowd that was rushing out of the courtroom. When he spotted John, he raised his voice to get his attention. "John. Wait up." When he heard a voice call out to him, John looked around. Seeing Frank motioning, John walked toward him. "John, what went on in there? What did I miss?" Frank asked as John approached him.

"You know I can't tell you that," John admitted. "Look, Frank, the judge broke for lunch earlier than usual. We don't have to be back here for two hours. Why don't you go home and get some rest. You won't be any good to Darin if you're too sick to be here when we need you to testify on his behalf." Not needing an excuse to rest, Frank nodded in agreement, turned, and walked away in his now normal slow pace.

As Frank reached the front door of the courthouse, he overheard the district attorney talking to Rusty. "I agree, Rusty, and it doesn't take a rocket scientist to know that the burglaries stopped the minute you locked up Darin. Given the fact that Darin laid low for a few months, your bait brought him out of temporary retirement. This is a cut and dried case. I predict it will be over—" As soon as George spotted Frank, and felt he had overheard his conversation with Rusty, George stopped talking and waited for Frank to walk by.

As Frank passed, he looked at George then glanced over at Rusty. As if in slow motion, Frank shook his head. Rusty could see the sadness in his friend's eyes.

When Frank was out of earshot, George stated, "Blast it. I didn't know he was behind me."

"Sorry, I didn't seem him coming," Rusty apologized.

Reaching in his briefcase and extracting a large brown envelope, George handed the envelope to Rusty. "Would you have one of your officers rush this over to the Sharpin bank and personally deliver it to the president? I called him so he knows to expect it."

Taking the envelope, Rusty inquired, "What's in it?"

"Important papers. That computer disk you gave me from Jefferson Welk had some information on it, other than the financial accounts and dates data. Seems Welk left his property and all his possessions to his daughter and—" Scratching his head, George admitted, "I didn't know the man on a personal basis, but I sure never heard he had a kid."

"I did, but I've always assumed that she's dead. Maybe Welk had his Will drawn up years ago, George."

"No. The Will is dated just a few years ago."

"Interesting."

"I guess it won't make any difference. According to the bank, Mr. Welk died a pauper. They're still holding the property in probate. They're having some darn fool debate over who is to take the property, the bank or the government." Already aware of the probate issue concerning Jefferson's property, Rusty nodded. "All I can say is, I'm glad I'm a district attorney." George chuckled. "I wouldn't want to be handling that case for either party.

Remember that envelope of papers you found under the computer?"

"When we were searching Jefferson's house?"

"Yes. Well, I released that packet of papers to the bank because they are, at present, the executor's of the estate. The envelope had a handwritten copy of his Last—Listen to me. You're the one that pointed it out to me."

"Yes," Rusty agreed.

"That reminds me, I have that signed custody release paper for that envelope in my office." George pointed to the envelope Rusty was holding. "I'll get it to you later, Rusty. I'm getting off track here. We need to deliver that envelope to the bank because it contains a printout of the Will we found on the disk. The bank is going to compare its contents to the handwritten one."

Rusty rubbed his head in confusion. "I don't follow you. Why the personal delivery for a printed copy of the Will when the bank already has the original in his handwriting? Why would you want them compared to one another?"

"Because," George beamed, patting Rusty on the shoulder, "if they are an exact match, the printout and the handwritten one, that makes our computer disk authentic. In other words, our prestigious attorney, John, cannot throw the disk out of court. The comparison will prove that the disk was indeed made by Jefferson Welk."

"You're good, George. I just knew you would come up with a way to prove that disk was legit." Rusty smiled with joy.

"That's why I need to get that packet over to the bank, ASAP, and handed in person to the president, C. D. Shomond.

Also, there is our State's Chain of Custody, which I know you're quite familiar with. Instead of giving you all the legal mumble jumble, let me get right to the meat. Sheriff Luden retrieved the disk from Welk's home and placed it into evidence. Unfortunately, his death left the disk sitting there until its recent discovery by Sheriff Martin. Then he released the disk to you.

Lucky for us, Doug had you sign the release. Then you, in turn, had my office sign the release of the disk into our hands. So, the chain of custody from the time it was confiscated until today bears the proper signatures. Therefore, it becomes solid evidence against Darin."

"Pardon my legal ignorance, George. If this printed Will is so important, why wasn't it sent to Shomond before now?"

"I broke one of the biggest rules that an attorney lives by. I assumed, after John read the discovery evidence we had against his client, that he would plead out so we would never get this far in court." George shrugged. "I take full responsibility for letting the ball drop. Thankfully, Judge Swanson broke for lunch when he did. This break gives me the opportunity to redeem myself. But, I've got to find out the results of the comparison before court reconvenes at 1:00."

"You know, George, a two-hour lunch is highly irregular for court. I don't suppose you had anything to do with getting Judge Swanson to give you an extra hour to pick up that ball you dropped?"

Both men had a good laugh, as George replied, "Why, Chief Simmons, I don't know what you're insinuating."

Since time was of the essence, Rusty signed the release form, and they parted company.

Court convened again at 1:00 p.m. on the dot. Both the prosecuting attorney and the defense attorney's sides gave their testimonies.

The State proved that Frank Righter's father had special ordered a set of hand-carved tools direct from the manufacturer back in 1940. According to the manufacturer's marks on the tools, the FBI was able to search out old records to verify this was the same set of tools that Rusty had found in Frank's tool shed. The same maker's mark on the screwdriver discovered in Oscar Denton's house, proved the screwdriver belonged to the same tool set.

The slight broken edge of the screwdriver's tip was an exact match to the jimmy marks left on every block of wood that Rusty had taken into evidence from each of the burglary victim's homes, including Oscar Denton's home.

According to the FBI expert witness, Special Agent Leo Coats, the print casts taken from three of the victim's homes, and from Frank's farm, were exact matches to the worn soles of the rubber work boots that belonged to Frank. Rusty's testimony about witnessing Darin wearing the boots was another undeniable factor that the jury found hard to ignore.

Darin almost freaked out when hearing Jefferson Welk had written incriminating evidence on his computer. Not only had Welk confessed to hiding the money for Darin, but he also had recorded every monitory amount Darin had given him and the dates received. Most of the dates and the amounts of money taken from the Cole County burglaries matched Rusty's records as reported by the victims.

The one item not accounted for in Rusty's records was the item termed 'gold coins.' After Rusty's testimony, the D.A. concluded that there was a victim-at-large too embarrassed to come forward and state they had been burglarized. Therefore, the thief got away with his precious gold coins.

The cherry atop the whipped cream was when not one of Darin's alibis for all the nights in question had checked out. No one person could prove positive or state under oath where Darin was on those nights the burglaries had occurred. Because of Frank's health, neither John nor George called him to the stand. Darin's future was looking very grim.

Seemingly exasperated, John looked up at the judge. "Your Honor, if the court pleases."

"Yes, John."

"I would like to request a short recess so I can confer with my client."

Judge Swanson looked at his watch before he replied, "It's getting late. Court will be in recess until 10:00, tomorrow morning. Request granted. Court adjourned." With the tap of the gavel, court was over for the day.

John arranged to talk to Darin in the holding area. As John waited, he paced the floor, mulling over in his mind exactly what he was going to say to Darin. He had no more than taken a seat at the long conference table when Darin entered the room and sat across the table, facing him.

"Well, Darin, you're in what's commonly known as a world of dog crap. There's not much I can do for you." John leaned in and rested his arms on the table. "It's over, Darin. There's no doubt the jury will find you guilty and you'll be looking at a minimum of ten years. As I told you earlier in one of our consultations, you'll have to serve at least seven to be eligible for parole."

"Come on, John, isn't there anything you can do? I won't be able to handle seven years. Please, John, help me," Darin pleaded.

John sat back in his chair and looked Darin straight in his face, eye to eye. "We may be able to work something out with the D.A. and then, I hope, get the judge's approval on it. If you will change your plea, right now, I can try to get you four years. In all probability, you would have to serve three and then be eligible for parole."

"No way, John! I told you that I'm not guilty. This is a crock," Darin yelled, slamming his fist on the table. Almost leaping from his chair, he waked over to the room's barred window. "You're all trying to friggin' railroad me. To hell with you and everyone else."

"No, Darin, *you* go straight to hell," John barked back "I've just about had enough of your childish fits. This is the best I can do for you. Take my offer, now, or you can go to jail and profess your innocence to your cellmates for the next ten years. This is the only option left on the table. Take it or leave it. But let me know, here and now, because I'm not waiting around for you to decide to grow up."

Darin stared out the window but was deep in thought. He didn't see a thing he was looking at. John sat in silence, waiting for Darin's response.

Damn Welk! With his help, they really built a case against me. I didn't think I would get any time over and above what I've already served. I guess I'm lucky if John thinks he can get me a shorter sentence. I'm almost positive the cops haven't found the money or they would certainly have said something in court. If I'm out of here in three, I'll still be young enough to enjoy my money.

On top of that, I'll have my trust fund waiting for me. I'll be rich, rich, rich, and in my prime of life. Best of all, they can't try me again. Rusty might be smarter than I gave him credit for, but I'll still have the last laugh when I'm living high off the hog. I've held the winning hand all along, so I win the pot. I better take the deal John's talking about. Count my blessings and take while the takings good.

Darin turned back toward his attorney. "I'm sorry, John. If you can make the deal, I'll stand on your judgment call."

"Glory be. That's the smartest thing I've heard come out of your mouth in a long time. Now, how about showing me a little respect, Darin. Come back over here and sit in your chair. Start acting like a gentleman, and save those childish outbursts for someone who deserves it." As Darin returned to his seat, he looked like a whipped dog. "There's one thing you have to remember when you plead guilty, Darin. There are no appeals.

It's over."

"I didn't know that, or maybe I don't remember you telling me. But, I understand. Will I get credit for the time I've already spent in jail?"

"I wouldn't count on it, but that's up to the judge. You spent how long in jail, nine months?"

"Ten."

"I'll have the officer take you back to your cell. Then I'll go see the D.A. You try and get some rest and I'll see you first thing in the morning."

John called George, arranging to see him, right away. Upon arrival at the district attorney's law offices, John was ushered into George's private office.

As they shook hands George asked, "What's on your mind, John?"

"Let's make a deal," John said rather light hearted, easing the tension of the day's trial. "I'll plead Darin out in the morning, if we can deal."

George laughed. "I don't know about that John. I think we have a pretty solid case against your client. Add that to the fact that the courts gave us permission to open his past juvenile records, the conviction is a done deal. But, since I'm the curious type, tell me what's in it for me?"

"Well, you're a public servant, George. No offense, but they don't give you a PR man to help build up your job or the responsibilities you have in your work."

"Quit beating around the bush, or as they say, cut to the chase. Tell me where you're going with this."

"Here it is. I know you're running for re-election this year. Wouldn't it be a feather in your cap if you could show the voters that you nailed a conviction on the Neat Nick Thief, and saved the county money by accepting a guilty plea instead of spending more of the taxpayers dollars for further court expenses?"

"John, you're something else," George expressed with humor. "You always were a promoter. I guess that's why you make the big bucks and I'm a public servant, as you so nicely put it. Okay, what do you have in mind?"

"Drop the Neat Nick Thief case against my client. He'll cop out on the Denton break-in. He takes four years, serves three and is eligible for parole. I admit that is saving about four years off Darin's time. Never the less, you're getting your guilty plea and saving the county a bundle of money. That would sure look good to the electorate."

"Okay, okay. You proved your point. A sure conviction on a plea bargain is better than—If Judge Swanson approves the plea then I'll go along with it. You know, John, you should have been a PR man, not an attorney." George laughed.

At 9:30, the next morning, John and George sat with the judge in his chambers. After informing the judge of their discussion the night before, both attorneys jointly requested the approval of the plea bargain. Judge Swanson accepted.

John took the legal papers for the plea bargain to Darin for his signature. Not bothering to read the document, Darin signed on the dotted line.

In the meantime, the bailiff, in accordance to the judge's orders, had gone to the witness room and excused all witnesses and those who were to give testimony in the trial. Once excused, the small group filed into the courtroom to find out why their testimonies were no longer needed. Frank took a seat behind John, who was already sitting at the defense table.

Escorted into the courtroom, Darin kept his eyes to the floor until he took his seat next to John. Frank patted Darin on the back just to let him know he was there. The arrogant, yet whipped Darin never turned to acknowledge Frank's presence.

Court started at exactly 10:00 a.m. All present took their seats after the judge entered the courtroom. His Honor dismissed the jury, explaining the defendant had changed his plea to guilty. He thanked them for their time. Next, the judge requested that Darin, John and George approach the bench.

As the three men stood in front of the bench, Judge Swanson addressed the defendant. "Darin George Righter, you have changed your plea to guilty. Is this decision to change your plea, your own?"

"Yes, your Honor, sir," Darin answered.

"Have you been coerced in any way to change your plea, and do you understand that a guilty plea forfeits your rights to appeal and that you will be sentenced today?"

Darin swallowed. He answered to the best of his recollection of what John had informed him. "Your Honor, this is my decision. I understand that I forfeit certain rights, and I am ready to receive my sentence."

"All right, Darin, this being your first offense, I sentence you to four years prison time. However, I will give you credit for the ten months you have spent awaiting trial. After two years, you will be eligible for parole. Your time is to be served-out in the State Penitentiary in Lincoln." Darin's heart sank to his feet. "Darin, I would like to hope that you have learned a valuable lesson, and that you turn your life around when you are released from prison." Having said that, the judge tapped his gavel, concluding, "Court adjourned."

Darin never said one word as the guard took him away.

Frank couldn't move. He seemed almost frozen to the hard, cold wood of the courtroom bench. Closing his eyes, he thought about his joke when Darin had made his birthday wish just a couple of years prior. *Be careful of what you wish for, Darin, because it may come true.*

John turned to talk to Frank and noticed his closed eyes. Deciding it was one of those moments when even he couldn't find words to console Frank, John took his briefcase and left the courtroom.

Rusty, also, left the courtroom without saying one word to Frank. Rusty's compassion for his friend brought about the thought, *Many times out of concern for the weary, silence is truly golden.*

Rusty was extremely upset that the D.A. settled for a plea bargain and for just one burglary. He knew the judicial system had Darin dead to rights as the thief he had been chasing. However, he was a law officer, not an attorney. Like it or not, he had to settle for the fact that at least Darin garnered a few years in the State Pen.

Even though court was over, Rusty's mind was not at rest. He had a puzzle to put together but there were a few missing pieces. There wasn't a doubt in his mind that Darin fit into his puzzle in a big way, he just didn't know how.

However, there was that question of uncertainty. If, per chance, Darin really wasn't the Neat Nick Thief, then who was it? Another issue bothering him was the taunting question of what happened to the missing money? If Darin was the thief, Rusty wanted to make sure Darin, when released from prison, never got his hands on it again. Was the money hidden somewhere or did someone else abscond with it?

Rusty didn't have the answers, but someone did. Perhaps if he could find that someone and the money, the puzzle pieces would fall into place.

THE UNKNOWN

Tapping the back of his fellow detective as he passed his desk, Joel said, "Come on, Steve."

Steve Kempel was a good detective, but hadn't been on the force as long as Joel. They had worked together for six years so they were very close during work hours and on their own time. Just two years earlier, Steve had married his childhood sweetheart. They were expecting their first child. Steve was a good cop but he knew how to leave the crime at the office. While at home, Steve set aside his badge and his gun until the next time he needed them.

Steve was talking on the telephone with his wife when Joel approached him. "Just a minute, honey." Placing the phone's receiver against his chest, he asked. "What's up, Joel?"

"Someone reported a dead body laying in an alley over in the warehouse district. Let's go."

Steve ended his phone conversation. "I'll call you later."

As Joel walked to the door, Steve followed. "Whose on lead?"

"The chief gave this one to me."

"It's about time. Do you have the address?"

"Yeah. That's why I'm taking the wheel."

Joel Applemeyer had worked hard to get from beat cop to a homicide detective on the Chicago Police Force. For the eight years he had been a detective at the 23rd Precinct, he had seen almost every tragedy known to man. Chicago was no different from any other large city— full of crime.

Married when he was still in uniform, the marriage soured not too long after he became a detective and started spending more and more time involved with the department's cases. Joel's wife divorced him after ten years of marriage. She felt he spent too much time living his job and not enough time paying attention to her. Joel was heartbroken but felt lucky there were no children involved. Since the divorce, he was free to dedicate his life to what he believed in—being the best detective he could be.

Now, finally given the opportunity to be chief investigator in a murder, Joel, as always, was determined to put his all into solving the crime.

"What do we know about the body?" Steve asked.

"Absolutely nothing. The call just came in."

"Who called it in?" Steve continued questioning as he got into the passenger side of the squad car.

Sliding into the driver's seat, Joel responded, "One of our favorite people."

As they drove out of the parking garage, Joel was laughing.

"Come on, Joel, who's one of our favorite—Oh, an anonymous phone call, huh?"

"You got it. I figure the tip came from one of our informants or the uniforms would have gotten the call instead me."

When Joel and Steve arrived at the alley, the scene of the body discovery, some of Chicago's finest in uniforms were already there. After a brief observation of the body from a distance, the two detectives spoke with the Sergeant in uniform.

"Thanks for getting here so fast and roping off the area from the snoopy spectators. We don't need any contamination in this area until we've had a chance to check the crime scene." The Sergeant acknowledged with a nod. Turning to his partner, Joel stated, "Okay, Steve, let's see what we've got."

Both detectives covered their hands with disposable gloves. As Joel and Steve approached the body, using care as to where they stepped, their immediate vision told them the victim was a female. She was face up with her arms folded across her chest.

"She doesn't look like she's any more than in her early twenties," Joel observed as he squatted next to the body.

Bending over next to Joel, Steve stated, "I don't know. To me, she looks like she was still a kid. I'd put her in her mid-teens."

"The crime lab techs should arrive soon. She doesn't appear to have any pockets in the dress she's wearing, so no possibility of her having any ID on her."

Steve started looking around, hoping there was a purse or a billfold close by that might belong to the deceased. Back in an upright stance, Joel joined in the search. They didn't wander far from the victim, not wanting to disturb anything until the crime techs could sweep the area. Their initial limited search brought them no clues as to the identity of the girl that was found lifeless in the dirty, cement-laden alley. As they waited for the crime techs, they made small talk.

Seeing a car drive up, Joel commented, "This should be—" Getting a look at the driver, Joel remarked, "Hey, that's not Jeff."

"No," Steve chimed in, "and it's sure not Erick, either."

As an attractive young woman got out of the car, Joel and Steve got their eyes full.

"Wow!"

Using the back of his hand, Joel gave Steve a quick swat on the arm. "Just remember, you're a married man."

"Hey, I might be married, but I'm not dead. From here, she's a real looker. Who do you suppose she is?"

"I don't know, but I'm about to find out." Joel walked toward the woman's car with Steve tight on his heels. "Hey, who are you and how did you get past the road block?" Joel demanded in a loud voice.

After closing her car door, the woman walked to the back of her car keeping her eyes on the detectives. As Joel and Steve approached her, she replied, "I guess I'm going to have to put a sign on my car. First, the police stop me, and now you. I'm Dr. Lea Brock, the new M.E."

Surprised, Joel responded, "You're a medical examiner? But what happened to the coroner's deputies?"

Lea opened the trunk of her car and pulled out her medical case. Not caring for any further protocol, she asked, "Where's the body?"

"Whoa, wait a minute. I'd appreciate it if you would answer my questions. Where's Erick or Jeff?"

"From what I was told, Erick quit a few days ago. Jeff is assisting the coroner. As if they didn't have enough bodies on ice, now they're bogged down with that family of five the police found in a car they pulled out of the river. Since the coroner is swamped, I was called in to assist in this case. What's the matter, do you have a problem with a female M.E.?" Closing the trunk, she asked, "Well?"

"Not at all," Joel stated. "I'm not a sexist. A female or a male medical examiner. is just fine with me. I've just never worked with a M.E. before."

"First time for everything, right? Where are the techs?" she asked, looking around.

"They're not here yet."

At that very moment, Steve spotted the crime lab van. "Here they are now."

Once the techs had their gear out of the van, they approached the area where Joel, Steve and Lea were standing. Joel told him what pictures he wanted and other pertinent information he felt was important to the case.

Leading the way, Joel stated, "Follow me. The deceased is right over here." As they neared the body, Joel stopped. Letting the techs go in front of him, Joel turned to Lea. "Oh, by the way, I'm Detective Joel Applemeyer. This is my partner Detective Steve Kempel."

"Nice to meet you, Detectives."

When the techs had completed their job, they waited for Lea's routine examination of the body. While Joel and Steve waited, watching Lea at work, a hospital ambulance showed up.

After her quick examination of the deceased was completed, Lea gave Joel and Steve her first educated guess about the victim. "I can't give you much right now, but I don't see any noticeable marks on her. Until further examination, I would rule out a gunshot or stab wound as the cause of death. There doesn't appear to be any noticeable marks on her neck, so, in all probability, I would rule out strangulation, also. I'll do a toxicology report and let you know what I find out. I work out of County, so that's where the body will be."

"County Hospital," Steve remarked, as if to confirm her statement. "I rather guessed that when I noticed the sign on the ambulance."

Joel asked, "Is this something new, having an M.E. do the autopsies now instead of the coroner?"

"Not really, Detective," Lea answered. "I've helped out a few times in the past when the police department has called me. I don't think I've ever worked with your precinct before."

Once the ambulance attendants placed the girl's body in a body bag, they loaded her into the ambulance. Lea removed her disposable gloves and booties that had covered her shoes, and headed back to her car.

Keeping up with her fast pace while walking beside her, Joel asked, "When can we expect your report?"

"As booked as our lab is, probably a month," she answered, opening the trunk of her car and placing her medical case inside. After tossing her soiled booties and gloves into a plastic bag, she slammed the trunk closed. She walked around the car opened her car door with Joel shadowing her.

He grabbed hold of the door while she got into her car.

"Is it Miss or do I call you Doctor or—"

"Lea is fine." Taking a hold of the car door to close it, she smiled. "Your report might take longer than a month if you don't let me get out of her and back to work."

"Look, Lea, if it's at all possible, could you try and get me a report earlier than a month?"

"I can only do my best, Detective, ah … " She hesitated to remember his name.

"Applemeyer. You can call me Joel."

"Okay, Joel. Now, please, let go of my door and let me get back to my job."

As the days passed, while Joel and Steve waited for the medical examiner's report, they canvassed the area where they had found the deceased girl. They questioned everyone who lived in the area, trying to find out the young girl's identity. With uniform help, they combed the area for any clue that could assist them with the case, but seemed to come up empty on both counts.

Four days after the discovery of the body, Joel got the call he was waiting for. When the phone on his desk rang, he answered it. "Detective Applemeyer."

"Joel, this is Lea. Your preliminary report is ready if you want to come downtown to my lab."

"I'm on my way."

After hanging up the phone, Joel and Steve hurried downtown to the County Hospital to see Lea.

Handing a folder to Joel, Lea explained, "I believe your young lady died from an overdose of drugs. No signs of suffocation or strangulation. And, just like I thought, there were no knife or gunshot wounds on her body."

"Any signs of rape?"

"No, Steve. Interesting enough, the young woman was a virgin," Lea answered.

With a quick glance over the report in the folder, Joel asked, "Any needle marks?"

"No."

"You don't think she could have died of natural causes."

Lea laughed. "Of course not, Joel. Do you?"

"Not the way she was laid out like a corpse in a casket," Joel handed the folder to Steve for his perusal, "but you haven't run any blood or body fluid tests yet. How can you be sure it was drugs that killed her?"

Walking to where the girl's body lay on one of the lab's cold slab tables, Lea said, "Look, Joel, I told you that was a preliminary report. I've put in extra hours around here so you could have that much."

Joining Lea next to the deceased's body, Joel replied, "I realize that, Lea. Believe me, we appreciate it."

"I didn't say that to get a pat on the back. It will take another couple of days for me to get the final results to you."

Not happy, Joel had no choice but to respond, "Okay."

"I also wanted you to know," Lea said, "there are no identifying marks on the girl. No moles. No birthmarks. There aren't even any scars on her body. From the looks of her teeth, she's never been to a dentist. It's doubtful you'll find dental records on her to assist with her identity.

The dress she was wearing has a pretty common label in it—a cheap cotton. There a dime a dozen in any local superstore. The same for her shoes and underclothes. Nothing that would give you any leads. However, everything is in a bag over there on the counter for you to take with you."

When he was through reading the report, Steve joined Lea and Joel. "She was a pretty little thing."

"Pretty!" Lea's objection gave both Joel and Steve a jolt. "Did either of you take a good look at her before now?" Both men shook their heads. "Even without makeup, this little gal was beautiful. Only a boneheaded, egomaniac wouldn't recognize the character in this girl's face." Standing over the body, Lea focused her attention on the deceased.

"Look at her bone structure. It's almost as if someone hand-molded those perfect facial features. For never having any dental work done, she has perfect, almost pearl-white teeth. From a woman's point of view, she has hair and a body to die for." Feeling the sensation of eyes penetrating into her brain, Lea looked up. Joel and Steve were both staring at her and smiling. "Okay," she replied with a return smile, "die was the wrong term to use."

"I guess we don't look at dead bodies the same way you do, Lea," Joel admitted.

"To be honest, it makes my job much easier if I don't study the face of the bodies I examine. This work would get the best of me, if I did. However, something about this girl compelled me to break my own rule."

Steve asked, "What's wrong with these kids today that they have to screw up their lives with drugs?"

Lea shook her head.

"I wish someone had the answer to that question," Joel chimed in. "I'd like to bring a tour of those pot-headed, drugged-out kids in here to take a good look at this young woman and let them see for their own eyes how they could end up here—just like her."

"It wouldn't do any good," Lea added to the conversation. So, what have you found out so far in your investigation?"

"Absolutely nothing," Joel replied. "We suspect she didn't die where we found her."

"It appears someone went to great efforts to place her in the alley," Steve stated, "then folded her arms across her chest on purpose."

"Like someone, at least, showed a little compassion for her?" Lea questioned.

"Could be," Joel replied. "Maybe her death was a suicide or an accident. It could be that the party or parties involved didn't want to get implicated and put their own nose on the line. So they moved her to where someone would find her."

"If that's the case, why didn't you find her ID?" Neither of the detectives had an answer for the medical examiner. "So for now, it's only speculation, right Detectives?" Joel and Steve nodded at the same time, acknowledging that Lea was correct in her assumption.

A week later, Lea had her final report delivered to Joel. Steve pushed his chair over to Joel's desk as Joel read the report.

After waiting a few minutes, Steve inquired, "Well, what's it say?"

"According to the lab tests, there are definite results of cocaine and amphetamine in the girl's system. Cause of death is verified as an overdose. Looks like my guess was right. Lea's report says she believes the girl was between eighteen and twenty."

"Shit, she sure looked a lot younger to me, Joel."

"Because of her petite size, no doubt. Damn, that's still too young to die. Lea's report says the girl must have been right handed and a writer of some kind."

"How did she draw that conclusion?"

"From a severe callus on the middle finger and traces of graphite on her right hand. Also, from the nicotine residue on the girl's teeth, she was a light smoker, probably cigarettes."

"Or, from smoking joints," Steve added.

Still reading the report, Joel continued. "No, Steve, there wasn't so much as a trace of marijuana found in Lea's tests. No tell-tale signs of wearing any rings, which indicates, most of the time, that she wasn't married."

"Pardon my ignorance, but I always wondered how they could tell if a deceased wore a ring, or not."

"Easy, my friend. Take off your wedding band. Chances are your skin is lighter under the ring than it is on the rest of your finger. Since the ring protects that small area from the sun, it's just seems natural that it remains lighter in color."

Just out of curiosity, Steve removed his wedding band. "Well, I'll be. You're right, Joel. I never noticed that before. But some people don't wear their rings all the time. They wouldn't always have this mark, would they?"

"I'm not sure. As far as the deceased is concerned, the girl being single is just speculation on a medical examiner's part." Joel handed the report to Steve. "You can read it over and see if I overlooked something of importance. Since we haven't had any missing person's reports that fit this girl's description, and no great leads, we'll have to just keep asking questions until we can get something meaty enough to go on. I still say the girl died some place other than that alley we found her in."

"I agree with you, Joel. She had no shoes on and the bottoms of her feet were clean. If she had been walking around in that area, there would have been dirt and, in all possibility, gravel stuck to the bottom of her feet."

"That also tells us that she was carried there, not dragged. As small as she was, almost anyone of average build could have lifted her without any great strain."

In deep thought, Joel sat back in his chair and stared into space. Steve read Lea's report. Placing the report back on Joel's desk, Steve asked, "What's on your mind?"

"Someone out there is missing a loved one. Yet, no one has filed a missing person's report on her."

"Come on, Joel, we see hundreds of victims that no one cares about locating. Half of the family members are happy the victims are out of their lives for one reason or another. Besides, you ought to be happy there are no loved ones to console in this case, at least for now."

"Why should that make me happy?"

"You can't fool me. I've been your friend and co-worker too long."

"Meaning what, Steve?"

"You might profess to be a hard-nose cop on the surface while you're doing your job, but underneath, you're a soft-hearted teddy bear. I know why your marriage broke up, remember? You take every case you work on as your own personal crusade to comfort the victim's loved ones."

"So?"

"So nothing, Joel. Just face it. You can't protect the whole world from crime, and you can't be Father Comforter to all who have lost someone in a homicide. Quit taking each case so darn personal. You'll live longer and be happier."

"Maybe we're too close, Steve. If my personal feelings are a thorn in your side, perhaps I should get another detective to work with me on this case."

Shrugging, Steve shook his head in disgust. "You know better than that. I'm just saying you'll work yourself to an early grave if you don't learn to leave these homicide cases in the files when you go home at nights. Okay. I can see from the look on your face that I've said enough. Let's get back to this case. What do you want to do next?"

"I was checking over some of my records, earlier today. We happen to have a snitch in the area where the girl's body was discovered. Maybe we ought to look him up and see what he can find out?"

"You don't mean Whitey, do you?"

"Sure do. He's perfect. The guy's been around that area of Chicago for years. He sees, hears and knows all that goes on down around that warehouse area. Don't you agree?"

"Yes and no. The last two cases we worked on, if you recall, Whitey was so drugged out that he wasn't one bit of help."

Standing, Joel tucked in the back of his shirt. "Well it's worth a shot. Let's go find him."

As they drove to the area of town where the warehouses were located, the men conversed.

"Hey, I've got some good news," Joel exclaimed.

"Don't tell me, you've finally got a date?"

"Look, wisenheimer," Joel stated, "I'll date when I'm good and ready and not until. So get off my case."

"Ease up, Joel. I was just kidding. So what's your good news?"

"Remember the guy I told you about that I roomed with when I attended the FBI Academy at Quantico?"

"Kind of. It's been quite a while since you mentioned him. Wait. Wasn't his name Joe something or another?"

"Joe Warner."

"Right. How could I forget? What about him?"

"As soon as he wraps up a murder case he's working on, he's coming to Chicago for a short visit. It will be good to see him again."

"Gee, that's great, Joel. Where does he live?"

"Mt. Pride, Colorado. He's in charge of the Detective's Unit at—I believe he said the 15th Precinct, but don't quote me. It's somewhere in a new area of town called High Cliff Estates. From what Joe tells me, it's like the ritzy part of Mt. Pride. Close to the mountains."

"Lucky stiff."

Whitey must have been either in hiding, or strung out somewhere high on drugs because Joel and Steve couldn't locate him. The word was out on the street, however, that they were looking for him. With no clues to further their investigation on the case, Detectives Applemeyer and Kempel could do nothing more but wait.

MAKING AMENDS

As days turned into weeks, and weeks turned into months, the pages of calendars seemed to change with the blink of an eye. With each passing day, tomorrow suddenly became yesterday.

The court convicted Darin on the last day of May. On the first day of June, he went to the State Pen in Lincoln where he would serve his time.

Darin's conviction and sentencing for his crime devastated Frank. In July, Frank gave up his search for Carole. In all of the responses he had received from all over the Nebraska, none were of any help. He resigned himself to the fact that he would never find Carole because too many years had passed since he had last seen her. The only things he had left to hold on to was a couple of pictures of her, some important documents, a piece of jewelry, some wonderful memories, and a very precious bond between them.

When September came, the Kidwell Police Department said farewell to their beloved Chief Simmons as he retired. Appointed by the Mayor, Officer Kelly accepted the position of Kidwell's new chief of police. Rusty gave up hope of ever putting his puzzle together concerning the missing money or the identity of the Neat Nick Thief. He took off for a month to Canada on a long awaited fishing trip.

In October, after Rusty returned home from Canada, he tried to see his friend Frank. He figured the four-month time span was long enough for Frank to forgive him for arresting Darin. However, either Frank wasn't answering his telephone or his doorbell because he wasn't home, or he was ignoring all outsiders. Rusty didn't know for sure. Finally, after many unsuccessful attempts, Rusty decided to back off and bide his time. He hoped Frank would get in contact with him. It didn't take long for Rusty to find out, through town gossip, that Frank, more often than not, stayed locked up in his house in solitude, shutting out the rest of the world.

Also in October, the bank in Sharpin discovered that some of their vital information had gotten lost in their record's system. Their discovery lead them to missing files, in particular, the complete financial records of Jefferson Welk. The bankers presumed this happened while installing their new computer system, several years previously. When the bank's board members found out the discrepancy in the accounts, they were determined to set the records straight.

Taking full responsibility for the enormous financial error, and realizing what an awful injustice had been done, the bank's board members took action. They paid back every one of Jefferson's creditors and all the back taxes, therefore releasing the government's hold on the Jefferson Welk properties.

On Halloween day, Rusty drove to the grocery store to purchase candy for his expected trick-or-treaters. When he left the store, he drove over to the local pharmacy to pick up a prescription the doctor had called in for him due to a minor shoulder strain he had received while fishing in Canada.

Standing in line at the pharmacy counter, Rusty waited his turn. Two men stood in front of him. While waiting, one of the men turned his head just enough for Rusty to see the side of his face. Rusty took a side step to get a better look at the man. He had a sudden tinge of double emotions when he realized the man he was viewing was Frank. The joy of seeing his friend, rushed through Rusty's body like a freight train. Sadness, however, almost derailed his excitement.

At one time, Frank weighed close to 180 pounds, and stood with his back straight and his shoulders soldier erect, which made him six feet tall. In the past few years, Rusty had observed Frank losing weight and looking a bit drawn. Not even then did Frank resemble the deteriorated physical state of the man Rusty witnessed standing in front of him at that very moment.

Frank looked as though he didn't weight more than a hundred pounds, soak and wet, like a skeleton with skin stretched over his delicate frame. Even with his scruffy beard, and wire-rimmed glasses with thick lenses, Rusty could see Frank's haggard face. There were but a few hairs left on Frank's head. His once broad shoulders were now slumped forward, causing his back to hump. The man, who was once so particular about the way he dressed, stood before Rusty in unkempt clothes which looked several sizes too large for him.

Rusty's heart seemed to be stuck in his throat as he approached the frail, unshaven man. "Frank, is that you?"

Turning, Frank acknowledged Rusty in a gravely voice. "Hi, Rusty."

"My God, Frank, I almost didn't recognized you. You look terrible." He immediately tried to change the subject, but after inserting one foot in his mouth, appeared to insert the second. "You know, I have been trying to contact you many times since Darin was sent to prison."

"I don't see too many people. Reckon I've become a hermit." After Frank paid for his prescription, he placed his small bag of pills into his coat pocket. "The only reason I get out anymore is to get my pills or a few groceries. It's been good to see you but I have to go home now."

As Frank turned to leave, Rusty took hold of his thin arm. "Look, old friend, I want to sit and visit with you. May I come over?"

"You know, Rusty, I don't think we have too much to talk about anymore. Besides, I'm not much for company these days."

"I won't take no for an answer. Are you parked out front?"

Nodding, Frank replied, "Same car I was driving the last time you saw me. Can't get in and out of the pick-up any longer."

"As soon as I get my prescription, I'll follow you home. We're going to mend this blasted fence, today," Rusty insisted.

Too weak to argue the point, Frank waited until Rusty completed his purchase. Then, Rusty shadowed Frank to his home.

When most people get very old or very ill, their bodies, their clothes, and their homes seem to emit an indescribable odor. Some call it the smell of death. When Rusty stepped into Frank's home, that distinct smell of death filled the air. After helping Frank off with his coat, Rusty forgot about his own pain as he eased his friend down into a big overstuffed chair in the living room. Rusty draped Frank's coat over one end of the couch. Then he sat on the opposite end within close proximity to Frank's chair.

"I'll be honest with you, even with that facial hair, I can see how drawn your face is. And those pants—my God, they look like they're three sizes too big for you. How much weight have you lost in these past few months?"

"Why don't you just say it? I look like death warmed over." Rusty shook his head. "This cancer is eating away at my body, faster and faster. I'm just waiting for the Good Lord to call my number," Frank said, straining to crack a smile.

"So, you're Mister Man of Leisure now, huh Rusty?"

Rusty tried hard to hold back tears. He went with the flow in the change of the conversation to divert his emotions. "You bet. You know, I was disappointed that you didn't make it to my retirement party."

"I didn't think it was my place to be there after everything that happened these past years. But, I'm happy you now have the time to do the those things you always wanted to do."

"Not quite, Frank. I recall, not too many years ago, that my best friend promised to go on some Canadian fishing trips with me when I retired. It seems like just yesterday when we confirmed bachelors made such wonderful plans to spend our golden years together. I guess a lot of us don't get what we want or wish for in this life."

"Be careful of what you wish for," Frank muttered under his breath.

"What's that?"

"What you said reminded me of Darin. It's not important. You know, Rusty, I have been meaning to contact you."

With a look of skepticism, Rusty remarked, "Sure you have, Frank."

"To be honest, I wasn't going to call or come visit you. I didn't have the guts to face you in person. But, I did write you a letter."

"You did, huh?" Rusty asked, still showing the disbelief in his voice.

"If you don't believe me, it's over there on my desk in the dining room." Frank pointed to a small room next to the living room. "I hadn't decided if I was going to mail it, or not. I seriously considered just leaving it on my desk for someone to find and see that you got it after my death. I never could make up my mind, that's why it's still sitting there."

Now trusting that Frank wasn't joshing him, Rusty got to his feet in anticipation. "May I get it?"

As Frank nodded his okay, Rusty headed to the small room. He was taken aback when he noticed close to twenty boxes still packed and sealed from Frank's move from the farm. Rusty didn't have to look very far because there on the desk in plain sight was a large manila, mailing envelope already addressed to him. He picked up the envelope and took it back into the living room where he sat back on the couch.

"Do you want me to open this now, Frank, or wait?"

"No sense in opening it while you're here. Actually, since you are here, I guess I can tell you what I wrote.

You know, I would love to have a cup of coffee. Don't suppose I could get you to make me one, could I?"

"You bet, Frank. I'd love one myself. I assume I'll find everything I need by just digging around in the kitchen cupboards?"

"Nope," Frank answered, as he started to get up from his chair.

Rising in haste, Rusty took a giant step, taking hold of Frank's arm to assist him. As he did, the envelope slid unnoticed between the cushions of the couch. "Come on, Frank, let me help you. You know I could've found everything in the kitchen without your help."

"Do you know," Frank said, as the two of them headed for the kitchen, "I haven't had a good cup of coffee since ... I don't know when."

In the kitchen, Rusty held steady, as Frank lowered himself to a chair. The kitchen, like the dining room, was stacked with packed boxes. The items on the counter consisted of a bowl, a coffee mug, a glass, a spoon, a small saucepan, and several bottles of prescriptions. From the looks of Frank, it was obvious to Rusty that his friend was not only deathly ill, but he wasn't eating properly. The items on the counter confirmed his suspicions.

Looks like Frank lives on soup. How much nourishment can that be. I don't dare bring up his bad eating habits right now, or he might kick me out of here. Somehow, I've got to make sure he gets something more beneficial to eat.

"Okay, Frank, tell me where everything is so I can get this brew going," Rusty joked, overriding his dismay.

"Right there in that top box to your left is the coffeemaker, the can of grounds and the filters. I've kept the can sealed so the coffee should still be fresh. I'm sure you'll have to rinse out the pot with hot water. It hasn't been used in quite a spell."

"Oh, yeah? Why's that, Frank?" Rusty asked as he took the coffeemaker out of the box.

"Too much work. Don't need to be cleaning a coffeepot when I can just put a cup of water in the microwave. Then I mix the hot water with some instant stuff. I have hot chocolate mix, instant coffee and instant soup. Shoot, they have all kinds of instant stuff on the shelves in the stores today, Rusty. Everything is instant. Don't that beat all? To tell you the truth, I don't even know why I bought the can of coffee. Just habit, I guess."

My God, Frank, they've had instant food products on grocery shelves for years. Your mind must be going along with your body. This is killing me to see him this way. As difficult as it was, Rusty knew he had to keep a smile on his face. He didn't want Frank misconstruing his deep concern for a look of pity.

Taking the can of coffee out of the box, Rusty attempted to make light of a sad situation. "No damn wonder you told me the coffee grounds were kept sealed. This can hasn't even been opened. Where do you keep the can opener?"

"Oh, let me think. Look in that little box next to the stove. I believe that's where I keep a few cooking gadgets."

With the lull in the conversation, the noise Rusty was making, preparing coffee was the only sound in the room. Frank sat in silence because he was trying to figure out how to tell Rusty everything he had written to him. Rusty was concentrating on what he could do to help make Frank's life a little easier.

While the coffee was brewing, Rusty took a seat at the table near Frank. He started the conversation going again. "My curiosity is killing me. What's in the letter?"

"Darn, once a cop, always a cop," Frank stated with a hint of a smile. The smile faded as he commented, "This isn't easy for me to say in person, that's why I wrote it all down in a letter to you. I'm sorry to have to admit this, but you were right. I'm referring to Darin. A person just doesn't want to believe his blood-kin is guilty of any kind of wrongdoing.

Loving Darin as I do, I—Shoot, no sense beating around the bush. I was in denial of the truth. Don't get me wrong, Rusty, I will still stand beside Darin, right or wrong. And I will until the day I die. I do, however, want to apologize to you. Pride kept me from admitting—"

"You don't owe me an apology, Frank. I've had a lot of time to think about this whole situation. If it had been Stu, who had been walking in Darin's shoes, I don't know what I would have done. But, if it makes you feel better, I accept your apology. However, there is a string attached."

"A string?"

"Yes. Let's bury the hatchet, right here and now, and put our friendship back in order. We are long overdue."

"No, you haven't heard everything yet. Since the coffee's almost done, how about you get us a cup and I'll tell you everything that's on my mind. As long as you're here, I need to talk about this to get it all off of my chest."

"Okay, Frank."

As Rusty poured coffee, he asked, "Don't you think you should have something a little more nourishing then instant soup to eat, Frank?"

"No. Soup is healthy enough. Besides, the old stomach doesn't set to kindly with too much more than that these past few months."

"Have you called the hospital to see if they could send you over a caretaker for a couple days a week?"

"What in Sam hill do I need a nursemaid for? I'm doing just fine on my own. I fix my own food, even if it is only soup. I get my own bath. Get dressed on my own. What's more, I can still drive my car.

Now, when and if I become incapacitated, well, then is time enough to get help in here. I don't want to get the hospital or none of them social services involved in my affairs." Getting teary-eyed, Frank doubled up his fist and shook it as he proclaimed, "I don't want to die in any hospital! I want to stay right here in my own home and die in my own bed. Promise me that, Rusty, please."

"Sure, Frank, what ever you want. Calm down, buddy. The last thing I wanted to do was to upset you. It's just that I care. If you want to live this way, then so be it," Rusty agreed, giving in to Frank's request.

Having set the filled cups on the table, and seated once again, Rusty said, "Okay, you wanted to tell me something more about the letter you wrote me."

Slurping his first sip of coffee, Frank expressed, "Umm, now that's a good cup of coffee. Ha! My grandfather used to call coffee jamoke, and my father called it java. That's funny, isn't it?"

"In the service we used to call it a cup of mud or a cup of brew. I don't remember that my grandparents or my parents called it anything but coffee. Today they have everything from espresso to something they call lattes, but I believe a cup of coffee is still called coffee."

Wrapping his hands around the cup, Frank held the cup close to his nose and inhaled the inviting aroma. He took another sip and rolled it around in his mouth, as if it were a fine wine. "Isn't the bouquet of coffee wonderful?"

"Frank, how long *has* it been since you've had a real cup of brewed coffee?"

"Probably since the day Darin cooked ... " Weepy-eyed, Frank thought about one of his last breakfasts with Darin. "No, that's not right, Rusty. It was back on the farm before I went to the hospital."

"Damn, Frank, that was almost a year ago."

"Yeah, I guess that's right. Well now, back to my confession."

"Your confession?"

"Darn it, Rusty. Let a person talk, will you?"

As Rusty sat drinking his coffee and listening with an attentive ear, Frank told him about Darin's books with the dog-eared pages that had highlighted and underlined phrases. In detail, he explained about discovering

Darin's hiding place where he found the mini-recorder and the mini-cassette tapes. He told of the many times that he had misplaced his gloves, but, like magic, Darin would find them right where they should have been.

When his mouth felt parched, Frank would take a breather and take a sip of coffee. Continuing with his confession, Frank explained how he figured out Darin was using him as an alibi by calling him at his Friday night poker games. He also went into detail about the grocery list still sitting on the table when Darin said he had gone grocery shopping; and about his missing money.

"Oh, there are many other things, but they aren't important now. You'll find everything I could remember, written in the letter. The fact is, Rusty, I know I could have made things a lot easier for you, and I am very sorry that I didn't. I wanted so much for Darin to be innocent on all counts. So, at the time, I didn't think any of these things were all that important. I'm grateful that you insisted on coming home with me. I was such an old fool to put a wedge in our friendship. Can you ever forgive me for being so stupid and pigheaded? I can't go to my grave unless I have a clear conscience."

Rusty shivered. "Stop. You're giving me the willies talking like that. As for Darin ... " Rusty bit the inside of his cheek, "well, today, I can say I understand. I know it's a fine line here but because you didn't know the truth for a fact—and you gave Darin the benefit of the doubt—you weren't legally obstructing justice. If you had known he was guilty at the time, then you would've been dragged into court as an accessory after the fact.

Anyway, Darin pled guilty to the one break-in. That's over and done with, okay?" *Thanks, Frank, you just reassured me that I was right about Darin being my Neat Nick Thief, and that he was a major player in the puzzle I tried to piece together.*

"No, it isn't, Rusty," Frank insisted. "I talk to Darin, once a week, and he still tells me how innocent he is, and how you and the D.A. railroaded him into pleading guilty. I told him straight out that I know he's as guilty as sin. I've even asked him—a number of times—to tell me where he hid the money.

He still claims that he doesn't know where any stolen money is because he didn't take it. Want to know what really puzzles me?" Rusty nodded. "Why wasn't Darin the least bit shocked when he was told that Jefferson Welk was dead? If Jefferson Welk was holding all that money for him, wouldn't you think Darin would have been a might worried about where the money went when the man died?"

"Believe me, Frank, you're not asking me questions I haven't asked myself, over and over again. I can only come up with a few reasonable conclusions. At first, I thought that Darin could have moved the money just before Welk died. I threw that theory out the window because that computer disk had the amount taken from the burglary just a few months prior to Welk's passing. Darin wouldn't have given him the money, I don't think, if he had planned on moving it right away. Of course with Darin, anything was possible."

"No, that doesn't make any sense to me. Darin didn't know Welk was going to die of a heart attack. So, he would have had no reason to move the money until he was ready to leave town. Right?"

"That's correct. My second theory involved the female farmhand that worked for Welk. Maybe, after Welk passed, she found the money and absconded with it. That was a lot of money for anybody. But for a poor female farmhand, that would have been the pot of gold at the end of the rainbow.

My third theory was that someone from the bank discovered the money when they were checking on the property, right after Welk died. That party might have sneaked back to the house and taken the money.

Of course, we have to take into consideration, Frank, with Darin's endless confession of his innocence and stating he didn't even know Welk, why would he give it away that he was shocked the man was dead. On the other hand—Oh, never mind."

"Go ahead and say it, Rusty. No, I'll say it for you. Do you think Darin could have murdered Jefferson Welk, then taken the money and hid it somewhere else?"

"I'm sorry, Frank, but, yes, that's what I did think. That is, until I remembered Sheriff Martin telling me that Welk died of natural causes. After my meeting with Doug, I spoke with Doc Shively. Welk died of a heart attack, just like you said. So that ruled the murder theory out in a hurry."

"Thank God for that. It's hard enough knowing Darin was an out and out thief. I couldn't bare the thought if I found out he was a murderer." Frank shuddered at such a horrible thought. "Back to the money. If Welk had the money hidden, how do you think the farmhand would have found it? Could she have just stumbled upon it?"

"I'm not sure. It's possible that she could have just come across it, since she cleaned the house for Welk. On the other hand, maybe Darin befriended and confided in her. I would be willing to bet that he knew right where Welk had the money hidden. Then, with the man's sudden death, she found the opportunity to betray Darin and helped herself. I hate to keep going back and forth like an old swing, but that theory could get blown right out the water too."

"Why do you say that?"

"I heard this young farm girl wasn't very bright. Your Darin, however, is a very intelligent, cunning young man. It doesn't make any sense that he would confide in someone with minor intellect, and expect that person to keep her mouth shut. Yet—You know, Doug also told me that he thought the farm girl was smarter than she let on the day Ward had questioned her. If that's the case, maybe she outwitted Darin?"

"What in Sam hill are you talking about, Rusty? When did Ward question this farm girl you're talking about?"

"You know what, let's forget about it, Frank. No sense in hashing this all over again. It certainly can't be healthy for you to keep worrying about things you can't do anything about. I'll tell you what bothers me right now, and that is what you just told me about the recorder."

"I knew it. I am so very sorry that I—"

"Oh, no, Frank, that's not what I meant. I'm just blown away that my men and I didn't find anything when we searched Darin's room. I know we tore the room apart. And, we did move the furniture, just in case something was hidden between a piece of furniture and the walls. We even checked under the furniture. But we sure didn't look for any loose floorboards."

"Don't be so hard on yourself, Rusty. I wouldn't have seen the loose boards, either, if I hadn't bent over to pick up the book. We both messed up. But like you said, Darin is in prison now. So, that's all water under the bridge as far as evidence against him is concerned. There's no sense in beating ourselves to death."

Tipping his cup to empty it, then offering it to Rusty, Frank said, "Never thought you would ask."

Rusty took Frank's cup to refill, chuckling over his comment. After Rusty returned to the table, Frank continued speaking. "Thanks, Rusty.

Now, let's get back to what I have in my letter to you. And I need to bring Darin back into the conversation. I want to pay back every cent Darin has taken. I would like you to get me a list of the victim's names and the amounts of money they had taken from them. This was something I wanted you to take care of after my death, but no sense in putting it off. I know, now, that Darin is, and was guilty as sin. As far as the finances are concerned, I want to make things right."

"That's all very decent of you, but definitely not necessary. If anyone was to make restitution, it should be Darin, not you."

"I understand that, Rusty, and I agree. I'm going to pay these people back out of Darin's trust fund. You see, he will be paying them back and the justice is that he—in a round about way—stole his own money. How much more justice could there be in that? I would say it was a bit ironic." Agreeing with the paradox in what Frank was saying made Rusty smile.

"The shame of it is, Darin could have just asked me and I would have given him the money. He would have saved himself time in prison, and saved everyone else all the grief he caused. I'm sorry to say this, Rusty, but I don't think those few years behind bars are going to teach Darin the lesson that losing his trust fund will do.

Somewhere along the line, as Darin grew up, he became greedy. I know most of it was my fault, so I'm the one who has to teach him that there is more to life than money."

"I have to admire you, Frank. I don't know if I would've been that smart to think of teaching Stu a lesson like that. Yes sir, I take my hat off to you. Now, as far as the list you want, well, your attorney should have a copy of the court's transcripts. Those transcripts have copies of my reports—I turned them over to the D.A.'s office during the trial—and all of the information you want to know. I'm sure John will advise you so you can do this all legally, and I know those folks will be most grateful."

"Shoot, gratitude I don't want, Rusty. I just want Darin to make right what he's done wrong. Now, I've got lots more to tell you, but I need to go lie down," Frank admitted, not even touching his second cup of coffee. "I think I overdid this visit."

Rusty got to his feet. He didn't let his own physical pain stand in his way to help an old friend. Even though he was much older than Frank, he felt twenty years younger as far as his own health was concerned.

"Come on, my friend," he said as he helped Frank to his feet. "I'll help you to your bedroom."

"Rusty, I need to tell you something that's very important, but you have to promise me it stays confidential until I'm gone," Frank said, as he leaned on Rusty for support.

"Okay, I promise. What is it?"

Frank's voice was weakening. "I'll have to tell you later after I nap first. Will you stick around?"

"Wild horses couldn't drag me away."

Frank was too exhausted to say another word. Rusty helped him to his bed. Frank's head barely hit the pillow before his eyes closed. The conversation about a promise would have to wait. Rusty removed Frank's shoes and covered him with a blanket.

After washing up the mugs and the coffeepot, Rusty went back to the living room. While he was waiting for Frank to awaken from his nap, Rusty decided to lie down on Frank's couch and take a short snooze.

A few hours later, the doorbell awakened Rusty. When he woke up in a startled state, his first thought in the semi-dark was confusion. Through the cracks in the window curtains the moonlight peeked through, casting a glow in the living room where he was napping. After realization set in, he turned on a lamp then went to the door. When Rusty saw it was a couple of children in costumes, he asked them to wait while he went to his car and retrieved the candy he had purchased earlier for the trick-or-treaters at his own house.

After he distributed the candy and closed the door, he checked his watch and noted the hour. He couldn't believe he had napped so long. Now both his back and shoulder were in tremendous pain after dozing on Frank's couch. However, he was more concerned about Frank than he was his own aches and pains.

Turning on the hall light, he crept into Frank's room. Noticing Frank's breathing was very peculiar, Rusty tried to wake him. Receiving no response, Rusty's immediate reaction was to call the paramedics. Frank was in a coma. The E.M. unit rushed Frank to County Hospital.

It was hard for Rusty to say good-bye. He kept telling Frank to wake up and come back to him because he needed his friend in his life. For the almost two months that Frank lay like a vegetable in the hospital, Rusty sat in a chair beside him. He held Frank's hand and talked to him as if Frank could hear his every word. Rusty took a few breaks to go home and shower, change clothes, and maybe catch a bite to eat, but for the rest of the time he was there with his friend.

On Christmas Eve day, Frank's conversation ran through Rusty's mind about the word denial. Rusty realized, right then, that he was in denial. As much as he hated to admit it, he knew in his heart that Frank wasn't going to come out of his coma. Even if he did awaken, he would have to endure more suffering and pain.

Rusty also realized how selfish he had been in telling Frank those words of encouragement. Over ruling his heart and his emotions, he told Frank that it was okay if he wanted to go. Rusty was ready to release his dearest friend to a better life. Somehow Rusty knew Frank had heard him. Frank died that evening.

"I'm deeply sorry, Rusty," Doc consoled, "but virtually every organ in his body was eaten away by the cancer. After his kidneys collapsed and pneumonia set in, his weak heart could no longer take the strain. I don't know what kept him alive this long."

"Yes, he was an amazing man, Doc. At least the suffering is over and he can rest in peace."

"If you don't mind I'd like to give you Frank's personal belongings. I know you will know what to do with them."

Rusty nodded. "I'll take them, but I don't really know what to do with them. As far as I'm concerned, you can trash his clothes. At least he can be buried in a decent set of clothes. I'll get him a nice suit and take it over to the mortuary."

To Rusty, losing Frank felt as if he had lost his brother all over again. He felt lucky that he was with Frank up until the end, but that didn't make his loss any easier. It was Christmas Eve. Frank's body had to stay in the hospital morgue until Rusty could make plans for the local mortuary to pick it up.

After his brief conversation with Doc, Rusty made his way to the hospital parking lot. He sat in his car thinking of his beloved friend, as the tears flooded his eyes and drenched his face. After sitting there, for who knows how long, it hit Rusty that he knew nothing of Frank's wishes for burial. He would have to find out tomorrow. Even thought the whole town was lit up with Christmas lights and decorations, Rusty never noticed any of them as he drove home.

On Christmas Day, Rusty made a special trip to the State Pen in Lincoln. He felt it was his duty to visit with Darin and inform him of Frank's passing. He also wanted to ask him about burial arrangements for his brother. He didn't know why he was surprised when Darin refused to see him. As angry as he was at Darin, he didn't want the little punk to hear about Frank's death from anyone else. So, he left a note with the warden to give to Darin.

As Rusty drove back to Kidwell, he was still wondering how he could find any information of Frank's burial wishes. Even as close as they had been for years, death never entered into their conversations. He thought, perhaps, he might find a clue in Frank's desk.

The night Frank went into a coma, Rusty was the one who had called 911. He still had Frank's keys, since he was the one who had locked the house. The thought never crossed his mind about going back into the house, until that moment, as his mind had been preoccupied.

With a sudden flashback, he remembered the envelope that Frank had given him. Up until then, he had forgotten about it.

As Rusty opened Frank's front door, that terrible sickening odor hit him, again, right between the eyes. He stood in the doorway for a moment remembering the last time he was there with Frank. Shivers ran up his spine. Since it was already dark outside, Rusty flipped on the overhead switch in the living room.

He looked around the room and under the couch for his envelope. What with all the commotion, paramedics running in and out that night Frank was rushed to the hospital, the envelope could have been picked-up, kicked or tossed anywhere. Rusty sat down and tried to retrace his steps that day. It was difficult for him to get past the mental block of that time.

Ready to give up his search, like a flash of lightening, Rusty thought of one last place to check before he left the house. Standing, he removed the sofa's cushions. There he found the envelope. Replacing the cushions, he sat down and opened the large manila envelope. Inside there were three white, legal-size envelopes addressed in big bold print: **MY LAST WISHES**, **MY CONFESSION** and **MY APOLOGY**.

He opened the envelope marked **MY LAST WISHES**. When he glanced through the enclosed documents, he knew Frank had gotten his affairs in order. Included in the envelope was a safety deposit key and bank records with Rusty's name still on all of his accounts. This was of little surprise to Rusty, since he and Frank had already discussed this matter.

What did surprise Rusty were other legal documents. Frank had not put Darin's name on anything of importance. There was Frank's Last Will and Testament in which he left the majority of everything to Rusty. There was a Power of Attorney that Frank had drawn up by his attorney, making Rusty the executor to his estate. Also enclosed in this envelope was a letter from Frank stating his intent to close the trust fund he had set up for Darin, in order to reimburse all of Darin's burglary victims for their stolen money. Included with all the other paperwork was the information that Rusty was hoping to find in regards to Frank's burial wishes.

Frank's information had no mention of his house. However, he left all of its contents—from furniture to personal belongings—to Rusty to do with as he pleased. Rusty also inherited Frank's like new car and pick-up.

"You were serious when you said Darin needed to be taught a good lesson, weren't you, Frank?" Rusty mumbled.

The hour was late. Rusty was experiencing complete exhaustion. Not having had a decent night's rest in almost two months, and having just made the long trip to Lincoln and back, he wanted to go home and get some sleep. Now that he had in his possession the most important information as to how Frank wanted his passing to be handled, Rusty knew he could read the contents in the other envelopes at another time. He picked up all of the papers and stuck them back inside the manila envelope. Rusty left Frank's house, locking the door behind him.

The day after Christmas, per Frank's wishes, Rusty had Frank's remains cremated. Rusty took Frank's ashes home with him in a small cardboard box that resembled an old cigar box. As Rusty placed the box of Frank's ashes on his living room end table, he somberly remarked, "Rest here in peace, old friend. One day, soon, I will take you to Canada and honor your last wish. It's not the kind of fishing trip we always talked about taking together, but it will be one I will never forget."

MAKING CONNECTIONS

Just before New Year's Eve, Rusty received a telephone call.
"Hello."
"Hi, Rusty, how are you holding up?"
Rusty hesitated for a second, trying to recognize the voice. He couldn't place it. "I'm sorry, who's this?"
"Oh, no, I'm the one who's sorry, Rusty. This is Oscar Denton. You know Pat's, I mean Kelly's brother-in-law? I guess it was pretty lame of me to think you would know my voice over the telephone."
"Oh, of course, Oscar. Gee, I'm sorry, but I just couldn't get a handle on your voice. I'm fine. How are you?"
"I can't complain," Oscar replied. "The important question is how are you? Kelly told me about Frank's passing. I guess I didn't know how close you two were."
"Yes, we were. I'm doing just fine. I have my bad moments when I get all teary eyed, like a child, but for the most part, I've accepted it. You said Kelly told you?"
"Yes, he did."
"I had the local newspaper do a nice write-up on Frank. I'm surprised you didn't read it."
"I guess you don't see much of Kelly anymore or you would have known that I've been out of town for the past three weeks. I tried to get in contact with you before I left. Since you were spending a night and day vigil at the hospital with Frank, it was difficult to get in touch with you."
"Yes, I'm sure it was. I didn't even bother to turn on my message machine, not that it works half the time anyway. To be honest, I didn't care about the outside world for those two months when—"
Not wanting to get maudlin, Rusty changed his direction of speech. "To answer your question, no. I can't say that I've seen too much of our

new police chief. Guess I'm going to have to stop by one of these days and see how he's doing. So, Oscar, if you've been out of town, where did you spend Christmas?"

"I went to Chicago. My wife and I owned an apartment complex there. After I moved to Kidwell, I had a real estate friend of mine in Chicago put it on the market. Anyway, the buyers just couldn't wait until the New Year to get all of the papers signed. I guess they wanted the tax break. It seemed like the complex took forever to sell, but when it did, everyone wanted everything done yesterday," he joked.

"So I had to cancel my holiday plans with Kelly and his family and fly out to Chicago. However, that brings me to the reason I called. I heard some news from an old buddy of mine, Joel Applemeyer. He's still on the force back in Chicago. I would like to talk to you about what Joel told me. I think you will find it of great interest."

"Me, have an interest in Chicago or the Chicago PD? No way, Oscar. Did that wind back there finally blow a hole in your head?" Rusty teased.

"Very funny," Oscar replied with humor. "But listen, Rusty, this is serious information. Could you meet me for coffee over at the Waffles 'N' More restaurant, say tomorrow morning around 10:00?"

"Sure. I don't have anything else in my life that's pressing right now. We can make it at 9:00, if you want?"

"Oh, no. If I know your old colleagues, they'll all be there for their morning coffee and donuts. I want to make sure they're gone before we get there. This information I have, well, I would rather you keep it under your hat for a while. It's best we don't have company around while we talk."

The following morning at the restaurant, Rusty was right on time. Oscar was a few minutes late.

"Good morning, Rusty. I apologize for keeping you waiting. But wouldn't you know it, Pat decided to come to my house for coffee this morning."

Rusty chuckled. "That figures. You know, you could've called me. We could've made this meeting another time."

"No, I can always have coffee with my brother-in-law. This is important." Oscar joined Rusty at the table and motioned for the waitress. "Have you ordered yet?"

"No. I was waiting for you. Besides, black coffee's all I want."

"Ah, come on, Rusty. This is still the holiday season. At least let me buy you a donut or a sweet roll."

"No, you go right ahead. Just coffee for me. Thanks anyway."

After filling their cups, the waitress placed a full carafe on their table. As she walked away, Oscar started the conversation.

"I'm a few years older than you, Rusty, and I've been off the force for quite some time now. Bear with me as I might be all over the ballpark with this information."

"That's fine. But you have me curious as all get out. Just start talking. If I get lost, I'll ask questions." Rusty laughed.

"To give you a quick background on my friend, Joel, he's the prime investigator for a homicide case at the 23rd Precinct in Chicago. He's quite a bit younger than I am, but we became pretty close while I was still on the force.

This past summer someone found a body of a young woman in a back alley in the warehouse district. The medical examiner's report said she died from an overdose of barbiturates. Since she had no ID on her, they ran her prints but came up empty.

After months of investigation, finally some crackhead—one of Joel's snitches—showed up at the 23rd. It seems this doper proceeded to rattle on and on about how he'd give up the ones that killed this poor girl in exchange for money. Joel said the guy was hurting for a fix.

I'm sure you're aware that we do things a lot different in the cities then you do in small town U.S.A.?" Rusty nodded. "In the city we use these snitches to help catch our mutts. Listen to me carrying on, like I'm still on the Chicago Force. Anyway, Joel decided to pay the guy a couple of bucks, but only after he had a chance to check out the guy's story. The story panned out."

"I hate to interrupt, Oscar, but are you sure this is a story I need to know about? I don't even know anybody in Chicago," Rusty admitted.

"Yes, and I'll tell you why. This involves Darin Righter, I believe. So please hear me out."

"Darin? I don't know how, but I'm all ears. Go ahead."

"Okay, I'll skip some of the details. When the cops raided the warehouse—the address the snitch had given them—they arrested a young Caucasian female. Joel said this girl's name is Michelle, but she goes by the handle Micky. They also arrested an Afro-American male about the same age as the girl. His name is Daniel. Joel said these two had enough drugs in their warehouse living quarters to keep the whole city of Chicago in drugs for a long time.

Anyway, this Micky plea-bargained, giving up her man-lover. So, she cops out to a lesser charge. In her confession—when she was asked about the identify of the deceased—she proceeded to tell Joel how she met this girl on a bus ride from Des Moines to Chicago. Seems the young girl was headed across country to New York. This Micky referred to the deceased as Daisy the Dip.

Like Joel said, they now refer to the deceased as Daisy for lack of a better ID. It seems Daisy was very naïve, and so uneducated and backward that Micky found her to be very amusing when she spoke. She convinced Daisy to stay in Chicago with her for a couple of days before taking off to New York.

After letting Daisy rest from the bus journey, Daniel slipped her a Mickey Finn in a soft drink just to get some information out of her. Micky said Daniel didn't believe anyone could be that naive, as what Daisy appeared to be on the surface. He thought maybe Daisy was a plant. A Narc.

Anyway, after the first drink, Micky said that Daisy did nothing but talk about all this money she had and how she was going to New York City to be a writer. Seems the time came when this Daniel fella decided that Daisy was far too stupid for her to be a set up. He became intrigued about all of the money she talked about."

Oscar paused long enough to take a drink of coffee. Then he continued. "Here's how it goes down, Rusty. The couple of days that Daisy was to stay in Chicago turned into over a year. After quite a lengthy period of time, and getting this poor innocent Daisy really hooked on drugs, they convinced her that she had to support her own habit.

Daisy was their houseguest, so she had no other expenses. Let me throw in something here, Rusty. During the investigation, Joel said he discovered that Daniel didn't have mail delivered to the warehouse. So, there was no way that Daisy could have received any mail there. Seems Daisy never left the place without Micky stuck to her side, like shit to toilet paper.

So, without the girl working, and not receiving any mail, Micky and Daniel couldn't figure out where she was getting her money. Each time Daisy wanted more drugs, she went to her room and brought back more cash. Daisy, from what I understand, called the drugs tickets for a roller coaster ride.'"

Rusty scrunched up his face. "What does that mean?"

"From the addicts we arrested, when I was still on the force, I can only assume it means the highs and lows some people experience when they're on drugs."

"You're probably right. Okay, go on."

"So, Daniel and Micky put their heads together. They figured Daisy must have brought a small bank with her in her luggage—a virtual goldmine of continuous wealth. Daniel wanted more than his share of it."

Raising his finger, Rusty said, "Wait a minute, Oscar. If this Daisy was a houseguest, what kept these other two from just going to her room—within that year—to search her belongings?"

"I'm getting to that."

"Sorry."

"When Daisy started talking about leaving and heading on her way to New York, that's when Daniel decided they should search her room first. Up until that point in time, according to Micky, they had respected her privacy. The main factor was, each bedroom in the warehouse had a key. Micky—"

"Whoa. Sorry to interrupt, but I've never heard of a bedroom in a warehouse. Is that something new?"

Oscar laughed. "You're behind the times, Rusty. For years now, people have been buying up old warehouses and making homes out of them. By the time the owners get through with the interior modifications and decorating, some of them are quite beautiful."

"I see. Okay, so each bedroom had its own key."

"Right. Micky said Daisy was a bit on the skittish side. Seems she was use to staying in hotels where she could keep her door locked. So, Micky and Daniel assumed there was no problem in giving her the key to the bedroom they gave her to stay in, allowing her to keep her door locked. Whenever Daisy was in the room, she locked the door. When she left her room, she locked her door. According to Micky, it was a game with the girl. Rather like a child playing with blocks." Rusty raised his brow. "I'm just repeating what Joel told me, Rusty.

Now, as long as she stayed and kept paying for drugs, they didn't care where she got the money. But when they felt threatened, losing their golden hen, so to speak, that's when they both turned against her." Rusty's investigative mind was shooting off fireworks in his head. He raised a finger, giving a wait-a-minute sign. Oscar's pickup on the gesture was immediate. "Question?"

"Yes. If you have a houseguest—throwing money around like water—why would you wait a year before deciding the person had a bundle of money in their room? And, why didn't this Daniel have a master key or get an extra key made?"

"I don't know, Rusty. There are a lot of street smart people that are lacking in common sense."

"True."

When Rusty picked up his cup, Oscar proceeded talking. "Once Daniel and Micky thought they had Daisy strung out—so she wouldn't know what was going on—that's when they took the key from her and started searching her room. They discovered she had some socks full of money in a large suitcase. Daniel started grabbing handfuls of bills and stuffing them in his pockets. Micky was shoving money down her blouse.

When Daisy stumbled into her room and discovered Daniel and Micky were helping themselves to her money, she started throwing a fit. With the mixture of the drugs, and Daisy's anger, Micky stated that a real frenzy occurred. Daisy commenced yelling about the money from Mr. Welk. She said Daisy was carrying on so, that she didn't understand who Mr. Welk was. Daisy was also ranting about someone she called Darin George Righter. Something about him being her buddy and she would tell him if they didn't leave her alone. Then Daisy started raging about how that money was for her to get to the world of New York so she could write books.

It seems that both the greed, and Daisy's outburst, got to Daniel. He wanted to not only calm her down, but to get rid of her for good. His greed took over. So he gave her a deadly overdose. Micky says she pleaded with Daniel not to kill Daisy—as she liked the girl—but he insisted that was the permanent way to shut her up.

Getting back to the money, this Micky said that after they moved Daisy's body into another room, they went back into Daisy's room to continue their search. Inside the large suitcase where they had discovered the first amount of money, there were also several small suitcases.

Micky said she and Daniel were shocked when they opened the small cases and discovered many were filled with more cash, plus a lot of plastic wrapped coins and a whole lot of gold coins." Trying to stay calm, Rusty knew he was sitting on the edge of his seat. "This Micky told Joel that Daniel insisted on counting the money without her around, so she couldn't even begin to guess how much it all added up to.

Up to the point of Daisy's demise, Daniel had been nothing but a small-time dealer. Micky said he had money of his own but wanted Daisy's money too. He wanted to become a 'kingpin' of dealers. He spent most of the deceased's money—according to this Micky—to stock up on drugs for his clients.

She said Daniel was going to take Daisy's gold ring so he could hock it. However, since it had initials engraved on the inside, he was afraid it would be traced back to him. When Joel asked her what had happened to the ring, she said Daniel threw it back into the large suitcase along with Daisy's other belongings. Many of Daisy's paper items and clothes were thrown into the fireplace because Daniel didn't want anything of hers left laying around.

It seems that Daniel wrapped Daisy in a sheet. In the middle of the night, upon Daniel's insistence, Micky was his lookout. She preceded him to make sure there was no one around while he carried the body a few blocks away from their warehouse. That's where he placed her body in an alley.

Feeling guilty, Micky said she couldn't sleep. As soon as she knew Daniel was in a sound sleep, she sneaked back to where Daniel had dumped the body. She took the sheet off the girl and folded her hands over her chest. Micky said she whispered a small prayer for Daisy, then made the anonymous phone call to the police so they would find the girl's body. Once she got back to the warehouse, she hid the sheet under a pile of dirty clothes so Daniel wouldn't find out that she had taken it off Daisy's body."

Oscar stopped to drink of coffee. This gave Rusty the perfect opportunity to comment on everything he had just heard.

"Mr. Welk? Darin? Bingo! The missing money! But who in the blazes is this Daisy?" It only took seconds for Rusty to answer his own question. "Oh, no! I'll lay you ten to one that she's the ignorant farmhand Doug told me about. Good Lord, Oscar, do you know any more about this dead girl?"

"Who's Doug?"

"Sheriff Martin."

"Oh. Well, Joel said they went back to the warehouse for their investigation. While there, they checked out the personal belongings that Micky said belonged to Daisy. Joel said they were fortunate that the suspect had been so busy spending the money on drugs, he hadn't disposed of the rest of the dead girl's property yet. They didn't find any money, of course, but they did find some different colored travel cases, a briefcase, and a large travel-all suitcase. I guess most of them were empty, but there were a couple with some personal items left in them.

Oh, just a minute ... " Oscar paused, taking a small piece of paper out of his pocket. "Here, these are some of the unusual items Joel said they found in her room. I jotted them down when Joel was telling me the story. Anyway," he laughed, "if I can read my own scribbling, I'll try and decipher it. This says an old metal cup, a gold ring, a worn greeting card, a lock of hair, a dried up flower, a rusty coffee can, and a birth certificate. There was something about coins, but I can't remember what it was, and I didn't write it down."

Rusty sat intent, devouring every word that Oscar spoke.

After placing the piece of paper on the table close to Rusty, Oscar went on to say, "Here, you take this. I hope you can translate my chicken scratching.

Now, Joel said they also found a briefcase full of what he called child's scribbles. This Micky said that Daisy swore she was going to be a writer some day, and always talked about how she had written stories ever since she had learned how to read and write.

Joel said there is a bunch of them, but he didn't take the time to read but just a couple. I should say, he tried to read a couple. He said even a child in first grade could write better stories and print better than this Daisy girl did. Joel did say, however, that most of the stories had titles. Stranger yet, all of them said they were written by the unusual name of Farm Girl.

I have to ask, Rusty, who is Welk?"

"If you don't mind, I can explain later. Right now, I want to know if your detective friend is concluding that Daisy and Farm Girl are one in the same."

"No, Rusty, not until he has further evidence."

"Did your friend, Detective Applemeyer, find any information to help with this girl's identity in the stories he tried to read?"

"No. He enlisted my help to see what I could find out here in Kidwell. I thought, since this is really your territory, that maybe you wouldn't mind helping me."

"I'll be more than happy to, but the guys at the station would be of more help to you. Why ask me instead of soliciting Kelly's help? Don't tell me you don't have confidence in your own brother-in-law?" Rusty joked.

"I know Kelly is competent, but I didn't know if this was a case for the police chief, or not."

"You're right there, Oscar. This should be placed in Sheriff Martin's hands, since it was a county case. You should contact Doug and—"

"Wait, Rusty. I really figured, since the Neat Nick Thief case had been your baby from the get-go, that you'd be the best one to ask for assistance. The truth is, when I heard Joel mention the name, Darin Righter, I volunteered to help Joel out. I figured, since you and I are both retired, that we would have more time than the uniforms to check out county records. Joel agreed to let me do some digging first, since locating the girl's ID wasn't an immediate emergency. Then, if I don't find anything that will help him, they'll have the deceased buried there in Chicago as Jane Doe."

"You lost me, Oscar. My brain hasn't had a chance to calculate everything you've been telling me. But from your information, I can pretty much put two and two together. The girl worked for Welk, knew Darin, and ended up with the missing money from Cole County. Unless I've missed something, none of this information says she would be on record here. Why check Cole County's records? What information does the Chicago Police Department have that connects this young girl, Daisy, to our area here in Nebraska?"

"Remember I told you that one of the items they found was a birth certificate?"

"Oh, right. So, it was hers?"

"Yes. It seems her birth certificate states she was born in Cole County, Nebraska."

"She was born here?"

"That's correct."

"Oh, now I see what you meant by it being my territory, and why your friend asked for your assistance. Excuse me, I mean why you volunteered."

"That and the fact of everything else that seemed to be connected to your Neat Nick Thief case," Oscar added.

"Let me get back to the girl's stories for a minute, Oscar. Why didn't Joel send these stories to an expert who could decipher them for him? They may be full of clues."

"Joel wanted to have the birth certificate checked out first. I know I've been rambling on and on with so much information to give you, Rusty, but let me back up and try to pull things together from where this all started.

When I was back in Chicago, I had lunch with Joel. In the course of conversation, I told Joel how I had helped you out here in Kidwell with Operation Ivy, and how the thief turned out to be one Darin Righter. I also explained that Darin pleaded out so he was not convicted as being the

Neat Nick Thief.

Just the mention of Darin's name and that's—in reality—how Joel's murder case was brought up in the first place. Also, I remembered Pat—I mean Kelly—telling me how much money Darin had gotten away with and that it was never recovered. It was all too much of a coincidence. Whew!

Okay, I'm through," Oscar said, as he picked up his glass of water, emptying it to quench his dry mouth.

Rusty attempted to pour some coffee, but the carafe was empty.

"Say, we, or I, went through that pot in a hurry. Let's get a refill." He held the pot in the air and motioned for the waitress. "Okay, Oscar, is it possible for me to get those stories? Call me stupid, but I would like to try and read them. Who knows, I might find the connection between Darin, Welk and this Daisy somewhere in them. I mean, from everything you've told me, they are connected. But I'd like to find out how this all came about. It's obvious, I can no longer recover the money if it was all spent on illegal drugs. Those stories, however, may help me get some answers. What do you think?"

"Joel said he's pushing hard to get this Daniel convicted soon. As soon as the trial is over, I'm sure you can have all of the deceased girl's papers. I'll bet you can even have the girl's body to be buried, I guess, here in Kidwell. I assume, if we find out who she is, that it would be our responsibility to locate her next of kin."

"Me? Why would I want to bury—Oh, on second thought, why not? Not that I want the responsibility of burying a total stranger, but I'm sure Frank would have taken care of it. Yeah, I think I'll probably do just that."

"Frank? Boy, you lost me on that one, Rusty. Why would this dead girl be Frank's responsibility?"

"I'm just assuming here, Oscar, but I knew Frank, like the back of my hand. Since Darin is in prison, whether he was convicted as the Neat Nick Thief or not, I'm sure Frank would feel obligated for taking care of the young girl who helped Darin get the money out of town. Frank always did the admirable thing.

Getting back to the money—There's still another theory that I've been contemplating in my brain. This Daisy girl could have found the money, taken it, and ran with it. I'm hoping something in those stories of hers, if I can read them, will give me the answer."

"You could be right," Oscar replied.

"Let's back up for a minute, if you don't mind. You said the deceased was called Daisy." Getting an affirmative nod from Oscar, Rusty continued. "Yet there are stories written by someone called Farm Girl. However, Detective Applemeyer says there is no conclusive evidence that proves these two names belong to the same girl. You also mentioned that there's a Certificate of Birth. I'm sorry I let that comment slip by me earlier, but it just hit me in the head. What's the name on that document?"

Reaching out to the paper he had earlier placed in front of Rusty, Oscar replied, "Let me look at my notes again." After scanning through them, he read, "First and middle initials with only two letters in last name. I don't remember now what that means or why I wrote it, Rusty. I'm sorry. I remember something about it that was confusing, but I guess I didn't write the whole thing down."

"Gee, Oscar, I hate to hurt your feelings but without a name, how did you expect us to check out court records?"

Quite by accident, Oscar had bumped the table as he was repositioning himself in his chair. When he did, some of the coffee spilled over the top of his cup. Lucky for Rusty, it didn't affect him, as his cup was empty. Oscar took a napkin from its holder as he answered Rusty's question. "For the same reason I didn't ask Kelly to help me on his own personal time." Oscar paused to wipe up the coffee off the table. It was almost as if he couldn't do two things at once.

After he put the wet napkin in the empty ashtray that adorned the table, he admitted, "My mind isn't as swift as it used to be, Rusty. I was trying to take notes on all the info Joel was telling me, but I just couldn't get everything written down. When I volunteered to help find this girl's ID, I was really volunteering you, not me, and Joel knew it. He said to have you call him for all of the details in the case. I'm sorry, Rusty. Guess it's a good thing that I don't work on the force anymore. I have a hard time, anymore, trying to keep up with my own personal dealings."

Feeling a bit down in the dumps, as if he was letting both Joel and Rusty down, he handed his paper of notes back to Rusty. Rusty could see the instant depressed look in Oscar's eyes, so he tried to lift his spirits with his usual humor.

"That's okay, Oscar, I guess this proves you weren't a secretary in your previous life."

It was obvious that Rusty's comment worked when both men broke into laughter.

"Look, Oscar, for your information, you've told me more details than I'm sure I would have ever gotten from reading a report. You have a better memory than you think you do. Besides, we're all allowed to forget some things, once in a while."

"Damn."

"What's the problem?"

"Not to change the subject about this Daisy whoever, but I'm coffee logged. I've also got a good case of TB. What do you say we get out of here?"

"Yes," Rusty agreed looking at his watch. "Look at the time. It's noon already. I've got a bit of tired butt myself, but how about letting me buy you lunch? I still have a million and one questions I want to ask."

"This from a guy who wouldn't let me buy him a breakfast roll? Well, I guess you can twist my arm, but let me get rid of some of this coffee first before my bladder explodes. I have to pee so bad my eyeballs are starting to float. I'll be right back." Oscar laughed as he left the table.

As Rusty waited for Oscar to return so he could continue asking questions, he couldn't stop the many thoughts that were whirling around in his head. *After what Frank had told me, I was convinced that Darin was my Neat Nick Thief. With the information that Oscar just laid on me, that cinches it. I've got Darin who steals the money and Welk who hides it, which was already proven.*

But now, enter another piece of the puzzle—an unknown girl. I don't know how she got involved with the money, but, at least, now I know where the money went. She's got to be the one and the same farmhand that worked for Welk, and the same one that Doug mentioned to me. Did she steal the money or was she helping Darin move it? Now that's the sixty-four thousand-dollar question! Good Lord, is this puzzle on my mind beginning to be a compulsion with me? Beginning? Who are you kidding, Rusty, old man. It is and has been a compulsion for years now.

Rusty broke into his own thoughts when he realized he was in a public restaurant, sitting alone at a table, bubbling from ear to ear.

IT'S A SMALL, SMALL WORLD

Immediately following the New Year, Rusty called the Chicago Police Department's 23rd Precinct to speak to Detective Joel Applemeyer. After the proper telephone introduction, Rusty explained why he was calling. Dropping protocol, they got right to a first name basis.

"So you see, Joel, Oscar filled me in on the whole wretched story about this murder investigation of yours. He also told me that he volunteered my services, since he thinks your case is tied into one I had worked on. To make a long story short, I believe you were expecting to hear from me."

"I sure was."

"Does the morgue still have this poor girl's body?"

"Yes, she's still on ice. It's a small world, isn't it, Rusty?" Joel commented.

"Boy, you can say that again. I'd like to come see you and discuss the information you have on this girl. Would that be a problem?"

"Heck no. If you want to make the trip, I'll be more than happy to make time for you. Besides the fact that I can use your help, it will be nice to meet you in person. According to Oscar, you were a top notch police chief."

"It's a shame he didn't say such nice things about you," Rusty stated, tongue in cheek.

After a moment of silence, Joel burst into laughter. "Oh, you almost had me. I almost forgot that Oscar said you also had a droll sense of humor."

The next day after their telephone conversation, Rusty showed up at the 23rd Precinct. He was pointed the way to Joel's desk. As Rusty approached the desk he saw two men sitting in chairs in close proximity of each other, involved in a conversation. He started to turn away when Joel spotted him. The man looked vaguely familiar, but Joel couldn't quite place where he had seen him before.

Raising his voice, Joel asked the stranger, "Yes, sir, may I help you?"

"I wanted to talk to Joel Applemeyer, but—"

"Say, from the description Oscar gave me, you must be Rusty?" Getting an affirmative nod from Rusty, Joel offered his hand "I thought you looked familiar. I'm Joel, Rusty, and it's sure good to meet you."

Shaking Joel's hand, Rusty offered, "For me too, Joel. Look, it's apparent you're busy. Why don't I—"

"Busy, that's a laugh. Rusty, meet my old pal Joe Warner." As the man sitting by Joel's desk stood to meet Rusty, Joel stated, "Joe, meet retired Chief of Police from Kidwell, Nebraska, Rusty Simmons."

Extending his hand, Rusty said, "Rusty will do. Hi, Joe, it's nice to meet you."

"Likewise, Rusty, and Happy New Year," Joe stated, shaking hands with Rusty.

"Thank you, and the same to both of you," Rusty reciprocated with a smile.

Joel grabbed a file folder off his desk. The three men went to a small conference room to talk, stopping by the coffee machine first to take coffee with them.

Joe asked, "How long have you been retired, Rusty?"

"Just since last September."

"I'd say semi-retired," Joel added, "since you're here to help me, and because you're still pursuing a case you worked on before retirement. You see, Joe, Rusty is here to get info on that homicide case I've been in charge of since last year."

"Oh, that unidentified girl you told me about?" Joe said.

"Right. Rusty is going to check out the public records back in his area in Nebraska, to see if he can come up with an ID for her."

"So, Joe, what do you do for a living?" Rusty inquired.

"I try to run a police unit back home in Mt. Pride, Colorado," Joe said with a half-cocked grin.

"He's being modest, Rusty," Joel interceded. "He's Captain Warner, Chief of Detectives."

As Joe laughed, he admitted, "There's nothing like a friend to blow up a man's ego. Actually, I'm just in charge of the 15th Precinct Unit."

"Joe and I were roomies at the FBI Academy, years ago. His wife kicked him out of the house so he came to Chicago to pester me for a few days," Joel said.

"That's only part truth, Rusty." Joe laughed. "Don't let this guy fill you with his BS. My wife did not kick me out. I just wanted to spend some time with my old buddy, here. She insisted I come alone.

Our original plans were to go to Canada and do some ice fishing, but with my wife's arthritis, we decided to cancel that trip. Instead, we spent a few days catching a few rays by the beach in Florida before I headed here. I have to admit, it was a little lonesome spending New Year's Eve without her." Realizing he was getting a bit too glum, he smiled and changed to a lighter side of conversation.

"Now, if you want some real truth from the past, I couldn't wait to get back to my wife after rooming with this bloke at the academy. My wife was always tidy, but damn, Joel was persnickety. He wouldn't leave the room unless his dirty clothes were picked up and his bed was made. That's not all, he made sure I did the same or he wouldn't let me out the door. I swear, it was like being home with my mother again," Joe teased as Joel's face turned red.

"Hey, I was in the military, Joe. That's my kind of roommate," Rusty offered with a laugh. "You know, Joe, I'm not much on geography, but Mt. Pride, if I recall, is a pretty good sized city."

Nodding, Joe responded, "Too big, sometimes."

"Joe just cleaned up a weird case not too long ago that he was telling me about when you came in, Rusty. Go on Joe, fill Rusty in. Then tell me why you said the homicide investigation ended so bizarre."

"No, I'm sure Rusty doesn't want to hear—"

Cutting in, Rusty stated, "Go ahead, Joe. We don't get as much excitement back home as you big city cops get. I'd love to hear about your case."

"I'll do my best to make this short. The case involved one of Mt. Pride's prominent psychologists—David—his childhood friend—Todd—David's wife—Ann—Ann's boss—Matt—and, Matt's wife—Renny. And, oh, Renny was also one of David's clients. When the uniforms found a dead body in the trunk of a car that had rolled over a cliff, that's when Detective Eddy Konklin and I got involved."

With a rap on the door, an important message took Joel out of the room. Rusty and Joe continued talking. After Joe finished telling Rusty the rest of the story about the case he had recently wrapped up, Rusty gave Joe details, in a nutshell form, of the Neat Nick Thief case.

It seemed that Joel had no more than entered the room, when there was another knock at the door. Since he barely had the door closed, Joel reopened it. It was his partner, Steve.

"Sorry to bother you again, Joel, but there's an important phone call from a Lieutenant Konklin for your buddy Joe. I had the Desk Sergeant put it through to your desk."

"Thanks, Steve."

Overhearing Steve, Joe took an immediate departure to take his call. Rusty and Joel conversed about non-essentials until Joe returned.

"What's up?" Joel asked, when Joe returned to the room.

"I have an emergency back home."

"I'm sorry to hear that," Joel stated. "It's not about your wife, is it?"

"No, but thanks for asking. My Lieutenant, Eddy Konklin, just informed me that our mayor is missing. I hate to cut this trip short," Joe apologized, "but I'll have to get back home, right away."

Joel and Rusty bid their farewells to Joe, then sat back at the table and got into the discussion of Joel's homicide case.

"I'll get right to it, Joel, do you mind releasing the girl's body to me?"

"Not at all."

"I would like the body shipped back to Kidwell. I'll cover the transport expenses, and see that she gets a decent burial and a modest headstone."

"According to all of my records and reports, I'm sure our medical examiner has already run every test we need to back up our case in court. I'm sure she would be more than happy to get rid of the body as soon as she can. That will, in all probability, be right after our perp's trial."

"Okay. Now, what about the birth certificate you found."

"As far as the birth certificate goes, we could make out some of the information, however ... " Joel hesitated as he looked a bit miffed at the manila file he had brought in with him earlier. "Sorry, Rusty. It looks as if I picked up the wrong folder from my desk. If you'll give me a minute here, I'll go get the correct file folder on this case."

"Of course," Rusty agreed.

Returning to the conference room, folder and note pad in hand, Joel laid a blank legal pad on the desk in front of Rusty. "I didn't know if you wanted to take notes, or not."

"Sure," Rusty stated, removing a pen from his shirt pocket. "Thank you."

"Unfortunately," Joel chuckled, "when Oscar and I discussed this case, it was in a fancy restaurant over lunch. They use cloth napkins, so

Oscar took notes on a small piece of paper he found in his pocket. It didn't allow him much room to take down proper details."

"So I found out." Rusty laughed. "Anytime I do something out of the ordinary, anymore, I blame age. I brought along a note pad, but I was smart enough to leave it sitting in the seat pocket in front of me on the airplane for the next guy to use."

"How very thoughtful of you Rusty," Joel teased with a grin.

Joel commenced thumbing through his paperwork in the file folder. "Now, where in the world—I know I kept a copy of that birth certificate. The original was singed around the edges from the fire, but, for the most part, it was semi-legible. Oh, yes, here it is. Okay, we can read the initials F.G., but the last name appears obliterated—either from a drop of ink or someone smudged the ink while it was still wet.

What we can make out of the smear in the last name are the letters ht. Now, we know the month and the year she was born, but we can't read the day recorded on this certificate. Since her murder occurred in June of last year, she was barely twenty when she met her maker. And, like you already know, she was born in Cole County, Nebraska."

No wonder Oscar didn't have a complete name to give me. And I thought he told me the girl was from Kidwell? Oh, well. "Okay, from what Oscar told me, the initials F.G. on the certificate would certainly fit with name Farm Girl that you found on the stories. So where did the name Daisy come from?"

"Who knows? If she was a runaway, she might have picked the name out of a hat so she couldn't be traced as she traveled. Just to fill you in, we've checked all of our missing persons and runaway files. To date, none of them are a match to the deceased."

"What about her parent's names. Aren't they on the certificate?" Rusty inquired.

"Well, yes and no. According to the certificate, her mother's first name is illegible out but her last name is recorded as Nobody. The father's full name is also illegible. It looked as though someone attempted to obliterate these names with an ink pen."

Rusty continued to converse as he took notes he thought would be important to him. "Nobody? That's a new one on me. I can tell you right off that the name isn't a familiar one to me. I'll check the courthouse back home just to be sure. The last two letters, 'ht', for the girl's name sure doesn't fit with the name Nobody." Joel agreed with the shake of his head. "So, we're in the dark as to the girl's last name or her father's name," Rusty stated with a question.

"True. Here's what I did. When I sent the girl's prints to the FBI Crime Lab back east, I sent the original birth certificate at the same time. I thought maybe one of those experts back there could get through the ink splotches and get me a name for the girl and her father.

The report on the prints came back, sometime ago, with no information on the girl. The lab is still working on the birth certificate, so I haven't heard back from them on it yet. This mutt that we've got locked up for the girl's murder is due to go to court on arraignment in April. I hope to have some word back from the lab by then. Just as soon as I find out her correct name, I'll give you a call and let you know."

"If I find out anything before then," Rusty commented, "I'll be sure and contact you, too."

"That reminds me, I need your phone number. I know I have your name written down on one of these papers." Joel found the paper with Rusty's name written on it. Taking a pen from his pocket, he stated, "Okay, shoot."

"It's 308-555-6731. Oh, if you can't reach me, I've got one of those answering machines. Problem is, half of the time it doesn't work right. Maybe it would be better if you contact Oscar. I know he'll make sure that I get the message. That is, providing it's okay with you?"

"That's a definite. I'll also let you know about releasing and shipping the body, and the ETA."

"Out of curiosity, why didn't you just contact the Cole County Courthouse by one of those computers? We might be a small area in Nebraska, but I know they have all their vital records on computers now."

"I did, Rusty, but they had nothing that could help me. I figured it would take manpower to literally go through archived data. You might find something that isn't recorded on a computer."

"If you don't mind my asking, Joel, you mentioned the birth certificate being singed. I'm assuming that it was meant to be burned the same time the deceased other items were."

"Yes. It seems our perp was attempting to burn as much as he could. According to his girlfriend, he didn't want the deceased's identity to show up anywhere after he killed her. He tried to burn most of her papers, handwritten stories, her birth certificate, and a small metal cup. We were fortunate the birth certificate managed to survive the fire with minor burned edges. We pulled the blackened cup from the ashes, too, and locked it up with the rest of her belongings that we recovered at the warehouse."

"It's strange he didn't burn the girl's stories," Rusty observed.

"He did manage to burn some of them up. According to his girlfriend, he had every intention in getting rid of everything. He figured the girl would never be traced back to him, so he felt he had plenty of time to get rid of her things."

"Well, he who hesitates hangs himself." Rusty laughed.

"If we're lucky, they do. We're very grateful to those offenders who drag their feet—thinking they're home free—and leave evidence laying around for us to find."

"I understand that."

"Say, I'm sorry about not being able to retrieve any of the money that was stolen from your community, if this case is in fact tied in together."

"I'd bet my life savings they fit together like a hand to a glove, Joel. It would certainly be a missing piece to a puzzle I've been trying to put together. There's been something so crazy about this whole thing, that my head just won't call it quits. You know the case has already been tried and the perp plead out, so he's in the State Pen doing his time. He copped out on a lesser plea, but at least he's behind bars right now."

"So Oscar informed me," Joel stated.

"Since my best friend's brother, Darin Righter, was Kidwell's Neat Nick Thief, I feel bound to locating and contacting this girl's relatives. I'd like to find out if this girl was in on the scheme of things, or if she was just an innocent who got caught in Darin's web. I figure if I could get those stories the girl supposedly wrote, that maybe I could read them and find a connection."

"Lots of luck." Joel laughed. "First of all, I tried to read two of them. I bet I spent a good hour trying to make out what they said. After I did, they were simple stories about clouds, fish, rocks, that kind of stuff. The stories had no bearing on my case, or any valid information as to her identity. Other than the name Farm Girl, I doubt, in all seriousness, if they would be of any help to you."

"That doesn't sound too encouraging. However, I've one up on you, Joel."

"Ha!" Joel laughed. "Outside of a few more years of law enforcement experience, what's that?"

Rusty grinned. "Time."

"That's true."

"Anyway, as far as the deceased is concerned—since I still have friends in law enforcement—I think I'll pull in a few favors to see what I can find out. The Neat Nick Thief case is in the cold case file, but with the right evidence, it could be reopened. Not that Darin could be tried again, but it would give us an option to look elsewhere in the remote possibility that he wasn't the real thief. *Not that I believe that, of course.* When you spoke of the money, Joel, you reminded me of something. Oscar mentioned something about coins. What kind of coins, and how are you connecting them to the deceased?"

"Once our female canary, Micky, started singing for her plea bargain, she told us a lot of details. Remember I told you that she and her boyfriend had found all kinds of money in one of the deceased's suitcases?"

Retired, or not, Rusty still had a sharp mind. He knew Oscar was the one who had told him about the money found in the suitcases. Not wanting to embarrass Joel, Rusty decided to let it pass by agreeing. "Yes."

"Evidently there were some socks filled with money in the bottom of a suitcase. Then, in some smaller cosmetic cases they found some loose change, wrapped coins, and quite a few gold coins. She remembered that Daniel told her he felt the wrapped coins were encased in clear plastic protectors because they were rare and worth a lot of money.

Seems Micky's boyfriend spent every bit of what he found on drugs. Our perp Daniel, of course, won't tell us what he knows. However, we added it all up. First, we never found any of the money or the gold when we searched the warehouse. Secondly, we did a complete record search and couldn't find any accounts in either of their names. Last, but not least, considering all the drugs we confiscated, we're concluding that the canary's telling us the truth. The perp spent every last cent to set himself up as local kingpin."

"Look, Joel," Rusty said with a wide grin on his face, "we aren't stupid or backward in Nebraska. But where I live, well, we're not real up-to-date on certain terms that you big-city cops use. I forgot to ask Oscar, when he mentioned it, so, do you mind explaining to an old coot, like me, what a kingpin is?"

"No, not at all. It's just a term for a head honcho of drug distribution. It's a real racket, Rusty."

"From what you've told me, you didn't find one cent amongst the deceased belongings."

"That's correct, Rusty. Not so much as a penny. Let's get back to those stories. As far as we know, the stories and the notes we found are, in fact, in the girl's own handwriting. I have to admit that we have nothing to back that up, just this Micky's word. She claims to have seen some of the deceased's papers, so I showed her some notes we found in the deceased's belongings." Looking back through his file of papers Joel pulled out a written report. After scanning it, he said, "To quote Micky, 'Yes, that's Daisy's goofy printing—never did go to school—so she never learned the proper form of writing.'

Oh, speaking of quotes ... " Joel didn't say anymore until he found another paper he was looking for in the file folder. "Here's a good one for you. This is what our perp, Daniel, said when we took his statement, and I quote, 'I did the world a favor. That sister was crazy. Use any cliché you want, but all she had to do was open her mouth and anyone could tell her elevator never left the basement.' Can you imagine spending thousands of dollars just on drugs, and most of all, killing someone just because you think they're stupid?" Joel paused to reflect back to a thought, then stated, "The main factor, however, is greed with a capitol G. No matter how you look at it, Daniel's a damn slime-ball in my book."

"Having had a few years of law enforcement under my belt, I have to admit that some people just have no regard for human life. I'm sure you've seen worse here in Chicago than I have in Kidwell, but no matter where it is in the world, murder is always so senseless."

"Amen," added Joel.

"Just out of the old investigative curiosity, is your perp from the Chicago area?"

"No, as a matter of fact, he's not. He won't give up any information on himself, but Micky told us all she knew about him. It wasn't much, of course. She said his real name is John Daniel Hobart. We verified that information on his driver's license. Seems that he came to Chicago on some money he had inherited. Evidently, it was quite a large sum to set him up in the narcotics business. Even before he took the money the deceased had, that slime made more money,"

Rusty's heart dropped to the floor, "in three months than I could make in—" Joel stopped in mid-sentence. Directing immediate attention to the disdain look on Rusty's face, he said, "Excuse me, Rusty, but are you all right? You look like you've seen a ghost."

"I thought it was a small world when I found out your victim was from my home area in Nebraska, and she knew ... " Rusty stopped to swallow. He rubbed his forehead as if he had a headache. "I have a gut feeling the world is much smaller than any of us ever realize."

Confused, Joel said, "I don't understand what you're talking about. Do you mind filling me in?"

"Sure. I could be dead wrong but the name John Daniel Hobart is very familiar to me. An old friend, Ward Luden, was the former Cole County Sheriff in Nebraska. He had supported a young man for years by that same name as your perp. When Ward died, he left quite a large sum of money to the young man. I sent him the vast amount of inheritance Ward left him. The Hobart I was in contact with, I thought, was either a senior in high school or had just graduated. I'm not sure anymore. Time goes by too swift. We may be talking about two different people with the same name, Joel, but it just all seems too coincidental."

"Good grief, Rusty. Do you think it could be one and the same person?"

"You know, the Hobart I wrote to lived down south, so it probably isn't him. At least, I hope not."

"I can take you to lock-up, if you want to ID him."

Shaking his head, Rusty declined. "That wouldn't do any good. I've never met the young man in person. I wouldn't know what he looks like. It's been well over a year since I've heard from him. I tried to keep in contact with John Daniel through mail correspondence, but my last three letters came back with addressee unknown." Rusty had another thought. "You mentioned his driver's license, so I assume your perp had his ID on him when you picked him up?"

"Yes, he had an Illinois Driver's License. He had a billfold with a few notes in it, but nothing that was of any importance to us. For the most part, it was a lot of numbers and dates. All we could do was to assume that they were some sort of code for his drug operation. Nothing that we could decipher."

"Maybe not to you, Joel, but if you don't mind, I'd like to see those papers. Perhaps something will ring a bell with me. If nothing else, it will make me feel better knowing it isn't the same person."

"You're sure welcome to take a look at them. I'll have Steve take you to personal property lock-up before you leave the station today."

"Did your perp, by any slim chance, have a sheriff's badge amongst his belongings?"

"No," Joel stated, shaking his head. "We went over the warehouse with a fine tooth comb, Rusty. If he had one, we sure never found it."

"Then your perp is probably not the same kid I'm speaking of, which is a relief. But I'll check out those papers anyway, just to be sure."

"Of course."

"I appreciate all the poop, but I won't take up any more of your time.

I'll be on my way," Rusty stated, getting to his feet. "Thanks for your time and your help, Joel."

Also standing, folder in hand, Joel headed to the door. "That goes likewise for me, Rusty. I'll appreciate any information you can get me on the deceased. Even if it is after my perp's trial, I'd like to know who she is for my own personal reasons. Just as soon as Hobart is tried and convicted, I'll get the girl's body and all of her personal belongings released to you."

"If you ever get to Kidwell, look me up."

"You know, I might just do that. I miss Oscar around here, so maybe I'll give him a visit sometime in the future. Then we can all get together and have a beer."

Steve took Rusty to personal property lock-up, so Rusty could go through the papers in Daniel's billfold. He found a torn piece of paper with a date written on it. It wouldn't have meant anything to anyone else, but to Rusty, it was devastating. The paper had been ripped out of Rusty's own letter to John Daniel. It was the date that Ward had died.

After the discovery, upon Rusty's request, Steve took him to John Daniel's cell. As Rusty looked through the bars at the prisoner, he was steaming mad. Although Rusty had never been a violent man, he wanted to go inside the cell and beat the living daylights out of him.

"So, you're John Daniel," Rusty stated in a resounding voice.

Daniel looked up from the cot he was sitting on. "You must be a stupid man to ask a stupid question," Daniel remarked with sarcasm.

"Yes, I guess I am stupid, right behind my good friend—him for supporting you, and me for sending you the money. I 'have no mercy' for punks like you. God forgive me, but may you rot in hell."

Daniel's eyes got as big as saucers. He looked like he had seen the devil himself. Neither spoke another word. Rusty turned and left, leaving Daniel in his own thoughts.

On the flight back from Illinois to Nebraska, Rusty sat in deep depression. His thoughts turned to Ward, as he stared out the window into the clouds below.

I'm so sorry, Ward. You worked hard your whole life, and lived a modest life so you would have a comfortable retirement. The unselfish person that you were, you not only supported the young man, but you left him all of your worldly possessions.

Send me a sign if I'm wrong, but I imagine the sin of your grandfather drew you into connecting with John Daniel. So, you supported the kid— I don't even know for how many years— trying to ease the guilt you carried on your shoulders and in your heart, and to prove that you weren't prejudice against skin color, like your grandfather had been. It's a shame the punk you befriended had to turn out to be a drug dealer and a murderer.

God, how does life get so messed up.

Rusty wondered how many more unexpected mysteries he would have to uncover before he could put his puzzle together, once and for all.

JOINING FORCES

John Daniel Hobart never made it to court. In mid-March a uniformed officer found Daniel hanging in his cell. Rather than go through a trial and face the consequences of his actions, he had committed suicide.

Around the first of April, after all the red tape of the judicial system was completed, Rusty received Farm Girl's body and her personal belongings. As promised, Rusty gave Farm Girl a decent burial at one of the local cemeteries. Not knowing her *true* identity, he waited on the headstone.

After a brief rummage through her package of belongings, Rusty pulled out a ring and a metal cup. Both of the items bore severe tarnish. He cleaned both items the best he could. The cup didn't seem to clean up as well as the ring did. The engraving in the inside of the ring was far too small for Rusty to read with his naked eye. He used a magnifying glass to assist him.

Having two clues to start with, Rusty then solicited the aide of Kelly and Janx to help him on their off-duty hours. The three of them sat in Rusty's living room, enjoying a cold beer, when Rusty disbursed the items for their mini-investigations. Until Rusty could prove without a doubt that Farm Girl was definitely connected to Darin by assisting him in getting the stolen money out of the area, he didn't want to give out detailed information, even to his friends and past colleagues.

All Rusty explained was that a Chicago Detective, one that Oscar Denton used to work with, asked for assistance in locating the identification of a murder victim. Since she was from the Cole County area, Oscar had solicited his assistance. Rusty also informed the men that the girl's first name could be Daisy. Even though she wasn't a published author, there was a remote possibility that she chose Farm Girl as her pen name.

"I appreciate you two agreeing to help me find out who this girl was."

"Okay, if you don't mind me asking. Why are we investigating an ID for a girl who was killed out of state?" Janx inquired. "And why is it so important to you to find out who this Jane Doe is?"

"Janx has a point," Kelly stated. "You only mentioned that you were soliciting our help as a personal favor to you. Don't you think we deserve a little more information instead of all this mysterious secrecy you seem to be hiding?"

"Sorry, fellas, but you'll have to trust me on this one. I don't want to give you all the details, yet, until I know what I'm looking for. You'll just have to take my word that this could be linked to a past case here in Cole County. Now, don't draw any conclusions with that statement, and please don't ask me for anymore pertinent information. I promise, when the right time comes, I'll fill you in with all the details.

And before you even ask, Kelly, I know you're the chief now. This has nothing to do with an ongoing case that either you or Sheriff Martin are working on. I'm sure you know that I wouldn't do anything that would break the law, especially withholding vital information."

"That never crossed my mind," Kelly replied with a shake of his head. "Okay, what do you want Janx and me to do?"

Rusty gave the gold ring to Officer Janx to see if he could come up with a jeweler, whom had either made the ring or sold it. And, if possible, any information as to a customer's name that had purchased it. "I want to know if that ring was the deceased's own personal ring. Was it a family heirloom? Was it just an old ring purchased at a pawnshop, or, has it ever been reported as stolen? I want any and all information we can get, Janx," Rusty stated.

The one thing they knew right then was that the ring had the initials C.N.R. engraved on the inside. Rusty was guessing that the ring was at least as old as Daisy was when she was murdered, give or take a few years.

"I'll do my best Chief, ah, Mr. Simmons, or—Rusty. Man, what do I call you now?" Janx asked, somewhat confused. "I can't keep ignoring calling you by name every time I see you." He laughed.

"Hey, you call me Chief now, remember?" Kelly joined in the laughter.

"I expect you to call me Rusty, just like Kelly does. I won't mind a slip of the tongue now and then if you call me Chief, but anyone who calls me Mister is done for," Rusty stated with humor.

Rusty gave the small metal cup to Kelly to see if he could find out any kind of information as to its origin. "Darn, Rusty, this one will be like finding that well known needle in the haystack," Kelly grunted.

"It's like I always told you when I was the chief. Any tidbit of info is more than we had before. Just do your best, Kelly. That's all I can ask."

After the off-duty officers left Rusty's home, he called his good friend, Special Agent Coats, at the FBI Crime Lab. Since it had been close to a year since the girl's death, Rusty asked if he could find out any information on Jane Doe's birth certificate that had been sent in by the Chicago Police Department's 23rd Precinct back in June the year before. Coats told Rusty that wasn't his department, but he would nose around and see if he could come up with any information, then call him back.

"Also, Rusty," Coats added, "remember this is a favor that could cause me some problems if someone knew I was giving out information to you. You know when you retired, you ceased being a cop anymore and lost the privilege of dealing directly with the Feds."

"You don't have to remind me, Leo. I'm quite aware that I no longer wear a uniform. But I'm asking as a friend, and would die before getting you in trouble," Rusty responded.

"Wait," Coats laughed, "you don't have to go that far. Just keep it under your hat."

"I hate to ask, but why would there be such a long delay in getting this birth certificate back by now?"

"It takes a lot of time and patience to first find out what was used to obliterate the original ink on the document. Then it takes careful testing to see what chemicals will remove the obliteration, if any, without destroying the writing under it or the paper. Add to the fact that this isn't a rush case, so it's possible that it's sitting on a back burner until the techs have time to get to it. At any rate, I'll see what I can find out and get back to you," Coats concluded.

Once Rusty had everything rolling, he called Oscar to update him.

"So you see, Oscar, we don't really have much to go on at this point."

"What do you want me to do?"

"It's best if you just sit tight for now."

"Okay, but keep me abreast of things, and let me know when and how I can help."

"Thanks, Oscar. I'll do that."

For the life of him, Rusty couldn't figure out why there was an old rusty coffee can amongst the deceased girl's belongings. Hoping it might be a clue in the girl's identity, somewhere down the line in his investigation, he set the can aside.

Rusty took the time to go through the deceased girl's stories to see if any of them had helpful information. Since the birth certificate held the initials F.G., Rusty decided to drop the Jane Doe and the Daisy, and call the unknown girl Farm Girl. While he worked alone in his house, Rusty sorted through the pile of her papers. He had to agree with Joel, Farm Girl's so-called printing was similar to a child's scribbling. Elated would be an understatement explaining Rusty's emotions when Darin's name popped up. That meant Farm Girl had written about Darin.

Rusty hoped his efforts would result in finding some important clues to his puzzle. He had the puzzle all put together with the exception of one small missing piece. The last puzzle piece, in Rusty's mind, was the answer to one question. Was the girl working with Darin, or did she take the money on her own? However, in order to find that answer, he presumed, he had to find out the girl's identity.

As he made a brief scan of the titles, he separated the stories into different piles. Many that he considered juvenile stories, he put into one pile. Any that mentioned the girl's growing up years, Mama or Jefferson's name, went into another pile. The ones with Darin's name, Rusty placed in yet another pile. There were some titles referring to both Welk and Darin. Rusty kept them in a separate pile.

Scattered amongst Farm Girl's stories were pages and pages of notes that detailed every event. To Rusty, it appeared obvious she used these notes to write each brief story. As Rusty separated this vast amount of papers from the stories, he could only imagine how long it would take him to decipher them. If more details were needed to put his puzzle together, these notes would be essential. But for now, they were set aside.

In his first review of the stories, Rusty tried to make out some of the words and make sense out of the sentences, which was difficult because of the terrible grammar Farm Girl had used. As he began to understand what he was reading, he figured out that most of Farm Girl's stories had a pattern, and that pattern became her weekly, if not daily, diary of her life. However, with no dates on many of the papers he scanned, there was no way to know when the deceased wrote them. Wanting to get to know Farm Girl, he just started reading.

Each time he finished a few stories, he sat and commented to himself about the life of Farm Girl that was unfolding before his very eyes.

"Mama, or whatever your real name was, you did one hellava number on your kid. After reading some of Farm Girl's accounting of you, I can see why you recorded your name as Nobody on Farm Girl's birth certificate. That was an inside joke, I assume. As for Farm Girl, I guess the girl's real name is F.G. Light, according to what I've read in her stories, thus far. I'll be sure to check that name in the courthouse archives for birth records. I suppose I had better check both names—Light and Nobody—just to be on the safe side.

A couple of things make more sense to me now. Being an orphan and not knowing your real name, other than Cheryl, gave you reason to keep changing your name to any name that suited you. If that's the case, Mama, then the name Nobody wouldn't be your real name, would it. To be on the safe side, I'll have to add the name Cheryl to my list with both surnames when checking court records.

If you're the woman that Ward questioned on the day that Welk died, then where was your daughter during that time? That doesn't make any sense. Doug said they spoke with a young girl that day. If you're Farm Girl's mother and Farm Girl was born in 1977, you weren't any spring chicken when Jefferson died.

No, something's wrong with this picture. Sure. I'll bet that was Farm Girl posing as her mother. Again, why, and, where was Mama the day Welk died? Damn, Farm Girl, I hope in these stories that I eventually find some more answers. As for right now, you're confusing the hell out me. If Farm Girl took the money on her own, where was Mama? Was she in on it, too? Better yet, where is Mama now?"

Once Rusty finished reading another group of stories, he sat back, going over his new speculations. He drew the conclusion that Darin must have discovered Frank was dying with cancer. "Oh my God! Was Darin planning on murdering Frank?" Rusty's words raced out of his mouth as his mind spun like a blender.

"All that talk about shooting a sick horse could have been a cover-up. If Darin could have found a way to do away with Frank, and make it look like an accident, then Darin would have received his trust fund. If this is true, then maybe we arrested Darin just in time before he could carry through with his heinous plans. I thought Darin was no good before, but this—If my speculation is correct, this makes him out to be pure evil."

Although Rusty was in a hurry to put everything together and solve the mystery that was eating away at his mind, his shoulder pain was getting worse, even with his pain pills. Due to time he needed for rest, it took Rusty over two weeks, at a snail's pace, to get through the stories. Other than a phone call, now and then, to check in with Kelly and Janx, Rusty shut off all contact with the outside world to work as diligent as possible in the solitude of his own home. Time was *not* of the essence. He could take all the time he needed to get all of his facts correctly documented.

He was still waiting for vital information, such as the original birth certificate from the FBI Lab in Quantico, and any information that Janx and Kelly could discover on the ring and cup. Moreover, with Darin behind bars, he didn't have to worry about where to find his perp when he finally put his evidence—his puzzle—together. Rusty had a difficult time waiting for the day he could confront Darin and throw the truth in his face.

One day Rusty found a story that shocked him down to his bones.

MURDER! Holy Mary, Mother of God!" Rusty shouted at the top of his lungs.

FROM SPECULATIONS TO FACTS

"My God of mercy, this mystery puzzle has become bigger and more complex then I ever imagined. Here I thought Darin wanted to kill Frank. When, all along, he was plotting the demise of both Mr. Welk and Farm Girl's mother."

The information was burning inside Rusty, but he had to scan through the remaining stories, just in case there was any more vital information he needed to know. Although Farm Girl's writing was getting a slight more legible, Rusty still found difficulty in scanning them at more than a slow pace. Every disgusting detail he was reading, sickened Rusty inside.

It was of great importance that Rusty find a copy of a document that proved Farm Girl had written the stories in her own hand. If not, Farm Girl's written confession may not hold up in court. At the moment, with Farm Girl dead, there was no way of having her write something new so a handwriting expert could compare the old with the new, therefore proving she *did* write the stories. Until now, there was only the statement from the crackhead female, Micky, that Farm Girl had in fact written them.

Leaving his dining room where he had papers scattered from table to floor, Rusty walked into his living room and picked up the box of Frank's ashes. "Sorry, old pal, but I'm grateful that you aren't alive and having to go through this ordeal. Finding out your brother is a murderer, would have devastated you even more so then Ward finding out about John Daniel. We sure don't live in a perfect world. But, to be crushed by loved ones we put our faith in, has to be the worst possible scenario life can hand us."

Rusty didn't get much sleep that night. He thought he had finally solved his puzzle when he found out what had happened to the missing money and the fact that Darin was now, without any doubts, the Neat Nick Thief.

However, the puzzle was not complete—not by any means. As Rusty would soon discover, it was, in fact, getting more complicated.

The next morning, Rusty was awake and out of bed before the sun came up. The murders had taken place outside Kidwell's city limits. That meant the ball was back in Doug's court. Rusty knew he was sitting on a keg of dynamite. However, there was no call to raise a red flag since the homicides had already taken place.

Rusty drank a full pot of coffee and paced the floor while waiting until, what he thought, was a proper time to call the sheriff's office. Just as soon as the big hand hit twelve and the little hand hit seven, Rusty was on the telephone.

"Sheriff Martin, please. Tell him it's Rusty calling."

After a brief silence, Doug responded. "Good morning, you old badger. I haven't heard from you in a coon's age."

"Good morning to you too, Doug," Rusty chuckled at the early morning teasing.

"See how you are? You retire, then forget your old friends in uniform who have to work for a living."

"I may be retired, but I've been busy. I've opened a hornet's nest, and I'm going to need your help in gathering up all of the hornets."

"What? Come on, Rusty, it's too early in the morning to play word games."

"Unless you get an emergency call, stay right there. I'm on my way over. Oh, in case you haven't already done so, put the coffeepot on," Rusty stated, hanging up the phone.

Rusty gathered up the few stories of incrimination, grabbed his coat and headed out the door.

At the sheriff's office, Doug greeted Rusty in his usual friendly, warm manner. "Rusty, come on in. Just as you requested, I've got coffee brewing."

"I hope it's good and strong. You're going to need it," Rusty said, tongue in cheek.

"Okay. Have a seat. Tell me about this hornet's nest."

"You are not going to believe this, Doug, but I've come across a double homicide."

"Murder? Hey, I thought you retired? Seems to me, I remember attending your retirement party," Doug joked. Noticing the look on Rusty's face, he added, "Okay, you're serious, aren't you? Who got murdered, Rusty?" Rusty didn't have a chance to respond. "No, wait. The coffee should be ready. Let me get us a couple of cups, then you can start at the beginning."

Doug left his office for a short time, returning with two full mugs. He handed one to Rusty and took the other with him back to his desk chair. "Okay, Rusty. Clue me in."

Just as a precautionary measure in case a visitor should arrive in the front office, Rusty got up and closed Doug's door. Returning to his seat, he commented, "I know your deputy is trustworthy, but that's just in case someone else comes into the outer office."

"No, problem. Come on now. Let's hear it. Don't keep me in suspense any longer."

When Rusty finished explaining what Oscar had informed him back in December, followed by his conversation with Joel in January, he went into detail about Farm Girl, her belongings, her burial, her stories and the double murder. After explaining that he had rewritten every story, just to be able to understand them, Rusty laid the few important stories he had brought with him on Doug's desk.

"If you look at the ones I've re-written, you'll find some words in parenthesis. Those are my words replacing the girl's words. After Doug acknowledged that he understood, Rusty continued. "We have to do several things, Doug," Rusty stated, very serious, then burst into a chuckle. He almost choked on his coffee.

"Rusty, are you all right? What's so funny about this information?"

Rusty shook his head and wiped the dribbled coffee from his chin. "I'm fine, and the story *is* dreadful. I was laughing at me. Listen to me— *we* have to—this is your baby. I apologize for appearing to take over."

"Oh, crap, we won't sweat the small stuff, Rusty. Look, I'll do my job, but I always did respect you as a law officer. Feel free to tell me what *you* would do. Now, if I happen to disagree with you, I won't hesitate telling you so."

"Okay, that's a deal. I believe we need to go back out to Welk's place and—wait. I should've asked first if it's still available for us to go on the property. The last I remember, the property was tied up in probate. Has the government taken it over, or did the bank get possession?"

"You know, Rusty," Doug sat back and grinned, "you need to spend more time reading the local newspapers. It appears you've let this case with Darin consume you. You don't seem to know what's going on around you anymore."

"As much as I hate to admit it, you're right. This case has become an obsession with me. Overlooking my obsession, I also feel that I have to do all of this for Frank. I feel, deep down inside my gut, that if the situation were reversed, Frank would be sitting, right here, doing the same thing for me. Plus the fact, I was on your end of the fence for so long, I guess getting to the truth is embedded in me. Now, what about Welk's place?"

"According to some bank officials—I won't mention names right now—but they thought some valuable bank records were destroyed when they installed a new banking computer system. That was back a few years ago. Consequently, this caused a mix-up of Welk's trust account visual records.

Seems there were only two employees at the bank who handled Welk's account. One was their main loan officer, Wallace Dodd. The other—surprise, surprise—was Darin Righter. They can't prove it, but they suspect Darin as the guilty party in hiding Welk's accounting records. Since you had cleared Dodd of all wrongdoing during your Neat Nick Thief investigation, well, that's why they're now pointing the finger at Darin. No one can figure out what Darin would have gained by such a carefully planned out catastrophe. He certainly didn't try to abscond with any of the money.

Once they restored the records, the bank could account for every misplaced penny. However, just to give you the flip side of the coin, there is also the speculation that this could have been just a human error on Darin's part but he didn't tell anyone. A month or so ago, when there was a major bank audit by the FDIC, that's when the information was found and restored. The ironic part is the bank has some sort of automatic back-up system on their computers. Have I lost you yet, Rusty?"

"Yes, and no. I realize Sharpin's bank isn't all that big, but why did it take so long to find the files? Don't they have someone in the bank that knows anything about the system they installed?"

"It appears they only had one person take the training course for the automated system—Darin Righter. That's why there's speculation that the mix-up may have been accidental. The bottom line is, Welk was still a very wealthy man when he died. Here's the fly in the crapper. Remember that Last Will and Testament on the computer disk?" Sitting on pins and needles, Rusty could barely contain himself to tell Doug everything he had discovered. However, he sat quietly, enjoying his coffee, and listening as Doug brought him up-to-date about Jefferson's Last Will and Testament, and the fact that he bequeathed his wealth to his missing daughter and his farmhand."

"I'm not sure, but think the D.A. already told me that, Doug. Talk about bad breaks in life. That poor farmhand probably worked for others all of her life, never having more than a couple of bucks here and there, and now she's dead—murdered by the hands of her own daughter. Then her daughter steals part of her own mother's inheritance money when she robs Welk."

"Whoa, you lost me there, Rusty. Back up and run that by me again."

"According to Detective Joel Applemeyer, Farm Girl had a suitcase full of money, rare coins and gold coins in her possession when she met up with her killers. That's why she was murdered. However, none of the victims in the Neat Nick Thief case ever reported the theft of any gold coins. If two plus two equals four, my guess is the gold belonged to Jefferson Welk. So, this little gal not only took Darin's money from him, but she also helped herself to everything Welk had saved and hidden in his home."

"Scuttlebutt has it that Welk owed a lot of bills when he died. If the gold belonged to him, why didn't he use it to get out of debt?"

"Who knows why some people do what they do, Doug? It's difficult to speculate what makes some people tick."

"God, Rusty, what a terrible world we live in, at times."

"That's an understatement. Which brings me to another shock I discovered in Chicago, but I'll explain that to you when we get finished here. We know for a fact that Welk is dead. What we do *not* know as factual is that her mother is also dead. All we have to go by is Farm Girl's stories. With both of Welk's heirs missing, the bank must still hold possession of the property." To keep their investigation legal, Rusty was more than aware of what the following procedure would be. However, Doug was wearing the uniform, not him. "So, Sheriff, what's our next step?"

"Since we're talking murder, we need to get a court order and go back to Welk's place."

"I agree. We need to search the total grounds. What we'll be looking for is a small log and stone shanty hidden in a wooden area and sitting close to the river. Back when my officers and I searched Welk's place, we never even thought to go roaming all over the back forty, looking for a shack or any other buildings. Of course, I wanted to look for the Welk's burial plot, but we never did.

That area close to the shack, according to one of the stories, is where we should find Mama Cheryl's body buried and some evidence the girl threw down a well. Incidentally, from Farm Girl's notes, that's the same shack built by Moses Welk."

"Oh," Doug responded with raised brow. "Now some of the pieces are beginning to come together in my mind."

"Welcome to my club." Rusty laughed. "That's an inside joke. Say, have they had any luck in finding the Welk kid?"

"Not to my knowledge, Rusty. From that heart-wrenching saga you told me last year, I don't give it much hope. Do you?"

"Not really. It's been too many years. I'm afraid, now, that all they will come up with is a lot of wannabes. When there is a search for a missing heir, involving a large fortune, all the kooks seem to come out of the woodwork," Rusty observed from his past law enforcement experiences.

"Look, we'll have to have the construction crew on stand-by so we can retrieve everything we can from that well," Rusty added. "Then we'll have the body, if we find it, and you've got the written confession in these stories. All—"

"Wait a minute. Why do you want the items out of the well?"

"Insurance, Doug. That no good bum, Darin, got off too easy this last time. He walked away with a few years and a smug look on his face. Then, he practically spat in the face of the one man who really loved him—Frank.

I understand Darin's still hollering about how innocent he is. He's not going to walk away from this one. Not if I have any say about it. I want every piece of evidence I can lay my hands on to nail that malicious, no-good excuse for a human to the wall. You might say, I'm on a personal crusade to see that Darin never walks the streets a free man, again, to hurt anyone else. Damn," Rusty clenched his fist, hitting it against the palm of his other hand, "that little bastard infuriates me."

"Understandable," Doug agreed.

"Back to the well. According to these stories, Darin sent some deadly substance to Farm Girl. In turn, per Darin's instructions, Farm Girl mixed this substance in Welk and Mama Cheryl's coffee. Whatever this substance was, we need to exhume the bodies of both Welk and the girl's mother, and have an autopsy performed on both of them.

Just in case nothing shows up, we need that thermos that Farm Girl threw down the well. If she screwed the top on tight, the thermos should be airtight. If that's the case, it should still contain some of the poisoned coffee inside. I know, I'm really reaching for a star, Doug, but I can only hope. Are you with me, so far?"

"Yes, and so far I agree with everything you're saying. Do you suppose we need to see if we can find anything else around Welk's house showing this girl's handwriting on it? And, hopefully, something with her name on it?"

"My thoughts exactly," Rusty agreed. "The only thing we have right now is the word of a crackhead. I'm hoping, since the girl spent a lot of time in Jefferson's house, that something she wrote got mixed up with his paperwork. We wouldn't have been looking for papers with scribbling on them when we were searching the place before. So, we might have seen something but just ignored, at the time."

"Anything else?"

Rusty explained all that he, Denton, Kelly and Janx, were doing to locate the correct identity of Farm Girl and her mother, including the fact the FBI Crime Lab was working on Farm Girl's Certificate of Birth. "Once we know the mother and the girl's *real* identities, we can find out if they have any living relatives." Rusty pondered a second. Then he replied, "Say. I wonder—if we do find any of this Farm Girl's living relatives—if they're the ones who will inherit part of the Welk fortune?"

"Only a lawyer can answer that, Rusty. Okay, let's—"

"Oh, no! Oh, sorry, Doug. Didn't mean to interrupt you, but I just had a horrible thought." Doug knew he had a questionable look on his face, but he never said a word as Rusty continued verbalizing his sudden thought pattern. "I was just wondering, if that punk, Darin, knew about the Will that Welk had, and met up with Farm Girl on purpose, knowing she would end up with that fortune.

Maybe he *did* plan to abscond with Welk's trust out of the bank, or had figured how to do it. Then he found out it would be easier to meet the girl whose mother was to inherit a fortune. Stealing from a girl—who is lacking in everything from good judgment to education—would be a far cry easier than trying to steal a trust fund from a bank. It makes sense, doesn't it? Jefferson leaves his fortune to Mama Cheryl, and with Mama dead, Farm Girl gets it all."

"Unless, of course, there are other siblings or there's another Will someplace that we don't know about," Doug interceded. "As long as we're being presumptuous here, maybe this Mama Cheryl also had a Will."

"Yes, you could be right. On the other hand, it sounds like something Darin would do just to get his hands on the trust money. Sorry I got so carried away, but I wouldn't put anything past Darin."

"You know, Rusty, you should write a book someday. You can really let your thoughts run away with you," Doug joked.

"You mean because I'm so full of hot air, have a wild imagination, talk a lot, and I have a tendency to keep repeating myself?" Rusty chuckled at the thought.

"No. I'm serious. I really think you should consider it."

"Me, write a book?" Rusty's chuckle became a roar of laughter. "Oh, Doug, that's a good one. If you only knew how much I hate writing, you would never even suggest such a thing, let alone think of it. Oh, that's rich."

After both men settled down from their moment of clownish remarks, it was back to business.

"Getting back on track, sit tight, Rusty, and let me make a few phone calls. Thank the good Lord for small favors. It's April and the weather has been halfway decent. I sure wouldn't want to have to go digging around if we still had six inches or more of snow on the ground." Doug laughed as he picked up the telephone receiver.

"Better cold then hot and humid, since Mama's body was never embalmed," Rusty added, making a sour-faced expression.

While Doug made his telephone calls, Rusty refilled their mugs and brought them back to the office.

Within an hour, the sheriff had a Search Warrant and a court order to exhume Mama's body, should they find it. After they got the key to Welk's house, Doug, his deputy and Rusty headed to Welk's farm.

As they drove, Rusty relayed the sad news about the identity of the young man who had killed Farm Girl. Doug was almost as shocked as Rusty had been when he made the discovery.

They also chatted on how unusual the winter had been. October through December had seen freezing temperatures and a lot of snow. Although the temperatures had been more on the mild side since the middle of March, the ground beneath the muddy exterior, in all probability, was still well frozen.

"When we get to Jefferson's house, let's start our search in the room where we found the computer. According to one of the stories, other than the kitchen, that's where the girl did most of her studying with Jefferson. If we're going to find anything in her handwriting, that room is our best bet. Besides, I have a wastebasket to check out for the discarded envelope."

"A discarded envelope? What for?" Doug asked.

"How about the envelope that housed the poison? As I told you back at your office, in many of Farm Girl's stories she explained every sorted detail of the murders. Darin mailed the foreclosure notice—along with a small packet of poison—in an envelope from the First People's Bank of Sharpin. She mentioned throwing the envelop in the wastebasket next to the computer."

"Say, that makes sense, now, why there was no envelope the day Welk died," Doug said.

"Okay, now *you* have lost *me*."

"The girl said Welk always opened his mail at breakfast. He died holding on to the bank's foreclosure notice but there wasn't an envelope anywhere in site. I don't think either Ward or I thought about it, at the time, because the girl mentioned she had cleaned the kitchen before we arrived."

Rusty nodded. "Covering her tracks. Darin told Farm Girl to throw away the envelope. Lucky for us, she told in a story where she had tossed it." After a bit of silence, Rusty had another thought. "I'm having one of those gut feelings, Doug. Going back to the girl's stories, she mentioned the enjoyment she got from the books Jefferson read to her. Which, of course, coincides with the fact that she liked to write. While I search through the wastebasket and the paperwork on the desk, why don't you start going through the books."

"Why the books?"

"I've never owned a bookmark. Often times, after I've read a number of pages from a book, I want to rest my eyes. I'll find a paper that's close by and use it as a bookmark. It's just a hunch, but a possibility that Jefferson or Farm Girl did the same thing."

"Yeah, I see what you mean. I lost an important document, once, for doing the exact same thing," Doug relayed, with an under the breath chuckle. "If I recall, Welk had shelves and shelves of books. That'll take some time to flip through them."

"Yes and no. Since the girl appeared to have a child's mind, I'd start with the children's books."

At Jefferson farm, Doug sent his deputy to scout around the property while he and Rusty went to the house.

"Didn't you board up the door when you were here last, Rusty?"

"We did. Someone else, obviously, removed the boards."

As they walked through the house on the way to the sitting room, stepping over items strewed about the floor, Doug remarked, "This place wasn't in this much of a disarray the last time you and I were here. Looks like someone's ransacked the place."

"Sorry, Doug, but I'm your guilty party. When my officers and I were here searching for evidence against Darin, we really made a mess of the place."

"Oh, yeah, when you came out here with your Search Warrant. Shame on you," Doug teased.

"Oh, well," Rusty replied. "Why do you suppose the door was no longer boarded up?"

"I'm guessing the bankers might have done it. I'll find out when we get back to town."

It didn't take very long for the discovery of vital evidence. After only a few minutes, digging through the wastebasket, Rusty remarked with joy, "Well I'll be—just where she said it would be. Take a look at what I found." He held up a used envelope, showing it to Doug. "We went through this wastebasket before, but overlooked this envelope from the bank in Sharpin. Of course we weren't really looking for it, at the time."

"Good work, Rusty."

"Could we be lucky enough to have some of the residue still in the bottom of this old envelope? What do you think?"

"It works for me," Doug agreed.

Doug reached in his pocket and took out one of the clear plastic evidence bags he had brought along with him. Rusty placed the envelope inside the bag. As Rusty went through the papers on the desk and in the desk drawers, Doug continued going through books. Finally, stuck in a book entitled *Bambi*, Doug pulled a piece of writing paper from the book's pages.

"Well, well, well. Look Rusty. I have here a paper that I think says, The Story of the Fly by Farm Girl. Since I didn't really look at those stories you brought to my office, does this chicken scratching look familiar?"

Walking across the room to where Doug was standing, Rusty looked at the paper. "It does," Rusty said, patting Doug on the back. "I've certainly seen enough of that scribble in the last few weeks to recognize it. Bag it. That's one we can send to the FBI Crime Lab for handwriting comparison."

Doug bagged the handwritten evidence. "So, what's next?"

"My guys and I made a pretty thorough inspection of the place the last time we were here. That's when we picked up the torn sock, a rag, and collected fibers from the metal bedsprings upstairs in the bedroom. At the time, we didn't know if they were evidence, or not."

"Were they?"

"According to the stories, yes. However, with our new prime evidence, we might not need them."

"Well, I think we've about recovered everything we need from the house."

"What do you say we go out and see what my deputy is up to."

Nodding in answer to Doug suggestion, Rusty's said, "Let's go."

Outside, they caught up with the deputy who informed them he found an old shack close to the river. After explaining he had almost gotten the patrol car stuck, he suggested they go back to town and get a 4-wheeler or a front drive pick-up truck because the ground was still very wet and muddy from the melted snows.

"How far is that shack from here?" Rusty asked, looking off into the distance in the direction the deputy had pointed out.

"Not far, sir. Maybe a quarter mile," the deputy answered.

"Did you find anything that looked like a grave over by the shack?" Rusty inquired.

"To be honest, I didn't get that close. Driving through that field, I noticed a path next to the trees. That's what I followed. When I came to a clearing, and what appears to be a narrow road, I turned in. I followed the road as far as I dared. It's really nothing but mud. Anyway, I only got a glimpse of the place."

"Doug, if you don't mind, I'd like to walk it. The two of you can go after another vehicle. I'll meet you over there. Oh, and maybe you should send for the crew to come out and exhume this woman's body, assuming we find a grave over there," Rusty suggested.

"I'm going with you," Doug stated.

Doug sent his deputy back to town to get a vehicle that could handle the muddy grounds, and instructions to notify the county corner and the stand-by maintenance crew to come out to Welk's farm.

"A bit soggy, but a nice day for a stroll," Doug commented, as they walked.

"The only bad thing with ground this muddy, you don't know for sure what you're stepping in—mud or cow pies." Rusty laughed.

"Thanks a hellava lot," Doug said, joining in on the laughter. "Leave it to you to ruin a nice walk in the sunshine."

With the shack buried amongst the shelter of the trees, the ground still showed signs of winter with snow mounds, here and there.

As they approached the small structure, Rusty pointed and remarked, "Look over there. That's the big old oak tree, I'll bet."

Doug looked in the direction that Rusty was pointing out. "Son-ofgunya, that's one huge tree. Refresh my memory, in case you've already told me. What significance does the tree have to this case?"

"First, I believe that's the tree the vigilantes hung Moses Welk from. Secondly, and I have to refer, once again, to the girl's stories, the Welk family members are buried under it's sprawling branches. And, most important of all, Mama is supposed to buried by this shack facing that tree." Rusty headed for the oak tree.

Doug didn't join him. Something caught his eye so he walked closer to the shack. He noticed that one snow mound sat fuller and higher than all the other mounds. Locating a twig, Doug started poking around in the large mound. Discovering the mound was mostly soil, he scraped off some of the top layer of snow. "Look here, Rusty," Doug yelled.

Turning back, Rusty responded, "What did you find?"

"There seems to be something written in rocks on this mound of dirt. Some of the rocks are gone so I don't quite understand if it's a design or letters."

In his usual stride, Rusty walked over to where Doug was standing by the damp mound of dirt. He bent over, bracing one hand on his knee. With his other hand, he carefully removed the rest of the snow that covered the rocks. In his heart, he already knew what it said, but he verbally spelled out each letter. "N-B-O-D. From the remaining rocks, I can only assume that two of those missing letters were the *O* and the *Y*. So, this is it, Doug. This is where Farm Girl buried her Mama—Nobody's Final Home."

"Excuse me?"

"It's the title of one of Farm Girl's stories. This is Mama Cheryl's grave." Standing upright, Rusty started looking around on the ground. "According to the girl's story about the murders, the shovel she used to bury her mother should be close by."

"Come on, Rusty, you don't plan on digging before the crew gets here, do you?"

"Ha!" Rusty laughed. "Not hardly. I just figured Farm Girl's prints might still be on the shovel. Laying out in the weather, I doubt it, but anything is possible."

Concentrating on finding the shovel, Rusty forgot about going back to the large oak. As the men looked around the area close to the grave, Doug used the twig he was still carrying, to poke around the ground.

Scraping his boot across the small areas of snow, Rusty commented, "You know, Doug, right this moment, I don't know whether to cry for this mother or to be very angry at her for the way she raised her daughter.

Here it is," he said, hitting the shovel with his foot. Picking up the shovel, careful not to touch the handle, Rusty walked back to the mound.

All of a sudden, Doug felt his heart pounding harder than usual as he experienced a horrendous flash back. "Oh, my God! We might have saved this woman's life."

Dropping the shovel on the ground next to Mama's grave, Rusty was quick to note the expression on Doug's face. He looked as if he were ready to pass out. Rusty rushed to Doug's side. "Calm down. You're as white as a sheet, Doug. What are you talking about?"

"That day at the farmhouse when Welk died. That little gal took a thermos of coffee with her when she left the house. She said it would help her to keep warm while she did chores."

"Yeah, I know. I told you about the thermos."

"It didn't hit me until just now. Did she happen to mention that Ward took the thermos and opened it, then had Doc Shivley check the contents just to make sure it was coffee?" Rusty gave a negative shake of his head. "I remember Doc saying something, like the coffee smelled strong enough to kill someone, or something to that affect. I never thought about it until this very second. We allowed that girl to take the thermos of poison to kill her own mother."

"She left out that part in her stories. Come on, Doug. You aren't responsible any more than Ward was, or even Doc was for that matter. You all followed good law enforcement procedures that day. How was Doc to know that what he smelled was nothing more than strong coffee? Come on, now, and settle down. We can be thankful that Doc didn't drink it or he might not be with us any longer either."

"I can't remember if Doc stuck his finger in the coffee and tasted it, or not, but I think he did."

"Quit beating yourself up, over it. None of you could have foreseen what was about to happen."

"Common sense dictates you're right, Rusty. But, it still gives me a terrible feeling in my insides."

Attempting to take Doug's mind off guilt, Rusty said, "Hey, let's go inside this shack and look around. You lead the way."

Doug headed for the door. Rusty followed. Stepping inside, Doug was appalled at what he was witnessing. "Jesus, Mary and Joseph! What a terrible way to live." As Doug looked around the small room, Rusty entered the shack. "I can't believe this, Rusty. One room with what looks like a bed of straw, and one small stone fireplace for heat and cooking.

Walls stuffed with straw and rags to keep out the weather. My God, do we still allow humans to exist this way today in the United States?"

"I guess so, Doug. The only consolation, if one could call it that, is that they at least had a roof over their heads and food to eat. A lot of people today don't even have that luxury."

"I have to admit, I'm ashamed of myself. When I grew up, they didn't have too many homeless people where I lived back east. Maybe they did and I never noticed. If you don't see it, you don't think too much about it. It doesn't hit you as reality. Shit, this hit me like a ball peen hammer right between the eyes. Let's get out of here."

Rusty's eyes met the floor. He bent over and picked up something, then stood erect. Holding the item, he remarked, "If my memory serves me correctly, this looks like a match to that sock we found on the floor in Jefferson's bedroom. I had forgotten that Farm Girl wrote she had just thrown the sock on the floor after she emptied it. She was pretty detailed, but this was a big error in her story."

"How's that?"

"She says she left the second torn sock on the floor of the shack because the sock belong to Welk. She felt, since it would be found on Welk's property, no one searching the place would be concerned."

"Makes sense to me, Rusty."

"It would seem that way if she hadn't been so detailed in her stories. According to her, they were the socks that Darin had taken from Frank. It doesn't really make a difference—other than forgetting whom the socks belonged to—because everything else Farm Girl wrote about is fitting into place. It's funny, though, how one little piece of evidence, like this sock, could have linked Darin to the girl and the money without everything else."

"Through Frank's DNA?"

"You bet."

After placing the sock in a small plastic bag, Rusty got back to what Doug had mentioned a few minutes prior. "You know, Doug, this place and your comments have got me thinking. Between you and me—and the proverbial fence post—Frank left quite a bundle of money to yours truly. When this is all over, I'm going to start a fund of some kind—maybe even build something, like a home for the needy—right here in Cole County. I'll put Frank's money to good use.

At my age, it's for darned sure that I could never spend it all before the Good Lord calls in my badge number. And you know, I think it would make Frank happy if he knew I spent his money on those less fortunate souls."

"It sounds like a wonderful idea, Rusty."

"Can you just imagine five people living in this tiny abode?"

"Five? Oh, you're speaking about Jefferson's ancestral family. No, I can't. I can't even imagine one person living in this hole."

The two men left the shack and walked around outside. Waiting for the crew to show up, they talked about fishing. Within a short time, they witnessed the parade of vehicles driving down the road toward them. The sheriff's deputy led the way in a four-wheel pick-up with an attached wench. Following the deputy was the digging crew driving a truck that carried a backhoe. Bringing up the rear was the ambulance that, if needed, would transport Mama's body back to town.

Wearing facemasks, the crew set up their equipment and began digging through the top layer of snow and muck, then into the frozen ground. They exhumed a body from the earthen grave. Amazingly to all concerned, the body had not deteriorated as much as everyone thought it would be since there had been no embalming or coffin encasement. As the stench of a dead body filled the air, Rusty and Doug covered their noses and mouths with their coats.

Once the ambulance took away the body, it was time to deal with the old well. Sheriff Martin and Rusty leaned over the side as they watched the lowering of one of the crewmembers into the well.

As the man got further into the well, he made a discovery. Hanging from a splintered plank of wood that formed the well was a piece of material. Realizing the material appeared to be holding something rather bulky inside its confines, he tried to pull the material loose from its resting-place when—

"Oh, crapola!" he yelled.

His voice echoing from the depth, Doug yelled, "You okay, down there? What happened?"

The man hollered back. "Some items obviously wrapped up in this old rag I found, fell out. Dammit! What ever it was has to be at the bottom of the well by now. I'm sorry, Sheriff," the man apologized. "There's something left inside of it. If it's okay with you, I'll bring this part up to you first?"

Looking at the crewmember standing next to him, Doug ordered, "Bring him up." With his attention back to the man in the well, Doug yelled, "We're bringing you up. Hold on to what you've got."

As the crewman got to the top of the well, the bundle he was holding unfolded, proving it was a woman's skirt. Out rolled a thermos along with an old fork. As the items hit the ground, both Rusty and Doug looked at each other and started laughing. The laughter turned into a belly roar of joyful hysteria.

Once they calmed down, Doug looked straight at his freckle-faced, Irish descendent colleague and spouted, "Of all the luck of the Irish."

"Yahoo! I would never have guessed that we could be *this* lucky. I thought everything would be buried a hundred feet down and laying on the well's bottom. Thank you, God," Rusty praised, as he raised his face to heaven. *And, thank you for your help, Ward. I know you had a hand in helping me out down here.* Rusty gave a wink.

As he turned back to Doug and the crew he said, "I don't care what fell out before. This is all we need for now. If our luck holds out, this will be major incriminating evidence against Darin Righter. Well, Doug, mission accomplished."

Doug nodded then turned to the crew. "Thanks a lot for your help. Send the county your bill."

Rusty and Doug left the area with thermos, fork, skirt, sock and shovel in hand. With these items plus the evidence items they had taken from the main house, along with Mama's body, they felt their exploration was successful.

In the car on their drive back to town, Rusty said, "Look, Doug, when we get back, you can drop me off at my car, if you don't mind?"

"No problem."

"I need to go to Frank's house and get a few things. I'll meet you back at your office before you pack up the necessary items to ship off to the FBI Crime Lab."

As soon as he got in his own car, Rusty headed for Frank's house. Because Frank had left him almost all of his possessions, and as executor of the rest, Rusty knew he didn't need a Search Warrant to enter Frank's house and take a few items.

At the house, he went through the boxes with Darin's name on them. Rusty discovered almost every book that Darin owned had marked passages in them just as Frank had said. Once he found the recorder and the cassettes, Rusty took what he needed to the living room. Sitting on the couch, he played one of the cassette tapes. What he heard were two voices who had identified themselves while conversing—Darin speaking with Jefferson Welk. He took the recorder, the tapes, and a few of the books and headed to the sheriff's office.

When Rusty entered Doug's office, Doug was busy dusting the shovel for fingerprints. Because the winter snows, spring rains, and the summer suns had washed off any existing signs of prints, other than Rusty's, the shovel was of no use as evidence.

The sheriff had his deputy store the holey sock in the evidence locker. Since they wouldn't be sending the recorder and the tapes to the FBI, Rusty set them aside on Doug's desk. The court could not use the cassette tapes unless Darin would agree to give a voice recording so the voices could be compared to prove it was Darin's voice on the incriminating cassettes.

Anyone could have made the tapes and used Darin and Jefferson's names while recording the conversations. With Jefferson deceased, he definitely couldn't verify that the voices on the tapes were in fact legitimate. However, Rusty and Doug still wanted to listen to them.

The main concern was to get evidence of poison from the bank envelope and the thermos, and to prove Farm Girl indeed wrote the stories in her own hand. Doug packed the items. Then he sent his deputy to the post office to ship the box of evidence, overnight express, to the FBI Crime Lab. In the meantime, Rusty called his friend, Special Agent Coats, and told him to expect the package.

Doug called Judge Simpson and obtained a court order to exhume Jefferson's body. Next, he got in contact with County Coroner Doc Shivley and gave him vital information. Both Mama and Jefferson's bodies needed an immediate and thorough examination for a poison that would have killed them. Once the results were known, if such a poison existed in their bodies, and if found and identified, the results could then be forwarded to the FBI Crime Lab for comparison to any findings in the envelope and/or the thermos.

After listening to the tapes, Rusty and Doug discovered how Darin had set up Jefferson Welk.

"Okay, Doug, I'll let you get back to your peace and quiet." Rusty laughed. "All joking aside, I really appreciate all you've done." Rusty offered his hand.

"Me?" Doug shook hands with Rusty. "I wouldn't have even known there was a murder, let alone two of them, if it weren't for you. You keep my life exciting."

When Rusty left the sheriff's office, he went straight home. It had been a full day and he was tired, cold and hungry. After a hot shower and a bite to eat, he went to bed.

Black Rosebud

The next morning, Rusty ran some necessary errands. Then he headed to his old stomping grounds, Kidwell's Police Department.

"Hey, Chief, how are you today?" Rusty asked of his replacement.

"Couldn't be any better if I tried, Rusty. How about you? Out bumming are you?" Kelly asked, grinning from ear to ear. "Or, are you checking up on me to see if I'm doing the job right?"

"Frankly, I don't give a—"

"Now, now, Rusty. You know I've got virgin ears," Kelly interceded. "Besides the fact that you don't look like Rhett Butler, and I don't bare even the slightest resemblance to Scarlet O'Hara, that comment has been overused and outdated for years. You're showing your age," he joked with a laugh, and a slap on Rusty's back.

"Okay, you big turkey, so you got me back good. Hey, have any of you guys found out anything on those items yet?"

"Sit down, Rusty, and I'll get Janx in here."

"He wasn't out there a second ago. Maybe he went to the can?"

"No, he's out on patrol. Nothing urgent or he would have called in."

Kelly stuck his head around the corner of his office door. He asked the desk officer to contact Janx and request that he return to the office. Then he went back to his desk and sat in his chair.

Somber faced, Rusty remarked, "Damn, Kelly. Don't you know that's what you have an intercom for? You just push that little button on it that says outgoing, to call out front."

Knowing Rusty, as he did, Kelly always knew when Rusty was trying to get one over on him. However, Kelly had a lot of practice in keeping up with his old boss. "What, and get all fat and out of shape and end up like you? No way. I walk to the door and yell around the corner. It's good exercise for my body and my throat. Besides, that way I can see what's going on out there behind my back."

"Don't tell me you don't trust the guys not doing their jobs while you're in here taking a nap?" Rusty continued to rib.

"Hey, we young chiefs don't need naps, like those old chiefs did."

As both men continued to pull each other's cords, they passed the time until Officer Janx joined them.

"Janx, thank heavens you're here," Rusty exclaimed with a huge grin. "Kelly's smart-mouthed remarks are about to get the best of me."

Janx grinned. "That'll be the day, you sly old fox."

"Janx, you're supposed to stand up for me," Rusty said with a pity-me look, "not pick on me too."

"Hey, when it comes to bullshit and pulling chains, we had a good teacher," Janx replied.

Rusty conceded. Giving Janx a friendly knuckle punch to his upper arm, the jesting stopped and serious talk took over.

Janx explained to Rusty what little he had found out about the ring. He had a local jeweler helping him. "The jeweler thinks it's a mail order piece. He said something about the gold band's simple design rings a bell. So, he's in the process of checking it out. He'll contact me if he finds out anything. As soon as I hear something, Rusty, you know I'll get it to you, ASAP."

"That's great, Janx. Thanks a lot for helping. How about you, Kelly, anything on the cup?"

"It just so happens, my neighbor does a lot of art work using all kinds of metals. So, here you have," Kelly reached into his bottom desk drawer and pulled out a shiny cup, "your basic, silver-plated, baby cup purchased in the 1940's with the initials F.G.R. on the front.

Ta-dah," he said, turning the cup for Rusty to see the initials. "My neighbor said that must have been some awful fire this cup was in, but luckily the heat didn't melt it—just singed it. He's been working on the cup since you gave it to me. I just got it back this morning before I left for work."

Staring at the cup Kelly was holding, Rusty related, "That doesn't make any sense. F.G. could definitely stand for Farm Girl's initials, but from the 1940's? That was way before her birth in the late seventies. The last initial R. doesn't fit either. According to her stories, Farm Girl's last name was Light. If her mother's name was Nobody, the last initial would be N. I'll be hog-tied, another puzzle piece. I'm going to have to figure that one out, but thanks, Kelly."

"There you go again, talking to us in riddles. Are you ready to give us more details now about the girl we're trying to identify? And, how about telling us about all of these mysterious stories you said you were reading and re-writing?" Kelly inquired. "You've been rather vague up to now, Rusty. Not to mention the fact that we all know how you hate to write. So, what gives?"

Janx thoroughly agreed with Kelly. "Sorry, Rusty, but the Chief is right. From day one, when we were at your house and you gave us the items to check out, all you ever said was that you were trying to identify a girl from a Chicago murder. Don't you think it's time we know what a Chicago homicide has to do with the personal investigation you have us working on with you?"

Getting to his feet, Rusty put on a somber face. Acting very serious, he stated, "You're both correct. I wanted to keep details to myself until I was sure I could put all of my speculations into proven facts. Look fellas, I'd like to buy both of you lunch today. Not only to show my gratitude for your help, but—"

Rusty could no longer hold a straight face. Turning his solemn face into an expression of joy, Rusty said, "Men, have I got a whopper of a story for you. I swear you two aren't going to believe it."

"Oh, give me a break, Rusty. When do you ever quit?" Kelly joked. "If this is another one of those Canadian fish stories, then you can buy me lunch— big one with desert."

"I guess I can sit through another one of your fish tales, if you also tell us about this girl you're referring to as Farm Girl. So count me in," Janx said, joining in Kelly and Rusty's laugher.

"Well then, let's go," Rusty stated. "Every good fish story has a great catch. Trust me. This is one huge catch you'll both be interested in. I guarantee it."

At lunch, Rusty told the guys every detail about his investigation. They were flabbergasted and as intrigued as Rusty had been from his first conversation with Oscar about the association between Farm Girl, Darin and Jefferson Welk.

Since Kelly and Janx had worked with Rusty from the very first burglary of the Neat Nick Thief, they were as anxious as he was to solve the mystery that seemed to evolve around one unidentified, deceased girl they referred to as Farm Girl.

HARD EVIDENCE

When the pieces started falling into place, the speed in which this complex and mysterious puzzle was fitting together was mind-boggling.

The same afternoon of the exhumation of Mama's body, the district attorney received notification of the circumstantial evidence suspecting Darin in the connection of two murders. The Sheriff's Department was the key investigator, since the homicides happened in Cole County. Rusty and all of the Kidwell Police Department were volunteering their time and services in follow-up investigations.

Sheriff Doug Martin had requested and received a court order to exhume Farm Girl's body for DNA testing. The FBI was working, hand in hand, with the sheriff's department and the District Attorney's Office in getting concrete evidence verified. All were busy closing any of the loopholes, and putting together an airtight case against Darin. The district attorney didn't want to charge Darin until he had all of the facts, reports, and bona fide proof in his hands. Besides, Darin certainly wasn't going anywhere since he was still behind bars.

Just a few years prior, the judicial system didn't recognize DNA testing as legal evidence in a court of law. However, times had changed. Today, DNA test results were admissible in the courts as concrete evidence. The DNA in this case was also going to be used to back-up all other admissible laboratory testing of body tissue and body fluids of the deceased: Farm Girl, Mama and Jefferson Welk. This was another added bonus for the District Attorney's Office in their case against Darin.

From time to time, Rusty would stop by the sheriff's office where he would bring Rusty up-to-date on the on-going investigation into Welk and Mama's murders. Most times, there was nothing new to report, but this day, Rusty got lucky.

"Anything new, Doug?" Rusty inquired.

"I just finished going over the latest reports. Here," Doug said, handing Rusty a file folder, "you can read it over yourself."

Rusty took the folder and sat in the chair near Doug's desk. He opened the manila folder and began quietly reading the reports that were enclosed. Skipping through the details, he selected those items that were important to him.

According to the coroner's inquest report, both Mama Cheryl and Jefferson Welk had strychnine poison in their body fluids. The coroner had sent fluid samples to the FBI Lab for comparison tests to any substance found in the coffee thermos or the bank envelope.

According to the FBI Crime Lab report, the technicians were able to test the coffee due to the airtight thermos. The coffee had been laced with poison. They also discovered traces of poison in the bank envelope. Both poisons were of the same substance: strychnine.

The heart-shaped locket pendant, found on Mama's person, had a picture of a young woman holding a small child. Sheriff Martin had taken the picture from the locket in order to blow it up for clearer view of the details. The locket had been pinned to Mama's undergarment with a 4-H Club pin.

As Rusty handed the file folder back to Doug, he commented, "It looks like things are getting accomplished in record time. So, Coats found strychnine, too."

"That's what it looks like, Rusty. I tried to call you when the FBI Lab's preliminary report came in, but you weren't home."

"Yeah, Oscar Denton and I have been busy at the courthouse and the library. One of these days, I guess, I should get my answering machine fixed or replaced."

"That would be a good idea," Doug joked, "especially if you aren't going to be home to get important news."

"I've got to get back to my record searching. Say, when will you have a blow-up of that picture from the locket?"

"I expect it in the next couple of days, Rusty. Stop by or I'll call you."

A couple of days later, Doug called Rusty to give him an update.

"Rusty, I received the preliminary report on the comparison test of Farm Girl's DNA against the DNA from Mama Cheryl Nobody."

"What did the report say?"

"The coroner's routine lab results were positive. I've shipped the results off to your friend, Special Agent Coats, for further testing."

"That's great, Doug. I appreciate your keeping me abreast of things."

As the days passed, Rusty was busy checking every avenue he could possibly think of to find out the identities of Farm Girl and her mother. Oscar, in the meantime, had checked public records. There wasn't a soul to be found with the name Cheryl Nobody or Cheryl Light. Both men had found a family in a nearby town by the last name of Light. After further investigation, it turned into a dead end lead.

In between Rusty's investigations, which were getting him nothing but frustrated, he continued to stop by the sheriff's office just to check on any new information. On one such visit, around the end of May, the sheriff had just received the enlargement copy of the picture from the gold locket taken from Mama's body. Doug was looking at the picture when he heard the bell on the front door ring from the outer office announcing a visitor, and soon followed by a familiar voice.

"Doug?" Rusty hollered.

Doug yelled back. "Rusty?"

"Who else?"

"Quit standing out there yelling at me and come on in here. I've got something to show you."

Rusty didn't wait for a second invitation. He immediately went into Doug's office. "How did you know it was me?"

"ESP," Doug joked. "I figured it was time for you to show up, again, so I took a wild guess."

"Your mother's ear. You recognized my voice."

"You're slipping, Rusty," Doug joked. "That took you a few minutes longer than most times to figure out."

"Son, you've been around me far too long. My bad traits are showing up in you," Rusty stated, tongue in cheek. "Okay, what have you got to show me? Something new in the murder case?"

"You might say that. I just received the blow-up of that picture taken from Mama Cheryl's locket. Come here and take a look. There's something about this woman's face that looks familiar to me."

Rusty walked over to Doug's desk, took the picture, and studied it for a few seconds. "Yes, you're right, Doug. She does look familiar. I can't quite place her though. Who is she?" Rusty handed the picture back to Doug.

"We can only assume it's Mama holding her alleged daughter Farm Girl," Doug answered. "Since her face was unrecognizable when we exhumed her body, we don't know for sure. According to those stories you handed over to the D.A., if this is her. She's also the farmhand that worked for Welk."

"Yes, of course. Our Cheryl Nobody."

"She's definitely not the woman Ward and I saw the day that Welk died. In fact, this woman was no where around when we were out there that day."

"But, Doug, if you remember what I told you about Farm Girl's story, then you should remember that she sent her Mama back to that shack with the money. So, how could any of you have seen her?"

In deep concentration, barely listening to Rusty, Doug managed to grunt out, "Yeah."

"What's the matter?"

"Oh, sorry, Rusty, but there's something about this woman's face that's driving me crazy. You know what's really weird is the fact that I would've never seen her before in my life. So, why is she so familiar?"

"How do you figure that?

"The date on the back of the original picture, Rusty. It's badly worn but you can tell that it was taken sometime in the seventies. I never lived around here until the late eighties. That's when I first came to work for Ward. What do you make of it?"

"I understand that Mama used to work in town when there was no farm work. If she worked in most communities she traveled to, you might have seen her in Kidwell or Sharpin," Rusty surmised. "Then, of course, we have the other possibility. They say everyone has a double. That could be the answer. However, I'm inclined to believe it's the first possibility because she's vaguely familiar to me, too. That reminds me, did Joel ever send you those pictures from his precinct in Chicago?"

"What pictures? Oh, wait a sec. I do remember seeing a large mailer envelope from the 23rd Precinct in this morning's mail. I haven't gotten around to opening the mail, yet, because I received this photo enlargement at the same time. Then you arrived. Let's see what we've got." Doug commenced searching through the mail in his in-basket on his desk. "It's in here somewhere. What pictures did he send to me?"

"Their police photographer took pictures of Farm Girl. Joel was going to send them to me when he sent the girl's stories and her other personal belongings, but he forgot. I called him and told him we now have a suspected dual murder case, so he should, officially, send them to you," Rusty explained.

"I thought *you* buried the girl? Didn't you look at her?"

"Yes, I did, but I've never seen her before. I wanted *you* to see a picture of her, to find out if she's the same girl you saw at Jefferson's house."

"Okay, here we are." Doug found the envelope and opened it. After taking out the pictures, it only took a moment for him to look at the first photo when he began to nod his head. "Okay, Rusty. That's the girl we interviewed the day Welk died. She was the one that was about to drive poor old Ward crazy the way she talked.

No wonder she disappeared so we couldn't ID her the next morning. She had just committed two homicides and had taken off with all of that stolen cash. You know, Rusty, she seemed to be crying genuine tears over Welk that day. I mean, she was heartbroken, like Welk was a member of her family. Man, we never know, do we?"

"According to her stories, she did love Welk, like he was family. In fact, both Farm Girl and her mother referred to him as Pappy. Following through with Darin's murder plan, the poor girl didn't realize—well, you're right, Doug. One never knows." Rusty sat quietly contemplating, then said, "What date did you say was on the back of that woman's picture?"

"It looks like nineteen seventy something. Why?"

"According to the date on the copy I have of the birth certificate, Farm Girl was born in seventy-seven. So it makes sense. Mama Cheryl is holding Farm Girl in that picture from the locket," Rusty concluded.

"I'm sure you're right."

"Look, unless you have anything else for me, I've got things to do and so do you. I'll catch you later."

Rusty exited Doug's office.

Even with the assistance of Denton, Kelly and Janx, Rusty had exhausted all leads when it came to finding any legal documents for Cheryl Nobody, Cheryl Light or F.G. Light. Outside of reading the final stories Farm Girl had written, just to see if he had missed anything, Rusty took a day to visit Jefferson's property. When he arrived at the burial area under the big oak, he sat under the tree making plans.

"Since Mama Cheryl is gone, it would be great if Jefferson's daughter could be found. If she is, I'd like to offer her a proposition. First off, she needs to bury her father here, next to her mother. I would hope that she spends some of her fortune on nice headstones for everyone that's buried here.

Also, if she has no plans for the property, I'd like to purchase it. The land would be perfect for building a home for the needy. Plenty of fields for growing crops and gardens, a river for fishing, small forest of trees for hunting and fresh air. Other than a place to eat and sleep, what could be better to help people feel like they belong in this world, or to help them get back on their feet? Nothing."

As busy as he was, Rusty couldn't believe how time swiftly passed. To him, time was like opening the front door to let the present in, then opening the backdoor for its immediate exit. Before he knew it, several weeks had passed since his last visit to Doug's office. He had called Doug, once a day, to check in, but there had been no new information until the phone rang in mid-June.

"Rusty, Doug here."

"Hey, you beat me to the punch this morning. This must mean you've got something juicy for me."

"I'm headed over to the D.A.'s office with a rather large box of information that I received from the FBI Crime Lab not thirty-minutes ago. I read the cover letter and it seems that your friend, Special Agent Coats, received plenty of assistance from his fellow workers on this case.

After I discovered what all the contents of the box consisted of, I called George, but he was in a meeting. He returned my call and I just got off the phone with him. George wants us at his office as soon as we can get there."

"Are you sure he wants me there, too?"

"You bet. I specifically asked him if you could come along to hear what the FBI has to say in their reports. After all, you're responsible for this whole case. George agreed. So, I'll meet you there, as soon as possible."

"I didn't start this, Doug, but thanks for the credit. I'm on my way."

At the district attorney's, the entire office came to a standstill as the results of the tests were explained. The D.A. did the official reporting, loud and clear.

"To save time, I'm only going to give you the basics. If anyone is interested in reading the long, detailed report, you can do so later. Since we're still lacking the official identifications of the two deceased females, we'll continue calling them Mama Cheryl and Farm Girl, for the present time.

In regards to the evidence sent to the FBI Crime Lab by Cole County, Nebraska's Sheriff Doug Martin, every test they ran at the FBI laboratory proved conclusive.

It goes, without saying, we had Darin Righter's prints on file to send to the FBI Crime Lab. From the prints of Farm Girl, sent to the lab from the Chicago police, and Mama Cheryl's prints sent to the lab from our coroner, Doc Shivley, the FBI Crime Lab was able to identify and match up several prints on vital pieces of evidence. They found both Farm Girl and Darin Righter's prints on the bank envelope. Both Farm Girl and Mama Cheryl's prints were on the coffee thermos. And, Farm Girl's prints were found on all the stories found in Chicago and on the story found in Jefferson Welk's house that had Farm Girl's name or initials on them.

Under substance testing—it states that they found traces of powder inside the envelope from the First People's Bank of Sharpin. The powder tested to be strychnine poison. Coffee left in the airtight thermos tested to contain a vast amount of strychnine poison.

As for the body fluid and tissue testing—the report states they found definite strychnine substance in both of the deceased victims, Jefferson Welk and Mama Cheryl. This testing backed up our own coroner's report. It is therefore conclusive that both victims died due to ingesting a large amount of the strychnine poison.

On the handwriting analysis—a comparison of handwriting from the stories taken from the crime scene of Farm Girl's murder in Chicago, to the story most recently taken from Jefferson Welk's farmhouse, proved that the same person wrote all. It was within reason to conclude that the handwriting of all samples was that of Farm Girl's."

The district attorney was ecstatic. Everyone in the office broke into a state of cheers. Rusty received pats on the back and his hand shaken more times then he cared to accept. As pleased as he was that they had an ironclad case against Darin, Rusty couldn't help feel sorrowful that it had to be Frank's brother.

"Rusty, you certainly have my gratitude for all your help in this case," George commented. "Darin would have tried to wrangle out of this one, I'm sure. He would have played it to the hilt, saying it was his word against the writings of a dead girl. Then he would have used the excuse that his fingerprints were on the envelope because it had been his job to send out foreclosures for the bank. Yes, I have no doubt that he would have tried every angle to prove us wrong. We've got him by the short hairs, thanks to the FBI Lab. I can guarantee you, Rusty, there will be no plea-bargaining this time.

We will want you to testify when the case gets to trial. Since you're retired, we can use you as an expert witness now." George laughed. Rusty wasn't laughing. He had something else on his mind and it showed with the far away look on his face. "You don't appear to be as happy as you were a few minutes ago, Rusty. What's bothering you?"

"Something just sunk into my head about the strychnine, George. That's not a poison in the market place for any John Doe to be able to purchase, like an aspirin for a headache."

Suddenly, George was worried. "Oh, no, Rusty, you're not going to throw water on these hot coals. We've got Darin dead-to-rights on this case."

Shaking his head, Rusty clarified his statement. "No, I didn't mean it that way. I was just putting some facts together in this old brain of mine. When we were chasing our Neat Nick Thief, one burglary didn't make sense at the time. That was the Trenton Reeves Exterminating Service. Reeves couldn't give us a complete list of all the chemicals that were missing, but a powdered form of strychnine poison was on his short list." George listened intently.

"At that time, I thought the thief pulled that job just to throw us off guard, or, Reeves was hit by someone other than our Neat Nick Thief. Now, it's as clear as day. Darin stole the poison to carry through with his murderous plot. Damn it, George, if only I had suspected—"

Patting Rusty on the back, George interrupted. "Look, you can't hammer yourself to death over something you never knew about before hand, Rusty. Shoot, I'm thrilled that you've just given me more vital evidence against Darin. That bit of information helps to seal our homicide case against the little bastard."

"Yeah, I guess you're right."

"You knew Shomond and Dodd lost their jobs over Welk's missing trust fund accounts, didn't you?"

"No, I sure didn't. I've been too wrapped up in this case. What's going on?"

"When the shit hit the fan during the bank's FDIC audit, Shomond blamed Dodd and canned his ass. Then the Bank's Board of Directors fired Shomond. And here's one for the books, Rusty. Along with the estate that the Welk family inherited years ago, Jefferson Welk owned the bank building.

I've since found out Welk's estate also includes every historical building in Sharpin and Kidwell, right down to the courthouse. Seems for years, only a handful of occupants have bothered to pay rent on these buildings, or inform Welk that the properties belonged to him."

"Knowing what little I did about Jefferson, I'm sure he knew every piece of property he owned. Just didn't know what to do about it," Rusty commented. "Wait a minute. If some of the occupants were paying rent, where did that money go?"

"Direct to Welk? No. It's a long complicated story, Rusty. The bank collected all rents and deposited the funds directly into Welk's account because the account always did and does exist."

"It's a shame they couldn't have found the computer problem before he died."

"True. The real shame, however, is the fact that Welk didn't go straight to a bank official to get the whole absurd problem straightened out from the get-go."

"Yeah. The poor man connected with liar, Darin Righter, instead."

"What I don't understand is where Welk got such a vast fortune to begin with. Someday, when I have time, I'm going to do some digging in the courthouse records."

Rusty knew he could have given George a reasonable answer. He chose not to. Instead, he changed the subject. "Just out of curiosity, did anyone check out the YMCA address I found with Farm Girl's papers? You know, the place where she was to meet up with Darin in New York."

"Yes, as a matter of fact, we called them for verification. After checking their back records, they found his name. Seems Darin had made reservations just before you arrested him the second time and put his butt in the can until his trial. Only Darin can tell us what he had planned next, once Farm Girl arrived in New York to meet him. Dread the thought, but probably another murder." Rusty had to agree with a nod.

"Well, Rusty, do you want to go with me to the State Penn to give Darin the good word that we plan on keeping him behind bars for the rest of his life, and watch me knock the pegs out from under his feet?"

"No thanks, George. I'll pass on this one. I tried to see the cocky little rooster and let him know that his only brother, Frank, had died. He didn't even have the courtesy to see me back then. Nope. You can have the pleasure without my company. Besides, I still have a puzzle to put together."

"Do you work those stupid things, too?" George inquired. "You know, my wife can sit for hours on end working on those one-thousand piece picture puzzles. She divides all the colors into different piles, makes her frame out of the straight edge pieces, then tries to fit all those crazy connections together in the middle. I swear, you both have to have the patience of Jobe."

"Patience I don't have. Determination, I've got lots of. I've been working on this puzzle since—well, let's just say a lot of years."

"I'm sorry to say this, Rusty, but that seems like too long of a time to work on putting one puzzle together. Why's it taking you so long?"

"Because the pieces have been scattered from here to Chicago and back, George. Just when I think I'm getting the full picture, I'll be darned if another piece doesn't show up in the most unexpected place."

Rusty knew George was a very intelligent man. So, without further explanation, he left the prominent D.A. to figure out exactly what he was talking about.

THE FINAL PICTURE

Elated with all the good news, but thoroughly exhausted from the entire investigation that mentally drained him, Rusty went home. Alas, everything seemed to be falling into place. Now all he needed was to find out the *true* identity of the mysterious Farm Girl. Then, and only then, would he consider his puzzle solved. When he checked his mailbox, he had some astonishing mail that assisted him.

Rusty's dining room table was where he kept his vital information on Farm Girl. Everything he had of Farm Girl's belongings cluttered the table. Because there wasn't an inch of unused space left on the tabletop, Rusty dropped the mail on the floor, next to the chair he always sat in. As he stood next to the table, he started digging through the clutter of scattered items. From under the papers, he uncovered the metal cup, the gold ring, and collected information on both items. Briefly, he went over the details on both.

The 1940-era cup had initials engraved on it, which he assumed belonged to Farm Girl. There were two problems to that theory. According to the information on the copy of Farm Girls' birth certificate, she was born in 1977 and her initials were different than the ones on the cup. According to Farm Girl's stories, the cup belonged to Mama. Maybe Mama Cheryl was born in the 1940's, but cup's initials were not even close to the name Cheryl Nobody.

The ring was 14k gold, a very popular catalogue order wedding band back in the 1970's. There was no clue as to what the engraved initials stood for.

Rusty placed the articles back on the table. After taking his seat at the table, he leaned over and picked up his mail. As he sorted through it, most

Black Rosebud

of it was junk. Recognizing the name and address on one particular envelope, he opened it. The letter was from his FBI Crime Lab friend, Leo. Before Rusty could read it, his phone rang. Dropping the envelope on the table, Rusty went to his phone and answered it.

"Hello."

"Rusty, this is Doug."

"Miss me already?" Rusty laughed.

"But of course," Doug teased in return. "All joking aside, Rusty, when I got to my office, I had a special delivery letter waiting for me. It's from your friend Coats."

"Leo must have been working overtime," Rusty joked. "I, also, just received something from him in today's mail."

"Mine seems to be a follow-up that was sent after the other final lab reports had already been mailed out. Do you want to hear it?"

"Sure do, Doug. I'm sure my letter from Leo is more on the personal side, so he wouldn't be sending me the same info he sent you. What is it?"

"Are you sitting down?"

"No. Should I be?"

"This one's going to knock the your socks off, Rusty. Hold on and I'll read the information Coats sent."

Stretching his phone cord, Rusty walked back to his dining room table, sat back in his chair, and waited for Doug to continue speaking.

"Are you still with me, Rusty?"

"Sure."

"Okay. This says, 'Special Note from the Desk of Special Agent Leo Coats. A new assistant in the crime lab wanted to do further DNA testing on the three main subjects (Welk, Nobody and Light) mentioned in a previous report, just for more experience in our lab techniques.

Due to the nature of her findings, we reran the tests and they came out positive. I thought you would be interested in the results. There is no doubt that Jefferson Welk fathered the female known as Cheryl Nobody."

"Holy jumpin-gee-hosafats!" Rusty blurted in full volume. "The missing daughter and the farmhand were both the same female?"

"Shit, Rusty, you almost broke my eardrum."

"Sorry for the outburst, Doug, but that's incredible."

"I'll say it is. I've heard of some strange coincidences in my life, but this wins the blue ribbon," Doug added.

"Unbelievable is all I can say. All those years of pain, after having his only child kidnapped—no wonder he took to Mama Cheryl and Farm

Girl. There must have been a special inner-bond that none of them could explain."

"Don't you think it's rather strange that Welk wouldn't have recognized his own daughter or granddaughter, Rusty? Wouldn't there have been some family resemblance?"

"I don't know. Maybe Welk did see a resemblance, but he put it out of his mind instead of getting his hopes built up."

"What about skin color?" Doug asked, a bit baffled. "Farm Girl, the day I saw her, was a little dark skinned, but it looked more like a weathered suntan look."

"Remember what I told you, Doug. Since Jefferson's grandmother was white, Jefferson was considered a mulatto because of the mixed blood. And, if you recall, Jefferson married a white woman, also. Mama, I mean, Cheryl could have very easily turned out more like her mother. And, if Cheryl married a white man, maybe only a hint of skin color showed up in Farm Girl.

Shit, Doug, I don't really know anything about human genes, so I'm only guessing. But, hell, the girl's origin or skin color isn't important here. It's a crying shame all three of them were murdered and went to their graves not knowing they were father, daughter and granddaughter."

"Yeah. Talk about your small world, huh, Rusty?"

"Seems I've said that very statement a hundred times lately, but in this case, that's an understatement. I'm still in shock."

"It's a good thing that new FBI tech is a go-getter, or this fact would have never been uncovered. At least not to us."

"Yeah. I say the tech deserves a huge pat on the back for this one."

"I agree, whole heartedly. Say, something just crossed my mind…"

When there was complete silence on the other end of the phone, Rusty asked, "Hey, Doug, you still there?"

"Yes. I'm digging through my paperwork, trying to find that report from Chicago."

"Which one?"

"From that Dr. Lea Thompson, I believe. She's the M.E. that performed Farm Girl's autopsy. I just don't remember seeing anything in her report about Farm Girl's race."

"If I remember correctly, Doug, she had a small note on the back of that report stating she sent the blood samples to the FBI Crime Lab for DNA testing. Her tests were inconclusive. Hey, did I lose you again?"

"No, I'm still here. I found the report and reading it. Looks like you're right on the money."

"And you doubted me?" Rusty joked.

"Well, that's my last mistake for today," Doug quipped in response. "Listen, Rusty, I've got to get in touch with the bank in Sharpin. They need to know this information so they can call off their dogs in their efforts to find the missing heirs. Looks like both of them have been found in one package. It's a shame neither Cheryl nor her child will be able to enjoy the vast fortune Welk left behind."

"Not half the shame as not knowing they were family. Jefferson's pain was bad enough, but think how that poor woman must have suffered all through life, not knowing who she was or where she came from. Oh, good gravy, Doug, I just remembered that Carol was the name the Welk's had given their baby. I'll lay you odds, since Farm Girl didn't know how to spell, that she wrote Cheryl instead of Carol."

"Unless you have a hearing impediment, I don't think they sound all that much alike, Rusty."

Rusty snapped his fingers. "Damn, Doug. You may have something there. That could be why she used wrong words, at times. For example, when she should have written concentrate, she wrote constipate, or, coroner in place of corner. That may have been a good share of her disability in learning proper English."

"Interesting. So, Carol Welk is the mother's *true* identity."

"That just proves that the name Nobody was a made up name. Although, it doesn't help me with the initials I still have staring me in the face. It does, however, make a great deal of sense about the orphanage story Farm Girl wrote about. Who ever kidnapped the Welk baby, didn't want to get caught. With all the publicity the kidnapping generated, I'm sure the perp had to get rid of the baby, fast. He or she probably took Carol out of state, then left her on the doorsteps of the orphanage.

Oh, well, all that isn't important anymore, since we know, now, who she really was. Look, Doug, thank you so much for sharing that information with me."

"No problem. I'll be talking to you."

Still in a daze from the news, Rusty hung up the phone. He picked up the envelope from Coats and opened it. Inside the envelope was a folded document with a note attached. Coats informed Rusty that a special process performed on the document to eradicate the ink-blotch, revealed the true lettering underneath. This was possible as the originator of the document used blue indelible ink in the original lettering. It appeared that someone wanted to cover the original writing, so they used soluble black ink to make the ink spots.

Rusty put the note on the table, opened the fold of the document, and looked at Farm Girl's Certificate of Birth. He was dumbfounded when he read the information on the document. In fact, no words could ever express what he felt when he read portions of the information aloud.

"'State of Nebraska—Department of Health—Division of Vital Statistics—Standard Certificate of Birth. Place of Birth, Cole County. Date of Birth, April 12, 1977. Mother of Child—Full maiden name, Carole Nobody. Father of Child—Full, Frank George Righter.'

Oh, my, God. This was your family, Frank." After the initial astonishment, he finally realized what went down. "Dear God, Frank, your own brother killed your daughter and your wife. What is this world coming to? It's a good thing I have a good heart because I don't think I could handle any more of these amazing bombshells that I've been hit with today.

It looks like Mama's name was Carole Nobody Righter. That's it!" Rusty exclaimed, as though he finally saw the light of day. "That's the picture that was in the locket. No wonder her face was so familiar to both Doug and me. That's the same face that Frank ran a picture of in the newspaper when he was looking for her. She must not have looked the same at all in her last years as she did when the picture was taken, or someone in town would have recognized her.

And speaking of newspapers, Jefferson Welk would have—No, he wouldn't have seen the newspaper picture. According to Farm Girl's stories, Jefferson never had anything like newspapers or magazines in his house, and didn't receive either by mail. Carole didn't know she was a Welk, so she elected to use the name Nobody. And how confusing. Frank was looking for a Carole, with an e. I was looking for a Carol without an e. That one tiny letter may, or may not have made a difference.

So, I was right. The baby Carole is holding in the picture was little Farm Girl. Good Lord, Frank, you had a wife and a daughter, and never even told me. What a shame they were living almost in your own backyard and you didn't even know it. So close, yet you never got to see them. With Carole traveling across country on foot, moving from here to there and using fake names, it's no darn wonder I couldn't locate her for you.

Besides, since you neglected to give me all of the pertinent details, Frank, I certainly wasn't looking for a woman with a daughter, either. Oh, and you certainly forgot to mention that you were married. Hell, she could have still been using her married name. Damn, Frank, if you had just told me everything.

Wait! If you hadn't seen Carole in twenty-plus years, then Farm Girl can't be your daughter. That's probably why you were never mentioned in any of Farm Girl's stories that I read. Something doesn't jive. Why is your name on Farm Girl's birth certificate if you aren't her father?

Drat the luck. Just when I think I've got things figured out, there's another mystery to solve. Dammit, Frank. If you had confided in me, like friends do, then I wouldn't be sitting here now, busting my ass trying to piece everything together."

Picking up the cup, Rusty muttered, "This was your cup, wasn't it Frank. I didn't even place the initials F.G.R. being the same as yours. It's only natural that I wouldn't have, since I didn't even think to put you and Mama together. Now I know why Farm Girl said the cup was part of her mama's worldly possessions.

As he set the cup back on the table, Rusty's eyes passed over the table of items. His attention rested on the brown envelope from Frank. He had forgotten all about the information Frank had given him, even though it, too, was laying on the same table. With too many other things on his mind for so many months, he never even thought to open the last two white envelopes. Now was the time.

Assuming the envelope marked **MY APOLOGY** contained the same information Frank had related to him during their last conversation, Rusty set the envelope aside. After opening the envelope labeled **MY CONFESSION**, a ring, two documents, two pictures, and a newspaper clipping fell to the table as he removed the enclosed letter.

"'Rusty, I hope, dear friend, that you will forgive my errors, but my fingers don't move as swiftly as they once did, and my vision isn't real good, anymore. I came to you once and asked for your help in finding the woman that I was once in love with.

You did what you could, with no luck, but I will always appreciate that you tried. I tried, too, Rusty, but like you, I couldn't find her either. However, I want you to know why I wanted to find Carole. Why she was, and is, so important to me. As I told you that day in your office, I was in love with her.

On the day I was to leave Allison's farm, I wanted to give Carole something special to remember me by. I had nothing. I ran into the house just as Allison was bringing in a Folgers coffee can, of all things, filled with freshly cut flowers from her garden. I convinced Allison to give me the can of flowers as a parting gift to Carole.

What I didn't tell you on the day I confided in you, Rusty, was that I had gotten Carole pregnant. When I found out she was carrying my child, thanks to a letter from Allison, I rushed to Carole's side. By then, she was already eight months pregnant. I took her to Kansas and married her. I will enclose our wedding certificate with this letter, and my wedding band. We stayed with Allison until after the baby was born.

If, per chance, you should ever find Carole, she should have the other half of the matched wedding set I purchased. I special ordered them out of a jeweler's catalog. Then I had her initials engraved inside her ring as a special gift to her. Since she never really knew her own birth name, we gave her the last name of Nobody. It was an inside joke with us since, from the day I met her, she had told me that she was a nobody.

Carole, she thought, was her real first name because she had remembered one particular woman from the orphanage kept calling her by that name. Of course, her story about being abandoned at birth is a whole other issue, which I won't go into since I know nothing more than what she told me.

Lucky for us that, years ago, two people in love could find a Justice of the Peace to marry them without asking for official identification papers. I gave her the first true name she ever had when I gave her my last name in marriage. We were so happy, Rusty—well, until my mother found out.'"

Finally, Rusty was getting answers to all the questions he had searched for. He looked across his table at the rusted coffee can. "So, Carole, at last I have the reason for you holding on to that old can. No wonder it meant so much to you."

Rusty had to take a small break from sitting. He got up and stretched. After making a trip to the bathroom, he got some chips and a cold beer. Then he sat back at the table. After opening the beer and chugging some good-sized gulps, he picked up the gold ring that had fallen out of the envelope from Frank. Inside the gold band were the initials F.G.R. He compared it to the ring that was amongst Farm Girl's belongings that had the initials C.N.R. engraved inside the band. No doubt about it, they were a matched set.

He also looked at the newspaper clipping and the two pictures that came out of the envelope. Rusty had been right. One picture was the original of the newspaper article Frank had placed to find Carole. The other was a larger photo of the picture that was in the locket found on Carole's body. After a few chips and some beer to wash them down, he picked up Frank's letter and continued reading.

"'One of my biggest mistakes was taking Carole and the child home with me to live with my folks. I will not bore you again with my disgust for my mother. But because of her, Carole left us. I didn't know, until years later, that Carole left because my mother used some lame threat that she could have her arrested and sent to jail. Carole was somewhat naive with the ways of the world, so she believed my mother could do such a thing. Then, my child was taken from me. As per my usual, I didn't have a backbone to stand up for what I believed in. So, I lost the battle.

One day, I was allowed to spend a full day with my child. We went to the 4-H County Fair. I ran into Carole quite by accident. It was quite a reunion between the three of us. We spent a wonderful day, together. Of course, it killed both of us that our own son couldn't know we were his real parents, but sometimes, as we all know, Rusty, life isn't fair.

Carole still carried the gold locket I had given to her as a wedding gift, but the chain had broken. So she could no longer wear it around her neck. I gave her my old 4-H pin, so she could pin the locket on her dress until I could get the chain replaced.

When I mentioned that I wanted a picture of her and our son together, she thought it was a great idea. She, too, wanted such a picture to put into her locket. I had a photographer from the fairgrounds take the picture. We got the small picture for Carole's locket, and I got a larger print. It was just another thing I had to sneak home and hide from my mother. She would have destroyed it.

For those few hours that the three of us were able to spend together as a real family, I was in heaven. I dreaded when the time came for us to split the family apart, again. I had to promise to get my son back home before dark or I wouldn't have been allowed to take him alone with me, ever again. When the sun started to set, I had some friends from the fair take him home. Carole and I stayed together and talked.

When she told me the truth, as to why she left me, I boiled inside with anger. I begged her to come back home. I really thought I had convinced her to do so. We spent the night together.

When I woke up the next morning, she was gone again. She left me a note telling me, since she had never known her own parents, she couldn't be responsible for putting an even bigger wedge between my mother and me. Oh, if she would just have realized that she was more important to me than my mother—but she didn't. July of seventy-six was the last time I ever saw her.

Well, Rusty, I didn't find out until my parents were killed in that car crash that I had a baby daughter. I was going through the desk drawers, gathering up my parent's important documents and other paperwork, when I found an opened letter. It was postmarked back in seventy-seven and addressed to me. I didn't recognize the handwriting, nor did I remember ever getting the letter.

I read it. It was a small note from Carole. She told me that we had a baby girl on April the twelfth of that year, and that she had given our daughter my initials. She told me the baby was our special *Black Rosebud*. You see, when she gave birth to our first born, we found out she had Negro blood in her. Not that I cared. Never in a million years would that have bothered me. I loved her, no matter if she were black, pink or purple. But I couldn't let my folks know, especially my mother—the bitch.

Back to my note from Carole, she said she was only a few miles away, working on a farm. The baby girl was delivered by a mid-wife, same as our son. She gave me the address and said she would wait for me so I could see my new daughter. She also said that she had given it a lot of thought, and if I really wanted her in my life, then I should leave my parent's home for good. The four of us could run away, somewhere, and make a fresh start of our lives.

My God, Rusty, do you realize, now, what a genuine old bitty my mother really was? I never got that letter. And, because I never got to read it back then, I never had the chance to see my daughter or be with my wife. My mother intercepted that letter, opened it, and kept the information from me for all those years. After reading that letter, I often wondered how long Carole waited for me to show up. What deep hatred she must have felt for me, thinking I didn't even want to see my own daughter.'"

Rusty's vision blurred with tears. He had to put the letter aside. After wiping his eyes with his shirtsleeves, he finished his beer. Even though Frank was deceased, Rusty's thoughts wailed out for his friend.

"Frank, I never knew. For years, all I did was cry on your shoulder about losing my brother, and here you had more hurt in your heart than any one human should be allowed to bear all alone. I'm so sorry. God, I am so sorry. And a son? Somewhere you have a son?

Wait a damn minute. Years ago, Frank always seemed to bring young Henry Lakey to town with him. Said he felt sorry for the kid since he was adopted and had no siblings. That's has to be it. Henry has to be Frank's son. Since Lakey isn't a common name, Henry should be easy enough to find. Casey bought their farm. Maybe he'll know where they moved to. Frank, I couldn't help you find your wife, but maybe I can find your son for you."

Trying to fit even more puzzle pieces into place, Rusty's mind was swirling like a top. He stood and stretched, rolling his head in slow circles in order to relieve some of the stiffness in his neck. After retrieving another beer, he sat back in his chair and picked up Frank's letter.

"Well, Carole, now I understand why you taught Farm Girl that love between a man and a woman only caused pain and sorrow. Just like Frank said, you probably figured Frank never showed up that day because he didn't want you and your daughter in his life. It's just a damn shame you never told Farm Girl that she had a father, and he was such a wonderful, warm human being. Maybe you three can all be a family now that your souls are together with God. I hope so."

Rusty finished reading Frank's letter, completing the puzzle, once and for all.

"'Rusty, I haven't written you this letter to lay all of my heavy burden on your shoulders. But, I am going to make you executor of my estate, so I figured there were quite a few things you should be well informed of in regards to my life. I will ask that you, verbally, give my son all of these details. I tried to tell him. But, each time I started, he didn't want to hear it. I figure you might be able to get through to him, at least I hope so. He will be out of prison in a few years and I want him taken care of.'"

Rusty dropped the letter, letting it fall to the table. His hand started shaking and he had to take a few deep breaths to compose himself.

"My God, it can't be! It's Darin? Darin is your son? No way."

After expelling his disbelief, he picked up the letter to finish reading. Rusty had to find out if he was right or not. Even though he didn't want to believe Darin was Frank's son, his heart told him it was true.

"'I don't want my son to have the large amount of trust money I had set aside for him, as I will explain in another letter to you. But, I don't want him out on the street, either. The house is paid for. It can be sold for a good price. Darin can have the money from the house to make his fresh start in New York City, where he has always wanted to go. Maybe he wouldn't have been in trouble, today, if I wouldn't have been so selfish in wanting to keep him on the farm with me.

Oh, I know too well what you are thinking, right now, Rusty, but, yes, I do take the blame. I blamed my mother for many years, since she was the one who scared Carole off, then took Darin from me and raised him as her own. Darin never knew the difference. From the time he could talk, he called me Frank, thinking I was his big brother.

I was the one at fault for not standing up to my mother. I should've been a man, taken my own son, and went in search of my wife the very moment I found her missing. It's no wonder she disappeared in the middle of the night when I met up with her, a few years later.

Anyway, no one can shoulder this blame but me. Maybe that's why I never went in for surgery or the radiology and chemotherapy. I felt God was punishing me for my life, so I deserved to die of the cancer I have in my body.

I have done everything I could to make up for Darin's life, but it is all up to him now. Yes, I spoiled him, and now, you know why. I just hope he has some good in him and, when he gets out of that State Penal Institution, that he keeps his nose clean and walks on the good side of life. I also pray that, someday, he will go in search of his mother and sister. I believe he will find a lot of peace within when that happens.

If Darin chooses not to believe the facts I have given you, then just show him his birth certificate, which I will enclose with my marriage certificate.

Thank you for being my friend, Rusty, and for doing this last huge favor for me. I know I don't have the right to ask, after the way I treated you when Darin was arrested, but I'm hoping you'll overlook my stupidity. I don't know that we will get a chance to visit again before my time is up, and I don't know if I will have the guts to mail this letter to you before I go. I can only hope that, if I leave it in plain sight, someone will see that you get it.

Please take care of Darin for me, and my wife and my sweet *Black Rosebud,* too, should you ever find them. I know this is a lot to ask, but the finances I'm leaving you should support all of you in a more than comfortable life style. It's really sad to think that Darin couldn't see beyond his greedy nose. He would have had all the money he ever needed—from me.

I've enjoyed our years of brotherly love and friendship that we had together. I'm only sorry that the last few years put a hardship on that friendship. Please understand that my son came first. Your friend, Frank.'"

Rusty laid down the letter and picked up the document that was Darin's Certificate of Birth.

"How does anyone tell a young man, close to the ripe old age of twenty-five, that he, when convicted in our penal system, will not only spend the rest of his life in prison for murder, but that the victims were his own immediate family?"

EPILOGUE

The next day, after he had read Frank's letter, Rusty received an unexpected, unwanted telephone call.

"Hello."

"Chief Simmons, this is Darin Righter."

Rusty clenched his jaws together so tight, he could feel the grinding of his teeth. His first impulse was to slam down the receiver. Then, he decided to wait and hear what Darin had to say.

"Mr. Simmons to you, son. What do you want?"

"I only have a short phone privilege, so I have to make this quick. I want to know if you'll come visit me. I would really like to see you," Darin's said in a polite tone of voice.

"I don't know what for, or what we would have to say to each other, Darin. If I recall, you wouldn't see me when I came to give you news of Frank's passing. Why should I want to come visit you now?"

"Please, come," Darin pleaded.

Out of respect for Frank, Rusty begrudgingly agreed.

Rusty knew Darin needed to know the truth about Frank. As long as he was going to make the trip, he might as well take all the important items with him in case Darin needed verification of the facts.

After he disconnected his phone call from Darin, Rusty called the district attorney. Upon his inquiries, the D.A. informed him that Darin knew he would be going to trial, again, and why.

Once Rusty had briefly explained the information he had recently discovered, George gave him the green light to show Darin any papers he deemed necessary. George felt, since their case against Darin was cut-and-dried, that any evidence he showed or told Darin, would not matter one way or the other. At this point, nothing could jeopardize the state's case.

Since he had official approval, Rusty gathered all the vital items and documents he felt he needed, and placed them in an empty shoebox. After dressing, he headed for Lincoln. As he made the long, tedious drive, he could only surmise why Darin wanted to meet with him.

"I just know you want money, Darin, now that you know you're up for a murder rap. Being the accessory before and after the fact, since you are the one who planned it all out, I imagine you're in need of a good attorney. Good defense attorneys, especially for murder trials, cost a lot of dough. Right Darin? I'll bet you think you can con me into giving you the money Frank left me in charge of. Well, if you think you'll get one red cent from me, you're sadly mistaken.

Damn, what would I do if that were my son in prison? I don't have any answers, right now. I hope I can come up with the right ones for Frank's sake, when I see Darin. That is, if money is what he wants. Frank asked me, more or less, to take care of him. So, I need to do what is right."

At the prison, Darin proved that Rusty's assumptions were right on track. Darin did want money. Rusty never gave in to giving him one penny of Frank's money because of his attitude. He did tell Darin about Frank's last bequest. His house would be there for Darin to live in when he got out of prison, or to sell and use the money to go to New York.

Since it was obvious to Rusty that Darin would be spending the rest of his life in prison, if he had any say about it, the natural conclusion would be for Darin to have the house sold for him. He could then use that money for a good criminal defense lawyer.

Having Darin's undivided attention, Rusty was able to tell Darin everything about Farm Girl being his sister, Carole being his mother, Jefferson Welk being his grandfather, and, like the cherry on the whipped cream, he topped it off with the fact that Frank was his biological father.

At first, Darin seemed to go numb. Then, like some deranged person, he started laughing and talking like a magpie. He joked about how Farm Girl could never be his sister as she turned his stomach. Darin called her a dumb cow. Most of all, he filled in the empty parts, conversations and his own thoughts that were missing in Farm Girl's stories. Rusty never showed Darin the stories—he had only mentioned them to him.

Rusty made mention he had seen Farm Girl's photo, and how pretty she was. Darin could only comment, "To each his own."

Almost four hours later, after confessing everything to Rusty, Darin went into hysterics. It was as if something exploded inside Darin's brain. The fact that he was a child of mixed blood, finally hit him. Rusty hadn't realized, until then, Darin's prejudice. Yelling four letter word obscenities, Darin picked up his chair and started smashing it at the window that divided him from Rusty. It took two prison guards to restrain and remove Darin from the visitor chambers.

Rusty's last words to Darin were, "I actually feel sorry for you. You could have had it all, you no good greedy … " Having second thoughts, Rusty didn't complete his statement.

In Rusty's eyes, the only remorse Darin showed, was not for the loss of lives, but for the loss of his freedom—of never being able to spend The Welk fortune he would inherit.

Once the court-appointed psychiatrist, together with the State Penal Institution's psychiatrist, agreed that Darin was of sound mind and could stand trial, the courts tried and convicted Darin. It only took the jury twenty minutes to bring in a verdict—Guilty. In the State of Nebraska, Darin's sentence was that he be executed in the electric chair. The last thing the judge said to him was, "May God have mercy on your soul."

Rusty called Detective Joel Applemeyer. In a brief synopsis, Rusty conveyed everything that had taken place on his end. Needless to say, Joel was very grateful for Rusty's help. As it turned out, Rusty was truly the grateful one.

After the state released from their custody Jefferson, Mama and Farm Girl's bodies, Rusty took charge. He had Jefferson's body buried next to his wife under the old oak tree. He had Mama Carole and Farm Girl laid to rest within close proximity to Jefferson. Rusty ordered head stones for each member of the Welk family.

Rusty took Frank's ashes with him on a three-day fishing trip to Canada. He kept the box of ashes by his side while he sat in the boat fishing. The morning before Rusty left Canada to return to Kidwell, he took his rental boat to the middle of the lake and scattered Frank's ashes, bidding him a fond adieu.

"Farewell, my friend. Now, you can finally be united with your loved ones. May your souls meet in heaven and you all have everlasting peace."

In order to settle the legality of his inheritance from Frank, Rusty had to go to court. The battle seemed endless. In short, due to Frank's hand-written letter to him, the court considered the letter as Frank's Last Will and Testament.

Since Frank and Carole were legally married, the inheritance that Carole would have received, as the Welk heiress, went to her only living relative, her son Darin. However, since Rusty was the executor of Frank's estate, and Darin was sitting on death row, the money was put in Rusty's hands to handle for Darin.

Then, the big surprise came. The only kind gesture Darin had made in his whole life, according to Rusty, was to completely sign over the Welk fortune to Rusty. Now Rusty did not have to answer to anyone. He could do anything with the money that he wanted to without recourse or circumstance. Rusty never understood why Darin had such a change of heart. But, it was his belief that Darin had come to his senses and felt remorse for what he had done—not only to the community but, above all, to this family.

After his trip to Canada to fill the last part of his obligation to Frank, and after getting the Welk and Righter Estates handled, Rusty did some traveling. However, this was not a trip for pleasure. He felt a story should be written about, Farm Girl, the vital piece of the mysterious puzzle he had put together. After all, she always wanted to be a writer and see her name in print.

Rusty decided he would try to honor that wish since she was Frank's daughter. He would write the story himself. Before he could do that, however, he had to travel to every place that Farm Girl had written about, interview each person she wrote about that she had come in contact and had a conversation with, and get her story in their words.

Before Rusty left on his trip into Farm Girl's journey of the past, he hired John Johnston to get things started on opening a home for the needy in Cole County. The money from Frank's estate and the Welk fortune would be spent for a good cause. Rusty utilized the scenic areas by the river on Welk's property to build the home.

The fields would be used for share cropping for those who could work but couldn't quite make it on their own. As far as Rusty was concerned, no human being who lived in or moved to the Cole County area, no matter what race, creed or religion, would ever again be homeless or have to live in a run-down, one-room shanty like Mama and Farm Girl did.

Even though Farm Girl was, by all rights, a murderess, she was ignorant of the fact that Darin set her up. Above all, she was Frank's daughter.

The home for the needy was built and dedicated in memory of *Black Rosebud.*

The End

BOBBY RUBLE

Award-winning author, **Bobby Ruble**, has served over twenty years in the US Marine Corps. He held the position of Tank Commander in Vietnam. Later he served ten years in the Criminal Investigation Division (CID). Upon retirement from the Marine Corps, he served in a variety of capacities for law enforcement agencies, capping his career as Chief of Police in Kennesaw, Georgia from 1980-1986.

While working fulltime as the Chief of Police, he enrolled in Brenau College in Gainsville, Georgia, at nights. Ruble earned his Bachelor of Science degree when he was 51 year old. He was listed in both the 1980 and 1983 editions of Who's Who in American Law Enforcement, and the 1986 edition of Men in Achievement.

Bobby has had his articles published both on the World Wide Web and in off-line periodicals. Because of a dream she had, Kam inspired Bobby to write his first novel, *Have No Mercy*. Together, Bobby and Kam wrote the article, *She Dreams It I Write It*, published in the Mystery Readers International, Partners in Crime II, Volume 17, No. 3, Fall 2001. Look for Bobby's story, *Strange Phenomenon Between Two People*, in the soon to be released *Romancing the Soul—True Stories and Verse of the Existence of Soul Mates From Around the World and Beyond*, of which Dorothy Thompson is the compiler and editor.

KAM RUBLE

A Nebraska native, **Kam Ruble** was born in Lincoln. She graduated from Westside High School in Omaha. Insisting she is not a world traveler, Kam has lived and traveled around several states and foreign countries.

Kam enjoyed writing short stories and poems from the day she learned to put words together to form a sentence. Her writing was put to good use when she wrote children stories and poems for her daughters when they were young.

Numerous careers throughout Kam's lifespan include everything from professional singing to owning and operating a gourmet coffee shop with her husband, Bobby. It was not until the mid-80's that she finally got serious about her writing. Kam, too, has numerous writing credits of her own. They include: poems published in Once Upon a Poet; The Poet's Hand, Volume I; The New Poets: Yes!; Voices in Poetics: A Modern Treasury, Vol. II; Hearts On Fire: A Treasury of Poems on Love, Volume V; Many Voices Many Lands: Anthology of Poetry, Volume 1, Number 1; Editor's Choice: A Selection of John Frost's Favorite Poets; Best New Poets of 1988; Lone Tree Literature; St. Paul's Pioneer Press; and, co-author of *She Dreams It, I Write It*, published in Mystery Readers International, Partners in Crime II, Volume 17, No. 3, Fall 2001.

Credits

© "LAYS" trademark:
Used by permission from Frito-Lay, Inc.

©"FOLGERS":
Used by permission from The Procter & Gamble Company.

William J. Doerr, GREYHOUND Web Support Team, for providing the bus schedule from Omaha, NE to Des Moines, IA; Des Moines to Chicago, IL; and from Chicago to New York, NY.

LeslyeAnn Rolik, owner of Professional Training Resources and PTR Books. First editing (of original title: Farm Girl)

GARDENIA PRESS: P. Elizabeth Collins, President; Trish Jankowski, Acquisitions Editor; Christy Lee, Associate Editor; Nancy Walker, Associate Editor; and, Georgio Feruentti, Accountant for their review comments.

FIRST NOVEL IN THE SERIES

HAVE NO MERCY
©Bobby Ruble 2002

Abandoned by his parents, deceived by his closest and only childhood friend, and scorned by his wife, David Epstein sets out on a journey to even the score. When David's wife is found dead, Colorado Homicide Detectives, Joe Warner and Eddy Konklin, enter the picture. Was Ann Epstein murdered, and if so, by whom? As the detectives dig deeper and deeper into their investigation of Ann's death, they discover plots of revenge gone wrong.

Review Blurbs

Owner/moderator/editor/reviewer for Sell Writing On Line, Dallas Franklin relates *Have No Mercy* - **"It could sit right up there in the top ten list and hold its own amongst any bestseller."** ©2002 Dallas Franklin

Reviewing for Word Weaving and Midwest Book Reviews, Cindy Penn advises *Have No Mercy* is "A chilling psychological thriller - Very highly recommended"

Harriet Klausner, top free lance reviewer for Amazon.com and an abundance of other on-line sites, raves *Have No Mercy* **"...is a very cleverly written crime thriller..."**

"Bobby Ruble has penned an interesting novel full of deceit and vengeance." Reports Kevin Tipple, reviewer for the Blue Iris Journal.

Dr. Labin, The Word Doctor On Line, regards HAVE NO MERCY as **"...A Best of Best Reads!"** ©2002 Dr. Linda L. Labin

As reported by Jonathan David Masters, freelance reviewer for Book Trees "…**Bobby Ruble has written a masterful read.**"

From the publisher and chief reviewer of Heartland Reviews, Bob Spear writes, "**The author demonstrates his experienced knowledge of investigation procedures to outline a story that catches innocent and not-so-innocent characters in a web of deceit and psychotic manipulation.**"

THIRD NOVEL IN THE SERIES

BLACK LILY: HAVE NO MERCY III
©**Bobby and Kam Ruble 2003**

The Mayor of Mt. Pride, Colorado, rules his family with the same iron hand he governs Mt. Pride as a top city official. It is only natural that this man of wealth and prestige has enemies. When the Mayor is missing, is it foul play by one of his enemies, or did he disappear on his own? It is up to Mt. Pride's top detectives, Joe Warner and Eddy Konklin, to find out the answer.

Scheduled for June 2004 G.A.P. publication, this will be another spell binding, psychological thriller with a shock ending.

For more information, visit -the Ruble's Website:
http://www.bobbyruble.com

Contact the Ruble's at
havenomercy@bobbyruble.com

Printed in the United States
1398000004B/124-129